THE WEATHERHOUSE

Anna (Nan) Shepherd was born in 1893 and died in 1981. Closely attached to Aberdeen and her native Deeside, she graduated from her home University in 1915, and went to work for the next forty-one years as a lecturer in English at what is now Aberdeen College of Education. An enthusiastic gardener and hill walker, she made many visits to the Cairngorms with students and friends and was a keen member of the Deeside Field Club. Her last book, a non-fiction study called *The Living Mountain*, testifies to her love of the hills and her knowledge of them in all their moods. Her many further travels included visits to Norway, France, Italy, Greece, and South Africa, but she always returned to the house where she was raised and lived almost all her adult life, in the village of West Cults, three miles from Aberdeen on North Deeside.

Nan Shepherd wrote three novels, all well received by the critics: *The Quarry Wood* (1928), followed by *The Weatherhouse* (1930) and *A Pass in the Grampians* (1933). A collection of poems, *In the Cairngorms*, appeared in 1934, and *The Living Mountain* was published in 1977. She edited *Aberdeen University Review* from 1957 to 1964, contributed to *The Deeside Field*, and worked on editions of poetry by two fellow North East writers, J.C. Milne and Charles Murray. She was awarded an honorary degree by Aberdeen University in 1964, and her many friends included Agnes Mure Mackenzie, Helen Cruickshank, Willa Muir, Hugh MacDiarmid, William Soutar, and Jessie Kesson.

Nan Shepherd

THE WEATHERHOUSE

Introduced by Roderick Watson

CANONGATE
CLASSICS
16

First published in 1930 by Constable & Co Ltd, London. This edition first published as a Canongate Classic in 1988 by Canongate Publishing Limited, 17 Jeffrey Street, Edinburgh EHI IDR. Copyright © 1930 Sheila M. Clouston. Introduction © 1988 Roderick Watson. All rights reserved.

The publishers gratefully acknowledge general subsidy from the Scottish Arts Council towards the Canongate Classics series and a specific grant towards the publication of this volume.

Set in 10pt Plantin by Falcon Graphic Art Ltd, Wallington, Surrey. Cover printed by Swains (Glasgow) Limited. Printed and bound in Great Britain by Cox and Wyman, Reading.

Canongate Classics
Series Editor: Roderick Watson
Editorial Board: Tom Crawford, J. B. Pick
British Library Cataloguing in Publication Data
Shepherd, Nan
The weatherhouse.—(Canongate classics).
I. Title
823'.912[F]

ISBN 0-86241-194-7

Contents

Introduction

Scottish literature is rich in novels which have taken the life of small communities for their setting: Dalmailing, Thrums, Barbie, Brieston, Kinraddie, Segget and many others, are memorably located on the maps of our imagination In modern times, however, these locations have been less than happy places, and in *Gillespie* and *The House with the Green Shutters*, they have been revealed as appalling microcosms of all that is mean, petty and cruel in the human spirit.

The spirit of Fetter-Rothnie in *The Weatherhouse* is more balanced from the start. As an account of Scottish rural life and character in the first decades of this century, it is a humourous delight. (Fetter-Rothnie is imagined to be near the coast, a few miles from Nan Shepherd's native Aberdeen.) As a social document, *The Weatherhouse* tells of a community of women—girls, widows, wives and spinster ladies—and of the many links which bind them together to make our world into a whole and humane place. Finally, as an exploration of human nature itself, and of the mysteriously personal and fluid well-springs which underlie what we think of as truth or reality, it is a small masterpiece, and a very fine modern novel in its own right.

This was Nan Shepherd's second book, published in 1930, and it is by far her most complex and subtle achievement. As with Chekhov, whose dryly compassionate wit she shares, there are no truly central characters to her story, for its themes are advanced through almost every person in the novel. There are no villains and heroes either, and what we are left with is a vision of mortal existence and human reconciliation which is transcendent, liberating, and even frightening at times. And yet all is achieved with the lightest of touches in what seems to be the most domestic and parochial of tales about poor Louise Morgan's fantasy engagement to David Grey (who has died T.B.), and Garry Forbes's determination to make her confront her self-delusion.

Shepherd keeps a wry distance from her world, as the section headings show: Garry Forbes's unseemly fervour and Louie Morgan's feeble untruths scarcely qualify as 'The Drama', after all, and the author's use of 'Prologue' and 'Epilogue' serves to place the affair even more ironically against the longer perspectives of time and local legend. Within the book itself the presiding genius of this detachment is Mrs 'Lang Leeb' Craigmyle, matriarch of the Weatherhouse and, at over ninety years old, 'an ironic commentator' with 'an intelligent indifference to life'. Her impudence is delightful, for there is 'no spectacle like what's at your own doors,' and as her creator observes, 'Life is an entertainment hard to beat when one's affections are not engaged.' Yet Lang Leeb's disinterestedness can strike a more sinister note, and this delicate and non-judgemental balance between the comic and the disturbing is characteristic of Shepherd's humour:

> Mrs Craigmyle had few gestures; she held herself still; only her eyes glittered and her lips moved, and often her fingers went to and fro as she knitted — a spider stillness. The film of delicate lace upon hair as fine as itself was not the only thing about her that betokened the spider. One had the sense of being caught upon a look, lured in and held.

The life that Leeb delights to observe is all around us in the book, for Shepherd has created a complex web of relationships in a community largely bound together by women in a tangle of connections through birth, friendship, work, debt, widowhood and marriage. The list of characters at the end of this introduction provides ample evidence of this web and will also serve, I hope, as an aid to understanding Nan Shepherd's most ambitious portrayal of how the social fabric is held together in small communities.

In this respect *The Weatherhouse* is a feminist text of considerable sensitivity, not least in its author's understanding of the position of women in a society where female status is still chained to bridal veils and apron strings. Thus the sweetness of Lindsay Lorimer's romance with Garry Forbes is countered by the sharper pains of Ellen Falconer's fantasies as she seeks to be the girl's mentor. At the age of sixty, Mrs Falconer is looking for vicarious fulfilment in Lindsay's youthful enthusiasms, and then again in the excitement of uncovering the 'truth' in the Louie Morgan affair. Finally, and most pathetically of all, she hopes to impress Garry Forbes, ostensibly on her daughter's behalf, but actually in her own right as a fellow idealist (as she sees herself) in a community of clods. What Lindsay sees, on the other hand, is 'a poor old thing', and later, 'a horrid old woman'. Nan Shepherd has the most piercing eye for the differences between how we like to think about ourselves and how others perceive us. Like Lang Leeb 'her cruelties [come] from comprehension, not from lack of it.'

Long widowed and isolated by her own dreamy, imaginative and uneducated nature, Ellen Falconer has to discover that she is just as sadly removed from the real springs of life (which she always thought to value so much), as the pitiable Louie Morgan. In fact their two fates are bound up in the most poignant fashion as Ellen, that 'shy, baffled soul', decides to visit Louie in a harrowing scene at the end of the book, only to recognise a mad version of herself. Yet reconciliation is possible, and she makes a kind of peace with Louie and Lindsay and herself. We, too, are kept from a more tragic sense of closure, for although the book ends with Ellen's death, the moment is lightened by a tribute paid to her by the bold Stella, who leaves a flower in her hands in memory of an unconsidered and unpretentious moment's kindness shown to her by Ellen long ago.

Garry Forbes has to learn, too, that things are not quite as they seem, nor as he would have them be. Shaken by grim experience and the trauma of the trenches, he returns to the parochial world of Fetter-Rothnie only to have his faith in the stability of the world undermined yet again, and at an even more profound level. Nan Shepherd uses a

destabilising imagery of light and dark and space to mark
the point at which Garry moves on from the simplicities
of his engineering trade ('making boilers and bridges as
stable as one could', with 'right and wrong as separate as
the bridges he helped to build'), to a perplexing vision of
ordinary life as something far more fluid, dynamic, dangerous and uplifting:

> Garry's thought went back upon the evening
> when he had seen the land emerge and take form
> slowly from primordial dark. Now its form was on the
> point of dissolution into light. And the people whom
> the land had made—they, too, had been shaped from
> a stuff as hard and intractable as their rock, through
> weathers as rude as stormed upon their heights; they
> too (he thought) at moments were dissolved into light,
> had their hours of transfiguration. In his aunt dancing
> her wilful reel on the kitchen floor, in Lindsay as
> she had grieved for Louie's hurt, he had seen life
> essentialised.

In such images Nan Shepherd manages to invest the
dourness of the Scottish land—a very familiar theme in our
fiction—with aspects of imagination and grace. For her the
natural world is full of such insights, and they are repeatedly evoked in brilliant descriptions of weather, light and
the North East landscape. In the realm of human affairs,
equivalent moments of generosity and delight are provided
by Shepherd's unsentimental affection for her characters.

Chief among these delights is Garry Forbes's maiden
aunt Barbara Paterson. Loud, boisterous and unconven-
tional, she is something of a natural force, 'elemental, a mass
of the very earth, earthy smelling, with her goat's beard, her
rough hairy tweed like the pelt of an animal.' Both Garry
and Lindsay (who is frightened of her at first), have much
to learn from 'Bawbie' Paterson's vivid enjoyment of the
moment, not least the grand carelessness with which she
sets fire to the roof of her farm at Knapperley, and then the
hilarious confidence with which she sets out to repair it. The
job is attacked with her usual gusto as she enlists the aid of
her untrained nephew and the hapless journeyman Francie
Ferguson. 'Up on the heid o' the house, like Garry Forbes

and his twa fools', becomes a local proverb on the strength of the event, and yet Garry comes to a crucial recognition (all the more timely since the bloodiest of wars is still being fought in Europe), that 'his folly on the housetop was a generosity, a gesture of faith in mankind.'

Such faith, like the imagery of light, fluidity and reconciliation, illuminates this extraordinary novel throughout, as Bawbie, at first an earthy 'boulder' in Garry's inner eye, finally becomes perceived by him as a 'dancing star'. Even Louie's pale and pathetic delusions are not without some saving grace in the end, for in the Epilogue, as Lindsay thinks of her childhood and happier days with the older girl, she seems to remember Louie's faithful whippet hound, Demon, who used to follow her wherever she went. ' "Nonsense!" rapped Miss Theresa. "Louie had never a dog . . . She wanted one . . . And after a while she used to pretend she had it—made on to be stroking it, spoke to it and all." '

Lindsay looked doubtfully.

'Did she? I know she pretended about a lot of things. But Demon –? He seems so real when I look back. Did she only make me think I saw him? He used to go our walks with us. We called to him—*Demon, Demon*—loud out, I know that.'

She pondered. The dog, bounding among the pines, had in her memory the compelling insistence of imaginative art. He was a symbol of swiftness, the divine joy of motion. But Lindsay preferred reality to symbol.

The last line returns us to common sense, but Nan Shepherd has already made her point. Once again she has managed a bitter-sweet and creative disturbance of our equilibrium, as she has done, so subtly and so memorably on almost every page of *The Weatherhouse*.

Roderick Watson

The Main Characters

husband (after 22 years engagement) to 'Peter Sandy's
Bell', already father to her children, Stella Dagmar and
Sidney Archibald Eric.

Mrs Barbara Hunter, of Craggie, ex servant girl and friend to
Bawbie Paterson at Knapperley; wife of crofter Jake
Hunter; mother of Dave, who returns wounded from the
war to re-educate himself as a graduate and a school
teacher.

Jonathan Bannochie, cobbler to trade, originator of the
phrase 'Garry Forbes and his twa fools', referring to Garry,
Bawbie and Francie.

The Prologue

The name of Garry Forbes has passed into proverb in Fetter-Rothnie.

One sees him gaunt, competent, a trifle anxious, the big fleshy ears standing out from his head, the two furrows cutting deeply round from nostril to chin, his hands powerful but squat, gift of a plebeian grandfather, and often grimed with oil and grease—hardly a figure of romance. Of those who know him, to some he is a keen, long-headed manager, with a stiff record behind him in the training of ex-service men and the juvenile unemployed, tenacious, taciturn, reliable, with uncanny reserves of knowledge; to others, a rampageous Socialist blustering out disaster, a frequenter of meetings: they add a hint of property (some say expectations) in Scotland; to some he is merely another of those confounded Scotch engineers; but to none is he a legend. They are not to know that in Fetter-Rothnie, where the tall, narrow, ugly house of Knapperley is situate, his name has already become a symbol.

You would need Garry Forbes to you. It is the local way of telling your man he is a liar. And when they deride you, scoffing at your lack of common sense, *Hine up on the head of the house like Garry Forbes and his twa fools*, is the accepted phrase. As the ladies at the Weatherhouse said, A byword and a laughing stock to the place. And married into the family, too!

ONE

To the Lorimers of a younger generation, children of the three Lorimer brothers who had played in the walled manse garden with the three Craigmyle girls, the Weatherhouse

I

was a place of pleasant dalliance. It meant day-long summer visits, toilsome uphill July walks that ended in the cool peace of the Weatherhouse parlour, with home-brewed ginger beer for refreshment, girdle scones and strawberry jam and butter biscuits, and old Aunt Leeb seated in her corner with her spider-fine white lace cap, piercing eyes and curious staves of song; then the eager rush for the open, the bickering around the old sundial, the race for the moor; and a sense of endless daylight, of enormous space, of a world lifted up beyond the concerns of common time; and eggs for tea, in polished wooden egg-cups that were right end up either way; and queer fascinating things such as one saw in no other house—the kettle holder with the black cross-stitch kettle worked upon it, framed samplers on the walls, the goffering iron, the spinning wheel. And sometimes Paradise would show them how the goffering iron was worked.

Paradise, indeed, gave a flavouring to a Weatherhouse day that none of the other ladies could offer. Round her clung still the recollection of older, rarer visits, when they were smaller and she not yet a cripple; of the splendid abounding wonder that inhabits a farm. Not a Lorimer but associated the thought of Paradise with chickens newly broken from the shell, ducks worrying with their flat bills in the grass; with dark, half-known, sweet-smelling corners in the barn, and the yielding, sliding, scratching feel of hay; with the steep wooden stair to the stable-loft and the sound of the big, patient, clumsy horses moving and munching below, a rattle of harness, the sudden nosing of a dog; with the swish of milk in the pail and the sharp delightful terror as the great tufted tail swung and lashed; with the smell of oatcakes browning, the plod of the churn and its changing note of triumph, and the wide, shallow basins set with gleaming milk; with the whirr of the reaper, the half-comprehended excitement of harvest, the binding, the shining stooks; with the wild madness of the last uncut patch, the trapped and furtive things one watched in a delirium of joy and revulsion; and the comfort, afterwards, of gathering eggs, safe, smooth and warm against the palm.

Of that need for comfort Paradise herself had no comprehension. Rats, rabbits and weakly chicks were killed as a matter of course. There was no false sentiment about Miss Annie: nothing flimsy. She was hard-knit, like a home-made worsted stocking, substantial, honest and durable. 'A cauff bed tied in the middle,' her sister Theresa said rudely of her in her later years, when inactivity had turned her flabby; but at the farm one remembered her as being everywhere.

It was Andrew Lorimer, her cousin, who transformed her baptismal name of Annie Dyce to Paradise, and now his children and his brothers' children scarcely knew her by another. Not that Miss Annie cared! 'I'm as much of Paradise as you are like to see, my lad,' she used to tell him.

The four ladies at the Weatherhouse, old Aunt Craigmyle and her daughters, could epitomise the countryside among them in their stories. Paradise knew how things were done; she told of ancient customs, of fairs and cattle markets and all the processes of a life whose principle is in the fields. The tales of Aunt Craigmyle herself had a fiercer quality; all the old balladry, the romance of wild and unscrupulous deeds, fell from her thin and shapely lips. And if she did not tell a tale, she sang. She was always singing. Ballads were the natural food of her mind. John, the second of the three Lorimer brothers, said of her, when the old lady attained her ninetieth birthday, 'She'll live to be a hundred yet, and attribute it to singing nothing but ballads all her life.'

Cousin Theresa cared more for what the folk of her own day did—matter of little moment to the children. But she had, too, the grisly tales: of the body-snatchers at Drum and the rescue by the grimy blacksmith on his skelping mare; of Malcolm Gillespie, best-hated of excisemen, and the ill end he came by on the gallows, and of the whisky driven glumly past him in a hearse. To Cousin Ellen the children paid less heed; though they laughed (as she laughed herself) at her funny headlong habit of suggesting conclusions to every half-told tale she heard. Cousins Annie or Theresa would say, 'Oh, yes, of course Nell must know all about it!' and she would laugh with them and answer, 'Yes, there I am again.' But sometimes she would bite her lip and

look annoyed. It was she too, who said, out on the moor,
'Look, you can see Ben A'an today—that faint blue line,'
or talked queer talk about the Druid stones. But these were
horizons too distant for childish minds. It was pleasanter to
hear again the familiar story of how the Weatherhouse came
to be built.

Mrs Craigmyle at fifty four, widowed but unperturbed,
announced to her unmarried daughters that she was done
with the farm: Annie could keep it if she liked—which
Annie did. Theresa and her mother would live free. Theresa
was not ill-pleased, when it became apparent that she was
to be mistress of the new home. Theresa could never
understand her mother's idle humour. The grace of ir-
responsibility was beyond her. But Mrs Craigmyle, whose
straight high shoulders and legs of swinging length had
earned her the family by-name of Lang Leeb, had been a
wild limb, with her mind more on balladry than on butter;
and her father, the Reverend Andrew, was thankful when
he got her safely married into the douce Craigmyle clan.
She had made James Craigmyle an excellent wife; but at
fifty four was quite content to let the excellence follow the
wifehood.

'We'll go to town, I suppose,' said Theresa, who liked
company.

'Fient a town. We'll go to Andra Findlater's place.'

Annie and Theresa stared.

Andra Findlater was a distant cousin of their mother,
dead long since. A stonemason to trade, he had lived in
a two-roomed cottage on the edge of their own farmlands.
When his daughters were seven and eight years old, Mrs
Findlater decided that she wanted the ben-end kept clear of
their muck; and Andra had knocked a hole in the back wall
and built them a room for themselves: a delicious room,
low-roofed and with a window set slanting.

'But if I could big a bit mair—' Andra kept thinking.
Another but-and-ben stood back from theirs, its own length
away and just out of line with the new room—now what
could a man do with that were he to join them up? Be it
understood that Andra Findlater had no prospect of being
able to join them up; but the problem of how to make the

houses one absorbed him to his dying day. It helped, indeed, to bring about his death; for Andra would lean against a spruce tree for hours of an evening, smoking his pipe and considering the lie of the buildings. He leaned one raw March night till he caught cold; and died of pneumonia.

Lang Leeb, as mistress of the big square farmhouse, had always time for a *newse* with her poor relations. She relished Andra. Many an evening she dandered across the fields, in her black silk apron and with her *shank* in her hands, to listen to his brooding projects. She loved the site of the red-tiled cottages, set high, almost on the crest of the long ridge; she loved the slanting window of the built-out room. A month after her husband's death she dandered down the field one day and asked the occupant of the cottage to let her see the little room again. 'It's a gey soster,' said she. 'The cat's just kittled in't.' Lang Leeb went home and told her daughters she was henceforth to live at Andra Findlater's place; and her daughters stared.

But Leeb knew what she was doing. She took the cottages and joined them. Andra's problem was, after all, easy enough to solve. She had money: a useful adjunct to brains. She knocked out the partition of Andra's original home and made of it a long living-room with a glass door to the garden; and between the two cottages, with the girls' old bedroom for corridor, she built a quaint irregular hexagon, with an upper storey that contained one plain bedroom and one that was all corners and windows—an elfin inconsequential room, using up odd scraps of space.

The whole was roofed with mellowed tiles. None of your crude new colourings for Leeb. She went up and down the country till she had collected all she required, from barns and byres and outhouses. Leeb knew how to obtain what she wanted. She came back possessed of three or four quern stones, a cruisie lamp and a tirl-the-pin; and from the farm she brought the spinning wheel and the old wooden dresser and plate racks.

The place grew quaint and rare both out of doors and in. One morning Leeb contemplated the low vestibule that had been a bedroom, humming the gay little verse it often brought to her mind:

> The grey cat's kittled in Charley's wig,
> There's ane o' them livin' an' twa o' them deid.

'Now this should be part of the living-room,' said she. 'It's dark and awkward as a passage. We'll have it so—and so.'

She knew exactly what she wanted done, and gave her orders; but the workman sent to her reported back some three hours later with instructions not to return.

'But what have you against the man?' his master asked.

'I've nothing against him, forbye that he's blind, and he canna see.'

She refused another man; but one day she called Jeames Ferguson in from the garden. Jeames was a wonder with his hands. He had set up the sundial, laid the crazy paving, and constructed stone stalks to the querns, some curved, some tapering, some squat, that made them look like monstrous mushrooms. 'Could you do *that*, Jeames?' 'Fine that.' Jeames did it, and was promptly dismissed to the garden, for his clumps of boots were ill-placed in the house. Mrs Craigmyle did the finishing herself and rearranged her curious possessions. Some weeks later Jeames, receiving orders beside the glass door, suddenly observed, 'I hinna seen't sin' it was finished,' and strode on to the Persian rug with his *dubbit* and tacketty boots. But no Persian rug did Jeames see. Folding his arms, he beamed all over his honest face and contemplated his own handiwork.

'That's a fine bit o' work, ay is it,' he said at last.

'You couldn't be angered at the body. He was that fine pleased with himself,' said Mrs Craigmyle.

But the house once to her mind, Mrs Craigmyle did no more work. Dismissing her husband in a phrase, 'He was a moral man—I can say no more,' she sat down with a careless ease in the Weatherhouse and gathered her chapbooks and broadsheets around her:

> Songs, Bibles, Psalm-books and the like,
> As mony as would big a dyke—

though, to be sure, daughter of the manse as she was, the Bible had scanty place in her heap of books. *Whistle Binkie* was her Shorter Catechism. She gave all her household dignity for an old song: sometimes her honour and kindliness as well; for Leeb treated the life around her as though it were already ballad. She relished it, but having ceased herself to feel, seemed to have forgotten that others felt. She grew hardly visibly older, retaining to old age her erect carriage and the colour and texture of her skin. Her face was without blemish, her hands were delicate; only the long legs, as Kate Falconer could have told, were brown with fern-tickles. Kate had watched so often, with a child's fascinated stare, her grandmother washing her feet in a tin basin on the kitchen floor. Kate grew up believing that her grandmother ran barefoot among tall bracken when she was young; and probably Kate was right.

So Lang Leeb detached herself from active living. Once a year she made an expedition to town, and visited in turn the homes of her three Lorimer nephews. She carried on these occasions a huge pot of jam, which she called 'the berries'; and having ladled out the Andrew Lorimers' portion with a wooden spoon, replaced the pot in her basket and bore it to the Roberts and the Johns. For the rest, she sat aside and chuckled. Life is an entertainment hard to beat when one's affections are not engaged. Theresa managed the house and throve on it, having found too little scope at the farm for her masterful temper. Her mother let her be, treating even her craze for acquisition with an ironic indulgence. Already with the things they had brought from the farm the house was full. But Theresa never missed a chance to add to her possessions. She had a passion for roups. 'A ga'in foot's aye gettin',' she said.

'She's like Robbie Welsh the hangman,' Lang Leeb would chuckle, 'must have a fish out of ilka creel.' And when Mrs Hunter told Jonathan Bannochie the souter, a noted hater of women, that Miss Theresa was at the Wastride roup, 'and up and awa wi' her oxter full o' stuff,' she was said to have added, 'They would need a displenish themsels in yon hoose, let alane bringin' mair in by.' 'Displenish,' snorted Jonathan. 'Displenish, said ye? It's a roup o' the fowk that's needed there.'

Miss Annie too, when she gave up the farm brought part of her plenishing. Ellen was the only one who brought nothing to the household gear. Ellen brought nothing but her child; and there was nowhere to put her but the daft room at the head of the stairs that Theresa had been using for lumber.

'It's a mad-like place,' Theresa said. 'Nothing but a trap for dust. But you won't take a Finnan haddie in a Hielan' burnie. She's no way to come but this, and she'll just need to be doing with it. She's swallowed the cow and needn't choke at the tail.'

Ellen did not choke. She loved the many-cornered room with its irregular windows. There she shut herself in as to a tower and was safe; or rather, she felt, shut herself out from the rest of the house. The room seemed not to end with itself, but through its protruding windows became part of the infinite world. There she lay and watched the stars; saw dawn touch the mountains; and fortified her soul in the darkness that had come on her.

TWO

Of the three Craigmyle sisters, Ellen was the likest to her mother. She too was long and lean, though she had not her mother's delicacy of fingers and of skin; and to Ellen alone among her daughters Mrs Craigmyle had bequeathed the wild Lorimer heart.

How wild it was not even the girl herself had discovered, when at twenty seven she married Charley Falconer. There was no opposition to the match, though Falconer was a stranger; well-doing apparently; quiet and assured: which the family took to mean reliable, and Ellen, profound. Her life had hitherto been hard and rigid; her father, James Craigmyle, kept his whole household to the plough; not from any love of tyranny, but because he had never conceived of a life other than strait and laborious. To work in sweat was man's natural heritage. His wife obeyed him and bided her time; Ellen obeyed, and escaped in thought to a fantastic world of her own imagining. The merest hint of a tale sufficed her, her fancy was off. Her choicest hours were spent in unreality—a land where others act in accordance with one's expectations. Sometimes her toppling palaces would crash at the touch of the actual, and then she suffered an agony of remorse because the real Ellen was so unlike the Ellen of her fancies. 'There I am again—I mustn't pretend these silly things,' she would say; and taking her Bible she would read the verse that she had marked for her own especial scourging: 'Casting down imaginations and every high thing that exalteth itself against the knowledge of God, and bringing into captivity every thought to the obedience of Christ.' For a day or two she would sternly dismiss each fleeting suggestion of fiction, striving to empty a mind that was naturally quick and receptive, and finding the plain sobriety of a Craigmyle regimen inadequate to fill it. Shortly she was 'telling herself stories' again. It might be wicked, but it made life radiant.

Concerning Charley Falconer she told herself an endless story. The tragedy of her brief married life lay in the clash between her story and the truth. Charley was very ordinary and a little cheap. He dragged her miserably from one lodging to another, unstable, but with a certain large indifference to his own interests that exposed his memory to Craigmyle and Lorimer contempt, when at his death Ellen could no longer deny how poor she was.

She came back to her mother's house, dependent, the more so that she had a child; at bitter variance with herself. She had been forced up against a grinding poverty, a shallow nature and a life without dignity. By the time she returned home her father was dead, the Weatherhouse built and Theresa comfortably settled as its genius. Ellen found herself tolerated. Power was too sweet to this youngest sister who had had none: the widowed and deprived was put in her place. Since that place was the odd-shaped upstairs room, Ellen did not grumble; but Theresa's management made it perhaps a trifle harder for her to come to terms with the world. Her own subordinate position in the house was subtly a temptation: it sent her back to refuge in her imaginings. After a time the rancour and indignity of her married years faded out. She thought she was experienced in life, but in truth she had assimilated nothing from her suffering, only dismissed it and returned to her dreams.

Two things above all restored her—her child and the country. It was a country that liberated. More than half the world was sky. The coastline vanished at one of the four corners of the earth, Ellen lost herself in its immensity. It wiled her from thought.

Kate also took her from herself. She was not a clever child, neither quaint nor original nor *ill-trickit*; but never out of humour. She asked nothing much from life—too easily satisfied, her mother thought, without what she could not have. Ellen, arguing from her own history, had schooled herself to meet the girl's inevitable revolt, her demand for her own way of living. But Kate at thirty had not yet revolted. She had wanted nothing that was not to her hand. She had no ambition after a career, higher education did not interest her, she questioned neither life nor her own right to relish it. Had she not been brought up among Craigmyles, their quiet domesticity was what she would have fancied. She liked making a bed and contriving a dinner; and since she must earn her living she took a Diploma in Domestic Science and had held several posts as housekeeper or school matron; but late in 1917 she entered (to the regret of some of her relations) upon voluntary work in a Hospital, becoming cook in a convalescent Hospital not far from her home.

Ellen had therefore carried for nearly thirty years the conviction that she had tested life; and mastered it.

At sixty she was curiously young. Her body was strong and supple, her face tanned, a warm glow beneath the tan. She walked much alone upon the moors, walking heel first to the ground with a firm and elastic tread. Her eyes were young; by cause both of their brightness and of their dreaming look. No experience was in their glance. She knew remote and unspeakable things—the passage of winds, the trembling of the morning star, the ecstasy of February nights when all the streams are murmuring. She did not know human pain and danger. She thought she did, but the pain she knew was only her own quivering hurt. Her world was all her own, she its centre and interpretation; and she had even a faint sweet contempt for those who could not enter it. The world and its modes passed by and she ignored them. She was a little proud of her indifference to fashion and chid her sister Theresa for liking a modish gown. She saw—as who could have helped seeing—the external changes that marked life during the thirty years she had lived in the Weatherhouse: motor cars, the shortening skirt, the vacuum cleaner; but of the profounder revolutions, the change in temper of a generation, the altered point of balance of the world's knowledge, the press of passions other than individual and domestic, she was completely unaware.

Insensibly as these thirty years passed she allowed her old fashion to grow on her. Fancy was her tower of refuge. Like any green girl she pictured her futures by the score. After a time she took the habit of her imaginary worlds so strongly that hints of their presence dropped out in her talk, and when she was laughed at she would laugh or be offended according to the vehemence with which she had created; but among the gentle scoffers none guessed the ravishment her creations brought her, and none the mortified despair of her occasional revulsions from her fairyland.

It did not occur to her that when Lindsay Lorimer came to Fetter-Rothnie her fairyland would vanish into smoke.

Lindsay came to stay at the Weatherhouse on this wise: her mother, Mrs Andrew Lorimer, arrived one day in perturbation.

'We don't know what to do with Lindsay,' she confessed. 'If you would let her come here for a little—? We thought perhaps the change—and away from the others. These boys do tease her so. They can't see that she's ill.'

'She's ill, is she?' said Theresa. 'And what ails her, then?'

Mrs Andrew took some time to make it clear that Lindsay's sickness was of the temper.

'Not that we have anything against him,' she said. 'He's an excellent young man—most gentlemanly. When he likes. But she's so young. Nineteen. Her father won't hear of it. "All nonsense too young," he says. But I suppose she keeps thinking, well, and if he doesn't come back. It's this war that does it.'

'It's time it were put a stop to,' said Miss Annie.

'Yes,' sighed Mrs Andrew. 'And let things be as they were.'

'But they won't be, said Ellen.

'No,' she answered. 'Frank'll never go to college now. He swears he won't go to the University and won't. And it's all this Captain Dalgarno. It's Dalgarno this and Dalgarno that. Frank's under him, you know. I wonder what the Captain means by it. He's contaminating Frank. Putting ideas into his head. He was only a schoolboy when it began, you must remember—hadn't had time to have his mind formed. And now he swears he won't go to the University and won't enter a profession. All my family have been in the professions.'

She sighed again.

'He wants to *do* things, he says. Things with his hands. Make things. "Good heavens, mother," he said to me, just his last leave—the Captain was home with him on his last leave, you know; it was then that Lindsay and he wanted to get married, and her father just wouldn't have it. "Good heavens mother, we've *un*-made enough, surely, in these three and a half years. I want to make something now. *You* haven't seen the ruined villages. The world will get on very well without the law and the Church for a considerable time to come," he said, "but it's going to be jolly much in need of engineers and carpenters." Make chairs and tables, that seems to be his idea. "Even if I could make one table to stand fast on its feet, I'd be happy. I won't belong to a privileged class," he said. "There aren't privileges. There's only the privilege of working." It *sounds* all right, of course, and I'm sure we all feel for the working man. But if Lindsay marries him I don't know what we shall all come to.'

Mrs Craigmyle, attentive in the corner, began to hum. No one of course heeded her. She sang a stave through any business that was afoot. She sang now, the hum developing to words:

Wash weel the fresh fish, wash weel the fresh fish,
Wash weel the fresh fish and skim weel the bree,
For there's mony a foul-fittit thing,
There's mony a foul-fittit thing in the saut sea.

And Ellen's anger suddenly flared. A natural song enough for one whose home looked down on the coast villages of Finnan and Portlendie; but it was Ellen the dreamer, not the sagacious Annie or Theresa, who had read in her mother that the old lady's was an intelligent indifference to life. She took no sides, an ironic commentator. Two and thirty years of Craigmyle wedlock had tamed her natural wildness of action to an impudence of thought that relished its own dainty morsels by itself. Her cruelties came from comprehension, not from lack of it. And had not Mrs Andrew said the word? 'Contaminating,' she had said. Ellen did well to be angry. She was angry on behalf of this young girl the secret of whose love was bandied thus among contemptuous women.

'But I know, I know, I understand,' she thought. 'I must help her, be her friend.' Already her fancy was off. She had climbed her tower and saw herself in radiant light, creating Lindsay's destiny.

She looked from under bent brows at her mother, who continued to sing, with a remote and airy grace, her long fine fingers folded in her lap. She sat very erect and looked at no one, lost apparently in her song. Ellen relaxed her frown, but remained gazing at the singer, falling unconsciously into the same attitude as her mother, and the singular resemblance between the two faces became apparent, both intent, both strangely innocent, the old lady's by reason of its much withdrawn, Ellen's from the enthusiasm of solitary dreaming that hedged her about from reality.

The Drama

ONE

Proposal for a Party

Miss Theresa Craigmyle opened the kitchen door in response to the knock, and saw Francie Ferguson holding a bag of potatoes in his arms.

'Ay, ay, Francie,' she said, 'you've brought the tatties. Who would have thought, now, there would be such a frost and us not to have a tattie out of the pit? It was a mercy you had some up.'

'O ay,' said Francie, 'and the frost's haudin'. There's the smell o' snaw in the air. It'll be dingin' on afore ye ken yersel.'

Miss Theresa took the potatoes, saying cheerily, 'And a fine big bag you've given us, Francie. But you were aye the one for a bittie by the bargain.'

Francie shuffled to the other foot and rubbed a hand upon his thigh.

'Well, ye like to be honest, but ye canna be ower honest or ye'd hae naething to yersel.' He added, spreading a dirty paw against the door-jamb, 'The missus is to her bed.'

'Oh,' said Miss Theresa. She said it tartly. The bag poised in her arms, she was judicially considering its weight. 'Not so heavy, after all,' she thought. Francie's way had formerly been, 'I just put in a puckle by guess like.' He hadn't been long at the school, he said, wasn't used with your weights and measures. But his lavishness, Miss Theresa could see, was receiving a check: beyond a doubt the work of the *missus*. Miss Theresa was not disposed to sympathy. 'She's a din-raising baggage,' she reflected, and heard Francie out with a face as set as the frost.

Francie was grumbling heartily at life. He knew fine that the potatoes were scanty measure. He did not confess it, of course, but since Miss Theresa was sure to discover,

17

he detailed the mitigating circumstances: a sick wife, a cow gone dry, forty barren besoms of hens and a daughter soft-hearted to the point of letting all the rabbits off the snares—ay, and giving them a bit of her *piece*, no less, any one that looked pitiful at her. Francie had remonstrated, of course, but might as well speak to the wind blowing by. 'A gey-like swippert o' a queyne, she is that,' he said, not without a certain conscious pride. And meat-whole, he added, 'They're a' that—the wife as weel.'

'She would be,' said Miss Theresa. 'She's about stotting off the ground with fat. And what is't that ails her, like?'

Francie laboured to explain.

'Oh, a stoun' of love,' said Miss Theresa shortly. 'It'll have come out at the wrong place. Wait you.' And laying down the potatoes, she brought a good-sized pudding from the pantry and thrust it on Francie.

'You can't take that before the court and swear to it that you're hungered,' she said, and shut the door on him.

In the parlour she repeated the conversation.

'He does all the cooking himself, he tells me. I wouldn't be any curious about eating it. He stewed a rabbit. "It was gey tough," he says, "it gart your jaws wonder." '

'Fancy the little girl and the rabbits,' cried Lindsay. 'That's the child we saw yesterday, isn't it, Katie? With the coal-black eyes. She looked a mischief! She's not like her father, anyway. You'd never suppose she was his daughter.'

'You never would, for the easy reason that she's not.'

'I'm glad to see he calls her his daughter, it's kindly of the body.'

'What other could he do? You can't give a gift a clyte in the mouth, and the bairns were her marriage gift to the craitur, as you might say.'

'They looked so neglected, these children,' cried Lindsay. 'And with their mother ill. Couldn't we give them a party? They can't have had much of a Christmas.'

'Oh, party away at them,' conceded Theresa. 'Would you really like it, Lindsay?'

Lindsay was aglow with eagerness. 'And a Christmas tree?' she said. 'Oh, I know it's January now, but I don't believe they've ever seen a tree. One of those big spruce branches would do.' She was given over entirely to her excitement. A mere child, thought Theresa. Well, and here was a change of countenance from the earlier days. The affair could not mean much when she threw it off so easily. The pale and moody Lindsay who had gone wanly about the house on her arrival, displeased Miss Theresa, who disliked a piner. Like many robust people, she resented the presence of suffering; pain, physical or mental, was an inconvenience that she preferred not to see. A Lindsay absorbed in trifling with a Christmas tree was a relief Miss Theresa might well afford herself; and she afforded it with grace.

'Have you time, Kate,' she asked of her niece Kate Falconer, who was spending her hour of leave at home, 'to go round on your way back to the Hospital and bid them come?'

'Why, yes,' said Kate, 'if we start at once. You come too, Linny.'

'Go in by to Craggie,' pursued Miss Theresa, 'and bid Mrs Hunter too. We've been meaning to have her to tea this while back. She'll be grand pleased at the tree. She's like a bairn when you give her a thing.'

Kate went to make ready, and Lindsay would have followed; but as she passed, her grand-aunt detained her with a look. Mrs Craigmyle had few gestures; she held herself still; only her eyes glittered and her lips moved, and often her fingers went to and fro as she knitted—a spider stillness. The film of delicate lace upon hair as fine as itself was not the only thing about her that betokened the spider. One had the sense of being caught upon a look, lured in and held.

Lindsay drew up to her, and stood.

'So, so, you are to turn my house into a market, Leezie Lindsay?'

'Why do you call me that, Aunt Leeb?'

Lang Leeb sang from the old ballad.

'Surely you know,' she said, 'that Leezie Lindsay came to Kingcausie with that braw lad she ran away with, and it's not far from Kingcausie that you've come, Mistress Lindsay.'

The scarlet rushed on Lindsay's brow and stood in splatches over neck and chin.

She pushed back her mop of curls and stared at the old woman; and her words seemed to be drawn from her without her will.

'Kingcausie? That's—isn't that the place among trees, a line of beeches and then some scraggy firs? Beyond the Tower there.'

'Hoots! Never a bit. That's Knapperley. Daft Bawbie Paterson's place. Kingcausie lies to the river.'

The scarlet had deepened on Lindsay's throat. 'Have I given myself away?' she was thinking.

She had discovered what she had wanted to know since ever she came to Fetter-Rothnie. Often as she had visited the Weatherhouse, she had not stayed there, and its surroundings were unfamiliar. It had seemed so easy, in imagination, when she walked with Kate, to ask it in a careless way, 'Isn't that Knapperley over there, Katie?' or 'What place is that among the trees?' But when the moment came her heart had thumped too wildly; she was not strong enough to ask. Now that she knew she sheered off nervously from the subject, as though to linger were deadly. And she plunged, 'But why a market, Aunt Leeb? I'm sure we shan't be very rowdy.'

'A lot you know about the fisher folk, if that's your way of thinking. It was them that cracked the Marykirk bell, jingle-janglin' for a burying.'

'But they're not fisher folk here—Francie?'

'She is.'

And Lindsay, because she was afraid to hear further of the lady who had brought the black-eyed bairns as a wedding gift to her husband, glanced rapidly around, and saw Mrs Falconer put her head in at the door and look at them. There was something pathetic about Cousin Ellen, Lindsay thought—her straying gaze, her muttering to herself. A poor old thing. And what was she wanting now, watching them both like that?

A poor young thing, Ellen was thinking. She must protect her from her mother's sly and studied jests. So she said, 'Kate must be off, Linny,' and the girl fled gladly.

Francie was shouting a lusty song as he worked:

I'll never forget till the day that I dee
The lumps o' fat my granny gied me,
The heids o' herrin' an' tails o'cats—

He broke off abruptly and cried, 'Are ye cleanin' yersels, littlins? Here's ladies to see you.'

The children hove in sight, drying their half-washed hands on opposite ends of a towel. Bold-eyed youngsters, with an address unusual in country bairns. Each hurried to complete the drying first and so be saved from putting away the towel; and both dropping it at one moment, it fell in a heap. The children began to quarrel noisily.

'Put you it by, Stellicky,' said the man, who stood watching the bickering bairns for awhile with every appearance of content. Francie had a soft foolish kindly face, and while the girl, with black looks, did as she was bidden, he swung the loonie to his shoulder and said, 'He's a gey bit birkie, isna he, to be but five year auld?'

'And how's the wife?' said Kate.

Francie confided in her that whiles she took a tig, and he thought it was maybe no more than that.

'They were only married in August,' said Kate, laughing, as the girls followed a field path away from the croft.

'Oh, look,' cried Lindsay. 'A bramble leaf still. Blood-red.'

'So it is,' Kate replied. 'And engaged for over twenty years.'

'I don't particularly want to hear about it, Katie.'

'But why,' said Kate, 'it's an entertaining tale.'

And she began to relate it.

Francie was son to old Jeames Ferguson, who had helped to make the Weatherhouse; and Francie's taking of a wife had been a seven days' speak in Fetter-Rothnie. He had been betrothed for two and twenty years. All the countryside knew of the betrothal, but that it should end in marriage was a surprise for which the gossips were not prepared. A joke, too. A better joke, as it turned out, than they had anticipated.

The two and twenty years of waiting were due to Francie's brother Weelum. Weelum in boyhood had discovered an astounding aptitude for craftsmanship. He had been apprenticed to a painter in Peterkirk, and in course became a journeyman. From that day on Francie referred invariably to his brother as 'The Journeyman.' Weelum's name was never heard to cross his lips; he remained 'The Journeyman,' though he did not remain a painter.

Weelum's career as a journeyman was mute and inglorious. He was a taciturn man: he wasted no words; and when his master's clients gave orders about the detail of the work he undertook he would listen with an intent, intelligent expression, and reply with a grave and considering nod. Afterwards he did exactly what he pleased. Folk complained. Weelum continued to do what he pleased. In the end his master dismissed him; reluctantly, for he had clever hands.

He established himself with Francie. There was not work on the croft for two men; but as there was no woman on it, Weelum took possession of the domestic affairs. He did what he pleased there too, and made much to-do about his industry. Francie could not see that there was much result from it all. 'He's eident, but he doesna win through,' he would sometimes say sorrowfully. 'Feel Weelum,' the folk called him. 'Oh, nae sae feel,' said Jonathan Bannochie the souter. 'He kens gey weel whaur his pottage bickers best.' To Francie he was still 'The Journeyman.'

When Weelum came home to bide, Francie was already contracted to a lassie in the fishing village of Bargie, some twenty miles away, down the coast. A bonny bit lass, but her folk were terrible tinks; they had the name of being the worst tinks in Bargie. Weelum had some family pride, if Francie had none, and there were bitter words between the brothers. The Journeyman set his face implacably against the marriage, and stood aggrieved and silent when Francie tried to thresh the matter out. 'He has ower good a downsit, and he kens it,' said the folk. Francie's respect for his brother was profound. On the Sunday afternoons when he cycled across to Bargie, he would slink out in silence by the back way from his own house. One Sunday the brothers came to high words. Francie mounted his cycle,

and trusted—as he always did trust—that all would be well
on his return. That Weelum did not speak on his return
gave him no anxiety: Weelum often *stunkit* at him and
kept silence for days. But this time Weelum kept silence
for ever. He never again addressed a word to his brother,
though he remained under his roof, eating of his bread,
for over twenty years. Through all that time the brothers
slept in the same bed, rising each in the morning to his
separate tasks.

One afternoon the Journeyman fell over with a stroke.
That was an end to the hope of his speaking. 'I some think
he would have liked to say something,' Francie declared.
He climbed in beside his brother to the one bed the room
contained, and wakened in the hour before dawn *geal cauld*
to find the Journeyman dead beside him.

Some months later Francie was cried in the kirk. A
burr of excitement ran through the congregation. So the
Bargie woman had waited for him! When the day of the
wedding came, Francie set out in the early morning, with
the old mare harnessed to the farm cart.

'Take her on the hin step o' yer bike, Francie, man,' cried
one of the bystanders. 'That would be mair gallivantin' like
than the cairt.'

'There's her bits o' things to fesh,' Francie answered.

'She'll hae some chairs an' thingies,' said the neighbours. 'The hoosie'll nae be oot o' the need o' them. It's
terrible bare.'

Francie had not dreamed of a reception; but when, late
in the evening, the bridal journey ended and the cart turned
soberly up the cart-road to the croft, he found a crowd about
his doors.

Francie bartered words with no man. He handed out
his bride, and after her one bairn, and then another; and
then a bundle tied up in a Turkey counterpane. The bride
and the bairns went in, and Francie shut the door on them;
and turned back to tend his mare.

'She'll hae been a weeda, Francie?' said Jonathan Bannochie. A titter ran round the company.

Francie unharnessed the mare.

'Weel, nae exactly a weeda,' he said in his slow way;

and led the mare to stable.

Next morning he harnessed her again and jogged in
the old cart to town. All Fetter-Rothnie watched him come
home with a brand-new iron bedstead in the cart. 'For the
bairns,' they said. 'He might have made less do with them.'
But the bed was not for the bairns.

'Aunt Tris was the first of us to see her,' Kate told
Lindsay. 'She invented an errand over. Aunt Tris would
invent an errand to the deil himself, Granny says, if she
wanted something from him. She came home and sat down
and took off all her outdoor things before she would say
a word. And then she said, "He was fond of fish before
he fried the scrubber." She told us about the bed. "She
won't even sleep with him," she told us. "Him and the
laddie sleeps in the kitchen, and her and the lassie's got
the room. It's six and sax, I'm thinking, for Francie, between the Journeyman and the wife." And she told us the
bairns' names.'

The bairns' names were a diversion to Fetter-Rothnie.
In a community that had hardly a dozen names amongst its
folk, Francie's betrothed had been known as Peter's Sandy's
Bell; but she was determined that her children should have
individual names, and called the girl Stella Dagmar and the
boy Sidney Archibald Eric. Bargie treated the names after
its fashion. The children became Stellicky Dagmaricky and
Peter's Sandy's Bellie's Sid.

'Granny sat and listened to Aunt Tris,' Kate continued.
'Licked her lips over it. Granny loves a tale. Particularly
with a wicked streak. "A spectacle," she said, "a second
Katherine Bran." Katherine Bran was somebody in a tale,
I believe. And then she said, "You have your theatres and
your picture palaces, you folk. You make a grand mistake."
And she told us there was no spectacle like what's at our
own doors. "Set her in the jougs and up on the faulters' stool
with her, for fourteen Sabbaths, as they did with Katherine,
and where's your picture palace then?" A *merry prank*, she
called it. Well!— "The faulter's stool and a penny bridal,"
she said, "and you've spectacle to last you, I'se warren."
Granny's very amusing when she begins with old tales.'

Lindsay's attention was flagging. 'Besides,' she thought,

'I don't like old tales. Nor this new one either.' They had come out of the wood on to a crossroad and the country was open for miles ahead.

'And that's Knapperley, is it, Katie?' she asked.

'Yes,' said Kate. 'But we don't go near it to get to Mrs Hunter's.'

TWO

The January Christmas Tree

Snow fell that night, and the night following, and the frost set harder than before. The guests were stamping at the doorstep, knocking off the snow that had frozen in translucent domes upon their heels, shaking their garments free from the glittering particles of ice that hung in them. The children eyed the house with awe, mingled in Stella Dagmar with disdain. 'It's a terrible slippery floor, I canna get traivelled,' she objected in the long, polished lobby. But the glories of the Christmas tree silenced criticism for awhile. Lindsay had made a very pretty thing of it; and when by and by she slipped from the room and Miss Theresa said ostentatiously, 'She's away to take a rest—she's been ill, you see,' the girl herself was as deliciously excited as any bairn. She giggled with pleasure as she draped an old crimson curtain round her and adjusted her Father Christmas beard. 'Now what all nonsense shall I say?' And she said it very well, disguising her voice and playing silly antics.

'My very toes is laughin',' Mrs Hunter declared.

The room grew hot, and Lindsay in her wrappings choked for air. She slid her hand behind the curtain that covered the glass door to the garden. But the door blew open at her touch. The wind and a woman entered together: a woman in the fifties, weathered and sinewy, clad in a rough, patched Lovat tweed and leggings caked with mud and battered snow. On her head sat a piece of curious finery that had been once a hat and from it dangled a trallop of dingy veiling.

'Bawbie Paterson,' cried Miss Theresa. 'Who would have expected that?'

Miss Paterson marched across the room.

26

'It's you I'm seekin', Barbara Hunter,' she announced. 'Will you send for Maggie? There's my lassie up and left me. The third one running. Will you send for Maggie? Maggie's the lass for me.'

'Barbara Paterson,' said Mrs Hunter, 'that I will not. Maggie's in a good place. I'd be black affronted to bid her up and awa'. And mair than that, Miss Barbara, nae lass o' mine'll ever be at your beck and ca'. Ye dinna feed your folk, Miss Barbara. I've seen my chickens hanging in to the bare wa's o' a cabbage as though they hadna seen meat this month an' mair, and your kitchen deemie, Barbara Paterson, had the same hungry e'e. Ye'll nae get Maggie.'

'And what am I to do wanting a kitchen lass?'

'Ye can tak the road an' run bits, Miss Barbara.'

'Since you are in my house, Bawbie Paterson,' said Miss Theresa, 'you'd better take a seat.'

'I'll not do that, Tris Craigmyle. You'd have me plotted with heat, would you? But I'll wait a whilie or I go in a lowe. And who might this be?' And she wheeled round to stare at Lindsay, who had dropped the curtain and was staring hard at her.

'A likely lass,' said Miss Barbara; and she clutched at Lindsay, who did not resist, but allowed herself to be drawn closer. 'And are you seeking a place? Can you cook a tattie? A' to dross?'

'Hoots, Miss Barbara,' cried Mrs Hunter, scandalised. 'That's nae a servant lass. That's Miss Lorimer—Andrew Lorimer the solicitor's daughter. Ye're nae at yersel.'

Lindsay's heart was beating fast. She said nothing, but stared at the great rough face above her. She had a feeling as though some huge elemental mass were towering over her, rock and earth, earthen smelling. Miss Barbara's tweeds had been sodden so long with the rains and matted with the dusts of her land, that they too seemed element-al. Her face was tufted with coarse black hairs, her naked hands that clutched the fabric of Lindsay's dress were hard, ingrained with black from wet wood and earth. 'She's not like a person, she's a thing,' Lindsay thought. The girl felt puny in her grasp, yet quite without fear, possessed instead by a strange exhilaration.

Held thus against Miss Barbara's person and clothes, the outdoor smell of which came strongly to the heat of the parlour, Lindsay, her senses sharpened by excitement, was keenly aware of an antagonism in the room: as though the fine self-respecting solidity of generations of Lorimers and Craigmyles, the measured and orderly dignity of their lives, won at some cost through centuries from their rude surroundings, resented this intrusion into their midst of an undisciplined and primitive force. The girl waited to hear what Miss Theresa would say, sure that it was Miss Theresa who would act spokesman against this earthy relic of an older age.

But before Miss Theresa could speak, Stella Dagmar, angry at her interrupted play and offended that no one noticed her, began a counting rhyme, running about among the women and slapping each in turn:

> I count you out
> For a dirty dish-clout.

Miss Theresa's wiry hands were on the culprit. 'A clout on the lug, that's what you would need. Francie hasn't his sorrow to seek.'

Stella dodged and screamed. The whole room was in an uproar. And suddenly Miss Barbara, loosening her grasp on Lindsay, broke into a bellow of laughter; and in a moment was gone.

Miss Theresa was scarlet in the face from fury.

'Saw you ever such an affront to put on a body?' she cried, cudgelling Stella to the rhythms of her anger. 'Coming into a body's house at a New Year time a sight like yon. Coming in at all, and her not bidden. And I'm sure you needn't all be making such a commotion now. You couldn't tell what's what nor wha's Jock's father.'

They were all talking together. Lindsay stood amazed. The voices became appallingly distinct, resounding in her very head; and the hot, lit room, the excited ladies in their rich apparel, burdened her. She wanted to run after Miss Barbara, to escape; and, picking up her crimson curtain, she said, 'I'll put this past.'

'I kent it was you all the time,' Stella flung at her. But Lindsay was already gone. She closed the door from the parlour and stood in the cold, still hall. Through the windows poured the light of full moon. And Lindsay had a vision of the white light flooding the world and gleaming on the snow, and of Miss Barbara convulsed with laughter in the middle of the gleam.

She threw the curtain about her, drew on a pair of galoshes, and ran into the night.

The night astonished her, so huge it was. She had the sense of escaping from the lit room into light itself. Light was everywhere: it gleamed from the whole surface of the earth, the moon poured it to the farthest quarters of heaven, round a third of the horizon the sea shimmered. The cold was intense. Lindsay's breath came quick and gasping. She ran through the spruce plantation and toiled up the field over snow that was matted in grass; and, reaching the crest, saw without interruption to the rims of the world. The matted snow and grass were solid enough beneath her feet, but when she looked beyond she felt that she must topple over into that reverberation of light. Her identity vanished. She was lost in light and space. When she moved on it surprised her that she stumbled with the rough going. She ought to have glided like light over an earth so insubstantial.

Then she saw Miss Barbara.

Miss Barbara Paterson came swinging up the field, treading surely and singing to herself. Her heavy bulk seemed to sail along the frozen surfaces, and when she reached the dyke she vaulted across it with an impatient snort.

'O wait for me!' Lindsay cried. She too was by the dyke, and would have leaped it, but was trammelled with her curtain.

'Wait for me,' she cried. 'I want to speak to you.'

But when Miss Barbara turned back, there was nothing she could find to say.

'Were you wanting over?' asked Miss Barbara. She leaned across the dyke, lifted the girl in her arms and swung her in the air. 'You're like the deil, you'll never hang, for you're as light 's a feather.'

'Oh, put me down. But I want to go with you. Will you show me Knapperley?'

'Ca' awa' then.' Miss Barbara, without further ado, made off up the top of a furrow, pushing the girl firmly along by the elbow. Lindsay kept her footing with difficulty, sinking ever and again in the deep snow that levelled the furrows. She wondered what her mother would think. It was like an escapade into space. Her safe and habitual life was leagues away.

Miss Barbara made no attempt to speak. They passed through a woodland and came out by a gap.

'There's Knapperley for you,' its owner said.

Lindsay stared. From every window of the tall narrow house there blazed a lamp. They blazed into the splendour of the night like a spurt of defiance.

'But the Zepps,' she gasped.

'They don't come this length.'

'But they do. One did. And anyway, the law.'

'That's to learn them to leave honest folks alone.'

A spasm of terror contracted Lindsay's heart. Miss Barbara had clambered on to the next dyke. She made little use of stile or gate, preferring always to go straight in the direction she desired. She stood there poised, keeping her footing with ease upon the icy stones, and pointed with an outstretched arm at the lights, a menacing figure. Then she bent as though to help Lindsay over.

'Will she lift me again?' thought the girl. The insecurity of her adventure rushed upon her.

'Will she kidnap me and make me her servant girl? But I couldn't live in a house with lights like that. There would be policemen if there weren't Zepps.'

She twisted herself out of reach of the descending hand and fled, trailing the scarlet curtain after her across the snow.

THREE

Knapperley

Meanwhile in the Weatherhouse parlour Mrs Hunter was discussing Miss Barbara.

'If she wasna Miss Barbara Paterson of Knapperley she would mak you roar. You would be handin' her a copper and speirin' if she wanted a piece.'

'O ay, she's fairly a Tinkler Tam,' said Miss Theresa. 'Coming into a body's house with that old tweed. But she hasn't any other, that's what it is.'

'That's where you're mistaken, Miss Craigmyle. She's gowns galore: silk gowns and satin gowns and ane with a velvet lappet. Kists stappit fu'. But whan does she wear them? That's the tickler. It's aye the auld Lovat tweed. And aye the black trallop hangin' down her back.'

'It's her only hat, that I can wager.'

'It or its marra. Wha would say? She bought it for a saxpence from a wifie at the door and trimmed it hersel' with yon wallopin' trash. "If you would do that to your hat, Barbara Hunter, it would be grander." "God forbid, Barbara Paterson, that I should ever wear a hat like that." But she's aye worn it sin' syne. Some says it's the same hat, and some says it's its marra and the auld ane gaes up the lum on a Sabbath night whan there's none to see.'

Mrs Hunter talked with enjoyment. She was entirely devoted to the spanking mare on whose land she and her husband held their croft, and entirely without compunction in her ridicule of Miss Barbara's departures from the normal. She liked to talk too—gamesome cordial talk when her hard day's work was over; and the Craigmyle ladies, with their natural good-heartedness, allowed her to talk on.

'Auld Knapperley gave her an umbrella and her just the littlin, and she must bring it to the Sabbath school as prood's pussy. "What'll I do with my umbrella?"—hidin' it in ahin her gown—"it's rainin'." "Put up your umbrella, Barbara." "I won't put it up, Barbara. I won't have it blaudit, and it new." And aye she happit it in the pink gown. Me and her was ages and both Barbara Paterson then, and she took a terrible notion o' me. If I had a blue peenie she must have a blue peenie as well. And syne I was servant lassie at Knapperley for a lot of years. I couldna but bide, her that fond of me and all.'

'But you won't let Maggie go, Mrs Hunter?'

'I will not that. She was queer enough whan the auld man was livin', and she's a sight queerer now. I was there whan he dee'd and whan Mrs Paterson dee'd an' a'. Ay, I mind fine, poor body, her thinkin' she would get him to mak her laddie laird o' the placie and nae Miss Barbara. She liked her laddie a sight mair than ever she liked her lassie. But she married Donnie Forbes for love and Knapperley for a downsit. And she thought, poor soul, that she had nae mair a-do than bid him say the word and Knapperley would be her laddie's. But she aye put off the speirin'. And syne whan she kent she wouldna rise again, she bids Knapperie in to her bedside. "What's that you're sayin'?" says he. "Say't again, for I'm surely nae hearin'." So she says it again. "And him a Forbes," she says, "a family of great antiquity." "O ay, like the shore porters o' Aberdeen, that discharged the cargo from Noah's Ark." "You're mockin' me," she says. "I'll grant you this," he says, "there was never a murder in this parish or the next but there was a Forbes in it. There was Forbes of Portlendie and Forbes of Bannochie, and a Forbes over at Cairns that flung his lassie's corp ahin a dyke. But there's been nae murder done at Knapperley and nae Forbes at Knapperley—" "But there wasna aye a Paterson at Knapperley, and some that kens," she says, meanin'-like, "says the first that ocht the place didna rightly owe the name." "It's a scant kin," he says, "that has neither thief nor bastard in it, and for my part I'd rather have the bastard than the thief. The lassie'll mak as good a laird as the laddie. The place is hers, and you needna set any landless lads on thievin' here. I'll keep my ain fish-guts for my ain sea-maws." She didna daur say mair, but aye

whan he gaed by her door there cam the t'ither great sigh.
"You can just sigh awa' there," he would say. And whiles
he said, "Jamie Fleeman *kent* he was the Laird o' Udny's
feel." Well, well, he was a Tartar, auld Knapperie. But
he's awa' whaur he'll have to tak a back seat. He dee'd
in an awfu' hurry.'

'And Mr Benjamin has never come back since.'

'O ay. O fie ay. He cam' back. But just the once.
"This is a great disappointment to me, Barbara. Bawbie's
getting near. You see the weather it is, and you could
hold all the fire in the lee of your hand. There's the
two of us, one on either side, and greatcoats on to keep
us warm. And nothing but a scrap end of candle to light
you to your bed." "You may thank your stars, Mr Benjamin, she didna stand and crack spunks or you were
in ower." So he never cam again. But he let his laddie come.'

'She'll be making him her heir,' said Miss Annie.

'I wouldna wonder. They're chief, Miss Barbara and
Mr Garry.'

'A halarackit lump,' Theresa said.

'O, a gey rough loon. Mair like auld Knapperie's son
than Mr Benjamin's. But a terrible fine laddie. Me and Mr
Garry's great billies. "Will you dance at my wedding, Mrs
Hunter? I'll give you a new pair of shoes." "I will do that,
laddie. But wha is the bonny birdie?" '

'Yes, who?' thought Mrs Falconer. She made a running
excursion into the past. Once she had fancied that Kate was
not indifferent to Garry Forbes. At one time they had been
much together, when he came on holiday to Fetter-Rothnie.
But Theresa's tongue had been so hard on the boy—the intimacy ceased. Mrs Falconer remembered her own impotent
fury against her sister. And, after all, Kate had given no
sign. 'Another dream of mine, I suppose,' thought Mrs
Falconer. And she sighed. It was not easy to include Kate
in any dream. 'And she's all I have to love,' thought her
mother wistfully.

Mrs Hunter ran on. ' "O, that's to see," he says. "I've
never found a lassie yet that I love like your ain bonny self."
"You flatterer," I says. "Unless it would be my aunt." And

we both to the laughin'. But he's fair fond of her, mind you. There's nae put-on yonder.'

'He would be,' said Theresa. 'Sic mannie sic horsie. She's a Hielan' yowe yon.'

Mrs Hunter bridled. 'She's a good woman, Miss Craigmyle. There's worse things than being queer. There's being bad. There's lots that's nae quite at themsels and nae ill in them, and some that's all there and all the worse for that. There's Louie Morgan, now—queer you must allow she is, but bad she couldna be.'

Whether because the affront put on her by Miss Barbara's rash incursion was still rankling, or whether by reason of the naturally combative quality of her mind, Miss Theresa stormed on the suggestion.

'Louie!' she said. 'Hantle o' whistlin' and little red land yonder. And you don't call it bad to bedizen herself with honours and her never got them?'

'Meaning' what, Miss Craigmyle?'

'This tale of her engagement,' said Theresa with scorn.

'Poor craitur! That was a sore heart to her. Losin' young Mr Grey that road, and them new promised. It'll be a while or she ca' ower't.'

'She never had him.'

'Havers, Miss Theresa, she has the ring.'

'Think of that, now.'

'She let me see the ring.'

'She bought it.'

'She didna that, Miss Theresa. It's his mother's ain ring, that she showed me lang syne, and said her laddie's bride would wear when she was i' the mools.'

Miss Theresa took the check badly. To be found in the wrong was a tax she could not meet. She had grown up with a hidden angry conviction that she was in the wrong by being born. As third daughter, she had defrauded her father of a son. It was after Theresa's birth that James Craigmyle set himself to turn Annie into as good a farmer as himself. He never reproached Tris to her face, but the sharp child guessed her offence. When he was dead, and she in the Weatherhouse had power and authority for the first time in her life, she developed an astounding genius for being in the right. To prove Theresa wrong was to jeopardise the household peace.

She was therefore dead set in her own opinion by Mrs Hunter's apparent proof of her mistake. The matter, to be sure, was hardly worth an argument. Louie Morgan was a weak, palavering thing, always playing for effect. The Craigmyle ladies knew better than to be taken in with her airs and her graces, that deceived the lesser intellects; but they had, like everyone else, accepted the story of her betrothal to David Grey, a young engineer brought up in the district, although David Grey was already dead before the betrothal was announced. Even Theresa had not openly questioned the story before. Irritation made her do it now, and the crossing of her theory drove her to conviction.

'It's as plain as a hole in a laddie's breeks,' she said. 'There was no word of an engagement when the young man was alive, was there?'

The whole company, however, was against her. The supposition was monstrous, and in view of Mrs Hunter's evidence upon the ring, untenable.

'And look at the times she's with auld Mr Grey,' said Mrs Hunter, 'that bides across the dyke from us, and him setting a seat for her that kindly like and cutting his braw chrysanthemums to give her.'

'She had sought them,' said Theresa.

'Oh, I wouldna say. She's fit for it, poor craiturie. But she wouldna tell a lee.' Mrs Hunter frankly admitted the failings of all her friends, but thought none the worse of them for that. 'She's her father's daughter there. A good man, the old Doctor, and a grand discourse he gave. It was worth a long traivel to see him in the pulpit, a fine upstandin' man as ever you saw. "Easy to him," Jake says. Jake's sair bent, Miss Craigmyle. "Easy to him, he's never done a stroke of work in his life." His wife did a' thing—yoked the shalt for him whan he went on his visitations, and had aye to have his pipe filled with tobacco to his hand when he got hame.'

'Where's Lindsay gone to?' Theresa cut abruptly across the conversation. 'She's taking a monstrous while to put away her cloak. And it's time these bairns were home.'

She pulled the coloured streamers from the tree out of Stella's hands.

They called for Lindsay, but had no answer. When it became plain she was not in the house, there was a flutter of consternation.

'Out?' said Miss Annie. 'But she'll get her death. And what could she be seeking out at this time of night?'

Only Mrs Falconer held her peace. A light smile played over her features, and her thoughts were running away by the upland paths of romance. She had a whole history woven for herself in a moment—a girl in love and escaping into moonshine on such a pure and radiant night as this: did one require pedestrian excuse?

She said, 'I'll put on my coat and take these children home. I'm sure to meet her on the way.'

Like Lindsay, she had the sense of escaping into light. She went along with a skipping step, her heart rejoicing; and almost forgot that she had come to look for a runaway whose absence caused concern.

She delivered over the children to Francie, who shut the door on them and said, 'I'll show you a sight, if you come up the park a bit.' Mrs Falconer followed, caring little where she went in that universal faerie shimmer. It seemed to her that she was among the days of creation, and light had been called into being, but neither divisions of time nor substance, nor any endeavours nor disturbances of man.

'What think you o' that in a Christian country?' Francie was asking; and Mrs Falconer saw, as Lindsay had seen, the blazing lights of Knapperley.

'What a strange pale beauty they have,' she said, 'in the moonlight.'

'Beauty, said ye?' echoed Francie, with supreme scorn. 'It's a beauty I can do fine wantin' in a war-time, and all them Zepps about.'

'Hoots, Francie,' said Mrs Falconer, recovering herself, 'it's as light as day. The house lights 'll make little difference in the sky tonight.'

'I've seen that lights, Mrs Falconer, in the darkest night o' winter. It's nae canny. She'll come by some mishaunter, ay will she, ay will she that.'

'A fine, maybe. Don't you worry, Francie. If she carries on like that the police 'll soon put a stop to her cantrips.'

Francie went away muttering. Mrs Falconer returned home, having forgotten to look very hard for the runaway. Lindsay was still absent.

'You can't have looked sore all the time you've been,' said Theresa.

Ellen did not, of course, confess that she had forgotten the girl. She said, 'What harm can she come to? She's gone out to see the moon.'

'Fiddlesticks and rosit! Everybody's not so daft about a view as you.'

'I'll go again,' said Ellen, nothing loth; but as she opened the door Lindsay arrived, running.

She was plainly in terror, and throwing herself on the sofa broke into sobbing.

'Whatever made you want to go there?' they asked when she told where she had been.

'I don't know,' sobbed Lindsay. She was like a little frightened child, and very lovely in her woe. They made much of her, and miscalled Bawbie Paterson to their hearts' content.

Lindsay told her story over again to Kate, when Kate had arrived home for the night and the girls were in the windowed room that Kate shared habitually with her mother. Ellen had yielded her tower to the guest.

'They wanted to know why I went, Katie, but they mustn't. Oh, I wish she weren't like that—she's dreadful.'

'But you needn't go near her, need you?'

Lindsay began to laugh and to sob. 'Katie,' she whispered, 'she's his aunt, you know.'

Kate was silent from astonishment.

She had heard her aunt's account of Mrs Andrew Lorimer's story—'Captain Dalgarno,' Mrs Andrew had said.

'I see,' she said at last. Captain Dalgarno was therefore Garry Forbes.

'Mother told you about me, didn't she? Didn't she, Katie? She had no right—they treat me like a child. She did say, didn't she?'

'I wasn't here, Linny. Yes, she said.'

'Said what? How much, Katie? Oh, I couldn't bear them to know that was why I ran after her. I wanted to see—Do you suppose they know, Katie?'

'I am sure they don't. But is it secret, Linny?'

'No. But running after her like that—' She began to writhe on the bed. 'I'm so unhappy, Katie.'

'Yes,' said Kate.

Kate was dumb before emotion. Her own was mastered and undivulged. She remained silent while Lindsay sobbed, and in a while the girl grew quiet, and fell asleep.

But Kate, after her young cousin slept, stole out of bed and crossed the room. Bending, she pulled the cover over Lindsay's naked arm. 'In this frost—she'd starve.' And for a moment Kate stood looking down on the flushed young face. So this was the woman whom Garry Forbes had chosen. Kate returned to bed and went to sleep. She had a long day's work ahead of her and a long day's work behind; and lying awake brought scanty profit.

FOUR

Coming of Spring

Lindsay's escapade on the night of the Christmas tree provided much matter for talk and for allusion. The ladies had their ways. Paradise, genial and warm, would cry, 'Out again, Lindsay. Stay you by the fire, my lass. But you don't seem to feel the cold, stravaigin' in the snow. You'll be stiffer about the hunkers before you come to my time of life. Put some clothes on, lassie, you'll starve.'

Theresa, hearing, would retort, 'She's not like you, rowed up like a sair thoomb. She's youth to keep her warm.'

'Ay, ay, here's me that needs the fire. And me to have been so active all my days.'

'Like Vesuvius.'

'Don't you heed her,' said Paradise, laughing. 'I could dander at night with the best when I was younger. O ay, frosty nights and all. Many's the lad that's chased me up the park and in by the woodie side.'

'But she aye took care of herself. Catch a weasel sleeping. You'd better have a care, Lindsay, going out alone by night, in a place you don't know.'

'There's somebody you would have liked fine to be meeting out there, my lady,' Paradise would add.

And Lindsay's face burned, as she watched them under narrowed lids. They had no mind to disconcert her, but had lived too long and heartily to remember the reticence of youth; and old Mrs Craigmyle, with her fine regard, Lindsay felt, enjoyed her young discomfort—not in a thoughtless frankness, like the others, but pondering its quality.

'Leezie Lindsay,' her grand-aunt would say—the very name made Lindsay's cheek grow hot—'you never ask the old dame for a song. When you were a littlin, it was, "And

39

now a song, my grand-aunt," and when she sang you danced and you trebled. You have other ploys to please you now.'

Lindsay, knowing that she avoided the old lady's presence, blushed the more. And there was nothing in the words, yet everything. Her rare low words had a choice insolence that astounded the girl; but she dared not take offence, so delicate was the insinuation, lest she had mistaken her grand-aunt's meaning and herself supplied the subtle sting she felt. She would leave Lang Leeb's presence bewildered, in a sorry heat of shame that she had a mind so tainted.

Mrs Falconer had other modes of leading to attack. She would make up on the girl as she tramped the long moor roads and walk musing by her side. An ungainly figure, Lindsay thought. And rather a nuisance. She could never get accustomed to Cousin Ellen's habit of muttering to herself as she walked, and when Mrs Falconer began to address her, in her low hesitating voice, it was hard to be sure that she was not still talking to herself. Hard, indeed; because Ellen had no plain path out from her dreams, and her queer ends of talk were part of the story she had woven around herself and Lindsay.

'There's hard knowing what to do,' she would say. 'I've had to suffer, too. I fought for my own way of seeing things.' That battle of thirty years before came fresh and horrible to her memory. 'One generation forgets another's war. But, you see, I came out the conqueror.'

She let her thought hover upon her own past. It was a glancing embroidery now, pleasant to sight. But Lindsay saw only a tarnished and tangled thread or two that had no connection with herself, and thus a scanty interest.

'So I didn't hurry you,' Cousin Ellen went on. ' "Seek her out," they said, "seek her out. There's danger." But I knew, you see. Oh yes, I knew. Not the danger *they* meant. So I didn't look sore. I let you bide your time. There's some sorts of danger you have to meet, and where better to meet them than under a moon like yon? Oh yes, I knew.'

'Knew what?' Lindsay pondered. 'Why I went out at night? But I am sure she doesn't. What danger was there?'

Only Kate, who knew, said nothing. Kate had no words. Lindsay thought her callous, and writhed angrily to remember how she had given her secret self away. But she could have given it to no better heart than Kate's. Kate took it in and loved it.

Lindsay, unaware of her devotion, had hours of embarrassment among these elderly women who barbed their chance words with a story half heard from her mother and an escapade whose reason they did not understand. The allusions were sufficiently rare, except on the part of Mrs Falconer, who continued to puzzle Lindsay with her air of secret communion; but their mere possibility was enough to alarm the girl and soil the pleasantness she had always expected of a Weatherhouse sojourn. When, therefore, the frost gave and the roads were filled with slush and the whole countryside was dirty, Lindsay went home without regret.

It was a black February, wet, with an east wind 'hostin' through atween the houses.' At the end of the month trains were blocked by snow and fallen trees, and March came in bleak and bitter. Lindsay found the time long. She had wanted to be a nurse and they would not let her—she was not strong enough, they said—and there was nothing else that she particularly desired to do. So she made swabs and waited at the Station Rest Room Canteen, and thought herself a little hardly used by fate, but would not confess it, since she saw others around her used more hardly. She was to think it shortly with more justice, for Garry ceased to write to her. She would not confess at home to the lapse, but searched casualty lists and grew pale and restless. Before March ended spring suddenly filled the world. Buds were swollen in a night. Crocuses and scilla broke from the black earth; and Mrs Andrew Lorimer, watching her daughter's thin, strained face, sent her back to the Weatherhouse. She knew well enough that no letter had come for Lindsay, but would show no sympathy in an affair of which she disapproved.

The Weatherhouse ladies had had time to forget Lindsay's escapade. It was no longer matter for stupid allusion. They seemed also to have forgotten the love affair. There were no covert allusions to that either. Perhaps the girl's bearing, a little proud, steeled to show no hurt even when hurt was taken, made a hearty farm allusiveness fall flat. Kate remembered in silence. Mrs Falconer again waylaid the girl with queer talk that she could not understand. Lindsay could have no idea of the rush of life that came to Cousin Ellen by touching even so distantly the vital experience of a young girl's love and growth. Ellen had touched no vital experience other than her own. Kate had apparently had none to show her. No one had opened a heart to her or shared with her the strange secrecy of living, and in the hours of remorse when she chid herself for the false fictions of her brain she recognised sadly that she created these because she had had so little of the real stuff of living to fill her mind. So Lindsay, coming to Fetter-Rothnie charged with the splendours of a real romance, intoxicated Mrs Falconer. The elderly woman watched her with a sort of adoration, and would have purchased her confidence at a price; but she did not know how to reach the girl's confidence. Lindsay thought her queer and avoided her.

The others she did not avoid. Suspense, she found, was easier to bear up here in the sun and wind, where no one knew that she was waiting. It surprised her to find how she slipped into the life of the countryside, learned its stories, its secret griefs and endeavours. She had not dreamed how much alive a few square miles of field and moor could become. Miss Annie taught her to understand the earth and its labourers—the long, slow toil of cultivating a land denuded of its men. She learned to despise Peter Cairnie, a shrewd shirker in a rich farm by the river, who ploughed Maggie Barnett's land to her at an exorbitant figure; and to honour Maggie, wife of a young crofter at the Front, who managed the croft and reared her three bairns alone.

'Do you hear from him often?' Lindsay said to Maggie.

'Whiles, whiles,' the wiry woman answered. 'But he's nae great sticks at the pen. I heard five weeks syne.'

Five weeks, Lindsay thought, and she takes it as of course. She watched Maggie whack the cow round in her stall and set to milking, and followed Miss Theresa a little thoughtfully to Mrs Hunter at Craggie.

Another croft; its man not gone this time, but slow and frail; Dave, the eldest boy, in the Gordons.

'And does he write?' asked Lindsay. It was something to say.

'Write!' cried Mrs Hunter in her glowing fashion. 'There was never a lad to write like our Dave. And money coming home to keep the loonies at the school. "Keep you Bill and Dod to their books, Mother," he says. "This war's bound to go over some time, and the boys'll need all the education they can get. I'll put them through college," he says. It's himsel should have been at the college, if I had my way of it. His heart was never in the joinering, but there, it couldna be. But the young ones, they're to town to the school, a gey lang way, and a gey lang day; their father could do fine with a hand from them with the beasts and about the place, but there you are, you see. "Keep them to their books, mother," says Dave. "They'll get what I couldn't get." And I can aye lend a hand with the beasts mysel.'

Lindsay went often to Mrs Hunter's. Mrs Hunter had been servant lass for so long at Knapperley, and she talked freely of Miss Barbara and Mr Garry, not suspecting the avid interest of her listener. Talk lightened the heart to Mrs Hunter. Good reminiscent unprejudiced talk was the salt of earth to her; and she had earth enough in her laborious life to require salting.

Lindsay would come in, swing herself to the table or squat upon a creepie, and manoeuvre Mrs Hunter to the subjects she desired. It was thus that she heard the story of David Grey. David had been Garry's friend. And he was dead. His father, John Grey, lived across the dyke from Mrs Hunter. This indomitable old man, approaching the seventies, spare, small and alert, lived alone except for the woman who kept his house. Son of a petty crofter in a Deeside glen, he had laboured on the croft, taken his schooling as he could, and fought his way to apprenticeship in an engineering shop. The master of the country school where he had spent his winters did well by him; in night school he rose steadily, until by the end of his apprenticeship he was teaching draughtsmanship and mechanics. He went out

early on Sunday mornings and took long walks in the coun
try, in the course of which he studied botany and learned
by heart the works of the English poets. He even wrote
verses, in Tennyson's early manner; and studied Carlyle
and Ruskin, John Locke and Adam Smith. His books were
bought from second-hand bookstalls; it was thus that he
became possessor of an eighteenth-century *Paradise Lost*,
leather-bound, with steel engravings of our First Parents in
a state of innocence. To these engravings he had added, for
Eve a skirt, for Adam short pants, of Indian ink. He married, became Works manager of the Foundry where he had
served his apprenticeship, settled within reach of town and
cultivated his garden. He rose with daylight, laboured in
the earth till the breakfast hour, made a rapid but thorough
toilet, went to town. At the end of his garden, the beauty of
which was celebrated through all the district, was a work-
shop: there was nothing connected with a homestead that
he could not make or mend. His fingers, clumsy, broad and
seamed, were incredibly delicate in action. His figure was
squat and plebeian, but redeemed by its alert activity and
by the large and noble head. The brow was wide and lofty,
the nose aquiline, shaggy eyebrows emphasised the depths
of the eye-sockets, in which there shone a pair of dark,
piercing and kindly eyes. Children loved him. His voice
was soft and persuasive. His men revered him and trusted
his judgment. He spoke evil of no man.

In youth his hair, brows and beard (which he never removed) were intensely black, but by the time of this story,
white; and so much of his forehead and temples was now
bare as gave a singularly lofty and serene appearance to his
head. One felt him as a man of peace. In the spring of 1914
he had retired from work and given himself with a child's
delight to his garden; but early in the war, feeling that
his specialised knowledge and training should be put at the
service of his country, he offered himself to the Munitions
Department of his city, and was engaged as a voluntary and
unpaid Inspector of Shells; he stipulated only that his travelling expenses should be paid—his salary had always been
small, and he had saved no more than would suffice for his
old age. The lifting and handling of shells was too much for

his failing strength. He toiled home at night exhausted; but was up on the following morning to work in his garden. He had even taken in another piece of ground and was growing huge crops of potatoes and green vegetables, which he distributed among the local hospitals.

His wife was dead. His only son, a brilliant boy, unlike his father in appearance and temperament, had inherited and intensifed his genius. David was tall, red-headed, fiery-tempered, wild and splendid, but with his father's capacity for engineering and his power over those who worked for him. John Grey saw his own dreams fulfilled in his son. The boy marched triumphantly through school and college, and, entering Woolwich Arsenal in the war, became night manager of a new fuse factory. His work was his passion. Brilliant, inventive, steady in work as his father, he lacked the older man's composed serenity. The artist's sensibility, the lover's exaltation, went to his work; and broke him. He developed tuberculosis, and in three months' time was dead.

John Grey took the blow in silence. He spoke to no one of his son, but went on his steady, quiet way. Only the professional books that he and the boy together had amassed ceased to interest him. He never read them again, and his tired mind had no further concern with the modern developments of which, for the boy's sake, he had kept himself informed.

When Lindsay learned, through Mrs Hunter, that David Grey had been Garry's friend, she placed both the old and the dead man in her shrine of heroes. This shy and undeveloped girl at nineteen had the Lorimer passion, exemplified in Mrs Falconer's day-dreams and the balladry of Lang Leeb her mother, for a romantic enlargement of life. Lindsay was given to hero-worship. On these spring evenings and on Saturday afternoons she would watch the old man at work in his garden. Sometimes, as he crawled weeding among the beds, in his old garments that had turned the colour of earth itself, with his hands earth-encrusted, he seemed older than human—some antique embodiment of earth. One could fancy a god creating an Eden. Steady and happy. Absorbed. Like a part of what he worked in, and yet beyond it. The immanent presence.

The stooping figure, moving back and forth like a great silent animal, would raise itself, the noble forehead come into view; and rising on stiff knees, the old man would greet the girl with a perfect courtesy, sit by her pulling at his pipe. Once, in the sun, he fell asleep as he sat beside her, nodding in an old man's light and easy slumbers.

Once or twice Louie Morgan came to the garden. Lindsay had heard her story too; how she was betrothed to young David Grey—an unannounced betrothal, to which she had confessed only after his death. One evening, walking away with her from the garden, Louie showed Lindsay a ring, which she wore about her neck.

'Why should I flaunt it for everyone to see?' she had said; and with her head on one side she gazed at the ring. Her face was all curious little puckers—a study for a Lady in Anguish. She made funny twists with her mouth. But Lindsay was excited. It was her first intimate personal contact with the bereavement of war, and she exalted Louie also to a place in her shrine.

So the spring wore on. There on the upland one saw leagues of the world and leagues of sea, all milky-blue, hazed like the bloom upon a peach. And how good it was to watch the country changing with the spring!

'Come,' Paradise would say. 'Tomorrow the chickens should be out. We'll sprinkle water on the eggs today.' Tomorrow came, and the shells broke—small, soft, delectable living things were there.

'Oh, how I love them! I have never seen them so young. Oh, it's running, it's running on my hand! But why can't I feed them?'

Paradise, taking the broken shells from the coop, told her they were too young for food; but Lindsay was not listening. She had heard somewhere a loud harsh cry.

'Look, look! Oh, there! See them! What can they be?' And she pointed far overhead, into the height of the blue sky. Birds were flying there, one bird, and others following in two lines that made an open angle upon the blue; but while one arm of the angle was short, the other stretched far out across the sky, undulating, fine and black.

'One, two three—twenty, twenty one—Oh, I have counted ninety birds! My neck is aching.' She held her hands to her neck, moving her head about to ease its pain. 'Paradise, tell me what they are.'

'Why, that is the wild geese. Have you never seen them fly before?'

'Never. Wild geese, wild geese! How wonderful the country is!'

When Cousin Ellen walked with her she assailed her with questions.

'And see, Cousin Ellen, this one. Look at him. Has he a nest there, do you think? Where do you look for nests? What kind is he? What is his name?'

Ellen shook her head.

'I hardly know their names, Linny.'

'But don't you love birds?'

'Oh, yes.' Ellen paused, gazing at the eager girl. 'They are a part of myself,' she wanted to say; but how could one explain that? Where it had to be explained it could not be understood. 'You are a part of me, too,' she thought, with her eyes fixed on Lindsay's where she waited for her answer. Her lips were parted and her eyes shone; and Mrs Falconer longed to tell her of the strange secret of life—how all things were one and there was no estrangement except for those who did not understand. But all that she could find to say was, 'I know hardly any of their names.'

The girl's clear regard confused her, and she dropped her eyes. She felt ashamed. 'Names don't matter very much, do they?' she asked hurriedly.

'Oh, yes. Names—they're like songs.' And she chanted in a singing voice, 'Wild duck, wild duck, kingfisher, curlew. Their names are a part of themselves. Can you tell me where to see a kingfisher, Cousin Ellen?'

'No . . . I'm afraid not.'

Ellen had been found wanting, Lindsay felt. To walk with her held no allurement.

Only once a spontaneous feeling of love for Cousin Ellen welled up in her heart.

Lindsay had come to the Weatherhouse bringing gifts.

'I've brought presents for you all. See, a poor woman made them. She can do nothing for the war, so she makes these lovely things and gives the money.'

Theresa and Paradise took their boxes, which were of embroidered silk exquisitely fashioned, and put them instantly to use. But Cousin Ellen's gift lay on the table.

'Don't you like your gift? I'm sorry you don't like it.'

'Oh yes, I like it. It is very beautiful. Please don't think because I don't use it that I am not grateful for it. I have never cared for many possessions. I have never had many possessions to care for,' she added, smiling brightly. 'A man's life consisteth not in the abundance of things that he hath.'

A week later Miss Theresa stamped into the parlour.

'Well, really, Nell! To give Lindsay's beautiful box away. Something commoner would have done, surely to peace, if you must be throwing things at that Stella Ferguson's head. A nice appreciation you show, I will say.'

'Yes, I gave it to Stella. Possessions mean a lot to her.'

Theresa continued to bluster; but Lindsay jumped from the stool where she had been seated with her book, and cried, 'Oh, I love you for giving it to Stella, Cousin Ellen.'

'Lindsay'—Miss Theresa changed the subject sharply—'you'll spoil your eyes, poring over these great books. You are quite wrinkled.'

Lindsay turned a flushed and troubled face, pushing the hair from off her brow.

'But I must be ready. The world will need us all. I'm doing nothing now, but I can prepare myself for afterwards. There will be ten years of trouble to live through.'

She quoted the phrases she had heard from Garry's lips, and set herself to study the books that he had read. 'We shall all have our part to play in the reconstruction.'

Into this life Garry Forbes came in the second week of April. All spring was in that week—its tempestuous disinclinations, its cold withdrawals, its blaze of sun, its flowers, its earthy smell. On all hands was a breaking: earth broken by the ploughshare, buds broken by the leaf. The smooth security of seed and egg was gone. Season most terrible in all the cycle of the year, time of the dread spring deities, Dionysus and Osiris and the risen Christ, gods of growth and of resurrection, whose worship has flowered in tragedy, superb and dark, in Prometheus and Oedipus, massacre and the stake. Life that comes again is hard: a jubilation and an agony.

Garry was at this time some thirty years of age. Tall, dark-skinned, black stubbs on his chin and cheek that no shaving would remove, with prominent nose and cheek bones and outstanding ears, the two deep furrows that were later so marked a feature of his appearance already ploughing their way from above the nostrils to encircle the mouth, and just now lank and haggard from war and influenza; he came to spend a brief sick leave with his aunt, Miss Barbara Paterson, at Knapperley.

'What do you want with a kitchen lass?' he said to her. 'I'll be your kitchen lass.'

Miss Barbara sat back in her deep chair and flung yowies from her pockets on to the blazing fire. She, who could spread dung and hold a plough with any man, disliked the petty drubs of housework.

'You're Donnie Forbes's grandson,' she said, watching her nephew as he washed the supper dishes. 'I'm a Paterson of Knapperley. A Paterson of Knapperley doesna fyle their fingers with dishwater.'

Benjamin Forbes, Miss Barbara's half-brother, son of the despised Donnie Forbes whom Mrs Paterson had wedded merely for love, had, like his mother, been timid and incapable in his relations with other people. He lived with his boy in the mean suburb of an inland town. When charwomen cheated and neglected them, it was the boy who found fault, dismissed and interviewed. The fiction was faithfully preserved between father and son that the father habitually did these things, but delegated them upon occasion to the son. Garry put a bold front upon the business, and won the praises of the women in the block for his assured and masterful bearing. They could not know that the child sometimes cried himself to sleep, and he would have perished rather than confess to it. When service was not to be had, Garry waited on his father;

and broke the nose of the boy who taunted him with it at school.

'I'll sweel out the slop-pail if I like,' he shouted.

He was a powerful fellow, able easily to wipe out insults, and far too proud to acknowledge his own secret abasement at doing a woman's jobs.

Benjamin talked often to the boy of Knapperley. 'Yon's the place, laddie,' he would say. Garry choked as he listened; he felt he must perish of desire for the burns and the rocky coast. But when he begged his father to let him go to Knapperley, Benjamin demurred. He shrank from a second encounter with his half-sister. One day, when Garry was twelve years old, Benjamin came home to find the boy on the next-door roof, mending a broken gutter-pipe, and learned that his son mended for all the women in the row—and took his wages. Shamefaced but voluble, Garry produced his money-box; he had not spent a penny of his earnings; all was saved—to pay his fare to Knapperley. Benjamin swore softly, but wrote to Miss Barbara; and though no answer was received, the boy set off alone as soon as his holidays began. He tramped the eight miles out from Aberdeen with his belongings on his back, and was dismayed at the ease of the journey. It was unbearably tame to walk in to Knapperley and sleep in a bed; and his secret hope (that his aunt would not receive him: a contingency for which he had made elaborate preparations) vanished like smoke when he saw the actual place. He was sure she would take him in and bid him wash his hands.

'That Knapperley?' he asked a man who was lounging against a gate.

'Who was ye seekin'?'

'Oh, nobody much. I just wanted to know.'

He walked away.

'Ay is't,' the man shouted after him

Garry did not turn.

He came in a little to the moor and saw the sea. That night was full moon. The boy wandered all night like a daft thing. He had drunk magic. At dawn he fell asleep, and the sun was well up when he awoke, furiously hungry, and made for Knapperley. He had no intention of telling where he had spent the night.

But the first person he saw was the fellow who had spoken to him by the gate. Miss Barbara was standing on a cart, forking straw from the cart into a great bundle beside the stable door.

'Ay, ay,' said the man. 'Ye've gotten your way. I tell't her ye was in-by the streen.'

'Let's see you with the graip,' said Miss Barbara, descending from the cart and handing the fork to her nephew.

Garry threw his knapsack from his shoulders and clambered on to the cart. He would not be outdone by anybody; but the horse moved and set the cart in motion; he lost his balance, plunged violently and swung his graip high in the air.

Miss Barbara and the man roared with laughter. A dozen dogs, as it seemed, arrived from nowhere and barked.

'I'll show you how to laugh at me!' cried Garry, recovering his footing. He was mortified to the soul, and began to handle the straw with all the skill and vigour he could command. Miss Barbara folded her arms and watched. Rabbie Mutch could be heard recounting the affair to the kitchen lass, and there followed a guffaw of laughter from them both.

'You'll be ready for your porridge, I'se warren,' said Miss Barbara in a little; and she led the way to the kitchen, where breakfast was ready for herself, her man and her kitchen girl. 'Where spent you the night?'

'Up beside a tower kind of place.'

'You never got in?'

'Oh no, just outside.'

'Gweed sakes!' roared Rabbie. 'Like the—nowt.'

'Dinna you do that,' said the kitchen lass earnestly. 'The moon'll get you. You'll dwine an' dee.'

Far from bidding him wash his hands, Miss Barbara let her nephew come to table with his clothes sullied from the moor. The rough free life she led suited the spirited lad. His manners grew ruder. Rabbie Mutch kept up on him the joke about his sprawling from the cart. He would say at dinner-time, 'O ay, ye can haud the forkie better'n the graip. Yon was a gey like way to haud a graip. Forkin' the lift, was ye?'

The sensitive boy was too proud to show his resentment. He retaliated in kind. Rabbie and he made rude jokes at each other's expense and became fast friends.

For his aunt, the boy admired her wholeheartedly. She knew so much that he had never heard. The country became a new possession. He was free, too, from the indignity that harassed him at home; the endless squabbling with washerwomen. Miss Barbara found fault often enough, but in a coarse and hearty manner, that was followed by guffaws of laughter from all concerned. Garry developed a poor opinion of his own and his father's assertion of authority, and determined to try Miss Barbara's methods on the next woman who offended.

He would secretly have preferred to leave these offenders unchallenged, but, being plagued with a passion for the ideal, could not let ill alone.

When, at the age of twenty nine, on leave at the Lorimer's house with the young Frank, he met and loved Lindsay, this passion had not abated. 'Well, I've done it now,' he thought. He rushed about the house, forgot his manners, played absurd practical jokes, swore himself to secrecy over his love, and blurted it out immediately to Lindsay. To his consternation she flung her arms around his neck.

'I've loved you for ever and ever so long,' she cried. 'You should hear how Frank talks of you.'

Her girl friends called him the Gargoyle.

'One could forgive the ears,' her mother declared, 'if he knew how to conduct himself.'

Garry's lapses from a Mrs Andrew Lorimer standard were not always due to ignorance. He resented those refinements that suggested privilege. This shy lover of the ideal, this poet who clowned away the suspicion of poetry from himself, burned in his heart with no less a fire than love for all mankind. A simple fool, not very fit for Mrs Andrew Lorimer's drawing-room, where such an enormous appetite was found ill-bred. The well-bred love with discrimination.

'Such waste of furrow,' said Mrs Robert Lorimer. 'Those architectural effects of feature. In a gentleman, how distinguished! A man of race and breeding could arrive where he liked with a face of that quality.'

Garry's race being that of the despised Donnie Forbes and his breeding of the back street, his ugliness was pronounced not distinguished, but common.

'You've got a rarity there, Miss Lindsay,' mocked her aunt Mrs Robert.

'I know he is rare,' the girl answered steadily. She and Frank alone appreciated the rareness. Both listened vehemently to his interminable plans for reconstructing the universe. They talked far into the night, until Mrs Andrew despatched her husband from his bed to round them up.

'Leave them alone,' he grumbled. 'There's a war on. Those boys'll be in the trenches again soon enough, God knows.' But he obeyed the mandate.

'Your mother thinks it's time you were in bed, Linny.'

He blinked in the glare of light. Standing there in his pyjamas and dressing-gown, an unimaginative man, he felt nevertheless the tense elation in the room.

'So courting's done in threes nowadays—eh?'

Lindsay flung back her head. 'O daddy, nights like this don't come again.'

She met her mother's morning eye with a clear regard.

'Europe is in the melting-pot, mother—is a slight alteration in one's bedtime of importance?'

'Ler her keep her phrase,' said Mr Lorimer. 'She'll outgrow that.'

Inflamed by Garry's letters, she continued to keep her phrase.

The letters ceased when Garry took influenza, after a day and a night's exposure in a shell hole, where, up to the thighs in filthy water, he had tried to suck the poison from another man's festering arm. The other fellow died where he stood, slithered through his fingers and doubled over into the filth, and Garry was violently sick. He stared at the horror beside him, and now he saw that blood had coagulated in the pit between the man's knees and his abdomen. Poor beggar, he must have had another wound . . . He must get out of sight of that, but his feet were stuck, they would never pull free again. He stooped, plunging his arm in the slimy water. Branches came up, dripping long strings of ooze. Now he had detached the other man's feet; the body canted over, a shapeless rigid mass, and he saw the glaring eyes, the open mouth out of which slime was oozing. He pushed with all his might, thrust the thing under; barricaded himself with branches against its presence. Rain fell, sullen single drops, that burrowed into the surface of the slime and sent oily purplish bubbles floating among the ends of branch that were not submerged. Clots of blood appeared, washed out from the body.

'A wound I didn't know of,' he thought. 'A wound you couldn't see.' Perhaps his own abdomen was like that— black with blood. Squandered blood. Perhaps he too was wounded and did not know it. 'I put him there—I thrust him in.'

Delirium came on him. A wind roared hideously. He knew it was an advancing shell, but shouted aloud as he used to do when a boy in the hurricanes that swept the woods at Knapperley. Again the rushing mighty wind. Night came at last. He knew he must escape. 'Can't leave you here, old man.' In some queer way he was identified with this other fellow, whom he had never seen before, whose body he had thrust with so little ceremony under the slime. 'Tra la la la la,' he sang, tugging at the corpse. 'Come out, you there. Myself. That's me. That's me. I thrust him in—I am rescuing myself.'

He was found towards morning in a raging fever, dragging a grotesque bundle at his heels—a corpse doubled over, with bits of branch that protruded from the clothing, plastered with slime. They had to bring him in by force.

'Don't take him from me, you chaps. It's myself. I have been wounded—here, in the abdomen. Here,' he shouted. And he put his arms round the shapeless horror he had dragged bumping from its hole.

He never knew what came of the body, nor whose it was. When he regained his senses he was in hospital, too weak to think or speak, but sure he had been wounded. 'Queer business that,' he said later, 'about my wound. I was convinced I had a wound. I saw myself. Oh, not a pretty sight. Obstinate old bag of guts. I had to haul myself out. I hauled for hours. And I knew it was myself and the other man too. I thrust him in, you see, and I had to haul myself out. Queer, isn't it, about oneself? Losing oneself like that, I mean, and being someone else.'

He lay pondering the hugeness of life. Sometimes he was so weak that he cried. Nurses said to one another, 'Poor fellow—that huge one in the corner. Crying like a baby. He has delusions.'

He fumed at their pity as he had fumed at ridicule in his boyhood; but in a gush of charity allowed himself even to be pitied. One could not refuse to meet other people halfway.

'It's because it's so big,' he tried to explain to one of the nurses.

'Yes, I know,' she answered, pressing his hand.

Of course she didn't know. It wasn't the war that was big, it was being alive in a world where wars happened—that was to say, in a world where there were other people, divinely different from oneself; whole Kingdoms of Heaven, clamouring to be taken by violence and loved in spite of themselves. No nurse could know that; but he permitted her to put her hand on his, and even when she pressed it he did not fling it off. But then he was so tired.

Some weeks later Garry left his valise at the station and set out to walk the four cross-country miles to Knapperley. Night had fallen—a night of war-time, unrelieved. Behind him, along the line of railway where the houses were clustered, dull blurs of light were visible; in front all was dark. Slowly the vast heaven detached itself from the earth. Trees took shape—bare, slender branches striking upward into the sky. It seemed as though out of the primal darkness the earth once more were taking form: an empty world, older than man, silent. In a while Garry became acutely aware of the silence. It burdened him. He stood to listen. A bird was stirring, dead dry leaves rustled in the beech hedge; far off, a dog barked. The lonely echo died, there was no wind, the world was still as dream. Life had not yet begun to be, man had not troubled the primordial peace. Strange stagnant world—he hated its complacency. Standing there on the ridge, dimly aware of miles of dark and silent land, Garry felt a sort of scorn for its quietude: earth, and men made from earth, dumb, graceless, burdened as itself.

'This place is dead,' he thought. The world he had come from was alive. Its incessant din, the movement, the vibration that never ceased from end to end of the war-swept territory, were earnest of a human activity so enormous that the mind spun with thinking of it. Over there one felt oneself part of something big. One was making the earth. Here there were men, no doubt, leading their hapless, misdirected, individual lives; but they were a people unaware, out of it. He felt almost angry that Lindsay should be dwelling among them. He knew from her letters that she was in Fetter-Rothnie, and, convalescent, had written her that he would come to Knapperley; but that her young fervour should be shut in this dead world annoyed him. She was too far from life. The reconstruction of the universe would not begin in this dark hole, inhabited by old wives and ploughmen.

But as he mounted farther into the night, the night, growing upon his consciousness, was a dark hole no longer. The sky, still dark, brooded upon a darker earth, but with no sense of oppression. Rather both sky and earth rolled away, were lost in a primordial darkness whence they had but half emerged. Garry felt himself fall, ages of time gave way, and he too, was a creature only half set free from the primordial dark. He was astonished at this effect upon himself, at the vastness which this familiar country had assumed. Width and spaciousness it always had, long clear lines, a far horizon, height of sky; yet the whole valley and its surrounding hills could have been set down and forgotten in the slum of the war territory from which he had crossed. All the generations of its history would not make up the tale of the fighting men.

He paused a little, contemplating that history. Fierce and turbulent men had made it: Picts and Celtic clansmen, raiders and Jacobites. Circles and sculptured stones, cairns and hill-forts, tall grim castellated strongholds, remained as witness to its past. In its mountain glens there were recesses, ledges at the waterside under overhanging crag a hundred feet in height, where fugitives had hidden from their foes; on its coasts dangerous caves, where smugglers had operated, caught the resounding seas. Craft put out and were tossed on the waters in adventures of piracy and merchandise and statesmanship. Fishermen knew its landmarks. Wrecks were strewn about its shores. Monarchs and chieftains had ridden its passes; a king had fled that way to his destruction, a queen watched the battle on which her fortune hung; and its men had gone to every land on earth following every career. Yet, a small land; poor; ill to harvest, its fields ringed about with dykes of stone laboriously gathered from the soil. Never before had Garry felt its vastness; and he paused now, watching and hearkening. A sound broke the stillness, faint bubble of a stream, the eternal mystery of moving water; and now the darkness, to his accustomed eyes, was no longer a covering, but a quality of what he looked upon. Waste land and the fields, in common with the arch of sky, and now a grandeur unsuspected in the day. Light showed them as they were at a moment of time, but the dark revealed their timeless attributes, reducing the particular to accident and hinting at a sublimer truth than the eye could distinguish. Garry felt for a moment as though he had ceased to live at the point in time where all his experience had hitherto been amassed.

He was recalled to his accidental point in time by a woman's voice, shrill and clamorous, carrying across the night. A man's voice answered, like a reverberating boom. Garry walked on. Knapperley was just ahead.

The dogs were on him as soon as he entered, but not before he had seen Miss Barbara, alone on the kitchen floor, in her swinging Lovat tweed, dancing a Highland fling. How she lifted her supple sinewy legs, and tossed her arms, and cracked her fingers! 'That's you, is it?' her nod seemed to say as she glanced towards her nephew and went on with the step. Garry laughed, weary as he was, and swung into the dance. How much of the character of the land had not gone into this vigorous measure, which a hard-knit woman of fifty five was dancing alone on her kitchen floor in the middle of a world war, for no other reason than that she wanted to!

But in a moment he caught his breath and sat down. Miss Barbara sat also, pulled a handful of raisins from her pocket and began to munch. She asked no questions of her nephew, accepting him as she accepted rain or a litter of pups.

'That's better than jazz, aunt.'

'And what might jazz be?'

'It's a thing some people do.'

'Don't you come here, my lad, with your things some people do. This is a decent house.'

The man lay back, face seamed and drawn, eyes sunken, and looked at the house. Since the war began he had not come to Knapperley till then.

'Not a mortal thing is changed. The war just hasn't touched you, has it, aunt?'

To which she answered with an indignant flash, 'Change and change enough. There's nae near so many bodies about the roads. Tinkler bodies. There's just nane ava, and they're a terrible miss. I aye liked them coming in about for a sup and a crack. Many's the collieshangie we've had in this very ingle—Jeemsie Parten that has nae teeth but on the Sabbath, and Tammas Hirn, he had aye a basket with trappin' and aye time for a newse, and an auld orra body that hadna a name—pigware he brought, bowls and bonny jugs. I hinna had a new bowl since I kenna the time. And Johnnie Rogie, a little shauchlin' craitur, but the king o' them a'.'

Garry went to his room and fell asleep; but awoke in a little shivering violently. The bed—he might have known it—was damp. He dressed and crawled shaking down to the embers. The dogs stirred, but soon were quiet. An owl called. Miss Barbara made no sign; and for the rest of the night Garry sat by the blaze that he rekindled, staring into its heart and attempting to reconcile his aunt's vivid enjoyment of the moment with the dark truth he had been thrust upon in his walk that evening, where time and the individual had ceased to matter.

FIVE

Problem set for Garry

Lindsay was on the moor next morning to meet her lover. She was glad that she had taken his letter herself from the postman, that the old women need not know. The five last empty weeks had collapsed, the moment was enough.

'There are tassels on the larch, Garry. Look, and purple osiers. And oh, do you smell the poplar? I forgot—you are laughing, you know all these places so much better than I. I have never been in the country in spring before.'

'But now that I think of it, neither have I.'

'Not here?'

'Why, no. They were schoolboy holiday visits. Once or twice since, in midsummer.'

'You've never bird's-nested here?—I am so glad. Then I can show you things . . . These are the osiers.'

'No matter what they are. They are too lovely to require a name.'

On the willows by the pool the catkins were fluffed, insubstantial, their stamens held so lightly to the tree that they seemed like the golden essence of its life escaping to the liberty of air. Once, as the two wandered in the wood, they saw a rowan, alone in the darkness of the firs, with smooth grey branches that gleamed in the sun. The tree had no seeming substance. It was like a lofty jet of essential light.

But farther into the wood, in a sheltered clearing, the sun blazed upon a woman, picking gleams from her feathery yellow hair. She was kneeling on the ground, her hands clasped together and her head thrown back. They could see that her eyes were squeezed close and her lips were moving.

'Saying her prayers,' cried Lindsay. 'It's Louie Morgan. She's pi, you know.'

Louie continued to pray. They could hear now the words that issued from her lips. Bowing and smirking to an audience that was not there, Louie was petitioning: 'I'm on the Fetter-Rothnie Committee—may I introduce myself? I'm on the Fetter-Rothnie Committee—may I introduce myself?'

Lindsay checked her gurgle of laughter. 'But it's a shame to laugh at her. Poor soul, she's had so hard a time.'

'How?' Garry asked, carelessly; amused at the creature's antics.

'But don't you know? Your friend David Grey.'

She told him the story of Louie's betrothal.

There began for Garry at that moment the tussle that made his name a byword in Fetter-Rothnie.

'Dave,' he repeated stupidly. 'Dave.'

He had shared rooms with David Grey when they were students at Glasgow Technical College. David's death had touched him closely. Lindsay knew little of the depth and strength of that affection, of which indeed he had never spoken.

'David Grey,' he repeated. 'That creature there.'

Louie was still becking and bowing, swaying upon her knees, with clasped hands and eyes squeezed close. The exhibition, which had been ludicrous, became offensive. But the eyes opened suddenly, and the antic creature scrambled, not ungracefully, to her feet.

Louie Morgan was a slight, manoeuvring figure, in the middle thirties. Her large eyes were melting and beautiful. She studied her movements of arm and throat. When a stranger asked the way of her, she heard him think, 'What a beautiful girl! What poise! I am glad I missed my way. That is a face one must remember.' She studied to have a face one must remember. She had solid respect in Fetter-Rothnie as the daughter of her father, who had been its minister; and of her mother, who made the tea at every Sale of Work and Social Meeting. As Jonathan Bannochie had said, in proposing her a vote of thanks at the last Congregational Meeting, 'It would be a gey dry tyauve wantin' the tea, and Mistress Morgan's genius lies in tea.' She had a further genius in her admiration for her only child. She thought Louie only a trifle less wonderful than Louie thought herself. Mrs Morgan was small, plain and collected. Louie, she said without a tinge of envy, took her charm and temperament from the father's side.

As became the daughter of her father, Louie was devout. She carried a pocket Testament and read it on ostentatious occasions. She wanted to hear strangers think, 'What beautiful piety! How fine the expression it gives the countenance!' And it was always in her prayers that the perfect lovers of whom she dreamed made their appearance. Always when she reached a certain point in her petitions they appeared. 'God bless father and mother . . . and all my little cousins . . . and make me a good girl—' She had a vision of herself as a good girl, a charitable Princess giving alms to footsore men, and one of them saying, out of parched and swollen lips, 'She is more radiant than the sun, and blesses what she looks on. It is she that the King my father sent me to seek.' As she grew older, *make me a good girl* changed its wording, but the sentiment remained and so did the vision, changed also. Her prayers had long footnotes, in which she had visions of herself in all the splendid roles she pleaded with Heaven to let her play; and always a hero came, whose comment on herself she heard, and whom she answered. She was a missionary in a dangerous land, and a ferocious chieftain knelt sobbing at her feet. 'You are more wonderful than all the gods of my people. Your God will be my God, and you shall be my queen.' She was a nurse in hospital, and the sick and wounded blessed her name. A great surgeon saw her pass, noted her touch. An emergency operation must be performed. The man's life hangs on it, he is delirious, fights, will not take the anaesthetic. 'You will come, hold him.' He is calm in a moment, his life is saved. 'Yes, the first time I saw my wife she helped me with a critical case. Saved the man. She has a wonderful touch.' Or perhaps the hero was diffident and would not speak. 'I'm on the Fetter-Rothnie Committee—may I introduce myself?' 'Ah, beloved, had you not had the courage to speak to me that fateful day, how drab life would have been.'

The immediate words that broke upon her prayer, however, were not these; were not, indeed, intelligible. Aware merely of voices, she opened her eyes; then rose and faced the two intruders, flushing with satisfaction. She had always wanted to be discovered at prayer in the woods. *Into the woods my Master went.* She composed the face one must remember, and heard Lindsay and Captain Forbes think, 'Her face is shining. It is by such devotion that the world is saved.'

Louie lifted her eyes from her subconscious play-acting to look at Captain Forbes.

'How ugly he is! It must be years since I've seen him.' Her satisfaction was marred. Garry's face was working. He was still thinking, 'That creature there.' She felt an antagonism. Was it not a waste of effect? 'The wrong sort of man to appreciate me. Life's like that—never the right people.' Distinctly, the wrong sort of man. Louie decided to have nothing to do with Captain Forbes; but immediately she tilted her head a little sideways and held out a hand. 'I am so glad. And what was doing at the Front? Oh, Captain Forbes, now that we have you here; you must say a few words at our concert. Next week. Comforts for the troops, you know.'

'Comforts? Oh yes, you protect yourselves against us with comforts, I believe.'

'Protect—?'

'Parcel us up your comforts, and then feel free to forget all about us.'

'But, Captain Forbes! Linny, do tell him he is absurd.'

'He always is. Garry, you'd better go to her concert and *tell* them about the comforts.'

'Tell them—Good Lord, I will! But it won't be a happy concert. You'd better not ask me, Miss Morgan. No, on the whole better not. Let's get on, Linny. Good afternoon.'

'So you won't come?' she called after them.

'No, no. Lin, where did that gossip get a start? I hope it hasn't spread far. What you told me, I mean. Who could have spread such a story? About David Grey.'

'But it isn't a story.'

'Isn't a story?'

'Not a story. It's true.'

'No.'

'Yes.'

'It'll need a jolly lot of comforts to protect me against that. Where did you get the tale?'

'But, Garry—don't you believe it?'

'Comforts. Believe it? Did you know David Grey?'

'No.'

'Well, I did.'

'But—'

'David was the cleanest thing on God's earth. And not killed, you know. Not a clean, sharp death. Rotted off. Diseased. To die like that! It's an insult. A stupid, sense-less, dirty joke. I wish they hadn't added this to it. These scandalmongers. They must always be at something. This tale about an engagement. Another dirty joke. Senseless and dirty. Accusing him of moral disease, as though the physical were not enough.'

'But she told me—'

Lindsay compelled him to understand that the story was no mere rumour. Louie herself asserted it.

'Of all the brazen— Clawed him up from the dead and devoured him. I wish her joy of the meal.'

'I can't understand you, Garry. Why should you dis-believe her?'

'Did you know David Grey?'

'You know I—'

'Well, I did. David was utterly incapable of fooling around with a woman he didn't mean to marry. And utterly incapable of marrying a woman like that thing there. It's ob-scene. See that tree there, Linny? It's like phosphorescence on decaying fish. Evil look, hasn't it?'

'Why, it's just the sun.'

It was the naked rowan they had seen before. Garry felt a poison in the air. He strode to and fro.

'But your precious Louie shall disgorge. I'll see to that. Give him back his character. In public, too.'

In their restless turning they came face to face again with Louie.

'Captain Forbes, I am sure you will reconsider. It would be such an attraction for our concert.'

Garry stood swaying upon his parted feet. A hand rumpled his forehead. He glared down. Like an ogre, Louie said. One did not fling liar at a woman: still, the thing had to stop.

'I thought perhaps a short address. Some aspect of life at the Front. Of course we want to know the truth.'

The truth, did they? That was easy. David was not cheap. He said aloud, 'Sorry. Been ill, you know. Really don't feel fit for that sort of business. And look here, by the way, this story that's going the rounds. About Grey. Couldn't we do something—fizzle it out somehow? They've got you mixed up in it too, I understand.'

He did not look at her. Louie's eyes melted into Lindsay's. She drew a long breath, then spoke with a guarded frailness in her speech. A mere trickle of sound.

'I don't quite follow, Captain Forbes.'

Lindsay was standing watchfully. A great unhappiness surged within her. Misery, she thought, had ended yesterday, when Garry's letter came at last, when he had said, meet me on the moor. Today had been so perfect that she had thought unhappiness was done with for ever. Why should it begin again? And when Louie's eyes melted into hers, she could have cried for the strangeness of life, its pain, its mystery. She, who had thrilled to her lover's denunciation (in the abstract) of injustice and hypocrisy, stood now aghast while he exposed one hypocrite. But Louie was true, that was the trouble. There was some hideous mistake.

'I don't quite follow, Captain Forbes.'

And then that Garry should say straight out the hideous thing! Now Louie was weeping, talking swiftly. 'But why should I say these things to a stranger? Oh, I know you were my dear David's friend, but some things are too sacred even for a friend's ear. Too secret. How could you know the secret sacred things I shared with David?'

It wasn't Garry's voice she heard. 'I'm sorry, Miss Morgan, I simply don't believe the story.' And Louie still weeping. Garry was going away. What! He could insult a woman like that and then march off and leave her! Louie's sad eyes were watching her.

'Men,' said Louie, 'never begin to understand what we

women have to suffer. The loneliness. The awful emptiness.'

'Oh, I know,' Lindsay cried, remembering her own anxiety. 'Tell me, tell me, Louie. He's quite wrong, isn't he? Oh, I don't know what he means by it. It's horrible. I'm so sorry, so sorry.' She began to sob.

Louie put her arms round the child. 'Ah, we women. We understand one another, don't we?' Lindsay let herself be comforted. There was a subtle flattery in Louie's accepting her as a grown woman, meet for a woman's suffering. She couldn't know all this if she hadn't been through it, thought the girl. Louie was like a priestess divulging mysteries.

'You *were* engaged, weren't you?' she whispered.

'I *am* engaged. As you call it. Betrothed, I prefer to say. My troth plighted unto eternity.'

'Forgive me for asking. Forgive me for asking.' In some deep fashion she felt that it was forgiveness for Garry that she requested.

To Garry the problem thus set seemed on the first evening simple, if a trifle disgusting. He had always disliked Louie Morgan. When he had first come to Knapperley, she, doubly entrenched as daughter of the manse and a young lady five or six years older than the boys, had administered reproof to David and Garry for their behaviour on the way to church. To Garry: 'Even though you do come from a godless house—' To David: 'And you should be all the more ashamed, a saintly man for your father.' The boys lay in wait for my young miss. On the day she wore her first long skirt they walked behind her, whispering and laughing. They sang in chorus, then in antiphon:

O wot ye what our maid Mary's gotten?
A braw new goon an' the tail o't rotten.
O wot ye—O wot ye—A braw new goon—
The tail o't—the tail o't rot-ten—

Louie could hardly wait till they desisted before ducking round to see that the tail of her skirt was in its place. A shout of laughter came from the ambushed boys.

Later they bribed a small girl to be their victim. In full view of the minister's daughter, they pulled her hair and punched her arms. The victim expiated all the sins of her sex in the way she wailed. Miss Louie was scarlet with indignation. She read the boys a homily they would remember. But suddenly all three had joined hands and danced round Her Indignation, whooping. The daughter of the manse spluttered with disgust. Assailing the victim: 'Are you not ashamed, you who come from a Christian home, to play deceitful tricks with these boys?' The victim (who was Kate Falconer) being sturdy and stolid, made a face. That night the boys took Kate to the harrying of a bike.

In the years of their apprenticeship the boys ceased to see each other. They served their time in different towns, and holidays were spent in camp. But with their Technical College Course they were again together. In the last of their student years David chanced to remark, 'Old Morgan's gone. Decent old soul.' 'And what's come of Miss Hullabaloo?' 'Oh, husband-hunting still, I suppose.' Garry could not remember that they had ever talked of her again.

He was therefore sure that the story, wherever it originated, was false. At first it had seemed a simple matter of gossip. That Louie herself asserted its truth made it hardly less simple, though more unpleasant. The claim was a lie, and must be exposed as such. Here was a small but definite engagement in the war against evil, and Garry's heart, on the first evening of the engagement, rose pleasurably to the fray. It was not often one could deliver so clear a blow against falsehood.

SIX

Tea at The Weatherhouse

In the course of the following morning Miss Theresa Craigmyle ran out of cornflour. Theresa made no objections
to running out of necessaries. It provided an excuse for
running out herself. Theresa's slogan—*A ga'in foot's aye
gettin'*—embraced more than what she purchased at a roup.
She would come home with all the gossip of the neighbourhood.

This morning she brought in the cornflour and
said, 'Mrs Hunter tells me that Bawbie Paterson's nephew is
come. Sick leave, she says. And a terrible sight. Influenza
and not got over it. All nonsense too thin. "Bawbie won't
fatten him sore," I says. "Oh, there's aye a bite and a sup for
him here," says she. "Mr Garry kens where to come whan
he's teem. He'll aye get what's goin'. The tail o' a fish and
the tap o' an egg, if it's nae mair." O aye, he would. He had
a crap for a' corn and a baggie for orrels, yon lad. He could
fair go his meat. You would have thought he was yoking a
pair of horse.'

'Well, well,' said Miss Annie, 'what would you expect?
A great growing loon. He needed his meat.'

Kate, who had come home that day with a week's leave
from hospital, heard and said, 'Better ask him to tea. Well,
why not? You ask all the young men home on leave, don't
you? Even if you do object to his aunt—well, even to himself, then—but I daresay he's sobered down by now. We
haven't seen him for donkey's years.'

Miss Theresa conceded the tea. It was one of her ways
of helping on the war. For every young man of the district
home on leave she baked her famous scones and gingerbread, while Miss Annie and Mrs Falconer asked the same
series of questions about the Front.

'I'll tell you what,' said Kate. 'Linny and I will walk round by Knapperley. She's never seen the place.'

'She's seen Bawbie. That should be enough. Well, Lindsay, don't you take her tea if she should offer you any. Spoot-ma-gruel.'

'He'll be waiting for me, Katie,' murmured Lindsay when they were outside.

'That's all right. I'll go away.'

'You'd better give the invitation— Or— As you please.'

Garry said, 'You, Kate— Remember the wasp's bike?'

'Why, yes, I do. Will you face my aunts tomorrow?'

'Will you face mine today? Yes, do come, Katie. Linny must see Knapperley. And I want to talk to you. How are we to set to work killing this lie about Davie? That Morgan creature, you know.'

'Is it a lie?'

'Oh, Katie,' cried Lindsay, 'do help me to convince him. He's taken such a dreadful idea into his head—that poor Louie has invented the whole story. He's hurt her so.'

'That sort doesn't hurt. Does it, Kate?'

'Why, yes. Very badly, I should fancy.'

'What! Hullabaloo? No. You thrust, and she closes up round. Unless she's changed a lot.'

'But why a lie?'

'You think David would have married that?'

'I don't know. Why not?'

'Lord, Kate!'

'Well, I don't see what's preposterous in the idea. She's a good woman. Feckless, a bit. Rather conceited. I'm not particularly fond of her. But David Grey may have been, for all I know. I presume he was, since he asked her to marry him.'

'But he didn't.'

'Didn't?'

'Garry, you don't *know*,' cried Lindsay.

'Look here, Kate, you wouldn't dishonour David, would you? You wouldn't think him capable of such meanness?'

'But why should it be meanness to marry a woman? Most men do.'

'But that Louie.'

'Louie's all right, Garry. I don't see why you should be so angry. I don't like her much, as I said, but lots of people do. You haven't seen her for so long. Of course, she was a bit—you know—self-important. Put on airs. But that sort of thing wears off. Or else one gets accustomed to it. She'd make as good a wife as another. I don't see why David shouldn't have chosen her.'

'David, Kate? As good a wife as another, yes. But for the other man—not for David.'

'David is merely the other man for me, Garry. Any man. I hadn't seen him for years. How could I know what he might or might not do? And a lot of men make fools of themselves when they marry, anyhow.'

'So at least you acknowledge that such a marriage would be folly.'

'No. I was talking of a general principle.'

'Katie, can't you see what is at stake? It's a lie. A blasted, damnable lie. She's false as hell. It must be killed. She must be forced to acknowledge there was no engagement.'

'But what an idea! You propose to put it to her?'

'Oh, Katie,' cried Lindsay, 'he isn't only proposing. He's done it.'

'And she acknowledged it, of course?'

'No, she denied.'

'Well, what more do you want? Why do you suppose it's a lie? I didn't know there was any doubt over it.'

'I suppose it's a lie because it can't be true.'

Kate stopped in the road and gave him a long, considering look.

'Because you refuse to believe it's true, you mean. Do you *know*? David ever say anything about it to you? You've no proof? Look here, Garry, you'd better be sure you're not doing this because you hate Miss Louie Morgan. You never used to miss a chance, you know, of tormenting her.'

'Of taking her down a peg, you mean. She needed it.'

'Yes. But it was good fun, taking her down.'

'Well . . . it staled. You never could take her down. Just what I said: you thrust and she closed up round. Oh yes, good fun enough. But you don't suppose there's any fun in this business about Grey, do you?'

'I think you are persuaded by your own dislike.'

'Katie,' Lindsay's clear, sharp voice rang out, 'you have no right to speak to Garry like that.'

'You don't want him to make a fool of himself in the countryside, do you?'

Garry winced.

'Louie Morgan is too much respected—her father—her mother. People would simply gape. It's your word against hers, isn't it? And they'll all remember the things you used to do to her. Even David Grey thought you went too far. That time you made on to be fighting, and she separated you and you carried her off and shut her in the old Tower.'

'And forgot to let her out.'

'A willing forget.'

'No, I don't think so. No, I'm sure we were doing something else. Queer how hard it is to remember. We did mean to let her out.'

'Do tell me,' said Lindsay.

'Nothing to tell. Horrid rumpus. Dr Morgan purple in the face. And David's father— That was something to remember. Davie said it happened only once before. Davie's father told him off. Six words, no more. No more needed.'

'No one could understand how you got in.'

'We pinched the key.'

'Are you quite sure you are not pinching the key this time? I'll leave you two,' Kate finished abruptly.

'But, Katie—about going home. I came out with you. They'd think it funny.' Lindsay did not wish the old women to understand Garry's identity. They would make uncomfortable remarks.

'Yes,' agreed Kate, 'they do chatter. Very well, I'll wait for you. Behind the spruce trees.'

'But,' Lindsay questioned as she watched Kate melt against the moor, 'need we go to Knapperley?'

Garry had been thinking of Kate: 'How she has altered! She's growing like her aunts. What, not go to Knapperley? But you must see my aunt. She is not fearsome,' he added, smiling.

'But I fear her.'

'Why?' he asked, smiling protectively down upon her.

'No, it's not that—I am not a child.' She could find no way to express her thoughts about Miss Barbara. They were not thoughts—that was it. They were something felt, apprehended in her dumb silent self. The image of Miss Barbara loomed above her, as she had appeared in the winter night, elemental, a mass of the very earth, earthy smelling, with her goat's beard, her rough hairy tweed like the pelt of an animal. She had thought John Grey too like a portion of earth, as he crawled on all fours weeding; but he embodied the kindly and benignant earth; Miss Barbara its coarser, crueller aspect . . . Has no mythology deified a bearded woman as its god of earth? Lindsay, unable to find words to explain her terror, which could not be explained by anything as yet within her experience, blurted, 'It was the lights. They were awful, Garry, truly. Every window blazing, in mid-winter, and it war-time.'

'What's this?' said Garry. 'Good old Barbara! She would win every war that ever was.'

'Win it? Keep it from being won. Defying orders.'

'But that's just it. The spirit of it. We shan't have won this war until we're all defiant. Haven't you understood that yet? My aunt's enormously herself. She'll never alter, except to get more herself. I don't suppose the lights mattered. The police would have seen to it otherwise.'

'But they did. She was fined, I think. Warned, at any rate.'

'Very well. Now come and see her after her warning.'

'You think I am a child, to be afraid.'

But perhaps she was. The warm glad sun danced over her. The earth shimmered away into idle space. And now she had seen a blue tit.

'What is he, what is he? I do so want to know his name. Garry, there are herons in the lower wood. I saw one yesterday with Kate. Flying. A great grey heavy one.'

'They are all like that.'

'Are they?'

'Then it had been herons we were hearing yesterday while we were talking.'

'Yes.'

'And are you satisfied now that you know?'

'Oh, to know makes me so happy . . . You think that strange?'

He took her through the high, bare rooms of Knapperley.

'But these are dreary rooms.'

'Not the kitchen. I don't know where my aunt can be.'

'No matter. Let's go out.'

'I was giving these outer doors and windows a coat of paint. Look how warped they are. The wood's shrunken. Do you mind if I go on?'

'How neatly you work, Garry! Do you hear that bird? I must follow.'

He gave himself to the consideration of Kate. She was wrong to be so sure: he was sure, moreover, that she was wrong. And to bring this ignoble motive in to a clean fight against falsehood! It was petty on Kate's part to suppose that he still harboured these boyish animosities. He fought for greater issues now. And if the victim in each case was the same, was he at fault? It was not as a person that he wanted Louie punished, but as the embodiment of a disgrace. He brought the brush down with neat furious strokes. But Mrs Hunter, when he had called the night before at Craggie, had scorned his suggestion of duplicity in Louie's tale.

'She has the ring, Mr Garry—his mother's ring that she showed me herself, and her dying, and said her laddie's love should wear. That's nae ca'ed story, Mr Garry. Louie fairly has the ring.'

'His mother's ring,' muttered Garry.

'I'm nae saying but it's a queer whirliorum, a matter like a marriage to come out in a by-your-leave fashion like that. Miss Craigmyle, now, was of your way of thinking—that she made the story up, But "Na, na," I said to her, "na, na, she has her credentials." And her credentials is more than the ring, Mr Garry. There's the name she has, and her family.'

Miss Theresa Craigmyle? Very well, then, he would go to their tea.

Lindsay came bounding back.

'Garry, your aunt knows—why didn't you tell me? Your aunt knows all kinds of things. There's a heronry in Kingcausie woods, my heron must have come from there. They have to shut the doors and windows at breeding time. Against the clamour. And there are oyster-catchers' eggs on that bit of shingle. Lying in the stones. You stumble on them. Oh, Garry, I like your paint. You have made a difference.'

'So you found my aunt.'

'I was watching a bird. I didn't know what it was, I am so ignorant. I crept in, under the trees there, following. She found me. I thought it was something wonderful. It was only a chaffinch. But even a chaffinch is very wonderful, if you know just nothing at all, like me.'

'Wonder what Aunt Barbara thinks of this Louie Morgan affair?'

'What does it matter, now? It's ended, isn't it?'

'Ended?'

'Surely Kate convinced you? Do you still think Louie made the story up?'

At the Weatherhouse, after tea that evening, Mrs Falconer followed Kate to the garden. How still the air, how shining pure the sky! Waiting—all waiting for the revelation of spring. But it was so hard to talk confidentially to Kate. Her mother stumbled, came in broken rushes against the girl's tranquillity.

'Garry is coming? I thought, I used to imagine—long ago—you were such friendly you two. I wondered sometimes—but then he went away. I used to think you cared.'

Kate knit her brows, considering the implications of her mother's insight; decided that the secret was not hers to divulge.

'Why, yes,' she said, unbending her frown. 'But there was no need for you to know.'

'And now? It hasn't altered?'

'No. No, I think not.' She thought, 'As good a way as any to cover Lindsay.'

Mother and daughter parted.

'Stop your bumming, Ellen,' sharply said Mrs Craigmyle. Leeb was accustomed to say, 'Not one of my daughters has tune in her, and there's Ellen would bum away half the time, if I would let her.'

Ellen laughed and forebore. She went out to the long brown Weatherhill, where no one would resent her bumming. It was that hour of waning light when colours take on their most magical values. The clumps and thickets of whin, that had turned golden in the few days of sun, glowed with a live intensity, as though light were within them. The colours of life had for Ellen the same bright magical intensity. She was more excited than she knew. Had Kate a hidden life her mother had not suspected? She was so placid, so contained; Ellen had schooled herself for so long to the disappointment of believing that her daughter was thus contained because there was nothing to spill over. Had she misjudged her Kate? Ellen's thoughts turned back to Kate's girlhood, and she remembered how the girl had run about the moor with this Garry Forbes—a great awkward lad, she had never seen much in him. Wild ruffian, Theresa said. Yes, they had all condemned his madcap ways, and Kate had suffered in silence. But Ellen had woven a whole romance around the two and hidden it in her heart, hardly believing it had more foundation than the hundred other romances that she wove. But it had, it had. Foundation, and a new miraculous lustre. Kate took on a new dignity in her mother's eyes—perhaps the grandeur of a tragic destiny. But no, that must not be—unless he were slaughtered. No, no, I must not fancy things like that. Kate's love would reach its consummation. They would be wedded. He would call her mother. The boy had had no mother—and now he would tell her the things that a son keeps for a mother's ear. 'Mother, it is so easy to tell this to you. You have a way of listening—' No, no. I must not fancy things like that.

But on the morrow, when Garry came to the Weatherhouse, Mrs Falconer tingled with her excitement. She pressed herself upon the guest, eager to know him. 'For Kate's sake, I must get to understand him.'

'You've no knives on your table, Nell,' scolded Theresa.

'No, no. No.' She *scuttered* at the open drawer, sat down again by Garry, smiling.

'See that your mother has those knives put down,' said Theresa to Kate. 'When my back's about I can't know what she'll do. She's been the deed of two or three queer things this day. I've got two or three angers with her.'

'She's tired today, I fancy.'

'Tired! Your granny in a band-box.'

Kate returned from the kitchen and set the knives herself. Mrs Falconer was smiling, looking up in Garry's face, asking senseless unimportant questions.

'You might have the wit to know *that*,' Lindsay was thinking, impatient at the trivial turns the conversation took.

'Mother, don't giggle,' said Kate, aside, passing her.

'Why shouldn't she giggle?' Garry thought, watching for the first time the elderly lady with interest. 'So, Miss Kate, you are growing like your aunt Theresa. You put people right.' He gave Mrs Falconer's questions a serious attention.

Theresa brought in the tea.

'There', slapping down her pancakes before the guest, 'you don't get the like of that at Knapperley. It's aye the same thing with Bawbie, a stovie or a sup kail.'

Garry drawled, 'A soo's snoot stewed on Sunday and on Monday a stewed soo's snoot.' And he did not look at Miss Theresa, whom he hated, with her air of triumph, her determination to show him that man must live by bread alone.

Miss Annie laughed delightedly. 'When did I hear that last? And whiles it'll be as tough's the woodie, I'm thinking, your soo's snoot.'

Lindsay cried, 'Garry, do you know them too, all these funny picturesque phrases? You must teach them to me.'

But Theresa muttered, 'Sarcastic deevil.'

'I would have you know'—he addressed himself mentally to Theresa—'I can't stand people who humiliate me. The pancakes are excellent, Miss Craigmyle,' he said aloud. 'And now please tell me, why do you suppose Miss Louie Morgan was not engaged to David Grey?'

'Did ever you suppose such a thing, Aunt Tris?' asked Kate.

'Garry has taken a dreadful idea into his head,' cried Lindsay, 'that Louie made the story up.'

'There!' cried Theresa triumphantly. 'Didn't I tell you that long ago, but you weren't hearing me. I was right, you see. I'm not often wrong.'

But was she right? Now, where did the tale begin? Let's trace it out. But nothing came of that, except to disturb everyone's sense of security. No, not a whisper before his death: that was plain. But shortly after, 'I haven't the right to wear mourning,' she had said to Mrs Hunter. And she had the ring. And Mr Grey received her often. But counter-balance that with her character: well, a good character, a moral character. But they all knew she was out after a man. Oh yes, a flighty thing, always ogling the men. 'Though there's lots that's taken in with her airs and her graces.' Would a man like Grey be taken in? His character against her known assertiveness, her pretty dangling. But where does all this lead? Since the man is dead, it can't be known for certain.

'Since he is dead, I must put it to the proof. His reputation must be cleared. And publicly.'

'Be wary, Garry,' said Kate. 'If you are wrong—no, accept the possibility for a moment—if you are wrong, you will have pilloried your friend.'

'Publicly,' Miss Annie cried. 'You wouldn't do the like of that. She's a harmless craiturie that nobody seeks to mind.'

'And it would hurt her. Garry, you don't understand—it will hurt her horribly,' Lindsay pleaded. 'Suppose he did love her, after all.'

'And David Grey,' said Miss Theresa, 'is hardly of the place now, as you might say. Since he went away to go to the college we've hardly seen or heard of him. Except his medals, to be sure, and prizes. But he might marry anyone you pleased to point at, and who would care? Not a soul would let their kail grow cold with thinking of it.'

'And anyway,' said Kate, 'now that he's dead, does it matter?'

'Captain Forbes matters,' said Mrs Falconer.

Ellen's hands were clasped tight together above her breast, and they shook rapidly from her excitement. They were like a tiny bald nodding head that gave assent to her speech. Her head nodded too, slightly and rapidly.

The gaunt young man looked across the table; and remained looking, his jaw down, as though, having opened his mouth to speak, what he was about to say had become suddenly unimportant.

'I mean,' she continued, 'honour matters. Whether people care or not, and whether she's to be hurt or not, you've to get the truth clear. Because of truth itself. Because of his honour. And it matters to you, because you feel his honour's in your keeping now he's gone.'

'Yes,' he said, 'that's why. Because of truth itself. It's good of you to see that.'

If one had never seen a bird before, never seen a flake of earth, loosened and blown into the air, change shape and rise, and poise, and speed far off, beyond the power of eye to follow; seeing one would understand the sharp delight that Mrs Falconer experienced at hearing the young man's words. She kindled, her face became winsome, like that of a young girl. She laughed—a low, sweet laughter. When he talked to her, words bubbled on her lips.

'But must you go so soon?' she pleaded. '—Yes, yes, a pack of women, we can't entertain you very hard.'

Indeed, as he walked away the man felt relief from the pack of women. On the other side of the dyke Francie Ferguson, slicing turnips, droned a song. Garry leaned his arms on the dyke and looked over.

'Ay, ay, you're having a song to yourself.'

Francie straightened his shoulders, pushed his cap farther back on his head, answered, 'Imphm,' scratched himself a little, added, 'Just that,' and returned to the turnips.

'Decent fellow,' thought Garry. Yes, that Morgan creature had to be corrected. Beside the honesty of Francie she showed unclean.

In the Weatherhouse: 'Stop your bumming, Ellen,' commanded Mrs Craigmyle.

'Mother, don't giggle,' said Kate apart.

As on the evening before, Mrs Falconer left them and walked alone on the Weatherhill. Again the sky was shining pure. Again the wide land waited. Annunciation of spring

was in the brown ploughed fields, the swollen buds, the
blackbird's sudden late cascade of song, the smell of earth.
A wood of naked birches hung on the hillside like a cloud of
heather, so deep a glow of purple was in their boughs. And
a bird had gone up out of Ellen's heart, pursuing its unac-
countable way into the distance. A flake from her earth had
risen. Life had a second spring, and it was opening for this
woman of sixty who had lived so long among her dreams.
The earnest young man, his brows drawn in that anxious
pucker, his eyes unsatisfied, roving from face to face, burdened with the pain and ugliness of life—yes, she was sure
that that was it, that haunted look of his betrayed a soul unhappy over the torment and mystery of life, its unreason and
its evil—this young man had brought her suddenly back into
its throng and business. She who had been content to dream
must now do.

And her fancy was off. She saw that it was she who
was to help the young man (she called him mentally her
son-in-law) to establish the truth, to rout Louie.

'How can I have lived among trivial matters for so long?'
she thought. 'This is real, and good. I feel alive.'

She wandered back slowly to the house. Light still lingered in the sky; the hills, that had been dissolved in its
splendour, like floating shapes of light themselves, grew
dark again. Ellen too, emerged from the transfiguring glory
of light in which she had been walking. What did her happiness mean? Why, of course, she was happy because of
Katie. This mysterious and tranquil glow that had irradiated life had its source in a mother's satisfaction. Kate loved,
Kate would be loved, Kate's mother would be satisfied.

But in the house there was no satisfaction. They were all
talking together. Lindsay tossed back her disordered hair,
angry tears were in her eyes. The leaping firelight gleamed
on her face, her agitated movements, and on Theresa's fingers as she put away the knives and silver, and on Leeb's
busy knitting needles and the glittering points her eyes made
in the gloom.

'Cousin Ellen,' cried the girl, 'Cousin Ellen, Louie is
true. Oh, she is! Garry is wrong, wrong, wrong.'

'It's not worth the to-do, Lindsay,' said Miss Theresa.

Ellen flamed magnificently from the exaltation with which she had been suffused. 'But yes. Always worth, always worth to follow truth. The young man is doing the right.'

'To hurt her? Even if it wasn't an engagement. If she just loved him—and never told?'

'She never did. She just couldn't stand being unimportant.'

Ellen said it suddenly. She had not known it herself till that moment. 'There's all the girls round about, they all had their lads, and some of them killed and some wounded, and everybody making much of them and them on everyone's lips. And Louie had nobody. She had a lot of talk one time about *missing, missing,* as though she wanted us to believe she had someone and him lost.'

'What an idea, Mother!' said Kate.

'But she had. "It's cruel, this *Missing, Presumed Dead,*" she would say. "It keeps one from starting fresh." '

'Yes, she said that to me.' Lindsay stared across at Mrs Falconer. 'She said, "It's the faithfulness that is unto death. It deadens you. Keeps you from beginning life anew." What a curious thing to say!'

'Always what we couldn't disprove, you see. And then she hit on David Grey. And so she paraded her tragedy. It made her important. They may say what they like about Louie looking miserable—she's never looked so *filled out* as she has of late. She was a starved sort of thing before.'

'But, Cousin Ellen, I can't believe that it's all a lie. If you had heard Louie talk about it. So tenderly. You can't imagine. A lie couldn't be lovely like that.'

'There's lots you can't believe in life, Linny. Angels of darkness masquerading as angels of light. I'm some afraid she's lived so much with her lie that she can't feel it a lie any longer. Her head must know, but her heart is persuaded.'

Lindsay's eyes, mournful and still, were fixed on her. 'Why, the child herself had some affair,' Ellen remembered. Surely it was over. This eager Lindsay, following bird song, catching at country ways and sights, gathering windflowers, was quite changed from the pallid girl who had come to them at Christmas. 'Yes, yes, she was too young. It must be over.' But the girl's eyes burned in the dusk; not eyes of light forgetfulness.

Theresa put the last of the knives away, and stood scratching the side of her nose.

'Such a to-do about a dead man,' she said, 'that can't come back to set the matter right. I've had an itchy nose all day—itchy nose, you'll hear of fey folk. It's to be hoped no more of you are doomed, the way you're carrying on. I always told you Louie made the story up. But to hold this parliament about it—'

'Cousin Theresa, don't you dare to mention it to anyone. Not anyone. That Louie made it up, I mean. Not till it's proved, if Garry ever does prove it. To disgrace her publicly— If *you* begin to talk, she'll have publicity enough.'

Mrs Craigmyle chuckled from her corner. 'Take you that to butter your skate.' Without lifting her eyes or altering a muscle of her face, she began to hum a little tune.

'You're turning as rude as that young man, Miss Lindsay,' retorted Theresa. 'But you will note that he enjoyed his tea. You needn't be in such a taking over Louie, bairn,' she added, more kindly. 'Grows there skate on Clochnaben? She was born with a want—you'll get no sense yonder. But *you* needn't turn your head about it. You greetin' like a leaky pot, and Nell with a great baby's face on her—I never saw the like. Worse than you's useless.'

The face that Ellen turned towards the fire was indeed strangely child-like. A soft smile played on it, pleased and innocent. She was still thinking, 'I shall help him to proclaim the truth.' But the sharpness of truth was not visible on her countenance. She had the look of the dreamer who has not yet tried to shape his dream from intractable matter.

In the firelit room Mrs Craigmyle's hum grew more audible. The words became clear:

Duncan Forb's cam here to woo,

sang Mrs Craigmyle, with a subtle emphasis upon the altered word:

Ha, ha, the wooin' o't.

Ellen looked up. Her face quivered. She began to talk loud and quickly.

'Hateful,' she thought, 'making it uncomfortable for Kate.'

Later she found her mother alone. Mrs Craigmyle raised her voice (but not her eyes) at her daughter's approach:

Duncan Forb's cam here to woo.

She sang gaily, her foot tapping the time, and her snow-white head, crowned with its mist of fine black lace, nodding to the leap of the flames. And her face was innocent of any intention. She was singing an old song.

'Mother,' said Ellen, with burning cheeks, 'you shouldn't do that. Hinting. In your song. It isn't nice.'

Mrs Craigmyle turned an amused, appraising eye upon her widowed daughter.

'You're right, bairn,' she answered blandly. 'The young man has a good Scots name that won't fit into the metre. You're right. I shouldn't spoil an old name as though I had an English tongue on me—feared to speak two syllables when one will do. I'll not offend again.'

She watched her daughter with a fine regard that had malice in it. Mrs Craigmyle, through her apparent uncon-cern, had noted Ellen, habitually so quiet and reserved, kindle and crackle, and it amused her.

'Well,' said Ellen, 'but if Kate doesn't like it.'

'That's right my lass, study you to please your family.'

Ellen went away, her cheeks still hot; and a mocking laughter followed her, faint, that seemed to echo from very far off, centuries away, in ancient story.

Lindsay was leaning from her open window. The spring night, hushed and dim, yet held a tumult. Out there, in every field, in boughs of the secret wood, life moved. Kate slept, but Lindsay could not sleep. Everything—the promise of spring in the air, an owl's call up the valley, the tranquil radiance that the young moon had left above the hills, water tumbling with a thin clear note, the shame and trouble of her nature—all conspired to keep her exquisitely awake. And Lindsay thought, 'I want everyone to be happy. It shouldn't hurt like this—all that beauty.'

She could not tell herself what the hurt was. All was vague and confused in her mind. Garry was different from what she had supposed him. But she had known him so little—only his kisses and those amazing talks, far into the night, until her father came and sent them all to bed. This Garry with the worried frown and haggard eyes was someone else. Worrying because he wanted to do a wicked thing—Lindsay was still convinced by Louie's phrases. Or—were her confusion and trouble because she was no longer quite convinced? Was Louie, whom she had set admiringly in her temple, no god at all, but brittle clay?

'I don't understand,' she cried, leaning to the night. 'Life's so strange. It isn't what you want.'

One grew and things altered, people altered, just being alive was somehow not the same. Spring was like that, changing the world, taking away the shapes and colours to which one was accustomed. Were seeds afraid, she wondered, and buds? Afraid to grow, afraid of life as she was afraid of it. Evil, and wrong—one knew there were such things in the world, but to find them in people, that was different. In people that one knew. Garry cruel, and Louie false; and all the while earth and sky brimmed with beauty. And she leaned farther into the tranquil night.

Below her on the grass someone was moving. Who should be in the garden so late? If it were Garry! How good to have him seek her presence in the dark, in the still, sweet April glamour! A very night for lovers.

But the figure on the lawn moved farther off. Now it was against the sky, and she saw that it was a woman's. Her eyeballs were stinging. 'I only want to be happy,' she cried. The sound of her own voice, breaking unexpectedly upon the silence, affrighted her. But Katie did not stir, and in a moment another voice was borne to her upon the air. She recognised it for Theresa's. 'Come in to your bed, Ellen.' The voice floated from the next window. 'Walking there like a ghost.' There was no answer, but the figure in the garden moved back towards the house; and Lindsay heard a stair creak. Cousin Ellen! Why should she walk in the night? Why should anyone walk in the night but the young and the untranquil and the lovers who cannot wait for morning?

SEVEN

Why Classroom Doors should be Kept Locked

Morning changed the temper of the spring. Plainly the lady had no more mind for honeyed promises. Her suave and gracious mood was done, and those who would win her favours must wrestle a fall with the insolent young Amazon. Sleet blattered against the ploughman's side as he followed the team; or, standing in a blink of sun, he saw the striding showers cross the corner of the field like sheeted ghosts. Never tell me, ghosts took to sheets for the first time in a Deeside ploughman's story, who, bewildered in an April dusk, saw white showers walk the land, larger than human, driven on the wind.

'Where are my birds today?' asked Lindsay. 'And oh, the poor thin petals! Look, Garry, on the whin.'

But Garry answered, 'I'm going to take you home.'

At the Weatherhouse door Mrs Falconer met them, running.

'Come in, come in. You must be wet.'

She did not pause to question why they were together.

'They never seem to guess,' Lindsay thought. 'Old people don't see.'

Doors flapped, sleet scurried along the lobby.

'Come in, come in,' Mrs Falconer cried. 'She will be angry at this mess.'

She drew them in and, stooping, plucked with her fingers at the melting flakes of sleet, and dabbed at the runnels with a corner of her skirt. 'There, she'll be none the wiser.'

'Not a whit,' Garry said. He had taken out his handkerchief and wiped a smeared wet patch from the hat stand.

But Theresa was safely in the kitchen, so they sat and talked by the living-room fire, with old Aunt Leeb spider-quiet in her corner, and Paradise in a happy doze. She opened her eyes and smiled at them. 'I'm dozened,' she said, and slid away again.

Garry began to talk of after the war. 'It will be a very different Britain before we're done with it.' He told them all that was to be accomplished to make life worthier. Lindsay glowed. This was the talk she loved to hear. Her young untried enthusiasms delighted in the noble. Above all she wanted her lover to be good. These splendid generalities were like the fulfilment of all her own vague adolescent aspirations.

Ellen also glowed. 'Why, what a barren useless life I have lived!' She felt a smoulder of shame run through her at the thought of the evanescent fancies in which her inner life had passed. 'But *this* is real. How I hate these shams and unrealities!' And, without noticing what she did, she began to form a new fancy. 'Katie loves him. If they should ever marry—when they marry I trust they will let me live with them.' How good that would be—to live in daily touch with men's enterprises, to know what was done and thought in the world. Hearing the young man speak, she would never slide again into these wicked imaginings. And she remembered how he had taken out his handkerchief and wiped away the smear of sleet. 'But when I live with them, I shan't need to go in terror of Tris.' She could open the door then, without fear of what came in, to strength and manhood and new ideas, and even to brave young folly that laughed in the sleet when it might sit warm at home.

All this she fancied at the very moment that Lindsay, lifting her eyes to smile into her lover's, was thinking, 'I thought if he came here there would be all their stupid jokes to face, but not one of them seems to notice.' Then she saw Miss Annie's eye upon her. But Miss Annie only said, 'I think I'm taking a cold. Lindsay, you've no clothes on.'

Lindsay ran behind the old woman's chair and put her arms round her neck. 'Girls don't wear clothes nowadays, Paradise, you dear.' And she wanted to tell Paradise that Garry was her lover. 'Because I'm sure you saw,' she thought. And, after all, it was pleasant that Paradise had seen. 'It's the others who would talk. Paradise, your hair's so soft behind. Paradisal hair.'

'It's got most terrible grey.'

'Silver, you mean. Silver of Paradise. Apples of gold and silver of Paradise.'

'You're a wheedling thing—what are you wanting now?'

'Only a kiss.'

She dropped a kiss in the nape of Miss Annie's neck and danced round the back of Garry's chair, running her fingers across his shoulders as she passed; but Cousin Ellen she did not touch. Even grand-aunt Leeb she had breathed upon, blowing a kiss so light upon her ancient head that the gossamer of her lace hardly trembled.

'How strange!' she thought. 'Last night I was miserable. And now today I'm glad. I don't know what to make of life.'

And Mrs Falconer, whom she had not touched, was unaware of the omission. A warm glow suffused her body. She was thinking, 'This false betrothal, that is something true. To expose the falsehood is something real that I can take my part in.'

Garry went away. The sleet eased off, but the roads were like mortar and the land looked bleak. An empty land—he remembered his vision of it as taking form from the primordial dark. Some human endeavour there must be: like Lindsay unaccustomed to a country year, he had hardly realised before today how much endeavour, skill and endurance went to the fashioning of food from earth in weathers such as these. His midsummer holidays had not told him of wet seed-times, of furious winds blowing the turnip seed across the moors, of snow blackening the stooks of corn. He saw a man lead home his beasts through mire, fields not yet sown were sodden wet again. He had never thought before of these things. There must be grit and strength in the men who sowed their turnips thrice and ploughed land that ran up into the encroaching heather. A tough race, strong in fibre. Yet since he came how little he had seen of them! Women mostly—Lindsay like whin blossom on the cankered stem of her people; his aunt like an antique pine, one side denuded, with gaunt arms flung along the tempest; Mrs Hunter like a bed of thyme . . . pleasant fancies, dehumanising the land.

Across them he felt suddenly as though a teasing tangle

had been flung—nets of spider-web, or some dark stinging noxious weed from under ocean. He had thought of Louie Morgan. He disliked the thought—no question as to that. And how this mean affair had tangled across his vision! Wherever he turned he saw it. Three days ago, when they came on Louie at her base devotions and he had heard the story first, it had seemed a simple thing to dispose of it. Now it was less simple. He had recoiled instinctively from the tale as something false, but his instinct was to be taken as no proof by other people. These women with whom he had discussed it insisted, moreover, after the fashion of women, on treating it as a personal matter, a matter of Louie Morgan, not of truth. His aunt, to be sure, had raised the issue to a matter of principle, but not one that helped him much.

'What's she wanting with a man ava?' was all he got from Miss Barbara.

The others saw it purely on the personal plane; and Kate's assumption that he himself was moved by a personal rancour smote him to wrath. Even Lindsay could not see that truth and justice were beyond a personal hurt—Lindsay, who had looked so sublimely lovely in her pleading that he resisted her hardly. Her eyes had been fixed on him, mournful and limpid. She was lovelier than herself. She had identified herself with Louie. She too, was hurt and was transfigured in her acceptance of another's suffering.

He had thought, 'But you can't ask other people to pay the price. You can't ask Lindsay.' Was truth, after all, more important than the pain you inflict on others for its sake? It was only that long, lean, nice Mrs Falconer who understood that truth and honour were at stake. A curious champion of truth. He remembered her furtive ducking in the lobby to dab the runlets of sleet with her petticoat. Well, he supposed, one could tilt at error even in petticoats and in spite of an abounding fear of one's sister in her domestic cogencies.

He had as yet, in these three days, had no man's opinion upon his problem. Not, for instance, John Grey's. But to visit John Grey, as he knew he must, David's father, was of necessity to find some expression for what he felt over David's death; and he could find none.

At that moment, through the darkening light, he saw Miss Morgan approach.

'The deil has lang lugs to hear when he's talked about,' muttered Garry.

Miss Morgan picked her way towards him along the puddled road, and her face was as puddled as the road itself. She was weeping. She stood with downcast eyes in front of the astonished young man and said, 'Oh, Captain Forbes, what shall I do? I've been a wicked woman. Help me, Garry—I may call you Garry? We are such old friends, we used to play together.'

A man stumped past and regarded them with curiosity.

'Well, we can't talk here,' Garry said.

'No, no. The school. I was going there. I have the key.' And she led the way, looking back at him over her shoulder with eyes that languished and saying, 'The concert, you know. For those comforts. Garry, I understand what you meant about comforts. We think our responsibility is over, and it isn't. Our responsibility is never over. We are our brother's keeper all the time. You must be my keeper.'

She unlocked the school door. 'I have a key. I am in charge, you see. A little sketch they are doing—there are so few hereabouts that understand these things.'

The school was a two-roomed building, built close upon the church. The church having no hall, and a vestry like a cupboard, the adjoining school was used for many parochial purposes. Miss Morgan went in. 'I have to measure something—curtains, you know.'

Garry followed in spite of a remarkable distaste. To chatter of curtains amid tears of contrition argued, to him, a blameworthy lightness. But were the tears of contrition? He waited.

'No, I think in here,' Louie was saying. She led him to the inner room, and with some ostentation locked the door. She had an indescribable air of enjoying the situation.

Then she came swiftly at him.

'Help me, help me. What am I to do? I've done such dreadful things. I've lied and I've stolen. I am a miserable sinner, and my transgression is ever before me.'

He stopped her torrent of words with a cold: 'It is easy

to bring such general accusations, Miss Morgan. We are all sinners. If I understood what you referred to—'

She darted him a glance of hatred.

'Of course you understand. But you will make it as hard for me as you are able. Oh, what shall I do? What shall I do? People must never know what I have done. Promise me that—they mustn't know. Promise me.'

'When I know myself—'

'Yes, yes, make it as hard for me as you can. It's right, it's just. I want to confess to the uttermost. Abjectly. I will tell you—I want to tell you everything. You. But no one else. Oh, do not make it public! My name, my mother, afterwards.—Yes, yes, I will tell you all.'

Garry stood in the dark schoolroom and marvelled. He had never seen an emotional abandonment so extreme, and it seemed to him as ignoble as her perfidious clutch on his friend. He would not have helped her out in the confession, determined that she should taste its dregs by telling all; but disgust drove him to shorten the affair.

'You mean that there was no engagement.'

'No, no, it's not like that.'

'You made it up.'

'No, no, I did not make it up.'

'What then?'

'It wasn't like that. Yes, yes, I made it up. Oh, how wicked I have been! Quite, quite wrong. Evil. I see that now.'

Suddenly she raised her head, listening.

'Yes, there's someone there,' said Garry.

He had heard before she did a sound of voices outside and of feet. Now the outer door of the school was pushed open and men came in. They heard their tramp and the noise of speech.

Louie's whole expression altered. She snatched her companion by the arm and whispered, 'Caught. It's a session meeting. I had forgotten it was tonight. What shall we do?'

He shook her off. 'There's nothing to make a fuss about. You have the right to be here, I suppose, since you have the key.'

At that moment someone tried the door of the inner room. The voices rose.

'But you,' said Louie, weeping. 'And alone here. And it's dark. Oh, what shall I do?'

'Do what you please. I should imagine you could invent a sufficient story.' He flung the window up and leaped out on to the ground. 'Better shut that window again,' he called back. Then he strode off.

Louie wiped her eyes and opened the door.

An oil lamp, new-lit and smoky, hung in the outer room. Louie blinked. Her eyes, bleared and tender, smarted in the smoky atmosphere; she stood shaking, thus ruthlessly thrust back from her attempt at truth to the service of appearances. To these men she was still Miss Morgan, daughter of their late minister. She put her head to the side and apologised, and in a minute speech came freely to her and with it relief: she had escaped from the terror of her attempted encounter with her naked self.

'I really didn't remember—that concert, you know. I was measuring. I didn't remember your meeting. But I'll go— Well, if you don't mind. I could get on with those curtains.' Aided by one of the elders, she took her measurements, which were in the outer room, and went.

Outside Garry stood in the gloom. It was lighter here than in the school. It was lighter than he had expected. Forms of men passed him and entered at the school door: elders of the kirk, on their way to deliberate. An odd idea seized him—to walk in upon their deliberations and state his problem. He remembered the old kirk session records: *Compeared before the Session, John Smith and Mary Taylor*—the public accusation and punishment. If he were to go now: *Compeared before the Session, David Grey and Louisa Morgan.* She was still there. Why should she not answer for her guilt, her moral delinquency? But to drag the dead man there—

He put the idea from him and walked on; but, considering that he had better have the interrupted matter out with Miss Morgan, returned towards the school.

Jonathan Bannochie the cobbler came from the school door as he hesitated.

'The birdie's flown, ma lad,' said Jonathan. 'Ay, she's awa'.'

Garry stared, but turned and walked on.

Jonathan kept step beside him. 'I'm for the same way mysel'. I've a pair o' boots for Jake Hunter's missus. They can just cogitate awa' wantin' me or I win back. Yon was a gey grand jump you took out at the windock. The laddies wouldna need to ken yon, or the missy'll hae her ain adae to haud them in. Ye're nae takin' us on? Man, it was a grand notion to get the door locked on the pair o' you. Ye're nae takin's on, I'm sayin'. Well, well, and what was the door locked for, my lad?'

'On a point of honour.'

'Eh? What's that? O ay, it's a gey honorable business, a kiss.' And he bellowed:

Some say kissin's a sin
But I say it's nane ava.

'Is the construction your own?' said Garry, stopping short. 'Or the finding of the Session?'

In the grey half-light he eyed his man. Jonathan Bannochie was a power to reckon with in Fetter-Rothnie. That the man had character was very evident: his mouth was gripped, a sardonic and destructive light glimmered in his eye. The man was baleful, yet not in action, but in speech. To have one's reputation on the souter's tongue did not make for comfort. If the souter's thumb was broad, in accordance with the rhyme:

The hecher grows the plum-tree
The sweeter grows the plums,
And the harder that the souter works
The broader grows his thumbs—

(and Jonathan was a smart and capable workman), the souter's tongue was sharp as the thumb was broad. He could destroy in a phrase, spread ruin with a jest. It was he who, in a few days' time, with a twist of mockery, was to make the name of Garry Forbes the common possession of Fetter-Rothnie speech.

Of this Garry could have no foreknowledge; but he saw in front of him a man of parts whose life's achievement had narrowed itself to a point of tongue. Undoubted that Jonathan had made his shoemaking a success, and Garry's philosophy set high the man whose common labour was achieved with skill and honesty; but that Jonathan's gifts would have been adequate to more than the cobbling of country boots he was very sure. The man had been dissipated, though by no overt system of dissipation. He did not even drink: in Mrs Hunter's eyes a downward step. 'I dinna ken what's come over him,' she said, 'he doesna even drink now. And a kinder man you needna have wished to meet when he had a dram in him.' His domestic life had come to grief. The wife whom Mrs Hunter could never understand his having chosen ('I dinna ken what gar't him tak her. A woman with a mouth like yon. The teeth that sair gone that the very jaws was rottin'. And nae even a tongue in it to haud her ain wi'.') moved early from the scene, and left him two daughters, both spiced with their father's temper. Both decamped. A few years later the elder girl, choosing her time with a knowledge of her father's habits, descended on the homestead, 'and up and awa' wi' the dresser under one arm and the best bed under the other.' Jonathan found the house stripped. In compensation a puny child was left on the kitchen bed. But Kitty did not prove another Eppie. She grew up scared and neglected, the butt of her grandfather's scorn, with rotting teeth like those of her grandmother, and her grandmother's lack of tongue.

In addition Jonathan Bannochie was an elder of the kirk, feared but hardly respected, a shrewd and efficient critic of other men's business and bosoms.

'Is the construction your own?' Garry asked, watching his man. 'Or the finding of the Session?'

'Ach, haud your tongue, Mr Forbes. A bonny lassie in ahin a door—we're nae the lads to blame you.'

There flashed across Garry's mind: *Compeared before the Session, Louisa Morgan and John Dalgarno Forbes.* Apparently, the finding was acquittal. He laughed.

'You've the wrong soo by the lug this time. Mrs Hunter, did you say? I'll hand over the boots. But as I've a matter to lay before the Session, I'll take it kindly if you'll step back with me now and hear it.' He stowed Jonathan's parcel away in his pocket.

EIGHT

Compeared before the Session

'Gentlemen,' said Garry, facing the assembled Session, 'forgive this interruption, but I see you have not yet begun your business. And I've some business of my own—yours too—I want to make it yours.'

He looked earnestly round the men. Some he knew, others were mere faces; one lined and puckered like a chimpanzee's, one spare and shrewd; one fat, without distinction, one keen and cultured; enormous brows; black beards; an oppression of watching eyes. He felt the impact of them like a mob; but as he talked, he scanned the countenances, swiftly computing how each would answer to his challenge. At his shoulder he was aware of the sardonic semi-grin of Jonathan Bannochie, that haunted him like an echo of all that grinned within himself, his contempt of his own sensitiveness to ridicule, his fear of the humiliation of failure. In front was the long, serious face of Jake Hunter, a crofter on his aunt's estate, husband to the jolly woman who was his aunt's old servant and faithful friend. Jake, too, was a faithful soul; a stern fighter against the odds of poverty, sour soil, bad harvests and uncertain prices. His bit of land was seamed with outcrops of rock and heather. He cut laboriously with the scythe, both because the land was too steep and uneven for the reaping machine he did not possess, and also because the scythe cut closer to the ground and no inch of loss on stubble could be afforded. Jake had fought his slow, obscure way upwards, quenching errant enthusiasms. Books had been one such enthusiasm. He was already a man over forty, toughened and worn by exposure and labour from his earliest childhood, when he wedded Barbara Paterson, Miss Bawbie's servant girl, and her uncle settled them on the meagre croft. Then for the first time Jake hoped to satisfy his craving for knowledge. He bought some books, a miscellaneous lot picked up from a second-hand bookstall, and settled it with Barbara that he would read for an hour each night. Barbara put the book for him and took her shank to sit and watch. But the reading did not thrive. A day's work is a day's work, and a man must stretch himself.

'I'm nae nane swacker o' anither day's wark, 'umman,' he would say; and then he would *ficher* with the pages awhile and nod a little. By and by it would be up to have a look at the weather.

'I'll just rax mysel' to be mair soople for the book,' he would tell Barbara, and coming back, dropped to sleep again. Not as you would say a real sleep. Still less of course, a feigned one. A sample, rather—three-four grains between finger and thumb for earnest of the wide fields of slumber that would be his at night. Waking from one of these offhand naps, he would stretch himself largely, move to the door again, and restore the book to the shelf before sitting down.

'I'll just be puttin' it by for the night,' he would say, smothering a mighty yawn. 'It's as you might say a habit, the readin', it beats you at the start. It'll come mair natural-like come time.'

Vain expectation. These habits do not grow on one. They have none of your fine Biblical ease in pushing, a man going to sleep and rising night and day while they adjust themselves to the requirements of the universe. Each year that made the rent queerer to come by and the stomachs of his hungry bairns harder to find a bottom to, made Jake swacker neither in the muscles nor in the wits. He stiffened by living. But his fervour for book learning passed to his eldest son Dave, who united the serious humour of his father with the drive of his mother's vitality. Dave, serving his time as a joiner, read far into the night, and fired by his new experiences at the Front, wrote home, as Mrs Hunter had told Lindsay, that he would put the younger boys through the University. As it happened, Dave, returning from the war with a single arm, went through the University himself on his pension and an ex-service grant, and turned schoolmaster, to his parents' great content.

Garry, in the rapid glance by which we can review at times many years' knowledge of a personality, saw the long, grave anxious face of Jake Hunter as that of a good man, a man upright in all his dealings, but too limited in the reach of his experience to understand the matter on which Garry desired a judgment.

His next door neighbour, John Grey, David's father, was not in the company. Garry felt freer to speak, but regretted not to meet him for the first time since David's death among other people.

The minister, who watched the young man curiously, was a latecomer to the district, not very old, pale and shrunken. To him, Garry felt, he was not speaking, but to these elder men who knew both Louie and David and had some pretensions to knowledge of himself.

'Gentlemen,' he said, addressing the pale young minister, 'I had a friend, a man you all knew and I believe respected—as you respect his father, Mr John Grey. He's dead. I lived with him—that tells you what a man is like. Well, I believe in David's honour with all my soul. I come here and I find—we make honourable images of our dead, don't we?—I find the image left of him in your memories defaced. By a woman. The woman who came out of that room there just now. I am given to understand you knew that I was in there too. Well, I was. In the dark. Locked in and all the rest of it. And I jumped out of the window, as I gather you also know. Because, gentlemen, I wanted to prove—I have every reason to believe'—he spoke very slowly, measuring his words— 'that her claim to be engaged to David Grey was an impudent forgery. She is a woman whose word is not to be trusted—'

'Tell her that, and seek a saxpence,' said Jonathan at his ear.

'I am convinced there was no engagement. The thing–the thing's immoral.' He began to talk wildly, blurring his words. Jonathan's interpolation angered him. 'It's an insult to my friend. Tell me—that's what I want you to do, once it was the duty of the Session to regulate the morals of the community, it doesn't seem to be so any longer—tell me what I am to do now.'

The men were embarrassed. The affair at issue was curious. But the man with the keen face, whom Garry did not know, and who was a petty landowner not always resident in the parish, said, 'There would seem to be the man to answer your question.' And turning, Garry saw John Grey, who had come quietly in while he was speaking.

It was a number of years since he had seen Mr Grey, and he was aghast at the change he saw. He was now an old man. His shoulders were bent, what was left of his hair had gone white; but the receding of the hair served only to expose still further the noble and lofty forehead and give his figure a serene dignity, a majesty even, that his smallness of stature hardly led one to expect. He had come in late. Weariness was in his bearing. He had lifted shells all day. But as he stood listening to Garry, his face was alert, and a deep still glow burned in his eyes. He came forward now, a pleasant briskness in his spare figure, and taking Garry by the hand, very courteously gave him welcome, neither mentioning what he had overheard nor inquiring the young man's business among the elders; but the former speaker pressed his point, saying, 'Mr Forbes has a matter here for your attention.'

'Let the matter rest.'

There was a stern authority in John Grey's tone. Without raising his voice, which was habitually soft, he yet conveyed in its intonation a settled finality that caused Garry to tremble. He had heard that note in his voice only once before, when David and he as boys had locked Louie in the tower.

'I know no more than you do,' John Grey said, 'the truth of this engagement. My son never mentioned it to me. The boy is dead. Let there be no more said about it.'

No more could be said. Garry felt a fool. He got himself out of that room and stood fuming on the road, having distinguished nothing in what was afterwards said to him but Jonathan Bannochie's whisper, 'Try her in the Tower, Mr Forbes.'

Inside the schoolroom there was an awkward moment. Most of the men resented vaguely this intrusion into the ordinariness of living. The landowner with the keen face said, 'A curious affair. Has the young man any grounds for his suspicion?'

Another man answered, 'Now here's a funny thing. Just yesterday my lassie had a letter from a friend, a boy in Captain Forbes's Company. Went queer, they said. Left out in a shell-hole and brought back clean off—raving mad. A corpse bumping at his heels that he insisted was himself. Wouldn't leave go of it. Touched, I'm afraid.'

'Is that the way of it? Poor chap! The war has much to answer for. He certainly looked raised.'

Garry, indeed, hollow-eyed, taut with the terrible earnestness of his purpose, breaking upon the Session to propound his riddle, looked hardly sane.

The pallid young minister wiped the sweat from his brow. A bookworm, he liked life plain. The promise of confusion among his people smote him to a sort of panic. Now, wiping his brow, he breathed deep in his relief. The threatened confusion to his peace was no worse than this, the meanderings of a poor fellow not quite responsible for what he said. He had never before seen Garry, but was ready to believe in any mental aberration in a nephew of Miss Barbara Paterson. John Grey interrupted his thoughts.

In his quiet, courteous fashion Mr Grey asked leave, if nothing demanded his presence in the meeting, to follow Garry.

'Yes do, do go,' the minister said. Sweat broke again upon his brow. He had come to this country parish to escape the impact of life, but there were moments when he recognised himself a coward. The sweat breaking on his brow bore witness to such a moment.

'Do go, Mr Grey,' he said.

Garry was still standing on the puddled road. All his boyhood's discomfort in the face of ridicule was working in him. At first he could hardly speak with civil tongue to Mr Grey; but the old man's quiet refusal to note that anything was wrong, as they walked and talked, in time restored him to a sense of deeper hurt than that to his own vanity; and he felt better. He went home with Mr Grey. Garry was unfed, and his host called for food. The room was shabby but gracious. All it contained, if old and worn, was good:

engravings after the Masters, some photographs of hills and of machinery, a Harvest Home, hung in oak frames of Mr Grey's own making. The bookcases, also of his making, were filled with books, like the furniture, good and worn. While Garry ate, the old man, seated by the fire, fell asleep; and awoke in a little to say, 'I'm getting to be a done old chap.' He stooped forward and picked a child's doll from the fender. Garry had observed it there, with china face and blue eyes that stared towards the fire.

'The eyes came out,' said John Grey, as he lifted the toy and examined it with care, 'and her little mistress brought her to me. She believes I can mend everything that breaks, but this was as hard a task as I have tried. I had to work the eyes back into place and fill the head up with cement to keep them fixed. See, it has set.'

Garry took the doll and examined the workmanship.

'Jolly neat. I saw a youngster, two evenings ago, as I went past, following you around while you were weeding. Slip of a girl. Her arms were round your neck as you knelt. Once I declare I saw her ride on you, bare leg across your shoulder, and you paying no attention.'

'That is the child.'

'Confident little sparrow, wasn't she just!'

'She was not in my way,' said the old man smiling.

Garry thrust plate and cup from him and buried his head in his hands.

'Perhaps I am not in your way either,' he said at last; and without waiting for an answer he began to talk, pouring out to David's father his bitter distaste at David's betrayal. 'You can't think that ever he meant to marry that woman.'

John Grey talked in his turn; but with reticence. It was plain, however, to Garry that Louie Morgan as a daughter was not a welcome thought. Yet he defended her, even, as it seemed to Garry, to the detriment of his son. He slowly gathered that the old man was unsure of what the brilliant boy, who escaped beyond his father's experience at many points, might not have done. Besides, David and Miss Morgan had certainly met, many times, not long before his death. She had been staying in the south, with friends, very near his lodgings. David's own letters had referred to her

presence, even to her quality. 'There's more in her than ever
I thought.' They had had long and intimate talks. No, David
had never hinted at love, certainly never a betrothal.

'But this confession she was making to me,' stammered
Garry. Death was in his heart. To find Mr Grey believing
that the thing was possible made Garry face it for the first
time, and the thought that David might indeed have kissed
that vapid mouth weighed on him like death.

'Think nothing of the confession. Never mind it. She
was overwrought. Leave the matter as it is. Let there be
no more said.'

Of what was he afraid, pondered Garry. Surely of something. He could not leave the theme, returning to his own
contempt of the woman. But the old man silenced his complaint. Garry felt uncomfortably that in his presence one
could disparage no human being; not even a woman for
whom he had confessed that he did not care.

'You are too good for this world,' thought Garry. 'Or
too simple.'

Mr Grey put the theme aside with decision.

'We'll just leave it where it is, lad.'

Garry was profoundly dissatisfied, but drew his chair
to the fire and smoked; and they talked for over an hour.
Garry would have enjoyed the talk (for he had a deep
respect for John Grey, and they had many tastes in common) had his secret uneasiness not kept growing. At last
its torment worked through even his interest in shells and
fuses, and he rose to go.

The night had cleared. Spring had danced her caper,
and sat now dreaming and demure. Under the wide dim
sky, where single stars hung soft, the man walked out his
torment. He had to face the issue he had evaded: someone
he must despise if his convictions were to go unchanged.
Was it John Grey, who could believe of a splendid son
that he would sully his honour? Or David himself, who
had sullied it? Had David loved—no, David could not have
loved this woman, but had he perhaps, incredibly, become
infatuated with her? Had the ancient madness worked, the
old invincible gods snuffed up their reek of sacrifice?
David's face rose before him, brooding, strong, ironic as in

life, and at the thought that he had lost not only the face
but what it meant to him, desolation fell so strongly upon
his spirit that David died a second time. His mouth was filled
with ashes, loathing took his soul. So it was the Cyprian John
Grey had feared, and, prudent man, stayed his eyes from looking
lest the goddess smite. It is not well for man to pry into the
doings of the gods. But as he paced in his bitter misery the
thought returned: what was this incomplete confession that
Mr Grey desired him to ignore? It must have had some
meaning, and he must know its end.

He had reached the gate of Knapperley when his hand
came against the bulge that Mrs Hunter's boots made in
his pocket. Jonathan Bannochie had told him they were
promised for tonight. He turned, then turned again and
took another road that came to Craggie by way of the house
inhabited by Mrs Morgan and her daughter.

The house, standing back from the road, was dark, but
against the shadowy trees a pale figure moved. Garry leaped
the wall and strode across the lawn.

Miss Morgan was as restless as himself. Her mother and
the maid had gone to bed, but she had come seeking into
the starlight—and found Garry.

'Let's finish that talk we were having,' he said.

She cried indignantly, 'What do you mean, breaking into
my garden like this, so late? You are as rude and wild as
when you were a boy. Haven't you done me harm enough
today already, locked in with me like that?'

'Don't be a fool. Who's to know I'm here?—Listen,
Miss Morgan'—he gripped himself and spoke less roughly—'you began tonight to tell me something. Will you
finish it?'

He saw, however, that he was dealing with another Louie.
Instead of tears he found defiance. Louie's attempted excursion into truth had been too hard. But he was determined
this time to hold her fast.

'Yes or no—were you engaged to marry David Grey?'

Louie twisted her hands together.

'What is it all about? Won't you tell me what you
meant this evening? Why are you a sinner? You said—'

'Yes, yes, I said! I said! Do you suppose words ever

mean the right thing? I said. And I suppose I meant it then. But you are to blame for what I said. You, by your suspicions and your accusations. I am too sensitive, that's what it is. I see other people's point of view too quickly. I said dreadful things about myself, and they all seemed true then. Because you had moved me and I was seeing with your eyes. Don't you understand? One can accuse oneself of any enormity under the stress of an emotion. You tell me how my conduct looks to you, and I see it. Yes, I see it. I acknowledge my sin and my transgression is before me. But that vision isn't me. When the emotion is over, I recover myself. I realise to what an enormity I have confessed.'

'But you haven't confessed to anything,' said Garry wearily.

'You think I made the story up—that David didn't love me. I will tell you what I meant, what I was trying to confess. But all those tears were quite wrong. I was too humble. It's nothing so very bad, after all. We were not actually engaged—no formal engagement, I mean. I could never bring myself to that—I wouldn't do as David wanted. Because, you see, I was not sure that he was saved. I couldn't say yes until his soul was safe.'

Garry was staring in the chill of horror.

'You think you knew David—you didn't know my David. You think I wasn't good enough for him. Perhaps I was too good. There was a side to him you didn't know. I developed it. I created him. My own part of him. And *you* can't take it from me. You didn't know how much we were to each other in those last months before he died.'

'I heard—something.'

'Oh, something. But no one knew. Do you suppose we blabbed? No, but we talked and talked—six weeks we talked. Oh, just in snatches, when he had the time. He slaved all those weeks. But when he had an hour—how we talked! We threshed out all the religions in the world, I think. You didn't know David cared for that. You thought his machinery and his music were all he thought about. But he did. I made him care. Only—he died so soon I never knew, never was sure that I had saved his soul. And now

I never can be. So, you see, I couldn't enter into a formal engagement, could I? But it would have come to that. Am I so very wrong to claim it before the world? To me it is like a proclamation of my faith in David—that his soul *was* right at the last. It is a mere formality I am assuming. But surely I am justified. The truth that was the truth of our hearts is expressed in it—that is all.'

Garry said slowly and with difficult utterance, 'That is a morality more involved than I am accustomed to.'

'Morality is always involved. Only truth is clear and one. But we never see it. That's why we must live by morality.'

Garry got up from the garden chair on which he had been seated.

'This is too much for me. I don't pretend to understand you. And was this what distressed you in the evening?'

'Yes, yes. You made me feel a cheat, to claim the reality without my formal right. But I do not feel a cheat now.'

'Then I suppose I had better go away?'

'Yes, go; yes, go.'

He went in misery. He could not disbelieve this tale of David. Talk they must have had. More of David—and more of Miss Morgan—than he had known became apparent: new stars slipping from the dusk. He walked bewildered.

In a little he came to Craggie. All was dark and silent. He rattled on the door, and the sound, rolling into the night, roused him to observe that all the countryside was folded. It must be late: he had not thought of time. He made out the figures on his luminous wristwatch—half past eleven. The Hunters were a-bed; he regretted having come and turned to go quietly away.

But shuffling footsteps were approaching, bolts were shot back, and the long knotted figure of Jake Hunter appeared in the doorway, trousers pulled hastily up over his nightshirt. His face was twisted in a look of apprehension.

'What's wrong, ava?'

'Nothing, nothing.' Garry apologised, explaining his errand.

'Man, it's a terrible-like time o'night to tak a body out o' their beds.'

'So it's you that's the death o' them,' cried Mrs Hunter,

coming to the door. 'And me callin' Jonathan Bannochie for a' thing—nae boots for Bill the morn's morn. An' it's nae like Jonathan to be ahin hand wi' his work. He doesna seek nae to put to his hand. And it's you that was poochin' my laddie's boots.'

'Man,' said Jake, 'you feared me, comin' in about at this hour.'

'O ay, now, Mr Garry, sir,' Mrs Hunter interrupted, 'what's this you were up to with Miss Louie? She came by this house with a face begrutten that you couldna tell it was a face, and when I but said "Good evening"—quiet-like and never lettin' on I saw the tears—ran as if she saw reek. Bubblin' an' greetin'—tears enough to make the por-ridge with.'

'Hoots, wumman,' said Jake, 'let the thing be. Seein' there's naething a-dae, let's to our beds. But man, you fair feared me. Would it be our laddie, I thocht, killed maybe or wounded.'

Garry apologised again.

'Miss Morgan's all right,' he told Mrs Hunter. 'I saw her a little ago. Very cheerful.'

The couple went in and shut their door. But Garry stood on the road, struck dumb. Mrs Hunter's voice had brought to his memory what he had forgotten—the assurance she had given him that Louie had her betrothal ring: the ring that David's mother had reserved for his bride.

Not betrothed to David, yet wearing his mother's ring: now what should that forebode?

NINE

The Andrew Lorimers go to the Country

The sleet had vanished in the night. Airs were soft as summer, and over the last golden clumps of crocus, wide open in the sun, bees droned and buzzed.

'A flinchin' Friday,' warned Miss Annie, who had a farmer's knowledge of the weather signs. 'There'll be storm on the heels of this.'

Storm! thought Ellen, bumming as she cleared the breakfast dishes. Youth was in her heart, she had risen up at the voice of a bird, and the world for her was azure. She could not understand this flood of new life that welled up within her.

The postman came, bringing the letters, and told them the story of Garry before the Session.

'He had no call to shame her like that,' said Miss Annie.

'Pity for her in her snuffy condition,' scoffed Theresa. 'The lad's as thrawn as cats' guts, he'll do as he pleases.'

'But it's not to laugh at,' said Ellen, with an unexpected heat. 'It was a noble thing to do.'

'Locking her in a schoolroom, the same as he locked her in the old Tower—where's your nobility in that? Well, well, Louie'll be having him next, wait till you see. The cow dies waiting the green grass, and if she can't get one to her mind, she's well advised to take what she can get.'

Lindsay thrust her thumb into the envelope of a letter and ripped it savagely open, and glared at Theresa above a trembling lip.

Ellen said, 'Tris, you're an old fool. As if the boy would mind her.'

'If he can't get a better, where's the odds?
  Are ye hungry?
  Lick the mills o' Bungrie,

Are ye thirsty?

Kiss Kirsty.

'What stite you talk!' said Miss Annie. 'The lad was scunnered at her.'

'There was once a lad that took a scunner at butter, and after that he could never eat it thicker than the bread.'

'Oh, they're coming here,' cried Lindsay, reading from her letter. 'The children—for a picnic.' She began to read aloud, hastily, to hide the trembling of her mouth, and even she was less indignant than Ellen at the monstrous suggestion that Theresa had made. The sisters were still bickering, and Theresa had just said, 'Oh, no, to be sure I know nothing. What should a silly tailor do but sit and sew a clout? It was me that had the right of it in the other affair, I would have you remember. I told you she wasn't engaged to him'—and was making for the kitchen, but paused to hear Lindsay read her mother's letter.

Mrs Andrew Lorimer wrote that as the holidays had begun the children were eager for a picnic. They were taking lunch out, and would the Weatherhouse ladies give them tea?

'And there's them turning in at the foot of the brae,' said Theresa. 'What a congregation! We'll need our time to tea all that.' She went to the kitchen and began to bake. Theresa liked nothing better than to provide a tea. Lindsay ran flying down the brae to meet the children, and as she ran the words spurted from her lips, 'Brute, brute, brute. I hate her. Brute.'

'She's never away in these thin shoes,' said Miss Annie, following Theresa to the kitchen. 'She'll be ill.'

'Fient an ill. She's that excited you would think she was a bairn herself. That's her that was so dead set on marrying. There's no more word of that affair, it seems. And she doesn't get letters from any at the Front but Frank.'

About the same hour Garry Forbes was walking up to Mrs Morgan's door. He was stern and ill at ease, but determined to go through with the task that he had set himself. Louie, too, was ill at ease. When she saw him her face crumpled up, puckering as though she were to cry, and she lowered her eyes and would not meet his. He was sure she had already been weeping.

'Forgive me,' he said, 'I haven't slept. I must know this: that ring you wear—it's David's mother's. How do you come to have it if you were not betrothed?'

'Why do you pursue me like this?' She sat down with a gesture of despair and motioned him to a seat. He saw the tears trickle between the hands with which she covered her face.

'I did try to tell the truth yesterday,' she said at last, looking up. 'Perhaps if they hadn't come in—and yet I don't know. Oh, must I tell you? Can't you understand how it is? I am so covered with shame—will you let me try to show you how it was? Will you let me try?'

He assented gravely.

'I think sometimes I can't tell the truth—can you understand that?'

He was embarrassed, not knowing what to answer.

'Yes,' she continued, 'truth to me is terribly hard. I am made like that. I live all the time—oh, I am going to scourge myself—in what I want other people to be thinking about me, until often I don't know—indeed, indeed I don't—what I really am and what I have thought they are thinking I am. I understand myself, you see. But I can't give it up, I can't. I've nothing to put in its place.'

Garry was looking in amazement.

'I should have thought the difference between truth and a lie was clear enough,' he said as she paused.

'Oh, no, it's not—not clear at all. Things are true and right in one relationship, and quite false in another. It's false, as a mere statement of fact, that I was betrothed to David, but true as an expression of—an expression of—' She faltered and burst into tears.

'I was going to say, an expression of feeling—our feeling. But it's my feeling. David—I am to tell you the truth now—David never mentioned love to me, or marriage. We had those talks—yes, yes, you must not think those were invented. We talked—all sorts of things, deep, intimate things. And I was always thinking: I am making an impression, I am altering his ideas. I wanted to save his

soul. I think—I think I wanted it to be *me* that would save
his soul, not just that his soul would be saved. I am trying
to be honest, you see. And then I thought: he will recognise how much I have done for him, I shall become needful
to him, and in time—in time—yes, I hoped that in time
he might marry me. Don't you understand? I think that
about every man. There have been so few—just none, just
none. No one ever before with whom I even had an intimate
conversation, like this with David. It was luscious, it was so
good! I wanted to be at the heart of life instead of on its
margins.'

'Yes, yes, I can see that. But I don't see that it justifies
you in grabbing David.'

'Grabbing! But I didn't grab. Oh, you haven't understood at all! That part of him is mine. I created it. No one
can touch it but me.'

'But you said he never—'

'No, no, he never did. I suppose it was all a tiny thing to
him—just some occasional talk. He liked it at the time. But
between times he was absorbed, he forgot. And I thought
and thought until that was all that was alive for me. And
yet he liked the talks. He would say, "Now there, what you
said last week—I've been thinking about that." He made me
feel, somehow, as though what I said was tremendously important, as though I were tremendously important to him.
And then I came to believe I *was* important. You see how
well I understand myself.'

Garry was at a loss. He felt as though a roof had blown
away and he was looking in amazement at a hive of popu-
lous rooms where things were done that he had never
imagined.

'So when he died it was myself I felt for, that my
hope would never come to be.' Garry made a motion of
disgust. 'Yes, yes, it was hideous. But don't you see my
desperation? "What are the men thinking about?" they
said. "Not about me"—I couldn't answer that. Don't you
understand? I had to save my self-respect. Confess no man
had ever wanted me? "What are the men thinking about,
that *you* are still unmarried?" "Ah, I could tell you that an
I would." You needn't tell a lie, you see. A hint is all. But

it saves you from humiliation—from yourself. Yes, I know it is in your own eyes that you are saved. The others forget, but you keep on remembering that they know.'

'So David had to suffer that people might think—the right thing about you.'

'To suffer! But I forgot. You think it is a degradation for David to be thought in love with me. That is why you have wormed all this out of me.'

He could not deny, and so was silent.

'But why should it be a degradation? I'm not wicked. I'm not ugly. I have charm. I'm thirty five—you wouldn't dream. I've kept astonishingly youthful.'

Juvenile, was the word that flashed across his brain.

'I have such girlish ways. Oh, God, what am I doing? Why did you let me go on? You can't expect me to acknowledge that it would have been a degradation. And yet I know it was only—what was the word you used?—*grabbing*. That I grabbed David. But it didn't feel like that to me. It felt like— Oh, I tried to explain it to you. Like the seal and signal of the great belief I had in him. A high and holy thing. I see now that it wasn't—that it was only—was bad and wicked. The human heart is deceitful above all things and desperately wicked. That doesn't mean that you tell lies. Self-deceitful. You think you are doing a brave thing, and it turns out mean. And you don't deliberately persuade yourself about it. You really are deceived. Only some people—like me, I'm one of them, you should pity us, we are of all men most miserable—, some people see the deceptive appearance and the deceit both together, as it were, only they can't quite distinguish. Or won't let themselves. Just now, for instance, I am hoping that I am saving your soul. As I hoped with David. I am saying, years after, he will look back on this hour and say, "My life was changed—that was a crucial hour for me. I had a new revelation of life given to me." That's what I meant by saving your soul. But you won't, will you?'

'No. No.'

'No, of course not. I know that. Only you see I go on thinking and acting as though I knew you would. There, I have revealed my innermost being to you. No one has seen it before. But you—you have forced me to see how vile it is. Will you not have mercy? Are you to make of me an outcast in the eyes of men?'

Garry found his thoughts in confusion; but remembered suddenly that she had not yet explained her possession of the ring.

She went very white, threw her head back and breathed deeply. 'I took it. Why don't you say something?' she added after a pause. 'I took it. *You* would say stole, I suppose. But it wasn't really that.'

'No?'

'Oh, you are cruel! You are saying, double meanings again. But I shall tell you how it came about. His mother wore that ring. I used to watch it when I was a girl—the strange old set and chasing of the gold. And I was with my mother when we saw her dying. She said, "It's not of value, it's only a square cairngorm, but the setting is old and rare. My son's bride shall have it." I thought nothing then, but you know how unimportant words like that may stay with you. You forget that you heard them, and then one day back they all come. It was Mr Grey himself that showed me it. I asked him, "Have you nothing for our jumble sale?" And he said there might be some useless odds and ends. He pulled out a drawer, and there was the ring. I knew it at once. He put it aside and some other things, and then he said, "If you find anything there of any use, just you take it." So I rummaged in the drawer. But afterwards I couldn't keep my thoughts off the ring. Nor off his mother's words, "David's bride." I said them over and over, and then I felt: if only I could have the ring a moment on my finger I should feel better. David's bride. It would feel real then. I thought about it till I couldn't keep away, and I went back to the house and opened the drawer and slipped the ring on. I felt so happy then, I can't explain to you. It seemed as though something had come true. I could have danced and sung. I couldn't bear to take it off again, and I went and stood by the window—it opens like a door, I had come in that way—and watched the light shine on it. And then I heard a sound, and there was his old housekeeper coming in at the door. So I slipped it in my pocket, meaning to put it back in the drawer, and I said, "Mr Grey gave me leave to take some things from that drawer for the Jumble Sale. I knocked, but you couldn't have heard. I'm glad you've come in, for I was just wondering if I could take the things away when nobody was here." Then I went into the room again and played about among the things in the drawer, always hoping I'd be able to slip the ring back. But she watched me all the time. So I had to carry it away. And I slept with it on that night. Oh, I can't make you understand—in a few days it felt like a part of me. All I had wanted of David seemed to be concentrated in that little piece of gold. I loved it. I couldn't bear to have it off my finger—though I was prudent, and wore it only when I was alone. He wasn't dead a month by then. Well, one day I had it on, and my glove was off, when I happened to meet Mrs Hunter. It was on my wedding finger, you understand, and she pounced at once, and said, "What, what!" and then she stood staring at the ring and cried, "But I've seen that ring before," and I felt like death and said, "Dear Mrs Hunter, it hasn't to be known. We hadn't made it public, and now—" "You poor bit bairn!" she said, and I began to weep. It was such a relief to weep, I felt so frightened. But then I recollected myself and told her on no account to speak of it. Especially not to Mr Grey. "You know that he never mentions David's name," I said. "And at any rate, since the betrothal had not been announced, it's better to keep it secret still. I prefer to suffer in silence." But I couldn't, you know. That was just it. I wanted everyone to know that I was suffering. Mrs Hunter promised faithfully to say nothing—'

Garry gave an involuntary exclamation and clapped his mouth shut on it at once.

'I know, I know. You are to say: she spoke to me, she told me. It *was* Mrs Hunter who told you the ring was his mother's, wasn't it? But you see she did not break her promise, it had got known without her, and she was free to speak. Got known, I say. I made it known, was what I mean. I couldn't keep it, you see. I gave other people hints—it was so sweet, oh, if you knew how sweet their pity was! No, not their pity—their admiration. For the way I bore my suffering, I mean.'

Garry sighed profoundly. The whole interview oppressed him. Her speech was an unseemly mockery of human pain. Yet she was terribly in earnest. He could not refuse to listen to the end. In some tortured and labyrinthine way she was revealing a soul. All was not sham. He sighed and listened.

But the door was opened, and Mrs Morgan came in, cordial but inquisitive. Louie's demeanour changed. She jumped to her feet, laughing, and said, 'Mother, I'm defeated. I've tried to persuade Captain Forbes to give a brief talk at our concert, and he refuses.'

Mrs Morgan sat down. She took possession of the room.

'Mother dear,' said Louie softly at last, 'Captain Forbes was so good—he called to—to tell me some things about David. Do you mind?'

Mrs Morgan did mind, plainly, but she rose and went. Garry sighed again. She was so enmeshed in falsehood, he supposed, that she hardly noticed when she told a lie.

'Now, where was I?' she was asking. Was it possible that she enjoyed this too, that her tale was one huge ostentation? She would have another invention for her mother's ears, of that he was sure. Mrs Morgan's knowing smile would invite till she received—received what? What had he to 'tell her about David'?

She continued. 'But I didn't dare to wear the ring, so I hung it round my neck and bought another not unlike it. I wore that, and trusted that Mrs Hunter, who was the only person who knew, would never notice the difference. It does sound deceitful, doesn't it?'

He did not reply.

'What are you to do now?' he asked after a pause.

'Do? Does anything need to be done?'

He rose and paced the room impatiently.

'At least I hope you will restore Mr Grey the ring.'

'The trouble is, how am I to get in without attracting notice?'

'Without— Good God, you don't mean that you would put it back and say nothing?'

'What can I say?'

'The truth, of course.'

He saw the sheer pain in her eyes.

'What I've told you?'

'If that is the truth, yes.'

'*If* it is the truth! Oh, do you not believe me yet?'

'Very well, of course you must tell it to him.'

'And then—then you'll proclaim it abroad. You'll tell everyone I am a common thief. That's what you wanted, wasn't it, to tell them all?'

He shook his head. To clear David's honour was one thing, but a very different matter to set the tongues wagging over such a sordid story. He would have felt it an indecency to expose her, and smiled a little soberly as he thought that those who could not see his point when he talked of his friend's dishonour would see quickly enough the point of a stolen ring. A profound sadness invaded him as he saw by what strange ties honour and reputation may be bound.

'No, no,' he said, 'this is not a matter for the public. But you must go by what Mr Grey decides.'

She was weeping now and said, pleading, 'Captain Forbes—Garry. I shall tell him, but need it be now? Listen. Our concert—it's just two days ahead. And I have so much to do in it. I'm playing. And there's that sketch. I've the curtains to finish, and final rehearsals. And if I tell—I'm so, so—I feel so keenly, it will kill me. I know I shall be ill. I feel I might collapse. Perhaps at the concert. I know that I'll be prostrate after I tell. Mayn't I wait? It's—it's a sort of public duty, to keep fit for the concert.'

Garry rose to his feet. Blind blundering emotions had hold on him. To his surprise he felt surges of pity where he had thought to feel only disgust; but it was a pity that it hurt him to give, as though some portion of himself had been rent to make the pity possible; and he was profoundly uncomfortable.

'Yes, yes, tell him when you please.'

'But you will say—'

'Nothing, nothing. Till your concert is over, then.'

She accompanied him to the door, talking loud and laughing. Mrs Morgan reappeared. He supposed she had come to hear what had passed. Louie, of course, would dissemble. He went rapidly out.

He was astonished at the pure sweet morning into which he walked—as though he had come from a murky den where the air oppressed. It was incredible that there could be a world as fresh and unashamed as that he saw around him. For a time he stood, breathing the sweet air, then rapidly climbed to the summit of the ridge. There space encompassed him. Space sang again its primal song, before man was, before the tangle of his shames began. Infinite sky was over him, blue land ran on and on until it seemed itself a ruffled fold of sky, a quivering of light upon the air; the blue sea trembled on the boundaries of space; and the man standing there alone was rapt up into the infinitudes around, lost for awhile the limitations of himself. He came back slowly. Strange how the land could be transfigured! A blue April morning, the shimmer of light, a breath, a passing air, and it was no longer a harsh and stubborn country, its hard-won fields beleaguered by moor and whin, its stones heaped together in dyke and cairn, marking the land like lines upon a weathered countenance, whose past must stay upon it to the end; but a dream, willing men's hearts. In the sun the leafless boughs were gleaming. Birches were like tangles of shining hair; or rather, he thought, insubstantial, floating like shredded light above the soil. Below the hills blue floated in the hollows, all but tangible, like a distillation that light had set free from the earth; and on a rowan tree in early leaf, its boughs blotted against the background, the tender leaves, like flakes of green fire, floated too, the wild burning life of spring loosened from earth's control. On every side earth was transmuted. Scents floated, the subtle life released from earth and assailing the pulses. Song floated. This dour and thankless country, this land that *grat a' winter and girned a' summer* could change before one's eyes to an elfin and enchanted radiance, could look, by some rare miracle of light or moisture, essentialised. A measure of her life this morning had gone up in sacrifice. Her substance had become spirit.

Garry's thought went back upon the evening when he had seen the land emerge and take form slowly from primordial dark. Now its form was on the point of dissolution into light. And the people whom the land had made—they too, had been shaped from a stuff as hard and intractable as their rock, through weathers as rude as stormed upon their heights; they too (he thought) at moments were dissolved in light, had their hours of transfiguration. In his aunt dancing her wilful reel on the kitchen floor, in Lindsay as she had grieved for Louie's hurt, he had seen life essentialised.

A shouting caught his ear. The swarm of young Lorimers, skimming the moor, hummed about him. He gave in gladly to their merriment, lunched with them beside the old tower, and led their games. Lindsay's gaiety, however, was assumed. She was still furious against Miss Theresa for her cynical suggestion of the morning; but though she tried to convince herself that her misery came from that, as the day wore on she was compelled to acknowledge that there was a deeper hurt in what Garry had done the previous evening in the school. After all, he had exposed Louie to public scorn. Her eyes sought his many times, reproachful and sad, but it was only on the homeward way that, lingering by common consent, the two could talk.

'I thought you would have done what I wanted you to do,' she said.

She did herself injustice by her complaint. She had no sense of personal grievance; but she had been quite sure that Garry would be good—that he would do nothing out of accord with her creed and standards. Her rebuke was the grieving of a bewildered child.

Garry kept silence. He could not tell her the collapse of Louie's story. The purloined ring had altered his attitude to the affair, and he almost hoped that Lindsay need never know of it. In any case he could not assert his knowledge of Louie's perfidy without revealing its proof. Constraint fell between them. They made up on the others, and reached the Weatherhouse in a bunch.

'What's *he* seeking here again?' said Miss Theresa, look-ing from the window.

Mrs Falconer looked from the window too, and saw Garry, as it happened, toss an empty basket laughingly to Kate. The bird sang in Mrs Falconer's heart—that fugitive bird, that flake from Ellen's earth that had escaped, far out into the blue air, across distant seas and islands of romance. She ran to set another cup and plate, thinking, 'How happy they look together!'

'You needn't bother yourself,' said Theresa. 'He's away.'

Ellen turned to the glass door, and saw him passing through the gate. She flung the glass door open and ran across the garden with hasty, unsure steps, her long angular body bent forward from the hips, and she reached the low wall before Garry had passed beyond it.

'Just a cup,' she panted. And when he would not come she continued to talk, leaning upon the stone crop that covered the wall.

'A pack of old women—I don't wonder. We must seem unreal to you. A picture-book house.'

'Well.' He stood considering. Unreal—he could not know all that she had put into the word, her lifelong battle against those figments of her fancy that had often held her richest life, yet it expressed what he had vaguely felt when he took tea with these women. 'After out there,' he said.

Mrs Falconer had the curious sense of having run, in her stumbling progress through the garden, a very long distance from her home.

'You're a dimension short,' he continued. 'Or no. You have three dimensions right enough, but we've a fourth dimension over there. We've depth. It's not the same thing as height,' he added, looking up. 'It's down in—hollowness and mud and foul water and bad smells and holes and more mud. Not common mud. It's dissolution—a dimension that won't remain stable—and you've to multiply everything by it to get any result at all. You people who live in a three-dimensional world don't know. You can't know. You go on thinking this is the real thing, but we've discovered that we can get off every imaginable plane that the old realities yielded.'

'We can perhaps imagine it a little.' She kept her adoring eyes upon him, and smiled at undergoing this initiation into a soldier's world.

'Imagination's no good. Imagination has to save the world, but the people who haven't it will never believe what the others say. Your sister's beckoning.'

Mrs Falconer turned and saw Theresa signal from the window. Cups clattered, talk and laughter eddied into the garden. Everyone had gone in: except old Mrs Craigmyle, who walked serenely to and fro on the garden path, knitting and carolling. Mrs Falconer looked, and turned back to Garry. She had a certain elation in disregarding Theresa's summons. There were plenty of them there to serve; but she was choosing a better part. She said, 'That's what I've always wanted—to have imagination.'

'You shouldn't. It's too cruel, too austere. You should pray your God of Comforts to keep you from imagination. Lead us not into imagination, but deliver us from understanding.'

Mrs Falconer shook her head, slowly, as though to shake away an idea that bemused her.

'They laugh at you,' Garry continued (he had not talked like this to anyone since his return, not tried to share, even with Lindsay, the thoughts that had haunted his delirium and convalescence), 'they laugh at you as foolish or pity you as not quite sane if you try to get past the appearances of things to their real nature. That's what they said about me: beside himself, cracked. I was in a fever, you see. But I'm convinced I saw clearer then than in my right mind.' He began to tell her of his adventure with the dead man in the hole. 'I wasn't rightly sure which was myself, you understand. And it's like that all the time. You do things, and you're not sure after they're done if it is yourself or someone else you've done them to.'

She was listening absorbed.

'Yes, yes, that Louie Morgan now. She did it just to please herself, but look what she has done to you. You were right to expose her, I think.'

But Garry was thinking (also of Louie) that in unmasking her he had done something to himself regarding which he was not yet quite sure. Nor did he want Louie on the public stage. He stepped back from the wall, said, 'But she's not exposed. Now I am keeping you from your tea,' and walked away.

Not exposed! thought Mrs Falconer, turning back across the garden. But she would be! A fire ran through her veins. Too austere! How could imagination be austere? Your God of Comforts. Another dimension. His words bubbled in her ears. She had run farther than ever from this idle garden, and the air beyond it was sharp and pungent to her nostrils.

The garden was not empty, after all. Lang Leeb still walked the path, serenely singing; and as her second daughter came near with wide unseeing eyes, Leeb raised her voice and sang on a gay and insolent note. She did not look at Mrs Falconer, but kept her fingers on her shank and her eyes straight ahead:

Auld wife, auld wife, will you go a-shearin'?
Speak up, speak up, for I'm hard o' hearin'.
Auld wife, auld wife, will you hae a man?—

The glass door slipped from Mrs Falconer's hand and clashed, and Mrs Falconer did not even apologise. She let Miss Theresa talk.

The children had finished tea. It was time they were off. There was noise and bustle.

'For the love of Pharaoh,' cried Miss Theresa, 'wash your faces. They'll charge you extra in the train for all that dirt.'

Mrs Falconer sat to her solitary tea. The children's voices came ringing up from the road, fading as the distance grew. Lindsay and Kate had gone with them.

'Your God of Comforts,' Mrs Falconer continued to think. The phrase brought Louie to her mind. 'Why, we must go to that concert. But how can she appear in front of them all? Not exposed, he said. Not. But she must be. And playing, they say. Well, if it's like the last concert, I'm sure I shan't care if I don't go. Terrible grand music, she said it was—just a bumming and a going on. But how can she face them? Your God of Comforts.' Her mind came back always to the phrase A comfortable God—what had the young man meant?

Lindsay and Kate returned. Night came. Lindsay leaned again from her window. She was trying to control her thoughts. They were like horses new let out to grass; brutal and beautiful; unbridled energies. She had never before had so many thoughts at once. Life was too intricate. New complications rose upon her. Getting to know Garry was not what she had supposed it would be like. And now the children would go home and tell that Garry was here, and there would be her mother's disapproval to be faced. She should have been more stern that afternoon, but he had kissed her, her throat was burning still where he had pressed it. Oh, where was she venturing? The sea grows more immense as the distance widens between us and the shore.

Kate was asleep. The whole house had withdrawn. Only she, awake and aware, tussled with life. She felt creep over her the desolation of youth, that believes no suffering has ever been like its suffering, no heart has been perplexed like it. 'They're all happy,' she thought, 'and I don't know what I am. They're all asleep, and I can't sleep.'

She did not know that through the wall, kneeling upon the floor, Mrs Falconer endured an agony of prayer. She too, wrestled, and as she wrestled a strange sense of triumph overwhelmed her, exultation filled her soul.

'Help me, O God,' she prayed, 'help me to overcome the evil and expose the wrong, that Thy great cause may be triumphant. Through our Lord Jesus Christ, Amen.'

The words sang to her spirit. No more for her the pallid shadows of her dreams. She would labour now for truth.

'Grant, O Lord, in Thy mercy, that I may be equal to that which Thou wouldst have me do.'

A shudder ran through her frame. The seraph with the live coal from off the altar touched her lips, and as she rose, chill and quiet, from her prayers, the dreamy innocence habitual to her face had changed to a high and rapt enthusiasm.

TEN

Andrew Lorimer does the Same

The following days deepened the furrows that became so characteristic a feature of Garry's countenance. Life had always been to him a serious affair, but, till the delirium of his recent illness, simple. One worked hard, making boilers and bridges as stable as one could, and played equally hard and sure; and men were good fellows. Evil there was, of course, but always in the next street—the condition that gave fighting its vehemence. The complexity of human motive and desire had not come home to him, and he supposed, without thinking much about it, that right and wrong were as separate as the bridges he helped to build and the waters over which he built them. But in what he had been irresistibly impelled to say to Mrs Falconer that afternoon, his discovery in the dissolution of the solid land of a new dimension by which experience must be multiplied, he was only giving articulate expression to thoughts that had for some time been worrying in his brain. Limits had shifted, boundaries been dissolved. Nothing ended in itself, but flowed over into something else; and the obsession of his delirium, that he was himself the dead man whose body he had lugged out of the slime, came back now and haunted him like the key note of a tune. But what a tune! How hard to play—rude and perplexing, with discords unresolved and a tantalising melody that fluted and escaped. His mind sounded the note again and again throughout that night, but always the tune itself eluded him.

The night was like the morning, soft and still. Earth floated in the radiance the young moon had left above the hills; stars, remote and pure, floated in the wide serene of heaven; nothing moved, yet all was moving, eternally sustained by flight; and Garry walked for hours in troubled impotence, angry at a world that would not let him keep his straight and clean-cut standards. To refute what he had thought a false conception of his friend's honour had seemed a simple and straightforward matter, but it had led him into a queer morass; and now, as he tramped in the night, he was filled with panic lest the story of the ring should become public through his agency. It would be a degradation to expose that. He was glad he had resisted the impulse to tell Lindsay, though her disapproval had been difficult to bear. He had longed to justify himself, and the frustrate longing had made him rough. He had caught her to him with violence, clutching at her throat until the mark burned upon her flesh. Her young primrose love had not yet learned to endure such heats.

In time he went to bed, but sleep did not come. Instead came fever and a new throng of disordered visions. He saw the solid granite earth, on which these established houses, the Weatherhouse and Knapperley, were built (less real, as he had said to Mrs Falconer, than the dissolution and mud of the war-swept country), melt and float and change its nature; and the people fashioned out of it, hard-featured, hard-headed, with granite frames and life-bitten faces, rude tongues and gestures, changed too, melted into forms he could not recognise. Then he perceived a boulder, earthy and enormous, a giant block of the unbridled crag, and behold! as he looked the boulder was his aunt. 'You won't touch me,' she seemed to say. 'I won't be cut and shaped and civilised.' But in an instant she began to move, treading ever more quickly and lightly, until he saw that she was dancing as he had caught her dancing on the night of his return. Faster and faster she spun, lighter of foot and more ethereal, and the rhythm of her dance was a phrase in the tune that had eluded him. And now she seemed to spurn the earth and float, and in the swiftness of her motion he could see no form nor substance, only a shining light, and he knew that what he watched was a dancing star.

It was already morning when he fell asleep, and he woke late, heavy-eyed and languid. Miss Barbara brought him a cup of tea—a visiting star, perhaps, but of peculiar magnitude. Thereafter she left him alone, and he lay swamped in lassitude and dozed again.

In the afternoon she went out. The house grew intolerably still. Not even a dog broke the uneasy quiet. He dozed, and struggled awake in a joyous clamour, a merry and tumultuous barking that did him good. Later he heard the stir around the ingle—sticks broken, fire-irons clattering, even, in the stillness of dusk, a sudden explosive crackle from the burning logs. He wanted food and a shave, the warmth and life of fire; speech, and the comfortable feel of paws and noses; and rising, he went downstairs.

To his surprise his aunt was just coming in. He had supposed her in the kitchen, where she, having seen the lamp lit, was supposing him. They pushed open the kitchen door together, and entered.

The fire was roaring on the hearth, the room was light and gay; dogs snuggled to the heat, tobacco smoke eddied on the air, the lid of the kettle danced and chattered and steam rose invitingly and bellied and wavered towards the chimney; and deep in Miss Barbara's favourite chair there sat a little man, as abundantly at home as if the place were his. As Miss Barbara and Garry came in he was in act of rocking back his chair, stretching his arms with a luxurious content, and singing to a merry tune:

> He took his pipes and played a spring
> And bade the coo consider—

'If it isna Johnnie Rogie!' cried Miss Barbara. 'Man, but you're a sight for sair e'en.'

The little man turned in the chair, nodded gaily to Miss Barbara in time to his music, beat vigorously with his arms and continued to sing:

> The coo considered wi' hersel
> That music wadna fill her—

Ay, ay, Bawbie, but I've the reek risin' and the kettle on, an' you shall hae your supper, lass:

> And you shall hae your supper.

'You'll have a dram first, laddie,' cried Miss Barbara. 'I've aye a drappie o' the real Mackay—none of your wersh war rubbish, dirten orra stuff.'

'We'll have it out, Bawbie.'

Miss Barbara fetched it running. She polished the tumblers and set them before her guest, who poured the whisky with the air of a god. Not more benignly did Zeus confer his benefits upon humanity than Johnnie Rogie the tramp handed Miss Barbara Paterson of Knapperley a share of her own whisky; and Miss Barbara took it with a gratitude that was divine in its acceptance, and called Garry to come forward and have his glass.

Unshaved, with hollow cheeks and sunken eyes from which the sleep was not yet washed, Garry came to the fire.

'Come awa', my lad,' cried Johnnie. 'Sojers need a dram like the lave o's.' He poured the whisky and conferred it upon Garry. 'Take you a' you get an' you'll never want.' And, raising his own glass, he let the golden liquor tremble to his mouth. 'And sojers need to live and sojers need to pray. Live, laddie, live? Ay, sojers need to live mair than the lave o's. Clean caup oot, like the communicants o' Birse'—his head went back as he drained his glass—'that's the way a sojer needs to live. Tak' you a' that life can give you, laddie. Drink you it up, clean caup oot. It's a grand dram as lang's ye're drinkin' it, and ye'll be a lang time deid.' And seeing that Garry had not yet emptied his tumbler, he added, 'But drink clean in, tak it a' at ae gulp. Life's a dram that's better in the mou' than in the belly.'

He poured himself another draught, and drank.

Apparently he found it good; for when he had swallowed it the sun-god himself was not more radiant, and when he spoke the words flowed out like song.

On Garry, too, unfed and over-strung, the golden liquor was having its effect. The shabby, under-sized man with the matted dingy hair and a little finger wanting, pouring the whisky and swaying his whole body to the rhythm of his chant, was hypnotising him, and with his will. He seemed a ministrant of life, bringing for a moment its golden energies within one's grasp, making the visionary gleam look true. Garry thrust his elbows on his knees and leaned forward, talking eagerly. Miss Barbara was moving from room to room upstairs. When she came in again her face was aglow and she slapped Johnnie heartily on the shoulder.

'And where have you been this long weary while?'

'Where you could never follow, Bawbie.'

'Nae to the wars,' she mocked.

'Just that.'

'Eh? And you near sixty, and a cripple muckle tae and but the ae cranny.'

'For a' that, an' a' that, I've been wi' the sojer laddies, Bawbie.' He reeled off into a popular soldier song. 'Ay, ay, the sojers need to live an' the sojers need to sing. An' wha wad sing to them if it wasna Johnnie? There's nae a camp an' nae a barrack but Johnnie's been there. An' whan the sojers are wearied an' whan the sojers are wae, wha but Johnnie wad gar them cantle up, wi' his auld fiddle an' his auld true tongue?'

He quaffed the golden fire again: Medea's fire, it made him young and reckless. He chanted more uproariously.

'An' mebbe whiles whan pay day cam, a sojer here, a sojer there, wad mind on singing Johnnie. Ay, ay, the sojer lads, they're free wi' their siller, the sojer lads, whan they ken the next march is the march to death. They've a lang road ahead o' them, a lang road an' few toons, the road to death; an' lads that wadna pairt wi' the dirt aneth their nails, in the ordiner ways of living, 'll gang laughin' doon to death an' toss the siller fae them like a lousy sark. What's the siller, what's the siller, give's a sang, they say.'

'You'll have a bonny penny in your pooch, Johnnie,' commented Miss Barbara. 'You'll have made your fortune.'

'Fient a fortune.' The little man ascended again to prose. He drew himself together, sat up straight and squared his shoulders. The reckless fire died down, the cadence of his voice altered. He talked of supper, and Miss Barbara made haste to prepare it.

Supper over, the dogs set up a barking.

'Did you hear a step?' said Miss Barbara.

She rose and let in Francie Ferguson.

Francie stood sheepishly in the glow of light. 'I didna ken ye had company, Miss Barbara. It was the lights. Yon's a terrible blaze, 'umman. I was feart you would dae us some hurt.'

'Ach!' said Barbara sturdily. 'What's in a puckle candles?'

The soldier and the tramp had tilted back their chairs and
with sprawling legs and arms flung easefully abroad, trolled
out old tales, recitative and chorus. Johnnie had slid away
again from prose. The boom of their laughter ceased when
Francie entered. Now Garry rose from his seat, crying, 'But
hang it all, you know, aunt—' and thereupon went off again
in a round of laughter. Recovering himself he said, 'I give
you my compliments. He's worth an illumination. Still, you
know, *noblesse oblige*. There are weaker brothers—prime
ministers and such-like fry.'

'I'm a Paterson of Knapperley, my lad, a Paterson of
Knapperley can please himself. It's only your common
bodies that need your laws and regulations, to be hauden
in about. The folk of race have your law within themselves.
Ay, ay, I'm a Paterson of Knapperley, but you're Donnie
Forbes's grandson and seek to make yourself a politician.
But go your ways.'

He went through the house, and found candle or oil-lamp
burning in every window; and put them out: with a queer
contraction of the heart as room after room was left dark and
dead behind him. The war was putting this out too—this
impetuous leap of exhilaration, this symbol of joy. When
he returned to the kitchen Francie had been drawn into the
charmed circle. He and Miss Barbara together were making
lusty chorus to Johnnie's song:

I saw an eel chase the Deil,
  Wha's fou, wha's fou?
I saw an eel chase the Deil
  Wha's fou noo, ma jo?
I saw an eel chase the Deil
Roon aboot the spinnin' wheel,
  An' we're a' blin' drunk, bousin' jolly fou, ma jo!'

Francie too, had drunk of fire, and was like one that
prophesied. Warmed by the whisky, heartened by honest
song, he began to talk of what sat closest to his own bosom:
what but Bell his wife and her incomprehensible trick of not
sitting close, of holding off. 'He doesna seek to kiss me.
I canna do with that kind o' sotter,' she had proclaimed

abroad. A libel on a man. 'A blazin' lee,' shouted Francie. 'Doesna seek to kiss her. Doesna indeed.' For what but that had he waited twenty years, to be thwarted in the end by a woman's caprice: a woman who had the impudence to say, 'Fingers off the beef, you canna buy,' to her own lawful spouse. 'But she'll be kissed this very night,' he shouted. He banged the table and swaggered home at last in glee. His habitual sheepish good-humour had turned to a more flaming quality. A man greatly resolved.

'He needs all his legs,' said Miss Barbara.

Garry went drunk to bed, but not with whisky. Again he had seen life essentialised. Its pure essence had been in Johnnie as he usurped the rites of hospitality and in Miss Barbara's extravaganza of candles; in Francie too, revolting against a niggard life.

He was interrupted in his soliloquy by the opening of the door. Johnnie shambled in, without apology, and asked for money: which Garry gave, amusedly, too much exalted still to resent this degradation in the golden godling; finding it indeed no degradation, but a glory the more. So few people had the grace to take what they wanted with such unabashed assurance. Oh, if all the world would turn audacious—! He fell asleep at last to the sound of Johnnie's voice on the other side of the wall:

There's twa moons the night
Quo' the auld wife to hersel.

Meanwhile for Lindsay the day had crawled. At every moment she had expected to see her mother arrive, and there would be an awkward moment when the ladies learned that the lover she had been sent here to forget was Garry Forbes. She detested the clandestine, yet merely to have sheltered from distasteful pleasantry was not a sign of guilt. She felt guilty nevertheless, and devised a score of speeches to convince her mother that the secrecy was not deceit. Her mother, however, did not come to be convinced.

Lindsay's feverish anxiety increased. She was ready to defend Garry against anything her mother might say, but as the day wore on she found it increasingly hard to defend Garry against herself. Always her accusation was the same—he had wantonly exposed Louie to the clack of tongues, without any proof that what he alleged was true. If he thought evil so readily of one woman, what might he not think soon of another, of herself? The child tossed upon dark and lashing waters, and was afraid. It had been safe and very beautiful on shore.

As dusk drew down she stole from the house, not unobserved by Kate, and shortly afterwards a car panted up the hill, and Andrew Lorimer himself came in.

Mrs Lorimer, as Lindsay expected, put it down to deliberate deceit on her daughter's part that they had not been told of Garry's arrival. Andrew refused to be annoyed.

'I'll talk to her myself,' he said. 'To the young man, too, if I clap eyes on him.'

Andrew Lorimer was a burly, big-nosed man, more like a farmer to the eye than a lawyer, thrawn and conservative, devoted to his children, but determined that they should have their good things in the shape that he saw fit to give them. He was quite willing that his little linnet should ultimately go to Miss Barbara's rough and rather ugly nephew, for he knew that the fellow had sound worth in spite of his execrable opinions; but the child was far too young. He wanted her for himself a long time yet.

'A nice condition you've cast my wife into,' he grumbled to the Weatherhouse ladies, 'letting that daughter of hers run round the country with her sweetheart at her tails.'

There was consternation and surprise. Andrew liked to hector.

'What,' he cried, 'you didn't know? So she takes you in, does she—cheats her mother on the sly?'

Kate looked up calmly from her sewing.

'There was nothing sly about it,' she said. 'Lindsay was perfectly frank. When she came at Christmas she told all there was to tell. And as we understood your objection was merely her age, what harm should we suppose in their meeting?'

And to Miss Theresa, who was still indignantly exclaiming, she said, with the same unmoved demeanour, 'Perhaps *you* may not have heard, Aunt Tris, but it wasn't because Lindsay didn't tell.'

'To be sure we knew,' put in Miss Annie with a chuckle. She remembered the day Lindsay had dropped kisses in the nape of her neck. 'And blithe we were to see the bairn so glad and bonny.'

Andrew Lorimer was in high feather. Theresa, disconcerted, took the check badly. He remembered how, from their childhood up, Tris had liked to be in the know, and he enjoyed her discomfiture. It was not unlikely that Kate also, calmly as she continued her needlework, with frank and placid eyes lifted to look at her aunt, relished the moment.

Theresa began to give Mr Dalgarno Forbes his character. 'You can just hold by his doors, then,' thundered Andrew.

Mrs Falconer sat stupefied. Her mind registered the incredible fact, but she could not feel it. And Kate, who on her own confession loved the man, sat there collectedly and sewed. She had known, even when she confessed, that Garry was Lindsay's lover. Mrs Falconer's dreams were dust.

Lang Leeb warbled from her corner. The fragile sounds were blown like gossamers about the room and no one heeded them, but Ellen moved her head impatiently as though they teased her face. Leeb sang:

My mother bade me gie him a piece,
    Imphm, ay, but I wunna hae him,
I gied him a piece and he sat like a geese,
    For his auld white beard was newly shaven.

Ellen turned and looked at her mother. The old eyes, bright and sharp, glittered like the reflection from a metal that has no inner illumination of its own. She was subtle and malicious, this old woman for whom life had ended save as a spectacle. Ellen, as she looked, read her mother's mocking thought. Theresa too, had said to her, when she ran across the garden to bid Garry stay for tea, 'Nell, you old fool.' What did they think—that she was running after the boy for her own sake? Dastardly supposition, so vile that she blushed, went hot and cold by turns. But wasn't it true? In a flash she realised it, that this sense of tragedy in which she had foundered came not from any grief for Kate, but for herself, because she loved the youth and wanted him near her. But it was life she wanted, strong current and fresh wind, no ignoble desire.

Theresa continued to sneer at the boy's expense. Leeb changed her song. The mocking voice teased like a gnat round Ellen's consciousness:

> She wouldna slack her silken stays,

sang Leeb.

What! Not be generous to this young man who had wakened her out of her unreal dreams? They could call her what kind of fool they liked, she would not be guilty of that cowardice. She would give. She cut across Theresa's denunciation with an incisive thrust.

'He is a very fine young man.'

Andrew turned and looked at his cousin, whose long lean cheek was from him.

'Very fine fiddlesticks. He's a very ordinary decent fellow, with some high-falutin ideas that ought to have worn themselves out by now. Better, I grant you, than the low-falutin that seems to be the fashion nowadays. I've no objection to an idealist, always provided he can keep his own wife when he takes one. And what ails you at Bawbie?' he added, swinging round again to disconcert Theresa. 'Bawbie's folk's as good's your own. A Paterson was settled in Knapperley as long since as the seventeen-thirties, and a Paterson was married on the son of an Earl, if you didn't know it, in 1725. A collateral branch, that would be. Let me see, let me see, it was the same branch—'

The door was opened, and Lindsay thrust unceremoniously in by a little wiry wrinkled man who bounced rapidly after her.

'It's yourself, Mr Lorimer,' said he, too excited even to greet the ladies into whose house he had thus bounded. 'Then pass you judgment, Mr Lorimer.' He rattled a tin pail under their noses. 'Pass you judgment. Here's me sortin' up the shop with the door steekit, and what do I hear but the jingle-jangle of my pail, that was sittin' waitin' me on the step. So out I goes and sees my lady here makin' away pretty sharp. "Ye're nae away wi' my pailie, surely," I says. Bang goes the pail and away goes she. So I puts on a spurt and up wi' her. "Ye needna awa' so fleet, Miss Craigmyle," I says.

"I see you fine. You werena needin' to send my pailie in ower the plantin'." But losh ye! It's nae Miss Craigmyle I've got a haud o', but this bit craiturie. A gey snod bit deemie, I wouldna mind her for a lass.' He turned the crunkled leather of his countenance towards Lindsay, in a wrinkled effort at a smile. 'But she would have been up and off with my pailie, Mr Lorimer, and nyod man, see here, the cloor it's gotten whan she flung it frae her into the plantin'.'

Andrew watched his daughter with amusement. Flushed, panting, near to tears, she stood in the middle of the room and threw defiant glances around.

'Clap it on her head, Mr Gillespie,' he answered to the indignant grocer, 'and up on the faulters' stool with her.'

'She has a gey canty hat there of her own,' said the grocer, whose wrath had fallen now that his grievance was recounted. 'But,' he added, glancing round the assemblage of ladies, 'it was Miss Theresa there I thought I had a haud o'. We a' ken she canna keep her hands off what she sees. She maun be inen the guts o' a'thing.'

Andrew bellowed with delight. Didn't he know the ancient habit of his cousin Tris, to appropriate all she fancied: failing roup, barter or purchase, then by simple annexation! The shades of sundry pocket-knives, pencils and caramels grinned humorously there above her ears. So the habit had not died, but was matter of common talk. To have seen his excellent cousin twice confounded in one evening was luck. He rose in fine fettle.

'Well, well, Gillespie man, but we can't let the lassie connach your goods like that.'

'Na, na, Mr Lorimer, sir,' answered the honest grocer, refusing the proffered money, 'I dinna want your siller. The pailie's nane the waur. It'll serve as well wi' a cloor in the ribs as wantin' it.' Mr Lorimer saw him out and came back to challenge Lindsay.

'Well, my lady, what have you been up to?'

'Daddy, I wasn't going to steal his pail—you know that.'

'What were you going to do, then?'

Lindsay looked round. They all awaited her answer. She wondered if they had been talking of Garry and her. Throwing her head proudly back, she answered, 'It's very silly. I don't know what made me do it. But Knapperley was all blazing with light. I thought—I really thought for a minute it was on fire, and I had a sort of panic. I saw the pail and seized it and began to run. I know it sounds absurd—as though my little pail could have helped any if there really was a fire. There wasn't, you know. The lights were blazing, right enough, but we saw them go out just after.'

'There's your Bawbie for you,' Theresa flung at Andrew Lorimer. Theresa was in a black anger. Her slogan, *A ga'in' foot's aye gettin'*, had covered numerous petty assaults on property, never (as of course one would understand) of magnitude to be called theft; but the grocer's calm recital of her obsession took her by surprise. She glared furiously at Andrew, and pounced triumphantly on Miss Paterson's aberration as a shelter from her own.

'Andrew's wanting a word with Lindsay,' Miss Annie interrupted in her pleasant way. 'We all know Bawbie's gotten a dunt on the riggin', Tris. Leave her alone. Andrew, I'm getting stiffened up like a clothes rope after rain. I'm terrible slow. But we'll all go through and let you talk to your lassie.'

'Indeed no, Paradise. Daddy and I will go through.'

Andrew trolled a song in his deep strong voice as he went to the other room. He had quite enjoyed the little episode. Theresa's exposure was part of the ruthless comicality of life. 'O ay, he's a comical deevil, your cousin Andrew,' Lang Leeb had been wont to say. 'He might laugh less if it was some of his own.'

One of his own was now involved. He had yet to deal with Lindsay's affair.

'Your mother,' he said, 'hasn't made the acquaintance of your proposed aunt-in-law. On the whole, we'd better keep this dark. She doesn't relish eccentricity in the family. What's this about the lights? And fined, was she? Well, you keep that to yourself. Your mother needn't know you were chasing round the countryside with the grocer's pail.'

'You're a dear,' said Lindsay.

'And you'd better tell me what to say about this man of yours. All fair and square, I suppose?'

'You bet.'

'What'll I say, then? Hurry up, I can't stay here all night. What am I to say to your mother? Lord love you, bairn, don't weep. Make up the triggest little tale you can.'

A burning tear splashed down upon his hand. Lindsay's face was against his coat, and he felt the shaking of her sobs.

'Daddy, daddy, I'm so miserable.'

'Here, here, cheer up. It's war-time, after all. Do you want to marry him?'

Lindsay raised her head and stared with blank eyes at her father.

'We'll bring your mother round,' continued Andrew.

Lindsay wept the harder.

'Well, well, that's settled,' said her father, drying her tears with his handkerchief, and he plunged exuberantly into talk of Theresa and the pail.

'But daddy, what could Mr Gillespie have meant?'

'Just what he said—your Cousin Theresa can't go past a thing she wants.'

'But taking things—? She's perhaps beginning to get old. Old people do things like that.'

'Don't you suggest it. Tris won't be thought old. No, no, it's not a sign of her decrepitude. Tris wasn't to be trusted with property at any time. If it was movable property that was concerned, she lee'd like a fishwife and thieved like Auld Nick.' He began to entertain his daughter with tales from his youth. 'But this won't do. What am I to say to your mother?'

'Why, daddy,' said Lindsay, with very bright eyes, 'it's your business to make up explanations for people.'

'What am I to say to your mother?'

'Don't eat me up! Are you to be everyone's advocate but mine?'

'What—'

'Well, say then—oh, say that he's a gruff old bear and you can't get a word in edgeways and it wouldn't have been safe to let her know that he was here. Say that he's a terror to the neighbourhood, that he has enormous ears, the better to hear you with, my dear, and perfectly enormous teeth, the better to eat you up. Oh, say what you like, daddy, I leave it to you.'

She clung about her father's neck, convulsively kissing the roughness of his coat.

Andrew fondled her.

'Well, if we let you marry him—you're not very old yet. Sure that you know your own mind? Quite sure you love the bear enough to spend your life with him? Eh?'

'Quite.'

Andrew enjoyed the arrogant lift of her head.

But later, hunched on her pillow, she queried in the dark of Kate, 'And you told daddy I was out with him, Katie?'

'And weren't you?'

'I said no, didn't I?'

'But I supposed—'

'You shouldn't suppose.'

'Oh, I'm sorry if I was wrong. But your father wasn't very angry, was he?'

'Oh, not particularly. It's mother that thinks he is not good enough for us. We're so grand, aren't we? Daddy only says I mustn't be turned into a woman too soon.'

'Well, neither you must, Linny.'

'Oh, you're all the same. As if age—Louie's the only one—'

'What about Louie?'

'Oh, nothing.'

'But it will be all right, Linny, when you're older? Your father won't make objections?'

'Oh, quite all right. It's perfectly all right, isn't it, not to make objections to an engagement that doesn't exist?'

'That doesn't— But it will exist when they give their permission.'

'I've broken it off.'

'But whatever—'

'Tonight. I wrote it. I was posting it when I was out, if you want to know.'

'But Lindsay, this is terrible. Whatever for?'

'Oh, for everything.' She slipped under the bedclothes and lay rigid, her face hidden. 'Don't speak to me, please, Kate.'

Kate held her peace.

'Katie.'

'Yes.'

'Life's so terribly strange, isn't it?'

'Is it? I don't know.'

'Don't *you* think it strange, Katie?'

'No, not particularly.'

Lindsay sat up again.

'But truly, Katie? Have you never thought life was tremendously queer? One day one thing, and the next day all changed. Don't you find yourself wanting one thing at one moment, and then in a trice you know that wasn't what you wanted at all, but something different? Don't you?'

'No, I can't say that I do.'

'Then is it only me that's unlike everyone else? How could I be anyone's wife, Kate, if I'm like that?'

'But—'

'Oh, it wasn't for that I broke it off. At least, partly that. He's—he's not what I thought quite, Katie, and I'm not what I thought, and I don't know what to do. I wish I had been like other people, but I don't know what to make of life. I don't know what I want. It's all so queer.'

'Lindsay, you're hysterical. Lie down and sleep. It'll all be right in the morning.'

'No, it won't. You don't understand. I don't seem to be like other people, Katie. I'm queer. It must run in the blood.' Kate smiled to herself at the thought of queerness running in the respectable Craigmyle-Lorimer veins. 'Look at Cousin Theresa,' continued the girl's impatient voice. 'That's her that cavils at Miss Barbara for being queer. I was never so ashamed in my life as when that grocer man shouted, "You hold your hand, Miss Craigmyle, we know you like to nab a thing fine." '

'In the house—I know she claims all she wants as hers. But outside— And so Miss Barbara's lights were up again, Lindsay? The police will be on her. She's been fined already, you know. Crazy old thing. A public nuisance.' Kate chatted on, in hope of distracting Lindsay's mind and persuading her to sleep. But the girl flared out, 'I don't see why you're all so bitter about it. I think she's splendid. She knows what she wants, and wants it enough to have it, too. She's magnificent. She's herself. She can burn her house up if she likes.'

'And it doesn't matter if other people suffer?'

'Not in the slightest. Oh, don't let's talk any more, Katie.'

Kate was silent as she was bid.

The night air grew colder. Lindsay tossed restlessly. The wind rose. A sough ran through the pines. Blinds shook, and somewhere in the house a door rattled. Lindsay shivered. How cold the night was now!

'Don't tell them I've broken it off, Katie. You see—we don't know yet what he may say.'

'Very well. Now sleep. It will be all right tomorrow.'

In the next room, preparing for bed, Theresa rapped out, 'Sleekit bessy she's been. And such a bairn to look at. Butter wouldn't melt in her mouth. And Kate's no better, Ellen, let me tell you that. To think of the two of them, and them up to such a cantrip.'

'They've done no wrong.'

'Ask Mrs Andrew as to that.'

'I can decide for myself without any Mrs Andrew.'

'Well, if you don't think it wrong, I'm sure—! Sleekit, I call it. And raking about with him like yon after dark—you never know what harm she might take.'

'Oh, pails are easy to come by,' said Ellen.

Theresa held her tongue and got into bed.

'Hist ye and get that light out,' she commanded in a while. Ellen raised her eyes from her Bible and said nothing. 'Your chapter's lasting you long tonight.'

Ellen dropped her eyes, but did not speak. She had read no chapter. One uncompleted sentence only: the sentence with which she had been wont, in her hours of abasement, to scourge her fleeing fancy. 'Casting down imaginations and every high thing that exalteth itself against the knowledge of the Lord.'

Imaginations! It mattered nothing to her what the commentators said, the word for her summed up those sweet excursions into the unreal that had punctuated all her life. She thought she had forsworn them, fired as she was by the glimpses that Garry had provided of man's real travail and endeavour. But all she had achieved was a still more presumptuous imagination; and as she saw the ruins of her palace lie around her, she realised how presumptuous, and at the same time how desirable it had been. Now she would never open the door of her dwelling to youth and arrogant active life. Desolation came upon her. The cold wind searched her and made her shudder. Her prayer was a long and moaning cry, 'Me miseram. I have sinned. I have sinned.'

ELEVEN

Garry and his Two Fools on the Housetop

Mrs Falconer awoke suddenly and could not remember what had occurred.

She knew that she had been hurt. Her mind was aware of its own suffering, but could not find the cause. She lay very still, grappling with memory. This impotence was horrible. It gave one a sense of calamity too huge for the mind to master. Her eyes went straying, and across the window she saw the passage of a falling star; then another, and another. 'That's someone dead,' she thought; but instantly came recollection. Her mind cleared and the weight of disaster lifted. Stars did not fall from heaven in the course of ordinary living; one's pain had other sources. Kate loved a man she would not marry: that was all. Kate— But Kate remained unmoved. The blackness of desolation was not for that, but was born of shame and of despair. There was no escape for her from unrealities to the busy world of men, and when she sought to break away she did shameful and presumptuous things. The gnat-bites of her mother's song had swollen now, poisonous and hateful seats of pain.

Outside, the shooting stars were still falling across the window. They could not be stars—so many, so continual. They eddied and fluttered. Mrs Falconer raised herself and stared. Sparks! Something must be on fire. She was fully awake now and her mind was alert and vigorous; as she got out of bed and crossed to the window she reviewed in a flash the whole story of the preceding days. 'There's no good not confessing it,' she thought. 'I do love that boy. I want to live the kind of life he would approve, to fight with real opponents for a real cause. I want to find the dimension that he said was lacking in our lives.' And then she thought, 'I can at least help him to expose

the falsehood about that betrothal. That is something real
I can help to do.'

Even if her fond dreams of his saying to her, 'Mother, no
one understands what I mean like you,' could meet with no
fulfilment, she must still do all she could to fight the evils
he detested.

All this passed through her mind as she hastened to the
window, at the same time as she was thinking, 'Can the fire
be in this house?'

When she reached the window she saw that the air was full
of large, floating flakes of snow. A shaft of light lay across
them and made them glow like tongues of fire. And now a
voice rose from the garden. Mrs Falconer leaned out, and
saw Francie Ferguson standing in the whirl of snowflakes,
moving a lantern.

'Ay, ye're there, are you? Ye're grand sleepers, the
lot of you, nae to hear a body bawlin' at your lug.'

'But what's the matter, Francie?'

'A dispensation of Providence, Mistress Falconer. Ay,
I tell't you whan a' that lights was bleezin' to the heav-
en, I tell't you the Lord would visit it upon her heid.
Knapperley's up in a lowe, Mistress Falconer—'

'What! But are you sure?'

'As sure's a cat's a hairy beast. Ay, ay, I've twa e'en
to glower wi' an' I'm gey good at glowerin'. And thinks
I, Miss Craigmyle'll never ca' ower it if there's a spectacle and she's nae there to see. So I e'en in about to let
you know.'

'But surely, in that snow—surely it won't burn.'

'The snaw's new on.'

Mrs Falconer roused Miss Theresa.

'What's that? Knapperley? It's just the price of her.'

Theresa was out of bed on the instant. As Francie knew,
she would have counted it a personal affront to be left out
from a nocturnal fire. Mrs Falconer too, put on her garments, with trembling and uneasy fingers.

'What can we do, Tris? We'll only be in the way.'

But though she offered a remonstrance, she was drawn
by some force beyond herself to complete her hasty dressing
and follow Theresa to the garden.

As they went out the snow ceased falling and they could see that dawn had come. The sky cleared. Francie put out his lantern, and in a while the sun rose in splendour, touching the leafless tangles of twigs, filigreed with snow, to a shining radiance. Snow coated the ground and the shadows cast along it by the sun glowed burning blue. Francie and Miss Theresa talked, but Mrs Falconer walked on through the sharp vivid morning, and the thoughts she was thinking were pungent like the morning air. 'All is not lost,' cried a voice within her heart. 'If I have been a fool in my imaginings, why, to be a fool may be the highest wisdom. If I have been a fool it was because I loved. To love is to pass out beyond yourself. If I pass beyond myself into the service of a cause, surely I can bear the stigma of fool.' And she was elated, walking rapidly over the melting snow. 'The thing,' she thought, 'is to find how I can help him to prove that Louie affair.'

At Knapperley there was shouting and confusion: but, thanks to the fall of snow, the flames had been mastered. A part of the roof had fallen in. Miss Barbara stood with her legs planted apart, hands in her jacket pockets, contemplating the destruction with an infinite calm. Garry emerged from the building, half-clad, pale and weary, the gauntness of his face emphasised by the black streaks and grime that smoke and charred wood had left on it. He came out brushing ash from his clothing with his hands and spoke in an anxious tone to Miss Barbara.

'Can't find a sign of him. Looks as though it began in that room, too. The bed's destroyed. But not a sign of the man.'

'Ach,' said Miss Barbara, unperturbed. 'He's been smoking in his bed again. He'll be far enough by now, once he saw what he had done. Many's the time I've said to Johnnie, "Smoke you in my beds again and we'll see." '

Garry gave vent to a whistling laugh. 'Well, we've seen.' He returned to his labour among the debris. The little crowd that had collected ran hither and thither, talking and making suggestions. Miss Barbara stalked upstairs. Garry thrust his head from the gap where an upper window had been. From beneath, with his blackened face and protuberant ears, he had the appearance of a gargoyle.

'Friends,' he shouted, 'my aunt is obliged to you all. There's not much harm done, but without your help it would have been much more.'

'You'll need to hap up that holie in the roof, lad,' interrupted one of the men.

'I'll do more than hap it up—I'll mend it. I've been talking to Morrison here, the joiner. He can't take on the job, he's short of men and too much in hand as it is. But he says I'll get the wood.'

'Ay, ay, Mr Forbes, fairly that,' said Morrison. 'But for working, na man, I'm promised this gey while ahead.'

'Well,' said Garry, 'my leave will soon be up. I mean to start myself this very day.'

At these words, 'My leave will soon be up,' Mrs Falconer felt a queer constriction of the heart. The folk began to move away, but Miss Barbara, thrusting her head in its turn from the blackened hole, cried, 'Step in-by, the lot o' you there, and get a nip afore you go.' Miss Craigmyle and Mrs Falconer, looking round a moment later for their escort Francie, and failing to find him, it was clear that he had been enticed by Miss Barbara's offer. Had he not drunk the golden fire the previous night? 'A cappie o' auld man's milk,' Miss Barbara said, pouring the whisky. The two ladies made their way indoors.

'I'll just be bidin', then,' Francie was saying.

Garry talked to him with earnest and eager gestures.

Francie had offered himself as a labourer in the rebuilding of the fallen portion of roof.

'You'll never take him on,' cried Miss Theresa. 'The body has no hands. His fingers are all thumbs.'

'His father, he tells me, helped to build your own house. And his brother was a noted craftsman.'

'You've a bit to go to fetch his brother and his father to your house. The fellow's never been a mile from a cow's tail, he'll never do your work. He's a timmer knife. I don't like to hear of you taking him.'

'You can like it or loup it. I've engaged him.'

'You're a dour billie to deal wi',' said Miss Theresa. 'There's no convincing you. But you'll be cheated. Wait till you see if I'm not right. Your fine fat cash will be gey lean work. But I see you don't care a craw's caw for anything I may say.'

Francie's foolish, happy face remained unmoved throughout her diatribe; but when she added, 'We'll go in-by and tell your wife where you are,' he bounded to his feet, thumping the table till the dishes rang.

'Na!' he roared. 'That's what you wunna do. She can just sit and cogitate. She can milk the kye there and try how that suits her and muck the byre out an' a'. Such a behaviour as she's behaved to me! Past redemption and ower the leaf. Dinna you go near, Miss Craigmyle. She'll maybe sing sma' and look peetifu' yet.'

Mrs Falconer said in a low, hurrying voice to Garry, 'If there is anything that we could do—'

'Nonsense, Nell,' came brusquely from her sister. 'Keep your senses right side up. What could you do?'

The sisters went away.

At the Weatherhouse Lindsay came disconsolate to breakfast. She hardly heeded the excited talk about the fire. 'It's no affair of mine,' she thought impatiently, and going to the window she gazed into the chilly garden.

'It's like winter come back. At this time of year, to have snow.'

'Hoots, bairn, it's only April. Did you never hear of the lassie that was smored in June, up by the Cabrach way?'

The sun had not reached the garden. The grass was covered with a carpeting of snow, except for dark circular patches underneath the trees; but the carpet was too meagre to have the intensely bright and vivid look that snow in quantity assumes. Birds had hopped over its surface, which was marked by their claws. The delicate crocus petals were bruised and broken, and early daffodils had been flattened, their blooms discoloured by contact with the claggy earth. Only the scilla and grape hyacinths, blue, cold and virginal, stood up unmoved amid the snow.

And how cold it was! Although the sun shone beyond the garden, melting the foam of snow that edged the waves of spruce, yet the air was bitter, searching its way within doors, turning lips and fingers blue.

'The milk's not come,' said Kate. 'Oh, that's the way of it. I always said Francie did the milking. Well, we've enough to last us breakfast.'

When breakfast was over, Miss Theresa put on her outdoor things.

'Now really, Tris, where are you off to? Haven't you had enough of gallivanting for one morning?'

'To see about the milk,' said Theresa, who was agog to discover how Bell was taking her husband's mild desertion.

'Well—I'll come too.'

Mrs Falconer hardly knew why she wished to go any more than she had known why she rose from her bed to see the fire. She seemed to be driven by a force outside herself.

'These things are real life,' she thought. 'That must be it. I ought to pay more heed to what other people are doing, not wrap myself up in my wicked fancies.'

The sisters made their way along the soft, wet cart-road. The first member of the family they came upon was the young boy Sid, who hodged along the road, hands in his pockets, spitting wide, in perfect imitation of Francie's gait and manner.

'Poor brutes, I don't believe they're ever milked,' Theresa said.

Bell greeted them with fine disdain. When Francie had first courted her, twenty years before, she must have had a bold and dashing beauty. Even yet she was handsome, in a generous style, and her black eyes had lost nothing of their boldness. Until Francie had wedded her, after the death of his brother Weelum, she had had a rude appetite for life but no technique in living. The spectacle, however, of her faithful and humble lover, claiming her in steadfast kindness after his long frustration, gave Bell a rich amusement. For the first time she ceased to follow her momentary appetites, and studied in a pretty insolence how best to take her entertainment from her marriage. She was therefore furious at Francie's disappearance.

'You can whistle for your milk,' she said. 'I wasna brought up to touch your kye, dirty greasy swine. Guttin' fish is a treat till't. The greasy feel o' a coo's skin fair scunners me.'

'Stellicky's milkin' the kye,' interrupted the little boy, who was keeking at the visitors round the edge of the door.

'Haud yer wisht, ye randy. Wait you or your da comes back.'

'But where is he?' gravely inquired Theresa.

'Whaur would he be? On the face o' the earth, whaur the wifie sowed her corn. Up and awa and left me and his innocent weans in the deid o' night, that's whaur he is. America, he's been sayin' gey often, I'll awa to America. I'll let him see America whan he wins back. I'll gar him stand yont. If he's to America, I'll to America an' a'.'

It was evident that she had received no hint of Francie's whereabouts, and the absence of the devoted drudge had wrought upon her finely. She was purple with wrath. The sisters went to the byre, where the small Stella, clad in an enormous apron, with a brilliant red kerchief knotted over her black hair, was milking the two cows. Stella saw the ladies, but paid not the slightest attention to their advent, and continued to milk with an important air, manoeuvring her little body, slapping the cows and addressing them in a loud and authoritative voice. Stella was in her glory.

'When you're done, we'll take our pailful,' said Miss Theresa sharply.

The girl looked round in an overdone amazement, kicked her stool from under her, swayed her little hips beneath the trailing apron and shoved the nearest cow aside. 'Haud back, ye—' she commanded, using a word that made the Weatherhouse ladies draw in their breath.

'You can bring that milk as fleet's you like,' said Miss Theresa. 'I'll give you your so-much if I hear you speak like that again.'

Stella tilted her chin and jigged her foot. In the darkness of the byre, clad in the old apron and the turkey-red kerchief, she glowed with an insolent beauty. Miss Theresa returned to the house, but Mrs Falconer remained at the byre door, watching the girl. Stella finished her milking, but instead of carrying the pails to the milk-house and giving the waiting customers their milk, she thrust the

cows about, flung her stool at the head of one that refused
to budge, and began with frantic haste to clean the byre.
Mrs Falconer made no remonstrance. There was something
in the impudent assurance of this nine year old child that
frightened her and saddened her. When she heard the same
wicked word tossed boldly from the childish lips, she thought,
'Well, this is reality, indeed. Why did I never think before
of all that this implies?' and she began to talk to the child.

Stella was ready for an audience.

'And do you often milk?' Mrs Falconer had inquired.

'Oh, he learned me, but he never lets me. I did it all
myself,' she added, with a gleaming toss of the head. 'She
said'—she jerked her elbow towards the house—'she said,
"Let the lousy brutes be." And she padlocked the door and
wouldna let me in. But I waited till she went out to the yard,
and I after her and up with a fine big thumper of a stick.
"Give's that key," says I. But losh ye, I had a bonny chase
or I got it out of her. Round and round, it was better'n tackie
any day. "Deil tak ye, bairn," she said, "you fleggit me out
o' a year o' my growth." "If it comes off you broadways," I
says, "you needna worry." '

Mrs Falconer did not ask for the milk. She continued
to watch the bouncing child.

Stella made the most of her audience. She talked large.

'Ken whaur I got my head-dress?' she asked, flaunting
the Turkey cotton. 'I got it frae my Sunday School teacher.
I'm in a play. I've got to speak five times. Ay, gospel truth,
I hae! Molly Mackie has only four times. Gospel.'

She struck attitudes, strutting about the byre and mouth-
ing her words.

'Ken this, I have that handky on my head in the play.
Ay have I. Teacher she says, "Now, girls, fold them all up
and we'll put them in this box." ' (Whose voice was she
mimicking, thought Mrs Falconer. The little brat had put
an intonation into it that was curiously familiar.)

'But Stella, how have you the handkerchief here?'

The girl burst into noisy laughter and went through a
rapid but effective dumb show. Mrs Falconer gathered that
she had brought the handkerchief away thrust into the neck
of her frock.

'But Stella, that was naughty. Your teacher will be disappointed.'

'She hides things herself,' said Stella carelessly. 'Ay does she. Gospel.' When she said *Gospel* Stella breathed noisily and crossed her breath with her forefinger. 'I'll tell you,' she rattled on eagerly. 'Teacher has a ring she keeps hine awa' down her neck. She's another ring that she keeps on her finger, just its marra. Twins!' The girl giggled with delight at recounting her story. 'Ken how I found that out? She aye bides ahin whan we're learnin' the play, a' by hersel. So one night I thought I'd see why, and I leaves my paperie with the words in ahin a desk and then goes marchin' back to look for it. So I sees her standin' there and one ring danglin' on a ribbon kind of thing, and the t'other ring aye on her finger. And she stuffs the ring intil her bosom, and my, but she got red. She's right bonny whan she blushes.'

The girl grasped her little nose with her fist and squinted, laughing, over the top of it to Mrs Falconer, who said severely, 'You are a naughty girl, Stella. You should never spy on people.'

'Tra la la, la la la la,' sang Stella hopping about the byre. 'I wunna tell you any more.' But she could not keep it in. Immediately she began again.

'Ken what it is she does whan she stays ahin? My! She's play-actin'. Just like us in the play. I think she'll be to say her piece at the concert an' a'. It's awful nice. It's just rare. I've found the way to climb up and see in at the window, and I've seen her ilka night, and naebody else has had a keek. They'll get a rare astonisher at the concert the morn, ay will they. Well, she pu's off the ring that's aye on her finger and dirds it down on the floor. "You hateful thing," she cries. Syne she jerks the other one up out of her bosom, louses the string, and puts the ring on her finger. This way.' The child was an astonishing little mimic. Her pantomime was lifelike. She began now to kiss the imaginary ring, holding her head to the side and rubbing the third finger of her left hand to and fro against her lips.

'Syne,' continued Stella, 'she turns the ring round, so that the stone's inside. And then she makes on to shake hands with somebody, and she says, "Do you take this woman to be your wedded wife?" "I do." Whiles after that she starts to greet and whiles to sing. I dinna ken which it really is, but we'll see the morn. I hope she'll be dressed up. She kens it rare. It's auld John Grey's ring,' she added carelessly.

'Whose?'

'Auld John Grey's, him that's head o' the Sunday School.'

'Surely, Stella, you call him Mr Grey.'

'What for? He's just auld John Grey. He's a rare mannie. You can scran anything off him. If you go in about whan he's delvin' he gives you sweeties and newses awa' to you. Ae day I was newsing awa' and the rain cam on. Loshty goshty guide's, it wasna rain, it was hale water. The rain didna take time to come down. So he took me in to his hoosie and the body that makes his drop tea spread a piece to me. And syne he gied me a pencil that goes roun' an' roun' in a cappie kind o' thing. It was in a drawer with preens and pencils and orra bits o' things—some pictur's that he let me see and bits o' stone wi' sheepy silver. And away at the back o' the drawer there was a boxie wi' a window for a lid, and yon ring was in there. I kent it fine whan I saw it again. She had scranned it off him, same's I did a preen wi' a pink top.'

'But when was that, Stella?'

'Oh, a while sin'. I dinna ken. Afore the New Year.'

'Was it before his son died, do you think?'

'The chiel that made the guns? Na, na. A long while after that.'

'And who is your Sunday School teacher?' asked Mrs Falconer.

'Miss Morgan, of course,' Stella answered, with a contemptuous stare for her visitor's ignorance.

The long lean woman positively shook where she stood.

'Stella, my dear,' she said, swallowing hard, 'you know you shouldn't take away Miss Morgan's handkerchief. What will she say when she doesn't find it in the box?'

Stella gave a loud and scornful laugh.

'Bless your bonnet, she'll find it there all right. I'll have it back afore she sees. Though, of course, after the play's done—' She broke off laughing, and leaping about in fantastic figures through the byre, she sang, 'It's half-past hangin'-time, steal whan you like.'

'So young, so shameless and so smart,' thought Mrs Falconer sadly. The warm byre oppressed her and she stepped to the door, opening her collar to the chilly air; but seeing Theresa at the same time step from the door of the house, she went back to the byre and lifted the two pails of milk.

'Is that milk not ready yet?' cried Theresa, appearing in front of the byre.

'Just ready,' Mrs Falconer answered, and balancing her body between the pails she carried the milk to the milk-house.

Miss Theresa had had a good fat gossip.

'It seems Francie's hinting at leaving them,' she told her sister. 'All talk, I fancy. If he goes to America, the wife says, I go too.' Miss Theresa laughed. 'They'll need a good strong boat and a steady sea before they take that carcase across the ocean. She had made the ground dirl, chasing round like that and the lassie after her. I'm glad to hear somebody can keep her in her neuk.'

Mrs Falconer walked home in troubled soliloquy. Reality had pressed too close. Her thoughts swirled and sounded in the narrow channel of her life, crashing in from distant ocean. Lindsay's betrothal, the fire, the young man's imminent return to the war, Francie's revolt, the pitiful spectacle of the child Stella in her vigorous vulgar assault upon life, the mystery of Louie Morgan's play-acting with the rings, her own shame, her mother's cruelty—smote her like thunder. From the hurly-burly of her mind one thought in time detached itself, insisted on attention. What had Louie done? What did the strange story of the rings imply? If the ring that had been David's mother's was indeed lying in the box in John Grey's drawer some time later than David's death, how came Louie to possess it? She turned the theme about in her head, puzzled and afraid. If it was true, as Garry maintained, that Louie had never been betrothed to David Grey, could she have given colour to her story by clandestine appropriation of the ring—in short, by stealing it? Mrs Falconer felt like a country child alone for the first time in the traffic of a city. What am I to do? she thought, what am I to do?

In the afternoon Mrs Falconer went to call on John Grey's housekeeper. This elderly woman, deaf and cankered, had few intimates and knew little of what went on beyond her doors. Gossip passed her by. 'And as for the master himself,' she would say to Mrs Hunter, 'he says neither echie nor ochie. I've seen me sit a whole long winter night and him never open his mouth.' She had therefore heard nothing of the interrupted Session meeting, nor of the speculation that Mr Garry Forbes had set going with regard to Miss Morgan.

Mrs Falconer bundled some wool beneath her arm. 'I can give her a supply for socks,' she thought. It made an excuse for her call. But the mere need to summon excuse put Mrs Falconer to the blush. How mean a thing it was to lurk and spy, in hope of proving ill against one's neighbour! Truth must be served, but if this were her service, surely it was ignoble. She sighed and rang the door bell; rang again; then knocked loudly on the panels. At last a step shuffled to the door.

'I'm that dull,' the old woman said. 'Folk could walk in-by and help themselves or ever I knew they were about.'

'I don't suppose many people would want to do that.' Strange point of departure for the interview!

'You never know, Mrs Falconer. Folk's queer. And Mr Grey, good soul, thinks ill of nobody. There's nothing in this house under lock and key. Forbye the meat-safe, Mrs Falconer, and for that I wouldna take denial. Since ever my dozen eggs went a-missing, that I found a hennie sitting on in the corner of the wood, and them dead rotten—I put them into the bottom of the safe, till Mr Grey would dig a hole and bury them. And in-by there comes a tinkey. "No," I says, "my man, I've nothing." But when I went outside, lo and behold, my eggs were gone. He had had a bonny omelette that night. Unless, as I said often to Mr Grey, he sold them for solid siller to some poor woman in the town. Poor soul, she had had a gey begeck. So after that I says, I'll have a key to my safe. If it's rotten eggs the day, it may be firm flesh the morn.'

She had led her visitor in, and rambled on, paying little heed to interpolations, which had, in any case, to be shouted at her ear. Mrs Falconer therefore gave up the attempt to talk, and sat listening.

'And you think nobody would want to help themselves? I'm not so sure, I'm not so sure. I'll tell you what I found here one day. My fine miss, the old minister's daughter, Miss Louie Morgan, right inside the parlour, if you please, with the master's drawer beneath his bookcase standing open and her having a good ransack. A good ransack, Mrs Falconer, minister's daughter though she be. "The master gave me leave," she says, "and you didn't hear me ring, so I just came in." He gave her leave right enough, I asked him. For the Jumble Sale, she says. "The things are no use to me," he said, "she is very welcome." He would give away his head, would the master, you could lift his very siller in front of him and he would be fine pleased, but don't you touch a flower. Pick a rose or a chrysanthemum and you needna look him in the face again.'

Mrs Falconer's mouth was parched, her lips were shaking. She had asked nothing, but the answer she desired had fallen directly in her ears. She was sure now that Louie had taken the ring. The Jumble Sale took place three months after the death of David Grey. But perhaps Mr Grey himself had given her the ring, to seal a betrothal left incomplete at the young man's death? Mrs Falconer put the thought away. No, no. The concealment of the ring, her stealing to the drawer unseen, Garry's certainty, all convinced her; and she was overwhelmed besides by the thought that she had been led straight that day to the discovery. The sense of urgency that had driven her to Knapperley in the night, and to Francie's croft in the morning, so that Stella's remarkable story came to her knowledge, and now the immediate relation by the housekeeper of Louie's conduct, amazed her like a revelation of supernatural design. 'I have been led to this,' she thought.

She rose to go, shouting at the old housekeeper an excuse for her unusual visit.

'There would be no mistake though you came again, Mrs Falconer.'

'But what must I do next?' she pondered as she went away.

Kate, bringing home the messages that same afternoon, overtook Louie Morgan on the road.

'I'm thinking of applying for a Lonely Soldier,' said Louie. 'To write to, you know. Wouldn't it be splendid?' And without giving Kate time to reply she hurried on, 'We must all do something to help the poor men. Or a war-time orphan to bring up. I've been thinking of that. Two of them, perhaps. Uplands is so much too large for mother and me—we'd easily have room for two. Isn't it a splendid idea for people to take these poor orphans and bring them up?'

'Excellent,' said capable Kate; but privately she thought, 'Heaven pity any child that is brought up by you.'

Louie blurted, 'I suppose you think I am making a fool of myself.'

'No. Why should I think so?'

Without answering, Louie burst suddenly into a side road and walked away.

She had just come from Knapperley.

Garry had laboured hard all day. Knowing that unless he saw the repairs completed before he left, the house would remain as it was and rot, he set to work at once to clear away the damaged material. Miss Barbara, keen for a space, volunteered her aid. She was strong as a man. Francie too, worked manfully. As the morning wore on people came in twos and threes to look at the scene of the fire. Miss Barbara's eccentric ways, above all her curious taste for lighted windows, gave rise to many explanations of the outbreak. Nor did the sight that met the eyes of the inquisitive lull the tales; for through the gap in the roof, moving about among the beams and on what was left of the flooring of a low attic, could be seen three figures, the tall lean soldier, the clumsy crofter and the brawny woman, sawing, scraping and hammering to the rhythm of an uproarious song:

I saw an eel chase the Deil
Roun' about the spinnin' wheel.
And we're a blin' drunk, boozin' jolly fou, ma jo!

Garry, swinging through the work in his enthusiasm, shouted as lustily as the other two:

I saw a pyet haud the pleuch,
Wha's fou, wha's fou?
An' he whussled weel eneugh,
Wha's fou noo, ma jo?

He broke off, however, at the sight of Miss Theresa Craigmyle among the spectators below. Theresa had hastened back, to lose nothing of the excitement, and found herself well rewarded.

'They had had a dram,' she declared later at the Weatherhouse. 'Bawling out of them like that.'

'And what more fitting?' inquired Lang Leeb from her corner. 'My tuneless daughters don't understand that work goes sweetest to a song. Did you never know that they built a pier in the harbour of Aberdeen three hundred years ago to the sound of drum and bagpipes? They don't work so wisely now. Knapperley roof will be a wonder.'

A wonder it bade fair to be. Miss Barbara tired soon and went to the stable. Francie fetched and carried, but the young gaffer having left him alone for a spell, he began to follow his own devices—which were various. Garry returned from attending to some matter on the ground and saw Francie, without plan or instruction, cut gaily into the new wood that he had brought from the carpenter's shop. He had hacked and hewed recklessly, but, like his father in the Weatherhouse parlour, though without his father's justification, was so highly pleased with himself that Garry stood abashed, unwilling to remonstrate. It was part of his creed that a man should take pleasure in the work of his hands, and to quench Francie's pleasure gave him the same sense of constricting life that he had felt in quenching Miss Barbara's candles. He set Francie's haggard boards aside.

He was called to the ground again, and before his return the post came in and he found Lindsay's letter. The note was curt: 'Garry, I can't marry you. I'm sure I'm not the right kind of wife for you. I'm sure I'm not.' Garry pocketed his scrap of paper and climbed to the attic. Francie had mismanaged his tools again. Garry cursed and set to work himself, hoping to prevent further mischief by adroit advice and order. As he worked, however, his heart grew cold. Lindsay's note settled hard upon it like a frost.

He worked dourly on; but nothing prospered. In his first enthusiasm to restore, he had been sure of what he had to do. Now he found checks and miscalculations. He had to stop and realise that he was uncertain how to proceed.

Just then he saw, foreshortened on the ground below him, the figure of Miss Morgan. She beckoned. He turned his back. But she called, 'May I not speak to you? Indeed it is urgent.' He went down.

Miss Theresa Craigmyle came near at the same moment. 'Can't you keep away?' he thought angrily. He knew that her visit was an idle curiosity, and had enough regard for the reputation he wished Miss Morgan to retain to ask Louie to enter the house.

'I want you to understand,' Louie began, 'I'm sure I didn't make it clear: in allowing my possession of the ring to become a symbol, a kind of rite, you realise that I had passed beyond the material vehicle to the spirit. Can I make you see? The material symbol was of no moment. I mean, it's some justification for my keeping the ring. I simply didn't see it as a piece of someone else's property. It was just an agglomeration of matter that symbolised what was unseen. I wonder if you understand?'

'I understand,' he said slowly, 'that you want to talk about yourself. But I am busy.'

'Yes, I want to talk about myself. I know, I know I do. To you. Not to anyone else. I can have no peace until you understand that I am not a common thief. You are doing yourself an injustice if you think that. You degrade yourself by your misjudgment. I have to make you see. I feel that I am needful to you, to open your eyes to new ways of judgment—'

He turned away. 'Excuse me, I am very busy.'

'We are all needful to one another. Even I to you. But you don't think so.'

'Excuse me.' He went away.

Louie went home, and meeting Kate Falconer on the road, proposed to adopt an orphan.

Garry returned grimly to his task. He was inexpressibly weary. The muddled disorder of the garret oppressed him.

Mrs Hunter came in her comfortable way and tried to make him eat.

'You never lippened to yon craitur,' she said, spying out the disorder of the land. 'Pay the body and send him hame.'

Later she recounted the affair to her neighbour John Grey.

'That Francie Ferguson—he wouldna cut butter on a hot stane. What a haggar' he's made. You would be doing a good deed, Mr Grey, to give the laddie a hand. He's dirt dane. I took him a bowlie of broth, but he's never even lippit it.'

John Grey went round to Knapperley and said to Garry in his quiet, unassertive way, 'You'd better let me give you a hand there.' He craned over among the rafters to look at Francie's mismanagement. 'Tchu, tchu, tchu,' he said, and began to work rapidly and surely.

Behind his back Garry paid Francie twice the sum he should have had for the completed work, and dismissed him.

'Your wood's unseasoned,' said Mr Grey. 'It's too dark to work tonight. Tomorrow's Saturday. I'll give you a hand in the afternoon.' He showed the younger man with a quiet tact where he had gone wrong in his work and how to remedy the faults. 'You haven't handled wood very much.' It was impossible to feel resentment. Garry swallowed his pride and set himself to learn.

But when at length he went to bed he was overwhelmed in a sense of failure. He could not mend a roof, nor chose a workman, nor love a woman. He could not now even vindicate his friend. He relit his candle, to read once again Lindsay's letter, which he knew by heart. All the self-distrust of his nature, inherited from a timid father and the grandmother whose utmost remonstrance was a sigh, had risen in him at the reading of her note. In vain, from boyhood up, he had sheltered under a bravado, a noisy clowning or proud assumption of ability where indeed he felt none; nevertheless at moments, suddenly, this ogre of self-distrust rushed out and bludgeoned him. He had never discovered how much he was indebted to the ogre. His later reputation as a man with surprising stores of curious knowledge had its foundations there. The shame he felt at being found at fault or ignorant sent him furiously to learn, and he never forgot what was bludgeoned in; but his sensitive heart, wroth to show a wound, suffered in the process. So now tonight, when Lindsay had found him at fault, he was overcome with shame.

'She thinks I'm all wrong about Louie, and I can't tell her. What a confounded mess everything is in!' He wished he was back at war. This land he had thought so empty was proving unpleasantly full. Wisely he slept on it and woke refreshed in a windy sunrise to think, 'I'm blest if I let Lindsay go like that.' Less than ever in the sanity of morning did he wish to see the mob gaping over Louie's theft; for all the subtlety of her excuses, theft it was. But Lindsay had to know, and should know, well and soon.

In the same wind of sunrise Mrs Falconer lay, very still beside her sleeping sister, and prayed, as she had prayed at intervals throughout the night:

'Help me, O God, in all that I may have to do.'

She was sure that she had been divinely led to her strange discovery, and in spite of her shrinking from the public stare, had made the dedication of herself to Garry's service. Her knowledge must be used to help his cause. She had prayed till she was worn out.

TWELVE

Concert Pitch

Breakfast was just ending when Miss Theresa remarked, 'And a pretty picture they made, the three of them, bawling out of them on the head of the house. He's as daft as Bawbie herself. He had a real raised look, they said, at that session meeting. Oh, I forgot, Lindsay, he's your young man. I haven't got accustomed to that yet.'

'Then you may spare yourself the trouble.' Lindsay's voice was curt.

'Eh? Now, Lindsay, you needn't be so short. You know I always say just what I think. There's no manner of doubt that the young man is strange. They are all saying it. So it's just as well to know what you are taking in hand if you're taking him.'

'Which I don't happen to be doing.'

Kate gave the girl a curious look. Lindsay continued, 'Oh, go ahead, Cousin Tris, tell us all you saw and did. He's not my young man. Say just what you think.'

'What I think,' said Miss Theresa, 'is that he's a young man you'd be better without. That Louie Morgan's setting her cap at him and like to get him, I should say. Not a soul did he pay heed to, and him up there on the roof, but as soon as she came in about, down he comes and goes straight to her. Never even saw that any other body was there. O ay, Louie knows what she's about, gazing at him with all her eyes. He had her into the house right away, and him so busy with his roof. No saying how long they stayed there.'

'Brute!' Lindsay pushed back her chair and walked out.

'What would you make of that?' asked Theresa. 'Is she marrying him, or is she not?'

Kate knit her brows and said nothing.

'Of course she's marrying him,' said Miss Annie. 'You've such an ill will at the boy you can't see the good in him. You scare the bonny birdie with your clapper of a tongue.'

The bonny birdie could be heard upstairs, banging a drawer shut. Kate followed her.

'You mustn't take Aunt Theresa too hard, Linny. It's just her way. She's got into a habit of speaking like that.'

'Damned impudence. And I was a damned ass to tell her what I did.'

'What language, Lindsay!'

'I know it's what language. I've been brought up to use tidy language, haven't I? My mother would be finely shocked if she heard me. But life isn't tidy, you see, Kate, and that's what I'm discovering. Louie making up to him indeed.' She jammed her hat on her head. 'I'm going to Knapperley.'

'But Linny, that was only Aunt Theresa's idea—'

'Idea or not, it's abominable. Making eyes at Garry? Someone will pay for this. I could face the devil naked.'

'My dear, don't be so upset—'

'Do you never feel about anything, Kate? You should fall in love. Then you would understand.'

She banged the door, crashed like a cataract down the stair, collided with Paradise, shouted, 'Sorry, sorry,' as she ran. The house door slammed.

Kate, left alone in the bedroom, pressed her hands upon her breast. Her lips drew together in a line of pain. But in a moment she relaxed and began carefully to make the beds.

Halfway to Knapperley Lindsay met Garry seeking her with the same fury of decision with which she was seeking him.

Later, as they walked towards Knapperley, a mournful Lindsay said, 'I can't believe it yet. She talked so beautifully. Made life seem so strange and big. I can't explain. It wasn't like anyone else's world. But Garry—I like the ordinary world best. Only—listen, that hateful Cousin Tris. Oh, I know I shouldn't hate her, but she's always right, always right. And since that grocer let out about the way she sneaks things, she's been on her high horse—you can't imagine! She's just aching for a chance to be splendidly right in front

of everyone. And I was ass enough to say I'd given you up.
Idiot! And now she'll crow and say she always knew it
wouldn't last. Listen, you must take me to that concert
tonight, claim me in front of everyone, let her see if all her
havering about you is right or wrong. You will come, now,
won't you?'

The afternoon sped by. In aiding John Grey, Garry
worked happily and well. At fall of dark, Mr Grey said,
'That will have to do tonight. I've promised to look in at
the concert. It's not much in my line, but the children will
be acting. They are expecting me to come.'

Garry called in the approved fashion at the Weatherhouse
door to convoy Lindsay to the school.

'Going off with him, Lindsay,' said Miss Theresa. 'I
thought you said you had given him up.'

'Given him up? Who? Garry? But what an idea,
Cousin Tris.'

'What were you saying this morning, then?'

'Oh, that—really, if you can't understand a little quiet
irony!' Miss Annie listening remembered the slamming of
the doors. 'I don't think much of your sense of humour,'
concluded Lindsay gravely, and walked away.

'People should say what they mean,' rapped Miss Theresa. 'I always say what I mean myself.'

She set out for the concert with Mrs Falconer and Kate.
Ahead of them on the road skipped Stella Dagmar, accompanied by her mother.

'She's fatter than ever,' commented Theresa.

'It's here's-an-end-and-I'll-be-round-in-five-minutes if
you wanted to measure yon. As I live, she's wearing
a new scarf.' She whipped round on the road, and saw
Francie following with the *loonie*.

'So there's you, Francie. You've been giving your wife
a present, my man.'

Francie rubbed the side of his nose and sniffed.

'What other would I do with the siller he gied me?'
he asked apologetically; and added, with a happy sheepish
grin, 'It sets her grand.'

The play went well. Stella flaunted her scarlet kerchief,
Miss Morgan 'managed' both visibly and audibly, there

was ample applause. The children scattered to their parents among the audience, and Louie took a curtain to herself, bowing and posturing. She had a charming mien, and her dress of filmy green set off the soft gold of her hair. As she stood in the packed, hot classroom savouring the clapping and the cheers ('Oh, we'll give her a clap, just for fashion's sake,' said Miss Theresa), Louie's spirit floated out into its own paradise. To be admired—she craved it as one of her profoundest needs. She threw back her head and smiled at the noisy crowd. The moment seemed eternal, it was so sweet. Slowly and dreamily she turned away and sat to the piano, striking a chord. Now she would play.

But between the striking of the chord and the first note of her music (which was never sounded), Mrs Falconer stood up in her place. She had not known herself what she was to do. White, erect, stern, she had sat through the entertainment like a woman hewn from stone; but suddenly, at sight of Louie posturing and smiling, her teeth began to chatter. 'False, false, false,' she thought. She was not conscious of getting upon her feet, nor did the voice that cried aloud above the chattering and the laughter seem to come from her throat; but the astonished assemblage saw the rising of the white stern figure, saw the thin lips move, and listened as she cried, 'Friends, there has been a wrong done here amongst you. That woman yonder is a thief. Round her neck you will find a ribbon, and on it she carries a ring. Will you ask her where she got that ring?' Louie's face was ashen. She was conscious of the glare of eyes, but all she could do was to shake her head and smile. 'The ring is Mr Grey's,' cried Mrs Falconer, and sat abruptly down. Her knees had given way.

Into the moment of astonished silence Stella's voice broke shrill. Stella had clambered up and was dancing on the seat in her excitement.

'It's a blue ribbon,' she shrieked. 'Oh, Miss Morgan, say your piece. "Do you take this woman to be your—" '

Her voice was drowned in the hubbub that arose. Someone pulled her off the seat and put a hand across her mouth. Stella battered herself free with two strong and skinny hands.

And then John Grey stood up. He had been seated with both hands laid on the head of his staff, a stout cherrywood staff, short, tough and seasoned like himself. He rose in his place and stretched a hand over the turbulent assembly.

'Now, now. Now, now.' His gentle voice would not carry. He stood with a hand stretched out and made a half-articulate sound of grieved annoyance, then rapped on the ground with his staff. In a moment the noise fell.

'There was no need for this bustle. I knew where the ring had gone to.'

Louie gave a gasping cry and made blindly for the door. A hulking overgrown farm lad, a *halflin* not yet old enough for war, thrust his clumsy boot across the passage to trip her. She stumbled and recovered; but John Grey, leaning from his place, hooked the handle of his staff into her filmy clothing and detained her. He detained her long enough to work his way out from among the people, then took her arm in his and led her from the room in courteous silence.

The hubbub recommenced; but Garry leaped to a form and shouted above the din.

'Friends, I'm sorry this has happened, but Mr Grey is sure to have some explanation. Don't let's spoil the concert, since we're all together. Let's sing something.'

He began to sing a rattling song, then another. The chorus was taken up with a will. That concert was remembered for years in Fetter-Rothnie—Garry Forbes's concert, they called it. They sing his songs and repeat his yarns today.

'I did myself ill with laughin',' declared Mrs Hunter.

As Miss Morgan herself had requested, Garry said a few words about the Front. But such words!—droll, gargantuan, unforeseen. Each tale was greeted with a hurricane of laughter, each chorus shouted in a lusty heat. The folk trooped out at last into the night, laughing and warm.

Garry wiped the pouring sweat from his face.

'That *was* fun,' Lindsay said, linking her arm in his. 'Garry, how can you keep so solemn when you tell those ridiculous stories? You didn't laugh once.'

'Never felt less like laughing in my life.'

She looked at him, and grew suddenly grave.

'You mean—you were doing it to keep them from—'

'From talking about her. Yes, of course. Fill up their heads with something else. It's an off-chance that they won't say quite so much about it as they'd have been sure to say if the concert had gone to bits. Good God, the thing was indecent! Do you realise what I feel like? I began it, of course. But to throw the common theft to the mob was mean. What on earth induced her?'

'She's a horrid old woman, thrusting herself into the limelight, that's what she is,' cried Lindsay, in her hard, clear, indignant voice.

Mrs Falconer, walking behind them, heard.

She had not yet ceased to tremble. From the moment when her knees had given way beneath her and she had sat down, her body had shaken without remission. She was deadly cold. Garry's quips, the laughter and the choruses, had passed over her like winds. They sounded in her ears, but brought no meaning. She was wholly given over to one idea, that at last she had achieved something in the world of real endeavour. Its results, its value, she was incapable of considering. All she could feel was that she had made the thrust, though the mere bodily effect upon herself was beyond belief. Yet, though her flesh was shaken, her mind was not. She felt as an arch-angel might who, returning from an errand on the earth, reports to God that his mission is fulfilled: no angel could be surer of the divine compulsion.

When therefore Lindsay's clear indignant cry, 'She's a horrid old woman, that's what she is,' came upon her ear, she did not at once understand its significance. She was, indeed, still wandering in her own pleasaunce. But instantly Theresa began to talk. Theresa had only a moment before made up on her sister on the road, having had words to exchange with sundry other curious persons. Now she demanded news. Ellen had to speak; and Theresa's impatience would not let her wait until the Weatherhouse was reached: she must needs call the lovers back to hear and to discuss.

So it was that Ellen was forced at last out of her dream, and learned that she had done the very thing that Garry was working to prevent. Standing there on the road, in the chill spring night, she heard him say, 'I'd give a good deal for this not to have happened.' The spring sky was hard and clear as Lindsay's voice.

'I meant to help you,' stammered the old woman. Old was what she felt, she who had been so young, feeling the spring in her coursing blood upon the moor. They talked interminably. Even in bed, Theresa's tongue ran on. But Ellen lay impassive. She had not even prayed that night. She was dumb.

THIRTEEN

Proverbial

The throng that passed out from the schoolroom singing Garry's songs and repeating his stories took away also a lively curiosity over the incident he had striven to make them forget, and inevitably it was linked with the earlier incident of Garry's outbreak before the Session. Matters so strange were worth the breath it cost to thresh them out. The wars had little chance of a hearing in Fetter-Rothnie for the next forty eight hours, by which time, thanks to Jonathan Bannochie, Garry's reputation was established in a phrase.

Out of the cold, clear night a wind came blowing. It gathered strength all day, till in the late afternoon nothing was at peace upon the earth. Trees and bushes swirled. Boughs were wrenched away and tender leaves, half opened, sailed aloft or drifted in huddled bands about the corners. Twigs and sand battered against the windows and struck the faces and necks of those who went outside. One had no sense of light in the world. The smooth, suave things from which light habitually glisters were wrinkled or soiled in the universal restlessness. Blossom was shrivelled. 'I can't hear a single bird,' Lindsay complained. 'Only the crows.'

Lindsay stood by the window, where she had stood the other morning to watch the snow upon the garden. Now the garden was changed anew. But while it had lain sealed and mute beneath the snow it was less hard to believe in the life within it than now, when this frenzy of motion tormented it from end to end. This was not the motion of life. How just, that Dante in his vision of love that has strayed from its own nature should see it punished by the blare and buffeting of such a wind as this. No silence, to hear the myriad voices, no quietude, to contemplate and recollect. No fineness of

160

perception. A wind of death.

But Lindsay felt only that the garden was ugly, and the howl and clatter set her teeth on edge. She could stay no longer in the warm room. She could not stay even in the garden. The fury of the wind within its enclosure, where the daffodil trumpets were flattened like paper bags and the air was full of strippings from the branches, seemed more withering and ruthless than on the open moor. On the moor the blast swept on without obstruction. The whole grey sky tore forwards to the sea. Even from the hill-top one saw the huge white bursts of foam that grew fiercer and more numerous from moment to moment. Lindsay ran all the way to Knapperley. She could not keep herself from running. When she turned aside her head she could hardly breathe, the wind drove her nostril in with such violence. But she wanted to run. She wanted to dance and to shout above the clamour of the hurricane. Nothing could have pleased her better than to fly thus upon the wings of the wind towards her lover—faster and faster, riding the gale like a leaf. She was glad to merge her will in the larger will of the tempest, for she knew now that she had merged it in her lover's will. Since the morning when he had told her of Louie's perfidy and she had recognised that her own judgment had gone astray, she had had no more desire to trust herself. She had wept, indeed, for the revelation she had had of the evil that is in life; but now, how free and glad she felt! Running thus before the wind, she had entered into the peace that is beyond understanding: she was at one with the motion of her universe.

At Knapperley she pushed open the door and ran upstairs. She felt free of the house now. She had accepted Miss Barbara. What a child she had been to fear her! As she had been a child to fear Garry's love. The sea was, after all, not so very wide; and earth, primitive, shapeless, intractable (as exemplified in Miss Barbara), was everywhere about one, and could be ignored. Roots, if one thought of it, must grow somewhere—in the customary earth.

She ran singing up the narrow stairway, and found Miss Barbara shaking with a jolly mirth beside the ruins of the tinker's bed.

'There's wounds,' she said, 'and growths and mutilations, bits rugged off and bits clapped on to the body
of man that is made in the image of his Maker. Them
and their war up there'—she nodded upwards to where
her nephew was at work—'they mutilate their thousands,
they chop off heads and hands and fingers, they could take
Johnny's cranny from him, but could they make another
Johnny? What's the use of your war, tell me that. You're
making tinklers right enough, I'll grant you. They'll be all
upon the roads, them that wants their legs and them that
wants their wits and them that wants a finger and a toe, like
Johnny. But ach! For all your shooting and your hacking,
Johnny's beyond you. Your war won't make him.'

'But you know,' said Lindsay, who had listened in amazement to this novel point of view upon the war, 'wounding
people isn't all that the war does.' She would have proceeded
to expound as best she could Garry's gospel of a rejuvenated
world, had Miss Barbara not cut her short with a decisive:
'Fient a thing does the war do that I can see but provide you
tramps to tramp the roads. Wounds and mutilations—that's
what a war's for and that's what it fabricates.'

'O Garry, may I come up?' Lindsay cried, turning
her back upon the crass earth without perceptions that she
divined Miss Barbara to be. 'May I come up the ladder?'
she cried, singing, and climbing, she thrust her head above
the attic floor and sang, 'Mayn't I hold something for you?
Or hand you up something? O Garry, mayn't I help?'

Already the gap in the roof was covered. Garry had
stripped a tumbled shed of its corrugated-iron roofing and
fixed the sheet upon the boards he had already nailed in
place. In the wild fury of the gale the iron sheeting had
worked loose, and kept an intermittent clatter above their
heads. The wind too, entering by nooks and holes, shrieked
desperately round the empty room. The old house groaned
and trembled.

'Garry, have you been at work all day? Garry, won't
you stop, one little minute—and kiss me? Now go on. I
love to watch you work. And I do love to be here. We're
so respectable. I went to church this morning, Garry—just
myself and Cousin Tris. Kate's back on duty, you know.

And—Garry, it was so strange. Cousin Ellen—'

She stopped, leaning from the top step of the ladder upon the garret planks, and was silent so long that Garry, dragging boards across the floor, stopped too and looked at her.

'Well, what of Cousin Ellen?'

She raised her eyes to his. Unshed tears were gleaming on her lashes. The tin patch rattled on the roof. The wind roared round the garret, raising the sawdust in whirlpools, and out of grimy corners the cobwebs streamed upon its current. And Lindsay said, 'I'm all afraid of life. I thought I wasn't, but I am. We're so cruel to one another, aren't we?' she continued. 'At least over at the Weatherhouse we are. I don't suppose we mean it, but we are. Cousin Ellen came down all ready dressed for church and Cousin Theresa said, "What! Nell you fool, you can't mean to go to church today. Show yourself off in public, after what you did last night." And Cousin Ellen said, "You would take my very God away from me." And she marched out on to the moor. "But what's worse in me than in your pails?" she turned back to ask. "If I'm not ashamed, why need you be?" They won't leave each other alone. Pails, pails, pails, and, Making yourself a public show, I never saw! It went on all dinner-time. I couldn't stand it any more, I ran away. And old Aunt Leeb sits there and chuckles. Oh, she's cruel! She's worse than they are. She's happy when she can say a thing that hurts. She's like the Snow Queen—she looks at you with those sharp eyes, and it's like splinters of ice that pierce you through. There's only Paradise that you can feel comfortable with.'

'Perhaps that's why you called her Paradise.'

'Oh yes, no one will be uncomfortable in Paradise, do you think? But I used to think no one could be uncomfortable in the Weatherhouse, and now it's all so changed. Garry, won't you marry me soon and let me be always with you? I feel so safe with you.'

But not, thought Garry, when later in the day, having taken her home, he was striding back across the moor: not because he was safe with himself. Her perfect trust was, of course, delightful: but oddly, in just those matters where she had yielded most generously to his opinion, he had himself become unsure. Even with regard to his aunt— 'But I'm not afraid of her any more,' Lindsay had said, 'I think she's splendid'—something of the girl's terror had gripped his own soul. While she, safe in his arms, had recounted her moment of panic, he too, had become afraid of his aunt: as of something monstrous, primitive and untameable, not by any ardours to be wrought into place in the universe of which he dreamed, a living mock to his aspirations. Yet how triumphantly herself! The corrugated iron clattering at that very moment on the roof of Knapperley was witness to that.

And over Louie Morgan also he was unsure. Lindsay was no longer her champion; but, strangely, she had championed herself. There was a queer twisted truth in what she had said. David too, had felt it. More bitterly than ever he regretted having thrown her to the mob.

Reaching Craggie on his homeward journey, spent with labour and thought, he suddenly turned aside and, bursting into Mrs Hunter's kitchen, cried, 'Feed me, for God's sake.'

'Weel-a-wat, laddie, come in-by.' Mrs Hunter thrust him in a chair and spread the cloth.

Food was never out of view in Mrs Hunter's kitchen. Enter when you would, plates were there, heaped high with girdle scones, oat-cake, soft biscuits. Jam was in perpetual relief. Syrup and sugar kept open state.

'A puckle sugar's that handy,' Mrs Hunter would say, throwing a handful on a dowie fire.

'I canna bide a room with nae meat about it,' she added. 'If Dave now came in at the door and him hadna had a bite a' the road frae the trenches, a bonny mother he would think he had gotten. And him sending hame his pay to keep the laddies at the school.'

Seizing the loaf, at Garry's request, and throwing to her youngest boy, seated at the fireside, the hearty hint: 'Will that kettle be boiling the night, Bill, or the morn's morning for breakfast?', she began to cut slice after slice of bread, until the whole loaf lay in pieces on the table. Jake, her husband, shook his head.

'There's nae need for sae mony a' at aince,' he said,

in a low voice. 'You can aye be cuttin' as it's called for.'

'I canna dae wi' a paltry table. If it were Dave now, in another body's house, you wouldna like it yoursel.' And she seized a brown loaf, slicing until it, too, was piled high upon a plate.

'I grudge nae man his meat, but there's nae call for sae mony a' at aince.'

Jake remained with his worried eyes fixed on the table. A lifetime of laborious need was in the look he bent upon the piles of bread.

'Never heed him, Mr Garry. I've a gingerbread here.' She cut that too. 'Are you feelin' like an egg, Mr Garry? There'll be a hotterel o' folks in here afore the night's out, see if there's nae. There's aye a collieshangie here on a Sabbath night. And I'll lay my lugs in pawn but it's you they'll have through hand, my lad. A bonny owerga'un they're givin' the twa o' you, you and Miss Morgan.—What kind's your tea, Mr Garry?—Ay, ay, there's been mair mention of you this day in Fetter-Rothnie than of God Almighty.'

Indeed, before Garry had well eaten Jonathan Bannochie came in, and with him others.

'Here's a young man has a crow to pick with you,' said Jonathan, pushing forward a half-witted lad in the later teens. 'You're terrible smart, a bittie ower smart whiles for us country chaps. What way now did you nae wait last night for the lads and the lasses that were ready with their sangs and suchlike? Here's Willie here had his sang all ready and him just waiting a chance to get it sung. But na, nae chance.'

'Indeed I am sorry,' said Garry, rising in confusion. 'I didn't suppose—I supposed Miss Morgan—well, that she had charge of all the programme, and when she was gone that it would fall to pieces.' He stammered an apology to the half-wit, who stared grinning.

'O ay,' said Jonathan. 'Anything to shield the lady. Ay, ay, the first thing that came handiest.'

Again, as when he stood before the Session, the young man felt a fury of rage against this mocker who could penetrate among his secret thoughts. Stammering a further apology, he went out.

'Try her in the tower, Captain Forbes,' quoth Jonathan, with a stolid face. A mutter of laughter ran about: the old story was remembered, had very lately been revived. Well out into the hurricane of wind, Garry could distinguish a louder laughter and Jonathan's voice clear in the general guffaw.

He walked into the anger of wind with his head down. Jonathan's parting barb was in, and rankled. At the moment he wanted to have Louie in the tower, wanted to have her alone, wanted simply to have her. And apology was not the need. She was in his blood like a disturbing drug. He knew that she had already turned to his pursuit, and his soul had sickened at the knowledge; but suddenly he realised that he wanted to seize her, to give her what she hankered after, make her taste to the dregs the cup she wantoned with. He went straight to the house of Mrs Morgan, and was shown in.

Louie sprang from a stool by the fireside and faced him screaming. Her lips were livid, her eyes blazed.

'How dare you come here?' she screamed. 'How dare you? How dare you? Haven't you done me enough harm already, exposing me like that? They all know now. You've ruined my name. And you promised not to tell, you promised.'

Her voice ran on, high-pitched, terrific in its morbid energy. Scarlet blotches showed upon the greyness of her face. Bags of skin hung under her eyes. The possession went from him. His fury of lust for strange knowledge was dead. He began to explain that his promise had not been broken.

She did not listen. The high-pitched voice screamed on. And now she was beating her hands against a chair and laughing because she had drawn blood.

'Oh, this is terrible! Oh, this is terrible!' moaned Mrs Morgan. The elder lady rocked her body back and fore, staring uneasily from her daughter to her guest. 'I shall never be able to give a hand with the tea again,' she moaned.

Garry shook the house from him and its dark sultry atmosphere, but in the howl of the wind he continued to hear Louie's hysterical screaming. He hated both himself and her. Sounds were swallowed in the gale. Nothing lived in the steady pouring noise but its own insistence. Even thought went numb. He let himself be driven before the blast as Lindsay earlier had done, but for him there was no joy of surrender. All that tormented—the whining shell, the destructive sea, lust, folly and derision, brute and insensate nature's roar—was in the cataract that crashed about his ears. To run before this enormous wind put him to shame, as though he had let himself be routed by unholy forces. Of purpose he overreached Knapperley and battled back, and in the tussle felt some control upon himself return. When therefore in the shelter of the house he distinguished voices, he was able to give them a wary attention.

The April night had almost come, but a drab gleam showed the figures of three or four men, curious like so many others, who were retreating from a survey of the burnt house. Unperceived, Garry heard the story of the fire recounted by a man who had indeed been present, but had rendered hardly the effective aid his boast suggested. The unseen listener smiled; but heard on the instant the voice of Jonathan Bannochie, who said, 'You would need Garry Forbes to you, my lad.'

Laughter greeted the sally. The braggart was known.

Garry remained hidden. The bandying of his name moved him to wrath.

'Well, well,' said another voice, 'he made's sit up over Miss Morgan, anyway.'

'Mrs Falconer did, you mean.'

'Ay, where got she her information, would you say?'

'Where she always bides,' said Jonathan. 'Hine up on the head o' the house, like Garry Forbes and his twa fools.'

Garry strode into the open.

'Good evening, gentlemen, you are having a look around. Rather dark, isn't it? Perhaps you'd like to see inside? Hine up on the head of the house, if you want to.'

And he suddenly began to laugh.

'Do come in,' he said. 'The night's young, and my aunt has a blazer of a fire. You're not so often round by Knapperley that you need to go so soon. Come away in.'

He ushered them suavely to the kitchen, lit a lamp and shepherded the party to the damaged room. A boisterous mirth took hold of him.

'Up you go,' he cried, pointing to the ladder by which Lindsay had climbed. It stretched into shadows, through the gaping hole above them that showed like a blotch of darkness upon the plaster. The wind still shrieked through the broken window and the sheet of iron clattered overhead.

Garry acted with a reckless gaiety. A fortunate mockery came to his aid, to assuage his own pain and bewilderment. He mocked at his aunt and Johnnie, Francie, himself, with a tongue so blithe and impudent that his guests felt its invitation to laughter and joined in his mirth. His laughter was quite unforced. The interlude had been high comedy; even his own part in it he could recount with appreciation of its comic values. He swaggered, sang again the drinking song. 'Garry Forbes and his twa fools,' he cried, laughing, and catching the noise of the sheet of iron that clattered on the slates, 'Hark to yon fellow—hine up on the head of the house, like Garry Forbes and his twa fools. The old house has got a dunt on the rigging, like the folk that bide in it. But you can't deny,' he added, with a persuasive gleam, 'that Francie showed spirit. I loved it in the man. A fine large folly we both showed, he to attack the thing he couldn't do, and I to let him. Ha, ha, we want more of that spirit in the world!'

They returned to the kitchen. Garry heaped wood upon the fire and fetched Miss Barbara's whisky. Only Jonathan refused to drink.

'Drink, man,' said Garry roughly, but turned away from him at once and talked to the other men. The talk flowed rich and warm as the whisky. Garry began to speak of the war, not in the sardonic humour of his overnight stories, but with the natural sincerity he used in speaking to John Grey. His guests gave him back of their best. They told him, in shrewd and racy idiom, how a countryside took war: food, stock, labour, transport.

'There's mair goes on here than the King kens o',' said one.

A very old man sat next the fire. His face was crunkled

and dry; he rarely spoke; but tonight, holding the glass
of whisky in a trembling hand, as the liquor slowly warmed
his old blood, he too began to talk.

'Your war—your war—surely it's gey near lousin' time.
What's come to a' the young men that they must up and to
the wars? In my young time we kent the way to bide whaur
our business was. I was fee'd for ane-an'-twenty year to sup
brose ane-an'-twenty times a week—nae gallivantin' frae
toun to toun whan I was a sharger. But there's nae haudin'
the young men in aboot the day. My lassie's loon, he's but
a bairn, he must be aff an' a'. "Come rattle in his queets wi'
the poker," I says to her. "That'll learn him to keep to his
work." War—it wunna let a body be. It's lousin' time, I
tell you.'

'It won't be lousin' time till we've won the field,' said
Garry. And he looked strangely at the very old man. How
easy, if one could regulate all life by a single duty: a ploughman his field to plough, a cobbler his boot to patch; a life
without glory and without failure, without responsibility
for oneself.

'Won!' mocked Jonathan across his thoughts. 'This
war will not be won. What's your belligerents? Twa fools,
playing Double Dummy and grand pleased with themselves.
Both'll think they've won, but there's neither won nor lost.
A farce all the ways of it.' He added, in a voice hardly
audible, his face to the fire and a smile playing about his
mouth, 'Twa fools, hine up on the head o' the house—'

Garry argued hotly. 'I don't know, I can't explain it,
but I believe we are in some way fighting the devil. Have
you no belief in the sanctity of a cause?'

'None.'

'And the rights of the small nations? National honour?'

Jonathan chanted:

> Peter my neebor,
> Had a wife an' couldna keep her,
> He stappit her in a hole in the dyke an' the mice
>   eat her.

And at Garry's impatient movement, 'You needna get hot,
Captain. You think much the same yourself at bottom. All
the mercy a war shows to any is to them that gets their

pooches filled. I'm told there's some that way,' he added, 'not that I know of it.'

Garry cried on a reckless inspiration, 'You would need Garry Forbes to *you*.'

The roar of laughter that went up from the others told him that the shaft went home. He watched Jonathan, throwing back his head and laughing too.

'Him!' said Mrs Hunter, when later he questioned her. 'He would skin a louse to get tallow. O ay, I'm told he's made a tidy bit out o' the war. A country cobbler—you would wonder, wouldna ye? But he must have a smart bit o' siller laid by and there's folks in debt to him round and round. There's places up and down that's changed hands since the war, folks bought out and businesses shut down, and some grand anes wi' new-got siller set up in their braw establishments, and Jonathan's got his nieve packed tight, ay has he that. He kens mair than he'll let on, but folk has an inkling. He kens the ins an' the oots o' maist o' the places that's come to the hammer hereaboots.'

Garry sat in Knapperley kitchen and watched the man. He changed countenance not at all, but laughed the matter by, saying idly, 'Garry Forbes would have his own ado.'

The phrase was established.

The following evening Jonathan said, in his own shop before a half dozen witnesses, to Mally Sandison who swore that she had paid the boots when she brought them to have the 'tackets ca'ed in,' 'What's that, mistress?' Jonathan said. 'Paid, said ye? You would need Garry Forbes to you, I'm thinking.'

The joke went round. It penetrated the more surely for being more than joke, or joke not fully understood. It puzzled the consciousness of Fetter-Rothnie, but remained on its tongue. The phrase became the accepted reproof of falsehood.

For the other phrase of Jonathan's coinage, 'Hine up on the head o' the house, like Garry Forbes and his twa fools,' that also passed into current speech, but baldly, a jesting reproach to those who attempted what they could not overtake. Like other phrases debased by popular usage, it lost the first subtle mockery it took from the brain of its originator. The intelligence of its victim alone apprehended it; he knew (as Jonathan did likewise, else he would not have mocked) that his folly on the housetop was a generosity, a gesture of faith in mankind.

Returning by the dark avenue when he had seen his guests to the gate of Knapperley on the Sunday after the concert, Garry heard a noise among the bushes that was not caused by the wind, and immediately a stone hit him on the shin-bone. He thrust his way among the bushes and dragged a captive to the open. His match flared in the wind and went out, but gave him time to see the half-wit whose song had not been sung. He spoke kindly to the lad, who wrenched himself free with evil words and made off.

The wind poured on—a south-wester like an elemental energy. Garry stood awhile in the fury. The shriek of wind brought to his mind the flying shells, and he thought of troop ships and minesweepers riding the storm. Only those without imagination, he felt, could love the wind. A tree crashed. He shuddered, and a longing seized him to have done with sick-leave and be again in battle. The danger that was abroad in the tortured night of wind cooled and braced him. 'I'm fit now,' he thought, 'I must get back. Damn that man and his talk of futility. It's a battle about something and I must get back.'

Jonathan's cynical smile recurred to his mind, and the roar of wind changed in his ear to the roaring of their ridicule as they made phrases of his name. That also seemed an elemental energy, and the screaming of a woman sounded through it, elemental too, destructive as the hurricane.

He slept at last, and the wind fell.

FOURTEEN

April Sunrise

He awoke before the dawn. There was no sound at all, no motion in the house or wood. The silence was unearthly, as though the wind had blown itself out and with it all the accustomed sounds of earth.

Birds brought back the normal world. Sounds began anew. Garry threw himself from bed and went outside.

The morning was like a flute note, single, high and pure, that for the moment of its domination satisfies the ear as though all music were in itself; but hardly has it sounded when the other instruments break in.

Life recommenced. Dogs barked, cocks crew, smoke rose, men shouted, women clattered their milk pails. Soon figures moved upon the empty fields. Somewhere a plough was creaking. Garry turned his head towards the noise and searched the brown earth until he saw the team. Seagulls were crying after it, settling in the black furrow, rising again to wheel around the horses. As he watched, the sun reached the field. The wet new-turned furrow was touched to light as though a line of fire had run along it. The flanks of the horses gleamed. They tossed their manes, lifting their arched necks and bowing again to the pull: brown farm horses, white-nosed, white-footed, stalwart and unhurrying as the earth they trampled or the man who held the share.

From where he watched Garry could see a long stretch of country. Jake Hunter's croft was visible. Jake was bowed above a heap of turnips, slicing in his slow, laborious fashion. Mrs Hunter sailed across the stackyard in a stream of hens. And on his steep, thin field Francie Ferguson walked, casting the seed. It was his moment of dignity. Clumsy, ridiculous, sport of a woman's caprice and a byword in men's jesting, as he cast the seed with the free ample movement of

the sower Francie had a grandeur more than natural. The
dead reached through him to the future. Continuity was in
his gait. His thin upland soil, ending in stony crests of whin
and heather, was transfigured by the faith that used it, he
himself by the sower's poise that symbolised his faith.

That gesture, of throwing the seed, seemed to the man
who watched the most generous of movements; and he was
glad to associate it with Francie, whose native generosity he
had seen and loved. His blind anger of the previous night
flared suddenly anew. 'Garry Forbes and his twa fools,' he
muttered. 'I had rather be Francie and capable of a generous folly than these others with all their common sense.' His
own wild mockery of both Francie and himself had had last
night a harsh wholesome savour; this morning it felt like a
disloyalty.

At that moment Mrs Falconer appeared among the trees.

The strong family resemblance among the Craigmyle
sisters had never seemed to him so marked as when he saw
Mrs Falconer walking towards him from the wood. She had
an almost truculent air. Theresa herself could not have put
him right with more assurance.

'So you like a sunrise, too,' she said in an abrupt, hard
way. 'Well, I wanted to say, I believe I crossed your
wishes the other night, letting them know about that Louie.
I thought you wanted them to know. But it seems you
changed your mind.'

'Oh well, you see—' The accusation in her tone annoyed
him. 'A matter of common theft—pretty low down to expose
that, don't you think?'

'Well, I'm sorry. But it was for—' She was about to
add '—your truth that I did it,' but something in his
face made her pause. He was grey and haggard. She left
her sentence incomplete. 'I'm sorry,' she repeated humbly.

'Her neck's thrawn now. Much good may it do us all.'

Mrs Falconer found nothing to answer.

'Don't you worry,' he continued. 'It amuses people.
One should be glad to add to the gaiety of mankind.
They've made a joke of it already. They seem to find me a
pretty good joke hereabouts.' With his arms folded on the
top of a gate he was leaning forward to watch Francie. 'See

that seed-casting machine over yonder?'

'What? Where? Machine—I only see Francie Ferguson.'

'What's he?'

'Mrs Falconer stared.

'Why, he's the crofter at the place by us, just over
the field. But you know Francie. It was him you—'

Again she left her sentence incomplete.

'Jerked up like a marionette on the roof at Knapperley,
for folk to laugh at. So it was.'

'You spoke of a machine—'

'Men like machines walking. Somewhere in the Bible,
I believe. I thought myself he was a man. I'm glad that
you agree.'

'Captain Forbes, I'm afraid I don't quite understand you.'

He straightened himself from the gate, stretched his
arms, and laughed.

'No, I suppose not. It's quite simple, though. I chose to
employ Francie because I liked the spirit of the man. He's
ignorant, he's clumsy, but—well, I love him. The men of
sense—oh, very decent fellows, I had a drink with some of
them last night—have made a laughing-stock of both of us. I
could forgive it for myself. I can't forgive it for Francie. And
I can't forgive them because I joined the laugh myself. Logi-
cal, isn't it? If you're laughed at, always join the laugh. It
takes the sting out. But then you see—I laughed at Francie
too. They made it seem, if I could put it so, a necessary
condition for my entering *their* kingdom.' He ended with
passion, 'They conspire together to prevent my loving men.'

Mrs Falconer turned away her eyes. His passionate face,
dark, unshaven, haggard, moved her with an emotion that
she dared not countenance. Gazing intently at the clear blue
hills she let fall the words, 'They too are men.'

And suddenly the man at her side, at whom she could not
look, burst out laughing. His laughter resounded through
the quiet morning. Jake Hunter, several fields away, lifted
himself from the turnips and shaded his brows with his hand
to search in the direction of the noise.

'It's Mr Garry up there,' said his quicker-eyed wife. 'He
has ways real like his aunt. I've seen her rumble out the

laughin' an naebody by. Well, a laugh's a thing for twa or for twenty, says I, nae for a man an' him himsel'.' Even her sharp eyes had not made out Mrs Falconer's sombre figure against the trees.

Garry stopped laughing and said to Mrs Falconer, 'It's such an obvious thing to say, isn't it? That's why it is so confoundedly clever of you to say it. Inspired, I ought to say. Clever is a stupid word. Yes, that is the brutal fact: they too are men. As much a part of things as I am. One knows it at the Front, but here—I'm angriest of all, you know, because I mocked at Francie. And yet I suppose I couldn't have mocked at myself without mocking at him too; and it was only when I had laughed at myself, last night, with these men, that I began to feel I was a part of things here.' He interrupted himself to say, 'But all this is boring you. And listen—this Louie business: of course I wanted David cleared. But when I found about the ring—well, any man would have shut up. I felt pretty beastly, I can tell you, when I saw them all agape. Anyhow, it was John Grey's business after that, not mine. I had told her, you see, that I would take no action. But you—I don't want you to—'

'I acted on an impulse,' she said, smiling bravely. 'It was cruel of me. I had just come to know. If I had thought about it longer, I'd have seen it was no business of mine.'

'Please don't blame yourself. Perhaps it's best—'

'Well, I'm glad I met you to apologise,' said Mrs Falconer calmly. 'I'll say goodbye just now.'

Garry went homeward thinking still of her reply: 'They too are men.' It seemed to him the wisest saying he had heard. He looked again at the wide leagues of land. And a curious thing happened. He saw everything he looked at not as substance, but as energy. All was life. Life pulsed in the clods of earth that the ploughshares were breaking, in the shares, the men. Substance, no matter what its form, was rare and fine.

The moment of perception passed. He had learned all that in college. But only now it had become real. Every substance had its own secret nature, exquisite, mysterious. Twice already this country sweeping out before him had ceased to be the agglomeration of woods, fields, roads, farms; mysterious as a star at dusk, with the same ease and thoroughness, had become visible as an entity: once when he had seen it taking form from the dark, solid, crass, mere bulk; once irradiated by the light until its substance all but vanished. Now, in the cold April dawn, he saw it neither crass nor rare, but both in one.

He looked again at this astonishing earth. And suddenly for the second time he laughed aloud. Mrs Falconer, gone not so far but that she heard him, stopped upon the road. She could not understand why he laughed, and she felt chill and sad.

'Both crass and fine,' he was thinking; but he was thinking no longer of the land, but of the men. Not irradiated by an alien light, but in themselves, through all the roughness of their make what strange and lovely glimpses one could have of their secret nature! 'Each obeying his law,' he thought.

Around him he noted that the woods were flaming. A fine flame was playing over the leafless branches, not gaudy like the fires of autumn, but strong and pure. The trees, not now by accident of light but in themselves, were again etherealised. For a brief space, in spring, before the leaf comes, the life in trees is like a pure and subtle fire in buds and boughs. Willows are like yellow rods of fire, blood-red burns in the sycamore and scales off in floating flakes as the bud unfolds and the sheath is loosened. Beeches and elms, all dull beneath, have webs of golden and purple brown upon their spreading tops. Purple blazes in the birch twigs and smoulders darkly in the blossom of the ash. At no other season are the trees so little earthly. Mere vegetable matter they are not. One understands the dryad myth, both the emergence of the vivid delicate creature and her melting again in her tree; for in a week, a day, the foliage thickens, she is a tree again.

For the first time Garry was in the country at the moment when this very principle of life declared itself in the boughs. 'As fine as that,' he thought, 'from coarse plain earth.' But if one surprised them at their moment, men had the same bright fire.

Mrs Falconer walked home.

Theresa asked, 'Where have you been stravaigin' to at this time of the morning? To get the air! Well, the work stands first, I always say. There's all the windows to clean after that gale. We can't see a thing for dirt.'

Lindsay was coming in from the garden. The grass was quite covered with twigs and torn leaves, with cypress berries, with pine needles and cones. And under one tree, an arm of which had been riven from the trunk, Lindsay had found a nest with an egg and three naked mangled nestlings tumbled on the ground. But saddest of all was the death of the bird she was holding against her body.

'Look, quite dead. I found it lying there. Oh, Paradise, could it be the mother of those gorbals? How pitiful—'

'No, no.' Paradise was touching the soft cold form with her misshapen fingers. 'This one was flying. See, his neck is broken. He had been driven by the wind against a bough. They're frail things, birdies. Many a one the gales bring down.'

'Oh! But can't they fly clear? Can't they see where they are going?'

Paradise shook her head. 'What's a fluff of air and feather against a hurricane? I've seen them rattle down in dozens.'

Lindsay held the dead bird against her breast, smoothing the silken wings and bosom. 'See, see.' She lifted a wing with gentle fingers and displayed a patch of warm bright russet in the hidden hollow.

'Such small, small feathers. Oh, its loveliest part is hid away.'

Mrs Falconer stood apart and watched. She had not offered to show the bird to Cousin Ellen.

'She loves the bird more than me,' thought the woman sadly. And she winced again at the remembrance of Lindsay's scornful words after the exposure of the theft. But as though she had divined a secret chagrin, the girl came softly to her side, holding the bird.

'See, Cousin Ellen.' She displayed the russet pool beneath the wing; and thinking that Ellen was sad because of Theresa's reprimand, she whispered, 'I'm cleaning windows, too—oh yes, I want to help.'

It was afternoon before she went to Knapperley. Garry was on the roof.

'Come down, come down. Have you been there all day?'

He nodded, nails in his mouth, and continued to hammer. Shortly he came down.

'Well, I've discovered a thing I never knew—how slates are put on.'

'Oh, you've slated it. Where's your iron sheet today?'

'Dangling by one tooth this morning. So I gathered what was left of the slates. No, I haven't slated it. Or only a bit. I'll have to get more slates. But I've fixed all that were usable. Come up the ladder and I'll show you. They go on like this—each one overlapping other two.'

'Yes. But stop for a little now, Garry.'

He came down, but almost at once began to clear away the drifts of rubbish that the wind had left.

'Will you be always like this when we are married, Garry? Always at work?'

'Expect so. There's so much to do. I'll tell you what, Linny, the war seems a colossal bit of work to get finished, but ordinary life's going to be a bigger. Coming back here, and finding all the queer individual things people do and think—it's frightened me. To get them all fitted in—I don't see how it can be done.'

The faces came on him in a mob–Francie, Jonathan, Jake, the tramp and the half-wit, Louie, Miss Theresa Craigmyle, Miss Barbara: the substance from which all his fine new kingdoms must be built. He would have liked to repudiate the knowledge he had just gained of human nature: how could one proclaim an ideal future when men and women persisted in being so stubbornly themselves?—And at that moment Miss Barbara rumbled round the corner of the house with a wheelbarrow.

'Build a house,' she said with scorn, as she set down the barrow, which was piled with earthy boulders. 'Build a house, mend a house, that's what your common bodies do. O ay, you're Donnie Forbes's grandson right enough. A Paterson of Knapperley never turned their hand to building houses.'

'And what are the stones for, aunt?'

'I'm putting up a cairn.' She stooped to the barrow handles and continued on her way.

'To commemorate the war?' shouted Garry.

'Deil a war. The fire, my lad, the fire.'

FIFTEEN

Whom the Gods Destroy

For Mrs Falconer, she watched Lindsay, all quick excitement, gather her possessions from the windowed bedroom
and drive away, rosy and laughing, by her father's side.
Then she climbed the stair and sat down in her empty room.
She had never felt so desolate. The past came freely to her
memory, and she recalled her dismal marriage, its ending,
her humiliation at Theresa's hands on her return. But none
of these things had troubled her as she was troubled now.
For many weeks she battled against a sense of guilt. But
what had she done wrong? Even if she had erred in her
public denunciation of the sinner, she had acted in good
faith, had meant well. The shame that overwhelmed her
was too deep and terrible to have sprung from that. The
weeks passed, Lindsay was married, and very slowly Mrs
Falconer began to understand. Lindsay's words rang often
in her ears—'a horrid old woman, thrusting herself into the
limelight'—and at first they made her indignant ('to think
that of me, to think that of me'), but after a time she saw
that they were true. She had accused Louie so that Garry
might be pleased with her.

During these months Mrs Falconer had grown pinched
and wan. She sat much alone, with hands interlocked, eyes
staring. When spoken to she started and spoke at random.
Lang Leeb's appreciation of these phenomena was delicate.
Fine barbs went quivering into Ellen's mind. A woman of
sixty, pining for a man not half her age, was a spectacle to
earn the gratitude of gods and men: so seldom do we let
ourselves be frankly ludicrous.

In August Ellen acknowledged to herself that her love
for Garry was an egotism. Her sense of shame and guilt
grew heavier, not because she had discovered its cause,

but because of the revelation she had had of the human heart, its waywardness and its duplicity. She had known quite well what her mother and sister had thought of her infatuation, and had despised them for the vileness of their thoughts. Now for the first time she herself felt evil. 'It was only myself I thought of all the time.' Her sense of escape, of flight into a larger world, was illusion.

She ceased to pray. Prayer, too, was an illusion. 'Your God of Comforts'—she understood it now. Her God had always been a God of Comforts from whose bounty, as she fashioned her petitions, she had taken precisely what she wanted. One could go through a long life like that, thrilled and glowing as one rose from prayer, and all the while be bounded horribly within oneself. The God who had constrained her in her flaming ecstasy of devotion, whose direct commands she had obeyed in denouncing Louie, was created from her imagination: a figment of her own desire.

She continued throughout that winter to go to church, because it did not occur to her to cease the practice; but the services were torture. She looked in horror at the people as they prayed. 'How do they know that there is anything there? Any God at all? I can never trust again what I feel within myself.'

One day in April as she walked alone, a bird flew low, alighted near her, pecked and tugged among the withered grasses, flew up in swift alarm, lit again. She watched, then sharply as though the words were spoken, she heard Lindsay's eager question, 'What is his name? But don't you love birds, Cousin Ellen?'

Yes, yes, I have always loved them, she thought—their grace, their far swift flight, the cadence of their song—as I have loved all beauty, that is a part of my undying self, possessed eternally, the kingdom within my soul. Yet because she could not name the bird that flew up and hopped in front of her, a miserable sense of failure came across her spirit. She went home and found her sister Annie.

'I saw a bird just now,' she began, then choked. She had not spoken all that year to anyone about the things that filled her heart.

'There's lots of them about,' said Miss Annie.

'Yes. It flew away and came back again. I wonder what it would have been.'

'What kind of bird?'

But Ellen could not answer. She knew neither its colour, nor shape, nor the length of wing or beak. She rose abruptly and went upstairs. The sense of shame and failure came over her with renewed intensity. It was absurd—because she did not know a bird's name; but as she sat miserably by her window she saw all at once that it was not only the bird's name of which she was ignorant: it was the whole world outside herself.

She had never felt so much abased, so lonely in the multitude of living things. It was spring, they were around her in myriads; but she did not know them. They had their own nature. Even the number of spots upon an egg, the sheen on wing or tail, was part of their identity. And that, she saw, was holy. They were themselves. She could not enter into their life save by respecting their real nature. Not to know was to despise them.

And so with men. One could not be taken into other lives except by learning what they were in themselves. Ellen had never cared to know. In her imaginings other people had been what she decreed, their real selves she ignored. 'I have despised them all.' She felt miserably small, imprisoned wholly in herself.

From that day her new life began; slowly, for she had consumed herself in shame, and at first had neither strength nor faith enough to live on new terms. Moreover, she was sixty one, and, from the monotony with which life in the Weatherhouse had passed, set in her habits. For a time she entertained wild projects: she would go away, work in a slum, learn life. But she had no money. The war was over, Kate was again in a paid situation. One day she drew Kate aside, mumbling.

'I can't make out what you're saying, mother.'

'If you could let me have some pocket money, dear. You know I've none at all.'

'But you never want for anything, mother, I hope?'

'No, no. It was only—just to have it, dear. But it doesn't matter.'

'Of course you shall have money, mother. I should have thought of it before.'

Kate gave her a few shillings.

One day she went to town. Excited, but calm through the magnitude of her purpose, she made her way to the Labour Exchange, and stood, fumbling among words, at the advisory bureau.

'No, that is not what I wanted. No, no.'

The woman who watched her with shrewd and kindly eyes guessed at a tragedy: a gentlewoman fallen on evil days. But when she understood what the worn, haggard old woman wanted, she was silent through astonishment.

'I thought there were so many openings for welfare workers,' stammered Mrs Falconer.

'But you have no training—and your age—but perhaps you must, you have nothing to live on.'

'No, it's not that—I just wanted to get away from home.'

'Oh! Then if you don't need the money, there is voluntary work that you could do.'

Mrs Falconer went bitterly home. Another fine fancy was smoke. She had pictured herself a successful social worker. 'And I wanted to get away from home because I couldn't bear to hear their remarks—to see me humiliated, that's what it is. Confessing that my life's been all amiss till now.'

These essays in sincerity hurt her. 'But it's only through sincerity that I can reach anywhere beyond myself.' She must be sincere even with the birds and the wild flowers she had begun to study, to know their real selves that she might enter their life. Kate's shillings had bought her certain textbooks, but her study halted. Birds moved so swiftly, she forgot so soon, her manuals were poor, and by her untaught efforts it was hard to identify these moving flakes of life and the bright, multitudinous flowers. Identify—discover their identity. She had never valued accurate information, holding that only the spirit signified, externals were an accident; yet when she found that by noting external details she could identify a passing bird or a growing plant, a thrill of joy passed through her heart. She was no longer captive within her single self.

These moments of bliss came rarely in a long, slow time.

That summer she ceased to go to church. God—was there a God? And where could one discover His identity? She had believed all her life in this comfortable God who revealed Himself to her spirit in ecstasy and beauty; but her ecstasies had been a blind self-indulgence. No sincerity in that. 'I can't find God in the forms of a religion that has let me go so terribly astray, that has shut me away from everything but myself.' '

Her sisters were aghast when she would not return to church. Annie's was a genuine distress. 'Ah, but you should go to church, you should go. We should all go to church as long's we're able.' Miss Annie herself, crippled and serene, set out each Sunday morning alone, an hour before the time of service, to make her slow, laborious journey.

'You might at least keep it up for appearance sake,' Theresa hectored. 'We've been a kirk-going family all our days. There's no need to be kirk-greedy to do the respectable thing. A pretty story they'll make of it, a Craigmyle and left the kirk.'

Some time after her rupture with the church, Mrs Falconer met the young Stella walking in dignified aloofness on the moor. Stella was in disgrace. Convicted of petty thieving, she had received a reprimand in face of the assembled Sunday School.

'Oh, Stella,' began Mrs Falconer, shocked at the bravado with which the girl flung out her story.

'Oh, yes,' interrupted Stella coolly. 'Tell me, like all the rest of them, that God is watching all I do. I don't believe it. There's not a God, He's just a make-up. So there!'

Mrs Falconer was silent. Stella, who had anticipated good game in the way of shocked remonstrance, inquired impatiently, 'Well, aren't you going to preach a bit to me about it?'

Mrs Falconer answered humbly, with her grieved eyes on the girl's face, 'I can't do that, Stella. I don't know if there is a God.'

Stella stared and cried, 'Well, you're a straight one. I like you for that.'

Perhaps I have done wrong, she thought, saying that

to the child. But no, nothing could be wrong that strove to establish truth. But I was striving to establish truth by exposing Louie. Life was past belief, complicated, huge. The God she had served judged all men by their motives. She had a glimpse now of a darker, more terrible God who judged results. How could it be enough to mean well? One came afterwards to repudiate one's own motives, to see that one was responsible in spite of them. One's true self, which one had not known, had worked. Surely if there was a God, it was one's real self that He judged.

Her mind turned to Louie. They had shut Uplands and gone away for a time. 'She'll get a man and not come back at all—see if she doesn't,' Theresa said. That was the kind of cruel thing that was said of her on all hands now. 'And I delivered her up to it,' thought Ellen. For years to come she was to see Louie degenerate because people knew her for what she was. But did they? She came to her deepest understanding of Louie when she saw that she was like herself, and built rashly on a foundation of her own imaginings. How could people understand that? 'But I understand. I know how it had all seemed to her.' She dwelt on the resemblance till she could hardly distinguish between herself and Louie. 'And people needn't have known her false pretences if it hadn't been for my false pretences.' She remembered Garry's tale of his delirium in the shell-hole. 'I thrust her in, I am rescuing myself.'

'Ah,' she thought, 'here is one person outside myself whom I really know.' And she went to seek Louie.

But some years had passed by then, and Mrs Falconer had made other attempts at knowing people.

It took her many months after the failure of her first grandiose designs to face again her need for entering other lives, and many months more to find a way.

One day she came home from town and said abruptly, 'Well, I'm going to help at the Working Girls' Guild. Tuesday evenings.'

'I'm sure it's a good thing, poor lassies!' said Paradise, who saw nothing incongruous in Ellen, with her old-fashioned dress and ideas, moving in the generation of post-war factory girls.

Nor did Ellen see her incongruity. Tuesday evenings were her excitement. The rude, boisterous life she met provided an experience. She came home too excited to sleep. 'Now, soon, I shall win the confidence of these girls. They will tell me all their lives, their secret thoughts.'

She did not guess that she was herself a problem to the leaders of the Guild. The girls made merciless fun of the hat that perched high above greying coils of hair, of the old-fashioned full skirt and the leather belt drawn tight to a meagre waist; still more of the smile with which she followed them about and the queer questions she put. And she could not do things. Each worker was armed with knowledge: one could guide the dancing, one tell stories, one teach gymnastics or dressmaking. Mrs Falconer had no asset.

'She's such a good soul,' the workers said, 'you don't want to hurt her, but really—she's in the way.'

'Oh, let her keep coming. She enjoys it. There's always something she can do.'

'The girls like her, though they laugh.'

'But she shouldn't be so tall. Old women oughtn't to be tall. They're not so lovable.'

They began to give her hints. She listened humbly, while students and youthful graduates told her how modern psychology decreed that working-girls should be treated. She took her lessons home and brooded over them.

For two years the centre of her life lay here. One evening she found Stella Ferguson in the Guild room, all staring eyes and open ears.

'I'm in a shop,' said Stella contemptuously. 'I'm fourteen. Ay, in the town: *I* wasn't going to your country shoppies, do you suppose.'

Some weeks later a bold girl burst indignantly up to the leader. 'Look here, I'm not going to have that old-clothes wife prying into my affairs. Cheek, I call it.' She let fly a stream of ugly oaths.

The leader was compelled to tell Mrs Falconer that she had been unwise.

'That girl, poor soul—her home and people don't stand

inquiring into. She's ashamed. One has to go very warily.'

Mrs Falconer understood after the conversation she had that evening with the leader that she had been of no great use at the Guild.

'You have been of great use to me,' she said humbly. 'I have been happy—but I won't come again.'

'Oh, please do! Come back sometimes and see us.'

Ruthless to herself, Mrs Falconer saw that her eagerness to know the intimacies of the girls' lives had been for her own sake, to quicken her life.

The following Tuesday she answered Theresa's, 'Isn't it time you were away?' with a proud plain 'I'm not going back. They think I'm too old for that work.'

The shy, baffled soul, entering upon her quest too late, with no key to open other lives, would take no consolation from deceit. It was about this period that she began to brood on Louie Morgan; and one day, though the two women had not spoken since the night of the concert, she set out to visit her.

The door was opened by the Morgans' servant, a middle-aged woman with sleeves pushed up to reveal enormous red elbows.

'It's Miss Louie you're seekin', nae the mistress?'

She led Mrs Falconer to the door of a room, within which someone was speaking.

'There's company—I won't go in.'

'Ach, she's just play-actin', ben you go.' The red-armed woman pushed Mrs Falconer in, but without announcing her, and shut the door.

Mrs Falconer stood amazed.

Louie held a teapot in her hand and was pouring tea. She moved with an elegant air around the table, filling cup after cup, and spoke to each guest in turn: but the guests were not there.

On the empty chairs Mrs Falconer seemed to see dark, menacing figures, guests with suave manners that covered a deadly leer.

A hot fervour took possession of her.

She cried aloud, 'Mr Facing-Both-Ways, Mr Two-

Tongues, My Lady Feigning.'

Louie set the teapot askew upon a chair in her aston-ishment.

'Oh, go away—my mother is out—what are you want-ing?' Her eyes glared, but in a moment she recovered herself and began to posture.

'I'm sorry. I didn't hear you announced, Mrs Falconer. Do sit down.' She waved her hand at the cups of tea. 'I was expecting guests. When I heard the bell ring I thought they had arrived, and I was pouring the tea to be ready. Do have some.' She thrust a cup into Mrs Falconer's hand. The tea was already cold.

She was extravagantly dressed, but the lace at her throat was torn and her fingernails were dirty. Her face, oppressed by powder, and her hair, which had straggled beyond its cut, gave her an air of sloven tawdriness; and she continued to posture and trill.

Mrs Falconer put the cup down and said, in a harsh, loud voice, 'I don't like the guests at your party. Don't pretend not to understand me,' she continued. 'I don't like your party, and I don't like the guests you entertain. You are entertaining ghosts, demons, delusions, snares, principalities and powers. You are entertaining your own destruction.'

The voice hardly seemed her own, but she could not check it. It poured on without intermission, crying a thou-sand things that she had brooded over, but to which she had given no language.

'Truth, truth—it must be truth. You mustn't compro-mise. If you would save yourself alive there must be no dallying with the false deities of the imagination. Things as they are. People as they are.'

Scarlet spots burned on Louie's face and throat. She began to retaliate, a fierce and insolent screaming.

'You—you—don't you know that you are to blame? You gave me away. *He* never meant them to know. It was you. And then you come and talk!'

'Yes, yes, I am to blame. We are both to blame. We must help each other to find the truth. No more compromise. But perhaps it's easier for the old not to compromise with life:

the young have so much longer to live. But you mustn't let yourself give in. Let me help you—'

'You fool!' burst from Louie's lips. 'I never want to see your face again.'

Mrs Falconer drew back in paralysed affright.

At that moment the big-boned servant came in to the room carrying a tray.

'Take your tea, the pair of you,' she said, and thrust the tray carelessly among the cups of cold tea upon the table. But Louie, ignoring the interruption, screamed miserably on.

Mrs Morgan's step and voice were heard.

'Not a word,' cried Louie. 'Not a word before my mother. Have you no sense of decency?'

Her whole demeanour altered. She laughed and chattered, a wild roguery possessed her. Gleams of graciousness returned.

Mrs Morgan accompanied Mrs Falconer to the door.

'Dear Louie! You must excuse her. She's so excitable. So natural in the circumstances. He may be arriving any day. Such a delightful man! We met him when we were staying in the south. Of course, we are not saying much, but you may be sure that I shall give my consent.'

The one elderly lady smiled benignly up into the face of the other; and Mrs Falconer, almost without her will, said softly, 'Yes, yes,' and patted the hand her hostess gave her in farewell. The round, pleased little lady smiled up again at her gaunt, tall guest.

'We mothers,' she murmured.

But Mrs Falconer went out on to the road shaking her head and muttering hard. All that evening she could not hold her peace. Words and broken sentences spurted from her lips, until at last Theresa said, 'What ails you, Nell, at all? If you want to say something, speak it out'; and Ellen, as though she had waited for the bidding, rose and spoke.

'I've been frightened of you all my life, Tris—I'm not frightened any longer. But I've seen a thing this afternoon that's frightened me. There's nothing to fear in all the world but deceit. Nothing at all. And I've seen it, I've seen it. I've seen a deluded woman—and he wakened her up from her idle dreams as he wakened me—despising truth, feeding herself on error, pouring her cups of devil's tea—'

'Where were you at all this afternoon?'

'At the Morgans'.'

'Oh, it's Louie you're meaning. Deluded, you may say. Their woman Eppie'll tell you the things she does.' Theresa prepared to expatiate, but Ellen cried, 'It's myself I mean. It was myself I saw. That's what I saw—myself. I'm inside Louie, and I'm a part of her deceit. God's in her, the God I can't get at—'

'You're raving, lass,' said Paradise. 'Feel her hands, Tris, she's in a fever.'

'—and for all my life to come I must proclaim it, that God's shut up inside us all and can't get out. I pushed her in, you see—'

Mrs Craigmyle, half rising in her corner, looked with sudden apprehension at her daughter. Ellen's face was chiselled now, its untouched innocence was gone; and as, for a moment, her mask of careless mockery let fall, Mrs Craigmyle bent forward to look at the raving woman, the old resemblance between the faces became strangely clear, both thin, both shapely and intent, and each significant.

Mrs Falconer's illness, which was tedious and severe, gave rise among the neighbours to such comments as: 'She's breaking up.' 'The poor old soul; they say she's terrible mixed.' 'Auld age doesna come its lane, but better the body to go than the mind, say I.'

Ellen's body in time recovered; but a change had come upon her. Nothing was in her head but the horror and sharpness of truth. She talked of it fiercely and incessantly to any who would listen. Her humble demeanour altered to one of angry pride. She could go to school to life no longer, since what she had learned was already more than her wits could rightly stand.

When her strength had returned she would slip away on Tuesday evenings and visit the Guild.

'Truth, my dear—no, no, I don't mean not telling lies. It's big, it's all one's life, all everyone's life, and no one finds it.'

They saw very quickly that all she wanted was to talk,

and let her be. One evening when she seemed more unsure of herself than usual they hesitated to let her go out upon the street alone; but one girl cried, 'I'll take her home, the craitur. She's real like my old granny. Many's the time I've taken her along. Come on, granny.'

They went off arm in arm.

The next time Mrs Falconer appeared in the Guild room Miss Theresa arrived on her heels, breathless, and apologised with many words; but paused, going, at the door, to indulge her natural inquisitiveness; and Mrs Falconer, stumbling back across the room, her head thrust forward, as she had run across the garden to intercept Garry Forbes, caught hand after hand that was held eagerly towards her, and patting them softly between her own, said, 'A little dottled, my dears, a little dottled. You must just forgive me.'

'Kate,' said Miss Theresa, 'you mustn't give your mother money. She wanders away.'

Kate gave her aunt a shrewd, considering look.

'I suppose she would wander away whether or not, Aunt Tris, and if she does, surely it's better she should have money to fetch her back. In any case, she's not so dottled as you would make out. A fixed idea, if you like, that's all.'

And when Mrs Falconer pulled her daughter aside, Kate gave her, smiling, what she wished.

At times a great bodily weakness came on her. She lay wasted and shrunken, very still, her face no bigger than an ailing child's, but the eyes shone out from it with full intelligence. She spoke seldom, unless her mother were in the room, when beckoning the old lady near, she would speak in a strong, firm voice.

On one such occasion she said, 'There is a God, but I have seen not even the shadow of His passing by. When one has found the secret being of all that lives, that is God. I have hardly begun, I have hardly begun. My life is ending and I have not seen Him.'

Another day she pondered, 'Am I old? I felt so young. I thought I had endless life ahead, and I have not. They say that I am old. I didn't believe that I could die, but I suppose I shall.'

Mrs Craigmyle answered, 'There's no need to get old, my lass. A body can be just the age he wants. For shame on you, get up, get up.'

Later, her strength come again, she would rise and stalk, erect and gaunt, upon the moor; or, gathering flowers, bring them to Paradise to name. 'That's tormentil,' said Paradise; or milkwort it might be, or eyebright; and Paradise would name them to her day after day. Or drawing her chair close in beside her mother's, she would talk with a strange wild clatter, by the hour.

In the last years of her life Mrs Craigmyle ceased to torment her second daughter, and when she died the old lady would not be consoled.

The Epilogue

Lindsay came by chance to the Weatherhouse on the day that Mrs Falconer died.

'Well!' thought Theresa. 'Nine years married and three bairns. Could one believe it?' She looked again at Lindsay's girlish figure and the happy candour of her eyes, veiled for the moment under a profound pity.

'Cousin Ellen,' Lindsay was thinking. 'Dying.' Death was remote and terrible. She had seen no one die; but there flashed back into her mind the recollection of a dead bird she had held against her bosom in this very room. 'I showed it to Cousin Ellen,' she remembered. 'That russet patch beneath its wing.' It comforted her vaguely that she had shown the beauty of the bird she mourned to the woman who was dying now. 'I didn't love her very much,' she thought. 'She interfered.' The gaunt, grey face upon the pillow horrified the watcher. 'I showed her my bird,' she thought, 'I showed her my bird.'

Mrs Falconer lay dazed and blank. 'Jumps out of bed!' thought Lindsay. 'She looks as if she could not move a foot.' But Theresa had explained that they had brought her down from her own high room. She couldn't be left alone a minute—would be up and running on her naked feet to the window. 'We couldn't be trotting up and down that stairs all day.'

'No, indeed,' said Lindsay, in her soft, commiserating voice. 'With Cousin Annie so lame, too—you must have so much to do.'

'Oh, not so much more,' answered Theresa tartly. 'If it's in the house you're meaning, all that Nell did in the house was neither here nor there. She's been about as much use this long while back as her mother, and less. Stravaigin' about on that moor at all hours. "You would need a season ticket, that's what you would need," I said to her. And muttering away to herself, you never heard! As wild as Bawbie Paterson herself, and she's a byword, though she be your husband's aunt, my dear.'

'Oh, you needn't tell me,' said Lindsay, with a glimmer. 'We can't stay in the house now. It's unspeakable. She's beyond everything.'

'It's a marvel to me that you ever stayed.'

'Indeed, yes,' said Miss Annie. ' "You must have taken her up wrong," I said to Tris, that first time after the war, when she came in and told us that Francie's wife had seen you arrive. And never to send us a line.'

'But that was Garry all over,' said Lindsay, laughing again. 'Up and away when he took it into his head. I couldn't have sent you a line.'

'Well,' thought Miss Theresa comfortably, 'I wouldn't be married to a man that's the byword and laughing stock of the place.' And she looked again at Lindsay with amazement. Happy—there was no doubt of it. Now who could have foretold that such a marriage would turn out well? 'It's these modern styles that does it,' she said aloud, with a nip to her tone, surveying the girl's lissome grace.

'I'm glad to see you don't show off your knees, Lindsay,' said Miss Annie.

Miss Annie had said, when the preparations for Lindsay's wedding were toward, 'I would like to hear that she was getting a good white wincey gown, but I don't suppose she will.'

'A byword and a laughing stock,' repeated Miss Theresa to herself. His name in everyone's mouth. *You would need Garry Forbes to you; Hine up on the head o' the house like Garry Forbes and his two fools*; and though *like seeking needles among preens* was an old phrase, *or sane folk among fools* had been added to it locally because of Garry. Mrs Craigmyle herself had made the addition, with a meaning eye upon her daughter Ellen. Theresa remembered the occasion well: an occasion when Ellen had said, unexpectedly, that Garry Forbes was liker a Christ than any other man she knew. A Christ—now what did she mean by *a* Christ? It gave them all a queer shock, coming like that from Ellen's gaunt, pale lips. Annie had said, 'Well, Bawbie now—she's never in the kirk from one year's end to another, and I doubt the young man's much the same.' Theresa remembered that she herself had cried, 'Well, there's no need for blasphemy about it,' and it was later the same evening that Mrs Craigmyle, using the phrase *like seeking needles among preens*, added *or sane folk among fools*.

'And indeed it's real hard whiles to tell the one from the other,' thought Miss Theresa complacently.

But there was no doubt of it, Lindsay was happy. Miss Theresa regarded her again. 'But when you've got your poke', she thought, 'you just have to be doing with the pig that's in it.' Even when the pig was one whose grumphs and squeaks made something of a family scandal. 'Old Garry's just hanging on for the next Coal Strike,' Frank Lorimer had said. 'Wait till you see—he'll come out strong, stronger than this time.' Some of his utterances had even been in the papers. A horrid disgrace. A mere asking for ridicule. Miss Theresa wondered that Lindsay would put up with it, but she didn't seem to care—just laughed and said, 'But that's the kind of thing that Garry does.' Well, she might repent it yet. Nine years was not so very long a time, and the wedding had been hasty enough, in all conscience. Theresa remembered how Mrs Robert Lorimer had come out to give them the news.

There they were, preparing for a marriage in the grand style a fortnight ahead; and that very morning, in the drawing-room at home, Lindsay had become Mrs Dalgarno Forbes; and the bridegroom was returning to the trenches the following day.

'Oh,' Theresa had said. 'Active service again. I thought he wasn't fit.'

Mrs Robert explained that it was his own desire. 'Would get himself sent. And it appears he was able enough all the time. It was just his nerves.'

So it had been a gey hasty affair, Annie supposed. And Mrs Robert told them that even the minister was not to be had in time, and so that old done man, the Reverend Mr Watson, tied the knot. 'And if he didn't forget the ring!—pronounced a benediction on them, and the ring still in the best man's fingers, and him fidgeting about and not knowing what to do. Such an unfortunate affair.'

'Well, well,' Theresa had said. 'Who will to Cupar maun to Cupar. That's her getting married in May. And the service all in a snorl. And no wedding frock and no party.'

'And her father,' continued Mrs Robert, 'he would blurt out anything, would Andrew. He said right out, "You're in a terrible hurry," he said, "come back and pay your loaf." And then they got the ring put on.'

'Sic mannie sic horsie,' old Mrs Craigmyle had said with a chuckle. 'Andrew's his father's son. You'll never see a Lorimer trauchled with overmuch respect for the kirk. And us all to come out of a manse, too.'

'And then,' Mrs Robert had proceeded, 'when he turned to kiss his wife, she actually skipped into his arms. Kicked her heels up—a regular dancing step. The trickiest you ever saw.'

'Oh, well,' Theresa had said, 'she grat sore enough about that wedding not so long ago, and she'll maybe greet again for all her dancing.'

'Yes, that was what I said,' she thought. 'And then mother began with her ballads.' She remembered perfectly what her mother had sung. She had sat aloof, as usual, just listening. One might be sure that in time she would put in her word. A song, most likely. She diddled away at old tunes most of the time. Hitherto, since Mrs Robert had arrived, she had spoken nothing but that chuckling proclamation of Lorimer disrespect. A gey life she and her brother must have led the old Reverend! But with her mind on the walled manse garden she reflected, 'He was real fond of a funnie himself.' Theresa was half a Craigmyle, a dourer folk than the Lorimers—dour, hard of grain, acquisitive; but even Theresa had spent hilarious days in her grandfather's patch of wood. And as she sat watching her sister die, Theresa's mind was a pleasant jumble of apple trees and the ploys of a pack of bairns, through which Lindsay's eager dance step and her mother's nine year old singing recurred like a refrain. The very tune came back and the mocking words:

He bocht an aul horse an' he hired an aul man

An' he sent her safe back to Northumberland.

It was then that Ellen had interfered. Opening her mouth for the first time, 'That's a cruel inference, mother,' she had cried sharply. Neither Theresa nor Annie paid much heed to what their mother sang. She was always singing, though there had been little singing since Ellen took ill. Dowie, the old lady was, peering anxiously. She wasn't in the habit of caring. Theresa thought it strange. 'It's the callow that worry,' she said to herself. A very old woman like her mother was past feeling strongly.

'What did the old ballads signify?' she thought, reverting to the wedding; but Ellen was always finding that her mother meant something—meant more than she should, Ellen intended to say. Well, and if she had meant to hint that the marriage might turn out ill, it was no more than they all thought at the time. 'But we were wrong, and it's a mercy,' she thought, daft Bawbie Paterson's nephew though he was. Would Bawbie have gone to the wedding now, she pondered; and with the black trallop hanging down her back? 'There was nothing amiss with the song, I'm sure,' Theresa said to herself. 'Mother had a rhyme about the ring too, if I could remember it:

a guid gowd ring
Made oot o' the auld brass pan, ay, ay.

But they had all cried out against that one—a sluttish thing, not to be associated with Lindsay. Mrs Craigmyle had let them cry, humming away at her tune, pleasuring herself with the unsavoury words.

The dying woman began to mutter restlessly. Miss Theresa put aside these ancient thoughts and went to the bedroom.

'How she speaks!' Miss Annie said to Lindsay. 'Such conversations as she holds, you never would believe. She's been taking a lot to your husband, my dear.'

'To my—to Garry? But how strange! Why, she hardly knows Garry. Talking to Garry?'

'Talking, my dear, and answering too.' Miss Annie broke off. 'But you never know what a body will say when they're dottled.' She sighed a little, looked towards her mother, and shook her head. The thought had come to her that to speak to Lindsay of Ellen's infatuation was less than kind. 'I re-member,' she began again, 'when I was but a little thing, an old, old man—'

Her pleasant voice ran on; but while she told her story she looked again, anxiously and in a puzzled way, at her mother. Lindsay, too, looked at her aged grand-aunt who at ninety four, straight as a pine-bole and with all her faculties unimpaired, was seated on the high-backed sofa, knitting at her shank; but her eyes, Lindsay noticed, never left her daughter's face—Ellen, her second daughter, dottled and dying at sixty nine.

The muttering continued.

'Poor old craitur!' said grand-aunt Craigmyle.

And her voice had still tune to it.

'Yes,' said Miss Annie, reading Lindsay's thought, 'it's the old generation that has the last in it, I say to mother. There's Mrs Morgan now, as blithe and active at her tea-makings as ever you saw, and Louie a poor wasted thing.'

Louie Morgan! thought Lindsay. Strange that she should be mentioned then. Lindsay's thoughts, like Miss Theresa's, had been travelling in the past. And Louie Morgan, as well as Cousin Ellen, had had her part in the singular drama that preceded that hasty marriage service.

She said aloud, 'I haven't seen Louie for—oh, such a long time.'

'And needn't seek to,' said Theresa, returning from the bedroom. 'She's not a sight for self-respecting eyes. The drink. She's drinking hard. Bleared. And her stockings cobbled with a yellow thread. That's you and your religion and no meal in the house.'

'Religion—is she so pious, then? She used to pray—'

'Oh, pray tonight and pray tomorrow. She would pray your head into train oil. But no one minds her—her big words and her grand speeches. They know what to make of *her* declarations.'

Lindsay had a movement of compassion for poor simple Louie, outcast from the love and reverence of the earth.

'But she wasn't saying them that time,' she thought and remembered how she and Garry, when she had stayed at the Weatherhouse before her marriage, had come on

Louie kneeling in the wood as though in audible prayer; but when they came behind her, what she was saying was ludicrous. 'I'm on the Fetter-Rothnie committee—may I introduce myself?' she was saying. And she smirked to an imaginary audience. They had laughed about it often afterwards, though Garry didn't like her to tell the story in public. 'Oh, leave her alone,' he always said. But what harm did it do, Lindsay would ask, with people who didn't know her? Aloud she said, 'Fancy Louie coming to that! Poor soul! I liked Louie,' she added in a moment. 'She used to take me for walks— long ago, when I was a little thing. And tell me stories. She had a dog—Demon, wasn't it? Oh, I remember how he could run. Through the wood. I can see him still.'

'Nonsense!' rapped Miss Theresa. 'Louie had never a dog.'

'But I remember. I can see him. A whippet hound he was.'

'Nonsense! She hadn't a dog. She wanted one—one of the Knapperley whippets, Miss Barbara's dogs. But old Mrs Morgan wouldn't have an animal about the place. Louie kicked up a waup over not getting it, I can tell you. And after a while she used to pretend she had it—made on to be stroking it, spoke to it and all. A palavering craitur.'

Lindsay looked doubtfully.

'Did she? I know she pretended about a lot of things. But Demon—? He seems so real when I look back. Did she only make me think I saw him? He used to go our walks with us. We called to him—*Demon, Demon*—loud out, I know that.'

She pondered. The dog, bounding among the pines, had in her memory the compelling insistence of imaginative art. He was a symbol of swiftness, the divine joy of motion. But Lindsay preferred reality to symbol.

'Queer, isn't it?' she said, coming out of her reverie. 'I remembered Demon was a real dog.'

She was unreasonably angry with Louie, as though by her own discovery of Demon's non-existence Louie had defrauded her of a recollected joy. And Garry had proved her a cheat. Lindsay's mind reverted to all that had followed that odd encounter in the wood, and so came back to Cousin Ellen. She shifted a little on her chair, bringing her eye into line with the open door and the muttering old woman who lay on the bed; and suddenly Mrs Falconer began to shout, 'They have despised him and rejected him. Cry aloud, spare not. A stubborn people who will pay no heed.'

Theresa stood over her, saying, 'Now, now. There, lie down again. Weesht ye, weesht. It's all right.' But Annie, who had caught the Biblical cadence of the words, folded her knotted and swollen hands together in her lap; and Ellen continued to shout, harshly and without intermission, tossing her long, fleshless arm above her head.

That evening Lindsay, who was on holiday at her old home, said to her father, 'Daddy, you must go out and see her. No, I don't mean Cousin Ellen. She wouldn't know you, of course. I mean old Aunt Craigmyle. She was always so fond of you. Perhaps you could comfort her a little.'

'Comfort!' grumbled Andrew Lorimer. 'The old lady never needed much comforting that I could see. You don't take things hard at ninety four, bairn.'

'Oh, I know, daddy. I know she never seemed to care about anything. She looked at us all as though she were reading about us in a book. But she is distressed—really she is.'

'Oh, well, we'll see.'

Andrew Lorimer took his car and ran out the nine odd miles that separated the Weatherhouse from the city, and by that time Mrs Falconer was dead.

'Oh, Andrew, I'm right glad to see you,' said Annie, who opened the door to him. 'Come away in. Mother's so dowie. I never saw her so come-at.'

'Eh?' said Andrew.

He remained standing on the doorstep.

'What a brae that is!' he grumbled. 'It's not fit for any car. I've a rheumatic here,' he added, feeling his shoulder. And because he wished to protract the moment before he must go in and talk to his aunt, he asked, 'How's your own rheumatism, Ann?'

Miss Annie looked down at her shapeless lumps of hands. 'It's as much as I could do to open the door for you,' she said. A gleam flickered on her pleasant face. 'I've aye been handless, Andrew, but I'm getting terrible handless among the feet forbye.'

Andrew allowed himself to laugh. He felt less constrained. He disliked heartily the job on which he was engaged; but he had always enjoyed Miss Annie.

'What'll I say to her?' he queried, following her across the threshold. 'You'd better tell me what to say.'

He sat down beside his aged aunt and began to tell her about his rheumatism, wresting his shoulder round to show her where the pain lay; but all the while he spoke his thoughts were on the woman who had just died. He realised that he was thinking of her as an old woman. 'But she can't be old,' he thought. She wasn't so much older than himself when they were all bairns together, the three Lorimer boys and the three Craigmyle lassies, and played in the Manse garden at Inverdrunie, and grandfather Lorimer gave them prizes for climbing the elm trees. 'To keep them out of the apple trees,' he explained to his wife. What a climber Paradise had been, with her long foalie's legs! Tris and he were of an age, and Ellen some three years older. Not yet seventy, then. Pretty near it, though. And he thought, seventy years without event. Oh, to be sure, there had been the episode with that Falconer chap who let her down so badly; but that must have meant four years at the most—long ago. Kate—why, Kate must be going on for forty. And at that moment Kate Falconer entered the room.

An able-looking girl—he had forgotten that she looked so well. Matron in some sort of Children's Home, and exceptionally capable, they said. Looked as though her wits were at her service. She could do well for herself, if she liked—marry well. There couldn't be much money in that Charity Home business, anyway, though he supposed Kate would take what she was offered and make no bones. She wouldn't push for her own advantage. Took that from her father. Couldn't hold off himself. Let any shaver cheat him. And then slipped out of it all and left his wife and child without a copper. Kate wouldn't have a penny but what she earned. Yes, she would marry.

'That's Stella Ferguson gone up the road,' said Miss Theresa, who was adjusting a blind.

A moment later came a sharp ring at the bell. Kate went to the door.

They heard the stranger ask in a loud, challenging voice, 'What are the blinds down for?'

Kate's soft answer was inaudible.

'She's not dead? Her? Lord alive!' The girl broke into noisy blubbering.

'Stella Ferguson?' said Andrew Lorimer. 'Oh, yes, old Jeames's grand-child. No? I remember, I remember.' With a movement of the head towards the noise of her sobbing, he added, 'I suppose that's the etiquette of mourning with that stamp.'

'No,' said Paradise, 'that's not a pose. Stella has a warm heart. A bold bessy but a warm heart. She's done well for herself, Stella has, she's a smartie. She's typist at Duncan Runciman's and making good money, though she's but eighteen. Quite my lady now, and keeps her mother in her place. But she has a warm heart. When Mr John Grey died—they found him dead in bed one May morning, a year past, and all the days he lay, you would have said a lying-in-state—not a cloud, not a breath of wind. Summer in its glory. Halcyon days they were—you would have thought his very garden knew. Well, Stella came and brought her flower. Gean blossom it was—black the next day. And so his cousin, that had come because he had none of his own, she threw away the shrivelled thing. Stella was like a play-actress—ramped and raged. Picked the very branch out of the rubbish heap and put it in his hand again. "I'll not take another," she declared. "I said a prayer over that, I did. I don't say a prayer so often that I want one wasted." So her bit of blossom went to the grave with him,' concluded Paradise. 'Quite right to leave it too, I think.'

Andrew Lorimer had gone only a little way down the hill on his journey home when the girl Stella, leaping from the dyke on which she had been seated, intercepted him.

'Look here,' she said. 'They don't like me much in there. My mother was a bad woman, and they think I'm a bad girl, but I'm not. Gospel.' As she said *Gospel* the girl breathed noisily and crossed her breath with a forefinger. 'But if I'm not a bad girl,' resumed Stella, 'it's to that precious saint lying dead in there that it's due. My eye! They don't none of them know the kind she was. Never goes to church, doesn't she? She was a stunner, I can tell you. Look here, she's got to get my roses in her hand.'

She displayed a cluster of hardy yellow scotch roses.

'Stella,' said Mr Lorimer, stepping from his car, 'if you were the worst sinner that ever was, you'd have the right to pay your tribute to the dead. But you're a good honest girl. Come with me.'

And, quite unconscious of the high scorn in the look that Stella cast on him, he led the way back to the Weatherhouse.

'You can come and put it in her hand yourself, Stella,' Miss Theresa said.

So Mrs Falconer lay that night, white and still, her face, beset so long with pain and darkened by failure, serene at last, and the rose of the girl Stella in her hand.

GLOSSARY

a'thing
  everything
begeck
  disappointment
begrutten
  tear stained
bide bydin
  stay, remain; staying
bike
  wasps' nest
bit
  little, scrap of
blithe
  happy
brose
  oatmeal and milk or hot water
cantle up
  brighten up
cantrip
  piece of mischief
canty
  lively, cheerful
chiel
  lad
cloor
  dent
clout
  rag
collieshangie
  animated talk
connach
  devour; spoil
crack
  gossip
craiturie
  little creature

a crap for a' corn and a baggie for orrels
  an appetite for absolutely anything and then some (literally: a bag for leftovers)
deil
  devil
delvin
  digging
dirds
  bangs (vb)
dirl
  ring (vb)
dour
  stubborn
dunt
  a blow
a dunt on the riggin
  not all there (dent in the roof)
(neither) echie nor ochie
  not the smallest sound
e'en
  eyes
fee'd
  hired
fey
  peculiar, other-worldly
ficher
  fiddle, fidget
fient
  never! not a! (lit: devil!)
fleggit
  startled
flinchin
  deceitful promise of better weather

205

forbye
  besides
fyle
  soil, make dirty
gar
  cause to
gey
  rather
a gey snod bit deemie
  a rather neat little maid
girned
  complained
glower
  scowl
grat
  cried
greetin
  crying
haggar
  clumsy hacking
halflin
  teenager
hap
  cover up
hotterel
  a swarm
hine awa'/up
  far away/up
ilka
  each, every
inen
  in among
keek, keeing
  peek, peeking
kye
  cattle
lift
  sky
to lippen to
  to trust
loon
  boy, lad
lousin time
  end of the working day
lowe
  blaze

lugs
  ears
neuk
  corner
newse
  chat
nieve
  fist
nyod
  (an exclamation, lit: God!)
orra
  odd, miscellaneous
pi
  pious, sanctimonious
pleuch
  plough
pooches
  pockets
preens
  pins
pyet
  magpie
queets
  ankles
rax
  stretch
roup
  a sale or public auction
sark
  shirt
scran
  scrounge
scuttered
  fiddled about
shank
  stocking being knitted
sharger
  half grown creature
sheepy silver
  flakes of mica (in a stone)
sic nannie sic horsie
  like master, like man
snored
  smothered (in snow)
snod
  neat

soo's snoot
  pig's nose

spoot-ma-gruel
  any unappetising food

steekit
  shut

stite
  nonsense

swacker
  more supple

tackie
  tig (child's game)

thrawn
  stubborn

timmer knife
  wooden knife (useless)

tinkey
  tinker

trig
  neat

wae
  woeful

wantin
  lacking

waur; nane the waur
  worse; none the worse

whiles
  at the same time

yon
  that

yowies
  pine cones

CANONGATE CLASSICS
TITLES IN PRINT

Since her explosion onto the publishing scene more than ten years ago, Suzanne Brockmann has written more than forty books, and is now widely recognised as one of the leading voices in women's suspense writing. Her work has earned her repeated appearances on the *USA Today* and *New York Times* bestseller lists, as well as numerous awards. Suzanne Brockmann lives west of Boston with her husband, author Ed Gaffney.

By Suzanne Brockmann and available from Headline

The Unsung Hero
Dark of Night
Hot Pursuit

SUZANNE BROCKMANN

THE UNSUNG HERO

headline

First published in 2009 by Ballantine Books,
an imprint of The Random House Publishing Group,
a division of Random House, Inc., New York and published
in arrangement with Ballantine Books

First published in Great Britain in 2009 by
HEADLINE PUBLISHING GROUP

First published in paperback in 2009 by
HEADLINE PUBLISHING GROUP

1

Cataloguing in Publication Data is available from the British Library

ISBN 978 0 7553 7105 1 (B-format)
ISBN 978 0 7553 5551 8 (A-format)

Typeset in Palatino by Avon DataSet Ltd, Bidford-on-Avon

Printed and bound in Great Britain by CPI Mackays, Chatham ME5 8TD

Headline's policy is to use papers that are natural, renewable and
recyclable products and made from wood grown in sustainable
forests. The logging and manufacturing processes are expected to
conform to the environmental regulations of the country of origin.

HEADLINE PUBLISHING GROUP
An Hachette UK Company
338 Euston Road
London NW1 3BH

www.headline.co.uk
www.hachette.co.uk

For the brave men and woman who fought
for freedom during the Second World War.
My most sincere and humble thanks.

Acknowledgments

Special thanks to Frances Stepp, who always knows exactly whom to call, and Mike Freeman, real-life hero and excellent friend. Thanks also to Charles Patrick of the Military History Research Center in Virginia (www.mhrc-va.com), who provided a wonderful source of information for creating my fictional Fifty-fifth Division. Hugs to Scott Lutz for sharing his vast knowledge of comic books and graphic novels, and to Deede Bergeron, Lee Brockmann, and Patricia McMahon – my personal support staff. Eternal thanks to Ed, my inspiration for all my heroes. Any mistakes that I've made or liberties that I've taken are completely my own.

Prologue

Spring

When both the Seahawk and its pilot took a direct hit, things went from bad to worse.

US Navy SEAL Lieutenant Tom Paoletti took over the controls and lurched the helicopter skyward as Jazz and Lopez worked to keep the pilot from bleeding to death.

The elite, eight-member SO squad had come into this latrine of a country to see to the safe departure of a diplomat's wife. The mission was important enough to warrant the presence of Lieutenant Paoletti, SEAL Team Sixteen's commanding officer. In fact, the order had come down from Admiral Chip Crowley himself.

Crowley had told Tom frankly that he hoped the CO's appearance, along with that of his executive officer, Lieutenant Junior Grade Casper 'Jazz' Jacquette, would make these fascist assholes behave like neither fascists nor assholes.

Maybe, just maybe, if Tom was there with his easygoing, let's-be-friends smile, countered by the

1

take-me-very-seriously rows of ribbons on his chest and his calm air of command, maybe these bottom feeders would actually do as they'd promised, and let them walk out with Mrs Hampton in tow.

And maybe, if Tom had Jazz standing beside him, six feet tall and nearly as wide across, very stern, very silent, very black, and very, very dangerous looking, this mission would, indeed, turn out to be no more than an eight-man escort job.

The local government had insisted up and down and backward and forward that Mrs Hampton wasn't being held against her will, so Tom and his squad had taken a commercial flight in, rented a van at the airport, and driven out to the hotel the Hamptons had been living in before Ronald Hampton had made the mistake of taking a day trip to a neighboring country without his wife. In the course of a single afternoon, without warning, the political situation in the area had changed so drastically that old Ron and his entourage weren't allowed back in.

Mrs Hampton was actually at the hotel – a fact that had caused Tom to pause and reflect on the possibility that they *were* simply going to escort her, without incident, to the airport. He'd considered it at some length as he and his squad sat sipping iced tea in a pleasantly cool garden courtyard while Mrs Hampton packed.

Her arrival in the lobby was announced by the presence of six enormous suitcases.

Mrs Wilhemina Hampton.

She was one of those leathery tan fifty-something women who looked as if she should be wearing tennis whites with the little panties under her skirt at all times, holding a racket in one hand, a martini and cigarette in the other.

She didn't look particularly glad to see her SEAL escorts, and when Tom gently suggested she ship most of her luggage home – that the local government's habit of extensive luggage searches might cause delays – she objected with the kind of whine that made him wonder why the United States was going to so much trouble to get her out.

He pointed out – slightly less gently – that temporary delays in this neck of the woods frequently turned into *permanent* delays. Although the whining didn't stop entirely, it lessened in intensity, and three of the suitcases were grudgingly left behind.

Tom handed her off to Petty Officer Third Class Mark Jenkins, squeaky young, complete with an earnest, angelic freckled face that belonged on a choirboy. Jenk was, in fact, a devious hell-raiser and the best professional liar Tom had ever met in all his years in the teams. Jenk gave Mrs Hampton his most adorable smile, asked her questions about her grandchildren, and led her to a seat safe in the middle of the van even as, in Tom's direction, he pointedly scratched the side of his face with his middle finger.

As they pulled out of the hotel parking lot, O'Leary was in the back, riding shotgun. 'A black sedan's on our six.'

They were being followed.

But Tom would've been surprised if they'd left the hotel *without* a tail.

Jenk and Lopez were oohing and aahing over pictures of Mrs Hampton's profoundly ugly grandchild when they heard the first of the sirens in the distance.

Ensign Sam Starrett, who was driving, met Tom's eyes in the rearview mirror.

'Steady,' Tom said. Until they knew for certain those sirens were coming for them, making a run for it would be foolish. Running would blow this entire charade out of the water. And right now they were still firmly planted in pretend. The government was going to let them get on that plane. Sure they were.

WildCard, also known as Petty Officer First Class Kenny Karmody, was riding up front, monitoring the radio, fine-tuning the signal for the benefit of Ensign John Nilsson, the team's language expert.

'Four cars and one army transport, L.T., carrying a full platoon, heading out from the airport, ready to intercept – ordered to use force if necessary,' Nilsson reported.

WildCard turned back to look at Tom with glee. But then again, there wasn't much WildCard didn't do with glee. 'Plan B, your holiness?'

Admiral Crowley had stressed the importance of using diplomacy over force in carrying out this mission. Tom knew if his squad fired the first shot, there'd be a hell of a lot of explaining to do. But he'd far prefer an uncomfortable few hours in front of Crowley's desk explaining *that* than having his entire squad and the delightful Mrs Hampton spend the next six years of their lives in some shithole prison cell, the subjects of an Amnesty International letter-writing campaign.

Plan Bravo was looking like a damn good choice.

'Let's do it.' The words had barely left Tom's lips before O'Leary neatly shot out the front tire of the black sedan.

4

Starrett took a hard right on two wheels, leaving both the main road and the swerving black sedan in the dust.

Mrs Hampton started screaming as they narrowly missed a head-on with a vegetable truck. 'What are you doing? What are you doing?'

Jenk raised his boyish tenor to be heard over her. 'Mrs Hampton, ma'am. Even though we were assured you'd be able to leave freely on a commercial airline flight, we made backup provisions for an alternative means of departure. We've got a Seahawk helicopter meeting us just outside of town. Lieutenant Paoletti believes our wisest course of action is to head for that alternative means of departure at this time.'

'L.T., my foot's on the floor,' Starrett shouted. 'This piece of shit's maxing out at forty-five.'

They were bouncing through the narrow, potholed side streets at a speed that seemed alarmingly fast. But Tom knew that if they were being actively pursued, it very quickly wouldn't seem fast enough.

It wasn't any wonder Starrett couldn't get this thing moving, though. They'd filled the beat-up passenger van with eight large men, a woman who wasn't exactly a lightweight, and three very heavy suitcases.

There was only one thing they could lose to try to lighten the load. Or rather, there were *three* things.

Tom met Jazz's gaze. His XO knew exactly what he was thinking, which was good, because he didn't have to say the words aloud. Mrs H. was already upset enough. But O'Leary, who was sitting in the back with the suitcases, wasn't on the same wavelength.

'O'Leary, help me jettison the ballast,' Jazz ordered the sniper in his sub-bass, Darth Vader voice.

5

Mrs H. had stopped screaming, but she was still clearly unhappy at the thought of flying out via helo. Thankfully she wasn't familiar with the nautical terms *jettison* or *ballast*. At least the protests wouldn't begin until it was too late to make a difference.

'I get airsick on anything smaller than a 737,' she complained.

Tom leaned over the back of his seat, turning to face her, hoping that what he was about to say would make her realize the gravity of their situation.

'We just heard a radio message that ordered four secret-police vehicles *and* a transport carrying thirty soldiers to stop us by any and all means,' he told her, getting right in her face, making it impossible for her to look anywhere but directly into his eyes. 'I don't imagine you had the opportunity to tour the central prison while you were visiting this country, ma'am, but picture, if you will, someplace dark and cold, filled with rats and the stink of unwashed bodies. If that sounds like a place you'd like to spend a few years, say the word, and we'll let you out at the curb.'

Mrs H. was quite silent. In fact, she didn't let out more than a strangled squeak as she noticed the draft from the opened back door and saw the last of her suitcases cartwheeling down the street like that old American Tourister commercial. Tom doubted anyone, including her very important husband, had ever spoken so bluntly to her in her entire life.

'I need you to stay close to Petty Officer Jenkins,' Tom continued. 'If he, or I, or anyone in this squad for that matter, gives you an order, you *must* follow that order without question, without hesitation. Am I making myself clear?'

She nodded grimly, her mouth tight. 'Abundantly, Lieutenant. Although you can be assured I'll be writing a letter directly to your commanding officer about this. Those suitcases were filled with designer clothing, all expensive, some irreplaceable.'

'Keep your head down and your mouth closed, ma'am,' Tom told her. 'We *will* get you out of here so you can write that letter. I promise you that.'

Mrs Hampton couldn't resist one last question. 'What's to keep them from shooting down your helicopter?'

'We've got full support from the US Air Force standing by, and an agreement that acts as a permission slip from NATO for our fighters to use force if necessary – a fact we'll start broadcasting across all channels as soon as we get into the air. They'd have to be crazy to fire on us knowing that. My best estimate –' he glanced at his watch, – 'has us landing on a US-friendly airfield in just under an hour. I'll see to it you get stationery and a pen when we arrive.'

'And if something goes wrong,' Mrs Hampton said acidly, 'is there a Plan C?'

'There's always a Plan C, ma'am.' C stood for creative solutions on the fly. It was one of the things Tom's special operations squad did best.

But Plan Bravo went like clockwork. With Nilsson monitoring the radio, Starrett keeping his foot to the floor, and WildCard navigating their way through the twisting streets, they made it to the extraction point right on schedule.

The Seahawk approached on schedule, too, dust swirling as the pilot touched all the way down so they would be able to toss Mrs H. on board.

The snafu came from a jeep full of patrolling enemy soldiers. It was one of those stupid-ass coincidences that set Tom's teeth on edge. The patrol had been in the exact wrong place at the exact wrong time. Obviously, they had seen the helo and come to check it out. If they'd been ninety seconds later, the helo would've been off the ground. Ninety seconds later, and the SEALs would have been moving quickly out of the soldiers' weapon range.

Instead, the patrol came around the corner, weapons locked and loaded. But Lopez had been watching for exactly that, and he reacted first, lobbing a grenade in the soldiers' direction as Tom and Jazz lobbed Mrs Hampton onto the helo.

The soldiers scattered, but one of them managed to get off a few wild shots.

It was sheer misfortune that one of those bullets went through the open door and directly into the shoulder of the pilot.

But Tom got them up and he got them away. It had been a few years since he'd flown one of these birds. If it wasn't quite smooth sailing, it was close enough.

'Christ, skipper,' Jenks shouted over the relentless din Mrs H. was still making, 'we're smoking!'

Shit, they were. The engine was sending out a plume of smoke like a signal flare. A bullet must've hit one of the two engines. Talk about a lucky shot. Son of a *bitch*.

They were already well outside of the city and moving fast toward the border, but they weren't going to make it over. Not with one engine gone. And, Christ, the fuel gauge was going crazy. They'd been hit in the fuel tank, too. A smoking engine and a leaking fuel tank didn't make for a good combination, unless, of course, you *wanted* an explosion. He had to bring this puppy down and he had to do it now.

The landscape below was barren and dry, a desert filled with unfriendly looking rocks and not much more than a whole lot of dust. It looked more like the moon than the lush New England countryside where Tom had grown up.

'Brace!' Tom shouted as he wrestled the helo down to the ground. The landing was bumpy – hell, it was just short of a crash. Anything not strapped down went flying. 'Jazz, get Mrs H. outta here! Move!'

His men were already in motion. Jazz and Jenks each had Mrs Hampton by an arm. As they lifted her out of the Seahawk and across the bone-dry ground to shelter behind an outcropping of rocks, she was shouting and struggling, her voice nearly hoarse.

Lopez and WildCard took the pilot, and Nilsson, Starrett, and O'Leary had already filled their arms with as much gear and water as they could carry away.

Tom was the last one out the door, and he hit the ground running, thinking, shit, that speech he'd given hadn't done a whole hell of a lot to shut Mrs Hampton's flapping mouth.

And then he heard what Mrs Hampton was shouting about. Her purse. She'd left her frigging purse behind.

'I'm sorry, ma'am,' he heard Jazz say, 'you'll have to do without it. That thing's a time bomb, it's going to—'

'My heart pills are in my purse!' Mrs Hampton's raspy voice seemed to echo against the rocks, slapping up among the walls of the gently sloping hills.

Heart pills.

Shit.

The world went into slow-mo. Tom saw Jazz step out from behind the rocks, heading back toward him, toward the helo. But Tom was at least thirty yards closer. He tried to execute a half-court pivot, but skidded in the dust, scrambling to keep his speed up as he raced now *back* toward the helicopter.

Ten steps, and he was inside, searching for the goddamned thing. It was invisible, like most women's handbags when you really wanted to find them fast. He dropped to the metal floor, searching under the seats and . . .

Jackpot. It was beige leather and it must've slid forward when he'd landed. He grabbed it and was out the door in a matter of heartbeats, running as hard and as fast as he possibly could.

Tom was at least twenty yards from the shelter of the rocks when he heard the Seahawk blow behind him, felt the force of the explosion send him hurtling through the air. The ground came up to meet him far too quickly.

Damn, he thought as he tucked Mrs H.'s handbag against him, protecting it with his body, this was going to hurt.

And then he stopped thinking as his world went black.

One

Tom swung his duffle bag down from the overhead rack and shuffled slowly with the other passengers off the commercial flight and out into Boston's Logan Airport.

Moving slowly was good, especially since – like right now – he still had bouts of dizziness from that head injury that had nearly taken him out of action permanently.

Outside the terminal, the city skyline was muted by the hazy morning sky. Welcome to summer in New England.

The humidity would lift, Tom knew, as he headed toward the tiny North Shore community of Baldwin's Bridge. The stiff ocean breezes kept the temperature down and the skies blue in the picture-perfect tourist town.

Tom was staying only until Sunday.

He had thirty days of convalescent leave to fill, which pissed him off. He didn't *want* thirty days,

11

dammit. He'd just spent far too much time in the hospital, too much time away from his command. Of course, thanks to Rear Admiral Larry Tucker, at this point he wasn't sure he even had much of a command to return to.

Was it any wonder he'd lost his temper when he'd found out that while he was in a frigging coma, Tucker had tried to make SEAL Team Sixteen a line item to be deleted on the upcoming fiscal year's budget? And when Tom had found out that Tucker had taken Sixteen's SO squad, the elite group of men that Tom had taken years to handpick – nicknamed 'The Troubleshooters' by some and 'The Trouble*makers*' by the non-SEAL brass like Tucker – and scattered them to the ends of the earth . . .

But Tom had only lost his temper with the rear admiral. He hadn't thrown the man through the fourth-story window of his DC office. He hadn't even slapped the self-satisfied smirk off the bastard's face.

All he'd done was list his objections perhaps a little more strenuously than he normally might have.

And for that, he'd lost another week of his life undergoing psych evaluations, as teams of medical doctors and psychiatrists tried to decide whether or not his outburst was directly related to his recent severe head injury.

Tom had tried to assure them that, indeed, his loss of temper was merely a side effect of dealing with Tucker.

But his doctor was a captain – Howard Eckert – who was up for promotion and eager to please Rear Admiral Tucker, and Tom's excuses didn't fly. Eckert gave him thirty days' convalescent leave in an attempt to recover further from the head injury. The doctor and the shrinks warned Tom that with such an injury it wasn't unusual to experience some temporary and slight changes in personality. Aggressive behavior. Feelings of persecution and paranoia. And of course there was the dizziness and headaches. He should try to stay calm and relaxed. Because after thirty days, when he returned to the naval base in Virginia, he would undergo a similar set of psychiatric tests, after which his fate would be decided.

Would he be given a medical discharge and cut adrift, or would he be allowed to continue his career in the US Navy?

Tom didn't want choice A, but he knew that Tucker would be pushing to have him safely retired. And *that* meant Tom needed to spend these next thirty days doing everything he could to get as rested and relaxed – and as sane – as possible.

He knew himself well enough to know that going home for more than a long weekend would be a major mistake as far as staying sane went. And Tuesday through Sunday made for a very long weekend.

But a short visit would be good. He wanted to see his great-uncle, Joe. He even wanted to see his sister, Angela, and his niece, Mallory. Mal had graduated from high school this year. Her teenage years were proving to be as rocky as his and Angie's had been.

Apparently it still wasn't easy to be a Paoletti kid growing up in highbrow Baldwin's Bridge, Massachusetts. Hell, there were members of the police force who *still* bristled when they saw Tom coming.

He was thirty-six years old now, a highly decorated and respected commanding officer in the US Navy

SEALs, yet all those old labels – troublemaker, fuckup, 'that wild Paoletti kid' – persevered.

No, as much as he missed Joe's solid company, a weekend in Baldwin's Bridge would definitely be long enough. But maybe he could talk Joe into going to Bermuda with him for a week or two. That would be cool. And if Joe insisted, Tom would even bring Charles Ashton along on this trip.

Mr Ashton was Joe's crotchety best friend or arch nemesis, depending on the two old men's moods. He was a contender for Mr Scrooge and the Grinch all rolled into one delightful, alcohol-soused package. But Joe had known the man since the Second World War. There was a lot of history behind his loyalty, and Tom could respect that. Besides, any man who'd managed to father Kelly Ashton couldn't be *that* bad.

Kelly Ashton. Tom thought of her every time he returned to Baldwin's Bridge. Of course, he thought of her when he wasn't there as well. In fact, he thought of her far too often, considering it had been more than sixteen years since he'd seen her last.

What were the chances she'd be visiting her father this week, while Tom was in town?

Slim to none. She was a doctor now, with a busy, full life that didn't include sitting around, waiting for Tom to come home.

And sixteen years was surely enough time for him to stop thinking about her. She'd obviously stopped thinking about him, considering she'd been married.

Of course, now she was divorced.

Which meant exactly nothing. For all he knew, she'd already remarried. Stop thinking about her. She wasn't going to be there.

Tom worked his way through the crowded airport, heading toward the overhang where the shuttle to the subway – called the T in Boston – would pick him up. He passed the luggage carousel, weaving his way through the throngs of people who were surging slightly forward now that the conveyor belt had started moving.

The crowd was made up mostly of vacationing families and older travelers waiting for their suitcases. The businessmen and -women had all packed lightly enough to carry on their bags and they were long gone.

But there was one dark-suited man in the crowd, about Tom's height, his light brown hair streaked with gray. He reached down to pick up his bag from the conveyor belt, turning to hoist it up onto his shoulder in a strange twisting move that made Tom stop short.

No way.

There was *no* way that, out of all the places in the world, Tom should run into the man known only as 'the Merchant' in Logan Airport.

His hair was too light, although that'd be easy enough to change.

His face was different – although it was roughly the same shape. But his nose and cheekbones were softer, less pronounced, his chin slightly weaker than Tom remembered. Could a plastic surgeon do all that? Was it even possible?

Tom moved closer to the man, trying to get a better look.

His eyes. The color was different. They were a muddy shade of blue and brown – that funky no-single-color that brown-eyed people could get when they bought blue-tinted contact lenses. But it didn't matter what color they were. Tom would have recognized those eyes anywhere. Still, he'd only gotten a glimpse.

God, was it possible? . . .

The man moved with his duffel bag still on his shoulder, heading for the door, and Tom followed more slowly, hampered by the crowd.

Now that he was walking, the man moved differently than the Merchant had, but a man who was the subject of an international manhunt would no doubt have worked to change his walk along with his face and his hair color. Still, that one twisting move . . . Tom had seen that many times on several different pieces of video – rare footage of the Merchant in action. And as for his eyes . . .

Tom still saw the Merchant's eyes in his sleep.

As Tom followed him, the man pushed open the door, heading toward a taxicab waiting at the curb.

Tom tried to get outside, doing some fancy footwork to keep from stepping on a toddler who'd escaped from his parents, then dancing around a pair of elderly ladies.

By the time he reached the door, his head was throbbing and the Merchant had gotten into the taxi and was driving away.

What now? *Follow that cab?*

There were no other cabs available.

Strains of the rock song 'Paranoia' echoed in Tom's head as he made a mental note of the departing taxi's ID number – 5768 – stenciled in black letters on its trunk. He glanced at his watch. Nearly 0800.

But if this really was the Merchant, calling the cab company to find out where cab number 5768 dropped his 0800 fare from Logan wasn't going to do a hell of a lot of good.

The Merchant wouldn't go directly from the airport to his final location. He would make sure he was dropped downtown, he'd wander a few blocks, then pick up another cab. He'd do this several times until he was certain he wasn't being followed, that his path couldn't be traced.

On the other side of the overhang, the shuttle to the T was pulling up.

'Paranoia' played a little bit louder until Tom shook his head, pushing away both it and the dizziness that still seemed to intervene whenever he stood up for too long.

Yes, it was going to sound frigging crazy when he tried to explain. 'Hi, I think I just saw the international terrorist that I spent four months tracking in '96 taking a cab out of Logan Airport. Yeah, that's in Boston, Massachusetts, that teeming hotbed of international intrigue . . .'

Yeah, right.

Tom got on the shuttle.

He would call. Crazy as it all sounded, he *had* to call someone. He'd call Admiral Crowley – a man who'd trusted Tom's crazy instincts before. But Tom would make the call from the comfort and privacy of his uncle Joe's cottage in Baldwin's Bridge.

He jammed his bag beneath his feet and sat near the window, putting his head back and closing his eyes. Rest and relaxation.

He could assume the position, but he couldn't keep his mind from racing.

Tom had no clue – *no clue* – what he was going to do

if Tucker got what he wanted and kicked him out of the Navy.

The tile was cold against his cheek.

It actually felt rather nice, but Charles Ashton didn't want to die, like Elvis, on the bathroom floor, with his pajama bottoms down around his ankles.

Where was the dignity in that?

'Come on, God,' he said, struggling to pull his pants up his legs. 'Give a guy a break.'

He'd been on a first-name basis with God ever since that day Joe Paoletti had driven him to Dr Grant's and the much too young physician had used the words *you* and *have* and *terminal* and *cancer* in the very same sentence. Charles had figured his and God's relationship was going to become far more personal and hands on in the very near future, so he might as well get friendly with the guy.

Death.

It wasn't a very fun or happy word, with any particularly appealing images attached. Charles preferred the more euphemistic expressions. Kicking the bucket. Belly-up – that was a particularly bouncy, friendly sounding one. And then there was the perennial favorite: shitting the bed.

No, strike that. He preferred the bare bones *dying* over *that* most unpleasant image.

The doctor had estimated that Charles had about four months before he'd pass on. Pass on – that was a stupid one. It made him think of passing gas, like dying was one giant, last-blast fart.

Of course, the precocious youngster with the medical degree had warned, he could be wrong and

18

the moment of truth could be far sooner than four months.

Like maybe this morning.

Charles wasn't afraid to die. Not anymore. Well, wait, strike that, too. He *was* afraid to die – on the bathroom floor. A thing like that would stay with a guy damn near forever.

'Remember Charles Ashton?' someone would say. 'Yeah, right, Ashton,' would be the reply. 'He died in his bathroom with his big bare ass hanging out of his pants.'

Forget about all the money he'd given to charity, all his philanthropic works. Forget the branch of the Baldwin's Bridge hospital dedicated to children's medicine, given in honor of both his own son who died from a ruptured appendix in 1947 as well as a little French boy killed by the Nazis, a little boy he'd never actually met. Forget about the war he'd helped to win. Forget about the trust funds he'd set up so that each year three promising young students from Baldwin's Bridge could attend the colleges of their choice.

Forget about everything but his big bare ass, dead as a doornail on the bathroom floor.

Dead.

It was a cold word.

Charles had suspected the news was coming when he'd first met the doctor, even before he'd had the full barrage of tests.

'When you're so old and your doctor is so young that you look at him and know you haven't had sex since before he was born, chances are, he's not going to have a whole hell of a lot of good news,' he'd told Joe grumpily as they'd driven home.

Joe hadn't said much – but then again, Joe wasn't a huge talker. Young Joe Paoletti – he was only seventy-six to Charles's exalted eighty – merely gave Charles a long look as they'd stopped at a red light.

And Charles had wisely shut up. It hadn't been the most considerate thing to say, considering Joe hadn't had sexual relations since 1944. The crazy bastard. He'd been a heartbreaker, with a face like a matinee idol. He could have had a different woman for every night of the week. Yet he'd lived like a monk since they both had returned to Baldwin's Bridge after the War.

The War. The one against the Nazis. Double-yew, double-yew, eye, eye.

He and Joe had met in France, of all places. Just after Normandy, that hell on earth. Joe hadn't really been much of a talker back then, either.

Theirs had become the kind of friendship that only a war could make. It was like something out of a storybook. Two men from completely different walks of life. One the poor son of a hardworking Italian immigrant from New York City, the other the wealthy son of a wealthy son from an old Boston family used to summers spent relaxing in the cool ocean breezes of the North Shore town of Baldwin's Bridge, Massachusetts. They'd fought together against Nazi Germany, and their relationship solidified into something beyond permanent, bonded together with Winston Churchill's own recipe for an indestructible tabby: blood, toil, tears, and sweat.

Tears.

Joe had wept when the doctor told Charles the C-word. He'd tried to hide it, but Charles had known.

You didn't spend nearly sixty years as someone's

best friend – even though you tried to deny it, even though you sometimes pretended he was only the gardener or the hired help or even just that stupid bum who'd followed you home from the War – and not know when he was hurting.

'You should've taken him first,' Charles scolded God now. '*I* could've handled it.'

With the last ounce of his strength, he heaved his pajama pants up around his waist. He lay there on the cool tile floor, his ass safely covered, coughing from the exertion, wondering if God could tell when he was lying.

Dr Kelly Ashton was running out of time.

She parked her subcompact in her father's driveway, next to Joe's four-hundred-year-old but still pristine Buick station wagon, and turned off the engine, sitting for a moment, her head on her arms, against the steering wheel.

What she was doing was stupid. *She* was stupid. Trying to maintain her pediatrics practice in Boston while living here, an hour north of the city at her father's house in Baldwin's Bridge, proved it. She should give the Harvard diploma back. Obviously it was a mistake. She was too stupid to have earned it.

And she was doubly stupid since her father made it painstakingly clear that he really didn't want her here.

He didn't need her help. He'd rather die alone.

Kelly pushed open the car door, gathering the bag from the drugstore and the sack of groceries she'd picked up from the Stop & Shop on her way home. This was supposed to be one of her days here in Baldwin's Bridge, but she'd gotten up at 4:30 to drive into Boston before the rush, to get some paperwork done. With her new schedule, she barely had time to think let alone do paperwork, and this morning she'd only managed to put a dent in the piles on her desk.

She'd also gone in early hoping that Betsy McKenna's test results would be in first thing.

Kelly suspected the frail six-year-old had leukemia. And if that was the case, she wanted to be the one to tell Betsy's parents, to talk about treatment, and to introduce them to the oncologist.

But at nine she'd called the lab and found out that Betsy's blood sample had been shipped in a van that had been totaled in an accident. In fact, the entire day's blood tests had to be redone. All those patients – Betsy included – would have to come back in. The results would be returned to Kelly stat. Tomorrow, they'd promised. Provided a new blood sample got to them today.

It was at that point she'd put the entire matter into the very capable hands of Pat Geary, her administrative assistant. And Kelly had given up on the paperwork and headed back here, to be near her father.

Who wanted nothing more than for her to leave him alone.

So she'd probably spend her day at home running around town, doing errands, trying to show him that she loved him in the only way she knew how. By being dutiful and obedient. By staying out of his way.

She gave the car door a hard push with her rear end, slamming it shut.

He'd always been a selfish bastard. What had he been thinking, anyway, having a kid when he was so damn old? He'd always been old – old and cynical and so jaded and sarcastic.

Kelly couldn't imagine what he'd seen in Tina, her mother, other than her youthful body and pretty face. She knew, however, what Tina had seen in him. Charles Ashton was an elegant, beautiful, seemingly sophisticated, and very, very wealthy man. Even now, at eighty, he was remarkably handsome. He still had a thick shock of hair – though pure white now instead of golden blond. And his eyes were still a bright piercing blue, though by all rights they should be bleary, watery, and shot with red, thanks to the gallons of alcohol he'd consumed through the years.

It was only his soul that was ugly and shriveled.

And it was only now, when he was dying, that he'd finally stopped drinking. Not because he wanted to be sober, but because he was having trouble eating or drinking just about everything. The gin that had once been his cure-all now was too harsh on his cancer-ridden stomach.

The irony was intense.

It took looming, imminent death by cancer to remove him from the clutches of the alcoholism that had been slowly but surely killing him. At one point, Kelly had been sure the DTs would do him in, but the old man was tough and he'd made it through.

And now, for the first time since Kelly could remember, her father was sober all the time and capable of carrying on meaningful conversations.

Except he didn't want to talk to her.

Charles didn't need her, but dammit, she needed him. He had three months left – if that. And she needed to use that time to reach some kind of an understanding, if not with him, then at least *about* him. Even if all they managed to do was sit in a room together without one of them getting a rash, that would be more than they'd shared in the recent past.

He might be stubborn, but she was stubborn, too. It wouldn't be easy, because she was, after all, an Ashton – raised to keep every emotion she was feeling carefully, politely inside.

Kelly went into the house and put down all her bags on the kitchen table.

The place was silent, but that didn't mean a thing. This monstrosity that had been the Ashton summer home for the past hundred and fifty years was so vast that Charles could be in his TV room with the set turned up deafeningly, and she wouldn't hear it in the kitchen.

Kelly began putting the groceries away as loudly as she possibly could, hoping – as futilely as the little girl she'd once been had hoped that her straight As on her report card would make her worthy of her father's love – that for once Charles would hear that she was home and come say good morning.

On the other end of the phone, Adm. Chip Crowley was silent. And when he finally sighed, Tom knew this was not going to be easy.

'Tell me again who this Merchant is?' Crowley asked.

Tom couldn't keep his voice from sounding tight. 'Sir. I'd appreciate it if you did not patronize me.'

'I'm not patronizing you, Tom, I'm trying to refresh my less than perfect memory. Will you please just answer my question? And I'll tell you right now to keep it at a decibel level that won't hurt my ears. Don't even think about giving me some of the same verbal disrespect that you dished out to Larry Tucker last week.'

Tom sat down at Joe's formica-topped kitchen table. 'Sir. Are you telling me you *support* Tucker's attempt to shut down Sixteen and the SO squad?'

'I'm telling you nothing of the kind,' Crowley said. 'Son, I'm behind your Troubleshooters two hundred percent. Team Sixteen's not going anywhere. You have my promise. What Larry tried to do was dead wrong. But what you did in response was *also* dead wrong. And I have to confess to being a little concerned. There are ways to deal with assholes like Larry Tucker that don't include going off half-cocked and getting yourself strapped down for a week's worth of psych evals. The man I chose to lead Team Sixteen a year and a half ago wouldn't have done what you did.'

Crowley was right. Tom's head was pounding and he rubbed his forehead with his fingers, trying to relieve the pressure. The kitchen wall was dingy, he noticed, and he looked around the room, realizing it needed fresh paint. *That's* what he should be doing with this weekend, not reporting sightings of dead terrorists, not putting his career even further at risk.

'Now why don't you do me a favor and answer my question?' Crowley said more gently. 'The Merchant. He had something to do with that embassy bombing back in, what was it, 1997?'

''Ninety-six,' Tom said. 'And yes, sir. He's an independent contractor – a mercenary who was the brains behind the car bomb that took out the American embassy in Paris that year. A Muslim extremist group claimed responsibility for the blast, but NAVINTEL put the Merchant there. It was definitely his work. The bomb had his cell's signature all over it.'

'You were part of a combined French-American force brought in after these terrorists were tracked to . . . London, was it?'

'Liverpool. The SAS played a part, too.'

They'd wasted a hell of a lot of time playing politics after the Merchant and his dirty band had been tracked to a warehouse in a particularly dank part of the English town most famous for being the home of the Beatles. In fact, Tom still believed that if they'd focused more on apprehending the terrorists rather than deciding the protocol of who got to kick down the door, they might've had five captured Tangos rather than four former terrorists in need of body bags and one terrorist – the Merchant – still 'at large,' as the Feds so aptly put it.

'We had security-camera footage of the Merchant being hit by gunfire,' Tom told the admiral. 'Through video analysis, his injuries were believed to be extensive. In fact, the word *fatal* was used. Even though he'd escaped, it was thought chances of his surviving were slim.'

Crowley was silent again, and Tom looked at the summer flowers Joe kept in a vase on the table. As far back as Tom could remember, Joe had had fresh flowers in his kitchen all spring and summer long.

It was one of the perks of being a groundskeeper, Tom supposed. Maybe that was what he could do after Tucker forced his early retirement. He could come back to Baldwin's Bridge and act as Joe's apprentice. Learn about roses and lawn grubs and all those things he'd been too impatient to pay attention to when he was in high school. He could eventually take over the position of the Ashtons' groundskeeper from Joe, and when Charles Ashton died . . . *If* Charles Ashton died. The old man was just ornery enough to be immortal out of spite. *If* Charles died, Tom could work full time for his daughter, Kelly, because she would no doubt inherit this humongous estate – the main house and grounds, and even this little cottage Joe had lived in for over fifty years.

Now there was a high school fantasy that had never died. Tom could be gorgeous Kelly Ashton's lawn boy. It was a fantasy that ran an awful lot like a cheap porno flick, starting with Tom slick with sweat from trimming the hedges around the house. Kelly Ashton, with her sweet girl-next-door face, those eyes that were unbelievably blue, and that sinfully perfect body, would be sitting on the screened porch. She'd invite him into the coolness of the house for a glass of lemonade, and . . .

'You're awfully quiet,' Crowley commented. 'I know what you're thinking.'

Oh, no, the admiral most certainly did not.

'You're thinking, if the Merchant's injuries really were that extensive, he wouldn't have been able to evade capture in the first place,' Crowley continued.

Not even close. But it was definitely what Tom *had* thought, both back in '96 and frequently over the past few years. That is, when he wasn't thinking about doing Kelly Ashton.

Which he did too goddamned often. Being back here, across the driveway from the house in which she used to live, wasn't going to help.

'Admiral,' Tom said, trying hard to focus, 'if the man I saw was the Merchant, he's had plastic surgery, changed his hair color. But he was the right height, had the right build. And his eyes . . . I know I'm failing to put this into words the right way, but I studied this man. Back in '96, for months he was the focus of my full attention. I memorized every photo in the task-force file. I spent literally weeks' worth of time staring at pictures of him, watching video footage, learning to think like him. Maybe I'm crazy but—'

'That right there is the problem, Lieutenant,' Crowley said. 'Maybe you *are* crazy. I've got a file of your recent psych evaluations on my desk, citing a list of side effects you could be experiencing from that knock on the head. I'm sure I don't need to remind you that the words *feelings of paranoia* are very high on that list.'

Tom ran his hand down his face. He had known this was coming. 'You don't need to remind me, sir. But I did see this man and I had to report what I saw.'

'What you thought you saw,' Crowley corrected him.

Tom wasn't going to argue with an admiral even though he disagreed. 'I guess I hoped you'd look into the matter discreetly – see if the Merchant's been mentioned in any NAVINTEL reports or, hell, in any Agency reports. I know you're connected, sir. I just want to find out if anyone else out there – someone who *hasn't* had doctors drilling holes in his skull in the past few months,' he added dryly, 'has seen this guy recently.'

'I'll put out feelers,' Crowley promised him. 'You just make damn sure you keep any other sightings of terrorists to yourself. If Larry Tucker hears about this, you'll have medical discharge papers in your hands so fast, you won't know what hit you.'

'I know, sir,' Tom said. 'Thank you, sir.'

'Get some rest, Tom,' Crowley said, and cut the connection.

Tom dropped the receiver into the cradle and pushed himself up and out of the chair. He had to stop, supporting himself on the table until the dizziness passed. Then, cursing his weakness, he went looking for Joe, to tell him he was home for the weekend – and that his kitchen needed a coat of paint.

TWO

'Kelly . . .'

Kelly froze, pulling her head out of the refrigerator to listen intently.

'Kelly . . .'

There it was again, barely audible. Her father's voice, sounding frail and weak. That is, more frail and weak than usual.

Kelly stuffed the quarter of a watermelon she was holding into the refrigerator and headed out of the kitchen at a run. She hurried down the long hallway that led to her father's bedroom.

The room was dim, the shades pulled down, blocking the bright early-afternoon sunshine. Kelly moved toward the bed, letting her eyes adjust, but Charles wasn't there.

She crossed toward the bathroom and . . .

Oh, God.

Her father was lying, facedown, on the tile floor.

Kelly knelt next to him, checking for his pulse. His skin was clammy and his eyelids fluttered at her touch, as if it were an effort to open his eyes.

''Bout time you got in here,' he wheezed. 'Usually check on me first thing in the morning. Figures today you'd decide to rearrange the cans of spinach in the kitchen cabinets.'

'I was putting away a few groceries,' she told him, her heart in her throat. Don't die now. Don't you dare die yet! She purposely made her voice sound matter of fact, knowing her upset would only annoy him. 'What happened?'

'Actually,' he said, 'I'm practicing for my audition for that commercial. You know – "I've fallen and I can't get up"?'

Kelly lost it. 'Daddy, for God's sake, will you *stop* being a *jerk* for just thirty seconds and tell me what happened? Did you slip? Are you having chest pains? Did you hit your head when you fell? Is anything broken?' Was it a stroke? If it was, he hadn't lost command of his speech center, that was for damn sure.

'If you must know,' Charles said almost primly, 'one minute I was on the commode, minding to my business, and the next I was on the floor. I don't think I hit my head. And it doesn't feel as if anything's broken – except for my pride.'

'We need to make arrangements to get a nurse to come in while I'm out,' Kelly said as she checked her father's eyes, checked his head. 'If I help you, do you think you can get up?'

'No,' Charles said. 'And no nurse. And don't you even *think* about calling the paramedics. If they come out here, they'll take me to the hospital, and I'm *not* going to the hospital. Remember Frank Elmer? He went in for minor chest pains – and he was dead the next day.'

'That was because he had a massive stroke.'

'My point exactly. Maybe he would have been fine if he hadn't gone to the hospital. I'll stay right here, thank you very much.'

His head looked fine. He must've somehow caught himself on the way down, thank God. She checked his arms and legs, and he managed to pull away from her irritably, even though he couldn't move far. 'Stop that.'

'I'm a doctor,' she reminded him. 'If you're going to refuse to go to the hospital when something like this happens—'

'*What* happened?' he asked. 'Big deal. I got dizzy, I still feel a little weak. That shouldn't surprise you. I'm a billion years old and I've got cancer. Something tells me that the bathroom floor and I aren't going to stay strangers.'

'If we had a nurse—'

'She would annoy me, too,' Charles finished. 'Get Joe,' he ordered. 'Between you, Joe, and me, we can get me back into bed.'

Kelly stood up, but she turned back to look down at him. Wasn't he even the tiniest bit glad that she was here? The question escaped before she could stop herself. 'Is that really what I do? Annoy you?'

Charles only briefly met her eyes. He opened his mouth to speak, but then stopped, shaking his head. 'Just get Joe and get back here, all right?'

Kelly hesitated, but her father closed his eyes, shutting the world – and her – out. God forbid they should ever actually *talk*. Trying hard not to let her hurt show – that would only make him more annoyed with her – she turned and hurried out of the bedroom, down the hall, back toward the kitchen.

She pushed her way out the kitchen door, letting the screen slap shut behind her. Joe's car was still in the driveway, thank God, and she hurried down toward the little cottage by the gate. 'Joe! Are you home?'

The shadow of a man was coming around the side of the cottage, and she changed her course, heading toward him, and . . .

It wasn't Joe.

It was *Tom* Paoletti, Joe's great-nephew.

It was a big, tall, full-grown, man-size Tom Paoletti, with far less hair and far more lines on his still remarkably handsome face. His shoulders were wider beneath his T-shirt, his face broader, but his eyes hadn't changed at all. Still hazel and still holding a hint of humor, keen intelligence, and an undercurrent of heat, his eyes belonged to the teenager she'd once known.

He stopped short at the sight of her, clearly as surprised to see her as she was to see him.

'Whoa,' he said. 'Kelly Ashton.' His voice was still the same – deep and warm and smooth, with only the slightest trace of blue-collar New England.

'Tom,' she said, feeling her world slipping, tilting out from under her feet. Remembering the dim glow from the dashboard of his car, exotically lighting his face as she'd . . . She pushed the thought away. 'I need to find Joe. My father's—'

She cut herself off, aware that this had happened before, an almost identical situation, back when she was in ninth grade and Tom was a soon-to-be-graduating senior.

She'd come home from school to find her father passed out in the kitchen, completely drunk. It was rare that it happened in the middle of the day, but there he was. Her mother had been due home any minute with some of the ladies from her tennis club.

Kelly had run looking for Joe, and had found Tom. Together they'd carried Charles to his bedroom and put him safely into bed.

'I don't know where Joe is,' Tom said now. 'I was looking for him, too. What's the problem? Can I help?'

'Yes. Thank you.' She quickly led him back to the main house. 'My father fell in the bathroom,' she told him. 'Even though he's lost a lot of weight, he's still too big for me to lift. I've been trying to convince him to get a nurse to come in, at least while I'm working, but he's so stubborn.'

God, listen to her. She was babbling. For the first time in sixteen years, her visit home had lined up with one of Tom's infrequent visits to Joe. Except she wasn't visiting. She was here to stay. Until her father died.

Tom followed her into the kitchen, into the house. 'Is your father sick?' he asked.

Kelly turned to face him, again struck by how much bigger and broader he'd become. 'My father's dying,' she told him quietly. 'Didn't Joe tell you?'

'Dying?' He was so surprised, it was obvious he *hadn't* known. 'Jesus, no. I mean, I haven't spoken to Joe in a while, but . . . Kelly, I'm so sorry. Is it . . . ?'

She nodded. 'Cancer. Lungs, liver, it's in his bones, his lymph nodes. You name it, it's metastasized there. They don't really know where it started or even exactly where it's all spread, but at this point it really doesn't matter. They're not about to do exploratory surgery on an eighty-year-old man. And chemo's out of the question, so . . .'

34

She had to clear her throat. Saying the words aloud always drove home the permanence of it all. One morning in the very near future, she was going to wake up to a world that didn't have her father in it. She wasn't ready for that yet. It was hard to imagine she would ever be.

Kelly led the way down the long corridor to Charles's room. 'Let's get him into bed, and let me make sure he's comfortable.' Maybe then they could talk. Maybe then she could sit down with Tom Paoletti, the subject of most of her teenage fantasies. And a few extremely adult ones as well.

She wondered if he'd say anything to her about that night. It was possible he didn't even remember.

'Hey, Mr Ashton,' Tom greeted her father as he went past her and into the bathroom. 'Looks like you could use a hand.'

'You remember Tom Paoletti, don't you, Dad?' Kelly asked.

As Tom crouched next to her father, he glanced up at Kelly. 'He okay to move? Nothing broken?'

'Yeah, I think he's all right. Nothing hurts more than usual, right, Dad?'

'Of course I remember Tom Paoletti,' Charles grumped, ignoring her other question completely. 'You still in the Navy?'

'Yes, sir,' Tom said. Even when he was in high school he'd been painstakingly polite. Always calling Charles *Mr Ashton* and *sir* despite the older man's obvious mistrust. 'I'm still with the SEAL teams.'

Back when Kelly was fifteen, she and Tom had struggled to carry Charles out of the kitchen and down the hall to his room. But in the past years, Charles had lost weight and Tom had gained muscles. He lifted her father seemingly effortlessly and carried him to the bed without her help at all.

'I'm the commanding officer of SEAL Team Sixteen.' Tom set the old man gently down.

'I know that,' Charles said. 'Joe talks about you all the time, you know. He's damn proud of you.'

'Can I get you anything?' Kelly asked her father, adjusting the sheets, trying desperately not to be jealous of Tom.

'I could use some eternal youth, if you've got any handy,' Charles said, at his charming, Cary Grant best for Tom's benefit. 'If not, maybe that Catherine Zeta-Jones, then I hear she goes for older men.'

Tom laughed, clearly charmed. Apparently, since he wasn't Charles's son, it was easier for him to forget the decades of slit-eyed anger and the half-slurred sarcasm.

But then he leaned closer to Charles, his smile fading. 'How's Joe taking this?' he asked the old man quietly.

Charles played dumb even though he clearly knew what Tom was referring to. He lifted one elegant white eyebrow. 'This?'

Kelly knew he was testing Tom, seeing if the younger man were brave enough to use the D-word in front of him.

Tom met her eyes across the bed and smiled slightly. It wasn't even a full smile, and just like that, she was fifteen again, her heart kicking into double time. God, he was even more good-looking than he'd been in his leather bomber jacket, astride his Harley, hair down past his shoulders.

These days, he wore his hair very short, as if he didn't give a damn about the fact that his hairline was receding. And it *was* thinning pretty drastically on top. But that was okay. Short hair looked good on him.

There was no doubt about it: in a few years, Tom Paoletti – the boy who'd worn a ponytail all through high school – was going to be the best-looking bald man in the world.

As Kelly watched, Tom turned and looked Charles directly in the eye. 'How's Joe taking the fact that his best friend is dying?' he asked.

Dying. There it was. The truth. Boldly, bravely tossed out among them, unveiled. So many visitors tried to push it away, but it would lurk, festering in the corner of the room, always present, putting everyone on edge.

'It's been hard for him,' Charles said, answering Tom with an equally rare honesty. 'Can you stay for a while? It would be good for Joe if you could stay for a while.'

What a liar. *Charles* hoped Tom would stay. Yet he would've preferred it if Kelly, his own daughter, packed her things and went back to Boston.

Tom made some vague sound that was neither yes nor no.

Like her father and despite her jealousy, Kelly, too, hoped that Tom would stay – but for entirely different reasons.

'When did your father grow a sense of humor?' Tom lowered himself into one of the chairs at the Ashtons' kitchen table.

Kelly was putting ice into a couple of tall glasses,

pouring them both some lemonade. She had her back to him, and even dressed as she was in wide-legged pants and a loose sleeveless silk shirt thing, Tom was hyperaware that the girl he'd drooled over had grown up into a woman who had a body to die for.

Now, as back then, she still dressed conservatively. Ever the good girl, she didn't flaunt what God had given her. But even now, as back then, nothing short of a heavy robe would've successfully hidden it. And even that was disputable.

'I think it reemerged when he stopped drinking,' she told him, bending over to put the lemonade back in the fridge.

Tom tried not to look at her ass, but damn, there it was, even more perfect than ever. As she turned to face him, he pulled his gaze away just in time, pretending to be fascinated by the clock in the microwave across the room. He looked up at her and smiled as she handed him the glass, as if he'd just noticed she was there. *Not staring at your body.*

She smiled back at him, no doubt still completely oblivious to the effect she had on him. He could remember her walking through the halls of the high school, totally clueless to the fact that heads turned wherever she went. At thirty-two, she still exuded that fresh innocence, that sweetness that made him want to protect her from the world – and from himself.

Mostly from himself.

'How's your mother?' he asked.

'Fine. Remarried. She's living near Baltimore.'

'Mine's in Florida. So when did you move back to Baldwin's Bridge?' he asked as she sat down at the table, across from him. 'Or is this just a visit?'

'I'm living half here, half in Boston, although the Boston half usually ends up being one night a week. My father refuses to let me hire a nurse, so I end up driving out here most nights. Thank God for Joe. He was the one who called me – about a week after they first found out it was cancer. If it were up to my father, I probably still wouldn't know.'

'How long has he got?' Tom quickly added. 'If you don't mind my asking so bluntly.'

Kelly shook her head. 'No, it's good,' she said. 'Really. Most people tiptoe around it.' She took a deep breath, as if bracing herself. 'He's got maybe a month before he'll need to start a morphine drip, before he's so weak he can't get out of bed. Right now he's handling the pain with pills. And he's got good days and bad days. On his good days, he's pretty mobile, although his hips give him trouble – that's a totally separate issue. An age thing, not related to the cancer. I got a walker; I just put it in his room. I'm hoping he'll just start using it. Maybe after today . . .'

For several long seconds, she faded out, staring into space, shoulders slumped, looking completely exhausted. But even tired, even sixteen years older, she had flawlessly beautiful skin. Sure, she had some lines – laughter lines around her eyes and mouth – but in Tom's opinion they made her look even more attractive, made her look less like a porcelain doll and more like a real, living, breathing woman. Her face was still heart shaped – maybe a little bit fuller, her cheekbones more pronounced.

Her blond hair was slightly darker, slightly longer than shoulder length. But as before, she wore it back from her face in a smooth, perfect ponytail. He'd once tried to get her to show him how she did that – his hair always lumped and bumped when he pulled it back.

He ran one hand over his buzz cut, aware of how different he must look to Kelly after all these years.

She looked exactly the same, with those ocean blue eyes a man could drown in. With those gracefully shaped, naturally red lips – soft lips he'd dreamed about kissing more times than he could count. Dreamed about, but never tasted.

Not even once.

Until that one crazy night he'd completely lost his mind.

Did she even remember?

For one moment, out on the driveway, when he'd turned the corner and was face-to-face with her for the first time in years, he'd sworn he saw an echo of that night in her eyes. But now . . .

It wasn't the kind of thing that could be brought up gracefully under normal circumstances, let alone the current situation. 'So, Kel, your dad's dying. But hey, remember that night in Joe's car, when we nearly . . .' Yeah. Real smooth.

And even if she did remember, it was probably something she wanted to forget. Still, he owed her an apology, and sooner or later he was going to have to bring it up.

As if realizing she wasn't alone, Kelly shook her head, and forced a smile. 'The commute's been tough,' she said. 'I'm sorry; I went in and back this morning already. I didn't mean to space out on you.'

'Living with your father can't be too much fun, either,' Tom countered. 'It never was a picnic for you, living here. And then to have to come back like this . . .'

She tried to make light of it. 'Yeah, right, that was me – the poor little rich girl.' She leaned forward. 'How are *you*, Tom? You look good.'

He let her change the subject. 'I'm doing all right.'

It was basically true – if he left out the part about the weeks spent in a coma, Rear Admiral Tucker's attempt to disband his SO squad, his thirty days of convalescent leave, and his spotting the Merchant at Logan Airport – a fact that made Admiral Crowley believe he was crazy. Sure, outside of *that*, he was peachy keen, thanks.

'Are you here by yourself?' she asked.

Was her question small talk or a polite fishing expedition? He answered honestly. 'Yeah, I'm still relentlessly single. I travel a lot and . . .' He shrugged and ran his hand again across his hair. 'Actually, I'm surprised you even recognized me, now that I'm hair challenged.'

She laughed. 'Aside from the hair, you look exactly the same. And I happen to like your hair short.'

'Thanks for lying, but—'

'I'm not lying.' She held his gaze, and something in his eyes – maybe another echo of that long ago night that Tom couldn't hide – made her suddenly look away, a slight flush on her cheeks.

She took a sip of lemonade, and he watched her delicate throat move as she swallowed, watched as she caught a drop from her lips with the very tip of her tongue.

Lemonade. His mainstay fantasy had always started with Kelly inviting him in for a glass of lemonade. One thing would lead to another, which invariably would lead to Kelly dropping to her knees

41

in front of him, usually right here in the kitchen of her father's house.

Kelly Ashton's fantasies no doubt featured a white dress, a veil, and a ceremony in church – the end result of a man getting down on *his* knees. She probably didn't even know what was implied by a woman doing it.

She was far too nice.

He stood up and set his empty glass in the sink. 'I should go find Joe,' he said. 'He doesn't even know I'm in town.' Coward. He should face her, right now, and apologize.

'How long will you be home?' Kelly asked.

Home. God, what a word. 'I don't know,' he admitted.

'If you've got the time,' she said, 'I know my father would love to see you when he's feeling a little better. Maybe you and Joe could come over for dinner – not necessarily tonight. I'm sure you want to spend tonight catching up. I know you're also probably planning to visit your sister, so tomorrow night's probably not good, either . . .'

'I was going to stay only until the weekend, but actually . . .' Once he admitted it, there'd be no turning back. Still, with Charles Ashton dying, how could he just desert Joe? So he said it. 'I've got thirty days.'

'Thirty!' Kelly stood, too, her face brightening. 'Oh, my God, Tom, it would be great if you could stay! You know, this thing for the Fifty-fifth is next week and I'm sure Joe would love—'

'Whoa. Wait. I *don't* know. What thing?'

'The celebration,' she said as if that explained everything. She laughed at the look on his face. 'Didn't

42

you see the decorations they've been putting up all over town?'

'Flags,' he remembered. 'I thought they were left over from the Fourth.'

'No, it's for this celebration thing,' she said. 'It's going to be a big deal – Senators Kennedy and Kerry are both coming for the opening ceremony. It's a four-day reunion of the Fighting Fifty-fifth. Hundreds of family members – descendants of the men who served with the Fifty-fifth in Europe – as well as the surviving soldiers are coming from all over the country. I think I read in the paper that there's fewer than a hundred of the men still alive. My father's one of them.'

'I knew your dad was in the Second World War.' Tom leaned back against the counter, watching her. He'd said he was leaving, but he couldn't seem to move any closer to the door. 'That's where he met Joe. In France.'

'You're going to love this,' she said, 'unless you already know, in which case I'm going to have to hit you for not telling me. But Joe's getting a special seat onstage at the celebration ceremony next Tuesday.'

'But he wasn't in the Fifty-fifth, he wasn't even Army.' It didn't make sense. 'He was Air Force – a rear-turret gunner on a reconnaissance plane.' Getting Joe to talk about it had been like pulling teeth and Tom had eventually given up. He knew far more about his own grandfather, Joe's brother, a man Tom had never met because he'd died at Anzio.

'Joe was shot down over France in '42,' Kelly told him.

Jesus, Joe hadn't told him that. His entire discussion with Tom of what he'd done in World War II was limited to a single sentence: 'I served in Europe.' Damn.

'I'm not sure exactly what he did – Dad doesn't talk about the war much, either – but it had *something* to do with the Fifty-fifth, something Joe ended up getting a Medal of Honor for.'

Tom nearly fell over, and for the first time in months his dizziness wasn't from his head injury. 'Holy shit, Joe's got a Medal of Honor? Excuse my language – I'm floored.' He had to laugh. 'You'd think he might've shown it to me at least *once*. I mean, forget about putting it on display in the living room . . .'

'The celebration starts August 15th, the anniversary of V-J Day, the official end of the war,' Kelly told him. 'The story I heard – through the newspaper, of course, God forbid either Dad or Joe tell me directly – is that on August 15, 1945, after the war was finally over, the men from the Fighting Fifty-fifth made a pact to meet fifty-five years later, in the year 2000. I think it probably seemed cosmic, the way the numbers added up. And 2000 must've seemed so far away back then. It truly was the future, you know? Yet there they were, part of millions of Allied troops who'd made the world safe for that future.

'They chose to meet in Baldwin's Bridge, because for many of them this was where it all started. Did you know there was an army training center here during the Second World War?'

Tom shook his head.

'This was where those men first came, where the Fifty-fifth was formed. The base was out where they built that new Super Stop & Shop about five years ago. There was a fire there just after the war, and they tore down the remaining buildings in 1950. By the time we were in high school, there were just woods out there.'

'I didn't know any of that,' Tom admitted.

'Joe and Dad still aren't talking about it, but they went to a celebration planning committee meeting last week,' she told him. 'You ready to hear something weird?'

He had to laugh. 'Like none of this is weird enough?'

Kelly smiled, too, but wanly. 'Maybe you *won't* think this is strange, but I did. Last week, when they came back from that meeting, they were arguing furiously. And Joe's been walking around in a snit ever since.'

'*Joe?*' Tom couldn't believe it. Joe had worked as the Ashtons' groundskeeper for nearly sixty years – ever since the two men had returned from the War. *Charles* was the snit master. He was quick tempered and opinionated. He'd spent a good portion of the past six decades in a snit. Tom had to smile. *Snit* was a good word for it.

'I was working on my computer,' Kelly told him, 'and I heard shouting, so I went out to see what was going on. Joe was really upset. I heard only a little of what he was saying – something about running out of time. He stopped as soon as he saw me. My dad stomped into the house, and no matter what I said, I couldn't get either of them to tell me what was wrong.'

Joe upset for an entire week. Tom couldn't believe it. His great-uncle Joe may have been quick to both laugh and cry, unafraid to show his emotions, but he'd always managed to keep his temper carefully in control. He was the king of patience, of reason, of careful, measured thought. Good thing, since he'd spent most of his life dealing first with Charles Ashton, and then with young Tom.

'Maybe I can get him to talk about it,' he said doubtfully. 'If I ever find him.'

'Tom! Tommy? Is that your bag in my kitchen?'

Tom smiled at Kelly. 'Looks like he found me.'

She smiled back at him. 'Tom, if it's really possible, stay for as long as you can,' she said. 'We could all use your company.'

No way could he leave, knowing that Charles was dying, knowing that Joe – a man who'd always been there for Tom – could probably use his support.

And with Kelly Ashton standing there, smiling at him, the idea of staying in Baldwin's Bridge for the full thirty days didn't seem so awful.

What could he say to her, except 'Yeah, I will.'

Still, when he went out the back door to meet Joe in the driveway, all he could wonder was what the hell he'd gotten himself into now.

Three

Mallory Paoletti paced the tiny living room, listening to her mother bitch about all the shit that was wrong in her life. No money, another crappy, demeaning cleaning job, this good-for-nothing kid who wasn't even going to college next year.

Except, oh, excuse me, Angela dearest, but you wanna rewind there to complaint A – no money? If there wasn't enough money to replace the effing water heater and pay the G.D. electric bill, how the *hell* was there going to be enough money for Mallory to go to college?

Her mother's brother, Tom, sat on the sofa, patiently hearing Angela out. But when Mallory looked over, he was watching *her*. He crossed his eyes just for a second. Just long enough for Mallory to know that he was still okay. He was still a cool guy, still on her side, despite the fact that he was losing his hair, big time.

Her mother was finally done. Or at least she made the mistake of pausing for breath. And Tom, as smart as he was cool, quickly took the floor.

'What about the Navy?' he asked, looking directly at Mal.

Her mother laughed breathlessly and lit another cigarette. 'Oh, that's a good one, Tommy. Can you really picture Mallory—'

'I wasn't asking you, Ang,' he said, blowing right over her. 'I was asking Mal. What do you want do with your life, kid? What do you like to do? If you want, I'll go down to the recruiter's office with you. It doesn't have to be the Navy. Between you, me, and the recruiting officer, we can match you up with the branch of the service that'll put you exactly where you want to be. We can negotiate four years of college for you. They like their recruits – even enlisted – to get an education.'

'Mallory wants to get herself pierced and tattooed,' Angela said. 'That's about all she wants to do these days. I know you probably don't believe it, Tommy, but beneath that awful cut and dye job, Mallory is a very pretty girl. She looks a lot like I did when I was eighteen.'

And *that* was a load of crap. Mallory was about six inches taller than her mother and built like an Amazon warrior, complete with size D cups, while Angela had been – and still was – model-slender and prettily petite. Willowy, it was called in books. Thirty-four years old, and her mother could go without a bra. Mallory hadn't had that option since fourth grade.

Tom was still looking at her, giving her that little half smile she remembered so well from his other trips home. *Take me with you*, she'd cried when she was eleven or twelve, when he'd blasted into town for a weekend or, worse, a too-short day.

He had been proof that a Paoletti could shake free from the shackles of this puritanical, narrow-minded, pointy-assed town. But nowadays, Tom was proof only of her own pathetic failings. Mal was more like her mother than her uncle. She was weighed down by all the bad shit, chain-smoking Winstons even though they couldn't find the money to buy milk, unable to break free.

'Think about it,' he told Mallory now. 'I'm going to be around for a while. Probably till the end of the month.'

She dropped her perpetually bored sneer, nearly dropped her own cigarette. 'Holy shit.' He was staying that long?

'Watch your mouth,' Angela murmured.

Tom was going to be in town for weeks. At one time, that news would've made Mallory ecstatic. Now it only made her more depressed. When it was just her and Angela hanging around the house, Mal didn't feel like such a loser. At least *she* had never spent her entire paycheck betting on the dogs at Wonderland. But with Tom in town as contrast, it was obvious she and her mother were in the same subset. Double losers. A mismatched pair of misfits. It was just a matter of time before she started buying lottery tickets with her last few bucks, just like Angela.

Tom stood up. 'Let me take a look at the water heater,' he said. 'If it needs to be replaced, I'll replace it myself. I mean, as long as I'm in town, I might as well do the work.'

That was a good idea. If he simply gave Angela a check, the money would be spent on anything *but* the water heater. She'd color her hair or get her nails done and buy a new dress, betting that the ridiculous makeover would help her snag a rich husband from the crowd down at the fancy-schmancy four-star

Baldwin's Bridge Hotel. She'd take the gamble, hoping the payoff would bring the end to all their money troubles.

Yeah, right.

Oddly enough, the times Angela did okay were when she had just enough money to scrape by. It was the large sums of money that got her dreaming, and it wasn't long until those dreams shattered, spiraling them down into the depths.

No doubt Tom had figured that out, too.

'It's in the basement.' Angela opened the door and led the way down the creaky stairs into the musty dank.

But Tom didn't follow, not right away. 'I'm right behind you,' he called to his sister, then turned back to Mallory, pulling a fold of bills from the pocket of his cargo shorts. 'Money for groceries.' He took out several hundred dollars.

But before he gave it to her, he took the cigarette out of her mouth and stabbed it out in an overflowing ashtray.

'Guess what,' he said. 'You're quitting smoking. As of today. When you join the Navy, first thing you'll do is get in shape. And trust me, it'll be easier if you're not a smoker.'

She sucked on her front tooth, giving him her best you-bore-me-completely look. 'You're nuts if you think I'm actually going to *volunteer* to let assholes like you order me around.'

He laughed, grabbed her arm, and gave her a zerbert on the inside of her elbow, the way he might've done when she was seven. It tickled and the farting noises were so realistic she couldn't keep from laughing.

'You're such a jerk,' she told him.

He slapped the money into her hand. 'It's a chance to get out of here,' he said, suddenly serious. 'And to do it completely on your own.'

To her horror, her eyes filled with tears. God, she wanted to escape, sometimes more than anything.

'Tommy, I'm standing down here in the dark!'

He turned away, pretending not to notice that Mallory was milliseconds from bursting into tears, giving her the space he thought she needed rather than pulling her into his arms.

God, she wished *some*one would hold her like she was five years old again and tell her everything was going to be okay. It was a lie, but it had always been a good lie, and for a minute, even for just a few seconds, she would feel safe.

'Think about it,' he said again, heading down the stairs.

Right. Mallory was going to do nothing but. Except thinking wouldn't bring her any closer to doing. Because if she left, if she wasn't around to buy groceries and sometimes even pay the rent with the money from her stupid paychecks from the stupid Ice Cream Shoppe, what would happen to her mother?

Mallory pushed her way out the door, angry as hell at the world. And angry at Tom for trying to give her hope when it was so effing obvious that everything sucked, and that nothing would change.

David Sullivan sat on a bench by the Ferris wheel, watching as most of the college-aged crowd of Baldwin's Bridge walked by.

He had his sketch pad and pencils with him, but despite the freak-show feel of the small-town church carnival at this hour of night, he hadn't yet taken them out of his backpack.

It was after ten, and he worked the early-morning shift at the hotel restaurant. He had to be dressed and ready to wait tables at 4:30 A.M. The room filled remarkably considering the hour. Golfers and sport fishermen. Leathery tan and rich, with big laughs and bigger wallets.

He had to move fast to get everyone on their way to the golf courses and the marina on time. Between 5:15 and 6:30, there was a bit of a lull, with a few golfers with slightly later tee times clogging their arteries with generous servings of steak and eggs. At 6:30, the women would appear, wearing tennis whites, sweaters tied around their necks. After 8:00, the sunbathers came and ordered coffee and toast. By 10:30 breakfast would be over. He would punch out, done for the day, having earned a small fortune in tips to add to his publishing fund. Another fifteen weeks, he'd have enough money saved, and *Nightshade* could become a reality. Problem was, there were only four more weeks before he had to be back at college.

He was thinking about getting a second job, maybe working more shifts, but he was already exhausted.

Almost every day he would vow to take a nap in the afternoon, but invariably something would catch his attention, and he'd start drawing. Before he knew it, it would be closing in on midnight again, and he'd be facing another very short four hours of sleep.

David stood, ready to be smart for once and head

for his summer rental – a studio apartment on the third floor of a house two blocks from the hotel – when he saw her.

He had to be honest with himself, it was her body that first caught his eye. She was wearing one of those little nothing, clingy, thin-strapped tank tops. It was black, and so was the bra she wore underneath, its straps clearly visible.

In short, she was stacked.

She was tall, with shoulders that looked as if she could consider playing pro football without the pads. The muscles in her arms were well-defined, and he would've guessed she was a weight lifter – except for the fact that she didn't have muscular pecs. Instead, she had real breasts.

And *that* was the understatement of the new millennium.

She had a jeans jacket tied by the sleeves around her waist. It helped gravity drag her baggy pants even lower on her hips, leaving a wide gap between her waistband and the bottom edge of her shirt. That gap revealed the soft smoothness of her stomach, and the fact that her belly button was pierced. The streetlight overhead made the bluish stone she was wearing sparkle.

Her face was hidden by a short, purposely ragged mess of dark black hair. Her chin and mouth – the only features he could see – were pixieish, her chin pointed and her lips delicate in direct contrast to her lush figure.

As David watched her from the other side of the church parking lot, she stopped walking and lit a cigarette, her movements quick, angry. She took a drag, then, still angrily, impatiently, she threw the cigarette down and moved swiftly away.

He shouldered his backpack, determined to go home, when she suddenly spun around. She went back to the cigarette, but it had rolled into a puddle.

'Shit,' he heard her say, her voice exactly as he'd imagined it – slightly husky, low pitched. Sexy.

She fumbled in her pockets, took out another cigarette, and lit it.

As she did, she turned slightly, lifting her head to look up at the Ferris wheel. Her hair fell back and the overhead street lamp lit her face.

And David stopped breathing.

It was the face he'd been looking for.

She was exotically pretty, with enormous eyes and wide cheekbones that tapered quickly down to that extremely pointed, delicate chin and almost tiny, doll-like nose and mouth. Her skin was pale, which made her dark eyebrows stand out. She looked otherworldly, particularly with the rows of glittering piercings in her ears.

As he watched, she took another long drag on the cigarette, and then threw it on the ground and crushed it with her clunky-heeled boot.

Swearing like a sailor, she stomped away, only to stop several feet away and light yet another cigarette.

Completely intrigued, all thoughts of a good night's sleep forgotten, David shifted the strap of his pack higher on his shoulder and followed her deeper into the carnival grounds.

Kelly was sitting in the backyard, on the tree swing, when the lights went on in Joe's cottage.

Tom was home.

Joe and Charles were still out at their weekly card game. Charles had awakened and had actually come into the kitchen at dinnertime, leaning heavily on the metal walker Kelly had put in his room for him.

She'd been preparing him a tray when he'd appeared. Chicken broth, a salad she knew he wouldn't touch, a power shake, and an array of his favorite, enticing desserts. He didn't say a word about the walker, and she clamped her mouth tightly shut and didn't mention it either.

He'd simply taken a few obligatory sips of the power shake she'd made him. Then he'd headed out toward the driveway, mumbling about the card game, grumbling something about how *some*one had to keep track of Joe, make sure he didn't go shooting off his damn fool mouth.

Kelly had seen no point in trying to talk Charles out of leaving. Even if lying at home in bed would extend his life by a minute fraction, at this point an extra week of staring at his bedroom ceiling didn't seem worth it. The man was going to die. He might as well do exactly what he wanted for as long as he possibly could.

As if Kelly could ever talk her father out of doing exactly what he wanted.

Besides, she had her pager on, and Joe had her number.

They'd left in the station wagon, and Tom had gone with them, getting a ride to his sister Angela's house.

Tom.

Kelly gazed at the lights blazing from the windows of Joe's cottage – lights Tom had turned on.

What was it about Tom Paoletti that got under her skin?

Just seeing him today had done something to her. It had woken her up, brought her back to life. The evening air smelled sweeter, the sounds of the crickets louder, brighter. The stars that were starting to twinkle through the hazy clouds overhead seemed close enough to reach out and touch.

Kelly had to laugh at the sheer poetry of it all – particularly since everything she was feeling could be traced to one extremely basic and base need.

Sex.

Fifteen minutes alone in a room with Tom Paoletti, and she couldn't keep herself from thinking about sex. One small smile from the man, and she was fifteen years old all over again, discovering the true meaning of the word *lust* as she sneaked a peek at his incredible body while he worked in the yard.

But the man had the power to move her in a way that was more than merely sexual. Just this afternoon, as she'd watched from the kitchen window, he'd greeted his great-uncle out on the driveway with an unabashedly unembarrassed embrace. The two men, young and old, had held each other tightly for a good long time.

Maybe it was their Italian heritage that set them apart from the cold-as-ice Ashtons, but Kelly couldn't remember ever seeing her father wrap his arms around *any*one – male or female – in such a public and emotional display of affection.

Worst of all, she couldn't remember the last time *she'd* greeted someone with a warm embrace. Even when she was married, she hadn't hugged or kissed

Gary in public. Even in private, unless they were in bed, he'd been aloof. He'd been a lot like her father – filled with chilly Beacon Hill propriety.

The lights went on in an upstairs window of the cottage, in the room that had been Tom's throughout his years of high school. Kelly well knew which windows were his. She'd spent most of those same years fascinated by him – that great-nephew of Joe's who came to live with him because he couldn't get along with his stepfather and because his mother couldn't control him. That wild Paoletti kid with his hair down his back and his penchant for getting all the teachers and administrators in school steaming mad at him. Kelly had been aware of his presence in Joe's little house down by the gate with every fiber of her being.

She looked up into the tree branches above her, at the tree house Joe had built with her the summer she'd turned ten. She'd spent many an evening up in her hideaway, dreaming about Tom Paoletti.

And the fact that from her tree house she had an unobstructed view into Tom's bedroom window had certainly helped solidify those fantasies. She'd seen Tom in only his underwear more times than he could imagine. And yes, once or twice she'd even seen him naked, too.

Kelly looked into the tree again. She hadn't gone up there in years. But she didn't need to climb a tree to know that Tom would still look beyond hot without a stitch of clothing on.

Tom Paoletti.

She could remember the magical day she'd spent with him the summer after freshman year as if it were yesterday. The day – and the night. Through the years, she'd followed the news Joe had shared with her about Tom. And yeah, maybe she'd paid particular attention to the fact that he'd never gotten married, that he'd never even so much as brought a woman home with him, that he always described all his many brief relationships to Joe as 'nothing special.'

He was, after all, Tom Paoletti. And as nice and kind as he'd once been to her, as many medals and honors and awards he won in the Navy, he still had a wild streak that ran deep.

Back in high school, she'd seen him out along the road by the beach more times than she could count, racing past on his Harley, the wind whipping his hair out behind him. She wanted to feel that exhilaration, taste that kind of speed. She wanted to fly like that with him.

She'd ridden on the back of his motorcycle just once. And she'd all but begged him to take her flying along that beach road. But he'd just laughed and kept his speed well beneath the posted limit.

Almost seventeen years had passed since then. And Kelly *still* wanted to fly with him.

She had to smile at the tackiness of that particular euphemism. Tom was home for thirty days – which would be just long enough for a perfect summer fling. At least she thought it would be. She didn't have a whole lot of experience in that area.

She'd never spent time with a man for purely selfish reasons. Every relationship she'd ever had had been fraught with meaning and potential, and damn near quivering with importance. Just once, *just once*, she wanted to be with someone who didn't give a damn about the fact that she'd graduated from Harvard

Medical School at the top of her class. Just once she wanted to date a man without wondering how that growing relationship would further his – or her – medical career. Just once she wanted to be with someone a little wild, a little crazy, a little rough. Someone who wasn't afraid of adrenaline rushes. Someone who would soul-kiss her on the beach and not give a damn who was watching. Someone who liked going dangerously fast. Someone like Tom Paoletti.

Someone *exactly* like Tom Paoletti.

Life was too short. Kelly was more aware of that now than ever, with her father's impending death looming over them. She needed to make some changes, take some chances with her own life.

And what better place to start than with Tom Paoletti?

She wanted comforting arms to hold her when the night got a little too long and dark. But she didn't want long term or heavy or complicated. She wanted simple, friendly sex, the likes of which she *knew* Tom could give her.

The fact that Tom was leaving in thirty days was a good thing. It set an end date to the affair – a boundary that would remind her constantly that she couldn't let herself love him more than just a little. She liked the idea of going in with her eyes wide open, with the relationship – and its ending – clearly defined right from the start.

And as for Tom, he'd probably jump at the chance for a no-strings, short-term fling. She knew he was attracted to her. At least, she *thought* he was attracted to her. Except for the fact that he'd turned her down before . . .

But that was then, this was now. And the new, bold, chance-taking Kelly Ashton was going to take hold of this opportunity with both hands.

She'd ask him out. To dinner. Just the two of them.

The worst that could happen was he could turn her down, right?

Oh, God, what would she do if he turned her down?

But guys did this all the time. They asked women out, facing the uncertainty and potential rejection.

How hard could it be?

Kelly headed back inside, knowing that if she were a man, she'd be turning out the light in her monk's cell in the monastery right about now.

Would she get the nerve to ask him? She didn't know.

The only thing she knew for certain was that this was going to be a summer she was going to remember for the rest of her life.

Four

Tom showered and turned on ESPN in an attempt to rid himself of his relentless headache. He was reaching into the refrigerator for a beer when he heard voices out on the driveway.

Joe and Charles were back.

It was earlier than Tom had expected. In the past, their card games had been notorious for going on late into the night.

Of course, in the past, Charles hadn't been dying of cancer.

'Have I ever asked you for anything?' he was saying angrily now, his voice reedy and thin, cutting through the quiet of the night. 'Have I?'

Joe's voice was softer, but no less intense. 'Yes! All those years I kept silent . . . ? You think I wanted that medal that's up in the attic? You think I don't think about her every time I walk past that attic door?'

Holy shit. Charles and Joe were arguing. Joe, who barely spoke in anything longer than a monosyllable, who never lost his temper, was spitting mad and speaking in paragraphs.

Tom put his beer down on the kitchen counter and pushed open the screen door, stepping out onto the back steps. The outside air was heavy with humidity, and he had to grip the railing as a wave of dizziness hit him. Dammit, when was this going to let up?

The two old men still sat in Joe's car, but the windows were open wide and their voices carried.

'Maybe you think I'm like you – that I've forgotten,' Joe continued hotly. 'Well, I haven't! I don't take a single breath without remembering!'

Charles looked apoplectic. His face was red and he was shaking with rage. 'How dare you suggest I—'

'It's time,' Joe shouted over him. 'Jenny's gone – the truth can't hurt her anymore. But you're the one who's afraid of that truth, aren't you? It never really had anything to do with your wife.'

Charles started to cough, a dry, racking hack that shook his body. 'Damn you,' he rasped between coughs. 'God *damn* you! I want you out of here! You're fired, you son of a bitch!'

'Hey, hey, guys . . .' As Tom moved toward the car, he realized that Kelly had come out of the main house. She approached from the other side, wheeling some kind of tank behind her. Oxygen.

'Stop this!' she said sharply. 'Right this minute! Both of you!'

Joe got out of the car, slamming the door shut. 'You can't fire me, you pompous, selfish bastard, because I *quit*!'

'Whoa,' Tom said, blocking Joe's path to the cottage. 'Everyone take a deep breath and count to ten. Let's rewind that last bit. I know you both didn't mean any of it. Let's just calm it down a little, okay?'

Kelly gave some kind of inhaler to her father. After he took a hit of the medicine, she helped affix a face mask to him, adjusting the tank, trying to make it easier for the old man to breathe. As his breathing grew less labored, she looked at Tom over the top of the car, shaking her head slightly, her eyes wide. This was as much a mystery to her as it was to him.

Her eyes widened even farther as she saw him standing there in – oh, damn – only his boxers.

She'd changed, too – into a pair of running shorts and a sports bra, sneakers on her feet. From the sheen of perspiration on her skin, it was obvious that she'd been interrupted in the middle of a workout.

He tried not to look at her trim, lithe body, but all that smooth skin was distracting as hell. Of course, he was one to talk, half naked as he was. But with Charles having some kind of attack and Joe quivering with anger, this wasn't the best time to go inside to find himself a pair of shorts and a T-shirt.

'What's this about?' he asked, shifting slightly left so that Joe couldn't go around him and escape into the house.

Charles yanked the mask away from his face. 'Seven, eight, nine, ten,' he rasped. 'You're *still* fired!'

'Dad!' Kelly said in exasperation as he started coughing again. She put the mask back on him, rolling her eyes at Tom.

He turned to his uncle, bracing himself against the side of the car as another wave of dizziness hit him. *Shit.* All this circus sideshow needed was for him to hit the deck face first. 'What's going on?'

Charles pulled his mask off again. 'You want to know what's going on? I'll tell you what's going on.

Judas here has agreed to give an interview with some stupid fool who's writing some stupid book about the Fighting Fifty-fifth.' He started coughing again and when Kelly reached for his mask, he pulled it away from her with a quelling look, putting it up over his mouth and nose himself.

'His name is Kurt Kaufman,' Joe said tightly, crossing around the back of the station wagon so that he could address Charles directly without having to peer through the interior of the car. 'And he's a professor of history at Boston College, so *stupid* probably doesn't apply, either to him *or* to his book.'

Charles pulled his mask away. 'Even better – he's some Kraut. What gives him the right—'

'His grandfather served beside you in the Fifty-fifth,' Joe told him. 'He died fighting the Nazis in the hedgerows outside of Normandy. He has every right.'

Charles put his mask back on with a *humph*, losing the point to Joe most ungraciously.

Tom followed Joe more slowly, keeping one hand on the car like a baby who could walk only while holding on to furniture.

He'd never seen Joe so angry before. The few times Joe had lost his temper had been quick explosions – short flashes that were over almost before they'd started. It had been nothing like this deeply burning, shaking fury.

'If he's writing about the Fifty-fifth,' Tom asked him, rubbing his forehead as a sharp pain suddenly grabbed him right behind his left eye, 'why does he want to talk to you? I've seen that picture Mom had of you with my grandfather after you enlisted. You were both in Air Force uniforms.'

Kelly was still crouched next to her father, but she was looking up at him, frowning slightly. 'Tom, are you all right?'

Great. He probably looked as shitty as he felt.

Aside from the fact that he had thirty short days to make this frigging dizziness and these damned headaches disappear for good, aside from the fact that his career was on the line and that the one relative he'd always counted on to be a port in a storm was crumbling with his own pain and uncertainty, aside from the fact that seeing Kelly again made him want her as badly and as foolishly as he'd wanted her all those years ago, aside from the fact that her father was dying – a man he'd never quite respected or admired, but that he'd cared for nonetheless . . .

Aside from all that, yeah, he was all right.

'I'm tired, I've got a headache, I'm standing here in my underwear, and I'm confused.' Tom let his exasperation show. 'I want to know what the hell's going on. Why does this writer want to talk to an Air Force veteran about the Fifty-fifth?'

Joe looked from Tom to Charles and shook his head. 'I'm sorry,' he said stiffly. 'This is private—'

'Like hell it is,' Charles snapped. 'You're the one wants to talk to this Kaufman. How private is that?' He glared at Tom. 'Kaufman wants to talk because Joe's the "Hero of the Fifty-fifth." The "Hero of Baldwin's Bridge." You know that statue by the marina? The one that lists the men from town who died in the war?'

Tom knew the statue well. He'd gazed at those long lists of names many times, thinking the stonecutter had screwed up by leaving the e and s off the word *hero*, thinking it should have read 'The *Heroes* of Baldwin's Bridge.'

He could feel Kelly watching him, and he forced himself to stand a little straighter.

Charles had paused to press the oxygen mask to his face, breathing deeply, but he now went on. 'Go down there and look at the face. That's Joe's face on that statue. He wouldn't let 'em put his name on it, but it's him. In France, a few weeks after the Normandy Invasion, he delivered information about a German counteroffensive that would have slaughtered thousands of men in the Fifty-fifth Division. Because of Joe, they were ready for 'em.'

The Hero of Baldwin's Bridge. Unassuming, quiet Joe Paoletti who loved his flowers was *the* frigging Hero of Baldwin's Bridge.

'Gee,' Tom said, turning to look at his uncle. 'How come you never told me? Knowing that might've come in handy back in high school, when I was sent to the dean's office for the fiftieth time.'

He was only half joking. God knows it would've helped his head, helped his low-as-shit self-esteem as he was growing up, to know that a Paoletti, a fucking *Paoletti*, wore not just the title 'hero' but '*the* hero.'

Joe just snorted. But he wouldn't meet Tom's eyes.

'The Nazis knew the terrain and planned to use it to cut off part of the Fifty-fifth,' Charles continued, 'isolate them from the rest of the Allied forces. The fighting was fierce – there would have been no prisoners taken.' He looked up at Kelly and Tom. 'Because of what Joe did, thousands of men from the Fifty-fifth were given a fighting chance.'

'Because of what *I* did,' Joe scoffed. 'That's not the

way it happened and you know it! I was wounded – I couldn't even walk. Without you and—'

'I was just along for the ride, and *you* know it,' Charles countered hotly, starting to cough again.

'Use that oxygen,' Kelly said sternly, 'or I *will* take you to the hospital.'

Charles had clamped the mask over his nose and mouth, but he started to pull it off as Joe countered with 'You were never just along for the ride. You wanted people to think you were—'

'Okay.' Tom held up his hand. He was starting to feel like a bad cross between a traffic cop and a referee. The sensation that the world was tilting was subsiding, leaving him to deal only with the pounding in his head. 'Wait a minute. I'm still confused.' He fixed Joe with his harshest commanding-officer gaze. 'In addition to this hero business, which is complete news to me, I find out a few hours ago – from Kelly, I might add – that you were shot down over France in 1942. But the Allied invasion didn't take place until the summer of 1944. What were you doing behind enemy lines in '42? Did you get shot down *twice*? Or did she have the date wrong?'

'No.' Figured Joe would pick now to go back into his monosyllabic routine.

'Yeah. See?' Charles said. 'You're all ready to start telling stories about *me*, but when it comes to yourself . . .' He glared up at Tom. 'He was shot down in '42. He was badly wounded – as is often the case when your airplane falls out of the sky like a brick. Lucky for him, he was found by the French Resistance instead of the Nazis. As a result, he was taken to a safe house instead of a concentration camp – you *did* know that it wasn't unheard of for the Nazis to send American prisoners of war to places like Auschwitz, didn't you? Geneva convention be damned.'

Joe shook his head. 'They don't want to hear this. *I* don't want to hear this.'

'What do you think this Kaufman's going to ask you about?' Charles asked him. 'It's not going to be questions about protecting your roses from early frost!'

'Dad,' Kelly said. 'You're both so upset. Maybe we should—'

'The Resistance found him and hid him and nursed him back to health,' Charles interrupted her. 'And spending time with—'

'Don't,' Joe said sharply.

'*Them*,' Charles said pointedly, 'the freedom fighters, Joe discovered his command of both Italian and French, combined with forged papers and his New York City *cajones*, gave him the edge he needed to wander the French countryside and target German military sites for Air Force bombing raids. It was far more effective than the airborne reconnaissance he'd originally been part of. In fact, he did such a good job, he was invited to stay in occupied France for the remainder of the war – to help provide information for the planned Allied invasion.' Charles took a hit from his oxygen tank. 'Joe started out Air Force, but he ended the war as OSS.'

Tom looked at his uncle. OSS. He'd always admired and respected his uncle, mostly for the kindness and respect he'd shown to Tom when no one else, including his own mother, had wanted anything to do with him. But he'd always been a little amused by Joe's love of his garden, and he'd imagined that Joe had gone through the war as a desk clerk or a cook or . . . Jesus, anything but OSS.

'My God, Joe,' Kelly said softly. 'You were a spy in Nazi-occupied France for two *years*?'

Tom himself had been on some tough missions, some extremely dangerous and covert missions that had required him to go deep undercover and walk among the enemy. He'd sat in cafés and had dinner surrounded by men and women who would have put a bullet in his brain had they known who and what he was.

But he hadn't done it straight for two frigging *years*. *Cajones*, indeed.

'It's over,' Joe said. 'It's done.'

'But you would do it again if you had to,' Charles coughed.

Joe fixed his friend with a grim stare. 'So would you.'

The two old men glared at each other. Neither of them blinked, neither of them moved until a cough racked Charles.

'You're going to do this interview, aren't you?' Charles gasped.

'I think so.'

Charles angrily covered his face with the mask, dragging in as much pure oxygen as he could. 'It doesn't matter anymore,' he coughed. 'Like you said – it's over. It's done. What's the use?' He coughed so hard his eyes watered and ran, and his lips were flecked with blood.

Kelly looked at Tom. 'I think I better get him inside. Would you mind? . . .'

'Good idea.' Tom picked up Charles, making sure

Kelly had the oxygen tank before he started toward the house.

But Charles wasn't done with Joe. He lifted his head to look over Tom's shoulder, pointing a shaking hand at his oldest friend accusingly. 'You hated me from the moment you first set eyes on me!'

Joe stood in the driveway, his heart aching, watching as Tommy and Kelly carried Charles into the main house.

The first time he'd seen Charles, nearly six decades ago, he was being carried then, too.

It was funny. Out of all the people Joe had met in his long life, Charles Ashton truly hated being helpless more than anyone.

Yet there he'd been, wounded and helpless, carried into the sanctuary of Cybele's house by Henri and Jean-Claude, bringing danger to them all merely with his presence.

He was badly injured and fading in and out of consciousness, his aristocratically handsome face pale and drawn with pain, his blond hair matted with blood and mud. A fallen prince. He'd needed Cybele's medical skills, so he'd been brought all the way here, from the front line, at great risk to them all.

If the Germans found him here, they would take him prisoner and hang them for harboring him.

Yet it was not hatred that had filled Joe's heart at that first sight of him, but rather hope.

The Americans had landed in France. The Allied invasion, which he himself had worked so hard for, had come about as planned.

It wouldn't be long before the fighting surged past them, and the small city of Ste.-Hélène was free from Nazi rule. It wouldn't be long until the few remaining Jewish families, hidden around the town in houses like Cybele's, could step out into the sunlight.

'Put him on the table,' Cybele commanded in rapid-fire French, tying her long, dark hair back from her face before she quickly washed in the kitchen basin. 'I need hot water. Marie, a fire. Pietra, bandages and soap. Get that uniform off of him. Giuseppe?'

She looked up at Joe with a flash of her dark brown eyes, and he nodded as the American soldier – an army lieutenant – was set down on the sturdy wooden table. His uniform – all his clothes, including his military-issue underwear – were quickly removed. Should the Nazis pay them a visit, without those clothes this man was merely a peasant, a farmer who'd been caught in the devastating crossfire of a war that was drawing closer every day.

Joe gathered the uniform along with the lieutenant's dog tags. 'Charles Ashton,' he read aloud before bundling it all together. The clothes were bloody, but he couldn't risk washing them clean, not right away. He'd have to bury them for now, deep enough so the starving dogs that wandered the town's streets wouldn't smell the blood and dig them up.

One of the Lucs – there were two in Cybele's private army – brought blankets to cover Ashton, but Cybele set them aside. The summer night was warm. His body was slick with sweat, and she certainly had no need for them.

She was barely twenty-one years old, but the sight of strange men, both naked and bloody, had become a common one in this house she'd once shared with her husband and their young son.

Ashton had been hit three times as far as Joe could see. Once in the shoulder, once in the side, and once in the upper leg. The wounds in the shoulder and the leg were bad enough, but being gut shot was a virtual kiss of death without a surgeon's skill available. Unless . . .

'He still has the bullets in him.' Cybele looked up from examining his wounds. 'That's a good thing. The rounds that hit him were spent. Maybe we can save him.'

Spent bullets meant that this lieutenant had been at the very edge of the German rifles' range when they'd shot at him. He'd been hit, but the bullets didn't have enough power left to pass through him. They'd merely lodged within him, their flight stopped by his muscle and tissue.

'If I can get these bullets out,' Cybele continued, 'and if we can prevent infection . . .'

As she met Joe's gaze, she suddenly looked weary and far older than she was. Infections had taken as many lives as German bullets. Odds were, without a hospital, without a real doctor, this soldier would die. The fact that the bullets were spent had merely moved his chance of survival from impossible to unlikely.

Joe touched her shoulder, squeezed the tense muscles in her arm. They'd gone up against unlikely before, and won. 'You can save him,' he told her.

Cybele took a deep breath and nodded. 'I can try. I'm going to need help holding him down, though, in case he wakes.'

They had no morphine, and removing bullets without the numbing effects of the drug would be screamingly painful. Joe himself could attest to that. Maybe, just maybe, Charles Ashton would remain blessedly unconscious until she was done.

Of course, he chose that instant to rouse. His eyelids fluttered and he groaned. And then he gazed directly up at Cybele with eyes that were the color of a summer sky.

As Joe watched, Cybele stared back at him, transfixed. He

was her first real American. Joe himself didn't truly count since he'd grown up in an apartment with an Italian father and French mother in a part of New York City that was more European than American.

Even naked, it was obvious Ashton was an American. He could have stepped right from the pages of a Hollywood magazine. Even injured, he was golden and gleaming, with chiseled features that provided a perfect frame for those unearthly blue eyes.

He stared back at Cybele, reaching up to touch her cheek. 'Angel,' he whispered.

Cybele jerked her gaze away from him, stepped back to avoid his touch. 'Tell him he's wrong.' She spoke only a small amount of English, but she'd understood his single word. She glanced at Joe again. 'Tell him that after I'm done he's going to swear I'm the devil.'

But Joe didn't get a chance to translate, because Ashton lifted his head, painfully trying to raise himself up. 'French,' he rasped. 'You're French, angel. Sister! What happened to . . . Oo et luh sare?' He could barely speak, but he struggled to sit up. 'You know, sare. Big hat, black dress? Mon Dieu, Jesus – luh sare?'

Whatever it was he wanted to know, it was vitally important to him. His eyes were all but rolling back in his head as he struggled to stay conscious.

Cybele shook her head, looking to Joe for help.

He stepped forward, but Ashton's head lolled back against the table.

'Quickly,' Cybele said to Marie and Luc Prieaux. 'Hold him for me.'

As she dug for the first bullet, Ashton groaned but didn't awaken.

'What was he asking?' she questioned Joe as she worked,

sweat beading on her brow and upper lip as the man continued to make those small sounds of pain.

'I don't know.' He shook his head, uncertain himself what the American soldier had meant with his atrocious, unintelligible, first-year schoolbook French. 'I'm sorry.'

'I won't be able to go with you tonight,' Cybele told him. 'I'll need to stay here to care for him. These first few hours are always critical.'

Joe was disappointed, but he hid it, as always. 'Of course.'

She looked up at him and gave him one of those sweet, sad smiles he'd come to know so well. 'You'll probably be safer without me.'

That much was true. She was fearless in her work against the Nazis. It wasn't enough for her simply to count numbers of troops and note stockpiles of ammunition. She had to get closer, close enough to overhear conversations, close enough to find out which warehouses held ammunition that her small army of freedom fighters could steal and use against the occupying forces. Close enough to guarantee a bullet in the head were they ever discovered.

Joe looked down at the bundle of clothing he still held in his hands. He'd have to rush to dig a hole deep enough for this, or he'd be late to the rendezvous point.

'Go,' Cybele said, well aware of the time.

Joe looked from her to the wounded American and tried his damnedest not to be jealous of a man who was probably going to die.

He caught Cybele's gaze one last time, losing himself just a little in the midnight darkness of her eyes. Then he turned, slipping out the door into the night, following her rule.

Since the occupation, Cybele had had only three rules. She'd told him about them once when they'd shared several bottles of wine. It was after a night spent making life a little less comfortable for the Nazis who controlled Ste.-Hélène.

Never turn down a chance to strike back at the Germans was one, she'd said. Never promise to meet again was two. And three was never, ever fall in love. Because love and war were a terrible combination.

That night as she'd gone up the stairs to her bedroom, alone as always, she'd made him promise to follow her rules, too.

As Joe silently took a shovel from the shed and began to dig in the postage stamp-size garden behind Cybele's house, inwardly he sighed.

Two out of three wasn't bad.

Cybele, he suspected, wouldn't agree.

'Thank you so much,' Kelly said to Tom as she closed the door to her father's bedroom. 'Again.'

The long hallway was only dimly lit. A lamp from down in the living room cast just enough light to throw exotic shadows across her face and body. It was alarmingly romantic.

But Tom's head was pounding, he was wearing only his boxers – his very thin cotton boxers – and this was Kelly Ashton standing next to him, not some bar bunny he'd fool around with for a few weeks and then cut free.

Although, the way the shadows fell across her face made her eyes seem almost hot. It seemed as if she was checking him out, as if she was running her gaze across his near-naked body appreciatively.

He looked good. Tom knew he looked good even though he was a little too skinny from those weeks in the hospital. The truth was, a man couldn't do as much PT as he and his SEAL team did and *not* look good.

Still, this was Kelly Ashton throwing those glances. Kelly class valedictorian, Phi Beta Kappa, Harvard Med School Ashton. Kelly Girl Scout, nursing home volunteer, church choir soloist Ashton.

Who had once kissed him as if the world were coming to an end. Kissed him and made it clear that she was his – if he wanted her.

Of course, that had been years ago. When she was fifteen.

'I'm glad I could help,' he told her now, remembering the way she'd looked at him right before she'd kissed him. Or maybe he was the one who'd kissed her. He didn't know – he hadn't known even at the time. All he'd known was it was late, they'd been together for nearly twelve hours, and he still wasn't ready to take her home.

They'd been sitting in Joe's station wagon – the same one that was out in the driveway – stopped at a red light down by the marina. Their conversation had lulled, and he figured she was probably tired. It was definitely time to call it a night. But when he'd glanced over at her, she didn't look tired. In fact, the look in her eyes had made his mouth go dry.

Now, he cleared his throat. 'You know, Kel, I owe you an apology.'

He saw from her eyes that she knew exactly what he was talking about. She turned away. 'No, you don't.'

'Yes, I do. That night before I left town—'

'It was just one of those impulsive things,' she said, still not meeting his gaze. 'We were both so young.'

She had been young. He'd been nearly nineteen. And maybe that first kiss had been impulsive, but what he'd done after, pulling into the darkness of the bank parking lot and turning off the engine . . . It had been the wrong thing to do, but if he were given a chance to do it over, he still wasn't certain he'd be able to resist her. 'Nevertheless, I've always wanted to apologize to you. I took advantage—'

'Oh, please!' She moved briskly down the hall toward the kitchen, clearly embarrassed. 'Don't turn it into something that it wasn't.'

'Still, I shouldn't have let it go as far as it—'

'Three kisses?' she said. 'Or was it four? For someone who had the reputation for deflowering most of the girls in town, I've always thought you showed remarkable restraint.'

'That reputation . . . I didn't really . . . We were friends and . . . Besides, you were way too young. I'm just . . . I'm sorry.' God, he was smooth. He tried again. 'I've missed having you as a friend, and now that we're both back here for a while, I didn't want that night hanging over us, making things awkward.'

'Apology completely unnecessary but accepted.' Kelly snapped on the glaringly bright kitchen light. 'Tell Joe he's not fired, will you? Tell him Dad didn't mean it.'

'I think he probably already knows that,' Tom said. 'But I'll tell him.'

'I keep thinking how awful it'll be if my father dies before he and Joe resolve this. This is hard enough on Joe as it is.'

The door was right behind him, and Tom knew he should move toward it. He should say good night and go. He'd apologized and it was obvious she didn't want to talk about it anymore.

The dead last thing he should do was put his arms

around her, no matter how lost and alone she seemed, no matter how amazing she looked in those barely there workout clothes.

He cleared his throat. 'I really should check on Joe. I'll try talking to him.'

Kelly nodded. She held out her hand to him. 'Thank you again,' she said. 'And please don't worry about . . . you know. That was a long time ago.'

Tom was afraid to touch her, but to *not* take her hand would've been rude. He braced himself and reached for her.

Her hand was small and cool but her grip was strong. No wet-fish handshake from Kelly Ashton, no sir. That was no surprise.

But then she did surprise him by lifting the back of his hand to her lips and kissing him softly.

'You *have* always been a good friend,' she said. 'I'm really glad that you're here.'

Tom was flustered. Funny, he'd pretty much considered himself fluster-proof prior to this very moment in time. But here he was. Completely uncertain what to do, what to say, what to *think*. She'd *kissed* his *hand*.

It was the perfect opportunity to pull her into his arms, yet he hesitated. Emotion hung in the air so thick he could feel it warm against his skin. He could kiss her, and maybe she'd be so caught up in the moment, she'd let him pull her with him into her room, into her bed.

Yeah, right – maybe he could take advantage of her. Again. After he'd apologized for doing just that.

If anyone else tried to take advantage of Kelly, he'd beat the shit out of the bastard.

Tom forced himself to back away from her. To pull his hand free. To smile at her as he pushed open the screen door.

'I'll see you tomorrow,' he said, and escaped with her virtue still intact.

Mallory regretted throwing away her lighter almost instantly.

It had been a perfectly good lighter after all, and she had only sixty-five cents in her pocket. Not including the three hundred dollars Tom had given her for groceries.

But spending that money on a lighter – after she'd just thrown hers away – seemed like a really wrong thing to do.

Matchbooks, however, were free. But the Honey Farms convenience store was a solid, ten minute, extremely inconvenient walk away.

Mallory spun in a slow circle, cigarette held in her fingers, searching for someone, *any*one she knew even remotely, who might have a match.

'I'd offer to light it, but even if I did have a match, you'd probably just put it out right away anyway. Why not save yourself the effort, skip lighting it, and just step on it now?'

Hey, ho. Geek alert! Motionless and mouth-breathing at two o'clock.

He was average height and skinny, with dark, painfully straight hair that he'd attempted to comb back behind his ears in a style that defied description. His wire-rimmed glasses were circa 1987 and too big for his face, giving him that scuba-diver look so popular among dorks. They were held together by both clear tape in the middle *and* a safety pin at the earpiece. She wondered if she should congratulate him for that major antifashion accomplishment.

He was wearing jeans, and Mallory wasn't sure which was worse, the fact that they were straight legged, or the fact that they were about a million inches too short, ending high above his shoes. Shoes. Who the hell wore *shoes* with their jeans?

'Hello!' she said. 'I see your socks.'

He blinked at her through his windshield. He needed wipers for those things. The breeze was wet, coming in off the ocean the way it was, and he was about to lose all visibility.

His shirt was a button-down short-sleeved plaid event that was made out of some kind of unnatural blend of completely synthetic fabrics. It fit him about as well as a cardboard box, and – just in case that wasn't awful enough – his collar was up on one side.

He had geek complexion type B. In Mallory's experience, geeks either had pizza face – type A for acne – or baby skin, type B, smooth and pale and perfect from all those years of building *Star Trek* models in the basement, away from the damaging rays of the sun.

Her new little friend's skin was smooth, but not quite alabaster – no doubt on account that he was at least part Asian-American.

He had that reverent look in his brown eyes as he gazed at her – that look that said he'd found paradise. However, unlike most of the other rejects who ogled her, he managed to keep his eyes on her face instead of glued to her megabreasts.

He held out his hand. 'Hi, I'm David Sullivan.'

She crossed her arms, leaving him dangling. 'Sullivan?' she repeated skeptically. 'Of the Tokyo Sullivans?'

'Adopted.' He smiled then, revealing straight, white teeth – no doubt the result of years of expensive orthodontics. Mallory couldn't keep herself from running her tongue over her own slightly crooked front teeth. God, it *so* wasn't fair. She hated him, and hated herself for being envious of an effing geek.

She lifted one eyebrow. 'Was there something you wanted?' she asked pointedly, omitting the word *loser* at the end. It was there, however, in her tone and attitude.

The geek didn't seem to notice. Or maybe he was just used to it. 'Yeah, actually,' he said, juggling his Day-Glo yellow backpack and opening the front zipper. 'I was watching you for a while, and I'm wondering if you might be interested in . . .'

Here it came. The disgusting proposition of the day.

He triumphantly pulled a rather worn-looking business card from his pack, but Mallory didn't let him finish.

'Let me guess,' she said. 'You'll give me twenty whole dollars if I put something else in my mouth besides this cigarette. Is that what you want, junior?'

David-the-geek actually looked surprised, and then embarrassed. In fact he even blushed. His baby-soft cheeks actually turned pink.

'Oh,' he said. 'Well, no, um.' He laughed. 'As, uh, lovely as that sounds that's not what I . . .' He cleared his throat and held out the business card. 'I'm an artist, and I was wondering if you might be interested in posing for me.'

Mallory didn't take the card. 'Posing. I suppose this is where you tell me I would do this posing back in your apartment. Oh, and by the way, you want me to pose naked, right?'

'Well, as much as I'd like that, it might make it hard for me to concentrate, so if you could wear a bikini—'

'What, do I look like some kind of fool to you?' She glared at him. 'I've heard a shitload of lines before, Einstein, but yours wins the stupid award. No way am I going anywhere with you. Not in this lifetime.'

She swiped the card out of his hand, pointedly tearing it in half and dropping it onto the puddled sidewalk as she walked away.

'Hey,' he called after her. 'I didn't get your name.'

Yeah, right. Mallory didn't even bother to look back.

Joe opened the bathroom door at Tommy's gentle knock. He made a show of drying his face with his towel so he didn't have to look the younger man in the eye.

'You all right?' Tom asked.

'No,' Joe admitted, feeling stupid. Charles was eighty years old. It was a miracle he'd lived *this* long. The fact that he was going to die shouldn't have been so distressing.

'You want to talk?'

'No.' Joe had his back to Tommy as he hung up his towel on the rack by the sink, but he heard the kid laugh.

'Now what made me guess that's what you'd say?' Tom asked. He sighed. 'Needless to say, I'm here. You know where to find me if you change your mind.'

Joe gave the kid an uh-huh sound as he made sure

his towel was spread out to dry, cut precisely in half by the rack, the corners neatly lined up.

'I figured I'd go pick up some paint tomorrow.' Tom deftly changed the subject. 'The kitchen's looking pretty gray. Between the two of us, we can slap on a few coats, have it done by Sunday, piece of cake. That is – if the Hero of Baldwin's Bridge deigns to do such menial labor as painting.'

Joe didn't answer. A comment like that didn't deserve any kind of response.

But Tom blocked his way out of the bathroom. 'You know, you could've at least told me that much,' he said mildly.

Joe couldn't have loved Tommy more if he'd been his own son. He looked at him for several good long seconds. 'No,' he said, shaking his head. 'I couldn't have.'

Five

'It's him, isn't it? It's Joe.'

Kelly was gazing up at the statue that was on the Baldwin's Bridge common – the picture-perfect lawn between the world-famous hotel and the town marina. But now she turned to find Tom standing behind her.

She wasn't one bit surprised that he should be here this morning, too. No doubt he had been as eager as she to take another look at the statue that was boldly labeled 'The Hero of Baldwin's Bridge.'

'Hey,' she said in greeting, trying not to blush, thinking of the way she'd kissed his hand last night. The way he'd run away afterward. Good thing she hadn't gotten close enough to kiss him on the lips.

'Taking the day off?' He didn't sound as if he were thinking about anything but here and now. He sounded . . . like Tom. Casual and friendly, with an undercurrent of sexuality he couldn't lose even when he was being casual and friendly.

'Hah. There's no such thing.' She tried to sound just

as casual, hoping he couldn't tell that every time she so much as saw him she started flashing hot and cold and having fantasies of him kissing her, right here, in public, on the Baldwin's Bridge common. 'I mean, yeah, this is supposed to be one of my stay home days, but odds are I'll be paged and end up going into Boston.'

Tom was wearing sunglasses and a baseball cap. Much of his face was hidden, but what she could see looked tired, as if he hadn't slept well or the headache he'd mentioned last night was still bothering him. He smelled great, though, like sunblock and coffee and fresh laundry. She resisted her urge to press her nose against the clean cotton sleeve of his muscle-hugging T-shirt and breathe in deeply.

'Check this out.' Kelly dug through her purse for the copies she'd made at the library from the microfiche machine. 'It's from *The Baldwin's Bridge Trumpet*.'

He laughed. 'We think alike. I was going to the library next.'

'I was there for over two hours and this was all I found,' she told him. 'Maybe you'll have better luck.'

'May 8, 1946,' he read as she handed him the copies. 'That's nearly a year after the end of the war.'

'Yeah, it was a year after VE Day. The town had a special statue unveiling. For *this* statue,' she explained, glancing up at it again. 'It was commissioned and paid for by Mrs Harper Baldwin to remember a son and a nephew who'd died in the war. According to what it says in the article, she had two other sons. Both served with the Fifty-fifth, and both survived, thanks at least in part to Joe, who risked his life to warn the division of a coming attack. Mrs Baldwin had the artist use a photo of Joe as the model for this statue, but honored Joe's quote unquote *most humble request* to leave his name off the statue.'

Kelly watched as Tom silently skimmed through the three pages of news articles and looked at the pictures. Joe, looking uncomfortable, standing stiffly next to Mrs Harper Baldwin, surrounded by a crowd of well-dressed townfolk. Joe in his uniform, impossibly young. He was twenty-two in 1946, after the war. When he'd first been shot down in France, he'd been only eighteen. *Eighteen.*

'The second article has a brief recounting of the incident in which Joe saved the division,' she told Tom. 'It doesn't say much more than what Dad told us last night. Although it *does* mention that Joe . . .' She moved closer to him to read over his shoulder, her arm brushing against his as she reached to point out the passage. She had to clear her throat. 'Here it is. "Joseph Paoletti, who is currently employed as the Ashton family groundskeeper in Baldwin's Bridge, met Charles Ashton, an officer with the Fighting Fifty-fifth, when Lieutenant Ashton was wounded in France in June 1944. Mr Paoletti helped hide the wounded officer from the Nazis after a German counteroffensive that pushed the battle line far to the west, leaving Lieutenant Ashton stranded deep within enemy territory."'

She looked up at Tom. 'My father was there, too. Behind the German lines. Did you know about that?'

He looked at her pointedly over the top of his sunglasses, and she laughed. 'Dumb question,' she said. 'Like either one of the silent twins would've told you. Sorry.'

As she watched, Tom looked from the blurred newspaper photograph of Joe – a young Joe, but still so serious – up to the grim-faced statue.

'It's definitely Joe,' Kelly agreed, gazing at the statue, too. 'He's got those Paoletti eyes.'

Tom laughed. 'You mean those *shifty* Paoletti eyes?'

She turned to face him, horrified. 'God, no! You don't have—'

'Whoa,' he said. 'Easy! I was just kidding.'

She was standing close enough to see his eyes behind his sunglasses. 'No, you weren't. There may have been people in this town who didn't like or trust you, Tom,' she said fiercely, 'but I was never one of them.'

He gave her one of his little half smiles. 'Yeah,' he said. 'I know. I . . . always appreciated that.'

Kelly was standing much too close but she purposely didn't back away. Her attraction for him was mutual. It had to be. When he wasn't around, she doubted its existence. But when she was with him . . . She wasn't imagining this electricity that crackled between them.

He'd apologized last night for kissing her all those years ago. But he hadn't apologized for leaving town the next day with only the lamest of goodbyes. She'd kept waiting for him to mention that, but he hadn't. Then all of a sudden he was about to go find Joe, so she'd reached out to shake his hand.

Way to initiate a seduction – with a brisk handshake. She knew she had to do *some*thing, and that was when – stupider and stupider – she'd kissed him.

On the hand.

Genius.

In retrospect, she came up with all kinds of snappy replies to his apology. Like, 'You don't need to apologize for something I enjoyed immensely and am dying to do again.'

Right – as if she'd ever find the nerve to say something like that to him.

'So explain,' Tom said now, glancing up at the statue looming above them. 'He's got Paoletti eyes. I'm dying to hear what that means.'

What was she supposed to tell him? That his version of those hazel Paoletti eyes had the power to make her melt? To make her heart rate increase? To fuel some pretty powerful fantasies, particularly when combined with the memory of a few stolen kisses in the front seat of a station wagon?

'Well,' she said carefully, 'I think it's probably a window-to-the-soul thing. Maybe it comes from being part Italian, but neither you nor Joe are very good at hiding your emotions. Which is really wonderful,' she added when it looked as if he was about to protest. 'And maybe it's because of that, but you both always look just a little bit sad. Even when you're smiling.' She gave him a sidelong glance. 'Probably comes from keeping so many secrets.'

He laughed and dimples appeared in his cheeks. 'I don't have any secrets.'

'Sure,' Kelly said. 'Aside from the fact that you're a Navy SEAL and everything you do is a secret, your life's an open book. But, whoops, you don't manage to come home to visit more than twice a year, because your career *is* your life.'

She had him there.

'And Joe,' she continued. 'All these years I thought he was just a gardener – turns out he's an international man of mystery. Every time I turn around, he's got another secret.'

'Only about the war,' Tom protested. 'There are plenty of men who returned from Europe and didn't say a single word about it to anyone. It's not that hard to understand.'

'What about his personal life?'

'What personal life?' Tom asked.

'See?' she countered triumphantly, smiling up at him.

He was silent then, just gazing down at her, still standing much, much too close. Kelly felt her smile fade. *Kiss me*.

She could see the sign for the bank from where she stood. Seventeen years ago, Tom had pulled into the dark bank parking lot, jammed his car into park, dragged her into his arms, and kissed her.

Right there.

Just a stone's throw from where they were now standing.

It had been, without a doubt, the hottest, most powerful sexual experience of her life. And she'd kept her clothes on the entire time.

For him, it had been only something for which to apologize.

He shifted slightly back, putting more space between them. Still backing away, even all these years later.

'Why didn't Joe ever get married?' Kelly asked. Why didn't *you* ever get married? was the question she *really* wanted to ask, even though she already knew.

He wasn't the kind of man who would willingly settle down. And that was a good thing, she reminded herself. If she *could* manage to strike a match and ignite their attraction, neither of them would get hurt.

She motioned toward the papers Tom still held, pointing at the picture of Joe. 'Look at him. He was delicious. And as if looking like this isn't enough,' she added, 'he just so happens to be one of the nicest guys in the world – *and* a war hero with a statue made in his likeness. I'm sorry, but the women in town *had* to be lining up to meet him.'

'You know, I asked Joe about that once,' Tom told her. 'I wanted to know why he didn't marry my grandmother – his brother's widow. She'd moved to Baldwin's Bridge a few years after Joe did. He got a job for her as a cook in your father's house after the war. It was obvious he liked her, and I've seen pictures – she was gorgeous. She must've married my grandfather when she was seventeen. So there she was, a war widow at the ripe old age of twenty-three, with a five-year-old kid in tow – my father. Joe helped her rent a house in town, helped her get settled, but that's as far as it went.

'When I was about six, she married the mailman. I didn't get it. I asked Joe why *he* didn't marry her, and he told me he loved my Gram like a sister. He was glad she was getting married – glad she'd found someone to spend the rest of her life with, glad she didn't have to be alone anymore.' He looked up at the statue. 'So I asked him how come he never got married, how come he didn't find someone so he didn't have to be alone.'

He laughed softly, remembering. 'I was only six, I

didn't have a clue about the boundaries I was stepping over with that one.'

'What did he say?' Kelly asked, intrigued.

'He told me he wasn't married because he'd met and lost his one true love during the war. I remember him saying that as if it were yesterday. His one true love.' He was silent for several long seconds. 'He told me that after he met her, there was really no point in looking any further, you know? No one could ever compare. And Joe, he said he wasn't the kind of man who was willing to settle. He'd rather be alone.'

Kelly stared up at the statue's grim face. 'Lost,' she whispered. 'Did she . . .' She looked at Tom. 'Did he mean that she died?'

'I don't know,' Tom admitted. 'Lost could mean a lot of things, couldn't it? Maybe she married someone else.' He looked down at the papers he still had in his hands, as if surprised by the sight of them. He stepped toward her, holding them out.

She exhaled her disbelief as she took them from him and put them back into her bag. 'God. It all seems so, I don't know . . . so romantic.' Yet Joe had always struck her as pragmatic and down to earth. He was a gardener, a handyman. To think that he'd spent all these years carrying a torch, refusing to settle for anyone else. Who would've thought? . . .

'Do you think he's right?' she asked Tom. 'That we each have only one chance at true love? Do you think there even *is* such a thing as true love?'

He shook his head. 'You're asking the wrong guy. I don't have a lot of experience with this subject. I don't really, um, do love, you know? It doesn't quite . . . fit with my line of work.'

91

'But you have an opinion, don't you?' she persisted. 'We all have ideas and beliefs about what love should or shouldn't be. In fact, your beliefs about love are probably behind your determination to avoid serious relationships.'

'Well, thank you, Dr Freud,' he said, amusement in his voice. 'Has it occurred to you that I might not be in a serious relationship because I know that with the combination of my, shall we say, restless temperament and the strains of my intensely relationship-unfriendly job, the odds of any relationship working out are zip?'

'So if your dream woman approached you – someone who fulfilled your every physical and emotional and mental expectation for what a life partner should be,' Kelly hypothesized, 'and she said, "Tom, here I am, ready to be your friend and lover forever, ready to stand beside you through bad and good, ready to play out your every sexual fantasy," you'd turn her down?'

Tom laughed. 'I don't know. You want to be more specific about those sexual fantasies?'

Yes. This was flirting. There was definitely an underlying current of attraction beneath his words. Now what *she* had to do was zing one right back at him. She could do this. She looked him squarely in the eye. 'You tell me. It's *your* fantasies we're talking about.'

Now it was his turn, but instead of pressing forward, he stepped back. He laughed.

'I'd feel kind of funny going into detail with Uncle Joe listening in,' he said lightly, glancing up at the statue.

'I don't think you'd turn your dream woman down.'

Kelly didn't want to laugh. She didn't want this conversation to turn lighthearted. She wanted to get back to that place where the very air between them crackled with sexual energy. Then all she had to do was ask him to dinner. She could do this.

Tom shook his head. 'I'd have to turn her down,' he countered. 'If she was that perfect . . . I wouldn't want to hurt her.'

'But if you were her one true love, you'd hurt her by not being with her.'

He rubbed his forehead as if he still had a headache even as he laughed again. 'Okay. Whoa. That's enough. You can't set up a completely fictional, no-chance-of-it-ever-happening scenario, and try to force a point of any kind with it. Let's get real here, Ashton. No "dream woman" is about to walk up to me and offer to—' He broke off, clearing his throat. 'Fill in the blank – I'll leave it to your imagination, but figure it probably involves whipped cream and black lingerie.'

Kelly couldn't keep from giggling. Black lingerie and . . . She took a deep breath and tried to pretend she wasn't blushing. Whipped cream and Tom Paoletti. My God. Somebody come take her order. She wanted a double.

'You *think* it's a no-chance scenario,' she argued. 'But what if Joe had actually met his dream woman? His true love?'

Tom shook his head. 'I don't know. Maybe he did.' But even that was too strong an admission for him, and he tried to back away from it. 'Look, Kel, all I really know for sure is whatever Joe felt, it had to be pretty powerful if it made him prefer to spend nearly sixty years of his life alone rather than settle for someone he didn't really love. And we're talking *alone* alone,' he added. 'Joe didn't have girlfriends, he didn't have lady friends, he didn't go out to bars and have one-night stands. He was Alone, with a capital *A*. No black lingerie. No whipped cream. Just Joe and his memories.'

God, that was sad. Had Joe simply quit looking at age twenty-two? Or did he hold on to hope for years, hope that he'd find someone to replace the woman he'd loved? If so, that hope had surely died slowly, painfully.

'In a lot of ways, I can understand his not wanting to settle,' Tom said quietly. 'There're a lot of things in my life I wouldn't be willing to settle for.'

Kelly's pager went off. She'd set it on silent when she went into the library, and the shaking made her jump. She checked the number.

'I'm sorry,' she said to Tom as she dug through her purse for her cell phone. 'I have to call my office.'

She dialed the number, turning slightly away from him. 'Hi, this is Dr Ashton. I was just paged.'

'Doctor, I'm sorry to disturb you.' It was Pat Geary. 'But the McKenna test results finally came in.'

Kelly closed her eyes. 'Please tell me it's some kind of weird anemia.'

'No such luck. It's about as bad as it gets,' Pat said grimly. 'Brenda McKenna's pretty anxious for the results. Should I call her back, schedule a meeting for tomorrow?'

'No, better make it today,' Kelly decided. 'And call Dr Martin. Let's get Betsy in to see the oncologist as soon as possible.'

'So much for your vacation.'

'It's not a vacation, it's a temporary partial leave.'

'Well, for someone who's taking temporary partial leave, you're sure here nearly all the time.'

'Schedule the meeting with the McKennas for about an hour from now,' Kelly told her assistant. 'I'm on my way in.'

She closed her phone and grabbed her keys from her purse before she realized. Her father. She swore and opened her cell phone again to call Pat back.

But Tom was already one step ahead of her. 'I was going from here to pick up some paint from Home Depot,' he told her, 'but that's a pretty low priority. If you want, I'll stay with your father.'

'You don't need to change your plans,' Kelly said, 'but if you wouldn't mind checking in on him when you get home . . .'

'No problem,' Tom said. 'Think he'd be up for a game of chess?'

'Oh, God, that would be *so* nice. I'm sure he'd love it.'

'Is there a number where I can reach you? I mean, I probably won't need it, but . . .'

Kelly dug through her purse for her business card. 'This has my office number – a direct line to my desk – and my pager, too. Please don't hesitate to call. And don't feel as if you need to stay with him the entire time. Just stick your head in every now and then.'

'Don't sweat it,' Tom said. 'It's not going to be a hardship. Believe it or not, I like the guy. And maybe if I'm lucky, there'll be a Red Sox game on, and I'll be able to get Joe to sit in the same room with him without fighting.'

Kelly had to hold on to herself to keep from hugging

him. 'If you can manage to do that, I'll love you forever. And if you can get them to make up and be friends and stop fighting for good . . . I'll bring home some whipped cream.'

Oh, my God, had she really said that out loud?

She had.

For about a half a second, Tom looked completely surprised, but then he laughed. 'Well, hey, there's incentive.' He pointed toward the nearby marina parking lot. 'Go,' he said. 'I'll see you later.'

She ran for her car.

It was him.

Right there in Home Depot on Route 1 in Baldwin's Bridge.

Tom had filled his shopping cart with cans of paint and rollers and was pushing it through the crowd toward the checkout when he saw him. The Merchant. Or at least it was the very same man he'd seen in Logan Airport by the luggage carousel. The man was pushing his own shopping cart to the exit, away from checkout number four.

Tom got a brief but very clear look at his face before he turned the corner. It was him.

Brown hair shot with gray, weak chin, slightly stooped shoulders as if he were trying to make himself shorter. It was *definitely* him.

What the *fuck* was the Merchant doing here in Baldwin's Bridge?

Shopping. He had an entire cart filled with his purchases. Tom could see a roll of electrical wire sticking out of his bag.

The hair on the back of his neck went straight up.

The man responsible for the 1996 Paris embassy car-bombing was buying electrical wire.

Tom left his cart right there, in the middle of an aisle, much to the displeasure of the shoppers around him. He deserted all his wayward thoughts about Kelly Ashton and whipped cream, too, as he pushed toward the same door the Merchant had used.

He fought the throng, silently cursing the time it was taking, the precious seconds he was wasting. He broke into a run as he hit a less crowded area. Hitting the sidewalk and the glaring brightness of the day, he skidded to a stop, shielding his eyes with one hand and fighting his dizziness as he quickly scanned the parking lot.

The Merchant was gone. The parking lot was busy, filled with cars, some pulling in, some pulling out. There were people walking to and from their vehicles, some with shopping carts, but none of them was the Merchant.

Tom scanned the area again. Come on, come on. Stand up and show yourself. No one could have pushed his cart out to a car, loaded up the trunk, and been inside it that quickly. Unless . . .

There were four cars heading for the entrance onto Route 1, a number of empty shopping carts left forlornly on the sidewalk outside the exit door. If the Merchant had had a car waiting for him, if he'd loaded it up right here from the sidewalk . . .

Tom looked again at the cars at the far end of the huge parking lot, waiting for the light to change so they could pull out onto the busy main road. Two were white subcompacts, one was a boxy red minivan, the last a blue sedan – probably a Ford Taurus. They were all too far away for him to see the license plates, and as he watched, the light changed and they all pulled away.

Shit.

Tom went back inside through the exit doors, back to the clerk working cash register four. She was an older woman, a senior citizen, probably looking to make a few extra bucks to bolster her Social Security checks. She was currently ringing up a whole cartful of plumbing supplies, her movements quick and sure. She glanced at Tom and he made himself smile at her despite the fact that his heart was still pounding. She looked as if she'd be able to multitask, so he didn't wait for her to finish.

'Excuse me, ma'am.' He read her name tag. 'Mae. There was a man who was just in here – he bought a whole cart of stuff? Some electrical wire? . . .'

She looked at him again, one eyebrow raised this time as she kept working, holding the various types of pipe and connections up to the scanner. 'You've just described nearly every customer I've helped since my coffee break at ten-thirty.'

She smiled at her own small joke and Tom took a steadying breath. Okay. She seemed friendly. At the very least she was good-natured and intelligent.

'This was just a few minutes ago,' he said. 'He had brown hair, going gray. About forty-five years old, about my height. He bought a roll of wire? . . .'

'Pleasant brown eyes?' she asked.

Brown eyes. But okay. 'Yes,' Tom said. If he *were* the Merchant, he would figure he'd call less attention to himself by not wearing the cheap blue contact lenses once he was away from the potential scrutiny at Logan

Airport. But Christ, what was he doing in *Baldwin's Bridge*?

Mae was looking at him, waiting for him to go on.

'He's my brother-in-law,' he said smoothly. Jenks would have been proud. 'My crazy sister just sent me down here to make sure he didn't forget a bunch of things we need. We're rewiring the house and ... But I just missed him. He pulled away before I could make sure he got everything. I saw he had the wire, but maybe you could tell me – did he also get pliers?'

'He bought quite a few items,' Mae told him as she worked. 'Wire, a wire cutter, needle-nose pliers, too. Let's see ... duct tape, lots of duct tape and electrical tape, a whole pile of switches and switch plate covers ...' She took a credit card from the man buying the plumbing supplies and ran the magnetic tape through her register. 'There was more. A bunch of doodads from our electrical department and a lovely hanging pot of impatiens from gardening that he said he just couldn't resist.'

Flowers. Why would a terrorist buy flowers? Tom could think of a few reasons without much effort. One – because no one would suspect he was a terrorist if he bought flowers. And two – because he wasn't really a terrorist, he was just some guy who looked like some other guy Tom had seen at Logan; and three – Tom was out of his fucking mind.

'How about a clock radio?' he asked. If he were building a bomb, the Merchant would need some kind of alarm clock to jury-rig. Provided he was the Merchant. Provided Tom hadn't completely lost it.

Mae shook her head. 'Nope, definitely not. But we

don't carry small appliances. You'll have to go to Radio Shack or Sears for something like that.'

'Did he pay with a credit card or—'

'Cash.'

It had been too much to hope he'd used a credit card. Of course, even if he had, it probably would have been stolen. 'Thank you, Mae,' Tom said.

'Good luck with your project,' she said.

Yeah, he definitely needed luck.

'A car bomb.' Admiral Crowley sighed.

Tom slowly sat down at Joe's kitchen table, trying his hardest not to sound insane, but even *he* didn't believe himself completely.

'He could pick up an alarm clock from anywhere. Sears. Bradlees. The CVS. Sir.' Tom chose his words carefully as he spoke into the phone. 'I know how crazy this all sounds. First I see this man at Logan, and then I see him here in Baldwin's Bridge. It doesn't make any sense to me, either. I mean, why Baldwin's Bridge? What's his target? Is it *me*?'

'That's the craziest thing you've said yet,' Crowley told him dryly. 'You weren't even in a command position when you helped go after the Merchant. Out of everyone on that task force, why should he go after you?'

'*How* could he go after me?' Tom pointed out. 'You know as well as I do that SEAL Team Sixteen's personnel records aren't exactly open to the public. And even if he had an inside connection with top secret clearance, he wouldn't find out much.' He rubbed his eyes, well aware that it had only been an hour since he'd last taken Tylenol. It wasn't working. 'I don't think he knows I'm here. It's hard to imagine he would go to Home Depot – right under my nose – and buy the tools and wires he'd need to build a bomb if he knew I was watching.'

'Tom.' Crowley sighed again. 'I've made some quiet inquiries, and none of our INTEL agencies report any movement from the Merchant. Nothing at all. Not a peep, not a breath. In fact, CIA's got him on a presumed-dead list. I'm finding it very difficult to get excited about this.'

'Sir, I understand your position, and I agree I'm not the most reliable pair of eyes right now, but I think it would be wise at least to take some precautions—'

'Tom. You need to use this next month to rest. To recharge. I'm going to be frank with you, son. You're going to have to be on your toes when you return from leave. Rear Admiral Tucker's actively trying to deep six you and your entire SO squad. And he's not the only one who wants you and your Troubleshooters gone from Team Sixteen. If you want to save your career, you're going to have to come back fighting. It's not going to help you one bit if word gets out that you've seen dead terrorists – or Elvis or aliens from outer space – in your hometown. I'm behind you, Lieutenant, you know I am, but there's only so much I can do to save your ass if you're determined to get it kicked.'

'Sir—'

'Get some rest, Lieutenant.' Crowley hung up, leaving Tom listening to the emptiness of a dead phone line.

He reached behind him to hang it up. If he wanted to save his career . . .

Tom did. His career meant just about everything to him.

But if that *was* the Merchant he'd seen, there was far more than his career at stake. The thought of the Merchant planting a car bomb somewhere in Boston's Government Center was chilling.

But why Boston? The Merchant had always targeted people and places for a reason. It didn't make sense that he should just randomly choose Boston now.

Unless he somehow *was* here because of Tom. Tom had been present, after all, when the Merchant's teammates – one of whom was his wife – were killed. And sure, while the records of the task force assault were top secret, even the most top secret information could be leaked or sold or stolen.

Maybe the Merchant *was* after Tom.

Christ, that sounded crazy.

In fact, it sounded frigging *paranoid*.

Get some rest, the admiral had ordered him.

He gripped the table with both hands, holding on as dizziness and doubt assaulted him relentlessly, making him giddy and breathless and sick to his stomach. This was new territory for him, this wondering if he could trust his judgment, wondering if he could trust what he'd seen with his own eyes.

He'd gotten where he was in the SEAL teams through his ability to take charge, to take command. Confidently. Completely. His men had faith in him. They trusted him implicitly – because Tom had always, without exception, trusted himself.

He'd seen the Merchant at Logan. It *was* the Merchant. He'd known, deep in his gut, with every cell in his body, that this was the man he'd studied for so many months.

But these strange feelings of doubt had crept in, and now he was wondering just who and what he'd seen.

What if he was wrong and it wasn't the Merchant? Well, okay, people made mistakes. He'd chalk it up to coincidence. With all the millions of people in the world, the man he'd seen just happened to pick up a bag with the same exact twisting motion that the Merchant had always used.

Unless Tom hadn't seen that telltale motion at all. Unless this goddamned head injury had only made him *think* he'd seen it.

And *that* was where the self-doubt was killing him.

Was he ever going to be able to trust his own eyes again?

That was enough to drive him fucking nuts – if he wasn't fucking nuts already.

But the sixty-four-million-dollar question was even harder to answer.

What if he *had* seen the Merchant? What if the terrorist was planning to hit some target in the Boston area?

And what if Tom just sat back in a lounge chair on the deck overlooking the ocean and did nothing except maybe take advantage of Kelly Ashton when she was feeling particularly lonely and in need of a physical connection?

Yeah, that would be great. He could be twice the asshole – ignoring the potential threat from a terrorist while deceiving a woman he liked and respected.

Kelly would end up hurt and people would die. Maybe a lot of people.

Head pounding, Tom reached for the phone again, leaning back to dial Jazz Jacquette's home phone number. Jazz had a key to Tom's apartment, where Tom still had files of information about the Merchant and his organization stashed on his computer's hard disk. It would take a matter of minutes for Jazz to send that info to Tom electronically. Jazz could also get in touch with WildCard, who could use his unique hacker skills to gather whatever new information had come in on the Merchant over the past few years – pictures, videos, reports, and even rumors.

Yeah, provided he could beg, borrow, or steal a computer with Internet access, Tom was about to get that rest Admiral Crowley recommended – while he caught up on his reading.

'What flavor do you recommend?'

The voice was familiar and Mallory looked over the Ice Cream Shoppe counter and focused on her five thousandth customer of the early afternoon.

What a surprise. It was the geek of last night past, come here to her place of employment to haunt her by rattling his pocket protector.

'A two scoop sugar cone,' she told him flatly. 'Plain vanilla.'

He blinked at her from behind his windshield, clearly surprised. But he'd asked, and in her opinion, none of the fancy, yuppified, rock- and twig-littered flavors ever beat the Shoppe's wicked awesome homemade vanilla.

'If that's too middle of the road for someone as obviously cosmopolitan as you,' she added, 'try one scoop vanilla, one scoop orange sorbet.'

'Like a Creamsicle,' he said. 'That sounds great. I'll take one of those.'

He watched through the glass as she leaned over and dug into the hard frozen vats of ice cream and sorbet – no doubt taking advantage of the opportunity to try to look down her shirt.

'You've been working here for a while, haven't you?' he said. 'More than a year, right?'

'A year and a half,' she told him. 'So what?'

There was actually nothing 'so what' about it. It was a year longer than her mother had ever held a job in her entire life. In the overall scheme of things, serving ice cream was stupid and meaningless, Mal knew, but when Carolyn had given her a copy of the key so she could open up in the morning, she'd been proud.

She reached across the counter to hand the cone to the geek and their fingers touched. It was hard to tell if it was on purpose. He didn't turn red or start stammering or fall down in a dead faint, so maybe it had been.

'Thanks,' he said with a flash of his perfect teeth, handing her a five that he had out and ready. 'When I first saw you, I thought maybe you lifted, but you don't have to, do you? You get that great definition in your arms just from working here – from scooping ice cream.'

Her *arms*. He was waxing poetic about her *arms*. It was almost funny enough to make her laugh, but she managed to restrain herself. Mallory turned her back on him as she made change at the cash register.

When she turned to face him, he'd somehow gotten a dab of ice cream on the tip of his nose. God, what a loser. She dropped the change into his hand from as distant a height as possible.

'Are you working all afternoon?' he asked.

Carolyn chose that exact moment to breeze out of the back room. 'Lunchtime, Mallory! You're free for an hour. Don't smoke too many cigarettes, girl.'

Oh, crap. It was bad enough Carolyn announced that she had the next hour free, but the real killer was that now the geek knew her name.

Mallory took off her apron, grabbed her bag lunch from the refrigerator, along with her book and cigarettes, and headed for the door.

Geek-boy followed with his ice cream – had she really thought that he wouldn't? Before she hit the door, she pulled a yooie, marching back toward the counter and grabbing a napkin. As ridiculous and pathetic as he was, and as scornful as she was of him, there was still no way she could knowingly let him walk out into the harsh streets of Baldwin's Bridge, among the snickering cliques of richie-rich yacht club kids, with ice cream on his nose.

'Don't move,' she ordered him, and swiped his face clean. 'And don't get excited. This doesn't mean anything except that you had ice cream on your nose.'

She tossed the napkin into the trash container outside the front door and kept going, pretending that he wasn't still following her.

'Actually,' he said, 'I did that on purpose.'

When he spoke to her, it made it hard to pretend he wasn't following her – especially when he said things that didn't make any sense at all. Mallory couldn't help herself. She turned and looked at him. 'What are you talking about?'

He smiled at her over his cone, a happy little geek

smile. 'The ice cream on the nose. It's my humanity test. You passed.'

'Yeah, well, fuck off,' Mallory said. She glanced at him. 'How do I rate now?'

He laughed. What do you know? A geek with a sense of humor. He followed her for a while in silence, eating his ice cream. 'Do you always have lunch down here by the marina?'

'Crap.' She'd forgotten to grab a soda from the Shoppe. And the only thing in the house this morning had been a stale loaf of bread and some peanut butter. Lunch was going to be a dry mouth fest.

'It's really beautiful down here.' He squinted as he gazed out over the glistening water, finishing up the last of his cone and wiping his hands and mouth on the napkin she'd wrapped around it. 'That was really good, by the way.'

'Look,' she told him, settling herself on the grass under the biggest shade tree on the lawn in front of the Baldwin's Bridge Hotel, 'I have only an hour, and I'm in the middle of this really great book. So if you don't mind? . . .'

He was bending into an odd shape, trying to see the cover of her book, and she impatiently held it out.

He shook his head. 'I don't know that author's name. Is she new?'

'Yeah,' Mallory told him, rolling her eyes. 'Like nearly ten years new. She's only the hottest romance author out there. God.'

'Ah,' he said. 'I don't read much romance.'

'Much?'

'Any,' he admitted.

She looked at him, at his mismatched socks, his

geekoid plaid shorts, his faded *Babylon-5* T-shirt, his bad haircut. David Sullivan, the Asian-American Irishman, could have been the spokesperson and poster model for bad hair days. And those glasses . . . Holy mother.

'Too macho for it, huh?' she asked him.

He answered as if it had been a serious question. 'No, just ignorant. I like to read science fiction.'

'Now *there's* a surprise. The fact that you're into *Babylon-5* was a clue.'

He looked astonished. 'How do you know I'm into *Babylon-5*?'

She pointed at his space vessel-covered chest.

He glanced down at himself as if surprised by what he was wearing. Actually, he was probably surprised by the fact that he had on clothes, period. 'Ah. And here I thought you were a mind reader. Instead, you're just a good observer.'

She rolled her eyes. 'Yeah, well, I've found it helps when you keep your eyes open and actually focus on something or someone. If you do that, you start to notice little details, like whether they're a human being or a Boston terrier.'

He actually managed to realize she was ragging on him. 'I notice details,' he protested. 'In fact, I'm good with details. It's just my own personal details I don't pay much attention to.' He tilted the cover of her book toward him again. 'Now that I know what to look for, I'm going to have to read a romance novel.'

'Yeah, right.' He'd pinned the bullshit meter with that one. He'd actually read a romance, and her mother would become the governor's wife. Mallory

108

opened her book, opened her bag, and started to eat and read, pointedly ignoring him.

He stood there for only a few seconds longer and then, to her complete surprise, he walked away.

Wonder of wonders. A geek who actually understood 'go away' body language.

But ten minutes didn't pass before Mallory saw him again, walking back across the lawn toward her. She braced herself, focusing all of her attention on the page of her book, hunching her shoulders, turning slightly away.

She didn't look up as he walked right up to her. She didn't say a word, didn't acknowledge him.

And again, to her surprise, he didn't stay very long. He didn't speak, didn't try to get her attention. He simply set something on the grass next to her and then walked away, toward the marina.

When he was finally far enough away and it was safe to move, Mallory looked up.

He'd brought her a can of soda.

As she watched, he sat down on a bench near the seawall, facing the harbor, and taking a book out of his bag, he began to read, too.

She opened the can of soda and took a long drink. It was cold and delicious. She lit a cigarette – one of her last three. This was going to be her last pack. After this, she was quitting for good.

As she savored both the cigarette and the soda, she looked over at David Sullivan.

He didn't look back at her, didn't do anything but slouch there and read.

What a complete weirdo.

Six

Joe finished watering the roses. He coiled the hose, gazing up at the rather ostentatious main house.

Charles was alone in there. The cleaning woman, Mrs Lerner, had pulled out of the driveway about thirty minutes ago. Joe had seen Kelly head into town early this morning and was surprised she wasn't back yet.

He should go check on Charles, but he was afraid that doing so would raise the man's blood pressure, ruffle his feathers.

It was funny, there was once a time when Joe had believed Charles to be unruffleable and completely unaffected by any of the drama and danger going on around him.

But that was years ago. That was back during the War, when they both thought they were men, but in truth they were little more than children.

Yet it seemed like yesterday. He could remember it with a clarity that was often disturbing. The 1950s through 80s were a vague blur of changing seasons, but his memories of the War were sharp and clear. He could close his eyes and live it over again.

He could still hear the drip of the water in Cybele's kitchen, smell the fear of the people hiding in the attic. He could see the brilliance of Cybele's smiles as she greeted the Nazi soldiers who patrolled the neighborhood, as she pretended to befriend the devil in order to give the angels a fighting chance in hell.

He could remember Charles, not stooped and dying but young and vibrant. He'd been wounded, sure, but the second time Joe met him, he was very, very much alive.

He was sitting up in Cybele's bed, his right arm in a sling, his side and leg bandaged. Sitting in Cybele's bed. Cybele, who worked tirelessly for the Resistance, who never shied from taking in, sheltering, and sharing her last turnip with any man, woman, or child in need regardless of race or religion, who would offer anyone who opposed the Nazis the warmth and relative comfort of a pallet on her kitchen floor, but who never, ever gave up the privacy of her own bedroom for anyone less than a woman in labor or a desperately sick child.

Yet she'd given up her bed for this man, this golden-haired American Army officer.

He was playing Hearts with the two Lucs and Dominique, and as Joe stood outside the doorway, watching, he won the hand with a grin. He was pale and slightly peaked-looking with a week's worth of beard on his chin and dark circles beneath his eyes, but nevertheless he was handsome in a way Joe himself would never be.

Charles Ashton had a certain magic to him. It infused him, lighting him from within, making his eyes seem even more blue and his hair even more golden. It was charisma. Or maybe it came from the money Joe knew he must have in the bank. Piles of money could give a wealthy man the kind of instant self-confidence that a poorer man would have to work hard to find.

As Joe watched, the American took a cigarette from a box on the bed. Dominique lit it for him, and he leaned toward her, smiling into her eyes as she blushed.

Yes, indeed, this one had some kind of magic.

Maybe Cybele hadn't given up her bed. Maybe she was sharing it with him.

The thought was an ugly one, but Joe was exhausted. His overnight information-gathering expedition had turned into a weeklong nightmare. It was very much a miracle he'd made it back at all.

'Guiseppe?'

He turned to see Cybele coming up the stairs, her face glowing with relief at the sight of him. She launched herself into his arms, and as always when he held her – which he didn't do often enough – he was amazed at how small, how slender and fragile she truly was.

She was one of their staunchest leaders, and her quiet ability to take charge, her intense calm under pressure, and her limitless stamina made her seem so strong and sturdy.

'Thank God,' she murmured. 'We'd heard rumors of your arrest, but I could get no one to tell me where they had taken you.' She pulled back to look at him, her eyes filled with emotion. 'Are you really all right?' She ran her hands across his shoulders, down his arms. 'All in one piece?'

'I'm just tired,' he told her, also speaking her native French. 'And very glad to be back.'

'What happened?'

'I was stopped by the Nazis, and they demanded to see my papers.' His forged papers. If there had been a chance to run, he would have. But there was nowhere to go, no way to escape. Running would have meant death. Of course, being exposed as an American spy would mean death, too. Death – but only after gruesome torture as the SS attempted to extract from him the names of the brave men and women who fought alongside him, who opposed the Nazi occupation. But Cybele had assured him his papers were the best she'd ever seen, so he'd handed them over, praying she was right.

'I was detained,' he told her, 'but not because my papers didn't pass their scrutiny.'

He hadn't known that at first. He'd been led away at gunpoint by guards who'd barked at him in a Swiss-Italian dialect that he didn't understand. And then he was locked alone in a room, waiting for a deadly interrogation that never came. He didn't know what was going on until he was loaded onto an already too-crowded railroad car.

'The Vichies have become upset by the food shortages,' he explained to Cybele. 'Because my papers say I'm Italian, I was part of a roundup of nonnationals who were being deported.'

Cybele laughed in disbelief. 'What?'

'I was being sent back to Italy because the Vichies don't want me eating their Brie. And they're just stupid enough to think that as the situation gets worse, the Nazis won't take every little last bit.'

He'd been in the railroad car for close to nine hours before he'd had the chance to escape – by jumping from a speeding train. His bruises were nothing compared to the broken neck he might have gotten with a little less luck.

'After I got free, I had to travel carefully – my papers were still held by the Nazis, on the train. It wasn't easy.' That was an understatement, but he didn't have to go into detail. Cybele had traveled to places she wasn't supposed to be. She knew full well how dangerous and frightening that was. 'I'm sorry I couldn't get back here sooner,' he told her.

'It doesn't matter now,' she said. 'I'm just so glad you are back.'

She hadn't yet pulled out of his arms, and as he held her, gazing down into the bottomless midnight of her beautiful eyes, he couldn't help himself. He bent his head to kiss her, to actually taste the lips he'd dreamed about so many nights.

But Cybele turned her face away, pressing her cheek against his shoulder, and he ended up with his nose buried in her hair.

It had been a stupid move. But when she'd looked at him that way, he'd foolishly dared to hope she'd finally welcome his kisses. He felt doubly foolish as he looked up to find the blond American watching him through the open doorway, amusement dancing in his eyes.

'Nice try,' the man said dryly, the first American English Joe had heard in months that wasn't from a BBC radio broadcast or from his own mouth as he tried to teach Cybele the language. 'But she's definitely not interested. I'm not sure what the story is, since my French is sketchy, but I think there's a husband somewhere.' He looked from Joe to Luc Prieaux and Luc Lambert. 'And none of you have the foggiest idea what I'm saying. Not that it really matters – as long as no one's speaking Deutsch, we'll all get along just fine.'

Cybele had gently pulled free from Joe's arms, and she now looked up at him expectantly, waiting for him to translate.

But the American didn't give him a chance to speak. He pointed to himself. 'Charles Ashton,' he said, enunciating clearly. 'You must be the boss – the one who was missing.

Things got a little tense around here when your friends thought you'd been taken by the Nazis. You're a little bit younger than I expected, but c'est la guerre, right?' He lifted his right arm, then winced, and looking down at his sling, he held out his left hand. *'Let's see if you understand my high school French better than these other frogs. Germ appell Charles.'*

Joe stepped into the room. 'I know your name is Charles Ashton, Lieutenant.' He folded his arms across his chest, purposely not taking the other man's hand. *'I took your dog tags off you last week when you were brought in. These frogs saved your life.'*

Charles was completely surprised, but he only let it show for maybe a tenth of a second. He lowered his hand. 'Whoops. I guess you do understand me – a little too well.' If he were at all embarrassed, it was short-lived. *He shifted painfully so he was sitting up in the bed. Behind his lazy, half-closed eyelids, his gaze was sharp as he looked at Joe with intense interest. 'You have a New York accent. Where the hell did you learn to speak English like that?'*

'In Brooklyn,' Joe replied.

'My God, you're American.' Charles laughed. 'I never would have known from looking at you. No offense.'

'Unfortunately, I can't say the same about you.' Joe turned to look at Cybele, at Luc Lambert. 'Why isn't he up in the attic? If the Germans were to search the house . . .' He realized he was speaking English and repeated himself in French.

Luc shrugged expansively, looking to Cybele.

'The heat,' she told him. 'I couldn't bear to hide him up there. Not with his wounds. Not after what he's done.'

Charles followed her French. 'I've done nothing,' he

protested in English. It was obvious to Joe they'd had this discussion before. 'Tell her whoever she thinks I am, she's mistaken.'

'He's a hero,' Cybele told Joe.

'She's wrong,' Charles told Joe. He turned to Cybele. 'You're wrong. I've spent the weeks since Normandy keeping my head down. My goal is to get home to Baldwin's Bridge, Massachusetts, in one undamaged piece. I'm thinking the sooner you can get me back to my unit, the sooner I'll be shipped back to the States. I'm more than happy to let the rest of the Fifty-fifth chase Hitler out of Berlin. I just want to get back to my summerhouse, make myself a dry martini, and sit watching the sun go down.'

Looking at him sitting there, cigarette dangling between his fingers, it was easy to believe he meant every word. Even dressed in ragged clothes, he looked more like a wealthy aristocrat than a common farmer.

More often than not, it was the common folk, like Cybele and the Lucs and Dominique – and Joe – who were refusing to sit by and let Hitler and his vile SS have free run of Europe.

As he turned away in disgust, Cybele let loose a stream of French that nearly went too fast even for Joe to understand. But he managed to get most of it, and when she was done, he looked at Charles with new respect. He wouldn't have believed it coming from anyone but Cybele.

'She says you saved the lives of twenty-five children and two nuns,' Joe translated. This was not the act of a man interested only in keeping his head down and protecting his own skin. 'She said the sisters were hiding with the children in the basement of the Church of the Ascension, up north, believing it was far enough from the fighting. But the Allies

116

– the men in your battalion – pushed through the Germans' defense, and the battle line moved. Because of that, the church became a target. You and three other American soldiers risked your lives to go to the children's aid.'

For a moment, Joe thought Charles was about to deny it all. But then he shook his head, his mouth a thin line. 'It was a stupid move. Like walking onto a shooting range.'

'I am so sorry your friends were killed,' Cybele murmured, her attempt at English solid but atrociously accented.

Charles understood her nonetheless. 'They weren't my friends. They were just some poor suckers I ordered to come with me. I didn't even give them a choice.' He looked up at Joe, his eyes hard. 'Tell her that. Parlay voo en Fran-sez and make sure she understands that.'

Joe quietly translated, aware that he was merely an interpreter in this highly charged conversation between Cybele and this American.

'Tell him all the children lived,' Cybele ordered. 'Even that one little boy he went back for.'

Joe could see her heart in her eyes, and he knew she was thinking of Michel, her own son. No one had gone back for Michel when the two-year-old had been caught in the cross-fire during one of the few shows of resistance when the Germans first invaded France. His father, Cybele's husband, had been killed first. The poor child had surely been alone and terrified before the explosion that had ended his too short, so precious life.

Joe couldn't read the look that came into Charles Ashton's eyes as he repeated Cybele's words to him in English.

'Tell her not to look at me that way,' the American said grimly, still gazing at Cybele. 'I'm not a goddamned hero.

Tell her I don't know what came over me that morning, that I wouldn't do it again, not for a million dollars.'

As Joe translated, Cybele laughed softly. She turned away. 'Don't tell him,' she said to Joe, 'but I don't believe him.'

'I understood that,' Charles called after her as she left the room. 'Je comprende – but you're wrong. I'm not like you.'

She called to the others to come downstairs and let the American rest, and as usual, the room seemed much less bright without her in it. The very air seemed hotter and heavier. Silently, Dominique and both Lucs followed her out the door. Joe turned to go, too, but Charles stopped him with a hand on his arm.

'I'm not like you,' he said again. 'What are you, anyway? OSS?'

'The less you know about any of us, the better,' Joe told him. 'For you and for us.'

'Whoops, and I overheard Cybele call you Guiseppe. Hope you don't have to kill me now, Joe.'

'As long as this war's on and I'm here, I'm Italian, not American. Don't get in the habit of calling me Joe. If you do, that could get me killed.'

'You're definitely OSS.' Charles squinted from behind the smoke as he lit another cigarette. 'I've heard of you guys, living behind enemy lines, sometimes right next door to the Nazis. You're nuts. You wouldn't catch me doing that.'

'And yet here you are.'

'Not by choice. Maybe I got her wrong, but the girl – Cybele – she seemed to imply that as soon as I'm strong enough, your men'll help me get back to my unit.'

'This girl,' Joe said to Charles, 'owns this house that we're both guests in. And these men – and women – look to her for leadership. She's the "boss," not me. They work with me, not for me.'

The American lieutenant gazed out the bedroom door, into the hallway where Cybele had vanished. 'That's incredible. She's the general of this motley army? She's so . . .'

Beautiful. Feminine. Slight of stature. Yet beneath Cybele's captivatingly dark eyes lay determination that was harder than steel, surrounded by tireless strength.

'Some of the best saboteurs I know are women,' Joe told him. 'Cybele and her friends have helped us fight the Nazis by setting bombs that bend railroad tracks, by providing information about munitions dumps and troop movements. Even just by painting one of Churchill's Vs for Victory on the wall of the commandant's house to keep the Germans on edge.'

'It's a strange world we find ourselves in,' Charles said. He shook his head. 'I can't begin to imagine my wife, Jenny, blowing up train tracks. I can't even picture her able to open a can of paint.'

'You'd be surprised what people can do if they have to,' Joe countered. Charles had a wife. The knowledge relieved him a little too much. As if he really thought he himself had a shot with Cybele, provided Charles was out of the picture. It was ridiculous. She was unattainable, untouchable. She was Joan of Arc, burning with passion but married to her cause. She was an angel to admire from afar, floating high above base human desires, always out of reach.

'Will you talk to Cybele for me?' Charles asked. 'Tell her I don't want to wait. I want to get back to the Allied side of the line as soon as possible.'

'It's not going to be that simple. The line's way up to the north and west,' Joe informed him. 'Miles away. The *fighting's intense – the Germans aren't letting go easily. Getting you across, at least right now, could be pretty difficult.'*

'Damn.' Charles glanced up at Joe, his elegant lips twisting into a smile. *'If I don't get back there soon, I'm not going to be considered wounded enough to be sent home.'*

Joe looked down at the other man's bandaged leg. *'Until you can walk on your own – and quickly – moving you would be too much of a risk.'*

Cybele flowed back into the room then, bringing in a tray with Charles's lunch. Two precious eggs, a slab of dark bread, a bit of cheese, some of the ever-present turnips. *'Risk,'* she said, having caught the word as she set down the tray on the bed beside Charles. She looked at Joe expectantly. *'What are you planning now?'* she asked him, switching into her native tongue.

'Our guest is impatient. He wants to return to his unit as soon as possible.'

'He's too weak still,' she said, then spoke in her stilted English directly to Charles. *'You are not yet strong enough to go anywhere.'*

The lieutenant grinned at her. *'Can't bear the thought of my leaving, can you? I do seem to have that power over the girls. And you are a pretty one, especially for a four star. Your wish is my command, General.'*

Cybele looked at Joe, but this time he took liberties with the translation. He told Cybele, *'He'll go when you say he's ready to go.'*

Kelly sat behind her desk, completely overwhelmed. She knew she had to prioritize. She had to set up an administrative triage. But it was hard to get excited about paperwork when she'd just spent over two hours talking to Betsy McKenna's parents.

God, what a nightmare. Brenda and Robert McKenna had crumpled at the news that six-year-old Betsy's tests had come back positive. It was leukemia. And the fact that the survival rate was better than ever before didn't change the very real possibility that the McKennas could lose their precious child.

They'd finally left, but the dazed look in their eyes haunted Kelly. Dr Martin, the head of oncology at Children's Hospital, wouldn't be able to meet with them until six. Technically, Kelly didn't really have to be there, but Brenda had asked her to come.

That wasn't going to be fun – getting into the technical details of the treatment and its risks.

As Kelly sat at her desk, the paperwork in front of her seemed stupid and unimportant.

She rested her head on a pile of files. Yes, that was definitely a far better use for them.

Her phone rang, and she jerked upright. It was her private line. She picked it up apprehensively. 'Dad?'

'Uh, no, actually, it's Tom.'

'Oh, God, what happened? Is my father—'

'Whoa, wait, everything's okay . . . Jeez, I'm sorry, Kel, it didn't even occur to me that you'd assume there was some kind of trouble if I called.'

Kelly had been holding her breath but now exhaled in a burst. 'Sorry,' she said. '*I'm* sorry. My fault for overreacting.'

It was Tom Paoletti. He'd called her on the phone – but not because her father was ill and needed her. Her pulse began to race for an entirely new reason.

'Actually,' he said with a soft laugh, 'now I feel

really stupid because this is not an important phone call. I mean, it really could have waited until after you got home. I just wanted to find out . . .'

Time hung for a split second as countless possibilities spun out enticingly around her.

'. . . if I could use your computer to sign on to the Internet,' Tom finished.

'Oh,' Kelly said, as disappointment settled down around her like a damp blanket. He only wanted to use her computer. He didn't want to take her dancing, to see a movie, to go to dinner. To have wild sex all night long. 'Well, sure. Yeah. That's no problem.'

'I'll sign on as a guest, use my own account, of course.'

'Of course,' she echoed. 'Use it for as long as you like, whenever you like.'

'Thanks,' he said. 'I really appreciate it.'

'Actually,' she said, 'I'm not sure when I'm going to be home. I've got a meeting at six that could run for a while. I can call Mrs Lerner and see if—'

'Don't sweat it. I'll hang with your father for as long as you need me to.'

Kelly closed her eyes. 'Thanks.'

There was the slightest of pauses, and then he said, 'Well, I won't keep you . . .' at the exact same moment that she opened her mouth and said, 'You know, Tom, I was wondering . . .'

This was it. She was going to do it. She was going to ask him to have dinner with her. She was going to ask him out on a date.

'Whoops,' he said with a laugh. 'Sorry. What's up?'

Ice. Her entire cardiovascular system was suddenly filled with ice.

'Um, I was wondering if you knew that my computer's in my bedroom,' she told him. Chicken. God, she was such a chicken. 'I figured I better tell you where it is so you don't have to search the whole house.' She closed her eyes, wincing silently. Not only was she a chicken, but she sounded like an idiot. An idiot chicken. 'My room's on the second floor, west wing. White walls, blue curtains . . .' Big sign on the wall saying IDIOT LIVES HERE.

It was the same bedroom she'd used as a child – a spacious room with a private bath and French doors connecting to a balcony that looked out over the backyard and the pool. From her second-floor vantage point, she'd been able to see Tom wherever he was working in the yard. Between the balcony and her tree house, she'd pretty much had him covered.

Perverted idiot chicken.

'Oops,' he said. 'I didn't realize you kept your computer in your bedroom. I don't want to invade your privacy or—'

'Do you smoke?' she asked.

'No.'

'Then no problem,' she said. 'It's just a room I happen to sleep in. Brace yourself, though. It's a mess. Just kick aside the dirty laundry and ignore the fact that the bed's not made.'

He laughed again at that. He had an incredibly sexy laugh, low and husky and intimate. He could have made a fortune on one of those 900-number phone sex lines. 'I thought the cleaning lady was just in.'

'Mrs Lerner's under strict orders to stay out of my room,' Kelly told him. 'I happen to like my mess.'

'And you're sure you want me going in there?'

He didn't know the half of it. 'It's really okay.' Kelly flipped through her calendar, searching for the next evening she was available and . . . 'You wouldn't happen to be free Thursday – tomorrow – night?'

Dear God. She did it. She'd actually said the words.

'Yeah, sure,' he said. 'Why? You need me to stay with your father again? No problem. I'm there.'

Words he'd completely misunderstood. How on earth did men live through this time and time again? It was a wonder more of them hadn't simply given up and become monks.

'No.' She closed her eyes, braced herself. 'I was hoping you'd have dinner with me.'

There was complete silence for at least a solid second. But it was a very, *very* long second.

'Well,' he said. 'Wow. Yeah, that would be . . .'

Kelly waited.

'Nice,' he finished.

It wasn't quite the word she was hoping for. But it was far better than a lot of words he might've come up with.

'Okay, good,' she said. God, that had been easier than she'd imagined.

There was another brief moment of silence, during which she realized he could well have accepted her invitation simply because he was kind and he didn't want to hurt her feelings. Maybe even right now he was trying to figure out how he could get out of it. Maybe . . .

She started to stammer. 'Because, you know, I just thought it would be nice –' Oh, crap, there was that awful word again. – 'to go someplace that isn't work or home with someone who . . .' Looks like you. No, wrong thing to say. 'Someone who . . .' Has a penis. Oh, God . . . 'Someone who . . .'

'Isn't eighty years old?' he suggested.

'Well,' she said, 'yeah. Sort of. God, that sounds awful.'

'It's not,' he said. 'Everyone needs a break. A little distraction.'

God, yes. 'Although, to be honest, there's a chance I might have to cancel at the last minute. One of my patients . . .' She had to clear her throat, glad she was talking to him over the phone, glad he couldn't see the sudden very unprofessional tears that welled in her eyes at the thought of sweet little Betsy McKenna and what she was faced with simply to survive. 'She's starting chemotherapy, and she and her parents might need a little extra attention.' Her voice wobbled slightly, and she coughed to cover it. 'Excuse me.'

'Oh, man, that must be hard as hell,' Tom said softly.

Kelly closed her eyes, wanting nothing more than to lose herself in her nearly lifelong attraction to this man. She didn't want to have dinner with him tomorrow night. She wanted him to take her for a ride on his old motorcycle, the one that was still carefully kept under that drop cloth in the garage. She wanted to go fast, fast enough to blot out all her pain and anger and fear.

It was the fear that hurt the worst. Fear that Betsy McKenna would die despite the advances of modern medicine, despite the care of one of the best children's hospital staffs in the world. Fear that her father would go to his grave without reconciling with Joe, fear that Joe would never recover from such a terrible blow. Fear that she'd live the rest of her life wishing she'd had just a few more months with her father, wishing she'd had the nerve to look him in the eye and tell him that she'd loved him – even when he drank, even when he was cruel – and to ask him if maybe there wasn't a time when he'd loved her back, just a little bit.

Fear that she would die just as angry and just as tragically alone.

She needed a distraction, all right, but she wanted something a little more high octane than dinner and conversation. She wanted full body contact and hot, deep kisses. She wanted wild abandon, total, breathtaking full penetration. She wanted to feel nothing but pleasure, nothing but heat. And wild Tom Paoletti was just the man for the job.

She'd spent the past sixteen years waiting for a chance to kiss him again. Wondering if the reality could stand up to the perfection of the memory. Maybe tomorrow night she'd find out.

'How old is she?' Tom asked, his husky voice like velvet against her ear.

'Just turned six.' Her lower lip trembled as if she were no older than that herself. Come on, Ashton, get a grip.

'Damn.'

'Tom . . .' Kelly clamped her mouth shut. What was she going to do, just ask him to have sex with her? A dinner invitation was one thing, but, God . . . She could imagine his surprised response, his attempt to be polite. Well, sure, that would be *nice*, but . . . 'I'm sorry,' she said instead. 'I really have to go.'

'Kelly, I'm . . . here if you need anything.'

'Thanks,' she managed to choke out before she dropped the phone back into its cradle.

And then, although she wanted nothing more than to drop her head onto her paperwork-laden desk and cry, she steeled herself the way she'd done so many times before and got to work.

Her father would have been proud.

Seven

'What good is an apology if you're not going to stop doing the thing that you're apologizing for?' Charles's voice shook with anger. 'That's like saying you're sorry for hitting me on the head with a two-by-four, while you continue to hit me on the head with a two-by-four!'

'But I'm not hitting you on the head,' Joe countered hotly. 'If you want to use that analogy, then you have to picture yourself hitting *me* over the head with that same two-by-four since 1944! You're the one who should apologize to me!'

As Tom came into the room, he saw Charles had stuck his fingers in his ears and was singing at the top of his lungs, 'La, la, la, la, la!' to block out Joe's words.

'What the hell is going on in here?' Tom had to raise his voice to a roar to be heard over them.

The two old men both fell silent, although they still stood, facing off like a pair of ancient boxers, in the middle of Charles's vast living room.

Charles had his oxygen tank at hand, and he took a

hit off it, covering his mouth and nose with the face mask, glaring at Joe.

'Why don't you wear the nose clip?' Joe asked wearily. 'If you need the oxygen—'

Charles picked up his walker and flung it as far as he could across the room – which wasn't very far. '*That's* why,' he said bitterly, trembling with anger. 'I can't walk by myself, I can't breathe by myself. Why doesn't God just strike me with lightning and kill me now?'

'Because there are things left undone,' Joe countered.

'Like telling stupid stories to stupid interviewers?' Charles had to sit down, and as he lowered himself onto the sofa, Tom stepped forward to help. Instead of a thanks, he got a dark look and a frown. 'Stupid stories that mean nothing now? The past is the past, and the dead are dead, Guiseppe. Digging them up—'

'Guys,' Tom said. 'Exactly what happened during the war?'

As he'd expected, they both shut up. Dead silence.

Tom waited. He was in no rush. He had Kelly's permission to use her computer whenever he wanted. He could play referee for hours and still have plenty of time to scan his old files, to read his notes on the Merchant, to wade through his doubt.

Joe was the first to move, the first to speak. 'I have to get back to work,' he said, heading for the door. 'The roses—'

'Stop. The roses can wait,' Tom ordered in his toughest team-commander voice, and Joe actually obeyed him. What do you know? 'Look, gentlemen,

SUZANNE BROCKMANN

I'm not going to pry, so if you don't want to talk about it—'

'We don't,' Charles interrupted with another of his potent death-ray glares aimed at Joe.

'Fine,' Tom said easily. 'Then I'm not going to ask about it again. But answer this for me instead. Joe, this one's for you. How many days does Mr Ashton have left to live?'

It was a cruel question, but letting his uncle walk away, to let the rift between these two old friends continue, would have been even more cruel.

Joe's shoulders sagged and he turned so that Tom couldn't see his face, so he could barely hear his reply. 'I don't know.'

'Yes, you do,' Tom told him. His stomach hurt for both of them, but this had to be said. 'Kelly told me the doctors are saying three or four months, tops. I'm sure you both know this. And I'm certain neither of you are so old and decrepit that you can no longer do simple math.' He looked at Charles. 'How many days does three months work out to be?'

Charles couldn't stay angry in the face of Joe's pain, and he turned his glare on Tom instead. His crackly voice was tinged with ice. 'This isn't necessary.'

'Yes, sir,' Tom said as mildly as he could manage, 'I think it is. Please answer the question. How many days?'

Charles looked at Joe again. 'Maybe ninety,' he finally said. 'But probably fewer.'

'Ninety days,' Tom repeated. 'How many perfect summer days like this, with a clear sky and low humidity, do you think we'll have over the next ninety days?'

Neither of them said a word.

130

'Probably way fewer than ninety,' Tom answered for them. 'In fact, we could well be into the single digits with that one, don't you agree?'

Silence.

Again Tom answered his own question. 'Yes, you agree. So the next obvious question, gentlemen, is: What the fuck are you doing wasting this gorgeous day fighting over some stupid-ass fifty-five-year-old disagreement, when you could be out on Mr Ashton's boat, fishing?'

Charles looked at Joe and Joe looked at Charles.

'Here's the deal,' Tom said. 'This thing you're fighting about? You don't talk about it, you don't *think* about it. You go down to the marina, you pick up some bait, and you spend this day doing something you both love. You sit there in silence if you have to, but you take advantage of this beautiful, precious, God's gift of a day.'

More silence. But Tom stood there, feigning patience, waiting.

Joe finally cleared his throat. 'Shall I call ahead to the harbormaster's office?' he asked Charles stiffly. 'Have them ready the *Lady Luck*?'

For a minute Tom was afraid Charles was too much of a bastard to make this easy for either of them. He didn't answer for way too long.

But when Tom raised his eyebrows and said, 'Mr Ashton? . . .' the old man finally gave in.

'Oh, all right.' It was by no means gracious, but it was good enough for now.

'Listen up,' Tom said to the pair of them. 'Whatever this problem is, you need to work it out. Not today, but soon.'

131

'We can solve this in an instant,' Charles said crankily. 'Joe just has to promise to keep his big mouth shut.'

Joe's big mouth was set in a straight, grim line. 'So I'm just supposed to stand there on that stage and accept that Medal of Honor all over again?' he asked. 'I'm supposed to stand there, in front of national news cameras, and shake the hands of all those dignitaries who've come all the way from England and France, and pretend—'

'Whoa,' Tom said. 'Wait. Dignitaries from where? What are you talking about?'

'The ceremony honoring the Fighting Fifty-fifth,' Joe told him. 'I don't even want to go.'

'You *have* to,' Charles said.

Joe bristled. 'I don't *have* to do anything.'

'Wait,' Tom said. 'Rewind. Did you just say there're going to be dignitaries from *England*?'

'Some distant cousin of the royal family no one's ever heard of,' Charles said grumpily. 'You'd think they'd send Winston Churchill's great-grandson. Now *there's* someone whose hand *I'd* be honored to shake.'

'You don't even know if Churchill *had* a great-grandson,' Joe countered.

'Well, you'd think the organizers of this celebration would at least try to find that out. And who are they sending from France? Some politicians, probably descended from Nazi collaborators.'

'Kelly told me several US senators would be attending, too,' Tom realized. The United States, England, and France. The three countries that had worked together to catch the Merchant back in 1996.

The three countries responsible for taking out most of the Merchant's team – including his beloved wife. Baldwin's Bridge would be packed with revered war heroes and crowds of spectators. CNN cameras would surely be there.

'Holy shit,' Tom said. 'I've got to make a phone call.'

'So it's possible the Merchant's target isn't going to be Boston after all,' Tom told Jazz. 'It could be right here in Baldwin's Bridge. If you can believe that.'

'You're thinking car bomb,' Jazz said.

'You bet. It's been this bastard's MO in the past,' Tom told his longtime XO and friend over the phone in the Ashtons' kitchen.

'What kind of security they gonna have for this shindig?'

'I don't know yet. I've got my uncle making a call to the local police to try to find that out.' Charles and Joe had snapped to. They'd stopped their arguing in the face of this immediate situation.

Tom had told them about spotting the Merchant in the airport, leaving out the part about his recent injury and Admiral Crowley's intense skepticism. Joe and Charles had gone into Charles's home office to try to find out as much as they could about the security planned for the celebration's opening ceremony. It was amazing, actually. As they'd headed down the hall, Tom had heard them speaking entire sentences to each other without flinging a single accusation or petty insult.

'Crowley know yet?' Jazz asked.

'I called, but he wasn't in,' Tom reported. 'I didn't want to leave a message.' No, this was definitely not the kind of thing he wanted to tell the admiral through voice mail. He took a deep breath. This wasn't going to be easy to say, but Jazz had to be told. 'You need to know, he's not behind me a hundred percent on this one, Jacquette.'

'It does sound nuts, sir.' Jazz laughed, a low rumble of distant thunder.

'He's not behind me at all,' Tom admitted.

His XO wasn't fazed. 'So when do you want me out there?'

'Jazz – straightforward, no shit, I could be completely wrong about this. There's a real chance I've lost touch, that this goddamned head injury has made it so I can't tell fantasy from reality.'

'Just give me a day or two to tie up some loose ends,' Jazz told him, 'and I'll be there. I'll call the rest of the squad, too. See who can arrange for leave.'

Jazz was coming to help him. The relief was so intense, Tom had to sit down. 'Be up front with them,' he ordered. 'If they *do* come, if *you* come, it's completely off record, two hundred percent covert, and totally volunteer. It's got to be on your own time as well – and I know you've all got better things to do while you're on leave, so—'

'I always wanted to meet your uncle Joe. 'Sides, isn't there some kind of famous watercolor painting school in Baldwin's Bridge?'

'Since when do you paint?' Tom asked.

'Since two or three days from now, L.T.,' Jazz told him. 'Unless you think I'll stand a better chance of blending with the white folk sunbathing on the beach?'

'Good point.' Tom looked up to see Joe standing in

the doorway. He stepped into the room and handed a piece of paper to Tom, then disappeared again. There were several lines written in Charles's spidery, shaky-looking hand.

'Ah, Christ,' Tom said to Jazz. 'The complete security plan for the ceremony honoring the Fighting Fifty-fifth is the normal Baldwin's Bridge PD weekday staff – five guys. Plus two local rent-a-cops for additional crowd control.'

'In that case, we'll definitely need help. Hang on.'

Tom could hear Jazz rustling papers, heard him swear.

'WildCard's out of the picture, sir,' Jazz reported. 'He's in California on special assignment. Senior Chief Wolchonok's having knee surgery. And O'Leary won't be back for another few weeks. He's at a sharp-shooter's competition in Saudi Arabia.'

'Damn. I'm going to want a shooter of his caliber. I don't want to assume car bomb and then have this turn out to be an assassination attempt.' He closed his eyes. Provided the Merchant was real. Provided Tom hadn't simply imagined seeing the man who may or may not have been the terrorist. 'I'm going to want a sniper of my own set up and ready, too.'

'That's not going to be easy, sir. This competition has drawn all the best men in all the armed forces.'

All the best *men*.

'Find out if Alyssa Locke went to this competition,' Tom ordered. SO squadmember Frank O'Leary was only the second best marksman in the US Navy. Lieutenant Junior Grade Locke had outscored him every single time they'd competed. She was a robot when it came to taking out a target.

'I know for a fact that she didn't,' Jazz told him. 'She wouldn't have been invited. Not to Saudi Arabia. A woman? Not a chance.'

'Call her.'

Jazz paused delicately. 'Sir. Do you think that's . . . wise?'

Locke was outspoken in her desire to be allowed into the male-only ranks of the SEALs. She hounded Tom – and Jazz – every opportunity she got. All she wanted, she claimed, was a chance to prove herself.

'She's pretty career driven,' Tom told him. 'She may not want to take the leave – or the risk. Make sure she understands that this could well be a waste of time. Nothing may come of it at all. She may end up spending a few weeks at the beach, learning to paint with you.'

'With me? Oh, joy,' Jazz said with a complete lack of enthusiasm.

'Did you get a chance to download those files from my computer?' Tom asked.

'It's all there, L.T., ready and waiting for you.'

'Look, Jacquette, I've got to say this again. I don't want you to feel like I'm ordering you to—'

'Completely understood, sir. I'll email you with my flight and arrival time as soon as I've got it.' Jazz cut the connection.

David cleared his throat. 'Mind if I sit down?'

Mallory looked up at him, hostility flaring in her light brown eyes and in the tight line of her delicate lips.

Paoletti was her last name. She lived with her

mother in a house on the other side of town. It hadn't been hard for David to find out all about her from the kids who hung out down by the town beach.

All about her. More, in fact, than he'd wanted to hear.

Both she and her mother were well-known for putting out for money or drugs. They weren't picky. They didn't take credit cards, but a simple line of cocaine would do the trick. According to town legend, that would buy a guy a professional-quality blow job. A slightly larger amount would get that much more. Here in Baldwin's Bridge, a man could have his pick of Paolettis – young or older. And apparently the mother was just as exotically, trashily beautiful as the daughter.

While David was far from the most experienced man in the world, he'd been around enough to know that when rumors came in gift-wrapped packages like that, complete with a ribbon around them, it was unlikely they were true. Mallory *and* her mother. Highly unlikely.

It sounded like small-town pettiness and jealousy to David. He didn't believe a single word.

He'd gone back to the Ice Cream Shoppe to see what time she got off work, and the manager there had told him she was doing an extra shift today. Mallory was working until eight, but right now she was taking her dinner break.

David had known exactly where to find her, and sure enough, she was back under the tree.

'Don't you ever give up?' Mallory asked him. 'Haven't you gotten tired yet of me telling you to get the hell away from me?'

He sat down in the shade about four feet away from her, pretended to think about it. 'Nope.'

She made a point of turning slightly away from him and continuing to read. She had another of those pathetic-looking, dried-up little peanut butter sandwiches for her dinner, and she ate it slowly as she devoted all her attention to the pages of her book.

David couldn't keep from looking at the soft curve of her cheek, her delicate nose, the slightly exotic shape of her eyes, her flawless skin, and her mouth. God, Mallory Paoletti had a perfect mouth.

Her chin was perfect, too. She held it at a stubborn angle, unaware that the defiant pose exposed the soft, graceful lines of her throat and neck. She had a long, elegant neck, collarbones that could have inspired an entire epic poem, and truly magnificent breasts.

She was his Nightshade, come to life. Of course, dressed the way she was in wide-legged cargo pants and a tank top, she looked more like Nightshade's human alter ego, Nicki Sheldon.

David pulled his day pack onto his lap, unzipping it and pulling out his own book – a copy of the same novel Mallory was reading. He'd managed to pick it up in the Super Stop & Shop at a discount.

Four feet away, Mallory changed her position. He didn't look up, but he heard her put her empty sandwich Baggie back into the brown bag. He heard her crinkle that bag, heard her shift her position once again.

And then she spoke. To him. In a voice dripping with skepticism. 'Oh, come on. You don't expect me to believe you're really reading that, do you?'

He looked at her over the top of his book. 'Of course I'm reading it. I'm more than half done.'

The look on her face was so comical, he nearly pulled his camera out of his pack to get it down on film.

'You're reading a romance.' She looked around. 'Out here, in front of everyone?'

David looked around, too. There were about twenty people on the lawn in front of the hotel, more down by the marina. Not a single person was paying either of them the slightest bit of attention. He shrugged. 'Yeah. You were right about it. It's great stuff. Thanks for recommending it.'

'You're really reading the whole thing?' she asked suspiciously. 'You're not just flipping through and reading only the sex scenes?'

'Why would I do that?'

'Because you're a guy? . . .'

'I'm really reading the whole thing.' He smiled. 'But I have to confess, when I get to them, I read the sex scenes twice.'

Her lips twitched, curving up into a very small smile. 'Yeah, well, join the club,' she said. 'So do I.'

She smiled at him. She smiled at him! It was a real, genuine we-have-something-in-common smile, not an I-want-to-put-your-eye-out-with-my-finger smile.

Mallory was nearly done with her book. 'You read fast,' he said.

She looked at his book, at the place where he was using his finger as a bookmark. 'You do, too.'

'I've always loved to read,' he told her. 'As long as I've got a book, it doesn't matter where I am. I can instantly be a million miles away, in a completely different place, on a different planet even. I can be someone else, you know? When it gets too complicated to be myself.'

Mallory nodded, but then she looked away, as if she were afraid she'd given too much away with that one little gesture of agreement. 'God, I need a cigarette,' she breathed.

'It's hard to quit, huh?'

'You wouldn't happen to have one, would you?'

'I don't smoke.'

'You wouldn't.'

It was meant to be an insult, but David let it slide. Mallory Paoletti had created some pretty staunch defenses to keep people out of her world. If he wanted in – and he did – he was going to have to ignore the scratch of the verbal brambles and step lightly over the passive-aggressive minefields.

He unzipped his pack again and dug into it, searching for the book he'd put in this afternoon. He found it underneath his camera, and held it out to her. But she didn't take it, and he ended up just setting it down in front of her, an offering to the goddess.

'I started reading this book –' he gestured to the one he was reading, the book she'd recommended, – 'and it occurred to me that you might have never read anything by Heinlein. I thought you might want to borrow one of my favorites.'

Mallory looked down at the book he'd put in front of her but she didn't touch it. She just looked at the cover, looked back at him. 'What do you want from me?'

The question was so point-blank that David didn't quite know how to answer it. He couldn't answer it, not caught the way he was in the intensity of her eyes.

'Do you really think that if you sign me up for some

little private book club, I'll let you slip me something besides a book every now and then? Is that what this is about? You want to do it with me, geek-boy?'

Geek-boy. Ouch. But David didn't get a chance to respond. She was spitting mad and she wasn't done yet. He found his voice but all he could get out was 'N—'

She pushed herself to her feet, savagely kicking his book back toward him, gathering up her crumpled bag, her half-finished soda, and her own book.

David had envisioned himself taking days, weeks even, to make friends with Mallory. And only then, after they were friends, would he tell her about Nightshade. But he realized now it wasn't going to happen that way. It was now or never.

And so he stood, too, fumbling in his pack for *Wingmasters Two*, pulling it free. 'I do want something from you, Mallory. You're right about that. But it's not what you think. See, I want you to model for me, for my next project.'

He held it out and she stared down at the dark colors on the cover.

'*Wingmasters Two?*' she read. She looked up at him. 'A comic book?'

'It's a graphic novel. We try to make it higher quality than a comic book. But you better believe if we got an offer from DC or Marvel, we'd proudly become a comic book in an instant.' He pointed to names on the front. 'By Renny Shimoda and David Sullivan. Artwork by David Sullivan. That's me.'

She gave him a disbelieving look as she pulled the book from his hands to take a closer look.

'*Wingmasters One* and *Two* both had limited

printings – a few thousand copies each. We started our own publishing company to distribute them,' he told her as she flipped through it. 'We had to pay for the printing up front, but we've made back most of our initial investment. Unfortunately, the series didn't catch on quite the way we'd hoped,' he continued, 'even though it's a cult favorite.'

She was standing there, flipping through the pages, probably only half listening.

'For the past two months, I've been developing a new series. *Nightshade*. This one's all mine. The story's mine, too, not just the artwork. It's about this high school girl, Nicki Sheldon, who realizes she has these superpowers. Kind of Buffy meets the X-Men.'

Mallory frowned up at him. 'So I'm just supposed to believe that you're *this* David Sullivan. The one whose name is on the front of this thing, this *graphic novel*.'

David took out his wallet, took out his driver's license.

She took it from him, squinted at his name and his parents' address in Newton. 'God, this picture sucks.' She looked up at him again. 'Well, maybe it doesn't.' She handed it back to him, still unconvinced. 'David Sullivan's a common enough name.'

David knew how to prove he was who he said he was. He sat down on the grass, searching through his pack for a pencil and his sketch pad. He opened to a clean page, balanced the pad on his leg, looked up at Mallory, and started to draw.

'Do me a favor and sit,' he ordered her. 'My neck's going to break.'

She was watching his pencil moving across the

142

page, and she slowly lowered herself to the ground. She sat forward, on her knees, so she could watch him draw.

'Oh, my God,' she breathed. 'That is so cool.'

It wasn't *that* good. He could do a lot better when not under so much pressure. But it wasn't bad, either – a rough comic-book version of Mallory's face, complete with her trademark scowl. He added a body – an exaggerated, stylized, superhero type body, in a superhero pose. Hands on hips, legs slightly spread in a powerful stance, muscles rippling, chest out.

'Nightshade,' Mallory read aloud as he printed the name in block letters beneath his drawing. She looked at the similar drawings on the cover of *Wingmasters Two*, then up at him. 'Holy shit, you *did* draw this, didn't you?'

He turned his notebook around so that it faced her. 'What I'd like to do,' he told her, 'is take photos of you. All kinds of poses, from all angles. The hardest thing is drawing realistic-looking bodies – you know, anatomically correct bodies that move and bend and flex the way real people do. I took an anatomy class in school last year, and that's helped a lot. But getting the right perspective is hard, too. Still, if I can have a few hundred photos of you pinned up around my drawing table, it makes it that much easier.'

She laughed as she gazed at the drawing. 'That really looks like me. That's so weird.'

'Here,' David said, moving closer to her. 'Let me show you what I mean.'

He took his camera out of his pack and placed it gently on the grass as he dug for the pictures he'd just got back from the developers at the drugstore.

'Oh, man, that's one huge camera.'

'The camera's actually pretty small.' He picked it up again and handed it to her. 'It's the lens that's big.' He pointed to the viewfinder. 'Look through there. Check it out. And move this, here, to focus.'

Their fingers touched, and she didn't pull away. He was close enough to smell the sweet scent of peanut butter on her breath.

She laughed. 'This is one of those paparazzi lenses – the kind photographers from the *National Enquirer* use to get pictures of Fergie sunbathing topless from, like, five miles away.' She looked up from the viewfinder, and at this proximity, he could see flecks of green and gold mixed in with the light brown of her eyes. She was gorgeous from forty feet away, stunning from four feet. From four inches, she was heart stopping.

David felt his IQ drop into the single digits as he stared into her eyes.

'So who were you taking pictures of with this superlens?' she asked. 'Prince William in town?'

'No,' he managed to say. 'No one – I mean, not yet. I mean, I was going to take some pictures later this afternoon.'

Pictures. Right. He was going to show her his pictures. Come on, brain. Don't fail now. She was sitting here, she was listening to him, she was interested in his project.

She handed the camera back to him, and again their fingers touched. 'I was in media club in middle school,' she told him. 'I loved it – I got to borrow this really cool camera and take all these freaky black-and-white pictures. Well, I did until Mark Fritz stole the camera from my locker. He told me he took it, but then he denied it when I told Mr Marley. It was Mark against me, and he got straight As and was captain of the middle-school tennis team, so I was blamed. I wasn't kicked out of media club, but I wasn't allowed to borrow the equipment anymore, so what was the point? My mother bought me some little Instamatic piece of shit to try to make me feel better. She didn't know the difference between that and a Nikon.'

Both Mark Fritz and Mr Marley deserved a sound thrashing. 'You can do a lot with an Instamatic,' he said. 'Or even one of those disposable cameras you can pick up at the drugstore. Especially if you work with natural light. Do you still take pictures?'

She shrugged evasively. It was hard to say whether it was a yes shrug or a no shrug. She glanced at her watch. Damn, he was losing her.

'I have to head back to the Ice Cream Shoppe in about five minutes.'

David found the packets of photos in the front pocket of his pack. 'Here, let me just show you these really quickly.'

Some of them were pictures he'd taken here in town. But most were from his recent photo session with Brandon.

'I took these in my apartment,' he told her. 'This is my friend Brandon Crane. He's a lifeguard over at the hotel. Basically, what I do is have him come in, he puts on a bathing suit—'

'Oh, is that what you call that?' Mallory asked. 'It doesn't leave a whole lot to the imagination, does it?'

David laughed. 'It's a Speedo. It's legal. Guys wear 'em all the time.'

'Yeah, maybe in Provincetown.' She flipped through the photos. 'God, what are you going to have *me* wear?'

His pulse kicked into gear. The way she'd asked that question, it was as if it was already a done deal, as if she was ready to sign on. But he couldn't assume that. He had to play it cool, play it out.

'Do you have a bikini?' he asked.

She shook her head. 'I burn so I don't do much sunbathing.'

'I've got a costume box, with bikinis in just about every size. If you found one you liked, you could even keep it after.'

She went back through the pictures of Brandon, looking at them more closely. 'I'm not sure I'd *want* to keep it after. Besides, what if it was the one you like to wear?'

Was that lighthearted teasing or was her comment intended to belittle, to cruelly mock him? David couldn't tell.

'Personally, I'm fond of my pink ballerina tutu,' he said lightly, choosing to believe she was teasing. 'That and the chicken suit. As long as you stay away from those . . .'

She laughed. And then she held up a particularly buff photo of Bran. 'Is this guy really a lifeguard here in town? He looks like he belongs on a movie set in LA. How'd you talk him into doing this, anyway?'

'We've been friends since fourth grade. He got this summer job for me as a breakfast waiter at the hotel.

He poses for me for free – for something called deferred payment. We have an understanding that if I make it big, I'll pay him lots of money down the road. But I could pay you up front, if you want. Fifty dollars an hour is about all I could afford, with a two hour guarantee.'

She was suddenly intently studying the photos again, as if she didn't want to look him in the eye. 'That seems like an awful lot of money just for standing around in a bathing suit.'

'Professional models get more than that,' he told her.

She was silent.

'What I'd really like,' David said, praying that he hadn't just screwed this up by talking about money, 'would be to schedule a shoot with both you and Brandon. I'm going to want a bunch of individual shots of you, of course, but it would be good to get some of the two of you together. He can show you how it's done.' Maybe she'd be more comfortable knowing she wasn't going to be alone with David in his apartment studio. 'He's going to be Julian, your love interest in the graphic novel.'

'Just how graphic is this graphic novel?' she asked suspiciously.

'No,' he said quickly. 'Not that way. Not at all. I'm targeting as wide an audience as possible. Some of the artists like to be, um, well, explicit. And while I imply certain relationships . . . I don't . . . I mean, sure, I'll show the two characters kiss, but . . .'

She looked down at the pictures of Brandon again. 'So . . . you want to take pictures of me kissing your friend.'

'Well, yeah, I mean, a few shots, sure. Kisses are hard to draw, so . . .'

'Is he, like, unattached?'

David's stomach twisted as he gazed at her. The question was posed so casually. *Too* casually. Oh, damn. This had happened too many times before. He and Brandon would be out somewhere, he'd meet a girl he really liked – and Bran would take her home. It was inevitable.

It was a pain in his ass.

Still, this wasn't about him liking this girl. This was about convincing her to pose for him. This was about *Nightshade*.

'Yeah,' he told her, pushing up his glasses with one finger. 'He's unattached. A word of warning, though – one look at you and he'll be hitting on you.' He felt like some kind of backward pimp, trying to entice her to come to his studio with promises of a roll with his friend, Mr Incredible Pecs.

Mallory shook her head. 'No way. A guy like this only goes out with the Susan Thornridges and the Mary Beth Blacklys.' She put the photos back in the envelope. 'And even if he *did* ask, I wouldn't go anywhere with him. I don't need his kind of shit messing up my life, no thanks.'

'Well, then I'll make sure I tell him to back off.' David was ready to promise her anything. Whatever it took. Brandon or not. Of course he preferred *or not*, but she would probably change her mind with one face-to-face meeting with his charismatic friend.

She stood up, brushing off the seat of her jeans. 'I'm late. I've got to go.'

'How's tonight?' he asked, reaching into his pack

148

for one of his cards. 'I happen to know that Bran's got the night off. He could be at my place by nine. What do you say? Nine to eleven?' He wanted to drop to his knees and plead, but he knew he'd get further by staying at least relatively cool.

She took her time taking his card from him, but this time she actually read it. He'd written his summer address and phone number on it in clean block letters.

'The bathing suit stays on?' she asked.

'Swear to God,' he said. 'If you want, you can bring your father along as a chaperone.'

'How about I bring my uncle?' she said challengingly. 'He's a Navy SEAL, in town on leave.'

David fumbled his sketch pad, dropping it onto the grass. A *SEAL* . . . 'Really?' His voice cracked. 'That's so cool. SEALs are built like gods. Definitely bring him. Do you think . . . wow, do you think he'd pose for me?'

Mallory laughed. 'No,' she said. 'But I will. You just convinced me you're for real, Sullivan. God, your dork index is off the charts.'

Yes. Thank God for his dork index, whatever that meant. David grinned at her. 'Then I'll see you tonight.' Oh, man, he had to get home fast and clean his apartment.

She scowled at him. 'If I turn out to be wrong about you, I will kick you so hard your balls will come out your nose. Do you understand?'

David couldn't keep from laughing, the image was such an intense one. 'Absolutely.'

She glared at him one more time as if to prove that she was dead serious, then turned and walked away, heading back to work, carefully tucking his card into the back pocket of her jeans.

David waited until she turned the corner onto South Street, and only then did he do a victory dance around the tree.

She was his. She was *his*.

Well, on paper, anyway.

Eight

Just kick aside the laundry, Kelly had said.

It seemed easy enough in theory. Execution, however, was slightly more difficult.

Because it seemed to Tom as if most of the laundry that was scattered about the room was underwear. Lacy, silky, completely feminine underwear.

It was on the bed, on the floor, on the chair in front of the computer, spilling out of the open top drawer of Kelly's dresser.

Sure, there were jeans and shorts and T-shirts, too. But he had those things in his own laundry hamper. He was used to them. He could kick that aside, no problem – he had many times in his own room. But the bras and panties and pantyhose . . . Yikes.

And when he had actually tried to push the laundry gingerly aside with his foot, a pair of green satin and lace panties had caught on his sandal, the fabric decadently cool against his bare toes.

Kelly Ashton's underwear.

That alone would have been too much to deal with. But when he'd leaned over to pull the green lace free, he'd found out something he wasn't sure he wanted to know.

Kelly Ashton wore thong panties.

Tom sat at her computer now, head pounding, slightly nauseated from dizziness, breathing in the ghostly fragrance of her perfumes and lotions, still slightly shocked. Jesus, he didn't want that image in his head – Kelly in her underwear was bad enough, but Kelly wearing *that*?

Forget about his head injury – that image alone was enough to make him dizzy.

And it was definitely *not* what he wanted to be thinking about when he had dinner with her tomorrow night, God help him.

Kelly Ashton had asked him to have dinner with her.

Down boy. It was only dinner.

Or was it?

He'd assumed that whipped cream comment she'd made this morning had been a joke. But what if she'd been only half kidding? What if she truly wanted . . .

Don't go there, dirtbrain.

Kelly Ashton probably wouldn't have agreed to let him use her computer if she'd known that he'd sit here, ogling her underwear, imagining her naked and locked with him in heart-stopping, gymnastically energetic sex.

Or maybe not energetic sex. Maybe sex with Kelly would be pulse-hammeringly slow. Devastatingly lethargic. Like one of those pseudo-erotic, black-and-white fragrance commercials on TV. Except there would be nothing pseudo about it. He would surround himself with her infinitely slowly, losing himself in her body as surely as he lost himself in her eyes. It would be the kind of sex where just one touch, just one of her fingers trailed lightly down the length of his arm, would be enough to push him over the edge and . . .

Christ, he had to get out of here.

Because that wasn't going to happen. Not tomorrow night, not ever.

Even if she wanted it, he was in no position right now to begin anything with a woman like Kelly Ashton. He'd spent his entire life avoiding women like her – the sweet, the innocent, the *nice* women who deserved lasting, committed relationships with gentle, caring men – and Kelly was their queen.

But, sweet God, he wanted her. He'd always wanted her, even when it was illegal to want her. Back then, it was easy. If he had touched her the way he'd wanted to touch her, he'd go to jail. It was bad enough that he'd kissed her. He'd banished himself for that, forcing himself to face the hurt in her eyes as he left without any real explanation. Afraid to be alone with her, he'd written a note. 'I'm sorry. I can't do this.' He'd said nothing about her being too young, nothing about his fear that he'd be swept away by passion if he so much as faced her again.

He could still hear her whisper, 'Meet me later tonight. In the tree house,' when he closed his eyes.

He'd wanted to. God, he had wanted Kelly more than he'd ever wanted anyone or anything. But his passion had terrified him. He'd taken only the time to scribble that note and put it where she'd find it before he'd taken off on his motorcycle, riding hard and fast until he'd run out of gas, until he'd stranded himself far from home.

Until there was no possible way he could make it back to Baldwin's Bridge that night, to meet Kelly in her tree house.

But he was back in Baldwin's Bridge now. And she wasn't too young any longer. No, now the risks were far less well-defined, and mostly emotional.

But they were no less dangerous, because it was Kelly's heart he'd be risking.

As Tom waited for the printer to spit out the second of his pictures of the Merchant, he glanced around Kelly's room, trying to ignore the underwear.

Her bed was unmade. It was a colorful jumble of flowery sheets, an antique four poster complete with a blue canopy that matched the window curtains. It looked comfortable and cool, and he longed to crawl in, to soothe his aching head by closing his eyes and sinking back among her sweetly fragranced pillows.

Like a reverse Goldilocks and the three bears, he'd be there when she got home and . . .

Well, there you go. If he ended up getting kicked out of the Navy, he had a future writing scripts for porno flicks.

Jesus, what was wrong with him that he should be completely unable to stop fantasizing about Kelly this way? And the truly stupid part was that she wasn't just some low-wattage babe he'd spotted in some trashy bar. The truth was that he respected Kelly. He admired her. She was brilliant and bright.

Back when they were both in high school, he'd loved to talk to her, to watch her brain work. She wasn't afraid to disagree with him, although always politely, of course. She was one of the nicest, sweetest, kindest people on the face of the earth.

154

His instincts should have been to protect her, to revere her, to worship her from afar. To hold her in esteem, as she deserved to be – the way he did his grandmother, Mother Teresa, and Julie Andrews.

Sunlight streamed in through the curtains, through the French doors that opened onto a narrow balcony. It was pretty enough to look at, but completely idiotic when it came to Kelly's personal safety. Any fool could climb up to the balcony in half a second. And the locks on the French doors were bush league. A four-year-old could have kicked them in.

Tom made a mental note to go back to Home Depot, get some proper locks. Dead bolts. After all, he wasn't going to be in town forever.

Surely she knew. So why, then, had she asked him to dinner?

She was still attracted to him. He'd have to be a fool not to see it. But if he was a bad candidate for a love affair this morning, this afternoon he was even worse.

The fear that had grabbed him when he'd seen the Merchant at the Home Depot had lodged in his chest, solid and unmoving. What if he *was* crazy? What if he started seeing terrorists everywhere he went? What if, because of this, he really *did* have to leave the Navy?

Now, more than ever, he had to keep Kelly at arm's length.

But now, more than ever, Tom wanted to lose himself in the sweet comfort of her arms.

God, he wanted her. And if she wanted him, how the hell was he going to keep turning her down?

The printer fell silent, and Tom shut down Kelly's computer. As he crossed to the door, he had to shake another piece of silk and lace from his foot. Cursing, he took the pictures he'd printed out into the hallway, down the stairs, and into the dining room, only to find Charles and Joe smack in the middle of another argument.

'You're wrong,' Charles said hotly. 'That's too obvious.'

'Keep it simple, stupid,' Joe countered.

Charles glared. 'Who are you calling stupid?'

Pain knifed behind Tom's left eye and his stomach churned. 'Mother of God,' he ground out, and they turned to look at him. 'I leave you alone for thirty minutes and you're back at it. If you can't get along without fighting, I don't want your help.' He gazed sternly at his uncle. 'I expected better from *you*,' he told Joe. 'I mean, come on. Calling him names? . . .'

'Names?' Joe looked from Tom to Charles, clearly confused.

'*Stupid*, stupid,' Charles reminded him.

Dawn broke. 'No,' Joe said. 'It's that expression. Tommy, you say it all the time. KISS simple. KISS stands for Keep It Simple, Stupid. I wasn't . . .' He started to chuckle. 'You thought I was calling Charles . . .' He looked at Charles, sitting at the table, taking a grim hit from his oxygen tank. 'You thought it, too. I could call you a lot of things, Ashton, but I'd never call you stupid.'

Charles looked mollified. 'Well, thank you. I think.'

'We were trying to figure out the best place near the hotel for a terrorist to leave a car bomb,' Joe told Tom.

Tom saw that, indeed, they'd spread out a huge map of the town on the dining-room table.

Joe put one finger down on the map, directly on top of the circular drive that graced the front of the hotel.

'I thought this Merchant fellow would just pull right up to the front doors, but Charles thought that would be too obvious.' He looked at his friend. 'You went with us once, to take out the train tracks the Germans were using to send reinforcements and supplies to the front line. The Nazis were expecting sabotage. They expected us to sneak to some secluded part of the track, in the night. Do you remember what we did?'

Charles didn't answer.

'We went in near the town, near the German barracks,' Joe reminded him. 'They never expected us to come so close, so the tracks weren't guarded there. It was Cybele's idea—'

'Of course I remember,' Charles cut him off, suddenly looking every minute of his age. 'You *know* I remember. God damn it!'

'Was this back in '44?' Tom asked. He honestly wanted to know, but even more than that, he wanted to keep them talking. Who was this Cybele?

They both would have been impossibly young. Joe something ridiculous, like twenty, Charles barely twenty-four.

When Tom was twenty-four, he'd just finished BUD/S, the SEAL training program. He'd just been assigned to his first team, and he'd taken part in some dangerous covert operations almost right away. But he'd been trained. Extensively and exhaustively, for years. He was strong and fit, both physically and psychologically. He was prepared to deal with damn near anything.

And despite all his massive preparation, there had been times down through the years when he'd been scared shitless.

Joe and Charles had had a few short months, at best, of boot camp before they were tossed into the fray. Fate had dealt them a hand requiring them to fight a very personal war from deep within enemy territory – one of the very things Tom had been trained so extensively to do.

But they'd had no training in covert operations, no experience – not much more than an intense conviction that what they were doing was right and necessary.

Tom had grown up knowing Joe and Charles had fought in the Second World War, but he'd never known exactly what that meant before this. Sabotaging German trains. Going in close to the German barracks. *Cybele* . . .

Of course, he wasn't likely to find out any more details, since both were silent, neither of them answering his questions, Joe looking at him as if he'd said what he'd said only because he'd forgotten Tom was standing there.

His uncle sat down on the other side of the table as if he were suddenly feeling as ancient and ill as Charles.

'You want me to leave so you can keep talking about this?' Tom asked them quietly.

'*No.*' They spoke in unison, both vehemently.

'I've made a few phone calls,' Charles said, clearing his throat repeatedly, changing the subject. 'I figured we'd need a few more computers if we were going to catch this terrorist. I ordered three. We can use the east wing for our HQ. I ordered more phone lines, too. I had to pay out my butt to get them to come on Friday. And that was the absolute earliest they could get here.'

'Whoa.' Tom was dizzy now for an entirely new

reason. 'Before you start spending any money, you need to know—'

'That your superiors don't believe this man you saw is really the Merchant?' Charles fixed him with a gaze that was laser-beam sharp.

'There is that little problem,' Tom agreed.

'Figured as much. It *does* sound crazy. A terrorist planning to blow up a New England seaside resort? What drugs are *you* on?'

'Which is why you shouldn't be so quick to spend your money,' Tom countered.

'It's my money,' Charles said crankily. 'I'll spend it however I damn please. It's not like I'm going to be able to use it in a few months, so I might as well use it now.'

Tom sat at the table, wishing his legs didn't feel so weak, pressing his left eyebrow with his thumb. Christ, his head hurt.

'What I have to do,' Tom told them, 'is make my story sound less crazy. Tracking down this guy or finding this bomb I'm pretty sure he's making would help.'

'A photo of him,' Charles suggested. He reached for the telephone. 'I'll get us some cameras.'

Tom stopped him, gently moving the telephone out of the old man's reach.

'A photo won't necessarily help.' He slid the two pictures he'd printed off Kelly's computer toward the old men.

'That's him, huh?' Charles asked, fumbling for the reading glasses he kept in his shirt pocket. 'The Merchant?'

'I'm pretty sure this was the man I saw,' Tom told

them. 'But he doesn't look much like this anymore.'

'He wouldn't,' Joe commented. 'Considering half the world is after him.'

'The changes he's made to his face are subtle but it really does the trick,' Tom admitted.

'Any identifying marks?' Joe asked. 'Something that would give him away?'

'Nothing that he wouldn't have already changed. However, the extremist group he's associated with in the past all wore the same tattoo,' Tom told him. 'A stylized eye on the back of their right hands.' He drew the circular symbol of power and omnipotence for them on the back of one of the pictures. 'It's relatively small – no larger than a quarter, probably more like the size of a nickel. The Merchant I knew wouldn't have had that removed, but now, who knows. If he's still got it, he probably wears a Band-Aid to conceal it.'

'So we should look for a man about your height,' Charles clarified, 'graying hair, bad skin, with a Band-Aid or a tattooed eyeball on the back of his right hand.'

Charles was really getting into this. In fact, ever since Tom had shown them the pictures of the Merchant, the old man hadn't looked quite such a deadly shade of pale. While he didn't quite have color in his cheeks, it had been several minutes since he'd needed his oxygen tank, since he'd had one of his coughing spells.

Still, Tom couldn't keep from smiling, imagining Charles wandering up and down the streets of Baldwin's Bridge with his walker and his oxygen tank, glaring at every passerby, searching for a man with a Band-Aid on the back on his right hand.

'What we need to do is get this Merchant's fingerprints,' Charles declared. 'They'll believe you then.'

'Provided NAVINTEL or the CIA has a record of his fingerprints on file, getting a match would probably solve our problems,' Tom said cautiously. 'But before we can get his prints, we've got to find the man. We're going to need more than just three pairs of eyes for that. My XO, Lieutenant Jacquette, is coming into town Friday afternoon, along with Ensign Starrett and Lieutenant Locke.'

There had been email from Jazz. The rest of the men in the SO squad were tied down, but he and Sam Starrett could and would get leave. They would rent a car from Logan and drive out to Baldwin's Bridge, ETA 1500 hours. Oh yeah, Alyssa Locke would be with them, too, God help them all.

'They can stay here,' Charles decided. 'We've got plenty of room.'

'It would probably be a good idea to check with Kelly first,' Joe suggested.

'Why do I have to check with Kelly? It's my house—'

'Because she's your daughter and she lives here, too,' Tom cut him off. 'Although it would be good when you check with her if you could ask if she minds my *vacationing friends* staying in some of your spare rooms.'

'You don't want Kelly to know about this?' Joe asked.

Tom hesitated. Maybe Kelly *should* know everything. Maybe if she thought he was looney tunes, she'd back off and he wouldn't have to worry about finding the strength to push her away.

'I don't know,' he finally said. 'Let me decide what to tell her. In the meantime, *no* one knows.' He looked from Charles to Joe. 'We need to keep this to ourselves, gentlemen. I know you can keep a secret.' Obviously, since they'd been keeping *some*thing secret since 1944. 'And I'm serious about needing you to stop the bullshit quarreling. If you can't do that, then you better just stay the hell away. I don't need that kind of help. Am I understood?'

Charles looked at Joe, and Joe looked at Charles. They both looked at Tom and nodded. Jesus, it was reluctant, though. As if they'd been mortal enemies these past sixty years instead of best friends.

Tom stuck it to them mercilessly. 'From now on, I need you to be inseparable. Whenever you leave this estate, you go together, and you go with a cell phone. You see anyone suspicious, you stay out of sight. You follow them – if you can – and you call me. No heroics.'

'Do you want us to go over to the hotel, set up surveillance in the lobby?' Charles asked, enjoying this immensely. 'If this Merchant's in town, he's got to be staying somewhere.'

'I'll get the chess set,' Joe said. 'It'll be the perfect cover. This terrorist will never suspect that two old men playing chess in the hotel lobby are really looking for him.'

He disappeared into the other room, and Charles stood up, too. 'Better get my hat.'

Tom watched him shuffle from the room, his oxygen tank forgotten. And for the first time in his life, he found himself thinking, thank God for the Merchant.

*

After hearing at the farm stand that Mrs Ellis had seen her father and Joe playing chess in the lobby of the Baldwin's Bridge Hotel, Kelly had been in a real rush to get home. But now that she was here, she paused just outside the door. She could see Tom through the screen, sitting at the kitchen table, surrounded by piles of papers and file folders.

He was wearing reading glasses, half glasses that made him look completely paradoxical – the intellectual warrior, or the thug librarian – and he rested his forehead in the palm of one hand. As she stood for a moment, holding the bag of fresh fruit and vegetables she'd picked up, he closed his eyes and rubbed his forehead as if he still had that terrible headache.

She shifted her weight slightly, and the brown paper of the bag made only the very softest sound, but he looked up, looked out into the darkness toward her, instantly alert. He was up on his feet, moving toward the door in one graceful motion. Flipping on the outside light, he opened the screen.

Kelly stood there, blinking at him in the sudden brightness.

He grabbed the glasses off his face and all but hid them behind his back.

Hi, honey, I'm home. For a few brief seconds, Kelly let herself imagine what it could be like to come home after a hard day of work to someone like Tom Paoletti. He'd meet her at the door with a soul kiss, start stripping her out of her professional doctor's clothes before they even made it down the hall to the bedroom. They'd have sex right there on the kitchen table, or up against the wall outside her bedroom door,

163

or on the living-room floor, and all the struggles and pain and frustrations of her day would just slip away.

'Sorry,' he said, stepping aside to let her in. 'I wasn't thinking. I should've turned on that outside light earlier.'

'That's okay.' Her voice sounded breathy and she cleared her throat, afraid he'd somehow know the direction her thoughts had gone. 'It's not as dark out there as it looks from in here.'

She put the bag down on the counter as he started to gather up his papers, having neatly made his glasses vanish into one of his pockets. He was wearing a loose-fitting T-shirt and a baggy pair of shorts that tried to hide the hard perfection of his body. But she could see most of his legs – long and tanned, lightly covered with golden brown, sun-bleached hair. His calves were muscular, his taut thighs disappearing up into the loose legs of his shorts. It didn't take much imagination to visualize the way those thighs would keep going, leading up to the sculpted perfection of his rear end and narrow hips.

'You don't have to put that away,' she told him. 'You can work here as long as you like.'

'Thanks,' he said, 'but I'm pretty much done. Everything okay?'

She managed to smile. 'As okay as it can be when a six-year-old has a potentially terminal illness. Betsy's going into the hospital first thing in the morning. There's a few more tests to run before we start the chemo and . . .'

Kelly realized she could hear the sounds of a baseball game coming from the living room. The living room. When Charles was alone, he watched from his favorite chair in the room he called the TV room. But he usually watched in the living room on the big screen television when he wasn't alone.

When Joe was with him.

She pushed open the kitchen door that led into the darkened dining room and moved toward the archway that separated the banquet-size area from the enormous living room. There was only one lamp on, but the light from the big screen TV more than illuminated the large room.

It flickered across Charles's and Joe's faces.

They were sitting together, in the same room, on the very same sofa, watching the Red Sox play Baltimore, discussing Nomar Garciaparra, who'd just gotten up to bat.

As she stood in the shadows and watched, Nomar hit one, and both men shouted in excitement as the ball went clear out of the park. She didn't hear what Joe said then, but whatever it was, it made her father laugh.

Charles was laughing. With Joe.

Kelly felt more than heard Tom move behind her, and she turned to face him, putting one finger up to her lips. Whatever had happened between Charles and Joe today had to have been the result of some powerful magic, and she wasn't going to risk breaking the spell. Gesturing for him to follow, she quickly led the way out onto the deck, through the dining-room sliders.

Only when the door was shut behind them did she speak. 'What did you do?' she asked Tom. 'What did you say to them?'

SUZANNE BROCKMANN

'Don't get too excited,' he warned her. 'This thing they're fighting about – it's still not resolved.'

'But they're sitting there . . . How did you do it? Did you hypnotize them? I thought nothing short of a miracle—' Kelly's voice broke, and she turned away as her eyes welled with tears. It *was* a miracle.

'I didn't really do much of anything,' Tom said. 'I just told them about a . . . well, a project I'm working on, and I said if they wanted to help me with it, their arguments and fighting would have to stop.'

Kelly could feel him watching her, feel him wondering if she was about to experience emotional meltdown and burst into tears. But he needn't have worried. Ashtons didn't do meltdowns. They tried to stay as far as possible from such unpleasantly base things as emotions. She herself had been well-trained. Get a grip, her father had told her without passion back when she'd been small, burying himself behind his open newspaper. Come back when you're prepared to discuss this like a rational human being. Tears of any kind – even joy – were to be avoided at all costs.

She'd learned to distance herself from her emotions – to separate and partition away everything she was feeling so she'd be calm and collected. It was an ability that had proven quite useful in her medical career. In fact, she'd used it extensively just today when talking to Betsy McKenna's distraught parents.

The only problem was, it didn't keep her from feeling all those untidy emotions. And it didn't keep her from carrying them around with her until she reached a time and a place where she could unload. Or explode.

166

Now was neither the time nor the place.

'Are you all right?' Tom asked, his voice gentle in the growing darkness. 'Tough day, huh?'

'I'm a little . . . tired,' she admitted. Ashtons were the kings and queens of understatement, too, god damn it. But why was she being so careful, so polite? This was Tom she was talking to – the closest thing to a friend she had here in Baldwin's Bridge. So she told him the truth. 'Actually, I'm so exhausted I can barely see straight. It's been a complete bitch of a day.'

Her voice broke again, but she no longer cared.

'Or at least it was until I stopped at the farm stand and heard that my father and Joe spent the afternoon playing chess together in the hotel lobby.' Her voice wobbled as she turned to face him. 'I don't know what I can say or do to thank you for whatever it was you did.'

She wanted to embrace him, the way Joe had embraced him out on the driveway, but she didn't. She couldn't. She didn't know how.

Besides, she could see from the look on his face that she was scaring him to death – the same way she'd scared Gary back when they were first married, before she'd learned to hide everything she was feeling from him, too, the same way she'd scared her father when she was a little girl.

'Don't worry,' she reassured Tom. 'I'm not going to cry.'

Of course that was the precise moment she burst into tears. But it wasn't just tears – she was laughing, too. Laughing at her perfect timing, at the comical look on his face, at the thought of all those pure Bostonian

Ashtons rolling in their graves at the idea of their offspring emoting so loudly and violently.

She did the only thing she could do under the circumstances.

She excused herself – politely, of course – and ran for the privacy of her room.

Tom didn't follow.

She hadn't expected him to.

'She isn't going to show.'

David glanced up from putting a new roll of film into his camera to see that Brandon still had on his jeans and T-shirt. 'She'll be here soon. Get changed, will you?'

'No way, bro. Not until she's here. No point to it. I've got places to go, people to see – Sharon, that redheaded cocktail waitress who works the pool the same shift I do? She dropped a major hint that she was going to go see the Jimmy Buffett wannabe over at the Marina Grill tonight. She's definitely mine if I want her.' Bran wandered over to David's drawing table. 'Whoa. Is this Mallory?'

'Yeah.' David had done some preliminary sketches this afternoon, from memory.

'You're using her just for her face, right? I mean, this body – that's whatchamacallit ... artistic license, right?'

David adjusted the white sheet he'd spread out on the bare wooden floor. 'Nope.'

Brandon whistled. 'Yow. I hope she *does* show.'

He looked up at his friend. 'Don't hit on her, Bran. She's ...' Fragile. It was true, but no one would know that from the tough bitch facade Mallory had erected for the world to see. Most people wouldn't try to see what was behind that mask. 'She's too young,' he finally said. 'I don't think she's even eighteen yet.'

The doorbell rang.

'Please,' David said, heading for the door. 'Don't scare her off.'

He took a deep breath before he opened it, but then there she was. Standing out on the wooden steps that led up to his top-floor apartment, trying to hide the fact that she was having second thoughts about being here.

'Hi,' he said, coming out onto the little wooden landing instead of pushing open the screen door so she could come inside. If she was at all nervous, taking it slowly might help. 'Did you have any trouble finding this place?'

She shook her head. God, she *was* young. And incredibly uncertain.

'You know,' he said, 'it's okay if you've changed your mind. I don't want you to do this if you're—'

Scared. He was going to say *scared*, and he realized just in time that that would not be a word this girl would ever want used to describe her – even it if was true.

She lifted her chin and gave him a scathing look. 'I'm not, like, afraid,' she told him.

'She says she's not afraid,' Bran echoed from behind the screen door. 'But I *am* – because you have completely lost your mind. You're supposed to talk her into doing this, fool, not give her permission to run away. Mallory, you gorgeous thing, come in here and see what Sully's done just from memory.'

Brandon opened the door and, taking Mallory by the hand, drew her inside.

'Oh, my God, it's cool in here,' she said. 'You have air-conditioning.'

'You and me, babe,' Bran said as he led Mallory toward David's drawing table, 'we are going to be so freaking famous when Sul hits it big. Hasbro's gonna make little action figures with our faces on 'em. We'll go to comic book conventions and sign autographs until our hands hurt. It is gonna be *such* a blast.'

As David closed the door, Mallory leaned over his drawings, studying them carefully. And then she looked up at him, seeming to examine him just as completely. As she did, he could not for the life of him read the look in her eyes.

Self-consciously, he glanced down to make sure his fly was zipped – to make sure he'd remembered to put pants on in the first place. But he was still wearing the bathing trunks he'd thrown on after this evening's sweatfest – when he'd cleaned and vacuumed his apartment in the oppressive heat. He hadn't turned on the air conditioner until about a half hour ago – it cost way too much to run and he was saving every penny. He'd showered after cleaning, but putting on anything more than his bathing suit had seemed insane.

He'd finally pulled on a T-shirt when he'd gone out to get a pizza for dinner. He now double-checked the logo on the front to make sure he wasn't wearing something offensive or too strange. No, it was his 'Spock for President' shirt, faded and loose, with a small but growing hole in the shoulder, along the seam.

'Why don't you get new glasses?' Mallory asked.

'You know, there's one of those one-hour places down on Route 1.'

David wasn't sure what to say. Was she trying to feel more in control of this situation by pointing out his obvious flaws? Except why stop with his broken glasses?

'I don't have the money.' He answered her as if her question was sincere. 'Right now everything I've got is going toward getting *Nightshade* drawn and printed.'

'What about your parents?' she asked. 'Couldn't you call them and tell them your glasses broke? I bet if you went to visit them, the first thing they'd do would be to take you to get new glasses.'

She was right, except . . . 'It's one thing when they offer to help, but to call and ask for money . . .' He shook his head.

Mallory nodded solemnly. 'I know what you mean.'

'I'll be going home about a week before school starts,' he told her. 'I'll probably get new glasses then.'

Her question *had* been sincere, not a thinly veiled put-down. She was talking to him, having this conversation as if she cared what he said, as if his thoughts and opinions were valid, as if she actually liked him. David's pulse kicked into a higher speed as he stood there, gazing into her luminescent eyes, unable to look away, barely able to breathe.

He and Mallory and Brandon were in a room together, and Mal was talking to him, looking at him, liking *him*.

'What's the big deal?' Bran said loudly. 'They're your parents. They expect you to call and ask for money.' He yanked his shirt over his head and began unfastening his pants.

171

His gleaming golden abs and pecs seemed to fill the room, and Mallory turned away from David to stare. The look of awe on her face would have been funny, except for the fact that it completely killed the little seed of hope that had unfurled just seconds ago in David's stomach.

And as Brandon kicked off his sneakers and stepped out of his jeans, as Mallory turned, wide-eyed, to watch him walk across the room in his boxers, David felt himself return to his normal invisible, unnoticed state.

Which was just as well, since he had work to do.

Nine

Tom couldn't concentrate on the baseball game. And there was no point in reading his printed file on the Merchant again. He'd read all the information five or six times, and he could recite parts of it from memory.

What he wanted to do was to get back on-line and see if WildCard had emailed him a download of additional information. But the computer was in Kelly's bedroom, and her door was tightly shut.

He stood outside her room for several long seconds, just listening. There was nothing but silence. If she was in there, and he knew she was, she was probably asleep.

What he *really* wanted was to be in Kelly's bedroom with her.

It had killed him earlier tonight when she'd started to cry. Not pulling her into his arms had been one of the hardest things he'd ever done. But he knew himself too well, knew he couldn't be the kind of friend who offered casual physical comfort.

He wanted this woman too much. Holding her

would have pushed him over the edge. He wouldn't have been able to resist the temptation, and he would have kissed her. And she would have either kissed him back or pushed him away.

Tom wasn't sure which response would have been worse.

If he had kissed her and she *hadn't* pushed him away, he didn't doubt for one second that he'd be in Kelly's room, behind that closed and locked door, right this very moment. He was good with women – it was a fact. He could say that with very little ego involved.

He knew just what to do, what to say to make a woman set aside her doubts and embrace the moment. So to speak.

The problem was, when it came to Kelly Ashton, he couldn't get past his own multitude of doubts.

What if the man he'd seen at Logan and the Home Depot *wasn't* the Merchant?

He'd always hated the fact that the terrorist had escaped capture. That had chafed long after the other members of the counterterrorist team had accepted the fact that the man was gone. The CIA had tried to pick up the Merchant's trail, but they'd come up empty-handed again and again.

With WildCard's help getting reports and records that normally wouldn't have crossed his desk, Tom had followed their progress over the past few years – if you could call it progress when absolutely nothing happened.

WildCard had jokingly referred to Tom's interest in the Merchant as TLO – Tommy's Little Obsession. They'd both laughed about it, but Tom wasn't laughing now. Now the word *obsession* made him a little too uncomfortable.

He gets a serious head injury and starts seeing the Merchant every time he turns around.

As the leader of a SEAL team, he needed to know without a doubt that everything he saw was real. There was no room for trying to figure out what was real and what was a hallucination.

No room for him, not in this condition.

Tom went outside, but the night air was neither cool nor fresh. The beautiful summer day had become more and more humid until this heavy mass of heat now sat solidly on top of them.

Needless to say, the change in weather didn't help his persistent headaches at all.

He was restless and dizzy and far too keyed up to try to go to bed.

From out in the yard, he could see that the light in Kelly's room was off. She was asleep.

He went farther into the yard, all the way to the fence. That was the shortest route into town – provided you could make it over the fence. Dizzy or not, it took Tom about a half second to climb, and another half second to drop down into the neighbor's yard.

In the distance, he could hear strains of music from the carnival that was in town, set up in the Catholic church parking lot. He headed toward it, hoping that a brisk walk there and back would at least make him tired enough to sleep.

Despite her exhaustion, Kelly couldn't sleep.

She heard the water running downstairs after the baseball game ended and her father got ready for bed.

Slipping on her robe, she went out into the dark hallway and down the stairs. He'd left his bedroom door ajar, and she knocked on it as she pushed it open even farther.

Charles had managed to get himself into bed, but it wouldn't be long before he could no longer do that. Every day he seemed a little bit skinnier, a little more frail. He was disappearing before her very eyes.

'Can I get you anything?' Kelly asked through the lump in her throat.

He shook his head, and she knew he was uncomfortable.

'It's okay if you take one of the pills Dr Grant prescribed.'

He looked at her, only briefly meeting her eyes before he looked away again. 'I took one an hour ago.'

It was too soon to take another. 'I can call the doctor,' she told him, 'see if—'

'It's not that bad.' He nodded at her, dismissing her. 'Good night.'

Frustration bloomed, choking her from inside out, and she couldn't stand it anymore. She couldn't pretend to be the perfect Ashton daughter another minute longer – quiet and polite and careful not to be emotionally untidy for fear she'd upset her father. The man was dying. How bad could a little upset be compared to that?

'Aren't you at all curious about what I did today?' she asked him, her voice a little too loud, a little too angry. She didn't give him time to answer before she continued, pulling up a chair to the side of his bed and sitting down. 'Today I had a meeting with the parents of a little girl who's probably going to die of leukemia. Even though these days the odds of survival are high, this little girl is pretty frail. If the cancer doesn't kill her, the chemotherapy might be too much for her – she could die of an infection. She could catch a cold and her suppressed immune system might not be able to fight it off. I had to sit there and explain this to her parents, trying to give them hope while cautioning them about the potential outcome.' Her voice shook. 'I've done this before, but this time it was different. I know there's always a fighting chance, but this time . . . I honestly don't think this little girl is going to make it, and I knew her parents could tell. Daddy, it was one of the worst days of my life.'

Her father didn't say a word. He just sat there, leaning back against his pillows, staring down at the lump his feet made underneath the sheet and blanket as if he wished he were anywhere but there.

'I probably should never have become a doctor,' Kelly told him. She'd never admitted anything like this to him before. She'd never dared. 'I'm not cut out for this. On the surface, I look fine. But inside, I feel like I'm going to die.'

Kelly knew he wanted her to leave. He wanted her to take her whining and get the hell out of his room, leave him in peace. But she couldn't do that. She was running out of time. And if she wanted him to talk to her, then dammit, she was going to have to start by talking to him. Tough shit if he thought it was wrong. Tough shit if he found it offensive. *He* was the one who was wrong all these years – all those too-stoic Ashtons were. Hold it inside, don't let it show, try not to feel.

But you couldn't *not* feel. And keeping it trapped didn't make it go away. It would build and build, a terrible ball of pain and anger and joy – yes, even joy, because God forbid an Ashton should laugh too loudly in public. And nothing, not even the alcohol her father had soused himself with for years, could make those feelings disappear.

She just had to do it. She had to open her mouth and talk to him. It was exactly like asking Tom to dinner, the way she'd done this afternoon. She just had to grit her teeth and make an attempt. Because she knew for damn sure she'd never get what she wanted – a chance to truly know her father – if she simply and meekly continued to act the way she had in the past.

'I came home today completely wrung out,' she told him. 'All I wanted to do was curl up somewhere and cry. You know, I cry a lot.'

His gaze flicked up to hers, but then he quickly looked away again. *Cry.* It was one of the most obscene words in the Ashton dictionary.

'Don't worry – I usually don't let anyone see,' she added. 'But I completely lost it tonight, when I was talking to Tom.'

Nothing. No response. She didn't even know if he was listening, or if he was running mathematical equations in his head, trying to shut her out. She felt a deeper flare of anger and hurt.

'You know, I still have a crush on him. Ever since he's been back, I've been trying to figure out the best way to get him into bed.'

Her father started to cough. Yes, he was listening.

Kelly helped him with his oxygen, and when he was

finally breathing more easily again, he glared up at her. Eye contact. Jackpot. 'Why on earth would you say something like that to me?'

Honesty. Brutal honesty. She could do this. If she could ask Tom to dinner, if she could look Brenda and Bob McKenna in the eye and tell them little Betsy was probably going to die, she could do *this*. 'I want you to know who I am.'

'I know who you are!'

'You don't know even a tiny fraction of—'

'I know all that I want to know, thanks.'

'Really?' Kelly asked quietly, her heart tearing in half. How could he say that? 'You honestly don't want to know any of my secrets? You don't want to know things like ... like ...' She searched for something important, something she'd never told him or anybody. 'Like up until today I've had two absolute best, golden days with memories that I'll cherish until the day I die? You don't want to know that one of those was a day I spent with you? You took me out in your sailboat – I think I was twelve – and we got caught in a squall. Do you remember that?'

'No.' He did. She *knew* he did. She could see the memory of the wind and waves in his eyes.

'Instead of sending me below, you trusted me to help you get us safely back to shore,' she continued. 'And after the storm was over, that night when we finally got home, you gave me the Purple Heart you won in the war. I *know* you remember that.'

He didn't do more than stubbornly shake his head no.

'I still have it, you know. You told me I was a good sailor,' she said to him. 'I was so proud that you thought so. But then Mom never let you take me out on the boat again.'

God, Kelly had wanted to be part of her father's life so badly. She'd had this crazy dream that together they'd race his sailboat. She'd help him win first prize again and again, and he'd tell her how much he loved her.

'You didn't fight very hard to get her to change her mind. You didn't even argue at all. You just lay down and let her win. I was so angry with you – I thought you were such a loser.' Kelly couldn't believe those words had just come out of her proper Ashton mouth.

Neither could Charles. He opened his own mouth, then shut it.

'What?' Kelly said. Please talk to me, Dad . . .

'You never knew the seriousness of the situation that day on the boat,' he finally said stiffly, stiltedly. 'The truth was, I couldn't have made it back in without your help. It was sheer luck we didn't capsize. You weren't a strong swimmer and I was sure you'd drown, even with the life vest on. After that day, I didn't *want* to take you out on the boat again.'

Her father had been afraid that she would drown. Her father, *afraid*. It was hard to imagine. He'd been so calm, practically blasé, even during the worst of the storm.

But suddenly other things made sense. 'That was when you signed me up for those awful early-morning swimming lessons with the pool Nazis.' She'd thought – despite his momentary lapse when he gave her that medal – that he simply didn't care for her and wanted her out of the house as often as possible.

Charles actually looked at her now. 'Pool Nazis?'

'"Excuse me, Herr Commandant,"' Kelly said, making her voice that of a young child's. ' "But it's only sixty degrees this morning, and the water temperature is fifty-two. I've heard of this thing called hypothermia—" "You vill get into ze pool, unt you vill stay varm by doing zwei hunnert laps of ze breaststroke, ja?"'

Charles coughed. It might have been a laugh, but Kelly wasn't certain. 'I had no idea.'

'By the time I got my swimming certificate, the summer was over. And the next year, you sold the sailboat.'

He shook his head. 'I wasn't using it. And when someone made me an offer . . .'

'You weren't using it because you were drinking.'

Well, there was an ugly little truth that came plopping out and now just lay there between them.

Kelly spoke to fill the sudden, tense silence. 'My other perfect, golden day was when I wiped out on my bike at the bottom of High Meadow Road and completely bent the front wheel's rim.'

He harrumphed. 'I'm noticing an alarming correlation between your idea of a perfect day and near catastrophes.' His tone was less than pleasant, but God, at least he was still talking. After that drinking comment, Kelly had been certain he wasn't going to say another word.

'I had my first beer at a party that day,' she admitted, 'and I thought I was going to throw up. When I left, I took the hill too fast, skidded into the corner, and skinned my elbow.'

He sniffed. 'So naturally you remember it fondly.'

'I was sitting by the side of the road when Tom came

along on his motorcycle,' Kelly told him. '*That's* what I remember fondly. I spent the entire rest of the day and most of the evening with him, just driving around.' She smiled. 'We drove past this antiques fair, and we went in on the pretense of getting a soda, but I knew he really wanted to look at all the old stuff. He was so into the history of it, and so nice to me, all day long. I'll never forget a single minute of that day. It was perfect – even the scraped elbow, because that's what made him stop to help me.'

She could still remember the way it had felt to ride on Tom's motorcycle, with her arms wrapped tightly around him, her cheek against his back, her legs pressed against his thighs. She remembered later that same night, sitting next to him in Joe's station wagon, with her bike in the back . . .

'I'm going to add today to my list of special days,' Kelly told him. 'Because even though it started out really dreadfully, it ended wonderfully. Daddy, when I came home and heard that you and Joe spent the day together without fighting . . . When I saw you in the living room . . .' She started to blink back her tears, but stopped, letting her eyes fill. Let him see how moved she'd been, how moved she *still* was. Let him see. 'I was so glad you've realized how precious this time is – this time you've got left – especially for the people who love you.'

Charles closed his eyes. But he didn't order her to get out.

So she pushed even harder. 'I know you don't want Joe to talk to that writer, I know you're angry with him, but I don't understand why. I'm still so afraid you're going to argue more, that you're going to say something in anger and then die before you can get a chance to take it back. I'm afraid you're going to die wishing you could erase your angry words, without ever having found peace.' Her voice shook. 'Daddy, I wish you would talk to me. I wish you would tell me what you and Joe have been fighting about. How can I help if I don't know what the problem is? I don't understand what could possibly come between two people who've been friends for as long as you've been.'

Charles was silent for so long, Kelly knew he wasn't going to answer. In fact, as she sat there, she was certain he'd shut her out so completely that he'd fallen asleep.

'I love you,' she whispered, daring to say the words aloud. 'I want to feel as if I'm a part of your life. Even just a *small* part . . .'

But then he spoke, his eyes still shut. 'It was a woman,' he whispered. 'Her name was Cybele Desjardins.' The French name sounded musical on his lips, his French pronunciation flawless. 'She was with the Resistance. She saved my life – she saved dozens of Allied fliers, scores of Jews. Everything she did was dedicated to defeating the Nazis. She thought nothing of risking her life to sabotage German railroad shipments and ammunition sites. She was incredibly brave and remarkably beautiful. Such eyes . . . Such conviction . . .'

He looked up at Kelly, and she realized with a jolt of shock that his eyes were swimming in unshed tears. And his lip, that stiff Ashton lip, actually trembled. 'I was married,' he told her, 'and I *knew* Joe was in love with her, and . . .'

183

Kelly took his hand, and for the first time in what seemed like forever, her father actually held on to her. A *woman*. This fight between Joe and Charles was over a woman. She never would have believed it possible, never in a million years.

'I still can't talk about her,' he said, closing his eyes again. 'I can barely stand to *think* about her. What Joe wants to do will rip my heart out all over again – he wants to tell the whole story to the entire world.'

Kelly pushed her father's hair back from his face, aching for him, wishing he'd tell her more, knowing he'd already told her far more than she'd ever believed he would. A *woman*.

'Do you want me to talk to Joe?' she asked gently. 'Do you want me to see if I can make him change his mind?'

'I want what I can't have.' Charles didn't open his eyes. And when he spoke again it was so quiet, Kelly wasn't certain he'd actually said the words aloud. 'Fifty-six years, and still, all I want is to have her back.'

The baby oil was wicked disgusting.

Mallory had come out of the bathroom after changing into one of the bathing suits from David's costume box, to find Brandon smearing himself with baby oil.

It was amazing. He was even better looking in person, with golden brown hair that shimmered and a Ben Affleck-perfect nose. He was tall – at least five inches taller than she was, with broad shoulders and anatomy-textbook-model muscles.

His smile was a flash of quicksilver, his eyes a wondrous shade of blue.

He was one of those people who was always in motion, filled with a kinetic energy that could knock you on your ass if you accidentally stepped into his path.

She could picture him sitting in his lifeguard chair at the Baldwin's Bridge Hotel pool. Even slouched, he would be in motion, constantly swinging his whistle on its chain, wrapping and unwrapping it around his hand.

'The oil helps provide muscle definition for the camera.' Brandon handed her the bottle. 'I hate to be forward, but if you slime some on my back, I'll slime some on yours.'

It was weird to touch him in a way that seemed so intimate. Especially considering they were both wearing next to nothing.

The top of the bathing suit David chose for her was a little too small – two triangles of thin fabric that tied around her neck and around her back, barely containing her megaboobs. The bottoms were cut high in the back, not quite a thong, but not the kind of suit her grandmother would've worn, either.

'So, David tells me you live in Baldwin's Bridge year-round.' Brandon took the bottle from her and spread oil across her shoulder blades. 'That must be so great.'

It was the first time she'd ever heard her status as a Townie described as *great*, but she stayed silent. His hands felt too good against her skin for her even to open her mouth to speak.

But he was done far too soon and Mallory took the bottle back from him. She covered her legs and then the tops of her breasts and her stomach with the oil, aware that Brandon was watching her. David was glancing at her, too, but he was less obvious about it than his friend.

'I'm going to need to take a shower after this,' she said, suddenly terribly self-conscious. It was cold in here. She was freezing – a fact that neither of them could possibly have missed. God, she wanted a cigarette.

'That's no problem,' David said quickly. 'I have a shower you can use in the bathroom.'

He blushed as if he realized how stupid he sounded.

'I hope you've got a shower in the bathroom,' Mallory said. 'I mean, like, instead of in the bedroom closet.'

Brandon laughed as if she were Jerry Seinfeld. It wasn't *that* funny, still, his laughter was so infectious she couldn't help smiling back at him.

He took her hand – his was still slimy, but otherwise very nice – and pulled her onto a sheet that was spread out on the floor. They stood on it, in front of a bare white wall, looking like a thoroughly slimed-up version of Frankie and Annette from one of those campy beach movies. Except Frankie and Annette never wore bathing suits like these.

Brandon kept up a constant chatter as David looked through his camera and did things with his light meter.

'This is the boring part,' he told her. 'Once Sul actually gets behind the camera and starts shooting, it's a lot more fun. And tonight it's going to be even more fun than usual.' He winked at her. He was the first guy she'd ever met who could actually pull that off. Winking made most guys just look stupid. 'He's making sure he's got the right amount of light for every little last detail . . .'

David held the meter up to her face, then lowered it so his hand was nearly touching the tops of her breasts. He was completely focused on whatever that little box was showing him. He looked from the light meter to her breasts – completely dispassionately, though – then to the meter and to her breasts again.

'Every detail,' Mallory echoed. 'As in, every nipple? Excuse me, David, are you having fun down there?'

Brandon shouted with laughter, and David looked up at her in surprise, directly into her eyes. As she gazed back at him, she saw her words finally penetrate his intense concentration, saw as he realized what she'd said. His gaze dropped back to her breasts as for a fraction of a second he really looked at her before he forced his eyes up, guiltily, to her face. And he blushed. Again.

'I'm sorry. Honestly, I don't mean to be disrespectful.'

She believed him. He was painfully sincere. No one was *that* good an actor. 'Any chance we can turn down the instafreeze setting on the air conditioner?' she asked him.

'I'm sorry,' he said again, blinking at her from behind his windshield. 'Are you cold? I didn't realize.'

'Are you kidding?' she asked. 'Am I cold? Hello? You want to look at me again, Einstein, this time with your eyes open?'

Brandon laughed again as David did a quick about-face, lunging for the industrial-size air conditioner laboring in the window across the room.

'Bran usually complains about being too hot under the lights.' David adjusted the temperature control, his face pink again. It wouldn't take much to keep him blushing all night long. 'Maybe I should offer a complete apology in advance. I get pretty intense when I'm working. But please, I want you to know, I absolutely do not intend any disrespect.'

He was completely embarrassed; in fact, it was more like mortified. He didn't intend any disrespect. It was funny, but besides her uncle Tom, and her great-uncle Joe, Mallory couldn't think of a single person who actually intended to be respectful when they interacted with her.

'I think you're quite possibly the most uniquely beautiful woman I've ever seen in my life,' David continued, 'but I'm also well aware that there's substantially more to you than your body and face, and if at any point tonight I start to treat you like some kind of object, please let me know. And please keep in mind that it's not intentional. At all. Whatsoever.'

'Go, Sul,' Brandon said. 'Way to sling the woo.'

This time, it was Mallory whose face was heating up. She'd heard a lot of bullshit compliments in her life, all intended to get her into the backseat of some loser's car, but this was different. David actually meant what he'd said. He was serious. It was incredibly sweet. *He* was incredibly sweet.

For a dork, anyway.

'Well, thanks,' Mallory said. 'I think you're completely full of shit, but thanks.'

David laughed. 'Now, how did I know you were going to say that?'

She laughed, too. It was funny, his smile was nearly as nice as Brandon's. And when he looked at her like that, gazing into her eyes . . .

'Ditto all that from me, too, babe.' Brandon grabbed her hand and spun her in a circle, away from David. 'I'm definitely the copresident of your fan club.'

David cleared his throat. 'Maybe we should get started.'

'Absolutely. Once we start, it'll really warm up,' Brandon told her, waggling his eyebrows, his smile promising heat of a completely different kind.

She tried to pull her hand free, but Brandon held on to her tightly, despite the slippery oil.

'Have you done any acting?' David asked her.

'A little.' Mallory thought of all those times she'd walked through the halls of the high school, pretending that she didn't give a damn what the other kids said behind her back. Sure, a little – provided ninety-nine percent of her life could be defined as 'a little.'

'Nightshade – the character you're helping me with – is seventeen years old,' David told her. 'She's still in high school, and when she's her alter ego, Nicki, she's . . . well, a loner, I guess. With the exception of another character, named Hubert, she doesn't have any friends.'

Well, hey, *that* shouldn't be too much of a stretch for her.

'How old are you, anyway?' Brandon asked.

'Eighteen.'

'So doesn't that mean . . . You just graduated, right? Congratulations.' Brandon looked over at David and grinned. 'She's eighteen and she just graduated. Great news, huh?'

'I thought you were in a hurry to get out of here tonight,' David said evenly.

'Me? No way. I can't think of anywhere else I'd rather be than right here, wearing my lovely little Speedo, flexing my abs, playing superheroes with my new friend Mallory.' Brandon rubbed Mallory's arm, as if trying to warm her up. His thumb accidentally brushed against her breast. 'Let's do this before the woman freezes to death.'

Mallory stepped slightly away from him. 'What's Nightshade's deal?'

'She's got super X-ray night vision,' Brandon told her. 'And she can fly or something, right?'

'She can completely dematerialize,' David corrected him. 'What she does is kind of like what the transporter does on *Star Trek*, except she can change the state of her molecules at will. She doesn't need a machine to do it. When she's dematerialized, she can move more quickly from place to place, which, yeah, is kind of like flying. But when she gets to her destination, it takes about an hour for her to rematerialize. And while she's rematerializing, she can't fight. She's got none of her powers – except her ability to see in the dark. She's completely vulnerable.'

Mallory knew all about being vulnerable.

'When she's materialized, she's a kick-ass fighter,' Brandon volunteered. 'Martial arts, you name it – she's down with it. She's pretty much invincible. No fear, you know.'

No fear. Now, *that* would require some acting.

'Okay,' David said, retreating back behind his camera, 'let's do it.'

'Doing it with pleasure,' Brandon murmured, waggling his perfect eyebrows at her again.

The pain pills Charles was taking didn't blot out things the way a good, stiff drink used to.

With gin, a man could just keep pouring himself drink after drink until the memories faded into nothingness. But his pain medication was rationed, and he couldn't keep taking pill upon pill.

Well, he supposed he could, but Kelly, for one, would frown upon it.

Kelly.

She'd always tried to please him. Until tonight. Tonight she'd let him have it – everything he deserved. Well, not quite everything. She'd gone easy with the scorn and derision.

With his eyes closed, he could see her at three, at seven, at thirteen, with her bright eyes and her brilliant mind and that impossibly sweet face. But even Kelly, as much as he'd loved her, hadn't been able to take away the emptiness that rotted him from the inside out. Only gin could numb that, and far too often even the gin wasn't enough.

Charles kept his eyes shut, breathing as deeply as he could without coughing, pretending he was asleep. After three failed marriages, if there was one thing he was good at, it was pretending he was asleep.

Kelly kissed him on the cheek. 'Good night, Daddy. I love you.'

She loved him. After over thirty years of behaving

like a son of a bitch, his daughter still somehow managed to love him.

But it still wasn't enough.

God, what was wrong with him?

He heard the bedroom door close gently, and he opened his eyes, stared up at the ceiling. His room was dimly lit from the night-light Kelly'd left on in the bathroom.

The pill he'd taken an hour ago made him feel as if he were floating – just a little – above the bed. It took the edge off the constant pain, but it didn't stop the memories.

France.

1944.

The summer after Normandy.

He blinked and suddenly it was bright as midday in his room. He blinked again, and it wasn't his room any longer. It was Cybele's kitchen.

He wasn't eighty and dying, he was twenty-four and healing.

He was doing well. He could shuffle around with a cane. Cybele had taken out the stitches in his side and his shoulder, and he'd taken off his sling just the day before.

Cybele – who thought he was some kind of hero because he went back into that church for some child who'd been left behind. He didn't know why he'd done it. He couldn't even remember it clearly. The entire battle was a blur. When he'd felt the bullets hit him, he'd been sure he was dead.

Yet here he was. Still taking up space, although thankfully not space in a Kraut POW camp. Instead, he was the great American hero in this small-town French Resistance headquarters.

Joe Paoletti – Charles was supposed to call him Giuseppe – was one hundred times the man Charles was. He was OSS, for crying out loud, yet no one gave him an extra egg for dinner. And even if they did, he wouldn't have eaten it. He was too much of a hero not to give it to someone else who needed the nourishment more.

Despite the fact that Joe was an overachiever in the hero department, despite his intensity and too-serious nature, Charles liked the man. How could he not? It would've been like disliking Jesus.

It was only a matter of days before Cybele and Joe and the others were to smuggle Charles back to the Allied side of the line.

He couldn't wait to leave.

Compared to the alternatives – death and its second cousin, life in a Nazi concentration camp – Charles's life here in Ste.-Hélène was pleasant enough. He didn't dare set foot outdoors in daylight since Cybele's house was five doors down from one of the highest-ranking Nazis in town, but that was just as well. For him, as for most of the men, days were mostly lazy. Henri, the two men he'd dubbed Luc Un and Luc Deux, and the others rarely went out in the daytime. They did most of their movement at night, venturing forth only in the shadows, like ghouls or vampires. They'd return to Cybele's house before dawn and sleep on the kitchen floor until noon or later, hiding out from the Germans.

Cybele and the other women, however, lived two lives. They lived in the nighttime world of the men, often participating in their missions despite the dangers. But they lived in the regular world as well. Cooking for the small army of resistance fighters who dozed on the kitchen floor. Cleaning, doing the laundry. Fishing in the river.

Cybele took in mending to earn money to buy flour for

bread. She and the other women didn't sit still without a sock and a darning needle in their hands.

It seemed ironic – her best customers were the Nazi soldiers who patrolled the streets of the town. Their worn socks appeared in Cybele's basket again and again.

And Saint Joe was as tireless as Cybele. He spent much of his days – even those when he was up until dawn – out in the small plot of land behind Cybele's house. He'd turned every workable inch of dirt into a vegetable garden, and he tended it more carefully than a miser would tend to a chestful of gold, coaxing precious food from the soil. For a kid from New York City, he had one hell of a green thumb.

Charles's French was improving. Or rather, his understanding of what the others were saying was improving. He still couldn't speak the language, despite Cybele's gentle tutoring.

She would laugh at his attempts, though. Frankly, it was worth it to fail, just to hear her laughter.

He told her all about Baldwin's Bridge in English, about lazy summers by the ocean, about his years at Harvard, and she would tell him, in French, about life in Ste.-Hélène before the Nazi invasion.

Her husband and son had been killed by the Germans, and Cybele's heart was still broken. She'd never said as much, but Charles knew it was so. She'd asked him in turn about Jenny.

It had been one of those hot afternoons a week or so after his arrival when Charles had reached into Cybele's basket and pulled out a sock and a needle.

Cybele had laughed at him. 'Don't tell me they taught mending at your Harvard University,' she'd teased.

'No such luck. I'm going to have to ask you to teach me

to do this,' he'd said, and she'd laughed some more, as if he'd made the biggest joke of the whole war.

'I'm sitting here doing nothing,' he'd insisted, woman's work be damned. 'I'm going out of my mind. Show me how to do this. God knows I eat the bread you make from the money you earn darning these socks.'

Her eyes had grown wide as she realized he wasn't joking. 'Henri and the Lucs refused to learn. It was all I could do to get them to help with the cooking.'

'Henri and the Lucs are asses.' Charles put his finger through the hole in the toe of the sock and waggled it at her. 'Get over here and teach me. I want to help.'

Laughing again, she had. She'd had to sit close to show him what to do. Her work-roughened fingers were cool against his, her thigh soft against his uninjured leg. She'd pulled her long hair up into a haphazard pile on her head, and several dark wisps lay against the long, graceful paleness of her neck. Her dress was old and loose and made of patched and faded cotton, and she smelled of cheap soap. She was too skinny from years of giving most of her dinner away to the people using her attic as a temporary stop on their dangerous road to freedom, and her collarbones stood out starkly on her chest.

And when she turned and looked into his eyes from just those few inches away, it had been the closest Charles had ever come, at that point in his life, to a religious experience.

Yet he knew that if she'd walked past him on the streets of Baldwin's Bridge, he never would have given her a second glance. He never would have taken the time to look into her eyes and see who she really was.

She was everything he wasn't. Everything Jenny wasn't.

They'd sat on that bench for quite some time, heads close

together, hands occasionally touching as she corrected him, as he tried to make his too-large fingers move like Cybele's. It was hard as hell to do – women's work, indeed.

But finally, he'd finished. One clumsily darned sock to six of Cybele's. And yet she applauded him, her brown eyes sparkling with admiration and warmth.

He took another sock from the basket and doggedly set to work.

He could tell from the way she watched him that she'd expected him to stop after one.

But there were sixty more socks in that basket that needed mending. At his current pace, he'd be done by next Wednesday. But it wasn't as if he had a whole hell of a lot else to do.

He could feel Cybele watching him, but he didn't dare let himself look up again. He knew he'd see hero worship in her eyes. And, sure, while he wanted her to like him, he wanted her to like him for the man he really was, not because of some twisted misconception. Maybe he'd been a hero by accident, but those days were behind him now.

'First thing I'm going to do when I get back to Baldwin's Bridge,' he told her, 'is absolutely nothing. I'm going to sit on the front porch of my father's summerhouse, and for about two months I'm going to do nothing but eat steak at every meal and watch the tides turn.' He glanced up. Big mistake. He tried to bluster on, tried to make a joke. 'I'm going to talk Joe into coming with me, and I'm going to pay him thousands of dollars to plant a flower garden in my backyard. No turnips, no cabbage. Just flowers.'

He saw it coming, saw her lean toward him, saw her gaze drop briefly to his mouth, and his heart nearly stopped beating.

He didn't close his eyes until her lips brushed his in the

gentlest of kisses. It was achingly sweet, and over far too soon.

He didn't reach for her, he didn't move. He couldn't. He was married. He had no business kissing anyone but Jenny.

But, God, he wanted Cybele.

He might've given in to the temptation to haul her into his arms and kiss her again, hard, until the room spun, had she not stood up and moved halfway across the kitchen. She turned to face him, but she couldn't hold his gaze.

'Thank you,' she said.

Charles nodded. He even somehow managed to smile. He let them both pretend that that had been a kiss of gratitude, even though they both knew damned well it had been so much more.

Ten

'Okay, that's it.' David straightened up from behind his camera, suddenly acutely aware that Bran was still kissing Mallory.

His friend lifted his head just long enough to say, 'Aw, come on, take a few more,' before he kissed her again.

'I don't need more.' David managed to say it evenly instead of shouting, *God damn it, stop kissing her!* 'I only needed a few.'

Every time he'd drawn Marcus and Webster kissing in *Wingmasters*, Ren had claimed the picture was unidentifiable and had made him draw it over again. This time, for *Nightshade*, David was determined to work from a photo. But . . . 'It's not like there's going to be a lot of kissing in this story.'

He turned around so he wouldn't have to watch Mallory with her mouth locked on Brandon's and her fingers in his wavy blond hair. Somehow it had looked a little less real through his camera's lens.

'Besides, I'm out of film.' He may as well have

spoken Swahili for all the attention either one of them paid him.

He crossed to the refrigerator, grabbed himself a can of soda, and opened it with a loud crack. He drank nearly the whole thing with his back still turned.

'Wow,' he heard Bran murmur to Mallory. 'I kind of forgot where I was for a minute there.'

No shit, Sherlock. David drained the rest of the soda and crushed the aluminum can in his hands.

'Do you want to . . .' Bran laughed self-consciously. 'This is going to sound crazy, but . . .' He laughed again.

But from the first moment I saw you, I felt a connection. David tossed the can into the bag he had for recyclables and sat down at his drawing table, suddenly exhausted. It was after eleven, and he had to be dressed and at the restaurant, ready to wait tables, in less than five hours.

'From the first moment I saw you, I felt this incredible connection between us,' Bran whispered.

Destiny. It was destiny. Yeah, right. David had heard Bran use these particular lines far too many times. At the beach, at a college party, on that camping trip they'd taken when they were both eighteen. The really stupid thing was, if *David* ever tried slinging that kind of crap around, he'd probably be tarred and feathered and run out of town. But Brandon got away with it. When Bran used it, *he* got laid. Talk about destiny.

'It's like destiny,' Bran said now to Mallory.

Here it came: I've never felt anything like this before. David couldn't stop himself from glancing over at them as he savagely sharpened his pencil. Bran still held her loosely in his arms. She could have pulled away – if she wanted to. Obviously, she didn't want to.

'I've never felt anything like this before,' Bran said so sincerely.

Except for the four hundred and sixty-seven other times . . . Come on, Nightshade, use your super night vision to see clear through this son of a bitch.

It wasn't that David didn't like Brandon, because he truly did. They'd been best friends for as long as he could remember, but the thought of Bran taking Mallory home tonight, the thought of them together, making love in Bran's apartment just downstairs from David, was too much to deal with.

He knew all it would take to stop it was four little words in Brandon's ear – *I like this girl.* Bran would back off, but where would that leave David? With a girl who'd rather be with Brandon.

'Come out with me tonight,' Brandon murmured. 'Are you hungry? We could go get something to eat.'

David started to draw rough sketches of Nightshade after Nightshade, running, jumping, flying, fighting evil, at her most invincible. He tried not to listen, tried not to care when Mallory finally spoke.

'I'm kind of gross with all this baby oil on me.'

'Sully already said he didn't mind if you used his shower.' Brandon pushed her toward David's bathroom as if it were a given she'd agree to go with him. 'I'll run and use my own – I live right downstairs.'

She hesitated, glancing over at David. 'I'm not sure—'

'Hey, we can go over to that carnival, grab a burger, and take a ride on the Ferris wheel.'

She lit up, and David knew it was over. But then again, who was he kidding? He knew it was a given she'd spend tonight with Brandon before he'd even asked her to pose for him.

'It's still in town, isn't it?' Brandon asked. 'You know, that carnival in the church parking lot?'

'It's here until Sunday,' Mallory told him.

'Great. Come on, what do you say?'

David kept his eyes glued to his sketch of Nightshade. 'All right' was what she said.

'Well, all right,' Bran headed for the door. 'I'll be back in ten – de-slimed. Later, dude,' he called to David, slamming the door behind him.

David heard her hesitate, but he didn't look up. He just kept drawing. Finally, the bathroom door closed and locked, and he heard the shower go on. He put his pencil down.

There was a small mirror over by the door. He slipped down off his stool and crossed toward it, looking at his reflection.

After over an hour of shooting, his hair was standing up straight in places. He looked as if he'd put his finger in a light socket. He tried to push it down, but that only made it worse. And his glasses . . . The tape and the safety pin didn't add to the fact that his glasses were about fifteen years out of fashion. The lenses were huge and thick and heavy as hell, a far cry from the little oval-shaped frames he now saw people wearing all over the place. He hadn't noticed the new style until yesterday when Bran had pointed it out. David'd drawn a few sketches of his Julian character in civilian mode, with glasses on, and Bran had told him no one who looked like Julian would be caught dead in nerd glasses like the ones he'd drawn.

Nerd glasses.

They'd been just like David's.

It seemed ridiculous. Glasses were merely a valuable instrument he used to enable himself to see. Why should it matter what they looked like?

Why should it matter what *he* looked like?

He took his glasses off and leaned closer to the mirror, squinting at himself in the glass. It wasn't as if he were some kind of a horrible, deformed monster. His eyes, nose, and mouth were all in relatively normal places on his face.

Still, he was no Brandon, that was for sure.

But the flip side was that Brandon was no David, either.

And David wouldn't trade his intelligence and his innate drawing talent for Brandon's looks. Not in a million years. That was a no-brainer.

He had a hell of a lot going for him, and if Mallory was too shallow to see that, if she cared more about the kind of beauty that was only skin deep, if she was completely swept away by Brandon's body and face, well . . .

Hypocrite. He was a complete hypocrite.

The reason he'd followed Mallory around town for days had nothing to do with her sharp sense of humor and her refreshingly acerbic personality. He'd followed her because she had a great ass, world-class breasts, and a face that was the perfect mix of exotic woman and sweet child. He'd followed her because he'd been completely swept away by her body and face.

The shower went off, and he put his glasses back on, quickly crossing back to his drawing table. He sat there, pretending to be engrossed by his sketch when the bathroom door opened several minutes later.

Mallory had put her clothes back on, but her hair was wet. She ran her fingers through it as she stood just outside the bathroom, clearly ill at ease. Brandon wasn't back yet. It was just Mallory and David. Alone.

Again, David didn't say a word. He just kept drawing.

From the corner of his eye, he saw her square her shoulders. She came toward him. It was the dead last thing he'd expected her to do.

'Lookit,' she said, 'I know you probably think I'm an asshole, because I said one thing and now I'm doing another—'

'He only does short term.' David looked up at her. 'Sometimes not more than one-night stands. Don't expect more than that from him.'

She laughed. 'God, I'm not gonna—' She broke off. 'I guess you have no reason to believe anything I say, but I swear, I'm just going to ride on the Ferris wheel with him.'

'You don't need to give me any explanations. I'm not going to judge you for doing what you want to do.' David just kept on drawing. 'So you miscalculated your reaction to Bran. Big deal. If I were a girl, I would've slept with him a long time ago.'

She pulled his other stool up to the table. 'I'm not going to sleep with him.'

'That's not what he thinks.'

'My God.' She leaned closer to look at the sketches he'd done. 'You are *so* good.'

'Hold it right there, don't move,' he ordered her, pulling a fresh sheet of paper in front of him. She was looking at him with such wonder, such admiration, he wanted to capture it. With her hair wet, she looked both tougher and more vulnerable, her eyes enormous in her face. He drew her swiftly, and with just a few quick lines he managed to catch her energy, her soul – or whatever that life force was that burned so fiercely inside of her.

It was a selfish thing to do – drawing her that way, telling her not to move, forcing her to give him her full attention, to look at him while he took in every millimeter of her face.

He took longer than he needed, doing some shading, adding more detail than he normally would've. But finally, he was done, and still holding her gaze, he pushed it toward her.

Mallory stared at him just a moment longer before she looked down. She turned the sketch to face her, gazing at it for a long time before she looked back at him. 'Is this her?' she finally asked. 'Nightshade?'

He shook his head. 'No, that one's all you.'

She looked at the sketch again. 'This is really how you see me?' She shook her head. 'I don't know, but that's not what *I* see when I look into the mirror.'

He could hear Brandon's footsteps coming up the outside stairs, and he stood, turning away from her. 'Have fun tonight.'

'I just want to go to the carnival with him. Everyone from school hangs out there,' she said. 'I just want to show up there with him. I want those bitches to see me out with this guy.'

David turned back. She was leaning toward him, intensity in her eyes.

'It's a shitty reason for going with him,' she admitted. 'I know that. I'm a jerk. But just once, I want—'

The door opened, and Hurricane Brandon swept in. 'Ready, babe?'

'I want to be the one who's envied for a change,' Mallory whispered, her eyes begging David to understand, 'instead of the one doing the envying. It's stupid, I know. You probably don't understand—'

Brandon caught sight of himself in the mirror and made a slight adjustment to his still wet hair. 'Come on, I'm starving; let's blow this joint.'

Mallory stood up, folding the drawing carefully and putting it into her pocket as Brandon came toward her. He put his arm around her waist as if he had every right to touch her, his hand sliding possessively beneath the bottom edge of her shirt, his fingers touching what David knew had to be the warm softness of her skin.

As he watched, Bran pulled her toward the door, and then they were gone.

What Mallory had said wasn't stupid. And David *did* understand. Being best friends with Bran, he knew a thing or two about envy.

Tom was in the convenience store when he saw him.

The man at the counter buying a pack of cigarettes and a lottery ticket wasn't the Merchant. He was about the same height as the Merchant, but he was much younger. In his early twenties, with dark curly hair and average brown eyes.

Tom had made note of him – mostly that he wasn't the Merchant – when he'd come into the store to get a cola and some pain reliever. The brisk walk into town hadn't made him feel better. In fact, it had made his head pound even harder.

He grabbed a soda from the wall of refrigerators in the back of the store, wishing he'd taken something for his headache before he'd left the house, wishing he hadn't come quite this far, because now he had to walk all the way back.

All the way.

It was a mile at the most. What was wrong with him that he should be daunted at the idea of having to walk a mere mile?

He headed toward the checkout counter, and that's when he saw it.

The dark-haired young man left the store, pushing open the door with his right hand. And on the back of that hand he had a small, round, dark mark. A tattoo.

Tom wasn't close enough to see the details, see if it was, indeed, the Merchant's mark – the stylized open eye. But it was round and it was the right size.

He might've been mistaken. It might've been a coincidence. Except for the fact that he didn't believe in coincidences. In the very same small town where he'd spotted the Merchant, he also coincidentally sees a man with a round tattoo on the back of his hand?

Not a chance.

His head was pounding and he felt sick to his stomach, but he'd been a SEAL long enough to know exactly what he had to do.

He had to follow the dark-haired man covertly, without him knowing he was being followed. He had to see where this guy was going, possibly find out where he was staying. And he had to try to get close enough to get another look at that mark on his hand.

'Sorry, changed my mind.' Tom set the bottle of soda down on the counter as he swiftly moved past it toward the door.

His headache and nausea faded to a dull background hum as he stepped out of the store and into the humid summer heat. The night was sharper now, clearer. He had a renewed sense of purpose and the entire world had an edge.

He saw the dark-haired man walking across the convenience store parking lot to . . .

Shit.

As Tom watched, the man pulled an old touring bicycle from the bike rack, climbed on, and began to pedal away.

Tom jogged to the rack, but the only other bike there was securely locked.

Double shit.

He could follow on foot, but running after a bike didn't exactly qualify as covert.

Unless . . .

He was wearing shorts and sneakers, a T-shirt. As long as the dark-haired man didn't go too fast . . .

Tom took off down the street at the fastest pace he could get away with and still look as if he were out for a leisurely recreational run.

For a small town, Baldwin's Bridge was hopping. It

was 2330, and the downtown area from the Honey Farms all the way past the hotel and marina, all the way to the beach, was still brightly lit and crowded with people. Tourists and vacationers and high school students were out in droves, wandering the quaint brick-paved streets. The music from the distant church carnival down by the beach gave the town an even more festive air.

The dark-haired man on the bike was moving faster than most of the strollers, but not by much. Brick roads, even ones as carefully kept as those in Baldwin's Bridge, could be hell on a bike rider. Tom knew that from experience. Riding too fast could make a man feel as if he'd spent an hour with his balls being shaken by a hardware store's paint mixer.

But Tom had to push himself faster as the dark-haired man turned the corner onto Webster Street, heading toward the beach and the church carnival.

Webster Street had regular pavement and a slight downward slope to it. By the time Tom reached the bottom, he was running as fast as he could, and the dark-haired man was still pulling away from him.

He'd soaked his T-shirt through, and his legs and lungs were on fire. He hadn't run too often since his release from the hospital, certainly not this hard, never this far. And he hadn't run at all over the past few days, not with the headaches he'd been having. Still, this should have been nothing. This was a garden party compared to the running he'd done regularly with Team Sixteen. Jesus, take a few months off, and it's all over.

The pounding in his head had moved to a very prominent place in the foreground, directly behind his left eye, in fact. Tom staggered slightly as the road in front of him seemed to shift and heave.

He forced himself to keep his eyes on the dark-haired man. He'd slowed slightly because of the crowds around the entrance to the church parking lot, but Tom had to slow down, too.

His ears were roaring and the world was spinning.

One foot in front of the other. He'd done this before – he could do it again.

Music was blaring from speakers, and barkers trying to draw the attention of the crowd were shouting over it.

The bright lights, spinning dizzily with the carnival rides, only added to the chaos of the jostling crowds.

Tom could barely focus, barely see.

He searched for the dark-haired man, but he was gone. Completely swallowed by the crowd and confusion.

He lurched forward, unwilling or maybe just unable to give up. The frowning face of a disapproving mother flashed into his line of sight as a wide-eyed boy was yanked out of Tom's path.

He needed . . .

He wanted . . .

He had to get out of this crowd, and he pushed his way to a clearing by the side of a food stand, desperate for air, but able to fill his lungs with only the cloyingly sweet scent of fried dough.

Hands on his knees, he tried to catch his breath, tried to grab hold of his equilibrium, tried to make the world stop moving and the lights stop swaying.

And there it was.

A bike. Leaning up against the railing of the Tilt-A-

Whirl. It was quite possibly the dark-haired man's bike – although Tom wasn't completely sure. He couldn't seem to focus well enough to see it clearly.

Tom moved toward it, back out into the crowd, searching for the dark-haired man. Christ, where were those blinding lights when he needed them? The people lined up to ride the Tilt-A-Whirl were standing in the shadows, and because of that, they all seemed to have dark hair.

Tom looked instead for the tattoo. Right hands. Right—

He saw it!

But then he saw another. And another. And . . .

There were dozens of them. He was standing here, literally surrounded by dozens of members of the Merchant's secret organization.

Pain knifed behind his eyes.

Jesus, that didn't make sense. That was wrong. It had to be wrong. He fought the haze, searching for the reason and . . . Cell size. Yeah. He knew for a fact that the Merchant never operated with a cell of more than ten, usually more like six or seven.

Yet there it was. That round mark. The Merchant's eye. Everywhere he looked, everyone had one. He tried to look more closely, tried to see it more clearly, but his vision was blurred. He had to sit down. He had to . . .

One of the tattooed hands reached out to him. 'Tom? Oh, my God, are you all right?'

The hand was attached to an arm, which, by following it, led him to a face. A familiar, female face.

Mallory. Angie's daughter.

No, it was two Mallorys. They were both looking at

him as if from a very great distance. Since when had she been recruited by the Merchant?

He grabbed her hand, pulling it closer to his eyes and . . .

It wasn't an eye or even a tattoo. 'It's a fucking clown's face,' he said, his voice distant over the roaring in his ears.

It was a badly smudged ink stamp of Bozo the Clown. Everyone had a fucking clown face on their hand.

'You pay ten dollars for the stamp,' the Mallorys told him in eerie unison. How the hell could she sound so far away when he was holding on to her hand? 'And then you can ride all you want until the carnival closes at one.'

Tom sank to his knees.

'Jesus, Tom!' Mallory crouched down next to him as he let go of her hand and dropped to all fours. He just . . . needed to rest . . . 'You know this guy?' Another voice – male, almost as young as Mallory – came from just as far away.

'He's my uncle,' he heard her say. 'I think he's completely shit-faced. Bran, do you have a car? I need to get him home.'

'Um, no. Um, Mal, I, uh, I . . . think I have to go now.'

'Oh,' Mallory said. 'Well . . . sure.'

'This is just a little too weird for me, you know? No offense, but . . . I'll see you around sometime.'

'Right. Sure. I'll see you.'

'Asshole.' Tom didn't realize he'd said it aloud until Mallory laughed.

'You got *that* right,' she said. 'I'm sorry, but it would

be a little too effing weird for *me* just to leave you here to get rolled. Or picked up by the police.'

'I'm sorry,' he muttered through his haze of gray. 'I'm not . . .' But he couldn't remember what it was that he wasn't. He focused on a sorry-looking patch of grass directly in front of him, focused on not giving in to the grayness. There was a reason he couldn't just put his face on the ground and give up, wasn't there?

'Don't worry about it,' she told him. 'He was pretty much looking for a way to ditch me after I turned down his generous offer to jump my bones. Like that was my grand prize for going out with him.'

'Last of . . . the romantics.'

She laughed again. 'Come on, Tommy, back on your feet. Do you think you can walk?'

'Am I walking now?'

'Not exactly.' She tugged at him and he tried to help her, but his body was uncooperative. 'Come on, Tom, I'll get you home. Just lean on me.'

Kelly couldn't sleep.

She sat out on her balcony, pretending she wasn't gazing at the dark windows of Joe's cottage.

She wasn't gazing at just any windows. The windows she particularly wasn't gazing at were Tom's bedroom windows.

She willed him to get up out of bed and turn on his light. She willed him out his door, out of Joe's house, and across the driveway. She bet he could climb up onto her balcony effortlessly.

And she'd been waiting almost seventeen years for him to do just that.

She willed him to come to her rescue, to save her from this sleeplessness that haunted her, from her anger and her grief and her pain.

It wouldn't be the first time Tom had come to her rescue.

She'd been fifteen the first time he'd saved her. She'd arrived home from school to find that her father had consumed his physical limit of evening martinis about five hours too early and had crash-landed in the middle of the kitchen floor.

She'd searched for Joe, desperate to get her father to his bedroom before her mother came home – desperate to avoid the start of World War Three.

But it was Tom she'd found, gleaming with sweat, at his pile of weights back behind the garage. And after he'd helped her wrestle Charles into bed, Kelly had started in on her litany of excuses.

'I don't know what happened,' she said. 'He must've slipped on some water in the kitchen. Maybe he's not feeling well – the flu's going around. Maybe he had the flu and he was dizzy and he slipped on some water in the kitchen and—'

'Kelly, I know your father's drunk.' Tom hadn't let her get away with any of it. 'I could smell the alcohol on him.'

Kelly had been shocked. Charles Ashton was an investment banker. He'd never missed a day of work because of his drinking, but from the moment he came home till the moment he went to bed at night he always had a glass of something potent in his hand. He wasn't a public drunk, though. He'd sit out on the deck or in front of the TV and just quietly fade away.

You were safe if you didn't get too close. If you did, he would lash out with that acerbic tongue, that scalding sarcasm. Nothing was good enough, no answer was acceptable. There had been nothing she could say that wouldn't warrant the response of some belittling comment from her father.

So Kelly had learned to keep her distance. And she'd never, *ever* brought friends home with her. That was her rule number one.

She followed it devoutly, especially when Charles went into semiretirement. He worked from an office in Baldwin's Bridge from nine to twelve. And then he came home and sat in that same damned deck chair all afternoon, until he staggered off to bed shortly after dinner.

'I know he drinks himself to sleep every night,' Tom had told her all those years ago, gently lifting her chin so that she had to look into his eyes. 'I take the trash to the dump. I see the bottles. You don't have to pretend with me.'

Kelly was mortified. Someone besides her and her mother *knew*. Tom *knew*. 'Don't tell,' she begged, suddenly afraid that she might throw up, afraid she might make it even worse by bursting into tears. 'Please, don't tell anyone.'

'Oh,' he said quickly, 'no way. You don't have to worry about that because I wouldn't. I won't. That stuff's private. You can trust me.'

He was so kind, sitting next to her on the stone wall that framed one end of the driveway.

And for the first time that Kelly could remember, she'd actually been able to drop her upbeat pretense of optimism. For the first time, she'd finally had a chance to unload a little of her despair and anger at her father. None of her friends knew her father drank the way he did, and it was such a relief to finally have someone to talk to about it, someone she didn't have to – as he'd said – *pretend* around.

And for a few weeks, in the magical evenings of the early summer, when Kelly went out in the yard to her tree swing after dinner, Tom would often appear and they'd talk. Sometimes for hours. Sometimes about her father, but mostly about nothing. Anything. *Every*thing. Kelly's friendship with Tom was based on a soul-baring level of honesty she'd never had before, and it was incredibly precious to her.

For a while she even dared to hope he had a crush on her, too.

But one day he just stopped coming out to the swing – about the time she heard from her friends that 'that wild Tom Paoletti' was dating Darci Thompkins. Darci was a senior who owned a red convertible and had a reputation for taking her own top down as well on the deserted beach over by Sandy Hook.

It hadn't been until later that summer, that, once again, Tom had come to Kelly's rescue. That had been one of Kelly's precious, golden days.

She'd fallen off her bike and skinned her elbow miles away from her house, up by Lennelman's Orchards, coming home from a party at Ellen Fritz's.

Tom had come by on his motorcycle – probably on his way to Ellen's. But he stopped when he saw her sitting on the side of the road, her front wheel irreparably bent.

It was awkward at first, but it didn't take long for them to fall into their old, familiar, easy conversation.

They drove around for hours that afternoon and evening, first on his Harley, her arms tightly wrapped around him. God, that had been paradise.

Later, they rode around in Joe's station wagon, after going back to pick up her bike. They'd stopped to walk through an antiques fair that filled the streets of nearby Salem, and they'd shared a large order of fried clams and French fries from the Gray Gull Grill down by the water.

And they'd talked and laughed for hours and hours.

It had been a wonderful, magical day.

And when it was nearly midnight, they'd been down by the marina, stopped at a traffic light. Kelly could remember gazing at Tom, her heart in her throat, wanting him to kiss her *so* badly. And when he'd turned to look at her . . .

She didn't remember moving, but she must have. Both of his hands were on the steering wheel. Still, somehow, it happened. She was kissing him – finally, *finally* kissing him.

He made a low, desperate sound in the back of his throat as he pulled her closer, as he swept his tongue into her mouth.

Kelly had never been kissed like that before, and in the back of her mind she thought she should probably be shocked, but she wasn't. It was too perfect, too right.

He tasted like the chocolate ice cream they'd shared, like the salty ocean air, like freedom.

Kissing Tom was everything she'd imagined and more.

Someone honked behind them, and Kelly looked up

to see that the light had turned green. Tom hit the gas and with a squeal of tires pulled the station wagon into the bank parking lot, skidding to a stop. He killed the engine and pulled her back to him, kissing her again and again.

It was paradise.

'Oh, God,' he breathed, leaning back to look into her eyes. 'Make me stop. I shouldn't be doing this.'

His hands were in her hair and he was breathing hard.

She didn't want him to stop, so she kissed him the way he'd kissed her, deeply, fiercely, stroking his tongue with hers, sucking him with her lips.

He made that same low sound, and she knew despite her inexperience, she'd kissed him the way he liked to be kissed.

Still, he pulled away. 'My God, you're dangerous.'

She was instantly uncertain. 'Don't you . . . ? But that was how you kissed me.'

He made a noise that wasn't quite a groan, wasn't quite laughter. 'How many boys have you kissed, Kelly?'

She couldn't meet his gaze. 'I don't know exactly. I don't keep track.'

He didn't say anything. He just watched her.

'One,' she whispered, 'and it wasn't anything like this.' She melted into the beautiful hazel green of his eyes. 'Nothing's ever felt like this. I want to kiss you forever.'

'You're so sweet,' he murmured, and this time when he kissed her, he was gentle, his mouth soft, almost delicate against her lips. It was the most wonderful sensation she'd ever known.

'I really have to take you home now,' he told her quietly.

'It's not that late,' she dared to say. 'We could go down to the beach.'

That was where the high school lovers went to park, steaming up the windows of their cars. The bolder ones took a blanket and a dinghy out past Sandy Hook to Fayne's Island.

She'd never been there.

'You really want to?' His voice sounded funny, tight.

'Yes.' She dared to glance at him again.

The muscle was jumping in the side of his jaw. She slowly reached out and put her hand on his knee.

'God help me,' he said. 'Lord Jesus, save me.' He started to laugh.

At *her*. Kelly jerked her hand back, mortified.

But he somehow knew what she was thinking and was instantly contrite. 'Kel, no – I'm not . . . I'm laughing at *me*.'

She didn't get it.

'As much as I want to, I can't take you to the beach,' he explained. 'You have no idea what goes on down there.'

'Yes, I do.' He *wanted* to. His words made her bold again, and she kissed him, as sweetly as he'd kissed her. 'And what I don't know, you could teach me.'

She heard Tom groan again.

And then he pushed her back onto the passenger's side, fastening the seat belt around her, and started the car. And for several heart-stopping moments, she was both terrified and elated.

But instead of taking the road to the beach, he sped up the hill. Toward home.

'Tom—'

'Don't,' he cut her off, his voice rough as he took the turn onto their street. 'Don't say anything else.'

'But—'

'*Please*,' he said.

I love you. Kelly clamped her teeth tightly over the words.

Joe came out of his cottage as soon as Tom pulled into the driveway.

Her mother came from the main house, looking suspiciously from Kelly to Tom. 'Where have you been? Do you know it's almost midnight?'

'Meet me later tonight,' Kelly whispered to Tom. 'In the tree house.'

Her mother had swept her inside, but before the door closed, Kelly looked back at Tom. He was lifting her bike out of the back of the station wagon, but he looked up and directly into her eyes, and she knew from the heat she saw there that he'd meet her. She *knew* it.

But by two A.M., she was finally ready to believe the scribbled note he'd left for her. 'I'm sorry. I can't do this.'

Still, hope won out over doubt, and she went to sleep believing that he couldn't have kissed her the way he had unless he loved her, too.

But the next day, Tom had left town for good. To Kelly's complete shock, he'd gotten a buzz cut. He'd joined the Navy and was shipping out. She didn't even get a chance to speak to him without Joe and her parents overhearing.

'I'm sorry,' he told her quietly, as he shook her hand – *shook* her *hand* – and she knew it was true. He *was* sorry. He didn't love her.

She had been a fool even to think that he might.

Kelly had kept her distance from him the few times he came home on leave that first year he was in the service. She pretended not even to notice he was in town, hoping desperately all the while that *he'd* approach *her*. But he never did. And then, a few weeks before she turned seventeen, her parents separated, and she and her mom moved out of Baldwin's Bridge.

Kelly's visits to her father had never lined up with Tom's visits home to Joe.

Until now.

Tomorrow night she was having dinner with him.

With wild Tom Paoletti.

And this time she was playing his game, by his rules.

Charles drifted, dreaming about ice.

Dreaming about frozen daiquiris, in big, wide-mouthed glasses filled with crushed ice. He and Jenny'd gone to Cuba for their honeymoon. The trip had been exorbitantly expensive – the entire week had probably cost more than Cybele's house in Ste.-Hélène. The irony hadn't escaped him, even back then – he'd paid big money to travel by plane from the ice and snow to a place that was hot, and then he'd paid still more for a glass of that very same ice that had probably been shipped on the plane with him.

Not just ice. Ice and Cuban rum. It went down like sugar candy. And after a few glasses, even the idea of spending the rest of his life with the childishly selfish Jenny had seemed positively grand.

Charles awoke with a start, with Luc Un's foot jabbing him sharply in the side as the Frenchman muttered something dark he didn't quite catch. The meaning was unmistakable, though – you bum.

The two Lucs and Henri and Jean-Whoever – Claude or Pierre or maybe even another Luc, who could keep them straight? – were all still darkly unhappy with Charles for making them learn how to darn socks. In truth, Charles had done nothing. He'd merely made sure he was busy and working every chance he got. It was the only way he had to fight the Nazis – by freeing up Cybele and the other women so that they could do more dangerous work. Which, he told himself, was fine with him. If he had a choice, if he couldn't be shipped safely back home, then he'd stay here in this kitchen, thanks, right until the end of the war.

He was much faster with his needle now – not as fast as Cybele or Dominique, true, but certainly the fastest among the men.

Joe had been next. Charles hadn't been at it for more than a day before Joe had picked up a needle and joined him.

Trying to earn points with Cybele, no doubt.

As far as Charles could tell, Joe had earned only one of Cybele's luminous smiles.

No kisses.

Charles was the only one who'd received that particular prize.

Of course, Cybele had been careful not to be alone with him since then. And that was a good thing, he reminded himself.

He'd entertained her with stories about Baldwin's Bridge

221

– but only when Joe was around to act as interpreter. And chaperon.

Now Joe, he was a piece of work. He was so quiet, you'd almost forget he was there. But the beans and fresh greens on the table at dinner were courtesy of Joe. And whenever there was an uproar in town, whenever the Germans had a truckload of supplies stolen out from under their noses or a train was derailed in the night, whenever downed American pilots mysteriously escaped Nazi capture, well, chances were that was courtesy of Joe, too.

For all their differences, Charles liked Joe. He respected Joe.

And he didn't need his degree from Harvard to know that Joe was in love with Cybele.

It was a wondrously pure, worshipful love. The kind that a woman like Cybele Desjardins deserved. A saintly love. An honest, respectful, humble, and true love.

There was no doubt about it – Joe would do anything, anything for her if she so much as asked. Yeah, he would lay down his life for Cybele.

Who had kissed Charles a week ago.

Now, Charles had kissed a lot of women in his relatively short life, and on a scale from one to five, with five being that greatest number of inches an enthusiastic woman's tongue could go down his throat, that tiny little kiss had been a solid zero.

Not a single tongue had been involved. It was nothing. Zilch. It was the kind of dry, dutiful kiss he might bestow upon his elderly maiden aunt. It was completely platonic. It was . . .

Christ, who was he kidding? That kiss had been anything but platonic. It had trembled with emotion and barely contained passion. It had been a promise – the very slightest *whisper of a promise, true, but a promise of paradise, for sure.*

He'd thought about that single, tiny kiss for hours, days. He'd spent more time dreaming about it than any other kiss he'd ever partaken of in his entire life.

And when he wasn't thinking about that kiss, he was thinking about Cybele's eyes. Eyes that a man could lose himself in for an eternity. Eyes that saw so much, that knew so much. Impossibly beautiful eyes.

And her mouth. Graceful lips, full and moist. Slightly, charmingly crooked teeth she didn't try to hide when she smiled.

And yes, he'd thought about her body plenty, too. The slight curve of her hips beneath her skirt, the oversized dresses that both concealed and revealed her less than ample breasts. Compared to Jenny, she had the body of a boy. Or at least he'd imagined she did. He'd spent a hell of a lot of time imagining.

God help him, but he wanted her. He ached for her, he burned for her – Jenny and Joe be damned.

'Guiseppe!' Dominique burst through the kitchen door. She lunged for the man sitting across from Charles at the kitchen table, crumpling to her knees in front of him, erupting in a whispered explosion of undecipherable French.

Undecipherable to Charles, that is. Joe seemed to get what she was saying, his face tightening, his eyes suddenly hard.

He stood up, issuing orders rapid-fire. Charles could only make out some of the words. Market basket. Egg money.

Luc Un was the only other man in the house. The others had strayed too far the night before and hadn't been able to get back before dawn. But now Luc went one way, Dominique the other, gathering the market basket and the carefully hoarded egg money Cybele kept hidden in her wooden gardening shoes.

Joe found his hat and headed purposefully for the door.

Charles pulled himself clumsily to his feet. 'What's happening?'

'The Germans have shot Andre Lague. They're searching his house. Dominique fears that Cybele's there, that she'll be arrested, or—' He opened the door. 'I'm going out to find her. To warn her.'

Out. Into town. In broad daylight.

Was he nuts?

Charles grabbed the cane Cybele had given him and hobbled after Joe. 'There's four of us. We can each head in a different direction.'

Joe turned to give him a disbelieving look. 'You're not going out there. What if you're stopped? You don't have any papers.'

'Neither do you.' Charles knew for a fact that Joe's papers hadn't yet been replaced. He'd overheard Cybele – the forger that they'd used in the past had been arrested. Cybele was trying to get hold of the supplies needed to do the work herself.

'If she was at Lague's, she could well be dead already,' Joe said harshly.

'And if she wasn't, she might show up there at any moment,' Charles countered, 'and give herself away. I can help find her.' He pushed past Joe, out the door, into the bright sunshine for the first time in weeks.

The sky was brilliant blue, sheer perfection. Cybele could not be dead. Not on a day like today. God couldn't possibly be so cruel.

But Cybele had whispered to him that the sky had been a beautiful shade of blue on the day her husband and son had died.

Joe took off his battered hat and jammed it onto Charles's head, covering as much of his blond hair as possible. 'If you're captured, she'll never forgive me.' He shot off some orders to Dominique and Luc, who dashed away. 'I'm heading to the Lagues'. You should stay here in case she comes back.'

'Her friend.' Charles hobbled after him, whispering, suddenly aware he was speaking English. American English. Out on the street in Nazi-occupied Ste.-Hélène, France. 'Marlise. The one who's about to have a baby. Cybele said something this morning about bringing her fresh spinach from your garden.'

'In French,' Joe hissed. He didn't stop. 'Only in French. Marlise lives above the bakery. The bakery. Bread. Baker. Go there and come right back. Do you understand me?'

'Oui.'

Joe pointed up the street. 'That way. God help us all if you're caught.' And then he was gone, moving faster than Charles could manage, leaving Charles alone.

But not completely alone.

Holy God. There were people walking toward him, on the opposite side of the street. Two older women. One man in a dapper business suit, its cut straight from a Paris showroom.

Charles hunched his shoulders in the ragged shirt he was wearing, lowered his head, and, his heart pounding, hobbled past.

None of them looked up. None of them called out to him, or challenged him in any way.

The sidewalk was uneven, the cobblestone street in dire need of repair. He tried not to stare like an American tourist at the ancient stone buildings. Many of them were crumbling, yet they still had a fairy-tale air to them, a European magic, as if there should be a sign out in front of each, boasting 'Cinderella slept here.'

It was harder to walk up the hill than he'd anticipated, every step sending flames of pain through his leg. But that was a good thing. It counteracted the glacier of fear that threatened to turn his circulatory system into a solid block of ice.

Finally he was there. At the bakery.

Marlise lived above it, Joe had said. Looking up, Charles could see windows above the storefront. But there was only one door – the one leading into the shop.

He heard them before he saw them. The clatter of feet on the street that could only be made by German army-issue boots. The hair on the back of his neck stood straight up, and he turned. Four Nazi soldiers in full uniform. Heading straight toward him. Or maybe toward the bakery. He didn't wait to find out which.

A narrow alley separated the building from the one next door. He didn't slow down or speed up. He just kept on moving, as if that alley had been his intended destination. Dear, sweet Jesus. What if instead of helping Cybele, he led the Germans directly to her?

There was no door along the side of the building, and he went around to the back.

Again, there was only one door, and it belonged to the bakery. It was ajar, the fragrant scent of fresh bread floating out of the kitchen. He hobbled up the steps, and inside, and . . .

And there was Cybele. Sitting in the kitchen with a heavily pregnant woman.

The woman, Marlise, made a small squeak of surprise as he stepped through the door without knocking.

'I'm so sorry – we have no work today,' she said. 'Nor scraps to spare—'

Cybele's eyes widened only slightly at the sight of him. She stopped Marlise with a hand on her arm. 'He's a friend of mine,' she said quietly. 'I think it must be urgent.'

Marlise turned away, as if she didn't want to see and remember his face.

'A cup of water for my friend,' Cybele said, her eyes still on Charles's face, 'and then we'll go.'

Marlise pointed to the sink, and Cybele quickly washed out a cup, then filled it with water.

Charles realized he was dripping with perspiration. He wiped his face with the sleeve of his shirt, then took the cup, his fingers briefly touching hers. Her hand was trembling.

'Merci,' he started to say as he handed the cup back to her, but she put one finger to her lips.

Cybele set down the cup, then led him back out the door, watching, ready to reach for him if he had trouble on the steps.

She was silent as she led the way farther into the alley, away from the bakery door. But then she turned to face him.

'I know this can't be good news,' she whispered. 'So don't try to make it bearable, Charles.'

His name was melodious in its French rendition, soft and sweet on her lips.

'Just say it,' she begged him.

So he did. 'Andre Lague is dead. Shot by the Nazis.'

She closed her eyes, drawing in a deep breath. 'And the children?'

'I don't know,' he told her. 'I didn't hear anything about any children.'

'Andre and Mattise were hiding over a dozen children – Jews and Gypsies – in their attic.'

There was no way those children could have remained

undiscovered. Not with the Nazis searching chez Lague. He knew that, and she knew it, too.

She was still trembling despite her attempts to steady herself and he couldn't help it. He put his arms around her, pulling her close. She clung to him, and he was astonished by both her softness and her strength.

He heard his cane clatter to the ground as the entire world seemed to slow, as the earth itself seemed to grind to a halt.

She fit against him so perfectly, he wanted to weep. Instead he breathed in her sweet scent, closing his eyes as he felt the warmth of the sun on his face, as he felt his heart pounding.

Andre Lague was dead, but Charles was alive. And Cybele was alive, too.

He lifted his head to look down at her, at the way the sunlight shimmered on her eyelashes, the way it lit her delicate nose and cheeks.

Her eyes looked bruised and a little dazed, as if she weren't quite certain where or even who she was. She searched his face in surprise as he gazed at her, and he knew, at this moment, he was unable to hide anything he was feeling. It was all right there, in his eyes.

His fear, and his intense relief at finding her safe. His grief and his anger over the death of her friend. And all his smoldering, selfish desire, his petty physical needs. His weaknesses and his self-disgust, his very knowledge that to kiss her the way he wanted would be wrong. It was all there for her to see as surely as if he'd been stripped naked.

He saw something wild flare in her eyes, and she stood on her toes, pulling his mouth down to hers as she hissed, 'Kiss me! Quick!'

She nearly knocked him over, pushing him back against the brick building, out of the sunlight and into the shadows.

She had turned to fire in his arms, her mouth burning his, her arms entwined around his neck, one leg encircling his, the softness of her thighs open to him as if she wanted . . . As if . . .

Charles pulled her tightly against him, filling his hands with the soft curve of her rear end, angling his head to kiss her harder, deeper. Dear God. He found the edge of her skirt as well, as he kissed her again and again. Reaching up, he ran the palm of his hand against the silken smoothness of her thigh.

He felt her fingers on the buckle of his belt, and his heart nearly stopped. Did she want? . . . Was she going to? . . .

He heard it then, the sound of leering male laughter, and he broke free from Cybele's kiss to see three German soldiers looking out at them from the open bakery door.

Cybele pulled him back to her, kissing him again, her eyes open for a moment as she looked at him. And he understood.

She'd known the soldiers were there from the start. This wasn't real. She wanted the Germans to think they'd met here in this alley for a sexual liaison, rather than to discuss the devastating death of their comrade in the Resistance.

This wasn't real. His relief was mixed with a rush of disappointment so strong, he knew that if she'd actually unfastened his pants, if this hadn't been pretense on her part, he would have made love to her right there in that alley, without any thought to who might be watching, without any thought to the child they could well conceive.

And without any thought to Joe, who loved her, or Jenny, his wife, to whom Charles had vowed to be faithful.

But it wasn't real, and no matter how badly he wanted Cybele, he couldn't have her. All he had were these next few moments, this period of make-believe until the Germans tired of watching.

So Charles kissed her.

Not fiercely, as they'd kissed just seconds ago, not hungrily, not that explosive wrestling match of lips and tongues that had made him ache with wanting to thrust himself deeply and just as savagely inside of her.

No, this time he kissed her slowly. He made his lips soft and he took her mouth gently, almost lazily – but much more thoroughly than before.

This time he took his time and tasted her, memorized her. Loved her.

She melted, somehow managing to nestle herself even more completely against him.

He knew he should have been ashamed – there was no way she could miss his arousal. Her friend was dead, and here was Charles, clearly ready for a quick roll. He deserved a slap across the face for his insensitivity. But she didn't pull away. She just held on to him, kissing him slowly, sweetly, until long after the Germans had gone back into the shop.

Finally she stepped back, and he let her pull free from his arms. He stood leaning against the bricks with his eyes closed, waiting for her to speak. Dreading what she might say.

He heard her ragged breathing as she tried to catch her breath, heard her clear her throat. 'Please, Charles, forgive me—'

'Don't.' He opened his eyes as he sharply cut her off. 'You know damn well I don't need an apology from you. I sure as hell have no intention of telling you I'm sorry, because I'm not.'

'En français,' she whispered, glancing toward the bakery door.

He couldn't say what he needed to say to her in French.

230

He didn't know the words. But then again, he probably didn't know the words in English, either.

He refastened his belt and picked up his cane, silently cursing the pain in his leg. Funny how he hadn't noticed it at all with his hand up Cybele's skirt. He didn't know which was more awkward and unwieldy, his stiff leg or the fact that even now he was still almost completely aroused.

Maybe now she'd finally realize he wasn't any kind of hero.

'We need to get you home, back safely inside,' she told him, trying her best to sound normal, as if mere moments ago her tongue hadn't been in his mouth, as if her body hadn't been warm against him, as if her very soul hadn't touched his. Moving painfully, he followed her out of the alley. 'Then I'll go to Lague's—'

'That's too dangerous,' he told her harshly. Jesus Christ, did she want to die?

She didn't meet his eyes. 'I'll be careful.'

'If you're going, I'm going, too.'

'That's crazy!'

'Exactly.'

She was clearly dying to say more, but there were other people on the street, and Charles's French was too awful. They went down the hill as quickly as he could manage, through the front gate, and around to the back of the house. She all but pushed him through the kitchen door.

'Joe's already gone there, looking for you,' he told her. 'Let's wait for him to return before—'

'Those children,' she said. 'Two of them were mine.'

Two of them were? . . .

'They were staying here,' she explained. 'In my attic. Two girls. Simone and little Rachel – she's only four years old. But then, after you arrived, the weather was so hot, and I

was afraid your being here would put them in danger ...'
She was trembling again. 'I sent them to Andre's, to assure
their safety.'

Oh, God. *'Will they talk?' Charles gripped her shoulders*
and all but shook her. 'Do they know your name?'

'They're babies,' she said. 'They knew nothing. Rachel
called me Maman Belle.' Her lip trembled. 'I need to go. If
there's even a chance ...'

'There's not.'

Charles and Cybele both looked up to see Joe standing in
the door. He had tears in his eyes. 'I was just there,' he said
quietly. 'The children were taken away in a truck. All of
them.'

Cybele was silent, her face terrible. 'Where?' she
whispered.

Charles gazed at Joe, who met his eyes only briefly before
looking away. The news wasn't going to be good.

'Where did they take them?' she said again, her voice
paper thin in the stillness.

Joe wiped away his tears with the back of his hand. He
couldn't answer, couldn't speak.

'Where?' Cybele said, louder now, pulling away from
Charles. 'Where did those monsters take my children? I'll
kill them. I'll kill them! Every one of them!'

She tried to push past Joe, to get out the door, but he
caught her, held her.

She fought him, slapping and kicking, and he simply
endured until she collapsed against him.

Cybele, who never cried, was sobbing as if her heart were
breaking.

Charles couldn't move. He stood there, with his own
heart in his throat, unable to say or do anything.

As he watched, her knees gave out. She crumpled to the

floor and Joe went with her, his arms still around her. He was crying, too, rocking her in his arms. 'I'm sorry,' he said. 'I'm so sorry, Cybele. I don't know where they were taken. There's no way I could know such a thing.'

'But there must be rumors. There are always rumors.' She pulled back to look at him, her breathing coming in ragged gasps. She searched Joe's eyes, and her face crumpled. 'To one of the death camps,' she breathed.

'Cherie, it's only a rumor. We don't know for sure.'

As Charles stood there and watched Cybele cry, he knew there was nothing he wouldn't do to help stop this woman's grief and pain.

Nothing.

But there was nothing he could do.

Absolutely nothing.

Eleven

David had fallen asleep in his clothes.

Which was a good thing, because apparently he wasn't aware of the pounding on his door. He also wasn't aware when the door opened. But he sure as hell came to fast enough when the overhead lights switched on.

He must've been sleeping with his eyes slightly open. It was as if one second he was in a cave, the next he was on the surface of the sun. He shut them tightly. 'Jeez, Bran—'

'David!'

He squinted up at . . .

'Nightshade?'

He blinked, and sure enough, it was Mallory.

He reached down, checking to make sure he wasn't lying there spread-eagled and naked, the way he did nearly every night in his attempt to save money by not turning on the bank account-sucking air conditioner. His hand encountered clothing. Bathing suit, T-shirt. Thank you, God.

'You actually wear your glasses to bed?'

He sat up. 'No, of course not,' he said, then realized that he did, indeed, still have his glasses on. 'Well, not all the time.'

'David, I'm really sorry I woke you, but it's kind of an emergency.'

An emergency. His sleep-fogged mind was slowly coming back on-line. Mallory had gone out with Brandon after the photo shoot. He'd dreaded hearing her come home with him, knowing the two of them were in Bran's apartment downstairs, together.

But Mallory wasn't downstairs. She was here. Alone.

'Emergency,' he said, swinging his legs over the side of the bed and standing up. 'Are you all right? What do you need? What can I do?'

She smiled wanly. 'Brandon is such a jerk.'

Oh, God. David felt sick. 'What did he do to you?'

'He didn't do anything except ditch me when I needed help. I'm fine – it's Tom who's not feeling so fresh.'

'Tom?'

'Do you have a car?'

'Yeah. It's kind of old, but I can usually get it to start. Who's Tom?'

'My uncle.' She took his hand and pulled him toward the door. 'Remember, I told you about him?'

'The Navy SEAL.' Mallory was holding his hand. Was this some kind of weird, wonderful dream?

David caught a glimpse of himself in the mirror as she led him out the door. His hair looked like a bad accident. No way was this a dream. If he were dreaming, he'd at least let himself look more like James Bond and less like Jerry Lewis.

'He says he wasn't drinking, but he's, like, completely trashed,' Mallory told him as they went down the stairs. 'I don't know what he's taken. I don't know anything anymore. If you'd told me an hour ago that Tom was on something mind-altering, I would've told you you were full of shit. But he's like . . . he can't even sit up. I need to get him back to my uncle Joe's.'

David stopped short as he saw him. Tom was a big man, and he was sprawled on his side near the last of the tiger lilies. 'Maybe we should take him to the hospital.'

'Not if he's high,' Mallory said. 'He's career Navy. If he's using . . .' Her voice shook. 'If he's using . . .'

'If he's on something, Mal, the hospital is the best place for him to be.'

She nodded. 'Yeah, I know, but . . . Let's take him to Uncle Joe's first, okay?' She was really upset about this, on the verge of total meltdown.

'Absolutely,' David said. 'Let me pull my car up onto the lawn instead of trying to wrestle your uncle out to the street. He looks pretty heavy.'

'He is.'

He gently freed his hand from her death grip. 'I need to run upstairs and get my keys.'

He moved quickly and was almost at the top when she called to him. 'David.'

He turned to see her looking up at him. In the dim streetlight, her face was only a smudge of pale. Nightshade at her most vulnerable.

'Thank you,' she said softly. 'I know what a pain in the ass this must be since you've got to get to work so early—'

'Forget about that,' he said. 'It's no big deal. I'll be down in a sec.'

'Charles.'

Joe had left the light on in the hallway, and in the dimness, he saw Charles's eyelids flutter.

He spoke a little louder. 'Ashton, wake up.'

Charles's eyes opened, but they were glazed from the combined haze of painkillers and sleep. 'Another air raid?' he rasped, speaking in his horrendously accented French.

'No.' There hadn't been an air raid for close to sixty years. 'It's Tom.'

As Joe watched, Charles made the journey from 1944 to all the way to today. Who said there was no such thing as time travel?

'Tom.' When Charles looked at Joe again, his eyes were sharper. '*Your* Tom?'

'Mallory – my niece Angela's daughter – just brought him home.' Joe moved his friend's walker to the bed. 'He's in pretty bad shape, but he's refusing to go to the hospital. I'm going to need your help.'

Kelly sat up, her heart pounding, instantly awake as she turned on the light on her bedside table.

There it was again – a soft knock on her door.

Didn't it figure that as soon as she finally fell asleep someone would need her?

But who was it?

'Dad?' It seemed unlikely he'd make it up the stairs with his walker. Besides, she'd programmed the number for her private line into his phone. If he needed her, all he had to do was hit the speed dial.

'Dr Ashton?' It wasn't her father. The voice from the other side of the door was young and decidedly female.

But who the heck . . . ? Who would have come into the house? Who would have the key? Whoever it was, it definitely wasn't Mrs Lerner, the cleaning lady.

'Just a sec.' Kelly pulled back the covers and climbed out of bed. Her robe was on the floor, but the belt that tied it together was nowhere to be found. It was just as well – it was too warm for a robe, and her makeshift pajamas, an old T-shirt and a pair of red plaid boxers, covered her perfectly.

She opened the door, pushing her hair back out of her face.

'I'm really sorry to bother you, Dr Ashton.' The young girl standing self-consciously out in the hallway looked familiar. She was dressed in teenaged contradictions – a body-hugging tank top and a too-large pair of cargo pants that exposed both her glitteringly pierced belly button and the top edge of her underpants. Her hair was dyed an impossible shade of black, and her eyes were light brown, and . . . They should have been hazel. Of course. If her eyes had been more hazel than brown, Kelly would've recognized her right away.

'Mallory Paoletti,' she said. 'My God, I haven't seen you since you were in fifth grade. What are you doing here? Are you okay?'

There was a boy – a young man, really – standing just behind her, his clothes and hair rumpled as if, like Kelly, he'd been pulled out of bed. Or maybe he'd worked for hours with gel and hairspray to get that effect with his hair. It was hard to tell.

'There's a problem,' Mallory said. 'But it's not me, it's Tom.'

Kelly glanced at the young man again. 'Tom?'

'No, he's David,' Mallory said. 'Tom's downstairs with Uncle Joe and Mr Ashton. You know, *Tom*. My uncle?'

Tom. 'Yes, of course I know Tom. What's wrong?'

'They're arguing about what to do. Tom says he's not drunk, that he had an accident a few months ago, but he doesn't want to go to the hospital to get himself checked out.' Mallory gestured to David again. 'David thinks he should go see a doctor, because he was *really* out of it even just a few minutes ago, but see, David's not obsessed with being a macho he-man. He thinks with his brain, not with his penis.'

David winced, as if he suspected Mallory's comment hadn't exactly been a compliment, as if he wasn't entirely sure he wanted his penis to be the topic of this or any discussion.

Kelly didn't blame him. She was entirely confused. 'Tom's downstairs, and he's . . . *not* drunk, but . . . ?'

'You're a doctor, right?' Mallory persisted.

'A pediatrician,' Kelly told her.

'Perfect,' Mallory said. 'Because right now Tom's acting like a real baby.'

Tom was okay, as long as he sat with his head down nearly between his knees, with his hands clamped around the back of his neck.

The word *okay* was relative. At this point in time, it meant that the world wasn't shaking and shimmying, and he was no longer seeing that world doubled and blurred and through a haze of gray. The odds he was going to puke up his dinner were down to about fifty-fifty, and the roaring in his ears had dropped to a persistent but manageable hum.

'I'm okay,' he said for the fifty-thousandth time. And compared to the way he'd felt just a short time ago, he was. 'I just want to go to bed. I want to take a shower and I want to lie down for about eight hours.'

'You were in the hospital for *how* long?' Charles asked.

Joe was silent – too silent – sitting across from Tom at the cottage's kitchen table.

'Not very long,' Tom said, not daring to look up at Joe.

'Yes, I think that was what you said before, and I was actually looking for something a little more specific, like two days. Or overnight. Or three months. Or—'

'Not very long,' Tom repeated, enunciating as clearly as possible. 'Look, Mr Ashton, I'm okay—'

'Yes, I believe you said that before, as well. Forgive us if we're skeptical, considering right now you look like *shit* on a *stick*.' For an old dying guy hooked up to an oxygen tank and leaning on a walker, Charles Ashton was a real son of a bitch.

Joe stood. 'That's it. I'm taking him to the emergency room.'

Tom finally looked up at his uncle. 'Joe, please, you've got to trust me here.'

Joe took his keys down from the wooden hanger that hung by the door. It was in the shape of a giant key – Tom had made it for him in sixth-grade wood-shop with a lot of love and not much skill or patience. It still hung there, carefully dusted and cared for as if it were some kind of work of art. 'Get in the car, Tommy.'

'No.'

'*Yes*.'

'What are you going to do, Joe, carry me?'

'Don't think that I won't.' Joe was really mad, and just ready to try.

'Look, going to the hospital would just be a waste of time.' Tom tried to sound reasonable, hoping Joe would do the same. 'I know what the problem is – I pushed too hard, too soon. I'm getting older—'

'*He's* getting *older*,' Charles said darkly. 'Shall I hit him with my walker or my oxygen tank?'

'And it's not as easy to bounce back from this kind of injury,' Tom finished.

'From *what* kind of injury?' Joe exploded. 'You've been here for days and this is the first I've heard of any injury.'

'I'm sorry, but it's not that big a deal. I didn't want to worry you.'

'If it's really not that big a deal, then when you told me about it, I wouldn't be worried, would I?'

'Excuse me for thinking you had enough to worry about.' Tom couldn't help it, his voice started getting louder, too.

'Great, except now all I'm going to do is worry,' Joe countered. 'Because I know something bad happens to you, you're *not* going to call me!'

'Look, I'm *fine*—'

'*You* were in the hospital and you didn't tell me!'

'You were in the OSS and you won a fucking Medal of Honor, and *you* didn't tell *me*!'

Silence. Even Charles kept his mouth shut after that one.

Tom pressed the tips of his fingers against his

eyebrows, against the bridge of his nose. 'Shit,' he swore softly, 'I'm sorry, Joe. I'm just . . . I'm exhausted. I've had a tough night, and the last thing I want to do is go to some ER and get poked and prodded by some pain in the ass doctors all night long.'

'How 'bout I look you over, take your blood pressure? Does that qualify as poking and prodding?'

Kelly. Tom looked up to see her standing in the archway between the kitchen and the dining room. She was carrying her medical bag, and she came farther into the room, setting it down on the table. She was wearing what had to be her pajamas – an old Harvard T-shirt and red boxers that were about four sizes too big. There was nothing remotely sexy about it – except for the fact that she was wearing it. And that was enough. It gave a whole new meaning to the phrase 'house call.'

'Jesus.' Tom sat back. 'Don't touch me. I really need a shower.'

She was undaunted, leaning over to look at him, to shine a little light from an ophthalmoscope into his eyes. 'Just look straight at me,' she ordered, her fingers cool and firm beneath his chin.

He was still dripping with sweat, and it wasn't that fresh, clean, healthy sweat that came with regular physical exertion. It was sick sweat, cold and nasty and profoundly foul-smelling. He couldn't look into her eyes, he couldn't bear to. Instead, he focused on her forehead, just above her gracefully arched left eyebrow.

She put down the scope and straightened up slightly, touching him with both hands, her fingers moving gently but methodically through his hair, across his scalp. 'Did you fall at all tonight?' she asked. 'Hit your head?'

'Not tonight.'

She wasn't wearing a bra beneath her T-shirt, and as she reached around behind his head, Tom closed his eyes. He was definitely all right, his body returning to normal. Although that wasn't something he wanted to advertise. Hey, look, Joe, I must be fine because once again, with Kelly Ashton standing directly in front of me, I'm unable to keep from thinking about sex.

'I'm going to ask you some stupid questions, okay?' she said. 'Let's start with your name.'

'Thomas J. Paoletti. You want rank and serial number, too?'

'Nope. But today's date would be nice.'

'It's 9 August. Minutes from 10 August.'

'Very good. You want to tell me Joe's phone number?'

He rattled off the numbers, throwing in her private line at work for good measure.

Kelly looked up from wrapping the blood pressure cuff around his arm. 'Very impressive.'

'I retain numbers. I still know the phone numbers and addresses of every apartment I lived in as a kid – and we moved around a lot. I'll probably remember your work number when I'm eighty.'

'I'm hoping to retire before then,' she said as she pumped the cuff full of air. 'Why don't you plan to call me a few decades earlier? I mean, as long as you know the number, you might as well make use of it. Too tight?'

He shook his head. Was she actually flirting with him? *As long as you know the number* . . . That was

243

definitely flirting, in public, too. *And* while he stank to high heaven.

Across the table, Joe had sat down again, but it was only on the edge of his seat. He looked as if he were dying to speak. Mallory and a weird-looking kid he didn't really recognize but he vaguely thought might've been named David were hovering anxiously in the archway that led to the dining room. Charles sat with his arms folded, like the king that he was, actually wearing a satin smoking jacket, critically surveying all that he owned.

Kelly slipped the head of her stethoscope between the cuff and Tom's arm, pressing his hand between her elbow and her hip. It felt good there. It would've felt even better if she'd been naked.

She slowly let the air out of the cuff, listening intently. When she was done, she did it all over again.

'Your blood pressure's pretty close to perfect,' she finally told him, reaching down to take his pulse, her fingers against his wrist, her focus now on the face of her watch.

Joe couldn't hold it in any longer. 'He could barely walk in here when Mallory and her friend brought him home.'

'Pulse is strong,' Kelly reported.

'You should also know,' Joe continued, 'that he was in the hospital for some kind of head injury not too long ago.'

Kelly looked at Joe. 'It would probably be a good idea,' she agreed, 'if Tom were to fill me in on the details of his previous injury, as well as exactly what happened tonight. But that's up to him.' She turned to

Tom. 'Regardless of what you do or don't decide to tell me, I'd like to talk to you privately. You feel up to tackling the stairs to the second floor?'

'No problem,' Tom lied. This was it. If he could stand up and walk up the stairs without falling on his face, all talk about dragging him to the ER would probably stop.

He stood and the world shifted slightly. 'Mind if I take a quick shower first?' he asked Kelly, trying to draw her attention away from the fact that he wasn't quite as steady as he'd thought, that he was holding on to the back of his chair.

'Nope.' She didn't miss a thing. 'As long as you think you're up to it. I'll be up in five minutes.'

She followed him out into the hall, as did Joe, and watched him every step up the stairs.

Finally, he reached the top and he looked down at her. He'd started to sweat again, but she was too far away to see that. 'Ta da,' he said.

Or maybe she wasn't too far away. Her eyes narrowed slightly. 'Don't lock the bathroom door. You've got five minutes. Be out of the shower by then or I'm coming in after you.'

'That a threat – or a promise?' he asked.

God, what was he doing, saying something like that to Kelly? He'd meant to disarm her, to draw her attention away from the fact that climbing the stairs had damn near wrung the last of his energy from him. It was a tactic that had worked for him with female doctors and nurses in the past, designed to fluster and embarrass.

'Sorry,' he said quickly. 'That was ... That wasn't very nice. I beg your pardon.'

He beat a quick retreat before he could say or do anything else stupid.

Kelly took a deep breath as she stood outside of Tom's bedroom door.

Mallory had described the way she'd found Tom staggering through the carnival, as if he were drunk or high. He'd started to come around as Joe had helped bring him into the cottage, and apparently his first coherent words once he was home were 'No hospital, no doctors.'

When Tom realized Mal thought he was on drugs, he'd been quick to offer up the explanation of a relatively recent head injury and hospitalization, which had placated Mallory but sent Joe into a tizzy.

Throughout all this, at least after Kelly had made the scene, Charles hadn't coughed once. His color was good and he actually seemed to be enjoying himself, the old sadist. Or maybe it was being needed. Apparently Joe had awakened Charles, asking for his help.

She'd have to keep that in mind. But right now she had to deal with Tom 'No hospital, no doctors' Paoletti. She had to approach him as a friend, with the medical knowledge of a doctor, and convince him to go to a hospital. Not necessarily tonight – the fact that he was alert and coherent kept it from being a dire emergency – but certainly first thing tomorrow.

Kelly squared her shoulders and knocked on Tom's door.

'It's open.'

She turned the doorknob, and there she was, about to step inside, invited into Tom's bedroom for the first time in her life.

There he was, too. Sitting on his bed in a pair of shorts and a fresh T-shirt, looking like a dream come true, all hard muscles and heavy-lidded eyes, his hair damp from his shower.

He watched expressionlessly as she came in and closed the door behind her.

Her heart was pounding as she glanced around the room she knew so well from her days of tree-house spying. It looked different from this perspective. Less exotic. Less mystical. His desk was small and bare. His dresser was freshly painted a gleaming white, his reading glasses, his wallet, a handful of change, and a comb on top. His closet door was tightly shut, his towel hanging on the outside knob. There was nothing on the floor besides his duffel bag in the corner – no clothes, no pile of books.

This wasn't his room anymore. It was just a room he stayed in while he visited. She knew what that was like.

'Feel any better?' she asked.

He moved his head noncommittally.

God, she was nervous. She was used to patients she could charm with a stuffed animal or a funny hat. She was used to patients who didn't have hair on their chests.

Patients she didn't have a crush on.

She just had to be direct. To the point. 'Who do you want me to be right now, Tom? Dr Ashton? Or your friend Kelly?'

He smiled at that, a flash of those impossibly adorable dimples. 'Are the two really separable?'

'No, not really. But while Dr Ashton would politely pull up a chair and probably get nowhere in finding out what's going on with you, Kelly would sit Indian style on the end of your bed and stay until she wrestled the truth from you.'

'That could take all night,' he said.

Kelly sat on the end of his bed. 'Is that a threat or a promise?'

He looked over at her sharply as she flashed hot and then cold. Oh, God, had she really said that? What was she doing? Was she actually hitting on a man who'd barely been able to climb a flight of stairs on his own? Tom needed her, and this couldn't be helping. She stood up again. 'Sorry. Wow. Bad timing, huh?'

He was laughing incredulously. 'Holy God. Are you, like . . .' He laughed again, shaking his head slightly. 'You can't be . . . serious, right?'

Kelly couldn't stand the fact that he was laughing at her, and her embarrassment was replaced by a surge of indignation. 'Why can't I be serious? I've always found you . . .'

Oh, good grief, what was she saying? Her college roommate had had a word for men like Tom. *Fuckable.* Kelly and Evie had spent many nights near-hysterical with laughter, compiling a top ten list of men – mostly movie stars – who were one hundred percent fuckable. Which meant, they'd decided, that they'd fall into the arms and beds of any of those men without question, without comment, without objection. It was pure animal attraction, pure lust, pure sex.

Not that either of them had ever done such a thing. Not even close. Evie had been as cautious as Kelly when it came to men. But it had been fun to pretend to be so daring and bold.

And Tom Paoletti had been in Kelly's top ten every

single time. He wasn't the kind of man a woman should dare to love. She'd learned that too well, all those years ago. But as far as that other verb went . . .

Kelly pretended to be engrossed in the view from his windows. She could see the tree that held her tree house from one, see her own bedroom balcony from the other. So this was what it looked like from here.

'You've always found me what?' Tom asked.

Oh, drat. 'I suppose it's too late to say never mind.'

He laughed. 'Well, yeah. Unless this is a new doctoring technique. Giving the patient renewed will to live by increasing levels of curiosity and frustration.'

She turned to face him. 'I'm here as your friend, not your doctor. I don't want to be your doctor.'

'Great, then sit down.' When she started for the chair that was over by his desk, he added, 'Over here. Friend.'

He was watching her with those incredible Paoletti eyes, those windows to that wild Paoletti soul. The heat she could see in them was off the chart and she nearly tripped on the throw rug.

It was like some kind of challenge, as if he were testing her to see just how real her vague, almost come-on had been.

So she sat on his bed. Not as far away from him as she could be, but not too close, either.

'You've always found me to be . . .' he said again.

'Extremely attractive,' she said briskly. 'Big deal. You know what you look like. Let's drop this, okay? Tell me about your injury. What happened? How'd you end up in the hospital?'

He was silent for a moment, just looking at her. But

then he nodded as if he'd made up his mind to tell her the truth.

'All right. I was on an op with my Troubleshooters, the SO squad from Team Sixteen,' he said. 'These guys are the best, the elite of an already elite organization. I can't tell you where we were. I can't tell you what we were doing. All I can say is, we ended up clusterfucked – if you'll pardon the expression. Trust me, it's exactly what it sounds like. And once things started going wrong, they kept going wrong.'

He told her about the helicopter going down, about the blast that had sent him flying.

'Actually,' he added with a smile, 'that was the okay part. It was landing that caused the problem. Let's just say my dismount needs work.'

God, he could actually joke about it. 'Where did you hit?' she asked.

'Where didn't I hit?' he countered, then relented. 'Like I said, I don't remember much of it, but apparently I came down pretty hard on the left front of my head. I fractured my left temporal bone.'

Kelly moved closer. 'I know I did this downstairs, but . . . do you mind?'

Tom shook his head, and she reached up, gently touching his head, lightly at first then a little bit harder. Now that she was looking, she could see the tiny red scar from his surgery. It was so small, it was almost invisible. 'Let me know if anything hurts,' she murmured.

'It's mutual, you know,' he said suddenly. 'This attraction thing.'

His face was about five inches from hers, his leg close enough for her to feel his body heat. His gaze dropped to her mouth for several long seconds, and Kelly knew it. This was it. After waiting for a lifetime, Tom Paoletti was finally going to kiss her again.

'It's extremely mutual,' he said again. And then he pulled back, away from her. 'But there're a few more details you need to understand before this goes any further.' He ticked them off on his fingers. 'I was in a coma for weeks, this injury could well be career ending, and I think I'm losing my mind, big time.'

For *weeks* he was in a coma? . . .

'I've been seeing this guy,' he said. 'And I don't know if he's real or if he's some paranoid figment caused by –' he choked on the words, – 'brain damage from my injury. He's called the Merchant. He's a terrorist, Kelly.'

He was watching for her reaction, and she knew she gave him a big one there. 'A terrorist. You mean, like, a *terrorist*?'

'Yeah, I know,' he said. 'It sounds nuts.'

'Tom, are you—'

'I need to tell you all of it,' he said. 'Just let me get it all out, and then if you have any questions . . .'

Kelly nodded. Fair enough. A *terrorist* . . .

She listened as he told her about the Merchant, a man who delivered death for money. The Paris embassy bombing in '96 was apparently his handiwork. Tom had been part of a team sent to catch him.

'I lived and breathed him for months, preparing to go up against him. It was like a government approved obsession,' he told her. 'My team studied the son of a bitch until we'd be able to recognize him in a dark room at midnight while wearing blindfolds. I knew him so well, Kelly, I swear, I could think like the bastard – anticipate his every move. When his cell – his team – was tracked to England, we moved in, ready to take him down. We would've, too, if we could have operated without the restrictions from the bureaucrats. Instead, it was a goatfuck. Again, excuse me.'

Kelly laughed despite herself, despite the seriousness of what he was telling her. 'A *goat*fuck this time. Is that better or worse than a clusterfuck?'

'It's messier.' Tom's smile was rueful. 'I'm sorry. I don't mean to offend you. That language just kind of slips out when I talk about this shit.' He winced. 'Sorry.'

'Do I look offended?'

His gaze was almost palpable. 'You look . . .' He shook his head, looking away, exhaling a burst of air. 'I've got to tell you the rest of this before . . .' He cleared his throat. 'We went in – badly – and the shooting started almost immediately. That's my definition of a goat, you know, fuck. When the shooting starts. SEALs operate very quietly. We're trained to insert and extract covertly. No one knows we're there until long after we're gone – if then. But once you start firing an MP4 submachine gun, people tend to notice you. Our plan was to go in and grab the Merchant silently. I don't even know what went wrong – who started shooting first – but suddenly we were in the middle of a firefight. And the Merchant ran. The bastard escaped.

'According to allegedly reliable sources, he was seriously injured. And when he dropped out of sight – and it's been years since anyone's heard anything from him – a lot of people presumed he'd died.'

'But not you.'

'I try not to make a habit of ever presuming anything.' Tom rubbed his forehead as if his head was hurting badly again. 'So okay. Here I am. Years later. In the middle of an entirely new clusterfuck. The helo goes down, and the blast knocks me on my head. I come to a few minutes later, and even though I've got a headache from hell, I figure everything's cool, I can stand up, I remember my name – I'm going to be okay.'

'The lucid interval,' Kelly said softly. Even with extremely severe head injuries, there tended to be some amount of time, as much as an hour or two, before internal bleeding caused coma.

'Exactly. And right on schedule, a few hours later, my vision's tunneling. I'm checking out. My XO, Jazz Jacquette, literally carries me to safety, but it's fifteen hours before I hit the nearest ER, and by that time, I'm in a pretty deep coma. Apparently, there was both epidural and subdural hemorrhages putting pressure on my brain. The surgeon drills a little hole in my skull, drains whatever needs to be drained, ties off whatever needs to be tied off, monkeys around in there, doing God knows what. A few weeks later, I wake up.'

A few *weeks*? God, he was lucky.

'And I'm the miracle man, because everything still works. There's no apparent brain damage. I can talk, I can walk, I can read and write. I remember just about everything – there's no huge chunk of my life missing. I go through all the tests with flying colors. Except for one. And it wasn't even a real test.'

He'd pushed himself back so that he was leaning against the headboard of his bed, and he sat there now, with his elbows on his knees, head in his hands.

'First day back on CONUS,' Tom told her, 'that's Continental United States, in Navyspeak – I have a little run-in with a rear admiral who was trying to downsize and eliminate Team Sixteen.' He shifted, resting his head back against the wall. 'I got a little too angry.'

He told her evenly about the psych evaluations, the medical reports, the conclusion that his injury had caused his aggressive behavior, the required convalescent leave. Kelly knew it wasn't easy for him to tell her any of this.

'When I go back, I've got to convince the Navy shrinks and doctors that I'm up to speed or else it's thank you very much and welcome back to the civilian world, Mr Paoletti,' he said. 'I came here believing that my career is riding on my ability to get mentally healthy over the next thirty days.'

Tom sat forward, gazing directly into her eyes. 'But now that I've started spotting international terrorists in Baldwin's Bridge, I'm wondering if I'm suffering from some kind of weird injury-related paranoia. For the first time in my life, I'm doubting myself, Kelly.' His voice broke, and he faltered. 'I need to know if I'm fit for command, or if my career's over.'

Kelly didn't know what to say, didn't know what to do. But he wasn't finished.

'I'm telling you this for a couple of reasons,' he continued. 'Obviously, I need to find a doctor I can trust – someone I can have faith in to be dead honest with me about what's going on here. Also obviously, after tonight, I need another CAT scan, to find out if something's started bleeding inside my head again. I doubt it, but I have to make sure. I need to find out more about this paranoia crap, too. I need to know what the hell's real and what's not.'

He took a deep breath, letting it out in a rush. 'Okay. Lecture's over. Any questions from the captive audience?'

Questions. God. She had about four thousand.

'Terrorists,' Kelly said. 'Plural. You said you've spotted *terrorists* – more than one?'

'Oh, yeah, tonight's bullshit.' He winced. 'Sorry.'

'I know the word,' she told him. 'I've even used it upon occasion. I've used the other words, too, and . . . Just tell me what happened tonight.'

He did, in that matter-of-fact, reporter-dry manner, as if his career, his life weren't on the verge of destruction. The convenience store. The man with the eyeball tattoo on his hand. It was pretty gutsy to mark his people so visibly on the hand, but that was always part of this Merchant's deal. Apparently, just seeing that tattoo was enough to make most people scared to death.

As Tom went on, Kelly closed her eyes, picturing him running after a man on a bike, just a short time out of the hospital after a near-fatal head injury. He described the dizziness, the tunnel vision that had hit him at the carnival.

'All of a sudden, I realize I'm in a crowd of people who've all got the Merchant's mark on the back of their hands. It was like a nightmare, Kelly. For a minute, I was sure I'd gone completely insane.'

His hands were shaking, just from recounting it, and Kelly couldn't help herself. She reached out and held on to him.

'And then I realized,' he told her, his voice barely

more than a whisper, 'it wasn't a tattoo. It was a hand stamp from the carnival. I can only assume that the guy in the Honey Farms – that the mark on *his* hand was from the carnival, too. I see one thing, and my mind turns it into something else. Something sinister. Sounds pretty goddamned paranoid, huh?' His voice shook. 'If that's the case, then Admiral Tucker's right in wanting me gone. There's no room for me in the SEAL teams.'

He'd been holding her hand tightly, but just like that, he loosened his grip. 'Sorry,' he said. 'I didn't mean to get all weird on you.'

He tried to pull away, but Kelly wouldn't let him go. 'You spend an awful lot of time apologizing to me.'

Tom nodded. 'I have this overwhelming urge to tell you I'm sorry about that, but somehow I suspect that would be the wrong thing to say.'

Kelly laughed, emotion balled tightly in her chest. She was on the verge of tears. Again. How many times could a person cry in one night? Shouldn't there be some sort of daily limit to emotional outbursts? Although, if there were, she'd probably built up a lifetime supply from holding it all inside during those years she'd lived with her father and then Gary.

And after what Tom had just told her, this was not a time to be reserved. Reaching up, she touched his face. 'Thank you for telling me all this,' she said softly. 'I won't tell anyone – not even Joe. I promise. Not unless you want me to.'

His skin was warm, his cheek slightly rough against her palm. He'd shaved this morning, but this morning had been hours and hours ago.

'Kelly, you *did* hear everything I just said, right? I'm

probably crazy. And I'm twenty-eight days from being unemployed. And homeless. I live on base, so I'll have to move out, and—'

'But you're not alone,' she countered. 'I'll help you. I know one of the top neurosurgeons in Boston. In the *world*. He's brilliant – you can trust him, I promise. I'll go with you to see him, if you want. He'll schedule a CAT scan for you first thing tomorrow and—'

'But *you're* a doctor. I trust *you*.'

Oh, God. 'I can't be your doctor. You need a specialist. Besides, I don't want to be your doctor. I want . . .'

Kelly didn't think. She didn't plan. She didn't anticipate or analyze. She just leaned forward and kissed Tom Paoletti.

His lips were warm and impossibly soft. He tasted like toothpaste – he must've brushed his teeth right before she came up to his room.

It was a small kiss, a gentle, brief one, not deep and lingering, not soul shattering and near orgasmic, not at all the way she'd remembered kissing Tom had been.

She'd surprised the hell out of him – and out of herself as well.

She stared at him, and he stared back at her for what seemed like twenty minutes, but was probably more like twenty seconds.

Then he spoke. 'I'm crazy. Hello? Didn't you understand what I just told you?' His laughter was edged with a dangerous-sounding desperation. 'Christ, and then you kiss me anyway. Where's your common sense, Ashton? What were you thinking?'

She shook her head. 'You're not crazy. You might still be suffering side effects from your injury, but—'

'Those side effects could be permanent and you know it,' he said harshly.

Hearing the pain in his voice, Kelly reached for him again. She put her arms around him and held him close. Lord, it was like hugging an unyielding mountain. But this mountain had a heart. With her head against his shoulder, she could hear Tom's heart racing.

It didn't take very long for him to relent. He put his arms around her, too, tentatively, though, almost reluctantly touching her hair.

'I can help you,' she whispered. 'I don't know that much about head injuries as serious as the one you've had, but I can certainly look up the information. I'll find out whatever I can. And we'll get you that CAT scan, too.'

His arms tightened around her. 'Thanks.' He shifted, pushing her back so that he was holding her by her shoulders, a full arm's-length away. 'But, Kelly, look. I think—'

She knew what he thought. And it was time for him to find out what *she* thought. She took hold of his arms, too, all but shaking him. 'It's possible you've had permanent damage that's making you misinterpret and assign some kind of negative meaning to the things you see. But it's *also* possible that this paranoia, or whatever you want to call it, will fade in time – like the headaches and dizziness you've been having. It's probable that you simply need more time to recuperate. Maybe even more than thirty days.'

He shook his head. 'I don't have more than thirty days.'

'Tom, if you fractured your leg, you wouldn't be

kicked out of the Navy if it didn't heal in thirty days, would you?'

'No, of course not.'

'What's the difference?' she persisted.

He frowned at her as if suddenly just aware that instead of holding her at a full arm's-length, he was now gripping her by the elbows. Her thigh was pressed against his. She was all but sitting on his lap.

'Maybe you should go,' he said. 'I thought if I told you everything, then you'd . . .'

She gazed at him. 'What?'

'I don't know,' he admitted. 'But there are a hell of a lot of options to choose from besides kissing me. Jesus.'

God, he was back to that again. Kelly's temper flared. 'I'm sorry if it was that awful. I didn't think, I just did it, all right? If I'd been thinking, I would've just kept wanting to kiss you – without ever daring to do it. At least this way, I've done it. Now I know. And so what, all right? Obviously, in my memory, I exaggerated the reality. It was actually kind of pedestrian, if you want to know the truth.'

'*Pedestrian?*' Tom laughed in disbelief. 'Well, sure. You gave me absolutely no warning, no body language clues, nothing. It was like some kind of blitz-kiss. A hit and run. It was a bad excuse for *half* a kiss.'

That was it. She was now completely humiliated. Kelly tried to pull away, but this time he wouldn't let *her* go. She opened her mouth to say . . . what? She wasn't sure what she intended to tell him, but she suddenly couldn't speak.

Because he was about to kiss her.

And boy, did she see it coming. He gave her plenty

of warning. He moved slowly. He even stopped with his lips the merest whisper from hers.

'Now I know I'm crazy,' he breathed.

And then he kissed her.

He brushed his lips against hers in the most tinglingly delicate caress. He kissed her again, still gently, but parting her lips with his tongue, tasting her, sweetly claiming her mouth.

Kelly melted. *This* was the kiss she remembered. When he would've pulled back, she kissed him again, wanting more. For years, she'd wanted more.

There was a knock on the door, and it swung open. It was Joe, and there was no way in hell he could've missed Kelly's guilty leap back, away from Tom.

Kelly couldn't bring herself to look at either of them.

'Sorry.' Joe cleared his throat, as embarrassed as she was. 'What's the verdict?'

Tom cleared his throat, too. 'I'm fine.'

'I was asking Kelly.'

'Tom's going to go to the hospital,' Kelly reported as briskly as she possibly could, 'but not until the morning. I'm going to take him into Boston for a CAT scan then.'

'Good.' Joe looked from Tom to Kelly and back again. 'Good.' He started to swing the door closed again. 'I'll walk Charles back to the house.'

Kelly nearly leapt for the door. 'Oh,' she said, 'no, I'll do that. I was . . . just leaving.'

But Joe was already gone, and she was alone again with Tom.

'Why don't we go into Boston in the morning,' she said, still trying to be brisk, still unable to look at him, 'but not until rush hour's over. About nine-thirty?'

'Yeah,' he said. 'Thanks.'

She turned to leave.

'Kelly.'

'Don't apologize,' she said. 'Don't you dare. That was . . .' God, just say it. How would he ever know how she felt unless she opened her mouth and *said* it? She turned to face him, looked him straight in the eye. 'It was incredible. And I'm looking forward to doing it again. Maybe after we have dinner tomorrow night?'

Well, she'd surprised him again, that much was obvious. He didn't seem to know what to say, and Kelly tried not to die inside. It was possible he didn't think kissing her was so incredible. It was possible he'd only done it to prove a point, to make sure she knew he wasn't *pedestrian*. It was possible he had no intention of kissing her ever again.

As she watched, Tom rubbed his forehead, put pressure on the bridge of his nose. 'So, I guess crazy's not a problem for you, huh?'

Kelly had to laugh at that, despite the fact that she wasn't really sure which was worse – the idea that Tom might be imagining the Merchant, or the idea that there really was a terrorist here in Baldwin's Bridge. 'You always had the reputation for being a little crazy back in high school. Besides, side effects from a head injury don't really qualify as being clinically crazy.'

He looked up at her. 'I hope you don't believe everything you heard about me in high school.'

'Only the good stuff.'

Tom smiled. 'God, *was* there any good stuff?'

Oh, yeah. Not that her mother would have agreed with her definition of *good*. Kelly opened his door. 'I'll see you in the morning. But if you want to go to the hospital tonight, just call. I can be over here in a minute if you need me.'

'Kelly.' He stopped her again. 'Everything I told you – about the Merchant? I need you to—'

'I won't tell anyone,' she told him. 'You know that.'

He nodded. 'I just had to say it.'

She looked back at him, her hand on the doorknob. 'What if you're not imagining this?' she asked. 'What if you really did see this man?'

'Then I figure out what his target is, and I stop him,' Tom said.

He made the near impossible sound so easy. But he said it with such confidence, Kelly found herself believing him.

Believing *in* him.

'Until I know for certain that I *am* nuts, I've got to act as if the threat is real,' he added. 'I've got some . . . friends coming into town in a few days to help me out.'

'You've got friends here in town, too,' she told him.

'Yeah.' He smiled. 'I know.'

Twelve

10 August

It had been a very bad night.

The pain had kept rousing Charles from a deep sleep, and the fact that he had kept the light on had woken him up the rest of the way.

He'd been sleeping with the light on, like a scared four-year-old, because without it, he'd been certain he could see the dark shape of Death in the shadows.

Waiting for him. Sitting silently in the rocking chair in the corner of his room.

Charles had decided last night that he hated knowing he was dying. He'd wished at least a thousand times he hadn't gone to see that prepubescent child in a doctor's white coat who only pretended he was old enough to shave.

Of course, if he hadn't gone to see the seemingly twelve-year-old Dr Grant, he wouldn't have been given the prescription for the pills that at least took the cutting edge off his pain.

The pills that weren't working quite so well anymore.

If Charles could have his choice, death would come in a completely unsuspecting flash. One moment he'd be there, and the next – blessedly painlessly – he'd be gone.

He was starting to become a big fan of nuclear annihilation.

At 5:07 A.M., he dragged himself – literally – out of bed. Climbing the stairs up to the attic was a pain in the ass – also literally – but once up there, it took him about four seconds to find what he was looking for.

Even though he hadn't touched the damned duffel bag in nearly sixty years.

So now here he was, at not yet six A.M., sitting on the deck that overlooked the ocean – *his* ocean – cleaning the souvenirs he'd brought home with him after the Fifty-fifth had pushed all the way into Germany and crushed Hitler's army back in '45.

Souvenirs. Hah.

A Luger nine millimeter. At nearly two pounds, it was almost too heavy for his illness-weakened arms, but at one time it had fit almost perfectly in his hand. It was in mint condition – well cared for by the German officer who had owned it previously.

But the Luger, as sought after by collectors as it was, had no value to Charles – not compared to the beat-up Walther PPK he'd also brought back to the States. It was lighter than the Luger, smaller, easier to carry concealed beneath clothing. But unlike the Luger, it wasn't handmade. Side by side, the Luger was a work of art, the Walther no more than a functional tool of destruction.

But the Walther had belonged to Cybele. She'd touched it, held it, worn it beneath her clothes, close to the warmth of her skin. She'd taken it from the wreckage of a downed German plane, off the body of a German Luftwaffe officer, long before Charles had met her. She'd given it to him when . . .

Christ. He didn't want to think about any of that.

He'd wasted a lot of money shipping these guns home. Souvenirs. Bah. He'd put them into the attic right away, after he'd returned. He didn't need – didn't *want* – to remember anything at all about the time he'd spent in France.

But lately, he'd been unable to think of much else.

And it was going to get worse when Joe gave that interview. It was all going to go in some book – everything he'd been hiding from for all these years. Everything he'd done. Everything he didn't do. Every damn detail. Yes, it was Joe's story, but it was *his* story, too. It was his life, his secrets, his failures.

His grief.

Nearly sixty years of running from himself, from all his pain, all his heartache, and here he was. Still here. Still aching.

And Joe, by stirring it all up, was just making it worse.

Charles saw the shadow and didn't even bother to look up. He just kept on cleaning the Walther. It was either Death, looming over him again, or Joe. Who else would be up this early? And although he wasn't one hundred percent certain, he was betting it was Joe.

'I'm getting these ready,' Charles told him crossly, 'so I can shoot you if you make any more noise about talking to that damned writer.'

Joe sighed and sat down next to him, looking out at the nearly placid ocean. It was beautiful. It was the view Charles had dreamed about back in France. It was the view he'd spoken of to Cybele so many times, his words translated by Joe into softer, equally beautiful-sounding French.

Cybele had wanted to come to Baldwin's Bridge, to see his beautiful house, his beautiful ocean, this beautiful view. Charles had promised time and again that he'd bring them all over for a visit after the war. After the war. It had a magical ring to it. After the war, all of them – even Jean-Claude, Henri, and the two surly Lucs – would come to America, as Charles's guests. He had the money. After the war, he'd fly them into Boston, put them up at the Baldwin's Bridge Hotel.

'We promised Tom we wouldn't fight anymore,' Joe pointed out.

'Who the hell's fighting?' Charles countered. 'I'm merely threatening you at gunpoint.'

'Do you really want to talk about this now?' Joe asked. 'We *can* talk about it. But we *talk*, we don't shout. If you start shouting, I'll stand up and walk away.'

'Fine.'

'Fine.' Joe took a deep breath. 'You might as well know, then, that I got a call last night,' he said. 'Kurt Kaufman – that author – wants to interview me at the hotel, right after the opening ceremony on Tuesday. I want to do this, so I told him yes – that I'd be there.'

The Walther slipped, clattering on the table. Charles tried to catch it and ended up smashing his finger. *Dammit.*

'I was hoping you'd go with me. You could help me tell the whole story,' Joe continued.

'What?' Charles said tightly. 'That I not only cheated on my wife, but on my best friend as well?'

Joe just gazed out at the sunlight sparkling on the water, at the tumble of rocks that served as a breaker, at the still vibrant summer green of the trees at the edge of the lush yard.

Charles didn't have to look up to know what Joe saw. He'd spent nearly sixty summers gazing out at it himself, drinking his gin and tonics until the ocean turned into a distant blur or the sun set, whichever came first.

'I've long since forgiven you for that,' Joe said quietly. 'And I've forgiven Cybele, too. Not that I had the right to do any forgiving – she didn't belong to me, Ashton. At least not outside my own imagination. You know that as well as I do.'

Cybele.

Charles couldn't speak. After all these years of never mentioning her name, how could Joe speak of her so easily, so casually? And to Charles of all people. He himself couldn't even think about Cybele without feeling his throat tighten.

Yet here he sat, cleaning her precious gun. Joe had to have recognized it. Cybele had never left her house without it.

'You know, I've never tired of sitting out here,' Joe mused. 'You always were right about that – this *is* one of the prettiest spots on this earth.'

Charles didn't look up from the Walther. He knew damn well what the ocean looked like from this deck.

'When I die,' he told Joe grimly, 'this'll be yours. This house, this land, and a half-million dollars, as well. It was Kelly's idea – the will's already been written. But if you continue with this . . . this *nonsense* about this book –' his voice shook slightly, – 'I'll change my will and you'll get nothing. *Nothing*.'

'You really think I care about that?' Joe asked with a snort of disbelief. 'About your house? Your money? You think that's what I want?'

Charles could feel Joe watching him, feel the intensity of his old friend's gaze, and he made the mistake of glancing up. Joe's face was wrinkled, his skin leathered by years of sun and wind, his hair white and wispy. But his eyes were the same steady hazel they'd always been. His eyes were that of the twenty-year-old OSS officer Charles had met an entire lifetime ago.

'I don't want your house, Charles.'

Then, as now, it had been ridiculously easy to read Joe, simply from the so obvious emotions that flickered in his eyes. Joe had a poker face, sure – he couldn't have survived as an Allied spy in Nazi-occupied France without an ability to hide everything he was feeling. But when his guard was down, as it so often was when he believed himself to be among friends, he let everything show.

And right now, as he gazed from Charles to the gun on the table, Charles knew exactly what Joe was thinking about.

Cybele.

Slight and slender. Gleaming brown hair tumbled down around her shoulders. Deep brown eyes that had seen such sorrow and pain, eyes that seemed to beg a man to run away with her, to escape, if only for a moment, for a heartbeat . . .

'You can't give me the only thing I've ever wanted,'

Joe said softly. He sat back in his chair, staring out at the ocean, but this time when Charles glanced at him, he knew Joe saw nothing. Joe was lost in the vibrancy of a nearly sixty-year-old recollection that was more vivid and distinct than the already cloudy memory of yesterday's chess game in the hotel lobby.

Who had won, anyway? Damned if *he* knew.

Charles looked down at the Walther, and he, too, could almost see Cybele's slender, work-roughened hands. He could practically see her slipping the gun into the pocket of her apron or tucking it into a pouch she wore just inside the waistband of her skirt.

He could see Cybele's eyes, her face wet with tears. Cybele, who never cried. She'd cried that one time, though. Cried as if her heart were breaking.

Another of the Resistance fighters, a man named Lague, had been killed, and the Jewish children hiding in his attic had been taken away by the Nazis.

And Cybele had wept, silently now.

Joe had tried to hold her. He'd tried to comfort her.

'It won't be long now before the war is over,' Joe told Cybele as Charles had stood awkwardly in the kitchen, uncertain of whether to go or stay, wanting . . . what?

To hold her himself, the way he'd held her that afternoon in the alley behind the bakery. He wanted to lose himself again in the intoxicating sensation of her hands in his hair, her leg wrapped around his. He wanted to feel her body straining against his. He wanted to rid them both of this pain and anguish by the simplest of solutions. It seemed so obvious. What they'd felt in that alley had been good, despite all the complexities and confusion. It had been very, very good. What they were feeling right now, with Cybele on the floor, weeping as if her very soul was wounded, was bad.

Very, very bad. They could have pleasure. Or no pleasure. And watching her cry was definitely no kind of pleasure.

But of course it couldn't be that easy.

'The Americans have landed in France,' Joe told her, desperately trying to give her hope when it was so painfully obvious that the last of her hope had gone. 'It's only a matter of time – months, weeks – before Ste.-Hélène will be free from the Nazis once and for all.'

'And then what, Guiseppe?' Cybele asked quietly. 'When the Germans have gone, when there's no one left to fight, what then? What will I do? Where will I go? Will I stay here in this empty house, alone with the ghosts of my husband and child?'

She tried to pull away, but he held on to her.

'Marry me,' he said. Tears were running down his face, too, and Charles knew he loved her enough to do anything for her. If he could have, Joe would have suffered her pain, and gladly. 'Marry me, Cybele, and come home with me. We'll go to Baldwin's Bridge together. I've never been there, but I'll take you there if you want. We can live next to Ashton's beautiful ocean. I'll tend to his garden, you can work in his house. We can go there, cherie, after the war is over. When life is normal again.'

Cybele gazed wistfully at Joe through her tears, smoothing his hair back from his face almost as if he were a child.

'Don't you know?' she said. 'Don't you realize? Not even the end of this war will make life normal again.' She touched his face, her eyes brimming with a fresh onslaught of tears. 'I can't marry you. I can't just walk away from my life here, from everything I've been and done and—'

'Then I'll stay,' he promised her desperately. 'We can live here in Ste.-Hélène. I'll do whatever you want—'

'I can't have what I want,' she whispered. 'The only thing I want, the only thing I'll ever want, is Michel. My baby.' Her face crumpled and she began to cry again. Terrible, soul-wrenching sobs that made Charles want to double up from the pain. 'I want my Michel back. I want to hold my son! If you could give me my son, even just for a minute, just for one moment, so I could feel his arms around my neck again – I would go with you. I would follow you anywhere, for the rest of your life! But you can't! You can't! No one can!'

She pulled herself away from Joe, dragging herself to the corner, where she wept.

Joe tried to follow her, and Charles moved to intercept. But Joe was weeping nearly as much as Cybele, and he wasn't easily stopped. At least not until Charles sat down, with a clatter of his cane on the tile. Not until Charles grabbed him and held him back.

Joe's need for her was only hurting, not helping. There was no one who could help her. No one.

And there, on a beautiful summer afternoon, with the sky a brilliant shade of blue, Charles and Joe clung to each other because there was nothing else they could do. Neither of them could come even remotely close to giving Cybele what she wanted most in all the world.

One last embrace from her baby son.

Tom cleared his throat. 'Hi.'

Kelly looked up from putting a jacket and her briefcase in the backseat of her car. 'Hi.' She smiled at Tom, but it was a self-conscious smile, a little bit stiff. She was nervous.

She wasn't the only one.

He gestured down at his summer uniform. 'I wasn't sure what to wear. Technically, if I need medical attention, I should go to a military hospital. But this is kind of a unique situation. There are privacy issues, and . . .' He climbed into the passenger side of her car, put the can of cola he'd taken from Joe's fridge into the cup holder in the front. 'I mean, if it turns out I need some kind of surgery, I'll have to go to a military hospital. Unless it's an emergency. But it's hard to believe it would be an emergency at this point.' Great. He was babbling. Way to be cool, Paoletti.

'How are you feeling this morning?' she asked, starting the car. She glanced at him only briefly before she gazed into the rearview mirror to back up, maneuvering out of the driveway.

'Okay,' Tom said. 'I've still got a headache, but it's okay. It's manageable, especially with my sunglasses on.' He saluted her with his soda can, taking a sip. 'Getting some caffeine into my system helps, too.'

She glanced at him again. 'You do look . . . nice.'

Okay. Now what did that little hesitation before the word *nice* mean? God, this was killing him. It was his fault, too. He'd made the choice to be polite as he'd approached her this morning. He'd chosen small talk and a polite, discreet distance over a full-body-contact embrace with a tongue-down-the-throat, to-hell-with-this-appointment-let's-go-get-naked kiss.

But his distance was for good reason. Even if Kelly didn't care if she became involved with a man who was certifiably crazy, *he* cared. She didn't deserve to get hooked up with some nut job – even if that nut job was him.

And maybe she'd changed her mind. Aside from that slight hesitation before the word *nice*, she was in heavy polite mode, too.

But then she glanced at him again. 'What is it about a man in uniform?'

Well, okay. That was definitely an invitation to flirt. It was the conversational equivalent of a yellow flag announcing her interest.

'I don't know,' he said. Come on, Paoletti, use your brain. Say something clever. 'I've spent years around men in uniform, and it doesn't do a damn thing for me.'

It was lame, but Kelly laughed anyway. 'That's right,' she said. 'I remember. You're into black lingerie and whipped cream.'

Holy Christ. That wasn't just a flag, that was an entire team of semaphore men gesturing wildly.

Tom, for the life of him, didn't know what the hell to say in response.

Paradoxically, fascinatingly, Kelly's cheeks were turning an intriguing shade of pink. She'd embarrassed herself. Go figure.

She looked way beyond nice this morning. She was wearing a sleeveless dress with a skirt that ended many wonderful inches above her equally wonderful knees. Her legs were tan and bare and gorgeous, and she had sandals on her feet, nail polish on her perfect toes. She'd taken extra time with her hair and makeup today, too. God, she looked delicious.

And she'd virtually just told him . . . Jeez, he wasn't sure *what* she'd just told him. With any other woman he would have interpreted her words to mean that if he played his cards even slightly right, he would be exploring far more than the inside of her mouth tonight.

The thought made him dizzy. He and Kelly. Tonight? . . .

Was it possible she really wanted that?

'I spoke to Gary on the phone,' she told him as she drove through town, heading out toward Route 128. She was using that brisk, businesslike voice she'd slipped into last night. After Joe caught them kissing on Tom's bed.

Tom hadn't seen Joe yet this morning, thank God for small favors. His uncle had been up and out ahead of him.

He had no idea what Joe was going to say about the fact that he'd seen Tom kissing Kelly Ashton. He would say *some*thing, even if it was just a cautious 'Be careful.' That was for sure.

'He was able to pull some strings,' Kelly added. 'You'll be able to go in for the CAT scan right away.'

Wait a minute. He *who*? 'Gary . . . ?'

'Dr Gary Brooks. He's the neurosurgeon I told you about last night.'

The name was vaguely familiar. Had she actually mentioned his name last night? Tom had been completely distracted – yeah, there was an understatement – but he didn't think she had. So why would this doctor's name ring a bell this way?

'After the CAT scan, around eleven-thirty, we'll meet Gary in his office. It's right there in the hospital. And after that – I'm sorry about this, but I've got to go see a patient. If you don't mind, I'll drop you at the train station.'

'No problem. You going to see Betsy McKenna?' he asked.

She glanced at him in surprise. 'Actually, yes. She starts chemotherapy today. I can't believe you remembered her name.'

'I'm good with names.' Except for this Gary Brooks guy. 'Tell me more about Dr Brooks. How come he has time to see me today?' Tom asked. 'That's pretty lucky, huh?'

'Not really,' Kelly told him. 'I knew Gary was free at eleven-thirty because we had a date to have lunch together.'

Tom was completely surprised. Kelly had a *date* with *Gary*.

What the hell was she doing kissing Tom last night and talking about frigging whipped cream if she had a date with Gary today?

'So,' Tom said, carefully casual, 'Gary doesn't mind missing out on a chance to have lunch with you?'

She glanced over her left shoulder, checking her blind spot as she accelerated onto the highway, moving immediately into the left lane. She drove fast, one hand on the wheel, the other on the stick shift, with the solid, relaxed confidence of an excellent driver.

Funny, he wouldn't have been surprised if she'd been timid behind the wheel. In fact, he'd almost expected it, almost volunteered to drive before they got into the car.

'Gary's probably as relieved as I am,' Kelly answered him. 'We get together about once every two months. Just to stay in touch. It's an attempt to be civilized since we work in the same city. But after we get done bragging about the medical miracles we've been involved with, we run out of things to say. It was pretty much like that when we were married, too.'

Ding.

That's why the name was familiar. Gary Brooks was Kelly's ex-husband.

'Are you sure I should want your ex as my *brain* surgeon?' Tom asked. 'Like, he's not going to have a fit of unwarranted jealousy and lobotomize me, is he?'

'We've been divorced for almost eighteen months,' she told him. 'He's remarried, and his daughter just celebrated her first birthday.' She glanced at him. 'I figure, as a Navy SEAL, you're probably pretty good at basic math, right?'

He was. Twelve plus nine was twenty-one months. Gary had gotten wife number two pregnant before he and Kelly had split up. 'Ouch. That must've hurt.'

'Actually,' she said, and she said it so sincerely, he found himself believing her, 'it was a relief. Neither of us wanted to admit our marriage, well, sucked. We would probably still be married, still droning our way through our pathetic lives if Gary hadn't met Miss Tits.'

Tom choked on his soda.

And Kelly turned slightly pink again. 'Sorry. That's my private nickname for her. I probably just should have kept it private.'

'No, it's . . . It just caught me off guard, that's all.' Tom tried to cough cola out of his lungs.

'She's actually very nice,' Kelly said earnestly. 'She can't help it if she's got, well . . . you know. A body like that. Frankly, I'm still a little surprised Gary actually noticed.'

'Gary was a fool for failing to notice what he already had,' Tom countered.

She smiled at him, genuinely pleased. 'Well, thank you.'

'Are we still on for dinner tonight?' Oh, Christ, whatever made him ask *that*? He should be maintaining a distance between them, not putting ideas about tonight into her head.

Still, he liked her. He truly liked her. Each time he talked to her, he liked her more and more. She was different than he'd remembered, than he'd imagined. Spicier. Sharper. *Earthier*. Miss Tits. God. But he had to keep his distance. The last thing he wanted to do was hurt her.

'Absolutely, we're still on for tonight,' she said, clearly happy that he'd remembered, giving him a smile that made him want to ignore his plan to proceed with caution. 'Although ... do you mind if we get takeout and eat on the deck? I didn't count on being out of the house for this long today, and—'

'No problem,' he said. 'That sounds great. I mean, assuming old Gary doesn't feel the need to fill his monthly quota and perform immediate brain surgery on me.'

Kelly laughed. 'Good doctors don't have *quotas*. And he's a good doctor, I promise.'

'I'm trusting you,' Tom said. 'As awful as it sounds, I'm putting my brain in your hands.'

Kelly laughed again, as he'd hoped she would. But then she reached across and took his hand.

'I like that you trust me,' she said. 'I've always trusted you, you know.'

Tom looked down at their fingers, laced comfortably together, and something tightened in his chest.

She trusted him. But right now, she shouldn't.

Because he no longer trusted himself.

It was that same night – the night after Andre Lague was killed – that Cybele came to his room.

It wasn't even a room. It was a closet with a window. But it was private and it was big enough to fit his bedroll. And as long as it continued to be cool enough at night, Charles could sleep with the door closed.

The moon was out that night. It was shining in the window, silvery bright. He remembered lying on his back with his hands beneath his head, staring up at the backside of the stairs above him when she slipped in through his door.

She didn't knock. She just came in.

He was wearing only a pair of briefs, and he was lucky he had that much on.

He sat up fast, scrambling for his pants, and he ended up nearly knocking himself out as his head connected with the wood above him.

It was not the most embarrassing moment of his life, but it was close.

'Jesus!' he hissed, a word that was understandable in nearly any language, as he collapsed back on his bedroll.

'Oh, Charles, I'm so sorry.' She knelt down beside him, her fingers cool against his head as she checked to make sure he hadn't sliced himself open.

He hadn't. It only felt as if he had.

She was wearing only her nightgown. It was thin and cotton, and in the silver moonlight, with her hair down around her shoulders, it made her look like an angel.

Charles sat up, carefully this time, and backed as far away as he could, which wasn't far enough, considering the room was the size of a closet. Where the hell were his pants?

'What's wrong?' he asked her in his atrocious French. Had there been some mission that he wasn't told about?

Something that Joe and the other men had left to take care of? Something that had gone wrong? 'Where's Guiseppe? What's happened?'

She shook her head. 'Nothing has happened. Guiseppe is upstairs, probably asleep.'

Oh.

Oh, damn.

As Charles looked into her eyes, he knew the truth. He knew why she was there.

'I don't want to be alone,' she whispered. 'I'm so tired of being alone. Please, Charles, will you—'

'Cybele, please don't ask me—'

'Make love to me tonight?'

No. No, no. It was the one thing he wanted more than anything in the world. It was the one thing he couldn't have, even though she was right there, right within his reach. And he didn't even have to reach. All he had to do was open his arms and . . .

'It's time to be honest,' she said, as straightforward and direct with this as with everything. 'I want you, and I know you want me.'

He felt like crying. 'You also know I'm married.' He said it both in English and in French.

She didn't move. She just knelt there, her face illuminated by moonlight. God, she was beautiful. 'But you don't love her. Not the way a man should love a woman. When you speak of her, of Jenny, it's as if she's a child that you care for. That you're fond of.'

She was right, but that didn't make the vows he'd made any less binding.

'You don't burn for her,' Cybele whispered.

'She loves me.' And she did – as much as Jenny could love anyone.

'She loves that you take care of her. She loves your fortune.'

That was true, too.

'Tell me you love her,' Cybele challenged him, 'and I'll go.'

'I love her,' he lied, both in English and in French.

She didn't believe him.

'I do,' he said in English. 'I know when I talk about her it sounds as if I don't, but I swear, I do.'

Cybele understood him. He knew she did. But she still didn't move.

'What about Joe?' Charles asked, near desperate now. If she touched him, he wasn't sure he could be so strong. If she touched him, she would know the truth. He didn't love Jenny. He'd married her because she was having his baby, because she was the kind of woman that men watched and he liked being the cause of all that palpable envy. He'd wanted Jenny, he'd lusted after her, and he'd even thought he'd loved her, but he didn't. He'd had no idea what love really was, what love could be.

'You should be up in Joe's room right now,' he told Cybele. 'He loves you, you know. He's free to love you, completely.'

'You want me to go to Guiseppe. You want me to be with him tonight. Not you.' Tears of disbelief were brimming in her eyes, and he knew the next thing he said would matter the most.

She hadn't asked a question, but he answered it anyway. 'Yes.' He could barely choke the word out, but choke it out he did. God help him. 'Go to Joe. Because I can't give you what you need.'

'I see.' She wiped her eyes with the back of her hand, drew in a deep breath. And then she turned and left his room.

The door closed behind her, and Charles wanted to run after her, to stop her, more than anything he'd ever wanted in his life.

But he sat still, sick down to his very soul. He heard the stairs creak as she started to climb them, and still he didn't move. Her room was to the right of the top of the stairs, Joe's to the left. Her footsteps passed directly over his head, going up, and then he heard her pause.

Charles closed his eyes, praying, though for what he wasn't sure.

But when the floorboard in the upstairs hallway creaked as she went left, he knew. He hadn't been praying for that.

Charles opened his eyes and gazed out at the ocean. Last night's physical pain had been nothing compared to the pain he'd felt that night, nearly sixty years ago, when he'd pushed Cybele into his best friend's arms.

He'd spent a sleepless night, hating himself for being weak enough to want her, and yet not weak enough to have her. All night long, he'd seethed with jealousy and frustration, imagining Cybele in Joe's room, in his bed, lying there beneath him, and . . . God. He hated himself, hated Joe, hated Jenny. Hated Cybele. How dare she come to his room, tempting him to be unfaithful simply because she wanted someone – *any*one – to hold her. And that surely was the case if she could go from Charles's room to Joe's with hardly any hesitation. Apparently his arms had been interchangeable with Joe's . . .

But hating her hadn't made it any easier to bear. Especially not the next morning, when Joe had appeared at breakfast with a lilt in his step and the unmistakable light of heaven in his eyes.

Joe had that same soft, faraway look in his eyes now,

nearly sixty years later, as he sat next to Charles on the deck of this multimillion-dollar house, overlooking the prettiest piece of property and the most beautiful view of the ocean in the world.

And nearly sixty years later, Charles was still jealous of Joe.

Joe turned and looked at him. 'I think there's something going on between Tom and Kelly.'

Charles fought to return to the present. Tom? And Kelly? Well, well, maybe the girl had actually made a move.

'You *think* there's something going on,' he said crossly to Joe. 'Suddenly, after all these years of living like a monk, you're the local expert on romance?'

Joe gave him one of those long, steady, patient looks that always made Charles feel like some kind of legless larva.

'I know enough to recognize a kiss when I see one,' he said evenly. 'And to tell at a glance who's on the giving and who's on the receiving end. I know Kelly's been lonely.'

Kelly'd kissed Tom. Charles's first reaction was to laugh. His daughter's life was her own, but he'd never particularly liked those pasty, bespectacled, self-important blowhards she'd brought home from the hospital. But Tom Paoletti – now *there* was a man. But probably way *too* much man. The reality was sobering. He'd never expected her actually to try for him. 'They're completely wrong for each other.'

'I don't agree with you,' Joe said, 'but I suspect Kelly does. I was thinking it might be a good idea for you to talk to her, so she doesn't end up hurting Tom too badly.'

Kelly hurting Tom. Now there was a twist on the old sad story of love gone wrong. But sure, it was possible. Why not? After all, she was an Ashton, and Ashtons were known for having hearts of stone.

Thirteen

'Everything looks really good.' Gary didn't waste time with small talk as he breezed into his office. 'No trace bleeding, no swelling, nothing at all to indicate that there's any kind of problem. It's healed nicely.'

Kelly closed her eyes as he gave her a perfunctory kiss on the cheek. 'Thank God.'

Tom didn't seem to be as happy at the news. He sat forward as Gary slid into his seat behind his desk. 'So what's going on, then? What's with the headaches and dizziness? The paranoia?'

'I found no physiological explanation, other than that of the injury and surgery.' Gary looked tired, older, lines of strain giving his handsome face a pinched, anxious look. 'The symptoms you've been having are probably related.'

'No kidding.' Tom looked at Kelly, his frustration evident. 'Am I asking the wrong questions here?'

'I think what Gary's trying to say is that he doesn't really know why you're experiencing these things,' she told him.

'There's a great deal we're still learning about injuries to the brain, Lieutenant,' Gary admitted. 'And ten individuals with similar injuries will have ten entirely different recoveries, varying from death to complete return to preaccident condition. The problems you've been having are insignificant compared to, say, paralysis or damage to the speech center of your brain. And as for the feelings of paranoia and the slight personality change regarding your lack of control with your temper – these aren't outside the realm of normal for the type of injury you've had. Although, again, since we know so little, normal tends to be a pretty broad band.'

'Is there any way to know whether or not the paranoia's going to be permanent?' Tom asked. But when Gary took a deep breath and opened his mouth to speak, Tom held up his hand. 'That was a yes-no question. I'm kind of hoping for a single word response.'

Gary closed his mouth. He looked at Kelly, and she lifted her eyebrows, waiting. He sighed. Single word answers weren't his forte. 'No.'

Tom nodded, his face impassive. It was not the answer he'd been hoping for, and Kelly ached for him. She wished she were sitting close enough to take his hand. She wished, when they walked out of here, that she'd have the courage to put her arms around him and hold him close. And she also wished that her comfort would be enough to sustain him.

'Can you give me any statistics?' he asked Gary. 'Percentages of people with this type of injury who *do* achieve complete recovery?'

Gary straightened the files on his desk into a neat

little pile. 'Since I don't have your medical records, I can't be absolutely certain, but from what you've described – the severity of your injury plus the length of time between being injured and getting medical attention . . .' He shook his head. 'I don't know the exact number, Lieutenant, but most people would not have survived. Statistically, you're way ahead of the game.'

Tom was silent.

'If these side effects *are* permanent,' Gary tried to reassure him, 'there are steps you can take to make them easier to live with. There's medication that will help relieve feelings of anxiety. It may also help with any vague feelings of paranoia you might be having. If you want I can—'

Tom shifted his weight, giving Gary a big body-language no. 'That's not an option. Not if I want to stay in the SEAL teams.'

'Maybe it's time to consider retirement,' Gary said as gently as he could. 'Return to civilian life. Take a year or two off – relax. Play golf, do a little gardening. Let yourself heal.'

Tom stood up. An even less subtle rejection. 'I'm not ready to quit yet. I've got a few more weeks. Any suggestions on what I should be doing to speed along any kind of additional recovery?'

'Rest,' Gary recommended, 'lots of sleep. Keep life low-stress. Take everything slowly, avoid upset, don't push yourself physically. Lots of massage and other tension-relieving, ahem, activities.'

Kelly didn't dare look at Tom. It was too bizarre – sitting here with this man she wanted to sleep with, listening to her ex-husband recommend he use sex to relieve tension. It was all she could do not to giggle. She stood up, too. 'Well, that sounds good to me.'

Both Gary and Tom looked at her, and she carefully kept her face perfectly straight, her eyes wide. Little Miss Innocent.

Gary didn't give her a second glance, but Tom kept one eye on her, even as Gary stood and the two men shook hands.

Tom was, no doubt, remembering the whipped-cream comment she'd made back in the car. Well, good. About time he caught on.

Kelly took Gary's hand and air-kissed his cheek as Tom moved tactfully out of the office, giving them at least the illusion of privacy.

'How's your father?' Gary asked.

'Pretty frail. How's Tiffany and the baby?'

He forced a smile. 'Fine. Great.' Very unhappy with his workaholic schedule, she knew. Tiffany had called Kelly to find out if Gary's eighty-hour workweek was normal. It was. Kelly gave their relationship five years, tops. Tiffany was too smart to take his oh-so-important-me crap for longer than that. Yes, he was a good doctor, but he wasn't Albert Schweitzer.

'Thanks again for seeing Tom,' she told him.

He was still holding her hand, and he lowered his voice. 'He seems nice, but . . . a Navy SEAL? Aren't you a little young to be having a midlife crisis?'

'He's an old friend from high school.' Kelly pulled her hand free. 'Whom I still happen to find very attractive. There's no crisis. I'm single, he's single. He's going to be in town for a few weeks . . .'

Gary smiled. 'So it's purely physical. I can

understand that. Use birth control, sweetheart, or it might become permanent.'

The five years with Tiffany shrank to less than two, and Gary morphed into her father, richer than God, but dying alone and bitter after a string of failed marriages.

'Goodbye, Gary.' Kelly closed his office door behind her, more glad than ever that she had escaped when she did. Tom was already out of the waiting room, standing in the hall. 'Sorry about that.'

He glanced at her. 'No problem.'

They started toward the bank of elevators. 'Are you okay?' she asked.

He met her gaze, sighed, and then, to her surprise, shook his head no. 'I'm pretty disappointed.' He laughed. 'I don't know what I was hoping for. Some kind of low level internal bleeding, maybe. Something that we could all point to and say, "Aha, there's the cause of the problems." Something that could be fixed.'

He jabbed the down call button for the elevator.

'Through surgery,' Kelly pointed out, trying to speak clearly even though her heart was securely lodged in her throat. She'd never expected him to be so honest about what he was feeling, although it was clear that *disappointed* was an enormous under-statement. 'Through the doctors drilling a hole in your skull and . . . God, Tom, Gary's a good doctor, but brain surgery involves certain high risks. We're talking about someone poking around in your *brain*. Even if the surgery goes well, there are chances of infection and—'

'Right now I'd take the risks. Gladly.'

The doors slid open, and Tom stepped aside, letting Kelly into the empty elevator first.

'Of course, the point is moot,' she said.

'Right.' Discouraged, he rubbed his forehead as the elevator took them to the lobby.

'I was a little surprised you didn't go into more detail about your . . .' She wasn't sure what to call it. 'Your suspected paranoid episodes.'

Tom looked at her and smiled ruefully. 'Tactfully put.' He shrugged. 'I just didn't feel as if I wanted him to know.'

And yet he'd told her, in complete detail.

'Do you think I'm nuts if I continue to act as if my seeing the Merchant was anything besides a paranoid delusion?' He laughed again. 'Okay, let's see you answer *that* one tactfully.'

That wasn't so hard. 'I think you should do whatever you need to do in order to feel most comfortable with this situation – make it as stress free as possible. I think you should follow Gary's advice and relax.'

Tom was leaning back against the elevator wall, just watching her. She could see his unhappiness in his eyes, his frustration at this 'wait and see' advice. She tried to imagine what it might be like. What if she were told there was a chance that she couldn't be a doctor anymore? That everything she'd worked for, everything she'd strived to become would be gone? And, oh, she had to wait a month to find out her fate.

Her anxiety and stress levels would be pretty high, too.

'Maybe you should go to some tropical island for a few weeks, just drink strawberry daiquiris on the beach all day,' she said, knowing as the words left her lips that even if Tom could walk away from this ghostly terrorist he'd thought he'd seen, her own father's failing health made the option impossible. Tom wouldn't leave Joe until his convalescent leave was up. 'I'd give just about anything to go with you.'

There it was. She'd just served him a nice, fat, slow pitch. If he wanted to, he could step up to the plate and hit the ball clear out of the park.

He didn't pretend to misinterpret or misunderstand. He just smiled that little half smile that always made her knees feel weak. 'What am I going to do about you? You should be running away from me.'

'Why should I run away,' she said, her heart pounding, 'when what I really want is for you to kiss me again?'

He pushed himself up and off the wall, and Kelly knew that he was going to do just that. She'd seen that same look in his eyes last night, and in Joe's car, all those years ago. Her pulse kicked into quadruple time, and her mouth went dry, and . . .

The elevator doors opened.

A half-dozen people were standing there, staring at them, waiting to get on. Tom stepped back to let her off first, ever the gentleman.

'Come on,' she said, leading the way through the crowded lobby, trying her hardest not to be embarrassed. He *had* been about to kiss her, hadn't he? 'I'll take you to the train.' When they got into her car, dammit, she'd kiss him.

But Tom caught her hand, stopping her before she pushed open the door that led to the parking garage. 'I can get myself to the train. It doesn't make sense for you to drive me to North Station and then drive all the way back here to the hospital to see Betsy.'

'Oh,' she said. 'No. I don't mind. In fact, I'd feel much better if I could actually take you into the station and get you onto the right train.'

'That's ridiculous. I don't need you to do that. I'm not a child.'

'What if you get dizzy again?' she worried.

He laughed. 'I'll sit down. I'll wait for it to pass. If I do get dizzy, I promise I won't run several miles at top speed, like I did last night, all right?'

She gazed at him, unconvinced, and the amusement in his eyes changed to something softer, something warmer as he laced their fingers together and pulled her toward him.

'I like that you care about me, Kelly,' he said. 'It makes me feel good. But you know what?'

She shook her head, aware that he was moving even closer, aware that she wanted him even closer – their legs touching, their stomachs, her breasts against his chest.

'I'm a highly trained professional,' he told her. 'I think I can probably get from the hospital to the train station and back to Baldwin's Bridge on my own, even if I get a little dizzy on the way.'

His mouth was now mere inches from hers. He paused, though, gazing down at her before he closed the gap and kissed her, sweetly covering her lips with his own.

It was a see-you-later kiss, but it was unlike any other see-you-later kiss she'd ever received in the middle of a crowded hospital lobby.

He took his time with it, making a point to nestle

her body against his, to slowly drink her in. He was all solid muscles, and yet, somehow, his arms managed to feel so soft.

His mouth was soft, too, and beautifully gentle. He tasted like coffee and chocolate, like everything that was good and right with the world.

When he finally stopped kissing her, when he lifted his head, *she* was the one who was dizzy. But it was okay, because he still held her tightly.

More tightly than she'd ever been held before in a hospital lobby.

But Tom didn't seem worried about the fact that they were standing there in public. He didn't seem to care that there were dozens of people around them. He surely saw them, but from the way he was looking at her, he didn't give a damn about anyone else. Gary and her father both would've frowned at such a display of affection, but to Kelly, it was as good as she'd always dreamed it would feel. And if this was the way he'd kiss her in public, how would he kiss her when they were alone? The thought was heart stopping.

'You trust me, remember?' he said softly.

Kelly nodded. Oh, yes.

'Then trust me to be able to take the T to North Station. Trust me to get to Baldwin's Bridge. I'll see you back there. Believe me, I wouldn't miss having dinner with you tonight for anything in the world.'

He kissed her again, but just briefly. Just long enough to make her lips tingle and her pulse surge.

And then, with a wave, he went out through the revolving doors and onto the street.

Kelly watched him from the window as he crossed to the aboveground T stop that ran down the center of

292

the city street. Although the platform was crowded, he stood out, unique and splendid in his uniform.

Tom Paoletti.

Tonight.

Oh, my God.

When David got home from work, Mallory Paoletti was sitting on the wooden stairs that led up to his apartment.

She closed her book and stood as he climbed out of his car. 'Hey, I thought your shift ended at ten-thirty.'

She was wearing low-riding shorts today with her trademark black tank top, probably because of the heat. The ring in her belly button glittered with a red stone instead of her usual blue. Both that and her long pale legs worked nicely with the shorts. *Very* nicely.

'Hey, Nightshade.' He shouldered his backpack and started up the stairs. 'My boss asked me to stay and work part of the lunch shift. What time is it, anyway?'

'It's after one. You must be exhausted.'

Had she been sitting here since 10:30?

The thought was absurd. She couldn't possibly have been.

And yet there it was, a pile of gum wrappers – her substitute these days for cigarettes – on the steps next to not one but two soda cans and an empty coffee hot-cup.

David *had* been tired. Coming home, he'd wanted nothing more than to crawl into bed and sleep for the entire afternoon. But now he felt energized. He felt terrific. Mallory had been sitting here, waiting for him for hours.

'I'm doing okay,' he told her. 'Hardly even tired at all.'

She was wearing sunglasses and he couldn't see her eyes as she gazed at him. 'You're kidding, right? You couldn't have gotten to bed before one-thirty. And you said you had to be at work at four-thirty. That was less than three hours—'

'I'm fine.' He unlocked his door. 'Come on in. Did you have lunch? What time do you have to be back at work?'

'I'm not on today.' She picked up her things and followed him inside, closing the door behind her. 'I don't have to work until tomorrow at noon.'

Oh heartache, oh pain. David was working pretty much nonstop *until* tomorrow at noon. He was going back in just a few hours, at six, to help with an evening party. The money was all overtime, which was good, but money meant nothing when Mallory Paoletti was standing in his apartment and telling him she had the next twenty-four hours off.

'I sort of had a liquid lunch,' she told him, wandering toward his computer setup. She touched the mouse, waking the computer out of standby mode. It came on with a series of beeps and a blast of music from his speakers, making her jump back. 'Oh, my God, what did I do?'

David put his backpack on the table by the door, in the kitchen area of his studio apartment. 'It's all right.' He crossed the room and turned down the speakers. 'I've set it up to go right on-line, check my email first thing.'

'Isn't that an Internet camera?' she asked, pointing carefully, clearly afraid to touch anything else. 'Pretty kinky, David Sullivan. What do you do, dance naked in cyberspace?'

'Oh, God, no! I use it to show stuff – artwork – to Ren Shimoda, my former partner in California,' he quickly explained. 'When I draw, particularly for a graphic novel, the paper's too big to put in the scanner and . . .'

Mallory was laughing at him. 'Chill, I was kidding. I figured it was something like that. You're definitely the type to do your naked dancing off-line.'

David was standing close enough to smell her perfume. It was tangy and sweet and not at all subtle. He loved it. He loved the different flecks of color he could see in her eyes at close range, too. He loved the sheer perfection of her skin, the delicate shape of her collarbone, the curve of her shoulder, her over-abundance of earrings.

He cleared his throat. 'So. I was just going to make myself a sandwich. Want one? I've got some sliced chicken and rye bread.'

He turned away, ready to escape to the safety of his refrigerator, but she stopped him with a hand on his arm. She had nice hands – long, slender, graceful fingers – but she bit her nails nearly to the quick. Her less than perfect nails ruined the effect created by her hair, her clothes, and her piercings, making her seem vulnerable, softer, human.

She pulled her hand away fast, as if she, too, had felt a jolt of electricity at the contact. No, couldn't be. That was *his* fantasy.

'Lookit, I came over because I wanted to thank you for helping me last night. I know that must've been really weird for you, dealing with my uncle and my great-uncle, and . . .' She shook her head. 'It shook me up seeing Tom like that.'

'I'm glad I could help you,' he told her. 'It was my pleasure.' He realized she actually had tears in her eyes, and he tried to make it into a joke. 'How often will I have the chance to come to Nightshade's rescue, anyway, right?'

But Mallory didn't laugh. 'Brandon just walked away,' she told him flatly. 'We were still at the carnival, and he just left me there, with Tom practically unconscious on the ground.'

Damn Bran. David wasn't surprised, but obviously Mal had expected more from his friend. She'd expected Bran to be as bright and shining inside as he was out. She'd probably even fallen more than half in love with the person she'd imagined him to be.

No wonder there were tears in her eyes. This had to hurt.

'I'm sorry,' he said quietly.

'Why are you apologizing?' She wiped her eyes brusquely with the back of her hand. 'You were great. If someone came waking *me* up in the middle of the night, I would've pulled the blanket over my head and told 'em to go to hell. You should be given a sainthood or something.'

No, he very definitely didn't qualify for sainthood. Especially not when Mallory stood so close. 'Well,' he said, backing up a little. 'Yeah. Sure. Hey, sandwich?'

She shook her head. 'No, I'm not going to eat your food, too, on top of making you sleep deprived. I should go, let you do whatever you were planning to do today.'

'Gee, I was going to make a couple sandwiches,

then go over to the Ice Cream Shoppe, see if you wanted one.'

She gave him her death look. 'You were not.'

He took the chicken and mustard out of the fridge and put it onto the table. 'Saint David never lies.'

Finally, *finally* she laughed. 'Yeah, right.'

The bread was still soft, the sell-by date several days in the future – always a good sign. He tossed it to Mallory. 'Hey, you know, I got the pictures back from last night. I dropped 'em at the one-hour photo place – they should call themselves Photo Thieves. It's, like, three times as expensive as getting the pictures developed at the drugstore. But I didn't want to wait, so I dropped them off during my break this morning, picked 'em up on the way home.'

Mallory brightened even more. 'Are they any good?'

'Some of 'em, yeah.' He got two paper plates from the cabinet, two plastic knives. 'I'm out of mayo, but I've got some catsup.'

'On *chicken*? Gross. Stick with mustard. Can I see the pictures?'

'Only if you stay and have a sandwich.' He put the plates and knives on the table, unzipped his backpack. There were three packs of photos. He tossed them out onto the table, near the chicken.

But Mallory just stood there, still holding the bread. 'David, Bran told me how you're trying to save money. I really don't need a sandwich.'

'How about we trade? You eat one of my sandwiches, you treat me to a sandwich some other time.'

She thought about that and nodded. 'All right. But

you've got to promise that you'll really let me buy you one. Maybe tonight?'

He had to *promise* that he would let her take him out for dinner. How twisted was this? Like he wouldn't sell his little brother into a life of slavery for just a chance to spend time with this girl. 'I'd love to, but tonight might be a little tight. I'm doing an extra shift from six to close.'

'Tomorrow, then.'

'Actually, I was kind of hoping you'd agree to come over for another photo shoot tomorrow night. Some of the pictures are really good, but in some the lighting was wrong – they came out overexposed.'

She was looking through the first packet of pictures, her nose wrinkled. 'Oh, my God, I look—'

'You look great,' he told her. 'Anything bad is my fault.'

She pulled out a picture in which her eyes were half-closed. 'Your fault?'

'Well, yeah, obviously I waited right until you blinked. Definitely my fault.'

She laughed again as she sat down at the table, flipping through the pictures.

'Do you want mustard on your sandwich?' he asked, sitting next to her and pulling the paper plates toward him.

'Yeah, thanks.' She looked at him. 'Man, that's service – you're gonna make it for me, too, huh?'

He shrugged. 'I'm making one, I might as well make two.'

'Most people don't think that way,' she said. 'Thanks.'

He smiled at her. 'You're welcome.' Thank *you* for

staying and having lunch and fulfilling one of my fantasies. A tame fantasy, but a fantasy just the same. 'What do you say about tomorrow night? It won't take long, maybe just an hour.'

'God, Brandon's photogenic,' she said.

Brandon. Way to kill the fantasy. 'Yeah, I know.'

She didn't look up from the photographs. 'Maybe tomorrow night we could go out for a burger afterward. I mean, you know, just to even up the score.'

'Sure,' David said. 'Right. Just to even up the score.'

'Kelly said to scold you if you didn't call for a ride from the train station.'

Tom stopped short on his way up the stairs to the Ashtons' deck. The kitchen door was locked, but he'd spotted this open slider. Now he saw that Joe and Charles were sitting out here in the shade.

Charles was asleep in a lounge chair, a blanket tenderly tucked around his bony frame. Joe was awake and looking at Tom, frowning slightly.

'It's not that long a walk,' Tom told his uncle quietly so as not to disturb Charles. 'I took it nice and easy. I actually feel pretty good today.'

Joe glanced at Charles, then pushed himself up out of the chair, moving toward the sliding door, away from his sleeping friend. 'Kelly told me about the CAT scan, that you're okay.'

'Yeah.' Tom looked out at the sparkling blue ocean. 'That's one way of looking at it.' He met Joe's eyes. 'I would have preferred more conclusive results.'

'I would have preferred finding out you were in the hospital *when* you were in the hospital.'

'I'm sorry.'

Joe laughed. 'No, you're not. You know, I can remember being young. It feels like it was yesterday.' He glanced at Charles, shaking his head. 'We spent a few hours at the hotel again today. I'm not sure what to tell you – either no one's suspicious looking or everyone's suspicious looking. I've been trying to pay attention to who's here with their family, who's not, but it's a big hotel, it's not an easy job.'

'My XO's coming tomorrow afternoon,' Tom told him. 'We'll figure out the best way to watch the place. I mean, even if all it comes down to is checking cars in the parking lot on the day of the opening ceremony.' He met Joe's gaze. 'There's probably no threat. I'm probably wasting everyone's time.'

'Probably,' Joe agreed. 'But maybe not.' He smiled sadly. 'Anyway, I've got some extra time to waste these days.' He cleared his throat. 'So. You and Kelly.'

Tom shook his head. 'Joe, I really don't want to discuss—'

'I apologize for walking in on you last night.'

'Okay. Apology accepted. Great.' Tom turned to go into the house.

'You're having dinner with her tonight.'

Tom turned back. 'Yeah. But, funny, I don't remember sending out that information in a press release.'

Joe crossed his arms. 'Is there a reason you don't want me to know you're spending the night with her?'

'Evening,' Tom corrected him. 'Dinner. Give me a break.'

'She'll be home in a few hours. She called to ask if I wanted her to pick up something from the Lotus Blossom. That's the Chinese restaurant here in town.'

Tom nodded. 'Yeah, I remember.'

'Good food. No MSG.'

'That's good.'

'Nice people own the place. New people.'

Tom waited.

'Chinese people,' Joe said. 'Don't speak much English, but they sure can cook a mean moo goo gai pan. They actually know a little French, so I don't have any trouble communicating.'

For a man who was taciturn, Joe was talking up a storm. But Tom knew that Chinese food wasn't the subject he really wanted to discuss.

'Okay,' Tom said. 'Me and Kelly. Let me have it. Your uncensored opinion. You don't think I should have dinner with her. At least not alone. You don't think—'

'No,' Joe said. 'I think it's great. In fact, I think you should get decked out in your dress whites tonight and use the opportunity to ask her to marry you.'

Tom nearly choked. 'What?'

'You heard me,' Joe said. 'That's what a man does when he's in love with a woman. And since you've been in love with Kelly nearly half your life, it's probably time to marry the girl.'

Tom scratched his head as he chose his words carefully. 'I'm not sure *love*'s quite the right word for it. Yes, I've always been attracted to her, but—'

Joe smiled. 'You call it whatever you want, whatever label you're comfortable with, Tommy. But if you have even half a brain, you'll marry her while you've got the chance.'

'Um . . .'

'I know you've got some history,' Joe continued,

'you and Kelly. I know something happened, something that scared you to death and chased you out of town that summer you left for basic training a whole month early.'

Tom tried to hide his surprise and the older man smiled. 'You don't really think I didn't know, do you? That night you brought her home so late.' He laughed softly. 'You had a wild look to you, Tommy, and I was proud of you for going – for knowing she was too young. And I was disappointed when she wasn't here for you to come home to when she was finally old enough.'

Joe met his gaze steadily. 'She didn't understand when you left,' he continued, 'and it nearly broke her heart. Tonight you can explain and make it right. And ask her to marry you.'

'What, so I can break her heart again?' God, how'd he get into this conversation anyway? Tom edged toward the door. He didn't want to talk about this, didn't want to think about the emotion he'd seen in Kelly's eyes sixteen years ago as he shook her hand and said good-bye. He'd actually *shaken* her hand. Jesus. 'You know damn well that a man in my profession can't afford to have any serious relationships. Marriage isn't easy in the SEAL units. It's—'

'A man in your profession can't afford *not* to have a serious relationship. I was in your profession, you know. Not exactly, but close enough. Life is so short, and so precious. You and I both know that – more than most men. How can you hold happiness in your hands and not do everything in your means to keep it forever?'

Tom didn't know what to say to that.

'Besides, there's no such thing as an easy marriage,' Joe continued. 'I've seen a lot of 'em in my life, and the marriages that seem to run smoothly, the ones that last the longest, they're the ones that are worked on diligently, kind of like an old car. A Model T will last forever if it's properly maintained. But as soon as you start to neglect it . . .'

Tom leaned back against the railing. 'And yet *you* never got married.'

'No,' Joe agreed. 'I didn't. But it wasn't because I didn't ask.'

'Cybele,' Tom said.

Joe glanced over at Charles, who was still sleeping soundly. When he looked back at Tom, he just shook his head.

'I wish you would tell me about France,' Tom said. 'And about this Cybele, and about Mr Ashton and the Fifty-fifth, too. I honestly didn't know until a few days ago that you were OSS, and I'm—' He stopped, shook his head. 'I understand why you didn't tell me about what you did in the War. There's an awful lot that I've done that I can't talk about, and even more that I *won't* talk about. I'm not going to ask you about it, but if you ever do want to talk . . .'

'Thank you,' Joe said. 'But I have to tell the whole story to that writer after the ceremony on Tuesday. I don't think I can stand to do it twice.'

'You don't *have to* do it at all,' Tom countered.

'You know,' Joe said, 'you could go into town to the jewelers and buy Kelly a ring. Give it to her *before* you spend the night with her.'

Oh, God. 'Dinner,' Tom said. 'We're starting with dinner.'

Joe nodded. 'I won't wait up.'

'I've got work to do on the computer,' Tom told him, beating a hasty retreat into the house.

You don't have to do it at all, Tom had said about Joe's plan to talk to that author, Kurt Kaufman.

But Joe *did* have to do it. Because the story needed to be told before Charles died.

There was a statue in front of the Baldwin's Bridge Hotel with Joe's face on it. And it was about time this town knew that that face should have been Charles Ashton's.

Charles Ashton – one of the richest of the rich in a wealthy town. He could buy and sell almost anyone, coming into money that his grandfather's grandfather had earned, and doubling it with his fearless investments and his cutthroat financial wizardry. He came off as cold-blooded and standoffish, and few recognized the truth – that risking money meant nothing to him. Not after having lived through the War, after having watched so many risk their very lives, after seeing so many sacrifice so much.

As Charles had gotten older, he'd tried to buy acceptance in the town by donating generously to the hospital fund. But all that had bought him were vague mutterings that he'd probably bought himself a safe position far from the front lines during the War, as well.

Nothing could be further from the truth.

Charles was the real hero of Baldwin's Bridge. And Joe was finally going to tell the story.

But not the whole story. There were parts he'd never tell anyone. Like the night Cybele had come to his room.

Joe sat on the deck near Charles, who was sleeping more peacefully than he had in a long time. He checked to make sure the blanket was still tucked around his friend's feet.

This morning, when he'd seen Charles cleaning the guns he'd brought home from the war, he'd been thrown back into the past. It was strange, seeing Cybele's Walther PPK again after all these years. One look at the thing, and it was as if he'd seen Cybele just yesterday. The clarity of his memories astounded him. He could practically smell her kitchen.

He could nearly feel the roughness of the sheets on his straw-filled mattress.

He could taste her kisses.

He sat back in his chair, gazing out at the water. Looking without seeing.

Remembering.

He'd been asleep, and he'd woken to Cybele's soft touch. She'd slipped into his arms, begging him to hold her. He would have been content to do just that, only that, but she'd kissed him, she'd finally kissed him, and, oh . . .

The night air coming in through the window had been cool, but it hadn't been long before their skin was slick with sweat. He'd been delirious, certain that he'd found heaven at last.

After, Cybele had cried. He hadn't understood. Not then. Not till later. He'd simply held her close to his heart, whispering that he loved her, asking her – again – to marry him, to love him not just that night, but forever. She'd begged him not to speak, asked him just to hold her, and she'd finally fallen asleep, there in the circle of his arms.

He'd slept, too, but when he awoke in the morning, Cybele was gone.

He'd washed and dressed quickly, and went down to breakfast, his heart and step both light. Sure, there was a war on. Sure, the Nazis were still living right down the street. But the Americans were pushing toward Ste.-Hélène. And Cybele belonged to him. There was even a chance that his child – their child – was growing, right now, in her womb.

Henri and Luc Deux were at the table, eating stale bread softened with warm goat's milk. Cybele and Marie were preparing several baskets of vegetables from the garden. They would take them along when they returned the mending to the Germans, try to sell them, too, earn a few more coins.

As Joe sat at the table, he saw Charles sitting on a bench by the door. He was unshaven and haggard looking, as if he'd had a sleepless night. And he was staring almost sightlessly at Joe.

'Leg bothering you again?' Joe asked him.

Charles gazed at him with his red-rimmed eyes for several moments longer before he spoke. 'Yeah. That's it.'

'I'm sorry,' Joe said, but he was in too good a mood to sound as if he truly meant it. He turned toward the two women, unable to keep from smiling, too filled with joy to try to hide it. He wanted to shout and dance, but instead he merely said, 'Good morning, Cybele. You should have woken me to come help in the garden.'

Cybele glanced up at him, then glanced almost furtively at Charles.

'You're always up at dawn,' she replied, not looking up again as she put the freshly washed beans into the basket. 'I thought I'd let you sleep.'

Why wouldn't she look at him? 'I slept quite well last night,' he said, willing her to look at him, to meet his gaze and smile. 'Exceptionally well, in fact.'

Charles laughed as he stood up abruptly, turning away to look out the open door.

And Cybele rinsed more of the beans as if she were angry, her movements quick and fierce.

'I wouldn't have minded if you woke me,' Joe continued, looking from Cybele to Charles.

They were both tense, both tightly wound, both careful not to look at the other. Too careful.

His joy was no longer quite as bright. It was accompanied by a slightly queasy feeling. What was going on here?

Perhaps Cybele had once again turned down Charles's request to be returned to the Allied side of the line. They'd argued over that in the past.

'What did I miss this morning,' Joe lowered his voice to ask Henri, 'by sleeping so late?'

Henri shook his head. 'Dunno.'

Charles turned away from the door, using his cane to shuffle toward the front of the house. 'I'll be lying down.'

Cybele threw down the beans and stormed after him, out of the room.

Joe pushed himself to his feet, not certain whose rescue he was going to – Cybele's or Charles's. But he stopped, just inside the kitchen door, at the sound of Cybele's voice.

'How dare you?'

'How dare I what? Close my eyes? Try to rest?' Charles's voice got louder with barely restrained anger. 'Heal this goddamned leg so I can leave here for good?'

'How dare you act as if I've injured you in some way!' she cried. 'You told me to—'

She broke off as Joe stepped into the hallway, wishing she hadn't stopped and at the same time certain he didn't want to hear what she had to say.

'I told you,' Charles said as he stood by the closet he'd

claimed as his bedroom. Although he spoke quietly, his voice shook. 'But I didn't know it would make me feel like this.'

And as Charles looked at Cybele, Cybele looked back at Charles in a way that Joe knew she had never, ever looked at him. Not even last night, when she was naked in his arms.

And he knew the truth.

Cybele loved Charles. And it was glaringly obvious that Charles loved her, too.

Joe had merely been a pawn in a game he hadn't even known they all were playing.

He turned silently and walked out of the house. When he heard Charles follow him, he ran.

He couldn't remember much of that day, wasn't sure where he'd been, what he'd done. All he knew was that he came back. As much as he wanted to, he couldn't stay away. There were people depending on him, and one of them was Cybele.

Whom he loved. Still.

She was waiting for him in his room, curled up asleep on his bed, with all her clothes on.

He sat on the edge of the bed, and the movement of the mattress woke her. He hadn't lit a candle, but the moon shining in through the open window was bright enough to light her face.

'Giuseppe, I'm so sorry,' she said. Her apology was sincere. Not that it made it hurt any less. 'I'm not as terrible as you must think. I honestly thought last night would . . . I don't know . . . save me, maybe. Don't you see? I can have nothing I truly want. I thought if I could make myself want something I can have . . .' She bowed her head. 'It was wrong and I'm sorry. The last thing I've ever wanted was to hurt you.'

He was silent. What could he say?

'I do love you,' she whispered. 'Just not the way you want me to.'

'Not the way you love Charles.' He had to know for sure. Maybe hearing the truth would make him stop loving her. God, he wanted to stop loving her.

And she didn't deny it. 'I'm sorry.'

Anger sparked. Frustration. Jealousy. 'He's married.'

'I know.'

'Is it his money that—'

'No!' She was vehement. 'I don't care about that. It means nothing to me. I own this house now. I'm a wealthy woman, too.'

'I don't understand why—'

'I don't, either,' Cybele said. 'All I know is he pretends so hard not to care about anything or anyone. He says he doesn't remember going back into the church, risking his life for that child. He says he'd never do it again, but I don't believe him.'

'And you think he could . . . save you somehow?' His voice sounded rough and harsh to his own ears, but he had to know. He had to stop loving her.

'I don't know,' she admitted. 'But just sitting with him, just looking into his eyes, makes me feel both despair and hope. And it's been so long since I've felt anything but despair.'

Her breathing was ragged, as if she were crying, but her face and her eyes were dry.

'Every breath I take hurts,' she whispered. 'It's so heavy, so suffocating. If it weren't for the anger and the hate I feel for the Nazis, I'm sure I would die.

'And I know I'm not alone. I know I'm not the only mother who lost a child in this war. There must be millions of us—' Her voice broke. 'And oh, I think, what an army *we'd make. All that outrage, all the anguish making us invincible. But then what? After we completely crush the Third Reich, what then? What will we have won?'*

Joe couldn't answer.

'A chance for Marlise's baby to live more than two years. That's the best I can hope for. There's nothing I can do that will bring Michel back.'

And still Joe couldn't speak.

'I'll win this war against the Nazis,' she told him fiercely. 'I'll win or I'll die. But when I win, I'll die anyway, because without an enemy to hate, I'll be completely alone with only the despair.'

'You're not alone,' he told her. 'I'm here.' He reached for her, but she pulled away. She didn't want him. God, that hurt.

'I wish I could love you,' she said wistfully.

When Joe looked at Cybele, he, too, felt hope with his despair, despite his hurt, despite his anger. 'Maybe someday you will.'

She gazed at him a moment longer, her beautiful eyes ancient looking and weary, as if she foresaw her own future and believed she had no someday to look forward to.

She closed his door gently behind her, leaving him loving her still, and suspecting that he always would.

Fourteen

Kelly came into her bedroom at full speed, singing a pop tune at the top of her lungs – baby, keep me up all night.

And taking off her clothes.

Tom was at her computer, and he didn't have time to warn her he was there. She spotted him at the exact same moment she flung her dress over what should have been her computer chair, hitting him full in the face.

'Oh, my *God*!'

She snatched her dress back, holding it up in front of her like a shield. As a dress, it was exceptional. However, as a shield, it didn't function well at all.

'Sorry,' he said, nearly knocking the chair over as he stood up. 'I needed to get on-line, and I didn't think you'd mind. I'll get out of your way.' He turned back to the computer. 'Just let me—'

'Wait.' Kelly moved closer to the computer, looking at the picture of the Merchant that was on the screen. 'Is that . . . him?'

When she stood next to Tom, the dress worked even

311

less well as a shield. Her entire back half was exposed. He forced himself not to look, but his peripheral vision was too damn good. She was wearing her trademark thong. In dark purple satin. Against pale skin. Dear God.

Tom sat back down so that she was slightly behind him, out of peripheral range.

Yes, they were having dinner tonight. Yes, he'd kissed her again while they were in Boston. Yes, he was intending to kiss her again tonight. And yes, very big yes, he wanted to explore all the wonderful possibilities of where this mutual attraction could go.

One of the possible places was back here, in Kelly's room, with the door tightly shut the way it was, with Kelly in only her underwear, also the way she was.

But there was a lot of talking that needed to be done before they reached that place. And as much as every cell in his body was screaming for him to stand up right now and take her into his arms, to slide his hands all over all that smooth, perfect skin, communication was key. The talking part had to come first.

It *had* to.

She trusted him.

She was looking at the picture on the computer screen, waiting for him to answer her question. *Is that him?*

Tom cleared his throat. 'Yeah, that's um . . .' What's his name. 'The Merchant. Before plastic surgery.'

'Can I see what he looks like after plastic surgery?' she asked.

'No,' he said, 'I don't have any recent photos of him. He's been presumed dead since '96. I'm assuming he had his face changed sometime between then and now.'

She moved back into his peripheral vision range, looking at him instead of the screen. At this proximity, her eyes were an illegal shade of blue. 'Assuming?'

'It's what I would've done if I were him.' He tried not to sound desperate. 'Can you do me a huge favor and put on a robe?'

She gave him what he was starting to recognize as her innocent face. The wide-eyed one that really wasn't very innocent at all. She was enjoying this. 'You mean the one you're sitting on?'

Tom stood up, and she pulled something that might've been a bathrobe off the back of the chair, showering the floor with a rain of lingerie.

Of course.

It was bad enough to sit here surrounded by it when she wasn't in the room. But when she was there . . . It was like finding out that Pollyanna modeled for Victoria's Secret on the sly. And then being invited to a photo shoot.

'Whoops,' she said, 'that's the clean stuff.'

She slipped on the robe – if you could call something that was made of very thin cotton and came only to midthigh a robe – tossed her dress onto her bed this time, then gathered up the 'clean stuff,' throwing it into her top dresser drawer. 'I don't suppose you've seen the belt anywhere, have you?'

Dear Christ, there was no belt to this so-called robe. 'No, but I bet if you give Mrs Lerner a miner's helmet and forty-eight hours, she could find it.'

Kelly laughed. 'It's not *that* bad in here.'

'Do you keep anything in your closet? I mean, what's the point in even having a closet?'

'I'm very neat back home – in my apartment in Boston.' She rummaged through the piles of clothing on a chair next to her bed. 'I think I've been resisting putting my clothes away because if I do, that's like admitting I'm really living here again. Dealing with my father's illness is hard enough without having to focus on my personal failure issues at the same time.'

She found the belt – thank you, Lord Jesus – and threaded it through the loops of her robe, tying it shut in the front.

'Failure issues?' he echoed.

'Pass,' she said. 'That's too pathetic a topic – and I'm in too good a mood. *And* my mood got even better when I got home and found my father sitting out on the deck with Joe. Do you know they spent the entire day together – without anyone needing extra oxygen?'

Tom let her change the subject. He had plenty of failure issues of his own, and God knows he didn't want to talk about them right now. The fact that his CAT scan had come back normal, that there wasn't an obvious if not easy fix to his physical problems, was also high on his list of topics to avoid.

'Yeah, they spent the early part of the afternoon staking out the hotel for me again. I told them it could be just a waste of time, but they don't care. They sit in the hotel, playing chess, watching for any suspicious-looking men.' Tom laughed. 'Kind of a vague order, but they're okay with it. I think they like having an excuse to hang together. And I've told them I won't let them help me if they fight. So they don't fight. At least not in front of me.'

'Bless you,' Kelly said. 'I can't tell you how glad I am you're here.'

Her eyes were too warm, and that robe was too short. Tom tried not to look at her legs.

Talk about failure issues. He was failing completely.

He had to get out of here. Fast. Before he kissed her again. Which would be fine later, downstairs, when they were both fully dressed. But as for right now . . .

'Tell me more about the Merchant.' Before he could stand up and lunge for the door, Kelly blocked his way and sent the conversation rocketing back in another direction. 'Do you have any other photos? Anything that really shows his eyes?'

She came up right behind him, spinning his chair back so he faced the computer, resting her hands possessively on his shoulders. He liked that she did that. Too much. Yes, he had to get out of here.

'Even if he had plastic surgery, he can't really change his eyes, can he?' she asked. 'I mean, he could change the color, sure, but color's just a small part of it. The intensity would stay the same. Look at his eyes in this picture – scary.'

She started rubbing his shoulders, and Tom knew damn well that he wasn't going anywhere. Especially not when her hands were cool against the back of his neck, her fingers in his hair.

Tom used the mouse to click through a series of pictures. The aftermath of the Paris embassy bombing. Five devastating café bombings in Afghanistan, a bus bombing in Israel. And then the Merchant. Most of the photos were taken from a distance, slightly blurred. But the last one was again in close-up. WildCard had done his computer voodoo on it, enhancing it, sharpening the edges. It was definitely the Merchant, smiling at the woman who was to become his wife, taken about a year before Paris.

Kelly leaned closer, and he could feel the softness of her body against his shoulder. He could smell her sweet scent. It wasn't perfume – it was probably some kind of lotion or maybe her shampoo or soap. Whatever it was, it made her smell delicious.

'In this one, he doesn't look like a monster,' she said. 'He looks like a regular man. A man who likes this woman – look at the way he's looking at her. He's crazy about her. He can't be *all* bad.'

'He's claimed responsibility for the deaths of over nine hundred people,' Tom told her.

'God,' she breathed, taking an even closer look. 'No wonder you're worried he's still out there. I could see how someone like that might stay on your mind.'

'I keep thinking he's the perfect man to succeed with a full-scale, high death-toll terrorist attack here in the US. He's not some amateur – he knows what he's doing. Yet he's not being watched twenty-four-seven like all the other big league players we do know about. He's invisible because he's on everyone's presumed-dead list. It was probably laughably easy for him to get into the country.' He shook his head. 'Unless he's on everyone's presumed-dead list because he is dead.'

Which meant *Tom* was the dangerous one, the complete fucking nut job who was going to start killing innocent salesmen from Des Moines or Cincinnati, imagining they were hard-core terrorists.

Kelly was rubbing his neck again, her fingers strong and cool against the heat of his skin. It was definitely time to leave before his eyes started rolling back in his head, before he came to the conclusion that talking was way overrated, that what he really wanted was a whole lot of nonverbal communication, and who really gave a damn about trust anyway?

It took a great deal of effort, but Tom cleared the screen, signed off the computer, and slipped out of both her hands and the chair. 'I'm going to go take a shower.' His voice sounded as ragged as if he'd just run ten miles, fast.

Her robe met in the front in a V that was growing deeper every moment. He caught a flash of dark purple against the soft, pale swell of her breasts, and as he looked up into her eyes, he knew the battle was lost.

She knew it, too.

He lunged for her as she reached for him, and then, God, she was in his arms and he was kissing her.

And she was kissing him back just as hungrily, her soft body tight against his.

Tom caught himself before he peeled her robe from her shoulders, forcing himself to slow down, to kiss her more tenderly and less ferociously, to stay in control, to keep from devouring her whole.

She was everything he wanted, everything he'd always stayed far, far away from.

Dinner first.

Talking first.

She trusted him.

Breathing hard, he pulled back. He could see the promise of paradise in her eyes. But the woman *trusted* him, dammit. 'I'll meet you on the deck for dinner in about an hour, okay?'

She smiled at him. 'If that's what you want.'

Tom headed for the door, then took two steps back

317

toward Kelly. 'You know damn well what I want. I'm trying to be good here. I'm trying to do this right.'

She didn't say a word, didn't argue, didn't do a damn thing but just stand there in her barely-there robe, looking at him. Wanting him, too, and letting him see it in her eyes.

'See, there's no way this could work,' he told her. 'I'm going to be here for only a few weeks. And even if we could keep it going long-distance – and I've got to be honest here, Kelly, I've never been able to keep *any* relationship going for more than a few months – you deserve better than that.'

She took a step toward him.

'My future's . . . a little shaky right now,' he told her, 'but I *can* tell you that I intend to do everything in my control to hang on to my career with the SEAL teams. I can also tell you that a romantic relationship with a SEAL is something I wouldn't wish on my worst enemy. These next few weeks I'm here in Baldwin's Bridge – this is probably going to be the longest time I spend in any one place in the US this year. I'm always moving, Kel, always heading out someplace new, usually overseas. Deployment's usually without warning, so I don't even get a chance to phone home to say goodbye. I'm just gone. And when I come back, I can't talk about where I've been or what I've done. And there's always a chance I might not come back at all.'

She took another step toward him and another and she was close enough now to touch.

Tom couldn't stop himself. He touched her. Her hair, her cheek, the warmth of her neck. She closed her eyes, pressing her cheek into his hand, her lips slightly parted. Her skin was smooth and so soft.

'A woman's got to be pretty tough,' he whispered, 'to put up with that.'

She was touching him now, too, her hands skimming his forearms. And when she opened her eyes, they were filled with both heat and need. 'I'm tougher than you think.'

Tom didn't laugh – at least not aloud. He didn't even let his lips twitch. But somehow she knew he didn't believe her.

'I am.' She ran her hands up to his shoulders, down the front of his uniform shirt.

He kissed her. He couldn't help himself, not when she was gazing at him so fiercely and touching him like that. He kissed her as slowly and as sweetly as he could, careful to keep his own explosive desire on the shortest possible leash. He felt her melt against him, heard her sigh as he pushed her robe off one perfect shoulder.

Jesus, somebody stop him.

He pulled her robe back.

'Maybe we should take this a little more slowly.' He couldn't believe the words that had just come out of his mouth. But then again, he couldn't believe he was standing here in Kelly Ashton's bedroom, with Kelly Ashton in his arms, nearly naked beneath her thin cotton robe. God help him, the way she was pressed against him, she couldn't miss feeling his arousal.

He knew he should step back, put some space between them, but he was only human, dammit, and he kissed her again. He could feel his control slipping and he worked harder to make his kisses gentle. Respectful. Reverent.

The kind of kisses Kelly Ashton would want.

'Ah, baby, I don't want to hurt you,' he told her hoarsely. 'And I'm so afraid I will. Even under the best of circumstances, I don't have much to offer a woman like you. And right now . . .'

Kelly pulled his head down and kissed him.

Again, she felt him retreat. Oh, his lips were against hers, and his tongue was in her mouth, but she could practically taste the tightness of his self-control. He was being careful with her, as if she were fragile. As if she might break.

She remembered that ride she took on the back of his Harley all those years ago. She'd asked him to go fast, as fast as he would dare to go along the beach road. She'd wanted to feel the wind in her face and the dizzying thrill of the pavement rushing beneath them.

But he didn't do it. He'd been careful with her then, too.

Too careful.

That same night in Joe's car, she'd wanted him to take her to the beach, to take her places she'd never been before.

Instead, he'd taken her home.

Just now, he'd said he didn't have much to offer *a woman like her*. Implication: a *nice* woman like her. All her life, people looked at her and couldn't see past the goody-two-shoes image that had followed her around since she was old enough to walk. Even in college when she'd gone through her Madonna phase – perpetual lacy black with bra straps showing – no one had taken her seriously. Her cheerleader-cute looks were mostly to blame.

When most people looked, they didn't look closely,

and all they saw were rosy cheeks, freckles, and big blue eyes. They only saw *nice*.

So, okay, maybe she *was* a little bit nice. But so what? Weren't nice women allowed to want heart-stoppingly passionate sex? Wasn't she allowed to long for the exhilarating sensation of Tom's incredible body out of control inside of her? As if nice women would only want polite, careful sex . . .

As if nice women didn't sometimes have healthy, short-term, no-strings relationships simply for the sake of fulfilling a lifelong fantasy, for the sake of feeling that powerful carnival ride, stomach dropping, I've-got-a-crush-on-you attraction, for the simple sake of having someone to hold on to when the night got particularly dark and lonely.

Lately her nights were very dark and lonely.

Kelly knew Tom wanted her. There was no disputing that. She could feel him, completely aroused, against her. She wanted to reach for him, to unfasten the buckle of his belt. She wanted . . .

There was nothing careful or controlled about what she wanted. What she wanted would probably give him a heart attack, particularly if he was expecting *nice*.

God, the last thing she wanted was another careful lover.

She wanted someone who would treat her as an equal, someone who would let her be on top, let her set the boundaries – of which there would be practically none. She wanted someone who wasn't afraid of her, someone wild, someone a little selfish, someone who lived for the moment.

That was how she'd always imagined Tom Paoletti to be.

She tested him, kissing him again, harder this time, sucking his tongue into her mouth as she swayed against him, brushing her stomach enticingly against the heaviness of his erection.

She heard him groan – that was good. She felt his hands slide down her back as if he were going to cup her rear end and press her more tightly against him, but he stopped politely, halfway there. And again, she could almost taste his control. That wasn't so good.

She knew he had to work hard to be careful. It wasn't natural for him. It was something special he was doing – because he was with *her*.

Miss Nice.

Kelly kissed him again and again, long, deep, languorous kisses that practically begged him to throw her back onto her bed. She pulled out his shirt and skimmed her hands beneath it, against the heat of his skin. She slid one hand between them, her knuckles against the taut muscles of his stomach as she dipped her fingers beneath the waistband of his pants. Just a little, not a lot. Just enough to make him wonder if she was going to reach down his pants.

How about *that* for nice?

He was working even harder now, that was for sure, but he was still in careful control.

Oh, no way was she going to make careful, polite love with Tom Paoletti. No, she wanted dangerous. She wanted tempestuous. She wanted the man with the reputation for being a little rough, a little crazy, a little wild.

'Kiss me, dammit,' she said to him. 'I'm not fifteen anymore. You're allowed to kiss me like you mean it!'

He used the opportunity to try to step back, to

carefully move her hand from the edge of his pants. 'Kelly, I think we might want to—'

She used a single, crudely honest word that managed, quite nicely, to define exactly what she wanted. 'That's what I want to do, Tommy, but every time I kiss you, it feels like you're a little too worried about hurting me. Believe me, what I want is *not* going to hurt.'

He laughed at that, but she could see surprise in his eyes. He'd never, not in a million years, expected her to be so blunt in either her words or her meaning.

It was exasperating.

'I'm not a virgin anymore, you know,' she told him. 'I was married for years, for God's sake. And brace yourself, but Gary wasn't the first. Believe it or not, I like sex that's a little risky, a little rough. I like it loud, too, Tom, and frankly, I'm looking forward to making a lot of noise with you.'

He didn't know what to say, didn't know what to do. Kelly could relate – she was shocking herself, too. But it was all true. She'd just never dared to say it aloud before, and now that she'd started, it was exhilarating. And she wasn't done.

'I know you still think of me as the little girl next door, but I'm a grown woman,' she continued. 'I have about a million bad habits and just as many dark, awful thoughts. I've seen a lot of shitty things, Tom – death and godawful suffering and pain. I need you to see me for who I am – let me climb down from this pedestal of niceness you've stuck me on top of, because up here I can't live my life the way I want to live it. I can't reach you from here. I can't wrap my legs around you the way I'm dying to do.'

The look on his face would've been funny if it weren't contradicted by the heat growing in his eyes. He was paying attention, and when she was done, she knew he was going to give her exactly what she wanted.

No more careful. No more control.

'I'm not perfect.' Her heart was pounding, but she needed to make sure he really understood. 'I cry when I'm unhappy, I have temper tantrums when I'm angry, and I really wallow in it when I'm down. I say bad words. All the time. *All* the time. I have a tattoo.' She nodded at his expression of disbelief. 'Yes, I do. It's only a little one, but it counts. I'm too chicken to get my belly button pierced, but I really want to, so maybe I will. There are a lot of things I want, you know. I want to be able to really talk to my father. I want to go to bed at night knowing I lived my life to the fullest, instead of feeling as if I've chickened out again. I want to stop playing it safe! I want to do all the things I've always dreamed about but never dared to do – to get a really funky haircut and wear clothes that show off my body. I want to skydive and windsurf. I . . . I want to, I don't know, swim with the dolphins, bike across Europe. I want to go down on you at the movie theater.'

Kelly couldn't believe she'd said that. He couldn't either. But she was on a roll now. 'I want to make love to you on my father's boat, out in the harbor! I want you to take me to bed tonight and not let me out until noon tomorrow – no, noon the day after that! I want the kind of passion that you read about in books – sex on the kitchen table, on the stairs up to the bedroom, in the bathroom of the train into the city. I want to do it *every*where – in the closet of the guest room at a party, you know, where people come in and out, to throw their coats on the bed? I want you to sneak into my bedroom window at night to wake me up and make love to me, even though we just made love two hours earlier. God, I want to feel you inside me—'

Tom kissed her.

He couldn't take another second of her voice, her words, winding around him, making him completely crazy. She wanted to . . . At the movies . . .

Screw dinner. Screw talking.

He wasn't even remotely hungry, *and* they'd said just about everything they'd needed to. He'd told her he was afraid of hurting her, and she'd informed him that she wanted him, in all sorts of various creative places and ways.

They were both on the same page.

He picked her up, wrapping her legs around him as she'd so vividly described, molding her soft warmth against him, filling his hands with the smoothness of her derriere. He could feel her working the buttons of his shirt as he carried her to her bed.

She'd been right about him.

He'd been guilty of doing the one thing he'd hated most when it was done to him. He hadn't looked beyond neat labels and obvious appearances to the real person below. He'd always had a crush on the *idea* of sweet Kelly Ashton – but the real woman in his arms took his breath away.

The real woman was more than sweet. She was spicy, she was funny, she was brazenly honest, she was even a little rude. And she was far hotter than any woman he'd ever known, ever met, ever dreamed of.

She had his shirt undone in record time and the sensation of her hands and mouth against his chest made him laugh out loud.

Her dress was on her bed, and he grabbed it with one hand and tossed it over the back of the computer chair. He shook his shirt free from his arms as she did the same with her robe.

Lord have mercy.

The woman was beautiful. Tom had a deep appreciation for nearly all half-naked women, but Kelly was amazing. Her breasts were voluptuously full, her stomach and thighs smooth and soft, and he realized in that instant that she was his idea of perfection. Every woman he'd ever been with in his life had paled in comparison – even the leggy, hard-bodied supermodel wannabe he'd dated a few years back. He'd thought there was something wrong with him because she just didn't do it for him.

Now he knew why.

He used to watch Kelly swim in her father's pool. He'd seen her in her bathing suit many times. But he'd only dreamed of her in her underwear. Until now.

This was so amazing. He kissed her, touched her, ran his hands across the impossible softness of her skin.

She was touching him the same way, as if she couldn't get enough of him, couldn't believe this was happening.

He sank down with her onto her bed, and she was still on top of him. He kissed her throat, her shoulders, the tops of her breasts.

She took off her bra, and he wanted to weep or sing

or shout. Or laugh. He laughed as he buried his face in her, touching and kissing and tasting as much of her as he could, all at once.

She was laughing, too, as she pulled back to reach for the buckle of his belt.

She couldn't get it undone, so she covered him with her hand, touching him through his pants, and it hit him. He was really here. In Kelly's room. Making love with her. Finally finishing what they'd started all those years ago in the front seat of Joe's station wagon.

Did she know how long he'd wanted her?

He gently pushed her off him, rolling from the bed to kick off his shoes and quickly shuck his pants from his legs. She knelt then, watching him, her eyes hot, her full breasts tightly peaked with desire, like some kind of wild dream come true.

He'd wanted her forever.

'Oh, my,' she murmured as he pulled down his boxers. When he glanced at her, she smiled and widened her eyes.

Tom had to laugh. He knew damn well that he was just a man, but her obvious admiration for his body – and the fact that she had no problem showing it – was a total turn-on.

He slid back into her arms, entangling his legs with hers, kissing her deeply. The sensation of her breasts against his chest was incredible. And when she reached between them to touch him, to encircle him with the sweet coolness of her fingers . . .

'Kelly.' It was more a gasp than a word.

She laughed, pushing him onto his back as she kissed his mouth, his neck, his chest. She was heading south, her hair tickling sensually as it moved across his sensitized skin. He pushed himself up onto his elbows just as . . .

God! Oh, God! He realized as he struggled to breathe that he'd actually cried out.

It wasn't so much the sensation of her soft mouth on him that made him shout. But rather it was the sight of her, with those blue eyes and that angelic face, smiling up at him as she . . .

Dear, *dear* God.

And they weren't even at the movie theater.

What she was doing to him felt so good, *too* good. But this wasn't the way he wanted their first time together to be. He wanted to be able to make *her* cry out, too.

He reached for her, hauling her up and practically throwing her onto her back. She pulled him with her, kissing his mouth as hungrily as she'd kissed him before.

She was still wearing those purple thong panties, and he reached beneath them, touching her, and she shifted her hips, opening her legs to him as she moaned.

Loudly.

Tom loved it. She was ready for him, soft and wet and smooth and perfect and not at all shy about letting him know it.

He found her tattoo. It was a miniature peace symbol, smaller than a dime and on her left hip, hiding just below her panty line. It was the perfect mix of both sweet and sexy, and he loved it.

Kelly pulled away from him again, this time crawling toward her bedside table, where she grabbed a foil-wrapped condom from the drawer. He dragged her panties down her legs as she tore the package open.

She kissed him as he covered himself. She pressed her body against him, sliding her hands down his arms, running her fingers through the hair on his chest. No sooner was he done than she threw her leg over him, straddling him.

Kelly was moving fast, but Tom caught her, holding her by the hips, stopping her from ensheathing him. She made a sound of protest and stopped kissing him long enough to look at him.

'Hey,' Tom said to her. 'Last chance to change your mind.'

She laughed – a burst of disbelief. 'You're kidding.'

'Damn right I'm kidding,' he said to her. 'I just wanted your attention.'

Now that he had it, now that she was looking at him, he lowered her slowly down, surrounding himself with her heat just a little bit, then just a little bit more.

'See, I've always had this fantasy,' he breathed, 'that the first time we did this, I'd be looking into your eyes.'

It was incredible. Whatever he'd fantasized or imagined, it hadn't been even close to this. He released her completely as he lay back, pressing himself even more deeply inside her. Home at last.

Still holding his gaze, Kelly smiled tremulously. 'I've always loved looking into your eyes,' she whispered as she began to move on top of him. 'You have such beautiful eyes, Tommy.'

What she was doing felt too good and Tom couldn't speak. He could only pull her forward to kiss her, to touch her, to fill his palms with the satin of her skin.

She was driving him mad by moving that slowly, but he stood it for far longer than he thought he could.

Then he rolled them both over so that he was on top, hoping that would give him the composure he needed.

It didn't.

He was out of control as Kelly pressed herself up to meet him, welcoming his faster rhythm, kissing him fiercely. The world began to blur, but his dizziness wasn't from his injury. He'd never known such intense pleasure, such soul-permeating ecstasy. Her mouth, his mouth, her hands, his. It was hard to tell where he ended and she began.

Tom heard her moaning – or was that his voice?

He moved even faster, harder at her urging, even though he knew that doing so would push him over the edge.

'Kelly,' he said raggedly. 'Kelly . . . Kel, this feels too good. I can't stop myself from—'

She shattered.

Just like that, he felt the power of her intense release. And if he hadn't felt it, he sure as hell would've heard it.

It was the most wonderful, beautiful sensation he'd ever experienced in his entire life. She clung to him desperately, as her body shook with wave upon wave of pleasure, as she cried his name again and again and again.

He did this. *He* made her feel this way.

He would've laughed out loud, but the scorching rush of his own climax rocketed dizzyingly through him, and he couldn't breathe, couldn't think, couldn't do anything but *feel*.

Kelly.

His brain shorted out for several long moments after. And as he drifted in that strange place between intense mind-blowing pleasure and the intoxicating warmth of afterglow, bits and pieces of the last few hours, the last few days even, replayed themselves in seemingly random order.

He heard an echo of Kelly's voice. *I've always loved looking into your eyes. You have such beautiful eyes. Beautiful eyes. Paoletti eyes. A little bit sad. Comes from keeping so many secrets. Secrets. Secrets.*

Joe's voice. *You've been in love with Kelly nearly half your life.*

Then Kelly again. *I need you to see me for who I am.*

Christ, maybe Joe saw something that Tom couldn't see, because Tom had been blinded by Kelly's nice-girl facade – a facade he himself had helped to build. But it was gone now. Completely torn down.

Tom saw Kelly's face. Kelly's smile as she made love to him. He saw her. Clearly. No mislabels. No mistakes. She was beautiful, she was naked, she was funny and rude and fresh and so much more than he'd let himself see before.

In a blinding, glaring flash, he knew that Joe was right. Tom loved this woman with all his heart.

He jerked open his eyes, launching himself out of that drifting place and back to here and now. To Kelly's room, Kelly's bed. Where his face was buried in Kelly's hair. He was crushing her, and he rolled to the side, pulling her into his arms. This was insane. He couldn't possibly love her. And yet . . . 'Holy shit.' He was breathing hard for a whole new reason now.

She snuggled against him. 'What?'

'Nah,' he said quickly. 'Nothing. I'm just . . . you know, *holy shit*, you know?'

Kelly laughed softly, lifting her head to kiss his jawline, lazily playing with the hair at the nape of his neck. 'Eloquently put.'

'Seriously, though,' Tom said, afraid of falling into contemplative silence, afraid of suddenly blurting out something he still hadn't completely figured out for himself yet. 'And be honest now. Was I noisy enough for you?'

She laughed again. 'Don't tell me you're one of those awful guys who ask –' she lowered her voice, – ' "So, was it good for you?" '

'Nah,' he said. 'It's just that noisy's not something I've had much experience with, so . . .' He smiled. 'Besides, I know if it was only one one-thousandth as good for you as it was for me, that it was still probably pretty damn good for you.'

She propped herself up on one elbow. 'Really? It was that good for you?' She rolled her eyes. 'Oh, God, *I've* turned into one of those awful guys.'

Tom leaned forward to lightly kiss the tip of her breast. 'Oh, no, you haven't. And oh, yes, it was . . .' He tried to sound casual and matter-of-fact, as if this were no big deal. 'The best sex of my life.'

She sat up. 'Wow.' She wasn't laughing anymore.

'So about that movie theater thing,' Tom said, cursing himself for revealing too much too soon. 'You busy tomorrow? There are a couple of movies out that I have absolutely no interest in seeing.'

She laughed again, as he'd hoped she would. And then she kissed him. 'This,' she said, with her beautiful eyes sparkling, 'is really going to be fun.'

Fifteen

'Do you suppose my father and Joe are wondering where we disappeared to?' Kelly lifted her head to look up at Tom.

He looked over at the open French doors, realizing with a flash of alarm that they were wide open. But no. No way could Joe and Charles have heard them, no matter how loud they'd been. The two old men were sitting on the other side of the house, down on the first floor, on the deck. Still . . .

'It wouldn't surprise me one bit if your father came searching for me with a shotgun.' He ran his hand lightly down her bare back, unable to get enough of touching her. 'I feel like I'm breaking the rules by being here – in Kelly Ashton's bedroom with the door locked.'

He'd always imagined that would be better than paradise. He'd been dead right.

Kelly smiled at him. 'It's kind of strange, isn't it?'

'Strange and wonderful.'

'Speaking of strange and wonderful, I forgot to mention it to you this morning, but last night I actually got Dad to tell me a little bit about this argument he's been having with Joe. Believe it or not, it has something to do with a woman who was in the French Resistance.'

'Cybele,' Tom said.

Her mouth dropped open. 'You know about her? And you didn't tell me?'

'I didn't,' he said hastily. 'Know about her, I mean. That was just a lucky guess. Joe mentioned someone named Cybele, and Charles nearly had a heart attack. I couldn't get them to tell me more than that. Although Joe gave me a few more hints today – mostly from the things he *didn't* say about her.'

'They were both in love with her,' Kelly told him. 'I think my father's still in love with her.' She laughed softly. 'I didn't think he knew how to love anyone, and yet here he's been in love with this Cybele woman for nearly his entire life.' She settled back down, with her head against his shoulder, running her fingers through the hair on his chest. 'I don't know what happened to her. Do you?'

Tom sighed. 'No. And Joe's not talking.'

Tipping her head back, she looked up at him and touched his face. 'You look tired. How are you feeling?'

He felt a wave of giddy disbelief as he looked into her eyes. Kelly Ashton was lying naked, next to him. He still couldn't believe it. And he wanted her again. Already. He kissed her. 'Incredible, thanks.'

'Headache? Dizziness?'

'Help, there's suddenly a doctor in my bed.'

'It's *my* bed,' she countered. 'There's always a doctor in it. How are you feeling?'

She was serious. She wanted a medical report. 'I'm doing okay,' he told her.

She sat up and looked at him. The eyebrow raised in skepticism was made far less effective by her nakedness. Her hair was tousled, and it just wasn't long enough to do more than bend enticingly at the tops of her breasts. Her beautiful, naked breasts.

It was impossible not to smile at her, but that just made her frown at him.

'What?' he said. 'I'm not allowed to be doing okay?'

'I need you to be honest with me about this,' Kelly said with wide-eyed sincerity. 'I know you're tough and you've been trained to endure nearly anything, but when you're with me, don't just endure, all right?' She took his hand, pressed it to her cheek. 'Please? Promise me, Tom . . .'

He'd always found naked, begging women impossible to disappoint. 'I promise.'

'How are you feeling?' she asked again.

'Slight – very slight – headache. Almost nonexistent, certainly not bad enough to complain about. See, I really am doing okay.' He reached for her, but she backed away.

She wasn't done. 'Dizzy at all?'

'To be honest, I don't know for sure. You do things to me, babe, that turn my world upside down. But all the dizziness I've felt today seems physiologically appropriate.'

Kelly smiled and leaned forward to kiss him. He took full advantage, pulling her close, touching all that soft skin, drinking her in.

Her voice was breathless. 'Last question from the doctor. Are you feeling up to—'

'Yes.'

She laughed as he swiftly rolled her onto her back, as he pushed his way between her legs. 'Because as a doctor I'm very observant, and I couldn't fail to notice—'

He kissed her.

'Mmmm,' she said as she pressed herself up against him. 'I thought so. I could get used to this.'

Oh, baby, so could he. Three, four times a day, every day? For the next few weeks. After that, he didn't want to think about it. He couldn't bear to think about it. He didn't want to stay, but he sure as hell didn't want to go. Suddenly his life was even more complicated than it had been just a few short hours ago.

He closed his eyes as she reached between them, her touch banishing all thought as she drew him to her, as she lifted her hips and . . .

The phone rang. At first he thought it was in his head, some kind of red alert condom alarm. What the hell was he doing, about to enter her without a condom on? Was he nuts? Was he completely insane?

He pulled back as the phone rang again.

'Uh-oh,' she said. 'It's the Bat Phone. Trouble in Gotham City.'

There were two of them, Tom realized. Two phones on her bedside table. One was a regular Princess phone, the other – the one that was shrilly ringing – was cordless.

He let her slide out from underneath him, taking the opportunity to touch her every inch of the way as she reached for the phone. 'Kelly Ashton.'

But once she was listening and talking, he kept his hands to himself. Fun was fun, but business was business, and he'd had lovers try to distract him from the business of an important phone call. He hadn't found it sexy at all – only irritating.

Whatever the person on the other end of the line told Kelly, it made her sit up. 'Yes.' She swung her legs over the side of the bed, turning her back on him. 'Yes. And she's . . .'

She scanned the floor for her underwear, finding her bra and finally her panties. 'I see, uh-huh.'

Oh, hell. Kelly was leaving.

As Tom watched, she put on her underwear. Watching her do that was nice, but compared to what they'd just started, it didn't cut it.

With the phone under her chin, she pulled a pair of khaki pants from a pile of clothes and stepped into them, too.

She was definitely leaving. Every cell in his body was jangling, ready for another enthusiastically energetic round of sex, and she was leaving.

Tom had to laugh – the irony was intense. *He* was used to being the one who had to leave. And he'd never really understood before what it felt like to be left behind. It was frustrating and annoying. He felt cheated and wistful as well as hopeful that she'd come back soon.

But he understood completely about having a job that required her to get up and go at a moment's notice. And the last thing he was going to do was whine and guilt her out. He pulled the sheet up to his waist, hiding the hard evidence of his desire, as he propped himself up on one elbow.

Kelly turned and looked at him as if suddenly remembering that he was there. 'Hang on, Pat.' She

SUZANNE BROCKMANN

covered the phone receiver. 'It's about Betsy. She started chemo today and apparently the oncologist gave her an antinausea drug that didn't do the trick. She's been throwing up blood for the past hour and her parents are scared to death. I really need to—'

'Definitely,' he said. 'Go. And don't worry. Between me and Joe, we've got your dad handled.'

She exhaled her relief. 'Thank you so much.' She uncovered the phone. 'Pat, tell them I'll be there as soon as I can.'

She hung up the phone, pulled a dark-colored T-shirt over her head. 'I'm so sorry about this.'

'Think of it as forced anticipation. And later tonight, when we *do* get a chance? . . . Oh, baby, get ready for fireworks.'

She laughed. 'Promise?'

'Absolutely.'

She was standing there, looking at him as if she was about to change her mind. 'It's so stupid. My going in, I mean. Vince Martin and the rest of the staff at the hospital have this completely covered. There's really nothing I can do.'

'Except make Betsy's parents feel better by being there.'

'Except for that.' She pulled her hair into a ponytail, still gazing at him. 'You're really okay with this, aren't you?'

Tom lay back in her bed, his hands up beneath his head. 'I admit I would like it a hell of a lot more if you could stay. But I know all about getting a page or a phone call and having to go to work. It doesn't always happen at the most convenient time, and that's life. In

338

fact, I was just thinking how it's usually me who has to climb out of bed at an inopportune moment.'

He watched as she brushed a little makeup onto her face, put on some lipstick. 'I guess you probably have a lot of . . . inopportune moments, huh?'

She was jealous. She was trying hard not to be, but she was. Usually jealousy made him want to run away screaming, but this time, coming from Kelly, it made him feel undeniably pleased.

'Not really,' he said. 'Certainly not lately. And never anything special, you know?'

She glanced at him. 'I didn't mean to sound . . . I'm not trying to pry, or . . .'

'I don't have anything to hide,' he countered. 'I mean, yeah, I've had relationships, but . . .'

Never one that made him feel even remotely like this.

Jesus, he couldn't tell her that. It scared him to death, the intensity of his feelings and her potential reaction – or lack of reaction – to them. He'd never used the word *love* preceded by *I* and followed by *you*. Never. He wasn't even sure that was what he was really feeling, and not some hormonal imbalance caused by seventeen years of delayed gratification.

'I really don't want to know,' Kelly told him. 'Really. It doesn't matter. I don't know why I said that.'

Tom was just as glad to let it drop. 'Call me from Boston,' he said to her. 'I mean, if you have time.'

She looked at herself critically in the mirror. 'They're going to know, aren't they? Just from looking at me. I've got that whoo-whee, I-just-got-laid look.'

He laughed at that. 'No one's going to be able to tell that from looking.'

'Oh, yeah?' She looked at him, eyes narrowing. 'You've got it, too. If you go downstairs right now, Joe and my father are going to know. If you're not careful, we're going to find ourselves in the middle of a shotgun wedding.'

'Your father's not that old-fashioned.'

'No, but Joe is.' She lingered, her hand on the doorknob. 'There's Chinese food in the refrigerator. Just heat it in the microwave when you get hungry.'

'Hey, aren't you going to kiss me goodbye?'

She laughed. 'Are you kidding? I don't trust myself within six feet of you. I'll kiss you hello, later.'

'Fair enough.'

'I really need to run.' She still didn't move. 'Thanks for the best day I can remember. Ever.'

'Thank you, for . . .' Being you. Jeez, when had he turned into a sappy greeting card?

'God,' she said, 'I can't believe I've finally got Tom Paoletti in my bed, and I'm about to get in my car and drive away.' As she shut the door behind her, he heard her laughter.

She was gone.

Tom lay back, breathing in the ghost of her perfume. He had to laugh, too. That made two of them. He couldn't believe he was here in Kelly's bed, couldn't believe what he felt when she smiled at him, couldn't believe she'd wanted him so desperately, too, couldn't believe they'd finally made love.

He climbed out of bed and went out onto the balcony to watch her get into her car. She didn't look up, didn't look back. She just drove away.

In a few weeks, when he was the one who had to leave, he wasn't quite sure he'd be able to do the same.

*

Mallory looked at her living room, imagining it from David's perspective.

Shabby sofa. Shabby recliner. Worn and stained wall-to-wall carpeting. A small room, only one window – and it was covered outside by a rusting white-and-turquoise awning, succeeding in making the room even darker and uglier than it had to be.

Cheap-shit artwork hung on the walls, from the time Angela had that job at the chain motel off Route 128 in Beverly. The place went out of business and Angela – in a brilliant move – had accepted six awful oil paintings in lieu of her final check.

David gazed at the still life on the wall behind the couch, his face carefully blank. Mal knew he saw amazingly crappily executed art in a garish gold-painted baroque-style wooden frame. But she saw more. She saw a reminder of her mother's folly.

Why the hell had she brought him here? What was wrong with her, anyway?

They'd been sitting in David's apartment, looking at the photographs he'd taken of her and Brandon. Most of them were extremely good. And as weird as it was to look at herself in a bikini, *she* looked good, too. She'd made herself look the way she imagined this Nightshade character was supposed to look – strong and brave and invincible.

But the lighting *was* bad in some of the pictures. The kisses were overexposed. Didn't it figure? They were going to have to shoot the kisses over again. Just her luck.

The sandwich David had made her was delicious and while she ate it, she'd asked him about drawing

341

graphic novels. Did all comic book artists do it this way – by taking photos?

David told her everyone had their own method. There was no wrong or right way – although there were some people who thought taking photos like this was cheating. But it wasn't as if David actually sketched over them. He just used them to remind himself how the human body moved.

He'd shown her which of the photos he thought he'd use the most, which he'd pin up right over his drawing table. And she'd told him they were so much better than anything she'd ever taken.

David being David had picked up on *that* right away. And one thing led to another until here they were. In her crappy house in the low-rent part of Baldwin's Bridge. In her crappy living room. Where she was about to show him some of the crappy photos she'd taken with her crappy Instamatic over the past few years.

Angela had left a pack of cigarettes on the coffee table. It was all Mallory could do not to light one up.

David kept glancing back at the still life from hell, as if he were afraid it was contagious.

'My grandfather painted that,' Mallory told him. 'Pretty good, huh?'

David looked at Mallory, looked at the painting. 'Amazing,' he murmured. He leaned closer to look at the brush strokes. 'That is really awful. A true artistic nightmare. Your grandfather –' he pointed to the signature, – 'Mary Lou Brackett, is clearly a genius.'

Busted. Mallory grinned at him. 'Grandfather Mary Lou was something of an eccentric. Extremely brilliant, but tortured. Understandably.'

'His disturbed presence certainly radiates from his work,' David said, smiling back at her.

Behind his ugly glasses, beneath his terrible haircut, his eyes were warm and intelligent. He liked her. She could see that just by looking at him. He didn't have that slightly glazed look in his eyes most guys got when they spoke to her. He wasn't here, in her house, because he wanted to score. He liked being with her. He was here because he wanted to hear what she had to say, because he really did want to see her photographs.

David didn't care what her house looked like – so what if it was the smallest, shittiest house in all of Baldwin's Bridge. It didn't matter to him one bit.

'Do you mind if we look at your pictures in the kitchen, Nightshade?' he asked. 'Grandpa Mary Lou's fruit bowl is a bit overwhelming.'

'There's another one in there,' she warned him. 'It's even worse.'

'*Worse*.'

'There are six . . . heirlooms altogether,' she said. 'Naturally we hung the very best in the living room.'

David went into the kitchen. 'Oh, God,' she heard him say as he started to laugh. 'Grandpa Mary Lou signed this one Elizabeth Keedler. Either he had a multiple personality disorder, or he was attempting to break into art forgery.'

'By copying the style of the as-yet-still-unknown master of motel oil painting, Elizabeth Keedler?' Mallory raised her voice so he could hear her. 'He *was* extremely shrewd.'

David came out of the kitchen. 'And you have *six* of these, you say?'

343

'That's right. Come on, it's safe – at least relatively safe – in my room.'

She led the way down the hall. Her room was tiny, but it was all hers. She kept her photo albums in her bookcase. She pulled the latest one from the shelf.

David stood in the doorway, suddenly and obviously uncomfortable. 'You know, I was just kidding. I don't mind sitting in the living room.'

She watched as he looked around the room, at her narrow bed, the dresser, her little built-in desk, the slant to the ceiling. This had been an add-on to the back of the house, a former toolshed or pantry. One of Angela's boyfriends had put a window in about ten years ago. He hadn't quite finished it before they'd broken up, so Mallory had painted the sill herself. Gleaming black. It was still the best part of the entire room.

David looked at the movie posters and pictures that covered every inch of her walls, at the books that overflowed her bookcase and sat in precariously tall piles on the floor.

And then he looked at her, sitting there cross-legged on her bed.

'I don't mind if you come in,' she told him. 'I know you're not going to, like, attack me or anything.'

He nodded, suddenly as serious as if she'd just given him a medal for saving the Rebel Forces from the Death Star. 'Okay. Good. I'm . . . glad you know that.'

He left her door wide open, pulled her chair from her desk. He slipped his neon backpack from his shoulder, but instead of putting it on the floor, he sat with it on his lap. And he unzipped it. 'You know, I was thinking, you could borrow my camera if you want.'

'What?'

He took it out of his pack by the neck strap, the enormous lens reattached. 'My camera. There's a new roll of film in it. Color prints, thirty-six exposures. You've got this evening and tomorrow morning off – you could shoot this entire roll if you want.'

Mallory stared at him. 'You want to lend me your camera.' That thing had to cost at least four paychecks.

'Sure.' He held it out to her, and when she didn't take it, he set it down next to her on the bed. 'It's easy to use. Pretty much point and shoot. You may want to play around with the settings when the sun starts going down, but you probably remember all that from media club.'

He *trusted* her with his camera.

David put his backpack on the floor, then held out his hands for the photo album she was clutching. 'So let me see your pictures.'

She held it even closer to her chest, afraid she wasn't good enough, afraid he'd take one look and laugh. 'I took these with an Instamatic. They suck, so don't pretend they don't, okay?'

He smiled. 'Okay.'

Mallory's stomach did a slow flip as she handed him the album. He had the best smile. And the deepest brown eyes.

He opened the album, screamed, and slammed it shut. 'Oh, my God! These *suck*!'

Mallory laughed and kicked him with her bare foot. 'Don't be a jerk.'

'Whoa,' he said, 'let me see if I've got this straight. *I* say they suck, and *I'm* a jerk. *You* say they suck and . . .' He looked at her expectantly.

Mallory rolled her eyes. 'And I'm a jerk. All right, they don't suck, okay?'

'Aha. The truth comes out.'

'Just don't . . . expect too much and don't lie, okay?'

'Okay.' He pushed the camera back so he could open the photo album on the bed. And just like that, he was instantly involved and connected, leaning over the pictures.

'Some of these are really good, Mal. Look at this one.' He pointed right away to a photo she'd taken when she was baby-sitting the O'Keefe twins, a photo she'd always thought was one of her best. 'Look at the composition here. It's really great the way you use the swing set to frame the photo. And you caught these kids in motion – it's really dynamic, and you did it with an Instamatic.'

Mallory watched him as he talked. He was so enthusiastic, he spoke with his hands, with his eyes, with his entire body. He was so completely different from too-cool-to-be-anything-but-bored Brandon.

He was wearing kind of fashionable shorts that came down past his knees. The dork factor kicked in, though, because he was wearing really dweeby dark socks with his ratty sneakers. His shirt was a desperately ugly button-down short-sleeved plaid, but it didn't matter. His crappy haircut didn't matter, nor did his ugly glasses.

It was all superficial. An hour at the mall, a few fashion dos and don'ts, and David would transform nicely from nerd to kind of average-looking guy. But nothing anyone could do would change him into a superstud like Brandon.

Of course, it would take far more than a trip to the

mall ever to change Brandon into someone as smart and funny and nice and genuinely sweet as David.

Mallory had to laugh.

David just smiled at her and kept on talking – he didn't think it was weird she should just suddenly feel the need to laugh out loud.

It was ridiculous, though. Unbelievable. And incredibly cool.

She, Mallory Paoletti, was completely falling for David Sullivan.

'I thought I heard you come home.' Charles turned on the overhead lights. 'What are you doing sitting in the living room in the dark?'

Kelly didn't turn to look at him. 'I'm exhausted and I'm hiding. What are you doing up? Joe left a note saying that you'd kicked him and Tom out at around eleven because you wanted to go to sleep.'

'A white lie,' he said. 'I wanted to be alone. These days it seems as if the only time I'm alone is when I'm in bed – which is the exact opposite of the way it should be.'

Kelly could hear him using the walker to shuffle farther into the room. 'Better not come in,' she said. 'It's not going to take much to start me crying.' And God knows Charles hated crying.

He stopped. 'Oh.'

Betsy wasn't going to make it. Kelly had realized that tonight. The chemo was most likely going to kill the little girl. But without it, the cancer would definitely kill her. 'Most likely' came with pain and suffering, but 'definitely' was definite. That was one hell of a choice for her parents to make.

Kelly had sat with the McKennas and Vince Martin for hours discussing different medications that might ease or even eliminate the side effects of the chemotherapy. But trial was involved, and with trial came error. And pain.

The McKennas had looked to her for answers, and she couldn't help them. She had no answers, not even today with Tom's scent still on her, with the glorious perfection of their physical joining still warming her skin.

The knowledge that he was everything she'd ever dreamed of in a lover – and more – didn't help her as Brenda McKenna's dark brown eyes begged her to tell them what to do. Let their child die, or try to save her and watch her suffer. After which she'd most likely die anyway.

Kelly had all but promised Tom they'd finish what they'd started when she got home tonight. But right now, sex was the dead last thing she wanted. She couldn't bear the thought of celebrating life that way, not while knowing that the McKennas were facing death and struggling with such sorrow.

She knew Tom was probably upstairs, in her room, waiting for her.

She drew in a deep breath as she sat up, turning toward her father.

'Do you need something?' she asked Charles. 'Can I make you a power shake?'

'No.' He cleared his throat. 'Thank you, but . . .'

'Time for a pill?'

'Took one an hour ago.'

'Are you . . . okay?' she asked. 'Is it time for me to call the doctor for a stronger—'

He took one hand off his walker to wave away her suggestion impatiently. 'No, I'm fine. Relatively speaking.'

Had she done something to disrupt his carefully ordered world? Kelly couldn't think of a single thing except for . . . oops. Seducing Tom up in her bedroom in the middle of the afternoon. Had Charles somehow found out about that?

He seemed exasperated and annoyed, but more at himself than at her.

'Do you need me to change your sheets?' she tried.

Maybe he'd soiled them during a nap. He hadn't had that problem before, but she was well aware loss of control could happen at any time to someone with his deteriorating physical condition. She'd bought some Depends, and, like the walker, she'd simply put the box in her father's room. They were there if he needed them – he wouldn't have to ask.

But changing the sheets on his bed – that was something he wouldn't be able to do by himself. And she could understand his not wanting to ask Joe for help.

'No,' he told her crossly. 'I just wanted—'

She waited.

'I wanted to sit and talk for a minute. But if you're feeling . . . Well, later will be fine.' He turned away, started back down the hall.

Her father wanted to *talk* to her.

Kelly couldn't move, couldn't think. Why did her father want to talk to her? And then she couldn't do anything but think of reasons. Maybe to tell her he'd come to terms with dying, with the fact that he was running out of time, the fact that everything he'd left unsaid had better be said, and soon. Maybe he wanted to tell her more about that French woman he'd mentioned just last night. Had that really been only last night? It seemed like a million years ago.

Or maybe he *had* found out about her and Tom.

'Wait! Dad!' She hurried after her father. 'Dad.'

As he stopped and turned toward her, she saw that just that little movement required a great deal of effort and her heart sank. He was looking more and more fragile every day.

'Talk to me.' She pulled him back into the living room, practically pushed him down into a chair. She pulled up a footstool right next to him. 'I'm here. What do you want to tell me? I'm dying to listen.'

'It's not that important. I just . . .' He couldn't meet her eyes.

'Just say it,' she whispered. 'It's amazing how easy it is once you open your mouth and start talking. It's amazing the things that come out.'

He finally looked at her. He even briefly reached out to touch her hair. 'You always were a pretty child. I used to be afraid of Tom Paoletti, when he was living with Joe down at the end of the driveway. I saw the way he looked at you.'

Oh, my God. This *was* about Tom.

'You know, Dad, I'm a big girl now. I'm pretty good at taking care of myself.'

'You've always been good at taking care of yourself. It's . . . um, it's occurred to me that because of that, you might miss out on an opportunity to let someone else take care of you, if you know what I mean.'

Kelly didn't. She shook her head.

'Tom,' Charles said with a spark of impatience. 'We're talking about Tom here.'

'Ah,' she said. 'We are?'

'He's a good man, Kelly.'

Oh, my God. Did her father think . . . ? 'He is,' she agreed.

'I just wanted to make sure you knew I thought that,' he said awkwardly. 'I've never come out and said that before.'

'Dad, it's obvious you think very highly of him.'

'I've been thinking about it a lot lately,' Charles said. 'Since you told me, well . . . You know, you could do far worse.'

Oh, God. Her father thought she and Tom . . . 'I'm not going to marry him. We're not . . . He's not . . .' She shook her head. 'I'm sorry to disappoint you.' Again.

'Oh,' he said. 'I thought . . . I'd hoped . . .' He searched her face, then sighed. 'It was too perfect. I just thought that if Tom could take care of you, then the two of you together could look out for Joe.'

This was about Joe. Her father was worried about what would happen to his dear friend Joe when he was gone.

Heart in her throat, Kelly took his hand. 'I'll make sure Joe's okay,' she told him huskily. 'I'll take care of him for you, Daddy. I promise.'

He touched her hair again and his eyes were sad. 'But who'll take care of you?'

Tom sat at Kelly's computer, suddenly completely uncertain.

He'd heard Kelly's car pull into the driveway nearly an hour ago. It was hard to believe she hadn't noticed that the light was on in her room, that the French doors were wide open.

She'd come into the house, but she hadn't come upstairs.

She hadn't called him from Boston, hadn't called from her car, either.

It was probably no big deal. She'd probably just misplaced his cell phone number. And maybe she'd grabbed something to eat, gone in to check on her father. Those things took time.

He'd showered and shaved before coming back over here tonight, brushed his teeth, run his fingers through his hair.

He'd even practiced bringing up that goddamned unpleasant subject a few times. 'Hey, Kel, you know in three and a half weeks when I go back to California? What do you say we do that crazy-assed long-distance thing? We could give it a try. You know, email, phone calls, I could visit every few months or so? . . .'

Of course, there was the variation on the theme that went something like 'Hey, Kel, you know in three and a half weeks when I go back to California? Maybe you could go with me . . .'

Or, best yet, 'Hey, Kel, you know in three and a half weeks when I fail my psych evals and I'm kicked out of the Navy, when I'm homeless and jobless and certifiably insane, when I'm at my most pathetically, depressingly lowest – and oh, did you happen to notice it's definite that I'm going bald? – what do you say we get married?'

It was crazy. He was nuts – this proved it.

But oh, God, he wanted her. He truly did. Tonight and forever. All evening, he'd been waiting, half-aroused, wishing she'd come home, dreaming of the stupidest things. The most efficient ways to get their crazy schedules to line up. A plan for bicoastal living. A simple, quiet wedding with Joe and Jazz standing up for him. Names for their children.

Holy shit, he was in serious trouble here. He was naming their frigging children after one naked afternoon. Yes, the sex was beyond incredible. Yes, she made him feel things he'd never felt before. But that didn't automatically make what he was feeling *love*. That didn't mean it was going to last forever.

Jesus, how do you know? Did the uncertainty ever fall away? Maybe if she looked into his eyes and whispered that she loved him. The thought of her doing that was enough to make him dizzy. God, he wanted her to love him.

He wanted her up here. *Now.*

If it had been him pulling into the driveway, he'd've taken the stairs to her room three at a time.

Finally, *finally* the door opened, and Kelly stepped inside.

She closed it behind her, leaning against it. She seemed to brace herself before looking over at him.

'Hi.' She forced a smile.

She'd been crying. She'd dried her face, but Tom could tell she was still extremely upset. He stood, suddenly even more uncertain. 'I hope you don't mind that I—'

'Of course not.' She was brisk as she came into the room, setting her bag down next to her dresser. 'I said you could use my computer whenever you wanted.'

He wasn't here to use her computer. Surely she knew that. 'Is everything . . . Are you . . . ?'

She sat on the edge of her bed and untied her shoes. 'I'm fine. I'm ... My father's dying. It gets to me sometimes. That and the fact that an eighty percent survival rate for childhood leukemia means that twenty percent of the children who get it *die*.' She fired first one and then the other of her shoes into the closet with about ten times the necessary force.

Tom sat down next to her. Oh, damn. 'It doesn't look good for Betsy, huh?'

She shook her head tensely, tightly. 'No, it doesn't.'

He took her hand, massaging her fingers gently. 'I'm really sorry.'

She gazed down at their hands. 'God, Tom, I'm so tired. It's been an intense couple of days, and ...'

'You look like you need a back rub.' He wanted to help erase the strain he could hear in her voice. 'Joe's got a pretty nice collection of French wine. I could go grab a bottle and—'

She pulled her hand free and stood up. Her voice shook. 'Look, I know I promised we'd get together again when I got home, but I'm sorry, I'm just ... I'm so not in the mood.'

Tom didn't know what to do. But leaving her alone and upset was the last thing he wanted. He tried to keep things light. 'For a back rub?'

Kelly turned to face him. 'For sex.'

'I didn't say you look like you need sex, I said you look like you need a back rub.'

'Isn't it the same thing? I don't think I've ever been given a glass of wine and a back rub that hasn't ended with sex.'

She was very tired and very upset. And Tom was guilty. A little wine, a little soothing massage, and a little full-body, sensual comfort usually followed. His motives hadn't been entirely pure. But he could make them pure. 'There's a first time for everything. And I can tell you right now, I've never had sex with a woman who didn't absolutely want it, so . . .'

'And I have no doubt that after one of your famous back rubs,' she countered sharply, 'I'll be on that list with all the other women you've made to want it. And I just don't goddamn feel like wanting it tonight, all right?'

Whoa. She was actually pissed off. 'Kelly—'

Her voice shook. 'I know I'm being awful. Tom, I loved our afternoon together, I really did. But I don't want to mislead you into thinking I'm ready to do anything right now besides crawl miserably into bed and sleep. So maybe you should just go.'

Tom stood up. He was trying hard to be understanding because she'd clearly had a tough night with that sick little girl, but it was getting harder not to raise his voice. 'Are you implying that the only thing I want from you is sex – that I wouldn't want to spend time with you unless we're going at it?'

She did. Oh, Jesus, she *did*. She didn't need to say a word, he could see it in her eyes.

'You don't think that when you come into your room –' his voice was definitely getting louder, – 'after you've been *crying*, that I might want to put my arms around you and talk to you, stay with you for a while, find out what the hell's made you so upset?'

'And you don't think that if you put your arms around me,' she countered, 'we'll be going at it, as you so accurately put it, in a matter of minutes?'

'Not unless you want to,' he said tightly.

She was exasperated. 'But that's my point. I don't want to *want to*, but we both know that I will if you touch me.' She all but threw up her hands. 'You know, this is all really new to me. I've never had a relationship that's based purely on sex before, and the truth is, all I have to do is look at you, and a part of me forgets that I don't want sex tonight. I know it's completely my problem, but please, just give me a break, Tom. Just *go*.'

Tom stared at her. A relationship based purely on sex. Jesus. Had he missed something here? Is that what she truly thought they had going? He laughed in disbelief. She had no fucking clue. If their relationship were based purely on sex, they wouldn't have spent all those hours talking. Caring what the other said and thought and felt and . . .

This *so* wasn't some fuck-me-tonight, pure sex deal in which they'd have only exchanged names and maybe a sentence or two of small talk. 'I grew up in Albuquerque.' 'Yeah? I have a friend whose sister lives there. Let's screw.'

What he had with Kelly was a love affair. At least that's what he'd thought it was. Obviously, he'd been wrong. What he had was a one-sided love affair with a talkative woman who wanted only to fuck him. Come to think of it, she'd used that very word from the start.

His stomach hurt and his throat felt tight. 'Well,' he said. 'Great. Why don't you give me a call when you want to have sex? I'll be, just, you know, standing by.'

He went out the French doors and over the side of the balcony without looking back.

Sixteen

'Tom!'

He was halfway across the driveway, heading toward Joe's cottage, and he didn't break stride.

'Tom, *wait*!'

He stopped and slowly turned around. Kelly could see both anger and impatience in the way he was standing.

'I'm sorry,' she called down to him. 'I've done this all wrong, and . . .'

His face was just a blur in the dimness outside the circle of light thrown by the floodlight on the garage. He moved closer, taking his time, moving slowly, deliberately, until he was directly beneath her balcony. 'So this is just sex,' he said tightly. 'What we've got going here?'

'Isn't it? I mean, you're leaving in a few weeks. I thought . . .'

He looked over at Joe's roses. 'Have you ever had a relationship before that was just sex? *Only* sex?' He turned his focus on her, and his eyes were devoid of the warmth she loved. He was indeed very, *very* angry. It didn't make sense.

Silently, she shook her head.

'So I win the prize. Why's that, Kelly? Why am *I* the guy who wins the no-strings sex, huh?'

He knew. She stood there, looking down at him, and she knew that he knew. She couldn't speak.

'See me as I really am.' His imitation of her was a little cruel. 'You goddamn did the same thing to me that you accused me of doing to you. You don't want to spend the next few weeks with *me*. You want to spend it with that wild punk kid Tom Paoletti – the one who was always stirring up trouble. The hell-raiser. The one with the reputation for getting girls into trouble. Is that what you want, Kelly? You want to be in trouble? I'll get you into trouble.'

He started climbing up the trellis on the side of the balcony, and she backed away, her heart racing. 'Don't.'

Tom dropped heavily back to the ground. 'Great. *Great.* Now you're afraid of me. This is *so* perfect.' He turned to look up at her, his stomach churning and his teeth clenched. His chest ached. 'Fourteen *years* I've been with the SEALs. Fourteen years I've been a man that people respect and admire. I'm the commanding officer of the abso-fucking-lutely most elite SEAL team in all of the US Navy. But you look at me – *you*, who always, *always* treated me decently, like a real human being – and all you can see, all you probably ever saw, is some fuckup.'

'That's not true!' Kelly faltered. 'Well, it's not entirely true. I thought . . . '

He just stood there, waiting for her to go on, waiting to see if she'd even try to explain.

'I didn't want entanglement,' she whispered. 'I

didn't want to start anything that was going to be hard to end. I honestly thought you'd be glad to have that kind of easy relationship for the summer.' She leaned over the railing. 'Tom, you told me you don't do love . . .'

'You're right,' he said. 'You're absolutely right.' He *didn't* do love. Christ, he didn't know what the hell he'd been thinking.

'I'm sorry. And I'm not afraid of you. Don't ever think that. See, I'm afraid of *me*. If you get too close . . .'

He laughed harshly at that. 'Yeah, right, I'm that irresistible.'

'You are,' she told him, wiping her face as if she was crying. Jesus, that made his chest hurt even worse. He didn't want her to cry. 'Don't you feel it? Even with me up here and you down there? . . .'

'Yeah, I feel it,' he said as he walked away. He definitely felt it. Funny thing was, he'd thought what he was feeling was something else entirely.

11 August

When Kelly pulled into the driveway, there was a car she didn't recognize next to Joe's station wagon. It must've just arrived, because its occupants were climbing out.

The driver was an imposing African-American man who managed, without being the tallest man she'd ever seen, to be the absolute biggest. She was amazed his shoulders fit inside that little car.

A sleek, athletic-looking woman came out of the

front passenger side, and a long-haired twenty-something man with a handlebar mustache and goatee, mirror sunglasses, and chains on his boots emerged from the back, stretching his long legs and yawning.

For a moment, Kelly hesitated, completely blanking on who this could possibly be. She'd called the Visiting Nurse Association just this morning, ready to start the search for a good candidate to come in and help with her father. She was looking for someone strong with a solid sense of humor. But these three, although winners in the strong department, looked more like professional wrestlers than nurses.

And then she remembered. Tom's teammates. His friends. He'd told her they were arriving this afternoon.

God, she was exhausted. No wonder her memory was shot. She'd slept poorly last night, tossing and turning – that was no big surprise. This morning, she'd gone looking for Tom before she drove into Boston, but he was nowhere to be found.

Also no big surprise.

She still wasn't sure what she wanted to say to him besides the fact that she was horribly sorry, but something else definitely had to be said.

As she parked and gathered up the trash from the sandwich she'd had in the car on the way home, Tom came out from around the side of her father's house as if he'd been out on the deck and heard the car doors slam.

He glanced in her direction only once and only briefly. His welcoming smile was decidedly for his friends. 'Hey.'

As Kelly watched, Tom shook hands, first with the black man, then with the younger man, and finally with the woman.

A woman. Even her tired brain recognized that as odd. Last she'd heard, the SEALs were still an exclusively male organization. No women, no exception.

As Kelly climbed out of her car, Tom hung on to the woman's hand far longer than he had for his male friends. She was gorgeous, Kelly realized. Her skin was mocha colored, but her hair had red highlights and her eyes were a vivid green. And she had a lithe body that matched the sheer perfection of her face. She may not have been large breasted, but she was perfectly proportioned and athletically trim. And she had amazing posture. Positively regal.

'Thanks so much for coming,' Tom said to her and to the younger man as well. He glanced at the black man. 'I'm assuming Jazz gave you both a full sit-rep. You know there's a solid chance you're here for nothing?'

The woman's voice was melodically low and as smoothly beautiful as she was. 'Sir. As I told Lieutenant Jacquette, I'd willingly take unpaid leave to back you up even if only to protect you from your own shadow.'

Tom smiled wryly. 'That could well be the situation. And please, let's not stand on formalities, Alyssa. May I call you Alyssa?'

Kelly stopped short. Did he know he was turning on the charm, that he was oozing charisma and that solid, confident sensuality that had driven her crazy for going on two decades?

Alyssa smiled at Tom. She had a gorgeous smile, gorgeous white teeth. 'You can call me whatever you like, L.T., although I prefer Locke.'

Kelly watched Tom, waiting for him to see her, to introduce her, to let go of Alyssa Locke's hand.

He released Locke, but didn't even glance over at Kelly. 'Locke it is. From now on, this is Jazz, Locke, not Lieutenant Jacquette. And if you figure out what the hell to call this long-haired deadbeat –' Tom slapped the younger man's back, – 'let me know, okay? His given name's Roger Starrett but I've never heard him called either of those. He's Houston or Ringo or Sam. Occasionally Bob. He swears there's a logic to all the nicknames, but I can't keep 'em straight.'

'Sam'll do just fine, Miz Locke.' He had a thick Texas drawl. *Dew jist fahn*. That accent couldn't possibly be real, could it?

The woman stood up even straighter. Kelly wouldn't have believed it possible. 'Just Locke,' she said coolly.

'For the duration,' Tom said, 'I'm—'

'L.T.,' Jazz interjected. 'L.T.'s good enough, sir.'

'I'm Tom,' he said firmly. 'As of right now, erase sir from your vocabularies, too.'

Jazz looked as if he had an unpleasantly painful case of gas.

As Kelly headed up to the deck, to where Joe and her father were waiting, Tom pulled Jazz aside.

And the man called Sam sidled up to Locke. 'I just want to take this opportunity to remind you that just because you're working with us in this situation, doesn't mean you've got your foot in the door at Coronado. A woman in the teams is never going to happen.' His voice was low, but Kelly overheard quite clearly as she passed by.

'Gee.' Locke's voice was edged with sarcasm. 'It's so nice that you're concerned for me, *Roger*.'

'Oh, but I am,' he said completely insincerely. 'I'd sure hate to see you get your little hopes up way too high.'

'There are two things in life that I'm sure I'll never be,' Locke said far too sweetly. 'One is a SEAL. That I regret. I believe I'd be an asset to the teams. The other, however, is a redneck asshole. No regrets there.' She smiled at him. 'Too bad you can't say the same.'

'This is going to be one hell of a vacation,' Sam growled.

'I'm not on vacation,' Locke replied. 'I'm here to work.'

'Okay, grab your gear,' Tom said, leading the way to the deck. 'Come and meet the other members of our team.'

Now he was going to introduce Kelly. This was when he'd actually look into her eyes, and she'd try to send him a telepathic apology.

'This is my uncle, Joe Paoletti,' Tom continued, 'and Mr Charles Ashton, who has graciously volunteered the east wing of his house for our use. You'll be bedding down there, as well as helping set up a temporary HQ. Joe and Mr Ashton are veterans of the Second World War. Mr Ashton was with the Army – the Fifty-fifth – and Joe was OSS. They've volunteered to help us.'

And this is Kelly, who wants only sex from me. Yes, Kelly supposed there were worse things than not being introduced.

She stepped forward. 'I'm volunteering, too.' She

held out her hand to Jazz. 'Hi, I'm Kelly Ashton. It's a pleasure to meet you – Jazz, right?'

She shook with Sam/Roger/Bob/whoever, and with Alyssa Locke as well. Alyssa did more than shake her hand. She sized Kelly up with her cool green gaze.

That's right, Kelly tried to say with her smile and her eyes. Tom's mine, babycakes. Hands off.

Except Tom still didn't do more than glance briefly in her direction. Maybe he wasn't hers, not after the things she'd said last night.

'Dr Ashton's got a pediatrics practice in Boston,' he told his teammates. 'She won't be around a lot.'

'Oh, but that's going to change,' Kelly said. 'I'm taking the next three weeks off. I spoke to my partners this morning.'

Tom looked at her then. Direct eye contact for the first time that day. *I'm sorry, I'm sorry, I'm sorry . . .*

'I'll go in if the McKennas need me,' she told him, willing him to hold her gaze, to believe her silent message. 'But that's it for me for a while. I hit some kind of wall last night.'

She couldn't read his expression, and he turned away before she could say what she most wanted to say. *I'm so sorry you caught most of the fallout.*

'Well, great,' Tom said. 'We've got a doctor on the team. Not that we need one. Here's hoping we'll continue not to need you, Doctor.'

Kelly's heart sank as he led his friends inside. Her unspoken apology was apparently not accepted.

'Are you . . . alone?'

Tom looked up from one of the new computers that had arrived just that morning. He and Jazz, Sam, and

Locke had set them up in this room in the east wing of the Ashtons' enormous house.

Their new headquarters had once been the Ashtons' music room – it still held a grand piano they'd pushed into the corner. They'd moved in tables and desks and a bunch of corkboards from an office supply store.

Joe and Charles had spent a good hour using pushpins to tack up all the pictures Tom had of the Merchant.

'Yeah,' Tom said, spinning in his chair to face Kelly. 'I'm alone.'

She came in cautiously. As if she wasn't sure of her welcome.

'Where'd they all go?'

He leaned back, looking at her. She was wearing a sundress with a tiny flower print. With her hair up off her shoulders she looked cool and sweet. Almost angelic.

'Your father's taking a nap on the deck. Joe's sitting with him. My team's just gone out to get familiar with the town, particularly the hotel and the marina. Locke's probably going to check out the church tower. One of the tricks to stopping a terrorist attack is to occupy all the good sniper positions.'

'I thought you said this Merchant guy specializes in car bombs.'

'He does. I'm just covering all the bases.'

'Alyssa Locke and Jazz both called you ... was it L.T.?'

Tom nodded. 'It's short for *Lieutenant*. It's a little more respectful than *Tom*, not as formal as *sir*.'

She moved farther into the room, looking at the

pictures on the boards, looking at the computers. 'This is . . . pretty intense.'

'Do you want something, Kelly?' he asked abruptly. 'Because I'm in the middle of trying to track down a van.'

She gazed at him, her eyes wide. It wasn't her innocent face. This one was for real. She was uncertain, a little afraid. 'Yes, I wanted to . . . talk to you. I had the opportunity this morning to do a little research about patients who've suffered feelings of paranoia caused by severe head injuries.'

'Ah,' he said. 'You're here as a doctor.'

She shook her head. 'No, I . . .' She took a deep breath. 'I'm here as your friend.'

He didn't say a word. He just waited for her to go on, torturing himself by watching the way the light from the windows gleamed on the smoothness of her shoulders.

'The more I read,' Dr Ashton continued – it helped if he thought of her as Dr Ashton, 'the more I was convinced.' She took a step toward him. 'I really don't think that's what's going on with you, Tom. The paranoia most patients experience is less specific than what you described to me. It's more like waves of anxiety and vague feelings of persecution. I didn't see a single mention of the kind of severe condition that actually has people seeing a specific threat – and especially not a threat to people *besides themselves*. Paranoia generally means someone's after *you*. The way you described it, this guy doesn't even know you're here.'

'So either my case is so unusual, I should be written up in a medical journal, or—'

Kelly took another step toward him. 'Or you're not paranoid. Maybe you really did see the Merchant. I've been thinking about this all day and I think you should do more than this.' She gestured around the room. 'I think you should call someone. Tell the authorities that you've seen this man here in Baldwin's Bridge.'

She was close enough now for him to smell her subtle perfume.

'Yeah, well, I've already made that call,' he told her. 'I did it right away. But no one's taking me seriously. And if I persist in calling for help, I'll be putting my career in jeopardy. There's that rear admiral I told you about – Tucker. He's been after my ass for years. I have no doubt that he'd try to use this situation to force my retirement.' He laughed in disgust. 'Now *that* sounds like feelings of persecution, doesn't it? But it's true. Admiral Crowley said as much to my face. He's the one who warned me to back off.'

'How about the FBI, then? Can you call them?'

'Yeah, I might do that. There's also a guy I know in the SAS. I'm waiting to see if I can find any concrete proof the Merchant is here, though. Because if my own superiors don't believe me, why should anyone else, you know?'

'This must be hard for you,' she said softly.

Tom stood up. 'Let me see if I've got this straight,' he said. 'When you're my team doctor, that's when we talk. But when we're lovers, all we do is—'

'I want us to be friends,' she said, flushing slightly.

'That's not the way I understood it. You told me last night all you wanted was to—'

'I also came to apologize,' she said. 'Last night I—'

Tom moved closer to her. 'Apology accepted. Because you know, you were right.'

He stopped hardly a foot away from her. He was close enough to see it all in her eyes. Everything she was feeling. Anxiety. Hope. Desire.

Desire.

He knew Kelly had come here because she could no more stay away from him than he could stay away from her.

This conversation was just an excuse – a way to get her in the door. She didn't really want to talk to him. She was here because she wanted him, wanted sex. She was just too damned polite to admit it.

Tom touched her. Just one finger down the side of her face.

She trembled and he knew he was right.

'We've got a few weeks,' he told her, told himself, too. 'Let's not waste a second.'

He kissed her, and she exploded, kissing him back furiously, frantically, almost knocking him off his feet.

Jesus, had she really thought that if she came to him, wanting him so desperately, he'd actually send her away?

He kissed her harder, deeper, and she was right there, pushing him to the max. Her arms were locked around him, her body close to his. He pressed his thigh between her legs and she rubbed herself against him.

No, he wasn't crazy enough to push her away. And now that he understood, now that he knew exactly what she wanted, he was going to give her just that, and nothing more. Yeah, from now on, he was going to keep his heart to himself.

This time, and for ever after, it *was* going to be just sex.

Tom pulled down the top of her dress, and the elastic straps that held it up gave just enough to expose her breasts, pushing them up and out into his hands, his mouth.

He felt her hands on the velcro fastener at the waist of his shorts, felt it give, too, felt her reach for him, find him. Yes . . .

But, God, the door was wide open. Anyone could walk in. Still, she'd had the opportunity to close and lock it when she came in. Maybe she'd wanted it open. She liked risk – she'd told him so.

But being caught with his pants down by his teammates – or Kelly's father – wasn't quite Tom's idea of fun.

However, there was a closet in the room. It was a walk-in, filled with overcoats and out-of-style suits that Charles Ashton would never wear again. A closet could be very, *very* much fun.

Tom dragged her toward it, pulled her inside. It was dark and airless and smelled of mothballs.

But damn, the door didn't latch. The ocean air had warped the old wood and it hung slightly open, letting in just enough light and barely enough air and an enormous amount of highly charged risk. Anyone could still walk in.

But Kelly kissed him again so urgently, Tom didn't give a damn.

She pushed down his shorts as he pulled up her skirt and then—

She wasn't wearing any underwear.

She moaned as he touched her slick heat, pushing

herself down to drive his fingers more deeply inside her.

'Please,' she breathed, and pressed a condom into his hand. She must've had it in the pocket of her skirt.

No underwear. A condom. The woman had come here prepared.

For sex. Only sex.

She kissed him again, and again he found he didn't care.

Tom swiftly covered himself and lifted her into his arms. She pulled her long skirt out of the way as she gripped him with her legs and then, yes, *yes*, he was inside of her.

She moaned her pleasure as she clung to him, as he drove himself fiercely into her, setting both a pace and rhythm that was on the verge of too rough.

'More,' she gasped. 'I want more.'

Yeah, she'd told him that, too, that she liked it a little wild, a little bit rough.

Tom pushed her up against the back wall of the closet for leverage, thrusting deeply inside of her. She gasped. Maybe too deeply. 'Don't you goddamn let me hurt you,' he rasped.

'You're not, oh, God, please Tom, you're not—'

''Lo?'

He froze. Kelly froze, too, staring directly into Tom's eyes.

Someone had come into the office.

'He's not here.' It was Ensign Starrett's familiar Texas drawl.

Tom and Kelly were surrounded on both sides by winter coats wrapped in plastic. If he tried to pull her back, farther into the shadows, that plastic would crinkle loudly, giving them away. It was better just to not move. To stay completely still. With his body buried deep inside her.

God.

Tom felt a bead of sweat trickle down his back.

'Are you sure? I could've sworn I heard voices.' Locke was in the office, too.

Kelly was still gazing into his eyes. But then, slowly, she leaned forward to kiss him.

'Tom? Hey, Tommy, you hiding beneath the desk or inside that there piano?' Starrett laughed. 'Nope, he's not here.'

It was a slow kiss, a deliberately languid kiss, a white-hot but completely silent kiss.

The sweat down his back turned into a river.

Locke snorted. 'That's obvious. Like you'd ever dare call your CO Tommy to his face.'

Just as silently, Kelly pulled back. Gazing into her eyes, Tom could see heat. She actually liked this. She actually wanted . . .

So he moved. Slowly. Silently. Out. And in.

And Kelly smiled, catching her lower lip between her teeth, deep pleasure in her eyes. Oh, yeah, she liked this.

'We're actually pretty tight,' Starrett said. 'Me an' ol' Tommy.'

'Right. Just grab the map. Jazz is waiting in the car.'

Tom did, too. He liked it, too. So he did it again. Just as infinitesimally slowly. Nearly all the way out.

'At least Tom knows I've had experience shooting more than paper targets, sweetheart.'

Locke's voice was tight. 'I know we've been told to dispense with rank and respect due to the covert nature of this assignment, but from now on, when we're alone, Ensign, you *will* address me as ma'am or Lieutenant. Is that clear?'

And all, all, *all* the way back in. Kelly made the start of a small noise and Tom kissed her, covering her mouth with his, swallowing the sound.

'Yes, ma'am.' Starrett's surly voice faded as they left the room.

And just in time.

Because Kelly was coming. Right there, around him. In slow motion. He could feel her body's release as he kept that erotically, decadently, intensely slow movement.

She was trying hard to be quiet, but the small sounds she was making were enough to push him over the edge.

He moved faster – he couldn't help himself. His own release came with a rush of sensation, a flash of light, the roar of his blood surging through his veins.

Sex. It was sex. Just sex.

And once again, it was incredible sex.

Tom knew he should feel glad. He should feel sated and pleased that this beautiful woman had come to him, that she so obviously had wanted him, that she hadn't been able to stay away.

And hey, this was great. He didn't have to take her to dinner. He didn't have to say another word to her.

He could just clean himself up as best he could, fasten his pants, and walk away.

He almost did it. He almost made it out the door without uttering a single syllable.

But he made the mistake of turning around and looking back at her, still leaning there against the closet wall, still breathing hard, dress rumpled, hair mussed. And he wanted her. He still wanted her. It was physiologically impossible for him to have her again. Not this soon. And yet . . .

'Unlock the screens to the French doors in your bedroom,' Tom told her, his voice still unsteady, 'if you want me up there tonight.'

She gazed at him. 'Tom, please, can we—'

He didn't want to hear it, didn't want to talk. It was, after all, her rule. 'No,' he said, and got out of there, fast.

Seventeen

'Are they awful?'

'I didn't look at them,' David said as he stepped back to let Mallory into his apartment. He had the air-conditioning on in anticipation of tonight's photo shoot, so he closed the door tightly behind her.

'You didn't? Why not?' She looped her fanny pack over the back of one of the kitchen chairs.

'Because they're *your* photos. You should be the one who sees them first.' This past day had been torture. As he'd worked, he'd seen only glimpses of Mallory taking pictures with his camera around the hotel. And then when he'd finally had the afternoon off, *she'd* been on at the Ice Cream Shoppe. He'd gone in, ordered a cone, and watched her work as he'd eaten it. He'd gotten a cup of coffee, too, and sketched her as it had cooled. He'd stretched it into two hours, but he was so afraid of being creepy. Of being David Sullivan, the stalker.

'You didn't even peek?' she asked.

'No,' he said.

'Honestly? Not even a little?'

He laughed as he handed her the pack of photos. 'No. You look at them, and if you decide you want me to see—'

'I want you to see them. I wouldn't have minded if you'd checked them out.'

Why was she looking at him like that? Her eyes were soft, and as he gazed back at her she turned away as if she was suddenly uncertain or . . . shy. Mallory Paoletti, *shy*?

'So how was work?' she asked as she sat down at his kitchen table and opened the pack of pictures, pulling them out and flipping quickly through them. 'I was thinking about how tired you must've been all day – after working all those extra shifts in a row, after getting almost no sleep that night I came in and woke you up.'

David slowly sat down next to her, struggling to understand, afraid to misinterpret. Had she meant she'd been thinking about him all day, or that he must've been tired all day? It couldn't have been the first. Could it?

'It was okay,' he said. 'I'm a little tired, but I made a lot of money from tips. I don't have to work in the morning, but the boss wants me to come in for the lunch shift tomorrow. One of the room service waiters quit and they're short staffed.'

A week ago he would've jumped at the chance to make the extra money. Now all he could think was if he worked during lunch, he wouldn't be able to meet Mallory at the Ice Cream Shoppe and have a sandwich with her by the marina. He'd missed doing that these past two days. Funny how quickly lunch had become his favorite time of day. Of course, right now, *now* was his favorite time of day, too, since she was finally here.

'Room service,' she said. 'Cool. Are you going to do it? Take bottles of champagne up to all those lonely millionaires' wives who're looking for a little action while their elderly husbands are out fishing or playing golf?' She imitated a breathy, high-class voice, 'Hello, room service? This is Mrs Megabucks in room 260. I'd like a triple order of caviar, and can you send it up with that attractive David Sullivan and his great, big, *enor*mous . . .'

She glanced up at him, her eyes gleaming, and David found himself thinking, shy. Where on earth had he gotten the impression earlier that she was suddenly shy?

'Tray,' she finished, laughing.

It was too late. He was already blushing.

'You thought I was going to say something else, didn't you?' she asked.

'Actually, with you, Nightshade, I always expect the extraordinary. I wouldn't dream of trying to second-guess you. You're far too unique.'

'Too much of a freak.'

'No, that's not what I meant,' he said quickly. 'I mean that you're *special*. I think you're incredible and . . .'

Oh, God, way to go. Nothing like screwing up their friendship by cluing her in to the fact that he was completely infatuated. He grabbed her pictures and began looking through them, bracing himself, ready for her to make some excuse and leave. She had to go clean the bottom of her garbage can. She had to go brush her cat's teeth. She had to . . . Or maybe she wouldn't take the excuse route. Maybe she'd stay, but give him the Friendship Speech. 'Gee, I really like you, David, and I'm so glad we're friends. *Friends*. Let me say that again in case you didn't hear. Ferrr-ennn-ddd-sss.'

But when he glanced up at her, she was looking at him in that same odd way that she'd been looking at him before. 'That's really nice,' she said softly.

And then she did it. At least he thought she did it. At the very least – and probably far more likely – he only imagined she did it. Her gaze dropped for just a split second to his mouth before she smiled and looked away.

According to every body language book in the world, that meant she wanted him to kiss her. Except, of course, if he'd only imagined it. Then it meant that he'd imagined she wanted him to kiss her. Two vastly different conclusions.

He looked down at the photos in his hands. She'd taken pictures of people. In and around the lobby of the Baldwin's Bridge Hotel. She'd used the zoom lens, so they were all candids, taken without the subjects' awareness of her presence.

She'd caught a distinguished-looking man with his finger up his nose. A woman, her face contorted with anger as she spoke on a pay phone. A little girl, dreamily lost within the pages of an open book. A man checking in at the registration desk, holding tightly on to the rolling cart filled with luggage, caught in a tug of war as a bellboy tried to take it away. Several shots of David as he'd worked, smiling as he stopped to talk with an elderly man, Mr Torrence. She must've taken them through the restaurant window.

'These are really great,' David said, spreading them out on the table.

He leaned forward to point to the angry woman, and his shoulder brushed Mallory's.

She didn't move back. In fact, she moved closer. Their heads were almost touching, too, as they looked at the photo, and David's mind went completely blank.

Two seconds ago, he'd intended to tell her something about this picture, but right now, all he could think about was the fact that her shoulder was warm and solid against his.

From the corner of his eye, he saw her turn to look at him.

She smelled like the gum she chewed by the pack as a substitute for her cigarettes, sharp and spicy. Cinnamon today.

He turned toward her, too, his mouth suddenly dry, his palms suddenly sweaty, feeling completely uncertain and scared to death. He wanted to kiss her. Every instinct he had was screaming that she wanted him to kiss her, too. But if he was wrong, he could lose her as a friend.

And he couldn't bear that.

'Brandon's late,' he said through the parched desert that had once been his mouth.

Mallory sat back. 'Do you want me to get changed? Do I *have* to get changed? Since it's just a kiss, can we do it dressed – without the oil and bathing suit?'

'Oh,' David said. 'Yeah, well, I was going to take more than just a close-up. I mean, I was going to take close-ups, too, but I also wanted some full-length shots. Bodies and legs. And hands. Hands are so hard to get right. I wanted to see where they fall – naturally, you know? Do you mind?' he added. 'I know the baby oil's really gross.'

She'd already crossed to his costume box and was searching for the bathing suit she'd worn the last time. 'The baby oil's not half as gross as the thought of kissing that asshole again.'

'You don't have to do this,' he told her. 'I really don't want you to if—'

'Chill.' She found the suit and turned to face him. 'It's acting. It doesn't mean anything if you're acting, right? But if he tries to cop a feel again . . . well, we'll just have to take a little break while he recovers. *If* you know what I mean.'

Mallory went into the bathroom and closed the door. But she opened it right away. 'I'm going to need help with the baby oil,' she said. 'Can you do me a favor and help me put it on? I mean, instead of letting Bran put his hands all over me again?'

'Yeah,' David said. 'Of course. My pleasure.' He realized a fraction of a second too late just what he'd said, and how completely inappropriate – although baldly true – it was.

He opened his mouth to stammer some kind of apology, but Mallory was smiling at him. 'Mine, too,' she said, and shut the bathroom door.

As David stood there, he felt the pupils of his eyes dilate, felt his body go into a mild state of shock.

That had *not* been his imagination. Not that time.

'Joe, can you do me a favor?' Tom said. 'I've got to get to the train station in fifteen minutes.'

Kelly knew when he realized she was sitting out on

the deck with Joe and Charles, watching the sunset turn the ocean colors and the sky shades of red-orange. It was right when he'd said the words *train station*. Something changed, very slightly, very subtly in his voice.

She shook the ice around in her glass of lemonade before she glanced up at him.

He was looking at Joe, tension visible in his shoulders, in the muscles working along the sides of his jaw. He'd changed into jeans and a T-shirt. Sneakers on his feet. Baseball cap.

'I need to rent a cargo van with tinted windows – Jazz is going to rig it with surveillance gear,' he explained. 'I finally found what I'm looking for in Swampscott, but it's a first come, first served kind of place, and they're open only till twenty hundred hours. Next train's in twenty-two minutes.'

'Are you sure you should be driving?' Kelly asked. 'All the way back from Swampscott by yourself?'

He looked at her, his eyes taking in her sundress – the same one she'd had on earlier that afternoon, clearly noting the fact that she'd let her hair down. Or rather he had. In the closet. She'd combed it since then. Put on sandals. And underwear. Reapplied the makeup that had run when she'd cried.

She wondered if he even knew he'd made her cry by leaving the way he had. So coldly. So abruptly. As if . . . She cleared her throat. 'What if you get dizzy?' she asked.

'I won't,' he said.

Joe had been about to stand, but now he was giving it a second thought, too. 'You sure you're feeling up to this?'

Tom was exasperated. 'I feel fine. I've got a headache, but I've just spent three hours on the phone trying to find this particular make of van. If I didn't have a headache after that, it would be some kind of miracle. And if I don't catch this train . . .'

'Why don't I just drive you into Swampscott,' Kelly said, her mouth dry – afraid he would turn her down, just as afraid he'd accept. What would she say to him during the forty-minute drive? 'You can skip the train, Tom. I'll take you right to the rental place.'

But he was already shaking his head. 'Thanks, but no. I'm not going to ask you to drive me to Swampscott.'

'You didn't ask,' Kelly countered. 'I volunteered.'

Joe and Charles were looking from her to Tom somewhat warily, obviously aware of the under-currents of tension, but – hopefully – having no clue as to their origin.

'Thanks, but no,' he said again.

'I want to.' Her voice wasn't shaking. Yet. 'I haven't had a chance to apologize to you and—'

'You did,' he said. 'Before. I accepted your apology.' He turned away, a trace of desperation in his voice. 'Joe, can you please drive me to the train?'

Kelly stood up, nearly knocking her chair over. 'God *damn* it. When I said what I said last night, I didn't mean that we should never *talk* to each other again. I don't want us not to be friends, Tom!'

Tom didn't move, didn't react, didn't blink. He just looked at her.

Kelly couldn't stand it. She didn't care that her father and Joe were watching. She marched up to Tom and kissed him, long and hard on the mouth.

'My doors *will* be open tonight.' Her voice shook with emotion. 'But if you come in, you better be ready to talk.'

She swept into the house.

Charles went along, riding in the backseat as Joe drove Tom to the train station.

Since it took only three minutes to get to the train, they'd stopped at the Honey Farms on the way. Tom had wanted a bottle of Pepsi, no doubt to try to control his headache, which surely had to be a damn sight worse after that show Kelly had put on out on the deck.

Kelly, whose doors – presumably the French ones on her balcony – would be open to Tom tonight.

Charles tried to reassure himself that he was okay with that. It was, after all, the start of the twenty-first century. If his thirty-two-year-old grown-up daughter wanted to have a relationship with a man who wasn't her lawfully wedded husband, well, that was her business, not his. He should have done the same with his second wife – saved himself one hell of a lot of grief. Not to mention money.

Tom got back into Joe's car, Pepsi in hand, and Joe put the car into reverse.

'Wait,' Charles ordered. He tapped Tom on the shoulder. 'Have you got everything you need? Because if you don't, you might want to go back in there and buy it. Them. A box. Ah, Christ. You know what I mean.'

Joe and Tom both turned to look back at him.

Where had Jenny's father been with that kind of advice the night Charles had taken her to the Lennox

Ballroom in Boston, and driven home via back roads? Very dark, very deserted back roads. Dark enough to take a blanket out into the crisp autumn night, spread it out in the middle of a deserted field so they could share a bottle of wine and gaze up at the stars . . .

Well, maybe Jenny had done some stargazing, but Charles sure hadn't.

'Condoms,' he said now, crossly. 'Do you need me to spell it for you, too? Do you have some, son?'

Tom gazed at him, completely surprised. Charles could read this Paoletti nearly as well as he could read the senior one. It was obvious that Tom wasn't afraid of Charles, but he was taken aback by his frankness, unsure how to respond to the father of the woman he was probably intending to . . . intending to . . .

Yes, this *was* awkward.

'Just nod your head,' Charles demanded. 'Yes or no? If it's yes, we go, if it's no, you trot back into the store and—'

Tom nodded. Yes. But then he shook his head no. 'Sir, I'm not—'

'Not going to talk about this anymore,' Charles loudly cut him off. 'You told me what I wanted to know. Just promise if the opportunity arises, you'll actually use the damn things.'

Tom nodded again. Yes.

And then – smart young man that he was – he turned back around and sat facing the front. Probably praying hard that Joe got him to the train before Charles started questioning him about his favorite sexual positions.

Joe drove down North Street, making sure Charles

saw him rolling his eyes balefully at him in the rearview mirror.

Just what Charles needed after they dropped Tom off at the train. A lecture from the High Priest of Polite on the propriety of talking about condoms with the man his only daughter had just publicly invited into her bedroom tonight.

Joe would probably have preferred that Charles urge caution to the point of not needing condoms. He didn't want either of their children – grown-up children, but still their children – to get hurt.

And Charles and Joe both knew a thing or two about how easy it was to hurt the people you care about the most.

As Joe pulled into the commuter rail station, Charles couldn't help but remember another trip he took with Joe to the train, this one back in France. Cybele had been with them, along with Henri and Luc Un, the poor bastard. They'd received a coded message from a BBC French Special Broadcast, requesting aid in stopping German troop movement. The fighting in the French countryside was fierce, and anything they could do to keep the Germans from sending reinforcements and supplies by train would help the Allies.

Joe had asked Charles to go with them. They were short-handed that night. Luc Deux, Marie, and Dominique were nowhere to be found, and Joe and Cybele needed his help.

Charles's leg had healed enough that he could move without his cane. Ironically, that had been the very night Joe had planned to begin the dangerous journey taking Charles to the Allied side of the line. But with the BBC broadcast, all bets were off.

Things were still tense in the house – it had been only a few days since he and Cybele had fought in the kitchen, since Joe had realized Cybele had gone to his bed only because she couldn't have Charles. The entire dynamics of the household had been turned sideways. No wonder Luc Deux, Marie, and Dominique had taken a powder.

At first, Charles had refused to help. What could he do? He knew nothing about explosives or blowing up train tracks. Besides, he'd told them, he'd quit the hero business. He'd filled his lifetime quota of heroic acts already, thanks.

But by nightfall, when the time came, Charles found himself dressed and ready to go, unable to let them leave without him.

Cybele had matter-of-factly handed him an extra gun as if she'd been expecting him all along, securing her own Walther PPK just inside the waist of her trousers. She was dressed like a man, complete with smudges of coal on her face, and she quickly helped him blacken his own face, too.

Moving through the streets was terrifying. They had to hide several times from patrolling Germans, hardly daring to breathe, knowing that the slightest wrong move, the slightest misstep, would mean discovery and certain death. It was nerve-racking and exhausting. And Joe and Cybele had been doing it nearly every night for years.

Moving through the woods outside town was only slightly better. They traveled quickly south, still on foot, to a nearby village that sat on the train line. The entire track was being guarded – the Germans were expecting saboteurs.

But Cybele had proposed they plant their explosives along a section of track uncomfortably near the German barracks, near the station, right on the outskirts of town. And sure enough, although it was tricky to get to, once they were there, the area was completely unguarded.

Henri planted the explosives along a key length of track, while Luc Un set his bomb beneath a railroad car sitting dark and silent nearby. It was open and empty, but it was there. And if they blew it up, the Germans couldn't use it to carry food and water to their soldiers on the front lines.

As the two men worked, Joe, Cybele, and Charles kept watch.

Charles had been terrified. Not for himself. For Cybele. He didn't want to care. He didn't want to love her.

All he'd ever wanted was to be back home . . .

He gazed out the window as Joe pulled the car up alongside the Baldwin's Bridge station house and braked to a stop.

'Thanks for the ride,' Tom said.

Joe nodded.

Tom opened the door and climbed out of the car.

Charles put down his window. 'By the way. Something I forgot to mention earlier. If you hurt Kelly, I'll kill you. Slowly and painfully.'

It was true that Kelly had told him she didn't want to marry Tom, but for all Charles knew, that was simply a case of protesting too much. He himself flipped back and forth between wanting them to try to have a life together and wanting them to stay far away from each other.

Tom had the good grace not to laugh in his face. 'Mr Ashton, I can assure you, it's not my intention to—'

'I don't care about your intentions. I know you don't *intend* to hurt her. I'm just telling you *don't*.' Charles pushed the button and the window slid back up.

For a minute, Charles thought the young man was going to knock on the window and demand to continue this conversation. But the train came into the station, and Tom dashed for the platform.

Joe sat for a moment, watching him. 'He's a good man,' Joe said. 'And he loves her. I'm certain of that. I don't know what that was about tonight on the deck, but I'm pretty sure she loves him, too – although I don't think we could get either of 'em to admit it.'

For Charles, that wasn't good news. For Charles, love was no kind of answer.

'Great,' he grumbled. 'That means Tom's got the power to *really* hurt her.'

Who were those stupid musicians who'd written that song a few years back? The song with the refrain that went 'All you need is love'?

Bah. What did they know about love, anyway? Love was certainly not all *he'd* needed, back when he'd finally found it. It was a curse, a cause of pain for everyone it touched.

What he'd *really* needed was to avoid love, to put up that newspaper barrier between him and his little blue-eyed daughter, because opening his heart to her would have meant just that – opening his heart. And God knows what might have happened had everything he'd locked inside escaped.

Maybe Kelly and Tom would be lucky, and they'd keep their relationship casual. Casual lovers having casual sex. No love.

No complications.

No heartache.

No endless lifetime of what-ifs and might-have-beens.

*

SUZANNE BROCKMANN

Mallory closed her eyes as David's hands slid across her bare shoulders and down her back.

He was silent. The room was silent. She could hear the sound of his quiet breathing in the stillness as he put more oil on his hands and gently, almost reverently applied it to her lower back.

And then he was done. He stepped back, away from her.

Damn.

'Thanks,' she said, turning to take the bottle from him.

For a half second, the look in his eyes was pure male. It gave his face an edge that was both frightening *and* exciting. David wasn't just skinny, goofy David. David was a man.

But then he looked embarrassed and apologetic, as if he was afraid that what she'd seen in his eyes might have offended her. And she wasn't at all afraid anymore. Because this man was David. Kind, sweet, wonderful *David*.

The phone rang. He crossed the room, grabbing a paper towel to wipe his hands before he picked it up. 'Hello?' It came out raspy, and he cleared his throat. 'Yeah, where are you?'

It had to be Brandon.

David glanced at her. 'But Mal's already transformed into Nightshade and—'

As she watched, he laughed. It was not a gee-that's-a-funny-joke laugh. It was a boy-you're-an-asshole laugh. 'Yeah, great. You get what you pay for. I know. Look, Bran, next time you cancel, don't do it thirty-five minutes after you were supposed to be here. When it's just you and me, I don't mind. But

Mallory's here. If you'd let me know earlier, I could have called her and rescheduled. Instead she came all the way over and—'

He met her gaze, shaking his head slightly, an apology in his eyes. Bran wasn't coming.

David hung up the phone. 'God damn it, I really wanted to get these photos taken.' He ran his hands through his hair. 'Shit. *Shit*. Mallory, I'm really sorry. I'm—'

'It's no big deal,' she reassured him. 'I would have come over anyway to see the pictures and to, you know, hang out. I mean, if you didn't mind.'

He laughed as he turned away, as if he didn't want to look directly at her. 'Mind. Yeah, right. Look, why don't you take a quick shower and we can go get something to eat. I'm really sorry we didn't wait until we heard from Bran before you got oiled up.'

'You know what I think?' Mallory asked. God, she'd just had a flash of brilliance. David was so painfully polite, if she waited for him, they were both going to be a hundred years old before he even held her hand. What better way to do this? She took a deep breath. 'I think you should use a remote and stand in for Brandon.'

David laughed again. 'Oh, I'm *real* photogenic.'

'But you *are*.'

'What, are you kidding?' He gestured to himself. 'Look at me, Mal. Come on.'

She went to the table, found the pictures she'd taken of him yesterday. 'I happen to think you're extremely photogenic. You've got a good face. It's not beautiful like Brandon's, but so what? Why does Julian have to be beautiful? I think it's far more likely Nightshade would hook up with a guy who looks like you – a guy who's got a real smile. When Brandon smiles, it's so fake. When he smiles, you know what it makes me think?'

David shook his head.

'His smile says to me, "I love myself so much, I'd suck my own dick if only I could reach it with my mouth." '

He tried not to laugh and failed.

'Nightshade wouldn't waste her time with a guy like that.' She tossed the pictures back on the table as she went for the costume box, digging through it. 'Lose the glasses. I'll fix your hair – I've got some gel in my bag.' She found the Speedo and fired it across the room at him as if it were a giant rubberband.

It hit him smack in the center of his chest.

He caught it, held it up. 'I don't think—'

'Oh, no fair,' she said. 'I put *this* on. You're definitely putting *that* on.'

He shook his head. 'But—'

'Please,' she said, playing her trump card. 'This way I won't have to kiss Brandon again.'

Kiss.

As she watched him, she saw the word – and its meaning – register. For a guy who was one of the smartest people she'd ever met, it sure took close to forever for the old lightbulb to click on. But once it did, he was no fool.

'Of course,' he said. 'It's certainly worth a try.'

And he took the Speedo and made a beeline for the bathroom to change.

After Kelly showered, she cleaned her room.

Underwear and T-shirts in the dresser drawers. Other clothes in the closet. On hangers.

Who had she been kidding, anyway?

She was definitely living here, whether she pretended she was or not, whether she hung her clothes in her closet or not. She'd really done it – at thirty-two years of age she *had* moved back into her childhood home.

The circumstances were such that it wasn't quite as pathetic as it sounded. Her father was dying. She had reason to be here. Of course, the fact that she was divorced and child-free and completely available to move back in to care for him *was* pretty pathetic. If she weren't such a loser with her personal life, she wouldn't have been able to help.

And it had to have been at least *partially* her fault that Gary had cheated on her and gotten Tiffany Big-Tits pregnant. The theory being that if she, Kelly, had been such a top-notch, grade-A wife, Gary wouldn't have sought pleasure elsewhere. But Kelly had obviously failed wifeness. She was a great pediatrician, a decent cook, and an above-average personal assistant when it came to scheduling both hers and Gary's lives. But when it came to being a lover and sex kitten extraordinaire, she'd flat-out failed. She'd chickened out. She'd let Gary take the lead, waited for him to inch his way out on the tightrope of sexual adventurousness. Only Gary had never inched. There'd been no adventurousness. And after a while, there was barely any sex.

Because Gary had stopped seeing her as the babe he'd once worked overtime to get into his bed. Instead, he saw her as the nice, faintly familiar-looking woman who picked up his dry cleaning. Complacency had replaced passion.

Marriage was like that. It was a giant permission slip to be complacent. And Kelly was determined not to get herself caught in that trap ever again. She *would not* spend even an hour of the rest of her life completely invisible, with someone who'd learned to see right through her.

Of course, she'd done absolutely nothing to shake Gary awake. If she had bought the sexy underwear she'd wanted, if she'd pulled him with her into the phone booth-size bathroom on the train, if she'd gone to his office and locked the door behind her, there was a pretty good chance he would've been ready to sign on.

Tom sure as hell had.

She would never have believed she had the nerve to do what she did this afternoon. To go to him that way, intending to seduce him.

It hadn't ended the way she'd imagined it would, with his forgiveness, his understanding, and his agreement that their relationship was based first and foremost on passion, but also on their longtime friendship.

It hadn't ended with tender kisses and shared laughter, two old friends who were more than friends in bed.

It had ended with Tom zipping up and walking away as if she meant absolutely nothing to him.

That wasn't what she'd wanted. Or was it?

She'd wanted only to play at deep passion. She'd wanted only to pretend at a personal connection. She hadn't wanted to risk getting too close, risk falling in love, risk heartache.

Especially not the kind of heartache she'd felt the last time Tom had walked out of her life.

Who was she kidding here? Only herself, it seemed.

She'd defined the parameters of this relationship with Tom before it had even started. She'd built them a neat little box, and surprise! That box couldn't begin to contain this thing that they shared.

It was too big, too unwieldy, too dangerous.

The truth was, she was terrified of falling in love with Tom, of being devastated when he walked away again.

Yet even more terrifying was her fear of falling *out* of love with Tom. Even if some impossible miracle occurred and there somehow *was* a fairy-tale happy ending to this mess, complete with Tom as Prince Charming, standing at the front of a church in his dress uniform as she wore a white gown, there was no guarantee their happiness would last. In fact, it probably wouldn't.

And Kelly wouldn't be able to bear it if in eight years their conversation was limited to who was picking up the dry cleaning on the way home from work.

What she wanted was always to be the woman Tom gazed at with molten heat and burning need in his eyes, the way he'd looked at her today, in that closet.

Before he'd coldly turned and walked away.

God, there were no easy solutions.

Kelly unlocked the screen door that led to the balcony and went outside, breathing in the fresh ocean air.

Thirty minutes by train to Swampscott.

Fifteen to thirty to the car rental place, depending on its location.

Twenty minutes to fill out the paperwork, pay for the van.

Another forty, forty-five minutes home, depending on the traffic.

According to her calculations, Tom should be home pretty soon.

Kelly sat down on the balcony rocking chair to wait.

Eighteen

Mallory used about a half pound of hair gel and managed to glue down David's hair. She'd combed it straight back from his face, but there had been one lock that just didn't want to behave until now.

He was sitting at the kitchen table with a towel modestly wrapped around his waist. He didn't look as painfully skinny as she'd thought he would without his shirt on. In fact, he wasn't so much skinny as lean. He was built like a long-distance runner, with hardly any fat on him at all. His shoulders were solid, though, and his arms were actually muscular – a far cry from the pipe-cleaner appendages she'd imagined he'd have.

Not that she would have cared.

Well . . . Maybe she would've cared a little.

But not much.

He was sitting there so seriously. In fact, Mallory doubted he'd smiled once since he came out of the bathroom.

'Stand up,' she ordered him. 'And lose the skirt, Braveheart. It's time for you to experience the joys of baby oil over ninety-eight percent of your body.'

He smiled at that, but it was pretty wan. 'You know, Mal, I'm not sure about—'

She didn't wait to find out what he wasn't sure about. She just squeezed some oil onto her hand and started spreading it across his back. She knew it felt cool against his warm skin. Or maybe it was the sensation of her hands on him that shut him up.

'Come on,' she said. 'Stand up.'

He stood, but he held the towel with one hand, at his waist.

Mallory used both hands to put oil on his entire back. His skin was remarkably soft. She wanted to take her time, to make it obvious this wasn't just about putting oil on him for the photos, but she was nervous, too.

'Come on,' she said again, tugging gently at the towel. 'I'm starting to get oil on this.'

David took a deep breath and released a rush of air. 'Oh, my God, I'm just going to say it, all right?' He closed his eyes tightly, took another deep breath. 'I really like you, Nightshade, and I *suck* at acting, and there's a good chance that I'm really going to offend you because even though *you're* going to be acting, I'm not. I really want to kiss you, and with this little bathing suit, there's just no way to hide the fact that you completely turn me on, and I'm already more than half, you know, oh, God. I don't want to take this towel off and it's okay if you just want to be friends. I don't want you thinking it's only about your body because it's not, it's really not, I mean, it is, but it *isn't*, you know? And—'

Mallory would have liked him to keep going.

Everything he was saying was making her feel about as good as she'd ever felt in her entire life. It was okay with him if she just wanted to be friends. He *really* liked her – he wasn't kidding.

But as she turned him to face her, as she began putting oil on his chest, he stopped. It was as if she'd suddenly pulled his plug out of the wall. He opened his eyes and looked down at her, as if he were surprised to see her there.

'Oh,' he said. 'I can do that.'

She didn't stop. She just looked up at him, directly into his eyes. 'Yeah, well, I can do it better.'

He gazed at her. Didn't it figure that *now* he'd be silent? When she most needed his reassurance that she wasn't making a total ass of herself?

Her pulse was going so hard, she wouldn't have been surprised if he could hear her heart beating. She squeezed more oil into her hands, set the bottle back on the table, and ran her hands across the muscles in his shoulders. He had really nice shoulders.

Her voice cracked slightly as she said, 'Don't you think?'

He nodded then. 'Yeah,' he whispered. 'Oh, yeah.'

Mallory picked up the bottle again, and as she poured more oil into her hands, David reached for her. He touched her gently, the tips of his fingers trailing almost ticklingly lightly down her side, his gaze luminously hot as his eyes followed his hand. He touched her stomach, still lightly, touched her belly button ring.

It was all the reassurance Mallory needed. 'I'm not going to be acting, either,' she told him quietly. 'Not tonight. Not with you, David.'

'Yeah?' he whispered again, gazing into her eyes. 'Oh, my God.'

He smiled then, and her heart did a slow flip in her chest. It was impossible not to smile back at him. He leaned closer, and she realized he was taller than she was. Much taller. He had to lower his head to kiss her.

But then he was kissing her, and she didn't care how tall he was. All that mattered was David's mouth, David's hands, David's eyes. His lips were exquisite, his mouth soft and deliciously sweet. He kissed her slowly, taking his time. She could taste his hunger, yet he didn't try to inhale her completely, the way most guys did when they kissed her. And when he pulled her closer, he didn't grab at her butt or her breasts, the way most guys did – as if a kiss gave them permission to manhandle her. Instead, he kept his hands carefully high on her back, still skimming her bare skin so deliciously lightly.

She felt his towel fall off, felt it slide down her leg and land on her foot.

'I hope you don't mind,' he said as he opened his eyes and gazed down at her. His beautiful eyes were so warm. 'I didn't want the first time I kissed you to be for the cameras.'

He was romantic. David of the funny hair and awful plaid shirts was the most romantic man Mallory had ever met in her life.

When she kissed him again, he sighed his pleasure and she knew.

It was okay that she'd fallen in love with him. Her heart was safe in his gentle hands.

Charles had gone to his room, feigning fatigue.

Although, it didn't really count as feigning. He was tired. He was always tired these days. Less than three months left to live, and he was sleeping it all away.

He and Joe had arrived home to find the living room overrun with commandos. Tom's friends were a little daunting. The big black man named Jazz rarely smiled. And the Hell's Angel with chains on his boots and long hair kept circling the Vanessa Williams look-alike, pretending that he didn't want her around.

Hah.

If Boots and Chains had his druthers, they'd be sharing a bedroom before the night was out. But Vanessa, she wasn't born yesterday. She kept her head in her book, avoiding eye contact with Boots, clearly as smart as she was beautiful.

And she *was* beautiful. Charles had flirted with her a bit before he'd sought out the peace and quiet of his room. Her name was Alyssa. Even prettier than Vanessa. She'd smiled at him, and flirted a bit back, sweet beneath her drill sergeant facade.

Charles climbed into bed – a trick that could well have been an Olympic event among the nursing home set. He needed a hit from the oxygen tank next to his bed after achieving his nine point nine score. He figured he wouldn't get a perfect ten, because even after nearly sixty years, the German judges would still have it in for him.

God knows he'd given them reason enough to hate him – and that hatred was mutual.

Hatred and fear. It was a bad combination. Made for some really nasty cold sweat. And the Ashtons tried to avoid stinking whenever possible.

He'd spent nearly all of 1944 reeking. He could

remember standing in the dark by the train station on that uncomfortably warm summer night, certain that if the Germans didn't see him, they'd be able to sniff him out.

Every cell in his body was on edge as he stood there, watching and listening for approaching Germans as Henri and Luc Un planted explosives on that railroad track.

His heart was literally hammering in his chest. He couldn't see Cybele from where he was positioned, and it was driving him mad. He should have insisted she stay behind. He should have volunteered to go right from the first.

He should have made love to her when she'd come to his room.

And then it happened. Charles still didn't know what went wrong. All he knew was one second he was scanning the nearby woods for Germans, and the next he was on his face, spitting dirt out of his mouth, with the roar of an explosion ringing in his ears, and the heat and flames from the blast still singeing the back of his head.

Cybele!

He pushed himself onto his feet, only to go back down, hard. Christ, he'd somehow twisted – or broken, God help him – his ankle. Same goddamned leg he'd hobbled around on for weeks.

It hurt like hell, but he could do little more than grit his teeth as he crawled toward the spot where he'd last seen Cybele.

She was there, and she was alive, thank God. But in the light of the fire dancing up from the flaming railroad car, he could see that she'd been stunned, a trickle of blood escaping from her ear.

He had to get her out of there. He could already hear shouting in harsh German and the sound of barking dogs. The two sounded remarkably similar and equally terrifying.

Cursing steadily to fight the pain, he pushed himself to his feet, scooping Cybele up in his arms.

Joe materialized through the smoke. And Charles saw from his face as he looked at Cybele that he feared the worst.

'She's alive,' he told the other man.

Joe closed his eyes briefly. 'Thank God.' He drew in a deep breath, looking back through the smoke, toward the flames. 'Take her to safety,' he ordered. 'Henri's already scattered. I'm going back to look for Luc.'

Charles felt the heat, even from this distance. 'There's no way he could have survived that. Why risk your own life for—'

'If he's not dead, he's badly burned and probably dying. But if the Germans find him . . .' Joe's face was grim as he checked that his gun was loaded. 'There's only so much pain a man can take, and too many secrets to let escape.'

And Charles understood. Joe was going back out of more than loyalty to Luc. He was going back to protect them all. If Luc lived long enough for the SS to get their hands on him, Cybele's entire operation was in dire danger.

'You take Cybele.' Charles tried to pass her to Joe. 'I'll find Luc.'

But Joe moved back. 'Luc's my friend,' he said quietly. 'Keep Cybele safe.' Just like that, he was gone.

'Wait,' Charles said desperately. 'I don't even know which way to go, which way to take her . . .'

But the German voices were getting louder, approaching swiftly from along the tracks.

Charles faded back into the woods, limping into the darkness. Exactly where, he didn't know. Praying he wasn't heading directly toward more Germans, he moved as quickly as he could on his injured ankle, trying to protect Cybele's face from the branches whipping past them.

He hadn't gone far when he heard it.

A single gunshot.

Either Joe was dead or . . .

Or Joe had found Luc, still alive but beyond saving, and he'd . . .

Both thoughts were unthinkable. But it was hard to believe a patrol of German soldiers would have taken Joe down without a volley of machine-gun fire.

And then the bomb Henri had planted on the tracks blew, and Charles knew Joe was still alive.

Charles heard the tearing sound of the German guns, the shouting as Joe surely led the soldiers in the opposite direction from Charles and Cybele.

Joe was still alive. At least for the moment.

Charles pushed on, farther into the countryside, the night a blur of pain and fear. He was hopelessly lost, and even when he tried to chart his direction from the night sky, he wasn't sure which way to go. West and north to the fighting? Or away from it?

After what seemed like hours, he found a deserted farmhouse, its roof torn open to the sky. He'd found a tattered blanket, spread it on the dirt floor. And he'd held Cybele in his arms through the night, praying she wasn't injured more seriously than he'd thought, praying for Joe. Praying Joe had gotten away, praying for his soul, praying that he, Charles, would never have to do what he suspected Joe had done – fire that single shot and put an end to a good friend's suffering.

Tom was home.

He'd been home for an hour.

Kelly had been on the balcony when he'd pulled the van into the driveway. She'd watched as he'd parked alongside the garage, watched as he'd climbed out.

She'd watched as he went into Joe's cottage without even a glance up toward her windows.

She'd watched the light go on in his bedroom, watched it go out.

And still he didn't come.

He didn't want to talk to her. He'd rather stay away.

Kelly turned off her own light and climbed into bed.

She refused to be so pathetic as to cry herself to sleep.

So she didn't go to sleep.

They were supposed to be taking pictures.

But David couldn't bring himself to stop kissing Mallory.

They were standing in his apartment, both nearly naked, and the sensation of her fabulous body pressed so tightly against his was mind-blowing. Her breasts against his chest, her thighs against his, the softness of her stomach against his arousal, the silkiness of her skin beneath his hands.

Breathing hard, he pulled back from her. Or at least he meant to pull back from her. Somehow his hand got tangled in the string of her bathing suit top.

It was completely, entirely unintentional, but as he pulled, the string untied, and . . .

It had been tied so tightly that, with the bow gone, the knot slipped free. One second she was wearing the top of the bikini, and the next she wasn't. The next she was standing in front of him, completely bare breasted.

As a twenty-year-old heterosexual man, David had a natural affinity for breasts. He enjoyed them immensely, whether covered by a T-shirt or a sweater or a bathing suit. Breasts were like a happy, pleasurable living party. They were a blast of loud, pulse-racing salsa music in the otherwise too-solemn dirge of life.

Mallory's breasts were all that and more. So much more. She was beyond beautiful, with large rosy pink tips and milky white skin.

'Oh, God,' David said. 'I'm sorry, I'm—'

'I'm not.' She didn't move to cover herself. In fact, she reached up and untied the second string that was around her back. 'This suit's too small. It's really uncomfortable.'

She wasn't as matter-of-fact about this as she was pretending to be. David saw uncertainty and a trace of something else – fear, maybe – in her eyes. As if she wasn't sure he'd like what he saw.

Was she nuts? 'How could you not know how beautiful you are?' he whispered. He touched her. He couldn't stop himself from filling his hands with her, from leaning down and tasting her. 'Don't you know what you do to me?'

He suckled harder, and she gasped, pulling him closer, her arms around him, her legs opening to him, the soft, sweet inside of her thigh against his.

He couldn't believe this was real, that this was truly happening. Slow down, he warned himself. Don't push her too far. Don't assume this means she wants to go all the way. Don't make that choice for her. Be ready for her to change her mind.

But she put her mouth close to his ear. 'You know, I *do* know.'

He lifted his head. 'What?'

'I know what I do to you.' Mallory smiled at him

wickedly. She pulled apart from him slightly and pointed down between them and . . .

His skimpy bathing suit no longer covered him. There he was, in all his dubious glory, emerging from the top of the suit. He quickly reached down to tug up the suit, but that didn't help. The suit was too little and he was too aroused. 'Oh, God, I'm sorry, I'm—'

'Can I touch you?'

She was serious. She was actually *asking* if she could . . .

David nodded. He couldn't speak.

She reached out with one finger. One *finger*. Yet it was almost enough to make him lose it as she lightly ran it down his entire length.

'Whoa,' she said. She did it again. 'You ever, um, used this thing before?'

He found his voice at that. 'If you're asking if I'm a virgin, the answer is no. Believe it or not, I've done this before.'

'Hey, I didn't mean to imply that you hadn't or insult you in any way.' She touched him again.

David couldn't stand it. He kissed her, pulling her close, pressing her hand fully against him as he filled his own hand with her breast. Filled to overflow . . . He remembered the first time he'd spoken to her. If someone had told him then that he'd be doing this now . . . He laughed aloud.

She wasn't done with her questions. 'So who was she?'

'No one.' He kissed her again. This was *so* not what he wanted to discuss right now.

Mallory pulled her mouth away from his again. 'She had to have a name.'

'It was Janice.' David looked down at her and knew she wasn't going to stop asking until she got the entire story. So he told her. 'She was Brandon's girlfriend back in high school. The summer after freshman year of college, she used me to try to make him jealous. It didn't work.' The only one who ended up getting hurt was *him*.

And Mallory somehow knew. 'That really must've sucked. Did you love her?'

He looked into the softness of her eyes and told her the truth that he'd never told Bran, never told Janice. 'Yeah.'

'I'm sorry.' She nodded, so serious. 'Yeah, I didn't think you'd do it with someone you didn't, you know, love.'

He had to be honest with her. 'Mal, I'm a guy. There've been times when if I could have—'

'But *did* you?'

'No. I didn't exactly have the opportunity.'

'So how do you know,' she asked, 'if you really would've done it?'

That was a good point.

'This Janice bitch,' she said. 'You know, honestly, I'm *not* sorry she didn't love you, too. Because then where would *I* be? In love with some guy who's already got a girlfriend.'

David couldn't breathe. Did she just say in *love* with? . . .

Mal tried to hold his gaze, her chin at a challenging angle, but she couldn't do it. She looked away from him, briefly closing her eyes. 'Say something, David. Don't leave me hanging here like this.'

He pulled her chin up so she had to look at him.

'You love me?' His voice cracked, but he didn't give a damn.

She shrugged, her movement pure Mallory. 'What? You didn't think *I'd* want to do it with someone *I* didn't love, did you?'

Do it. She wanted to do it. Desire crashed into him, making his bathing suit even more ridiculously useless.

He was speechless again for just a little too long, and uncertainty crept back into her eyes. 'I mean,' she said, 'that's assuming we're going to . . . you know. Do it.'

And David knew. His entire life had been leading up to this very moment, this one night. Mallory *loved* him. She wanted him. He wanted to cry.

Instead, he took her hand and pulled her toward his bed. 'I love you, too,' he told her, fighting to get the words past the emotion that clogged his throat.

She kissed him, slowing them down. 'I know,' she said. 'I mean, I *hoped* you did . . .'

'I fell in love with you that day I first came to the Ice Cream Shoppe,' he admitted. 'I remember the moment I knew. It was when you told me to fuck off.'

She laughed. 'What?'

'You didn't really mean it. Well, maybe you did, but you said it to be funny, and I realized right at that moment that you had a wicked sense of humor and I . . . I fell in love with you.'

He couldn't wait another second, and he picked her up to take her the last few steps to his bed.

'Oh, my God,' she said, clinging to him, 'we're going to get oil on the sheets!'

'Do I look like I care?'

She looked down at his bathing suit and laughed again. 'Um, no?'

He kissed her as he sank back with her on the bed, ready to take his time. He wanted to worship her, make love to her reverently, explore every inch of her body with his eyes and his mouth and his fingers.

But she was in a hurry, tugging at his swimsuit, freeing him from its elastic confines. She struggled to get her own suit down her legs.

He helped her, and then they were naked. Both of them. In his bed. David laughed. He couldn't help himself. This was too good, too amazing, too damned wonderful.

'Do you have a condom?'

He stopped laughing. Oh, doom. He didn't. He wasn't at all prepared for this. 'No. Mal, I never dreamed—'

'I did,' she told him. 'I dreamed. And I stopped at the drugstore on my way over tonight.' She pointed to her bag, over by the kitchen table. 'Would you mind? They should be on the top.'

No, he *so* didn't mind. He pushed himself off the bed and found a box – an entire box! – of condoms. He tore the outer plastic, tore the little foil wrapper.

Mallory had pulled his sheet up over her body – how funny that she was so modest – and now she watched him cover himself.

But no sooner was he done than the sheet was off. She pulled him down alongside her and kissed him, long and strong and sweet.

He would've been happy just to kiss her all night, but she was the one who urged him on. 'Please, David . . .'

He'd been certain she would prefer to be on top, to take control, but she didn't seem to want that. So he shifted on top of her, gently pushing himself between her legs. She opened for him and he touched her with his fingers. She was so smooth, like satin.

Like heaven.

He couldn't wait. He pushed against her, sliding slowly into her, and then—

That was strange.

He pushed again, but he couldn't go any farther. It was as if he'd hit a barrier.

He pushed a little harder – resistance. Definitely resistance.

What the *hell*? . . . And then he knew. Realization dawned.

'Mal?' His voice shook.

She opened her eyes and looked up at him and he saw the truth. He was right.

Oh, God.

'You're a virgin.' Even though he said it, even though he could feel her tight around him, he didn't quite comprehend it. 'Why didn't you tell me?'

'Why didn't you ask?'

He'd assumed she was experienced. With her attitude and that *body*, he'd believed . . . And she knew what he'd believed. God, he was a jerk.

'You love me, David.' She searched his eyes. 'Right?'

He nodded, scared to death, humbled, ashamed, *exhilarated*. 'I don't know if I can do this. The thought of hurting you, even just a little . . .' He truly didn't want to hurt her, but the idea that he was the first – ever, only, because there was only one first time – was a total turn-on. She, Mallory, had chosen him, David.

She could have had anyone, *any*one, but she'd wanted *him*. And he wanted her, now, more than ever.

He moved inside of her, just the little bit he could.

'Tell me you love me,' she whispered. 'Please, David?'

'Oh, Nightshade, I do love you,' he breathed. 'With all my heart.'

He kissed her mouth, her face, her breasts until the room spun around him, until his need and his passion for her outweighed his fear, and then he thrust, hard and deep.

He felt the resistance give, heard her cry out, and he held her tightly, buried impossibly deep inside her.

He was trembling as much as she was. More.

'Are you okay?' she asked. 'Because I'm okay. I'm really okay.'

He lifted his head to look into her eyes. 'Are you sure?'

She smiled tremulously, then kissed him, raising her hips and pushing him even more deeply inside of her. 'Is this what I'm supposed to do?'

God, yes.

David moved with her. Slowly at first, then faster. He kissed her, touched her, loved her. *Loved* her. For her first time.

It was amazing – knowing, *absolutely*, that she loved him, too.

David could see the rest of his life, stretching out in front of him, a perfect, endless comic strip of laughter and song. And Mallory was there beside him, in every frame.

He felt her release, felt her cling to him as she exploded. It was all he'd been waiting for, and he crashed into her with such a surge of pleasure, his eyes teared.

'Oh, David, thank you,' she breathed.

She was thanking *him*.

David couldn't speak for fear she'd know he was crying.

But then she used the sheet to wipe her face, and he knew. Tough-as-nails Mallory was crying, too.

Because she wasn't tough as nails. She was soft and sweet. She was a total romantic – who had saved herself for love.

Charles was in pain.

It was enough to wake him up. Enough to bring tears to his eyes and keep him doubled over and gasping. Enough to make him grab the bottle of pills on his bedside table, to shake more than one into his hand and swallow them down with the glass of now warm water that was sitting there.

He also grabbed the phone. He clung both to it and to the knowledge that his daughter was just a speed-dialed phone call away as he waited for the pills to work.

He hated needing her. He hated needing anyone.

But it would take a while for the pills to kick in.

He groaned aloud. Maybe this was it. Maybe he was dying. Right now. Tonight.

He almost dialed the phone, but then he remembered. Kelly and Tom. Tom and Kelly. She'd invited young Paoletti to her room tonight. He was probably there right now.

Charles saw the way they looked at each other. Tom was *definitely* there right now.

More reason to call her. Stop them from going past the point of no return, from falling in love. It was so obvious they were dead wrong for each other. Either that, or they were a perfect match. Charles couldn't decide, couldn't deny that he both wanted them to marry *and* wanted them to run as fast and as far from each other as they possibly could.

Although, if they married, Charles wouldn't have to worry about Joe.

The pain grabbed him again. *Christ.* He clutched the phone. Joe. He could call Joe.

Yes, he could always count on Joe. Joe had been there for him, loyal and true, for an entire lifetime. Joe had forgiven him for all his indiscretions. *All* of 'em.

Charles was the one who had never truly been able to forgive Joe.

Or Cybele.

Cybele. He closed his eyes, praying for the pills to start working, trying to help along that drifting, free-from-pain feeling by remembering Cybele as she was in the sunlight.

He'd seen her far too infrequently in the light of day.

But that one day, that one bright, golden summer day, she'd belonged to him and he'd belonged to her – in the sunlight.

It was the morning after the explosion gone wrong.

Dawn had come and gone by the time Charles awoke, still exhausted, still in pain, still afraid of being discovered by the Germans.

He opened his eyes and saw the late-morning sunlight playing across the charred beams of the ruined farmhouse. He felt Cybele stir beside him and . . .

Cybele.

He'd been sleeping with his arms around her, her back to his front, his leg beneath hers, her head tucked beneath his chin, his hand possessively on her breast.

She turned now to look up at him as he gazed down at her.

He moved his hand, smiling weakly. 'Sorry.'

She didn't smile back. She just looked at him.

'Are you all right?' He asked it twice, once in English, once in his pathetic French.

She nodded as she pushed herself up, but then she sank back down, holding her head with both hands as if trying to keep it all in one piece. 'Where are we?'

He immediately missed the warm intimacy of her body next to his. 'Well, I've narrowed it down to . . . France.'

He wished he had water to offer her, but all he had was the whiskey in his hip flask. He took it out, and she shook her head. She had her own water, he realized, in a canteen left over from the Great War. The War to End All Wars. Hah. She took a sip, offered it to him.

He shook his head, preferring the hot jolt from the whiskey.

Cybele moved even farther away from him, leaning back against what was left of the kitchen wall. 'What happened?'

'Luc must've had a faulty fuse,' Charles told her, struggling with the French. Still, she understood from his sign language. 'His bomb went off too soon.'

'Luc Prieaux.' There was pain in her dark brown eyes. He wanted to hold her again, but he didn't dare. 'Is he dead?'

'I think so. I'm not sure, but . . .' He could still hear an echo of that single gunshot. Why raise false hopes? 'Probably, yes. I'm sorry.'

She took a deep breath. 'What of Henri?' she asked. 'And Guiseppe?'

'I think Henri got away,' Charles told her. 'As for Joe . . . I

SUZANNE BROCKMANN

don't know. Last I heard, he was leading the Germans in the other direction so I could get you to safety.'

She closed her eyes, and he wondered if she believed in God. He wondered if she were praying. For Henri and Luc. For Joe. For her own safety.

She was grimy, her face still streaked with the soot she'd used to blend in with the night. In the dark, dressed in men's trousers and a coarse work-shirt, with her hair tucked into a cap, she could pass for a boy – provided the person looking at her was old and half-blind. But in the sunlight her femininity was even more obvious. The graceful line of her neck, the delicate curve of her cheek. Her too-slender wrists, long elegant fingers.

If the Germans found them, they'd have plenty about which to question them, particularly with last night's sabotage fresh in their memories.

'We should wash,' Charles said abruptly. He wanted to get her to the safety of her home even more than he wanted to hold her again.

Cybele slowly pulled herself up, looking out the empty shell of a broken window. 'I think I know where we are. There's a stream nearby. If I'm right, there's a trail through the woods we can use to head toward Ste.-Hélène. We should go.'

'You should go. I can't even stand up.' He gestured to his ankle, now swelling out of the top of his boot. It looked awful. Christ, maybe it was broken.

'Mother of God.' She knelt beside him. Her touch was gentle, but still Charles had to bite back a curse. 'Did you walk all this way on that? Carrying me?'

'No,' he said. 'I ran.'

She looked at him, eyes wide, and he realized she'd misunderstood.

414

'I ran because I was afraid,' he explained. 'See, it's what I've been trying to tell you. I'm really good at running away. Fear trumps pain. I didn't feel a thing. Cowards usually don't.'

Her eyes turned stormy. She didn't understand half of what he'd said, but she understood enough. 'Why do you always pretend to be someone you're not?'

He was just as frustrated. 'Why do you insist on seeing some kind of hero when you look at me?'

'I see what I see.' Cybele stood up. 'Take off your boot. I'll check if there's water in the well in the yard. If so, it'll be cool. We can soak your ankle in it. If not, we'll figure out a way to get you to that stream.'

'I'll go to the well,' he said, struggling to pull himself up. 'Don't you go out there without me.'

'You said you can't even stand up.'

'Yes, I can. I was lying. See, I'm a liar, too.'

'I already know that,' she whispered, then turned away.

'Cybele.' Charles tried to follow, cursing and hopping.

She was back with a bucket of water before he'd painfully navigated his way around a pile of debris. His ankle wasn't broken. He wouldn't have been able to hobble on it if it were.

'Sit,' she ordered him back to the blanket he'd spread out on the floor. Her face was already clean, and she dipped the end of her shirt into the water.

'I can—'

'Be still.'

He let her kneel beside him and wash his face. He tolerated – yeah, sure – the sensation of her hands against his face, the sight of the softness of her belly as she pulled her shirt up slightly. But he couldn't keep quiet. 'You should go back alone. I can't possibly move fast enough. I'll put you into danger.'

'No,' she said with her customary, take-charge command. 'We'll wait until dark, and we'll go together. Slowly.'

'Cybele—'

She looked down at him. 'You want me to leave you here?'

'Once you get back, you can send Joe or—'

'Would you leave me?' There was no escaping the directness of her gaze, no denying that what he really wanted was to pull her into his arms, to kiss her, to love her. Would he leave her?

In a perfect world? Never. But this was no perfect world. 'Yes.'

She laughed. 'You are a liar.' But then her gaze softened, and she touched his face, gently pushing his hair back.

'I would. In a heartbeat.' He was desperate for her to stop touching him, but he couldn't make himself back away. He used words instead to try to regain the proper distance between them. 'Why do you think I'm in such a hurry to return to the American side of the line?'

It didn't work. She dried his face gently with the loose sleeve of her shirt, that soft look never leaving her eyes. 'Because despite what you think, you are a hero. Because you're torn between what you want and what you believe is right.'

Charles laughed. Or maybe it was a sob that exploded out of him. It was difficult to tell. 'A hero.' He grabbed her wrist, pulling her far too roughly toward him. 'Would a hero do this?' He kissed her bruisingly hard.

She wouldn't let him hurt her. She melted into him, taking his anger and returning it to him as passion. And it was. When Charles lifted his head to gaze down at her, only need – a powerful, burning need – remained.

He was going to kiss her again. He knew it and she knew it. It was wrong, but he was going to kiss her. And then . . .

'The world has gone crazy. Nothing makes sense anymore,' Cybele whispered. 'All I want – just for these few hours, this one single day – is to forget all the pain, all the horror. I want only you, and me, and this beautiful summer day. This makes sense to me, Charles. It makes so much more sense than anything I've known or done in years.'

She touched his face, leaned forward to gently press her lips to his. 'But I don't want this day angry. I don't want it filled with guilt and pain. I want it pure and clean and perfect, just this beautiful glimpse of what might have been.'

Cybele kissed him again. 'Please, Charles. Just this one day. It's all I'll ever ask of you.'

Charles caught her mouth with his, kissing her deeply, filling his soul with her light and life. With a groan of defeat, he pulled her back with him onto the blanket he'd found last night.

Their clothes fell away. She must've done it somehow. It seemed like magic, her smooth skin beneath his fingers, pale and cool against his heat.

She was beautiful, more beautiful even than he'd dreamed. He wanted to look, to touch, to taste. To slow time down. If he only had this one day, he wanted it to be endlessly long.

But she drew him to her, careful of his injured ankle, and he loved her with his body as well as his heart and soul – pure and clean and perfectly, just as she'd asked.

She whispered his name as her eyes burned into his, and he spilled his seed deep inside of her, knowing, for the first time in his life, what it truly meant to make love.

A shaft of sunlight streamed in through the broken roof, and it sparkled on her eyelashes, kissed the smooth perfection of her freshly washed cheeks, made her brown hair gleam. As she looked up at him, her eyes were dreamy, still lost in the *breathless wonder of their joining. She reached up and touched his hair, his face.*

'Angel,' she whispered.

Charles shook his head. What could he say? No guilt, no pain, no anger – yet they threatened to overwhelm him. He kissed her to banish them, then rolled over, pulling her into his arms.

He lay silently for a long time, holding her close, her heart beating against his. He watched the dust that hung in sunlight, refusing to think, just drifting.

Drifting.

Loving Cybele and drifting.

No pain. No anger.

Just Cybele in his arms, in his heart.

Just Cybele.

Kelly awakened with a start, sitting bolt upright in her bed, heart pounding.

And for good cause. Because there, standing in the balcony doorway, a dark shadow backlit by the waxing moon, was Tom.

He didn't move, didn't speak.

The clock on her bedside table read 3:38. Dear God, it was late.

She could hear it ticking as she gazed at him, as she willed him to come farther in.

But he didn't.

'I can't stay away,' he finally said, his voice low and rough in the darkness. 'I tried, but I can't do it.'

Kelly's heart was in her throat. She held out her hand to him.

But still he didn't move. 'I didn't come here to talk, Kelly.'

'I don't care,' she whispered.

He moved toward her slowly, one step at a time. As he drew closer, she saw he wasn't wearing a shirt, and the muscles in his chest and arms stood out in stark relief in the dim moonlight. He wore only cargo shorts, low on his lean hips. And he stepped out of them at the side of her bed.

'See, that's the problem,' he said softly. 'Because I do.'

She didn't understand, and then she didn't try to understand as he slipped into her bed, as he took her in his arms and kissed her.

And then neither of them said another word.

Nineteen

12 August

'Go home,' Tom said. 'Go someplace else – go *any*where else.'

Jazz sat in silence, rereading the email WildCard had sent just this morning. It was written vaguely enough to be sent through cyberspace, but for both Tom and Jazz, the meaning was perfectly clear. 'The subject of your inquiry is believed to have permanently left the building four days after the "Twist and Shout" clusterfuck. Reliable source cites eyewitness, also reliable, who claims to have been present at the departing event. IMO, it's the real deal. To quote my favorite doctor, he's dead, Jim.' He being, of course, the Merchant.

WildCard had found a reliable source who in turn knew someone else who claimed to have been present at the Merchant's death.

Jazz shrugged. 'Eyewitnesses been wrong before.'

'Yeah, but this time it looks like *I'm* the eyewitness

who's wrong.' Tom swore. 'I'm the eyewitness who's fucking crazy.'

Jazz thought about that for half a second. 'Maybe. Maybe not. We're here. Let's play out the maybe-not scenario. It's only a few more days until this celebration thing starts.'

Tom shook his head. He felt like shit. His headache was back, and he was exhausted. He'd slept only about an hour and a half last night.

In Kelly's bed.

He hadn't meant to stay. He'd meant to have sex with her and leave. But she'd collapsed on top of him, and didn't move. She seemed content not to talk – and for good reason. She'd fallen asleep. So he'd told himself he'd stay for just a little while. He'd wait until she was completely asleep before he moved out from under her. But a little while had stretched into a long while, and he'd woken up at dawn, still beside her.

He'd left then, afraid she'd stir, unable to face her when she awoke.

He still didn't want to talk. Even last night, with so little said, he'd managed to say too much.

Yet he'd lingered next to Kelly's bed, watching her as she slept. Wanting her still.

Today he knew for sure what he'd only guessed in the darkest hours of the night. He *had* to stay away from her. As much as he was trying to keep this thing between them just sex, he couldn't do it. And he was going to end up completely trashed when all was said and done.

Jazz had already gotten back to work, scaring up the surveillance equipment they needed to outfit the van.

This folly – *his* folly – was costing money.

'God damn it,' Tom ground out, 'let's just shut this down now.'

But the phone rang before Jazz could answer him.

Jazz picked it up, handed it to him. 'It's your sister.'

Perfect. Just what he needed. Some of Angela's crap. As if his day weren't already foul enough. 'Yeah,' he said, 'Ang. What's up?'

'Tommy, it's Mallory.' Her voice was shaking.

Tom sat up. 'What happened? Is she hurt?'

'She didn't come home last night.'

Oh, shit. He didn't need this now. 'What, have you two been fighting again?'

'No. Not at all. She left a note saying she was staying at a friend's house—'

'She left a note.' That was more than Angie usually did when *she* went missing. Tom shook his head. In the past, it had been Mal calling with a quiver in her voice, wondering if he'd seen Angela. 'What's the big deal?'

'The big deal is that this so-called friend is named *David*. He's that college boy she's been seeing so much of. The one who lent her that camera?'

What camera? 'David.' Tom vaguely remembered David. 'Dark hair, glasses?'

'I don't know what he looks like. You think she'd bring him home and introduce him to me? The only things I know for sure about him are that he works the breakfast shift at the hotel and he's male. He'll get her pregnant, Tommy, and then where will we be?' Angela started to cry. 'I wanted more for her, but it's so hard raising a child alone, without a man in the house.'

Jesus H. Christ. Tom sighed. 'Don't cry, all right? What do you want me to do?'

*

'Who's at the door?'

Tom could hear Mallory's voice from inside the apartment.

'Well, I guess I'm in the right place,' he said to the skinny young man standing wide-eyed in front of him.

He had to give David credit – he was only speechless for a few short seconds. 'It's your uncle,' he called back to Mallory. He held out his hand to Tom. 'How are you feeling, sir?'

Sir. Damn straight the kid better call Tom *sir*. 'I'm fine. But Mallory's mother was a little concerned about her.'

Mal pulled the door open farther. 'But I left her a note.' She was wearing one of David's button-down shirts and probably very little else. She smiled at him, smiled at David, and for David, her smile was radiant.

David wasn't quite so relaxed. Although he smiled at Mal, he glanced warily at Tom. Still, he touched her arm, as if he couldn't bear standing near her without some kind of physical contact.

'So I'm busted,' Mallory said, still cheerful. It was amazing. *Cheerful* and *Mallory* were two words Tom had never thought he'd use in the same sentence. 'I spent the night with David. Have you come to drag me home by my hair?'

David stepped back. 'Maybe it would be better to talk about this inside.'

Tom went into the apartment, finding himself liking the kid. He wasn't the kind of man Tom would've expected Mallory to hook up with. He'd expected someone more like Sam Starrett. A crazy biker type. Or maybe one of those drearily self-absorbed, dirty-haired, over-pierced counterculture poets, living in squalor allegedly because one had to suffer for one's art, but truthfully because they were too lazy or stoned to do the dishes.

David's apartment was remarkably clean – taking into consideration, of course, that he was a man in his early twenties who was living alone. His place was a studio, with a kitchen in one corner, a table by the door, covered with shiny, color photographs. He had some kind of drawing board in another corner, a camera on a tripod, and a state-of-the-art computer setup, complete with a scanner and video camera. It looked like something that WildCard, too, would've considered bare necessities for a summer vacation. Forget about packing clothes – just make sure you've got the computer.

Tom was bemused. He'd never have thought Mal would hook up with a computer geek.

'Do you want some coffee?' Mallory asked, going into the kitchen to take an extra mug from the cabinet.

'Yeah.' A jolt of caffeine would help his headache. Particularly as he stood looking at the double bed in the far corner of the room – the sheets rumpled, a box of condoms spilled onto its side, and opened wrappers scattered colorfully on the floor. Busted indeed. Busy night, kids.

He'd intended to come in to preach safe sex and throw a few intimidating looks in David's direction. But David was not intimidated, and they obviously had the safe sex part handled.

Besides, who was he to preach safe sex when over

the past few days he'd had the most dangerous sex of his life? Sure, he and Kelly had used a condom every time. Kelly was always prepared. No, their sex had been dangerous because Kelly didn't love him, would never love him. She'd planned *not* to love him, right from the start.

And realizing that had ripped the heart out of his chest.

Because he loved her. That was his big problem here.

He'd loved Kelly for as long as he could remember.

He'd figured that out last night, as he was lying alone in his bed, trying his damnedest not to go to Kelly's room.

So here he was now, a fool and a loser, about to put a frigging damper on the joy and enthusiasm and, yes, sweet love he could see in both Mallory's and David's eyes.

Maybe it wouldn't work out. They were both so painfully young. Maybe Mallory would end up ripping David's poor heart to shreds. Or maybe David would be the one to hurt her. But whatever was to come didn't matter. Because for now, anyway, they'd found heaven in this crappy little walk-up studio.

'I'll go home and talk to my mother,' Mal was saying quietly to David now. 'And then I'll meet you downtown. Under our tree.'

They had a tree. Tom could've cried, it was so damn sweet. He and Kelly had once had a tree. The tree that held her tree house. There was a swing tied to one sturdy branch, and he'd met her there, every evening after dinner, for more weeks than he should have, considering how young she'd been at the time.

'I'll go with you,' David said. 'I'd like to meet your mother.'

She rolled her eyes. 'No, you wouldn't.'

He caught her hand, pulled her toward him, gently touched her face. 'Yes, I would.'

It was so obvious. This kid wasn't taking advantage of Mal. He wasn't using her. He was crazy about her. And if Angela had any brains in her head – and Tom thought despite everything that she did – she'd see that, too, and welcome David Sullivan into their lives with open arms.

Tom cleared his throat, moving back toward the door. 'I'm going to skip the coffee. And the long lectures, too. Safe sex, all right? No exceptions, not even if you run out of condoms at three in the morning on the one night the convenience store is closed, is that clear?'

Mallory laughed. David nodded solemnly, holding his gaze. 'Yes, sir.' It was more than Tom had been able to do when Charles had given him a similar speech just last night.

Tom turned to make a quick exit, but then stopped.

Wait a minute. He stepped closer to the table, closer to the photos. The Merchant. His face – his surgically altered face – looked out at Tom from among the dozens of brightly colored pictures scattered there.

'Holy shit. Holy *shit*!' He picked up the shots, looked from David to Mallory. 'Who took these?'

'I did.' Mallory was looking at him as if he'd snapped.

'*When?*'

She shrugged, glanced at David. 'Yesterday? Some the night before?'

Tom fished through the rest of the photos. There were more than one of the Merchant. There were three separate poses, all taken at the front desk of the Baldwin's Bridge Hotel. Another of him in the lobby, speaking to another man, both faces clearly in focus.

'I've got to use your phone.'

David's scanner was super high quality.

Tom had taken one look at it, and suddenly David's entire apartment had become Antiterrorist Central.

Although Mallory couldn't quite shake the idea that Tom was here only to keep her and David from spending the morning making love.

But no. Tom had hugged her. After he'd found the pictures she'd taken of that man he called the Merchant. After he'd called in reinforcements to come take over David's apartment. After David had realized they were about to be invaded and he'd started running around, making the bed, hiding the box of condoms she'd brought with her last night.

Tom had held her tightly and whispered that he thought David was a good one, that he'd always known she was a smart young woman, that he was glad, deeply glad that she'd found someone who loved her.

Mallory was glad she'd found someone who loved her, too.

She watched David now, sitting at his computer, sending electronic versions of her photos back and forth to some other computer genius in California. Someone named WildCard. He sounded like one of David's characters.

And this whole scenario sounded like the plot of one of David's graphic novels, too. International terrorist comes to wreak havoc on small-town New England . . .

It seemed pretty fantastic, but all these people – the big grim black man, Mr Skeevy Cowboy, and the humorless woman with the most gorgeous skin and eyes who walked as if she had a long-handled rake lodged up her ass – they all seemed to think there was a real threat.

And as long as David was having a good time showing off what his computer could do, Mallory was happy to hang out.

They were trying to compare two faces – those of the Merchant before and after he'd had plastic surgery. They were trying to do a bone-structure analysis to see if the man in her photos could be the same as the man in Tom's.

The black man named Jazz sat down at the table next to her. 'You take these pictures with some kind of zoom lens?'

His shoulders must've been four feet wide. Mallory wondered how he fit in the seats at the movie theater or on a bus. 'Yeah.'

'Thought so.' He held her gaze. 'He see you take 'em?'
'No.'

He nodded. 'You're lucky. If you see him again, Mallory, stay away from him. No more pictures, you understand? If he knew you took the ones you did, he might've come after you. He's killed for less.'

Killed? For pictures? The hair actually rose on the back of her neck. 'Are you serious?' Dumb question to ask Mr Grim.

'In fact, I think your uncle would probably appreciate it if you just stayed away from the hotel for the next few days.'

Oh, God. 'But David – he works there.'

'He does?' He turned to look speculatively at David. 'Doing what?'

'He's a waiter.'

'Room service?' Jazz asked.

'No, although they've asked him to work some of the room service lunch shifts. They're really short staffed. Why?'

Jazz smiled at her. He had a great smile. He could've made a fortune acting in toothpaste commercials. 'David's going to help your uncle save Baldwin's Bridge from the bad guys.'

'Oh,' Mallory said. 'Is that all?'

Charles looked up as Joe came onto the deck.

'Kelly said you were looking for me?' Joe asked, his hat in his hands.

Charles nodded, suddenly strangely uncomfortable. As if he were the employer and Joe the employee. As if he'd sent for Joe. Which he had, in a sense. But he'd meant for this discussion to be between them as friends.

So he didn't mince words. He just brought it straight to the bottom line.

'Pain got pretty bad last night.'

Joe looked searchingly into his eyes as he slowly sat down. 'Is it better now?'

Charles kept his own face impassive. 'Comes and goes.'

'I'm sorry. Is there anything I can do?'

Charles looked at his old friend. 'Not now but maybe soon.'

Joe gazed back at him, his eyes narrowing slightly. He may have spent his life as a simple gardener, but it was by choice. He was a very smart man, that Joe Paoletti.

Still, Charles spelled it out for him. 'When the pain gets too bad, then you can help me.'

Joe was silent, and for the first time in years, his expression was unreadable.

'You remember Luc Prieaux. The one I called Luc Un?'

Joe was already shaking his head. He knew what Charles was asking, and his answer was either no, or no, he didn't want to talk about this. Charles didn't blame him. He hated having to bring it up.

'I never asked you about him,' Charles said. 'I never really knew for sure. I always just assumed that he was still alive when you found him. I . . . I heard the shot from your gun, you know.'

Joe stared out at the ocean, his face terribly old. Thunder rumbled in the distance. A storm was brewing. 'I've never spoken of this with anyone but God.'

'I'm the only one who knows, Guiseppe. Besides, you did what you had to do to keep the rest of us safe. And see, I thought if you could do that—'

Joe looked at him. 'I did what I did for *Luc*. He was beyond saving, beyond talking, *far* beyond giving us away. He should have already been dead, but somehow, he still breathed. He was my friend, so yes, I did it. I put an end to his suffering. And not a single day has dawned since then that I haven't remembered him, that I haven't seen those eyes in that burned face . . .'

'You did the right thing,' Charles told him, his heart aching for his friend. 'You showed Luc mercy and compassion. God would agree.'

Joe just gazed at the horizon, tears brimming in his eyes.

Charles looked out at the ocean, too, at his beautiful ocean. 'I'm your friend, too.'

Tears ran down Joe's weathered cheeks.

The pain stirred within him, an echo of last night, a hint of what was to come. It gave Charles the strength he needed to go on. To ask this impossible, terrible thing of this good man.

'When I start a morphine drip,' Charles said, 'it won't be too hard to just . . . turn it up and let me drift away. Don't let Kelly be the one to do it, Joe. I know you love her, too. Let's not make this long and drawn out. Let's make it as easy for her as we can.'

Joe wiped his face with the heels of his hands.

'I'll give you a sign,' Charles told his oldest, dearest friend. 'A sign so you'll know when I'm ready to go. Like . . . like that Carol Burnett. Remember we used to love watching that Carol Burnett? Funny as hell, and beautiful, too.' He tugged on his earlobe. 'She'd do this to sign off. To say good night. Do you remember?'

Joe nodded, just once, his gaze never leaving the ocean.

'That,' Charles said, 'will be my sign.'

A storm was coming. Kelly went into the garden to see if Joe needed help stacking the lawn chairs.

But Tom's friend Jazz had already beaten her to it.

He passed her on the way into the house, but then turned back. 'Excuse me, Kelly, got a second?'

'Sure.'

'The lieutenant's had something of a tough day,' he said. 'I don't know what's going on between you and him, and frankly, I don't want to know. That's not what this is about. I just . . . wanted to warn you, and maybe ask you to take it a little easy on him this evening. If you can manage that.'

'What happened?' she asked.

He shook his head. 'That's not for me to tell you.'

Great. As if Tom would talk about it with her. 'Where is he?' Kelly wasn't sure if she wanted to know so that she could find him or stay far away from him.

'Last I saw him, he was down by that old tree swing.'

The tree swing. *Her* tree swing. And Kelly knew. She wanted to find him. Because if he was there, *he* surely wanted her to find him.

'Thanks,' she said.

'Hey, is there a good pizzeria around here that delivers?'

'Mario's. Number's on the fridge. Will you order enough for me and Joe? And Tom?'

'Sure.' Jazz gave her one of his rare smiles as he headed into the house.

And Kelly went back, behind the cottage, toward her old tree house.

She slowed as she saw him sitting there. The wind was starting to pick up, and the leaves were showing their silver sides, dancing frenetically, noisily. But he still somehow managed to hear her coming.

He turned away from her, and she realized with a jolt that he was wiping his eyes.

Kelly stopped short, uncertain once more whether to stay or go.

She almost left when he said, 'Well, hey, look who's looking for me. What's the matter, babe, can't wait until tonight?'

She might've left, but his voice sounded so rough, so raw, she couldn't walk away. 'Are you all right?'

'Yeah, I'm just perfect, thanks.'

'What happened?'

'It's a long story,' he said. 'Too long to tell. Because after five minutes with me, well, you know what'll happen. We'll both have our clothes off.'

She deserved that, she supposed. She gazed at him, uncertain of what to say. She'd apologized, several times. But obviously an apology wasn't what he wanted.

She had no clue what he wanted.

'I think we'll be safe enough out here,' she told him. 'This is a little too high traffic. Even for me.'

He might've smiled at that, but she wasn't quite sure. It was getting darker by the minute.

Kelly sat down on her swing, pushed herself off, stretching her arms out and leaning back to watch the leaves as they whipped in first one direction and then the other. 'Remember that one summer we used to meet out here? I know, it was never official, we never planned it, but *I* always came out here hoping you'd be here, too. And for a while you always were.'

Tom was silent. She glanced at him to make sure he was still there.

'I always thought we had this unspoken agreement

that whatever we said here, it wouldn't go any further.' Kelly gazed at him as steadily as she could, considering she was swinging back and forth. 'So. What happened today?'

'What *didn't* happen?' He nearly kicked the tree in frustration. 'So much happened, I don't know where to start.'

How about after he left her bed last night. What had he been thinking? How had he felt? With his passion spent, was there only anger left? And *why* was he still so angry with her?

He blew out a burst of frustrated air on a pungent curse. 'I guess it started this morning, with Angela calling me because Mallory didn't come home last night.'

'Oh, God,' Kelly said. 'Is she all right?'

'Yeah, she's fine. She's got a boyfriend, and she stayed at his place. I don't know what Ang's problem is. Mal's eighteen. And she left Ang a note.'

'Eighteen's a little young.'

'Mal's chronologically young, but not emotionally. She's been the adult in that family since she was seven.' He paused. 'How old were you when you had your first, you know, sleepover at a boyfriend's?'

A personal question. Kelly couldn't believe the way that made her heart race. 'Nineteen. I was in college. I was . . . in love.' She rolled her eyes. 'He wasn't.'

'That hurts,' Tom said. 'Huh?'

She nodded, tipping her head back again to look at him. 'I don't think I want to ask how old *you* were.'

He smiled, but it was rueful. 'You probably think I'm one of those guys who started having sex when they were twelve.'

434

She closed her eyes. 'Oh, God, I knew it—'

'I hate to burst your little fantasy about me as some kind of teenaged Don Juan, but you're wrong. I was sixteen. And I was selective. Throughout high school, I slept with only four girls. Women, really. They were all in college, all more experienced than me, and all leaving town within months of when we first got together.' He paused. 'Kind of like what we're doing right now. Together with an end date.'

'Are we together?' she asked, her heart in her throat.

'I'm not sure,' he said, his gaze palpably hot as it flicked across her body. 'But I think so. I mean, we've been talking for over four minutes, and I've managed to keep my pants zipped. I think what happens in the next minute could be crucial in defining whether we're together or whether we're just two horny people who like to jump each other's bones.'

'So Angie called you,' she said.

He laughed, but it was low, dangerous. 'Yeah. Angie called and I tracked down David and went over to his apartment, intending to put the fear of God into him and to drag Mal's ass home. Only it was so obvious that he's completely in love with her, and she's happier than I've ever seen her. I mean, not since she was four have I seen her this happy. You met this kid, David, didn't you?'

Kelly nodded. 'Briefly. He seems nice.' She cringed at her choice of word. Poor kid. Saddled with the curse of niceness.

'He is. He looked me in the eye, and . . .' Tom cleared his throat. 'He's a good man. So I give 'em my blessing, and I'm about to leave the apartment when I see it. David's got a camera, Mal's been using it to take pictures, and on his kitchen table, scattered among all these other shots of people, are four photos of the Merchant in the lobby of the Baldwin's Bridge Hotel.'

Kelly skidded to a stop. 'Oh, my God, Tom, that's *great*.'

'Yeah. It got better, too, before it got worse.' He hunkered down, his back against the trunk of the tree, arms around his knees. 'We used David's computer to scan in the pictures and send 'em to a guy named WildCard. He's the SO squad's computer expert – he's in California right now.

'Turns out David's an artist, and he and WildCard managed to take these new photos of the Merchant and run a comparison with the old photos, to see if, through computer analysis of bone configuration, it's even possible this is the same man. And the answer comes up yes. Of course yes means there's a seventy-five percent chance that they're one and the same. There's a lot of room there for doubt. So I figure before I call Admiral Crowley and hang myself out to twist in the wind, I'll get more proof.'

'Like . . . what?'

'I figured getting my hands on the explosives he's using to build this bomb might be a good place to start. Or hey, the bomb itself would probably even do the trick. So Alyssa Locke put on a dress and high heels and took one of the photos to the same desk clerk who checked the Merchant and his raftload of luggage into the hotel. She flashed the picture, flashed her legs, and—'

'That is *so* sexist!'

Tom laughed. 'Yeah. And do you want to guess how long it took her to get the name?'

'She got the Merchant's *name*?'

'Only the name he used to check into the hotel. It's not his real name, you can bet on that. But in three seconds Locke and her legs find out he's going by Mr Richard Rakowski.'

'Locke and her *legs*. God, I hate that.'

'Yeah, well, it's the way the world works. Women can go places and do things to get information in ways that men just can't. Jazz and Sam are so opposed to letting women join the SEAL teams, but it's not because they don't think a woman can get the job done. They think their own abilities will be compromised because they'll be distracted.'

The wind blew, hard, and a shower of leaves swirled down around them. Thunder rumbled ominously. But Kelly didn't want to go inside. Not yet.

'So you've got his name,' she said. 'What next?'

'David went to work – literally. The kid's a waiter at the hotel, and they're currently short staffed, particularly for room service. So we shined up Sam Starrett, brushed his hair, washed his beamish little face, and sent him with David into the supervisor's office. While Sammy filled out a job application, and the supervisor kept a sharp eye on him to make sure he didn't steal anything off the desk, David covertly accessed the hotel computer and found that Mr Richard Rakowski was in room 104.'

'How could this be bad? It's *great* you know this. You don't have to wait for him to build a bomb. You can just catch him. Why not just bring *him* in?'

'Well, for starters, because this is America, and when someone with no authority *catches* someone and takes them someplace they don't want to go, it's called kidnapping.'

'But you're a SEAL, an officer in the Navy—'

'I have no authority here, Kelly. Which is why I need to bring some kind of proof to the attention of my superiors, who in turn need to bring it to the attention of the FBI, who will then apprehend this scumbag.' His voice hardened. 'Don't get me wrong. If I have to, I'll risk kidnapping charges and grab him up. Starrett and Locke are watching his room right now. But after what we found out this afternoon . . .' He exhaled in disgust. 'I'm sure they're just humoring me.'

'What did you find out?'

'After learning he was registered to room 104, I did a little more research, and I was *positive* we'd got him. I found out room 104 is on the marina side of the hotel, on the concierge level – which is a fancy name for the ground floor. Room 104 also happens to be directly over the hotel's oil tank in the basement.' Tom laughed in disbelief. 'If I were going to take out the Baldwin's Bridge Hotel, that's where I'd start. With the oil tank right there, you'd get the added oomph of all that fuel. And a ground-level blast would do the most structural damage. It'd bring down the whole front face of the hotel.' He looked at her, frustration in his eyes. 'I was so *sure*.'

'I don't understand. Why aren't you sure anymore?'

'We went into his room.'

He said it so simply, but Kelly knew it had been anything but. If Richard Rakowski was the Merchant, and a bomb was in that room, his door would have been protected in some way. Booby-trapped, maybe. She couldn't even imagine the kind of security or warning systems the Merchant might have set up, but she knew that Tom could. And Tom and his friends had no doubt taken precautions. *We went into his room*. They surely didn't just pick the lock, turn the knob, and walk in. It had, no doubt, taken grueling hours.

'There was nothing there,' Tom told her, his frustration tightening his voice. 'Locke watched the front windows from up in the Congregational church tower, and Starrett watched from the end of the hall while Jazz and I searched the place. No bomb, no explosives, no suitcase filled with semiautomatics. It was just . . . a really nice hotel suite. He had only one suitcase, filled with golf clothes. There was an open bottle of mineral water on the table; we took that – for fingerprints. There was a nice clear set on it, which we sent electronically to a guy I know – who found a match right away. The prints belong to – guess who? One Richard Rakowski.'

Oh, no.

Tom rubbed his forehead. 'I need a shower.'

'Tom, are you sure—'

He stood up. 'I'm not sure of anything anymore.'

'Jazz is ordering pizza.'

'Great,' he said. 'Because I don't think they serve pizza too often in the nuthouse.'

He started toward Joe's cottage. She hurried after him. 'Being mistaken isn't exactly the same thing as being crazy.'

He stopped and looked at her, the wind whipping the trees crazily around them. 'I still believe this guy's the Merchant. I still think there's a threat. I'm still scared out of my goddamned mind about what a man like that could do in a town like this.'

439

She took a step back from the vehemence in his voice.

He smiled, but it didn't touch his eyes. 'Well, there we go,' he said much more quietly. 'There's the way to keep our distance. Crazy's okay, but obsessed doesn't do it for you, huh, babe?' He made a *tsk*ing sound. 'Too bad.'

Twenty

At 2315, Tom gave up and dialed Kelly's private line. He knew she was still up. He could see the light on in her bedroom window.

'Ashton.'

'It's only me. It's not about Betsy.'

'Oh, thank God.' Relief was thick in her voice.

'I'm sorry.' Tom felt like a complete ass. 'I didn't want to call on the house line and risk waking your father, but I . . . How *is* Betsy?'

'Much better,' Kelly said. 'She's been doing much better with this new antinausea drug that Dr Martin's trying. I mean, her long-term outlook is still touch and go, but . . .' She laughed softly and he clung to the sound. 'Is this really why you called me at quarter after eleven at night?'

He'd called because he'd wanted to talk to her, *had* to talk to her. But he didn't just want to show up in her room. They'd restructured all their boundaries this evening out by the swing, and he no longer had a clue about what she wanted or expected from him. But God, he was desperate. His hands were shaking.

441

'No.' He had to clear his throat. 'Look, I know I've been a complete bastard, but I . . .' He managed to stop before his voice shook. *Shit*.

'Tom, are you all right?'

The silence stretched on as Tom fought his tears, fought even to say one word. Fought and lost. *No.* Dammit, *no*, he wasn't all right. 'I'm sorry,' he said, and hung up the phone.

Kelly carried her medical bag as she ran across the driveway in her nightgown and a pair of her father's old boots that had been sitting in the mudroom off the kitchen.

Joe's house was dark, but the front door was unlocked. Nothing to steal, Joe always claimed. Besides, who'd rob his little house when there was that great big treasure-filled Ashton estate right next door?

She'd thought the rain had let up, and it had, but it was still coming down enough to make her drip as she stepped into Joe's living room. She pushed her wet hair back from her face, kicked off her father's boots, and took the stairs to Tom's room two at a time.

His door was tightly shut, and she stopped outside of it, suddenly scared to death.

She leaned her forehead against it, just listening, clutching her bag to her chest.

She heard what she was afraid of hearing, what she'd dreaded hearing. Choked sobs. Ragged breathing.

Tom was crying.

Oh, God. Oh, God. What should she do? She *had* to go in there, to make sure he wasn't physically hurt. The doctor in her wouldn't let her walk away.

But the woman in her knew that the last thing Tom would want was for her to see him cry.

Still, she'd been reading about head injuries. Even though his CAT scan had come back looking good, there could well have been a blood vessel in his brain weakened by the injury or the operation. She needed to talk to him, to look into his eyes, to take his blood pressure. To make sure his very life wasn't suddenly in danger.

And she needed that more than he needed her not to see him cry.

She knocked on his door.

There was dead silence from inside the room.

She knocked again. 'Tom?'

'Don't come in.' His voice sounded raw.

It was all she could do to keep from crying, too. 'I have to.'

'Just go home.'

'I can't.' She tried the knob. His door was unlocked.

His room was dark, but she could see him sitting on his bed. He stood as he realized she was coming in, tried to wipe his face. 'Jesus! Do you mind? Get the fuck out!'

Her voice shook. 'You can't call me, asking for help, and then expect me to ignore you.'

'I didn't ask you for help!'

'Then why did you call me?'

'Kelly, please, just *leave*.'

She went into the room, closed the door behind her. 'Oh, *Christ*!'

'Tom, I have to make sure you're all right.' She set her bag down at the end of his bed. 'Are you dizzy? Is—'

'It's not my head. It's my fucking life, all right?

Everything I've worked so hard for – and tomorrow I'm going to flush it down the fucking toilet! But I don't have a choice!' His voice cracked. 'I don't have a goddamned choice!'

He broke down, and Kelly's heart broke for him. She pulled him into her arms, holding him close.

'I'm sorry,' he sobbed. 'Oh, Christ, I'm sorry.'

'Oh, Tom.' She was crying, too. 'I wish I could make it right.'

Mallory woke up alone in David's bed.

It was still raining. She could hear it coming down on the roof directly overhead.

The lamp was on in the corner, by David's drawing table. He was sitting there, leaning over his work, his left hand holding his hair back from his face.

He'd put on a pair of boxers, but that was it, and the muscles in his shoulders and back gleamed in the light.

Mallory could feel her heart. It seemed to fill her chest with a calm warmth even while it sent her blood surging through her veins. Desire and peace. How could one person make her feel both of those things, both at the same time?

Angela hadn't understood. After she'd met David, she'd had only two things to say. Mallory's babies would have slanted eyes. And at least this one – meaning David – would never leave her, implying that he was a loser.

It wasn't quite the complete acceptance Mallory had wished for, but she was glad her mother had waited to make the crack about the eyes until David was in the bathroom. He'd find out about Angela's ignorance at some point, but now was just a little too soon.

As for her mother's other comment, Mal hoped with all her heart that it was true, that David would never leave her.

Angela looked at him and saw a guy with bad hair who was uncomfortable and awkward inside his own body. Mallory saw a beautiful man who loved her.

She didn't think she'd moved, but he glanced up from his drawing. 'I'm sorry, is this light bothering you?'

'No.' Mallory got up, wrapping the sheet around her, still uncomfortable with the idea of walking around naked the way David did so easily. 'What are you doing?'

He sat back to let her look, reaching for her, pulling her close to him, his hands warm and gentle.

She felt him watching her as she looked at the still-rough sketches he'd done. It was Nightshade, and she was in superhero mode, scowling at the leader of a mangy, cyber-looking gang.

'If I turn out to be wrong about you,' Nightshade was saying in David's perfect block letters, 'I will kick you so hard your balls will come out your nose. Do you understand?'

Mallory laughed as she looked at David. 'That sounds very familiar.'

He smiled back at her. 'It was too good not to use.'

There was heat in his eyes, but he didn't move, didn't kiss her. He just looked at her.

And Mallory looked back, losing herself in that falling elevator feeling that took her breath away.

She wanted him again. Wanted to make love. But ... 'The box of condoms says they're not one hundred percent effective. But it doesn't say how effective they are. I mean, God, are they ninety-nine percent effective or *ten* percent or—'

'I think it depends,' David told her. 'I think I remember reading that it varies from somewhere in the high eighties—'

'*Eighty* percent? Holy shit. That means that *twenty* percent of the time . . .'

'That's if you use them the wrong way,' he added quickly, 'or if they break.'

'Break.' Oh, God. She hadn't thought about that. Condoms could break. It was true. She'd learned that in health class.

'But if you use them correctly, they're close to ninety-eight percent effective.'

Mallory looked at him. That meant best case scenario, two percent of the time . . .

'You know, if I get you pregnant, I won't leave you the way your father left your mother.' David kissed her. 'If I get you pregnant, I'll marry you.'

'I don't want you to *have* to marry me. I don't want to do it that way.' She kissed him, too. 'I want to make love to you all the time, except that two percent scares me. Because that means for every hundred times we make love, then at least two times I'll be at risk to get pregnant, right? And all you really need is one time – I'm living proof of that. And if we make love three hundred times, then that's *six* times, and—'

David laughed.

'It's not funny. I'm serious!' But it was hard to keep a straight face, his laughter was so infectious.

'I'm not laughing at you,' he told her with a kiss. 'I'm laughing because you told me you want to make love to me three hundred times – which is really great news. It does things to me you can't even imagine. But right after telling me that, I'm supposed to try to explain percentages and probability to you?'

He kissed her again, longer this time, lingeringly. 'I can't get enough of you, either, Nightshade. I'm willing to take the risk – even if that box said fifty percent effective. But this isn't just about me, it's about you, too, and if you don't want to . . .'

Don't want to wasn't even close.

Mallory let the sheet drop.

Tom lay on his back on his bed, one arm around Kelly, the other up, elbow bent, over his eyes. He couldn't remember the last time he'd been this tired.

He couldn't remember the last time he'd broken down and cried. When he was fourteen, and his soon-to-be stepfather had beaten the shit out of him for something ridiculous, like a glass of spilled root beer at dinner, and his mother hadn't said a word in his defense?

When he was fifteen, and his mother had packed up all his things and told him to move into Joe's house for good, when she'd chosen that vicious bastard she'd married over her own flesh and blood?

When he'd found out that Angela had gotten pregnant and would probably never escape from this soul-sucking town?

When not-even-sixteen-year-old Kelly had whispered for him to meet her later, in her tree house, when she'd turned and looked back at him, letting him see in her eyes that she wanted him to kiss her again, that she *wanted* him, and he knew like a rock in his gut that he had to leave town as quickly as possible, or else he'd never leave at all?

Because *that* was really why he'd left. He'd told himself it was about her not being old enough. But he could have waited until she was old enough. He could've done it. For Kelly, he *would* have waited forever. He could have slowed things down, kept them both from going too far until she was ready.

She'd been in love with him. He *knew* she'd been in love with him. And if he'd stayed, they would've had what Mallory and David had found.

They'd have children by now, because he *would* have married Kelly. He'd be lying here on this bed with his wife, instead of his sometimes, almost lover.

Sure, he probably wouldn't be a SEAL, but hey, in a few weeks, he wasn't going to be a SEAL anymore, anyway.

If he had known then what he knew now, would he have left?

'The what ifs can really kill you,' he said.

Kelly lifted her head slightly to look at him. 'Don't play that game,' she said. 'You can't win.'

But he had to. 'What if I hadn't left that summer, Kel? What if I'd met you in the tree house that night?'

She laughed softly, lowering her head back to his shoulder. Her hand was warm against his chest, against his heart. 'I would've lost my virginity a lot earlier than nineteen.'

'I'm in love with you.'

He felt her freeze. It was funny, because she wasn't moving to start with. But he felt her get even more still.

Not a good sign.

'I didn't say that expecting any kind of response,' he

told her. 'It was just something I had to, you know, say.' Definitely time to change the subject. 'I went back to room 104 tonight, and I dusted for fingerprints. You know what I found?'

'No,' she said faintly.

'I found prints for Maria Consuela, Ginny Tipten, Gloria Haynes, and Erique Romano – all employees of the Baldwin's Bridge Hotel. I found some old, smudged prints for George and Helena Waters and Mr Ernest Roddiman, all previous patrons of the hotel. But I did not find one single other print for Richard Rakowski. There was nothing on the outside or inside of his suitcase, nothing on the buckle of a belt that was packed with a pair of plaid golf pants in that suitcase, nothing on the closet door or the TV or the telephone. Nothing.'

It had taken him hours to dust, hours to clean it up, all the while aware that the man calling himself Richard Rakowski could return any moment. His team was watching, and Tom was wired with a radio so he could talk to them. But their heads-up wouldn't give him much time to get out or even hide.

He pushed the pillows behind him, pushed himself so that he was sitting up. Kelly sat up, too. 'Yes, that's very suspicious – no other prints of his in the room except the ones that probably were planted on that bottle,' he continued. 'I know exactly what you're dying to ask. You're also dying to find out what the hell aka Richard Rakowski is doing away from his two hundred and eighty dollar a night hotel room at nine o'clock at night. Right?'

Kelly nodded. Her hair had gotten wet in the rain, and it was curling around her face as it dried.

449

Combined with the white cotton nightgown, it made her look impossibly young.

Tom reached for the alarm clock on his bedside table, turning it to face them. 'You're wondering why at nearly midnight I *still* haven't received a call from my team telling me our man's back in his room. And you're right to wonder. It's some kind of decoy room, some kind of . . . hell, I don't know. Maybe he's going to bring the bomb there at the last minute. Maybe it's a precaution designed to throw people like me off his track. Maybe *he's* the goddamned paranoid one.'

He gazed into her eyes. 'It's him, Kelly, I know it's him. I have these moments where I'm so completely convinced, I can taste it. And I know the celebration for the Fifty-fifth is his target. I know I have to tell someone. Only they're not going to believe me. I have no proof, I have nothing but an empty hotel room without any fingerprints, a set of pictures of a man who's basically got the same shape skull as the Merchant did.' His voice shook. God, don't let him start crying again. 'And then I start to wonder. Maybe I *am* nuts. Maybe it's the injury that makes me so blindingly certain it's him. But I've decided . . .' He had to stop and clear his throat. 'I have to call Admiral Crowley.'

He'd made up his mind tonight. Or rather, he'd resigned himself to making the call first thing in the morning. There really wasn't a decision to be made. There was only one right thing to do in this situation, and he had to do it.

Even if it meant giving up his career, his entire life.

'If I'm wrong about this . . .' He had to stop for a

second because his goddamned lip was trembling. 'If I'm wrong, if I'm seeing dead terrorists when I shouldn't be, then I don't deserve the command of SEAL Team Sixteen. If I'm wrong, I should accept a medical discharge. It's not what I hoped for, but there's no shame in it.'

'There's not.' She moved to push herself even farther up, to kneel beside him on the bed. 'But there's also a chance, with a few more months of rest, you'll be—'

'No,' he said. 'Once I call Admiral Crowley in the morning, once I sound the alarm, I'm not going to be given a few more months. My doctor's a captain who's wearing a choke collar – and Rear Admiral Tucker's on the end of his leash. I'll go before a medical board almost immediately, I can guarantee it. And seeing dead terrorists in Massachusetts isn't something even a bipartisan board is going to take lightly. If I do this – *when* I do this – there's a good chance that not only will I be discharged, but I'll be psych evaled to death – and confined for the duration.'

Kelly had tears in her eyes.

'But I can't not tell anyone,' Tom said softly. 'I can't just ignore it. And I'm running out of time.'

'Is there anything I can do to help?' she asked. 'To make it any easier? Is there someone I can talk to, or call for you, or . . . ?'

He shook his head, afraid to reach for her, especially after she'd pulled back, after she'd almost seemed to make a point not to touch him.

I'm in love with you. It was a stupid-ass thing to have said. He'd scared the hell out of her, even more than he'd done with his crazy talk about terrorists. It should have scared the hell out of him, too, but tonight he'd gone out to a point way beyond fear.

'Tom.' She was going to talk about it. She was going to let him down gently. She was going to try to explain everything that he knew was crazy about him loving her. 'About what you said—'

'No.' He stopped her. 'I can't talk about that. Can we please not talk about that right now?'

She nodded, silent. She wanted to go, she wanted to stay – he didn't know. He couldn't read her body language at all.

'Do you want me to stay for a while?' she asked, exactly as he said, 'You probably need to get back to the house.'

'Yes,' he said, while she said, 'Oh.'

'No,' she added. 'My father has Joe's phone number, so . . .'

'Just . . . For God's sake, don't stay out of pity,' he told her roughly.

Kelly leaned forward and kissed him. And when he reached for her, she slipped into his arms, as if she knew that was where he wanted her, where she belonged.

What if she never left him? What if he'd cut her off too soon and she'd actually been about to tell him that she loved him, too? What if he awoke in the morning to find her in bed, beside him?

She pulled her nightgown up and over her head, and then she was naked, his hands skimming the softness of her skin.

The what ifs *could* really kill you. He wouldn't play that game. He couldn't win. The future would play itself out. There was no way to know for sure what was to come.

Tom helped Kelly help him out of his shorts.

And then he lost himself in the here and now.

13 August

Charles stopped just inside the sliders that led from the living room to the deck. Kelly was already up and out there, sitting on the railing, her knees pulled up to her chest.

She was dressed oddly – in her white cotton nightgown and . . . his old boots?

She was gazing out at the ocean, watching the sun rise.

It was still windy from the storm that had blown through last night, and the skirt of her nightgown flapped. She looked tired. Dark circles beneath her eyes. Her normally healthy cheeks slightly pale. The boots didn't help.

He tried to turn around quietly. He knew the haunted look of a person who wanted to be alone. He'd encountered it often enough in his own mirror.

But quiet wasn't an option that came with his walker. The metal frame hit God knows what, and Kelly looked up.

She tried to smile. It didn't work. 'You're up early. Couldn't you sleep?'

She wanted to play it normal. She'd been sitting there looking despondent, as if she were about to break into some operatic aria of doom and despair. But now she was playing the 'Fine' game.

He tested her. 'Are you all right?'

'Sure. I'm fine.' She forced another ghastly smile.

'Right,' he said. 'Me, too. I'm just fine.' Dying, but doing it just fine.

Truth was, he'd been up for quite a while in the night, with the pain. His new bedfellow.

She looked at him closely. 'Are you sure? You look . . .'

She was too polite to finish the sentence. Like hell. Like pig crap. Like an eighty-year-old man who had cancer of the everything.

Now was not the time to tell her he needed to get his medication upgraded to first class. She was strung pretty tightly, as if she were about to burst into tears any minute.

'I'm fine,' he told her. He was good at it, too.

'Listen to us,' she said. 'My God, would you listen to us? Neither of us are goddamn *fine*.'

Uh-oh.

She slid down from the railing – a good way to get splinters in her butt. But she didn't seem to care. She'd snapped. If he knew his daughter, full detonation was imminent.

'You're dying,' she told him, 'and I'm . . .' Her lip trembled, just the way it had when she was a little girl. 'I'm scared to death of living.'

'That doesn't sound so fine,' he agreed.

'No. It's not. Tom loves me.' Her tears overflowed, just the way they had when she was a little girl. 'But I don't love him. I don't want to love him. I *refuse* to love him again.'

She ran from the deck, just the way she had when she was a little girl.

'Well, that's stupid,' Charles said even though she was already gone. 'I didn't realize I raised you to be stupid. You can't choose who you love. Where the hell did you get that idea?'

Tom took a gamble. He bypassed Admiral Crowley's office and called the FBI directly. He'd worked with Special Agent Duncan Lund a few years ago. And although they hadn't kept in close touch, he knew Dunk wouldn't have forgotten him.

He called the man at home and he spelled it out in detail – head injury, paranoia, doubt. It was two days to the ceremony and he was out of time. But Tom knew, from the way Dunk got more and more quiet, that he'd lost before he'd even begun.

Dunk had listened to all of it, though. And when he'd signed off, he'd told Tom he'd see what he could do to get people out there for Tuesday's ceremony.

But Tom didn't need a tracer on Dunk's phone to know the next number the FBI agent dialed was that of the US Navy.

He was screwed. But what had he expected? His entire day had started badly right when he had woken up alone in his bed.

Kelly had been long gone. He'd told her he loved her, but she hadn't even stayed until dawn.

Tom punched in Chip Crowley's home number, hoping he'd connect with the admiral first.

But he was put on hold for an awfully long time.

'Well, you fucked yourself good this time,' the admiral said in the form of a greeting as he came onto the line. 'I just spoke to Larry Tucker, who wants to send the shore patrol out to bring you in. Seems *he* just got off the phone with the head of the FBI's counter-terrorist division, who told him—'

'Sir, this threat's real,' Tom interrupted Crowley. 'This celebration is going to start with a high profile ceremony in two days, and I'm alone out here. I need help.'

'That, Lieutenant, is God's truth. You *do* need help. But right now, I fear you have put yourself in a position where you are beyond any help I can give you.'

'What can it hurt,' Tom argued, 'to bring in the FBI? There are going to be US senators here. Representatives from England and France. If this bomb goes off – no, Admiral, *when* this bomb goes off—'

Crowley spoke through gritted teeth. 'God damn it, Tom. Haven't you had enough? Can't you hear how crazy this sounds?'

'Sir, what if I'm right?'

'Son, you've had a serious injury that's affecting your judgment. What I want you to do is check yourself into the nearest military hospital.'

'Yes, sir,' Tom said. 'I will do that, sir. Next week, after this celebration is over, if I'm wrong about this, I'll go. But until then . . . Well, sir, there are people in this town I care a great deal about, and I'm not leaving them until I'm dead certain the threat has been neutralized or proven nonexistent.'

Mallory was still in bed when Brandon unlocked the door of David's apartment.

'Wow,' he said, as clearly surprised to see her as she was to see him. 'I'm sorry, I didn't know you were here.'

He pocketed his key, but didn't turn to leave. Instead, he went into the kitchen. 'I came to steal some of Sully's milk.'

'There isn't any,' Mallory told him, hiding the note David had left her on his pillow.

'Damn,' Brandon said.

The sheet was up to her chin, but she was naked beneath it. She pulled her arms under, too, hoping he wouldn't notice, hoping he would leave as quickly as he came.

But he didn't. Instead, he sat on the edge of the bed.

'Who would've guessed?' he said with one of his stupid-ass smiles that she'd once thought made him look so handsome. He may have been good-looking, but it was so superficial. His eyes were rimmed with red, as if he'd been out too late, drinking and partying. 'Gorgeous Mallory in our little Sully's bed.'

'He's not little,' she said coldly. 'Do you mind? I was sleeping.'

He didn't move. 'You know, Sul's been in love with his Nightshade character for years,' he said. 'Now that he's given her a face, it's only appropriate he should live out the complete fantasy and get to sleep with her, too.' He laughed. 'So tell me honestly, babe. Does he make you put on tights and pretend to fly around the room when you get it on?'

Mallory didn't laugh. She didn't even smile. 'Very funny, Bran. Go away.'

'You sure?' Bran winked. She couldn't believe she'd once liked the way that he winked. What had she been thinking? 'He's not going to be back for another few hours. And it looks awfully comfortable in there . . .'

He tugged at the sheet.

Mallory gripped it more tightly to her. '*Don't!*'

'Whoa, hey, relax, I was only kidding.' He stood up, headed toward the door, thank God. But he turned back to look at her. 'Sully's a lucky dude – living out that fantasy, you know? Kind of like getting a chance to sleep with Princess Leia or Counselor Troi. Yow! See you later, Nightshade.'

As he shut the door behind him, Mallory pulled the note David had left her up from under the sheet.

He'd drawn a picture of her, asleep in his bed, drawn himself leaning over to kiss her good-bye. And in a thought bubble over his head, he'd written, 'Can't wait to get back from work to make love to Nightshade again . . .'

Nightshade.

He called her Nightshade, all the time. *I love you, Nightshade.*

Oh, God. What if Brandon hadn't been kidding? What if David wasn't in love with Mallory? What if he was in love with Nightshade?

And she wasn't Nightshade, that much was clear. She only shared the character's face and body.

Nightshade was brave and strong and confident. She was a superhero.

Mallory was the illegitimate child of the town screwup.

And she knew with a sudden flash of fear that while David would never leave Nightshade, he'd probably soon grow tired of Mallory Paoletti.

Tom threw the telephone across the office.

Jazz didn't look up at him, didn't flinch, didn't even blink. He just finished his own phone conversation, ending it more traditionally by dropping the handset into the cradle.

'I got Jenk, Nilsson, and Lopez.' He spun in his chair

to face Tom as he reported. His 'sir' was silent, but it was there. 'However, none of them can get here before early Tuesday morning.'

'Shit.'

'Better we have them then than not at all.'

Tom rubbed his forehead. 'I'm not so sure about that anymore. In fact, if this thing goes off without a hitch, if I've been wrong about the Merchant from the start, I want you and Starrett and Locke to leave town immediately. I don't want you getting hammered for helping me.'

'There are worse things, Tom.'

Tom looked into the eyes of the man who'd been at his side for years. A man he'd want beside him if he had to go into hell and back. And there had been times over the years that they'd done just that. 'If I'm out, I'm going to push to have you take over the SO squad. You probably won't be given Team Sixteen. Not yet. But maybe someday—'

'I'm in no hurry for you to leave,' Jazz said evenly.

'Yeah, well, Tucker is.' Tom shook his head. 'Wherever I call for help, his staff has been there first. The state police had been warned I might be calling, and were ordered to ignore me. Even the local police don't want to talk to me. In fact, the Baldwin's Bridge chief of police had the frigging audacity to order me away from the hotel until the celebration is over. He told me if I'm seen there, his men will pick me up and escort me to the station.'

Jazz lifted an eyebrow. 'Gee, I'd almost like to see them try.'

'We're on our own,' Tom told his XO.

Jazz actually smiled. 'More power to us.'

*

Kelly found her father curled up in his bed, gasping for air.

At first she thought he was having some kind of attack or stroke. And then she realized it was pain. Charles was in awful pain.

She slipped the nosepiece from his oxygen tank over his head to get him breathing easier. And then she opened his bottle of pain pills and . . .

There were only three left.

He must've been double and even triple dosing for going on days now.

'How many did you take, Daddy?' she asked. 'How long ago?'

'Three,' he told her. 'Twenty minutes.'

Twenty minutes he'd been like this, bent in half in agony.

'Why didn't you call me?' The question was out of her mouth before she realized the answer was unimportant. She was here now. She could help him as best she could now, which, after he'd taken three pills – three! – wasn't going to be much. She put her arms around him. He was so skinny, so fragile.

But to her surprise, he actually responded. 'Didn't need to call. Knew you'd be down to say good night in a few minutes. Knew you'd come.' He closed his eyes tightly as if a particularly terrible wave of pain washed over him, clutching at her arms with hands that had once been so big and strong, but now were skeletal and gnarled. 'Can I . . . Christ, can you call the doctor for me? This stuff isn't working too well anymore.'

Kelly wanted to cry. 'There's nothing he can give you – not after you took *three* of these pills. You're going to have to wait. They may not be working to stop the pain, but if you take too many, they'll make you stop breathing.'

'Okay,' he said. 'Okay, then.' He opened his eyes as he let go of her, pushed her away. 'You don't need to see this. You should go, then—'

'The hell I will. I'm not going to *leave* you.' Kelly planted herself against the headboard of his bed, holding him close, as if she were the parent and he were the child.

'Cybele wouldn't, either,' he told her. 'You're a lot like Cybele – so strong and sure of yourself.' He closed his eyes again, his words coming in gasps. 'I'm not sure how much longer I can take this, but I just don't seem to die. Not last night, not today, probably not tonight. I'm not afraid of dying anymore – I'm afraid of this godawful pain.'

Kelly couldn't help it. She started to cry. 'I wish I could help you.'

'You can. You can promise me you'll look out for Joe.'

'I will,' she promised. 'I told you I would. I'll see he always has a place to live and—'

'Not that way,' he said. 'I know he's not going to be homeless or starving. I've left him enough money to take care of that. I mean the other. Take *care* of him. Try to make him understand that he really *was* the Hero of Baldwin's Bridge. He was ten times the man I was, Kelly. A *hundred* times. I don't know why Cybele couldn't love him, why she had to go and fall in love with me instead.'

Kelly had seen her father's picture, taken at age twenty-three, right before he'd left to join the US Army, the Fighting Fifty-fifth. He'd smiled into the camera, his eyes dancing with life and amusement. Joe had been a good-looking man, too, but Charles had had a magical air about him. He still had it, even at eighty. Even back when he was drinking and at his most cruel and verbally abusive, even then, the spark didn't quite go out.

She was not at all surprised that this Cybele would have chosen Charles, even over Joe.

'All I know is this,' he whispered. 'Listen. Are you listening?'

'Yeah,' Kelly said. 'I'm here.'

'I know you're here, but are you *listening*?'

'You don't need to talk right now.' As much as she wanted to hear what he had to say, she knew it was difficult for him to get these words out.

'It helps,' he said. 'Besides, you need to know. Because this is important, Kelly. You can't choose who you love. You can't say "No, I will not love you; yes, I *will* love you." You can't do that. When I met Cybele and Joe, I knew he was in love with her. And after about a week, probably even less than that, I was in love with her, too. Only, I was married. I had a kid. I had no business falling in love with Cybele or anyone who wasn't Jenny. But it happened, and I couldn't stop it. And Cybele was drawn to me, too – I still don't know why. I tried so hard to do the right thing, to stay away from her, but in the end I failed. I gave in, and do you know, I would've sold my soul to the devil to be free to love her, to spend my life with her. I loved her that much. It was that strong, that powerful.'

He was silent then for a moment, and Kelly prayed

the pills he'd taken were starting to work against his pain.

'Only I refused to admit it at first,' Charles said quietly. 'For more than a week, I let myself wallow in my failings – the fact that with my embracing this wondrous thing, this love, I hurt my wife, I hurt Joe. But I ended up hurting myself and Cybele even more, because I wasted the precious time we had together.

'Cybele once told me that on the day that her husband and son were killed, she made them breakfast, but she didn't take the time to sit down at the table and eat with them. She told me she would spend the rest of her life wishing she'd given herself those extra moments with them. She wished she'd watched her boy eat his porridge, wished she'd kissed her husband good-bye. She wished she'd held her son close instead of merely wiping his mouth with a wet cloth. She wished she'd told them she loved them before they left her kitchen and her life for good.

'She told me all that,' Charles said to Kelly, 'and I *still* didn't understand. It wasn't until it was too late . . .'

He was starting to relax. Kelly could tell from the way he was leaning against her. She helped him down, into his bed, beneath the covers, but she didn't leave. She sat with him, gently stroking his hair, holding his hand.

'It was the night we found out about the German plan to crush the Fifty-fifth.' His voice was softer, weaker, but he seemed to want to keep on talking, and God, she wanted to hear this.

Her father, giving her advice of the heart. It was

unbelievable. It was more than she'd ever hoped possible.

'I'd hurt my ankle again about a week before, and I was finally strong enough to travel. I was going to leave Ste-Hélène, cross the line, get back to the Fifty-fifth. Joe was going to take me as far as he could.

'I didn't say good-bye to Cybele. I think I probably knew if I'd so much as spoken to her, I would've admitted how much I loved her. I was afraid of making her promises I wouldn't be able to keep when sanity somehow returned.' Charles smiled sadly at Kelly. 'I fully expected sanity to return, but it never did. Never.

'So we left Ste-Hélène, Joe and I, just after dark. It was a clear night, a warm night, and we headed north and west along a trail through the woods both Joe and Cybele often used. Each step of the way, I remember thinking, how could I leave? How could I have gone without saying *some*thing? How could I return to Baldwin's Bridge without gazing at least once more upon her face? And I realized then that I must've somehow known. I must've done it on purpose, left without saying good-bye – so that I'd *have* to return to Ste-Hélène before I went back to the United States for good. I *would* see Cybele again. And I knew right then, at the lightness and joy in my heart at the thought of going back, that I loved her beyond all else. The house in Baldwin's Bridge – this house – that I'd spoken of and longed to return to so often throughout my ordeal in France, my fortune, my family, my wife, my life. It all meant nothing to me compared to the love I'd found with Cybele.'

He was silent then, his eyes closed, and as much as

Kelly wanted him to sleep, she found herself hoping he was only resting.

'What happened?' she whispered. 'Why didn't you stay in France, Daddy?'

The pills he'd taken were working now, and working well. As he opened his eyes to look up at her, he seemed to look right through her, as if he could see all those years into his own past.

'We hadn't gone more than seven miles, Joe and I, when Cybele caught up with us. She'd been running all that way after us, but she still had the energy to slap me, hard, across the face, when she found us. I, of course, kissed her. She was so angry, but I kissed her, and I told her all that I'd realized. That I was coming back to Ste-Hélène after the war. That I loved her. That I would do anything for her. Even die.'

Her father laughed softly, his eyes still so distant, and Kelly knew he saw her – his Cybele.

'She cried, and told me that was something she never wanted – for me to die for her. She would not allow that. Not ever.' He shook his head. 'Poor Joe. It must've been torture for him to stand there and listen to us declare our love – he loved her just as much as I did. Probably even more.

'But then Cybele told us why she'd followed. It wasn't to slap me across the face, although she'd been happy to get a chance to do that. She told us of a coming German counter-offensive. She had papers she'd been given, papers that spelled out the attack, that needed to get into Allied hands before dawn.

'So we went. The three of us. There were Germans everywhere as we moved toward the line. It was impossibly dangerous – I've never been that afraid.'

His voice shook. 'Then Joe was wounded, and things went from bad to worse. He slowed us down, but we couldn't leave him. How could we leave him? We were moving through a town – I never even knew its name, but the houses were all rubble, the streets impossible to pass through.

'We were trapped there,' he said flatly. 'We were hiding in the debris, hiding from a patrol of Germans. They were coming straight toward us. It was over. I knew it was over. But I had my gun drawn. I was going to take out as many of them as I possibly could, and dammit, at that moment, I could have done it. I could have killed them all, and we could have gotten away. The hell with the fact they had machine guns, and I had only that little Luger. But I didn't get a chance to try because Cybele, she handed me those papers and her gun, her Walther PPK. I didn't understand. God, I was so stupid.'

There were tears in his eyes, and Kelly's heart was in her throat.

'She kissed me,' he whispered. 'She looked into my eyes, and she said, "I love you." And then, before I could stop her, she ran. Back the way we'd come, as fast as she could – and she was fast.'

His lip trembled and a single tear escaped, rolling down his gray cheek. 'The Germans chased her. They opened fire. I saw their bullets hit her, I saw her fall. I knew she was dead, just like that, she was *dead*! But I also knew that unless I moved fast, I wouldn't get those papers and Joe to safety. She'd died so I could do that, so somehow I did. To this day, I don't know how I managed it – to evade the Germans and carry Joe across the line. I left him where he would be found, made sure those papers got into the right hands. Then I grabbed a gun and joined the fighting. I think I probably tried to die, but I didn't. God knows I wanted to. It wasn't until the war was over that Joe managed to find me. He knew he hadn't crossed that line on his own, but when they came to talk to me about that Medal of Honor, I denied being there. I didn't want it. I didn't deserve it.'

He was silent for a moment, and Kelly was, too. There was nothing she could say.

'For a long time I hated Joe – for having been wounded, for keeping us from moving quickly and being trapped in the first place. I've never forgiven him for that. I've never forgiven Cybele, either.'

'How about yourself?' Kelly asked softly. 'Have you forgiven yourself?'

He shook his head. 'Look what I did with this life that Cybele gave me. Fifty-six years, and I failed to live up to what she expected from me. I was her hero. Yet I went home and couldn't even keep my marriage to Jenny together after little Charlie died. Two more marriages, both total flops. Some hero – sitting on the deck drinking himself to death, lazy son of a bitch.

'Cybele gave me the most precious gift of all, the gift of life. And here I am, lying in this bed, looking at the single good thing I ever did – and it happened by accident. *You* happened by accident. You're an amazing woman, Kelly, and I'm deeply proud of you, but who you are is no thanks to me.'

Kelly couldn't speak, could barely see through the tears in her eyes.

'I love you,' Charles told her. 'You and Cybele. All my life. You know, if she'd lived, I would've given up my future to be with her. I would have dealt with Jenny's pain and anger. I would have handled my father's shame. I would have done anything. I would have faced my biggest fears.

'You can't choose who you love, Kelly, but you *can* waste it. Why on earth would anyone want to waste it?'

His eyes closed.

His breathing was slow and steady. He was free from pain – physical pain – at least for now.

Twenty-one

14 August

The traffic was crazy.

Kelly pulled into the parking lot by the movie theater, planning to walk the rest of the way to the drugstore to pick up her father's newest prescription.

Baldwin's Bridge was bursting with the usual summer tourists as well as all the people flocking into town for the Fifty-fifth celebration tomorrow.

The marina was crowded, too. There were lots of people coming in via sailboat and pleasure yacht. Even more people were taking advantage of the beautiful weather and going out for day trips, resulting in an overabundance of little boats on both sides of the stone breakers at the harbor's entrance.

Over by the hotel, she could see containers of folding chairs ready to be set up on the lawn first thing in the morning. Workmen were constructing a portable stage for the dignitaries. And there, off to the side, parked on the street, was the SEAL mobile. The van with tinted windows that Tom and his friends had outfitted with high-tech surveillance equipment.

So this was where they all were.

Kelly had awakened this morning to a silent and empty house. Even Charles, who'd had such a tough night, had been gone by the time she went downstairs.

She'd been disappointed.

She'd hoped to see Tom. She'd *wanted* to see Tom.

But his makeshift office had been empty.

Just as empty as his bedroom had been last night when she'd crept into the cottage, hoping to find him, hoping to tell him . . . what? She still didn't know.

All she knew was that she wanted to be with him. She wanted to be near him.

And right now she wanted to help him. In any way that she could.

She headed for the van, knocked on the back door.

She sensed some kind of movement behind the darkly tinted glass, but the door didn't open. Nothing moved.

She knocked again.

'It's Dr Ashton.' Mallory's voice came in loud and clear over Tom's headset.

Kelly. 'What does she want?' he asked.

Charles's voice came over the radio from his lookout position on the harbormaster's deck. 'If she's smart, she's looking for you. If she's not so smart, she's looking for me.'

'Let's keep radio chatter down to a minimum, people,' Jazz's voice cut in.

'I don't know what she wants,' Mallory reported. 'Should I let her in?'

'Yes.' Tom tried to keep his impatience and frustration from ringing in his voice. Yes, let her in, because forcing Kelly to stand outside the parked van and knock on the windows is only drawing attention to you. 'Get her in there quickly. And shut the door behind her.'

He heard the sound of the door opening, heard Kelly's voice. 'Hey, Mallory. What are *you* doing here?'

'David and I are helping Tommy.'

'Oh, hi, David. How are you? Hey, I like your haircut.'

'Thanks. Mal did it.'

'Can I come in?'

'Yeah, Tom says to get in. Quick.'

Tom looked at Starrett and rolled his eyes as he finally heard the door close. 'Mal, can you put me on over the speakers so Kelly can hear me?'

'The van's speakers aren't working really well,' David replied, 'but we've got an extra wired headset here that she can use.'

'Great,' Tom said. 'Can you give it to her?'

'Tom?' Kelly's voice said. David was a little more on the ball. He'd already gotten the headset to her.

'What's up, Kelly?' He tried to make his voice matter-of-fact. Casual. As if she hadn't absolutely shredded the last of his hope by running and hiding after he'd told her he loved her. As if he hadn't particularly noticed that she'd stayed far, *far* away from him all day yesterday. I love you, too – *not*. 'Something you need?'

'Where are you? You sound so close.'

'I am so close. I'm in the hotel.'

'Locke's watching room 104 from the Congregational

church tower,' Mallory told Kelly. 'Jazz and Sam are helping Tommy do a room-by-room search, looking for a bomb.'

Mallory made it sound easy. As if they could simply knock on every door, explain that there might be a bomb in the room, would it be too much trouble to ask if they could take a look? . . .

No, they had to do this covertly. With Starrett dressed in a billion-dollar suit, hair swept back in a leather ponytail holder, pinky ring on his finger, pretending to be the rather effeminate 'Mr Sam' of the hotel staff, and Jazz impressively dressed in his summer uniform – posing as preliminary security for tomorrow's event. Lt. (jg) Jazz Jacquette had even introduced himself to the desk clerks on his way in.

Tom wore surfer shorts with a big overshirt to hide the small arsenal Jazz had scrounged up from God knows where. His job this morning was to search the rooms in which no one was home.

So far so good. They were on the third floor – two more to go. And the higher they got, the less likely they were to find a bomb. Someone with the Merchant's experience and knowledge would know that a bomb on the fourth floor would do far less damage to a building than one on the first floor.

But Tom had realized last night that while they had a photo of the Merchant checking into the hotel with a cartful of luggage, room 104 contained only one small suitcase. Where was the rest of his stuff if not in one of these other rooms?

Tom signaled for Jazz and Starrett to go on up to the fourth floor as he let himself into the last room at the end of the hall.

'I thought the chances of there being a bomb in the hotel itself are slim.' Kelly's voice sounded as if she were right there, whispering into his ear. 'I thought this guy's MO was a car bomb.'

The room looked as if it were being occupied by a family with a small child. Baby toys were everywhere. But that didn't mean Tom didn't search it thoroughly. If *he* were a terrorist planting a bomb, he'd scatter a Bite Me Elmo doll and bright-colored blocks on the floor, too.

'Today we search the hotel,' Tom told her as he moved efficiently through the room. 'Tonight and tomorrow, we'll be out in the parking lots.'

'What can I do to help?' she asked.

'Not a lot,' he said flatly. 'If you want, you can hang with Mal and David – help them man the van. But like I told them, I don't want you inside this hotel, not under any circumstances.'

'I was kind of hoping I'd get a chance to talk to you,' Kelly told him. 'When are you going to take a break?'

'Wednesday.' She wanted to talk to him. Great. She wanted to tell him it was probably best if they kept their distance from each other until he left at the end of the month. She didn't want to hurt him and . . .

'Are you serious?' she said. 'You're not going to take a single break between now and—'

'No.' He let himself out of the hotel room, making sure the door was locked behind him. Room 375 was clean. He made a little checkmark on his list, stuck it back into his pocket.

'You're not even going to go to the bathroom?' she

asked. 'There's not even a time when I can come in and talk to you while you pee?'

'Kelly, I'm a little busy now,' he said tightly. 'Do you mind saving the humor for another time?'

'I don't want to wait until Wednesday to tell you that I was wrong from the start.' She lowered her voice. 'What we've got between us is more than just sex. But I was scared, Tom. I'm still scared, but after last night, when I looked for you and you weren't there, now I'm more scared about losing you.'

'Um, Kelly—'

She lowered her voice even more. 'I miss you. I miss the time we spent together. I miss talking to you. Believe it or not, I love talking to you as much as I love—'

Tom quickly cut her off. 'Yeah, I know what you love. And now that the entire team – including your father – has heard it—'

'*What?*'

'Everyone's listening,' he told her, unable to keep from laughing. Jesus. Of all the things she might've said to him, he hadn't been expecting this. And despite the fact that she was going to be very embarrassed, he was glad. It wasn't 'I love you, too,' but it was good enough for now. 'This is a very open channel.'

Kelly laughed, too. 'Oh, my *God*. It *is*?'

'Please don't stop,' Starrett's voice drawled. 'Personally, I'm finding this a million times better than *The Young and the Restless*.'

'Thanks,' Tom said dryly, 'but I think she's probably done.'

'I'm not,' Kelly said. 'Because I still have to tell you that I love you.'

'See?' Starrett said. 'She's not done.'

'I didn't want to have to wait till Wednesday to say that,' Kelly added.

'Although, on Wednesday, you wouldn't've had to make it a public service announcement,' Tom pointed out. She loved him. He wasn't sure whether to be happy or scared to death.

'I don't care who hears,' she told him fiercely. 'I love you, and it's a good thing.'

She sounded as if she were still trying to convince herself of that fact. Tom knew exactly how she felt.

'I mean,' she faltered, 'as long as you still love me, too . . .'

Silence. There was dead silence.

Kelly flashed hot and then cold and then hot again as she waited an eternity for Tom to reply.

'How about we plan to take a break in about an hour and a half?' he finally said. 'When we're through with the fourth floor?'

'I'm sorry,' she said softly. 'I didn't mean to embarrass you.'

'I'm not embarrassed. I just want to continue this more privately, that's all.'

'Okay,' she said. 'So in about an hour and a half—'

'Tom, we've got a small commercial helo approaching the hotel roof,' Locke's cool voice cut in. 'Is there some kind of landing pad up there?'

'Anyone know?' Tom asked, his voice instantly that of a team commander.

'Yes,' David said. 'The hotel has facilities for rooftop pickups and drop-offs of guests.'

'This one's coming in with only a pilot,' Locke reported. 'Probably a pickup.'

'Activity in hallway,' Starrett said quietly. 'Tom, stay out of sight. Jazz's in room 415, dark-haired man coming out of room 435, carrying a small overnight bag, looks like . . . Tango, tango – I've got visual, team, it's our man.'

Tom took the stairs three at a time as he heard Starrett say, 'Excuse me, Mr Rakowski—'

'Shit, no, Sam,' he said. 'You just gave yourself away.'

He didn't see it, but he heard it. Three gunshots. It didn't take much to picture what had happened. Starrett called the Merchant Mr Rakowski, the name he'd used to check into that decoy room down on the first floor, and the man turned around with his weapon already out and firing.

'Jazz, report!'

'Starrett's down,' the XO's deep voice said. 'We need medical assistance – he's bleeding pretty badly. The Merchant's in the far stairwell, and yes, sir, we've got a bomb in room 435. Holy Mother of God, it must've been rigged to the door opening because the timer's just switched from oh-nine-thirty tomorrow to twenty minutes from *now*. It's homemade, L.T., but it's a big motherfucker. Our man definitely knew what he was doing. Someone better start evacuating this building. I'm not sure I can get past all these booby traps in time to keep this thing from blowing.'

'Medical assistance is on its way,' Mallory's voice cut through. 'Kelly told me to tell you she's coming to help Sam.'

'No!' Tom shouted as he kept going past the fourth floor, toward the roof. 'God damn it, you tell Kelly to stay in the van!'

'But she's already on her way.'

'*Shit!* Jazz, call WildCard,' Tom ordered. 'He's standing by. Use him, however you can, to help you with that bomb. Mal, call the police, tell them we found something real. Locke, be ready for anything.'

'Always am, sir.'

He burst onto the roof, out into the brain-splitting brightness of the morning. Weapon drawn, he ran for the other access door.

And then there he was.

The Merchant.

He saw Tom, saw his weapon, and raised his own side arm.

He was just a little too late.

Tom kicked it, hard, from his hand, like a game-winning soccer kick. It went flying back through the open access door. Tom heard it rattling down the stairs. Goal!

But the Merchant was already swinging his briefcase, and it landed hard against the side of Tom's head, then hard against his right wrist. His weapon dropped, too, and the Merchant dove for it.

Kelly took the stairs to the fourth floor. Starrett had been shot. Please, God, don't let him have been *shot* in the chest or the face or . . .

He was slumped on the floor, bleeding heavily from a bullet wound in his shoulder. Two and a half inches lower, and that bullet would have hit his heart. Two and a half inches lower, and this man would be dead.

As it was, he was unconscious, and Kelly saw there was blood on his head as well. A second bullet had grazed his temple. She took off his headset and put it on. She had far more use for it than Sam did right now.

The door to 435 was open and as she went inside to get some towels to use to stop his bleeding, she stopped short at the sight of the bomb.

Dear God, Tom had been right all along. Tom, who was no doubt *chasing* the man with the gun. Please, God, keep him safe!

'Seventeen minutes and counting down,' Jazz was saying grimly to someone on the hotel telephone. 'I'll try to describe it completely, but I sure as hell wish you could see it for yourself.'

David sat up. Lieutenant Jacquette wanted WildCard, out in California, to see the bomb that was in room 435.

He could do it. He could help. With his Internet camera. His laptop.

He opened the van door. 'Don't go anywhere,' he said to Mallory. 'Stay right here, all right?'

'But—'

'I've got to get something,' he told her, and ran for home.

Mallory couldn't get through. She'd used the cell phone to dial 911, but she kept getting freaking disconnected.

Don't go anywhere.

Don't leave the van.

That rule was supposed to apply to David and Kelly as well as herself.

So why was she the only one left sitting here like a big idiot?

Her job was to warn the police about the bomb. Start the evacuation of the hotel. Fifteen minutes now before the bomb went off.

Screw this. How could she warn anyone with a cell phone that didn't effing work? She switched off her lip microphone, left the van, and ran for the hotel.

It was amazing. There were people playing Frisbee on the lawn, workmen building a stage. And in the hotel lobby, it was as poshly, snobbishly too-elegant-for-the-likes-of-you as it always had been.

That was going to change, and fast.

There was a line at the front desk, a line at the concierge's counter. But there was a security guard, gun strapped to his side, chatting up the woman working at the gift shop.

Mallory skidded to a stop in front of him.

'No running in the hotel,' he said sternly.

'Yeah? How about when there's a bomb set to go off in fifteen minutes?'

The guard got even more stern. 'Bomb threats are a felony, young lady. Even when said in jest.'

'This isn't a threat or a joke, Jack. It's in room 435. We need to start evacuating this building *now*.'

'Paoletti, right?' he said, eyes narrowing. 'Yeah, I know you. You're Angie Paoletti's kid. You know, we got a call from the police department, warning us that Tom Paoletti was hallucinating some kind of terrorist threat. Do me a favor, kid. Go home, and take your nutball uncle with you.'

'I'm serious. Sir. Officer.' Mallory gave respectful a try. 'Please, will you at least go up to room 435 and—'

'You got ten seconds to get the hell out of here,' the security guard told her. 'And the only reason I'm being nice and letting you leave without calling the police is because I'm friends with your mother.'

'Friends. Right,' Mallory said. 'Does your wife know?'

He reached for her, but she was already gone.

Charles stood gripping the railing on the deck of the harbormaster's house, Joe beside him. 'What do you see?' he said. 'Alyssa, please. *Shoot* the bastard.'

'Tom and the Merchant are fighting,' Alyssa Locke reported from her perch in the church tower. 'Hand to hand. Believe me, sir, if I could get a clear shot . . .'

'Kelly,' Charles said. 'Where are you?'

'She's here,' David answered the old man. 'With Sam. The mike on her radio headset broke. She can receive but she can't send.'

He stepped over the fallen SEAL, trying not to look at the blood on the towel Kelly held pressed to the man's shoulder. God, Sam Starrett had been shot. This all had seemed like pretend back in the van, but it wasn't. It was real.

'Get out,' Tom's voice rasped over David's headset. 'Get her the hell out of there, *now!*'

'I'm not leaving Sam,' Kelly said calmly. 'He's already lost too much blood.'

David repeated her words as he carried his laptop and camera into room 435.

And there it was.

A bomb.

It looked a whole lot less assuming than the bombs he'd seen on TV and in the movies. It had a timer, counting down minutes and seconds. There were thirteen minutes and forty-seven seconds left. Forty-six. Forty-five. Forty-four.

Jazz was dripping sweat. The hotel telephone was tucked under his chin as he looked at all the wires.

'God,' David said. 'Those wires are all the same color. How do you know which is which?'

Jazz glanced up at him. 'Yeah, what? You really think the Merchant's going to color code them for our ease in defusing this sucker?'

'But in the movies . . .'

Jazz shot him a withering look.

David set up his laptop. 'I brought my Internet camera. You said you wanted WildCard to see this bomb. Well, now he can.'

The withering look vanished, fast.

Kelly prayed. Dear God, don't let her save Sam only to have them both blown up. Dear God, keep Tom safe.

She could hear Locke from the church tower, describing Tom's fight with the Merchant. 'I can't get a clear shot,' she kept saying. 'They're all over the place. I can't risk it.'

Then, 'Uh-oh,' she said. 'We got some trouble. The pilot's getting out of the helo. He's armed.' Her voice was tight. 'I could use some orders.'

Tom was silent. Kelly applied pressure to Sam's shoulder and knew that Tom's silence was not a good thing.

Mallory ran into the middle of the lobby, scrambling up onto the top of a table as she heard a shot ring out.

She took advantage of the sudden lull.

'Excuse me, rich people, I need your attention! There's a bomb in this hotel, up in room 435, and it's set to go off in about twelve minutes! That sound you just heard was a gunshot. Someone should definitely call the police. And everyone else who wants to live better grab their wallets and head for the door and—'

She didn't see who grabbed her and pulled her down from there. Whoever it was, she didn't like the hand over her mouth, didn't like the way he held her by the chest as he dragged her across the lobby and into an elevator.

She elbowed him hard in the ribs as she bit his hand, and he released her. But the elevator doors had already closed, and they were already going up.

She turned to face him, ready to fight, and found herself gazing into the barrel of a very deadly-looking gun.

And the man holding it had a face she recognized. He was in that picture she'd taken of the Merchant. He was the man she'd captured on film, talking to the terrorist. His face was ugly, distorted with anger. And on the back of his hand, just as Tom had described, he had a small tattoo of a single, staring, creepy-as-shit eye.

'Who the hell are you?' he asked. 'I should kill you right now!'

Mallory refused to cry. Instead she stood tall, chin high, just like Nightshade would have. 'Surrender now, asshole, and it'll go easier on you.'

*

Tom was dizzy.

The Merchant was strong, and Tom struggled to stay in control, to keep from rolling back to where his weapon had landed on the gravel rooftop.

He fought to keep the Merchant's hands pinned, knowing full well that the man was carrying a knife, knowing he wouldn't hesitate to shove it hard into Tom's chest if he had the slightest opportunity.

Tom was winning, though. He'd started winning the moment Locke had fired the shot that had chased the pilot back into the helo. He'd started winning big when the pilot and helo took off, leaving the Merchant behind.

'Pin him, sir,' he heard Locke say. 'Pin him, and I'll take him out.'

Easier said than done, particularly when his head was throbbing and his equilibrium was off. Still, Tom had his arm around the Merchant's neck as they flopped about on the roof. He was cutting off the man's air. He could feel him starting to fade, his kicks growing weaker.

'Eleven minutes and counting,' Tom heard Jazz report. 'And L.T., if you're listening, it's occurred to me that there might be a reason our little Merchant purchased two alarm clocks. I've got two empty boxes here, but only one is used in this particular piece of performance art. If you've got this guy's ear, you might want to ask him where he's put the second bomb.'

Oh, *fuck*.

Tom let go of the Merchant, scrambling back to grab his weapon and hold it with both hands, aimed at the man's forehead.

He pulled himself to his feet and administered

scumbag resuscitation by kicking the terrorist hard in the ribs.

The Merchant drew in a shuddering breath.

'Get up,' Tom said. 'Hands on your head.'

The man couldn't do more than push himself onto his hands and knees for several long moments. But time was running out. 'Get up!'

'Drop the gun.'

Tom did nothing of the sort. He kept his weapon trained on the Merchant as he turned slightly toward the access door.

It was Terrorist Number Two. Tom recognized him from the photo Mallory had taken. And, oh, double fuck. He had Mallory, his weapon held to her head.

'Drop it or I'll kill the girl.'

How the hell had *this* happened?

'Jesus, Mallory,' Tom said.

'Mallory?' David's voice cut through. 'Mal, where are you? Did you leave the van?'

'I'm sorry,' Mal said, too softly for Tom to hear her, but he could read her lips. Her microphone was broken. Jazz was going to hear about these cheapshit headsets, that was for sure. She had a scratch on the side of her face, no doubt from the broken piece of plastic. Her lip was swollen, too. The bastard had hit her.

'Drop. The. Gun.' T2 was starting to lose it.

'Please, Tom, do whatever he says,' David begged him over the headset from down on the fourth floor. 'Please don't let her die.'

'Drop it,' T2 ordered.

If Tom did, they were both dead. He kept his own weapon on the Merchant. 'You drop *your* gun, asshole, or your boss checks out. And the next bullet's yours, I promise you that.'

'Lieutenant Paoletti, please step a little to your right.' That was Locke's cool voice. Locke, who was in the church tower with a sniper rifle and the best aim in the US Navy.

Tom stepped right.

He felt the shot whizzing past his cheek, heard it crack, and T2 crumpled lifelessly to the ground.

'Mallory!' David's cry was anguished. Of course, he didn't know. He couldn't see, could only hear the sound of the gunshot.

Mallory was sprayed with blood, but she didn't faint, didn't fall. She scooped up T2's weapon before it even had time to bounce. She held it in both hands, like Tom, aimed directly at the Merchant, also like Tom. Only she aimed the barrel lower, much lower than the man's forehead.

'Tell David I'm still alive.'

But David was already in the doorway. '*Mallory.*'

'He called me Mallory,' she said to Tom. 'Did you hear that?' She was crying, covered with tears and snot and blood, but she didn't waver. 'David, go back and help Jazz. I'm all right.'

He was crying, too. 'I just . . . God, I love you and I thought—'

Mal smiled. 'I know. Go.'

'Both of you go,' Tom ordered them. 'Get out of here. *Now.*'

Mallory shook her head. 'No, I think I'll back you up a little longer. You don't look very good, Tom.'

'Yeah, but I'm the one with the gun.' He looked at the Merchant. Both of the Merchants. Double fuck,

485

indeed. He fought his dizziness. 'Tell me where the second bomb is.'

The Merchant's gaze shifted. Just a little. Just enough. Out to the harbor.

And with a blazing revelation, Tom knew. As he gazed into the son of a bitch's eyes, he knew the whole plan. He knew how this asshole's mind worked. The bomb was on the fourth floor, not to do the most structural damage, but rather to act as a shepherding device to push the crowd away from the hotel.

Away from the hotel and down toward the marina.

Where all those little boats were sitting, all in a row. The Merchant had to set only one bomb in one boat, and the rest would blow sky-high, like a chain of firecrackers, one right after another. The entire marina would go up into the biggest terrorist explosion in US history, and anyone within hundreds of yards would go with it.

The Merchant looked up at the blueness of the sky. And then, without warning, he rushed Tom's gun.

But Tom didn't need warning. He knew this man too well, knew he'd choose death over capture.

He squeezed the trigger of his weapon and ended the Merchant's too-long life.

'Locke, Joe, Charles!' Tom's voice rang clearly over Charles's headset. 'The second bomb's on a boat, possibly underwater, under the hull, where you won't even be able to see it.'

Charles could see Alyssa already running across the lawn from the Congregational church. Joe, too, was already down the stairs that led to the boat slips.

But even though Charles's legs weren't moving

as quickly, his brain was doing just fine. He pushed open the door of the harbormaster's office and appropriated the guest register, checking the names of all the boats that were currently docked in the visitor slips. It was premium real estate, those visitor slips, bringing a hefty amount of income into the marina, making it possible for regular folks to dock a boat there without having to quadruple mortgage their houses.

He used his finger to go down the list and . . .

There was nothing that jumped out at him. No boat named *Merchant's Prize* or something equally obvious.

But there *was* one thing that caught his eye. The *Sea Breeze*. At the start of the week, it had been docked in slot A-3. But halfway through, it got moved over to B-7. Now, that was odd, because as far as convenience and ease, A-3 was a better slot. However, as far as blowing up things went, B-7 was smack in the middle of the marina.

'Alyssa, Joe, check B-7,' he said over his radio headset.

But just to be safe, he took all the spare copies of all the keys that were hanging on the harbormaster's wall.

Dottie, who worked behind the counter, stood up. 'Mr Ashton, what are you . . . ?'

'Stealing all the visitors' boats,' he told her crossly. 'What do you think I'm doing?'

Navigating the stairs with his walker wasn't happening, so he tossed the damn thing to the bottom, and went down like a little kid, on the seat of his pants.

Joe searched the inside of the *Sea Breeze*. And there it was. A bomb. In the head. The timer read seven minutes and twenty-eight seconds, exactly three minutes behind the bomb in the hotel.

Alyssa Locke was right behind him, and she tossed him her radio and headset and dove headfirst into the murky waters of the harbor. She came up coughing, grabbed a lungful of air, and went back down.

He could see Charles, making his way down the steep ramp that led to the B slips.

Alyssa came up, gasping. 'He's right. Tom's right. This thing's rigged to blow. The entire hull is wired with explosives.'

'There's a bomb in the john, too,' Joe told her.

She reached a hand up, and he helped haul her onto the deck. She was heavy for such a little thing. Or maybe he was just getting too old for this.

'It's probably the timer,' she said, slicking her hair back from her face and going to take a look. 'Yeah. See how this wire runs down here and over the side. But this one's rigged with a failsafe – we cut this wire, and this smaller bomb blows. Which will set off the other bomb.'

She put her headset and radio back on. 'L.T., are you there? We've located our second bomb, and we're in serious trouble.'

'I've got at least two more minutes to go before I neutralize *this* bomb,' Jazz's voice came back. 'No way can I get down there and take care of that one, too.'

'I'm on my way,' Tom said.

Charles tossed his walker into the recessed deck of the boat, then swung himself on board. It wasn't graceful, but it got the job done. 'Alyssa,' he said. 'Dearest. Jump back into the water and see if the bomb is attached to the inboard motor.'

'What are you thinking?' she asked.

'You're not going to make *me* do it, are you?'

She took off her radio again and, with a hard look at Charles, she went over the side.

'What *are* you thinking?' Joe asked.

Alyssa came back up, sputtering and coughing. 'It's not connected – at least not as far as I can tell.'

Cybele. Charles was thinking about Cybele.

'I have the *Sea Breeze*'s key,' he told his oldest friend.

He could see understanding in Joe's eyes. 'I'll come with you.'

'Why should we both go?' he said as gently as he could.

'No one's going anywhere.' Tom's voice rang over their headsets. 'Just wait for me to get down there.'

'I got it,' Jazz's voice was thick with relief. 'Timer's stopped running, L.T.'

Joe swung himself down below. 'This timer's still going. Four minutes and counting.'

'Is someone going to help me out of the water and back onto that boat?' Alyssa called.

They were out of time. If Charles was going to do this, he had to do it now.

'Kelly, you made me proud this morning,' he said into his microphone. 'I love you. I'm glad you found Tom, glad you recognized what you found.'

Joe had tears in his eyes. 'I'm coming with you,' he said again.

'You can't,' Charles said, and for the first time in nearly six decades, he embraced his best friend. 'Tell the truth to that writer – that *Cybele* was the real hero of Baldwin's Bridge.'

He'd caught Joe completely off guard with his embrace, and when he finally pulled back, he was able to push his friend neatly over the side and into the water.

Charles started the motor with a roar, and the boat didn't blow up. That was good.

'Daddy, I love you!' Kelly had gotten herself to a headset with a microphone.

'I know,' he told her. 'That's the one thing I never doubted ever in my life, Kelly. You loved me, and Cybele loved me. It was more than I deserved.'

He backed out of the slip, and he could see Alyssa and Joe, still there in the water.

He could see Joe's face, Joe's eyes, Joe's anguish.

And Charles touched his right ear, giving Joe his sign.

He was ready to go.

Tom turned to see Kelly running toward him across the lawn.

Out in the harbor, Charles had opened up the throttle, breaking all the posted speed limits as he headed for the open sea, moving quickly out of radio range.

Kelly slowed, her chest heaving as she cried.

Tom reached for her, and she went into his arms.

Down on the dock, Locke helped Joe out of the water.

In the hotel, Jazz sat with Starrett, eyes closed as he waited for the ambulance.

Mallory and David stood at the window, watching the *Sea Breeze* grow smaller and smaller.

And there, on the deck of that boat, Charles finally

knew. He finally understood why Cybele gave her life for him and for Joe and for the Fighting Fifty-fifth.

And he finally forgave her.

She had been in pain, and weary of life. It wasn't that she didn't love him, because she did, oh, he knew that she did. But unless she'd acted when she had, Charles would have sacrificed himself to save her. And then, once again, Cybele would have been left with her heart turned to ashes. She loved him so much that she didn't want to live without him.

She was an amazing woman. She saw in him a hero, and when he was with her, he was one.

Charles aimed the bow of the boat toward the distant horizon, at peace with himself for the first time in years, knowing that he'd managed, one last time before he died, to once again become the man that Cybele Desjardins had loved.

On the lawn between the Baldwin's Bridge Hotel and the marina, near the statue honoring the men who gave their lives in the Second World War, Tom held Kelly close.

On the dock, a bedraggled Joe saluted the far-off boat as beside him, Lt. Alyssa Locke bowed her head.

The explosion was distant, but still loud enough to make everyone in the harbor and on the hotel lawn look up and out to sea.

For several seconds, there was a hush. A moment of silence.

But then life resumed.

Laughter.

Children shouting.

An ice cream truck approached, its bell ringing.

Tom stood there with Kelly for a good long time, letting her look into the faces of the many people whose lives her father had saved that day.

Twenty-two

15 August

Tom left the debriefing in Washington with just enough time to catch the tail end of the ceremony honoring the Fifty-fifth.

The celebration had gone on as scheduled – with heightened security, and with nearly everyone in attendance unaware of the previous day's drama.

The United States' government's counterterrorist policies included keeping attempted terrorist attacks low profile. Since terrorists tended to be after media coverage even in failed missions, it was US policy to try to give them none.

But Tom didn't care if no one ever knew – no one except for Adm. Chip Crowley. And Rear Admiral Tucker, who ground out a not very sincere-sounding apology to Tom in front of Crowley's staff.

As Tom watched from the edge of the crowd, Kelly took the stage to graciously accept a special medal from the French, British, and US governments for her father's part in the war.

The ceremony ended shortly after that.

He tried to fight his way through the crowd to Kelly, but succeeded only in finding Mallory and David.

'How's Sam?' Mal asked.

'Already out of ICU and annoying the hell out of the nurses,' Tom told her. 'How are *you* doing? It's not everyday someone holds a gun to your head and threatens to kill you.'

'I'm okay,' she said. 'Still a little shaky.' She laughed. 'Still a *lot* shaky. When you see Locke, thank her for saving my life.'

'Yes,' David said. 'Please.' As Tom watched, David pulled her into his arms, as if he couldn't bear not to hold her.

And Tom had to ask. 'What happens with you guys in September?'

'I'm going to go to school part-time,' Mal told him. 'I'm not going to do the Navy thing – no offense, Tommy, but it's not my speed.'

'We were thinking Mal could try to get a job in Boston as a photographer's assistant,' David added.

'David lives in this big place, a six-bedroom apartment, and they nearly always need housemates, so I wouldn't really be living with him. And I'll be close enough to home, in case Angela needs me.'

'In three or four years, we'll think about getting married,' David said.

Married. The kid said the word in a sentence including the word we, and he didn't faint or make the sign of the cross or show any kind of fear at all. In fact, he smiled.

'You really think you'll still be together in three or four years?' Tom asked.

Both David and Mallory nodded.

'Absolutely.'

'Definitely.'

Their confidence awed him. Still, he had to ask. 'And if you're not? . . .'

David looked at Mallory and smiled. It was loaded with meaning, laced with a healthy dose of 'can you believe how stupid this guy is?'

'If we're not still together,' David told him, 'it won't be from lack of trying.'

Kelly waited for Tom in the dark.

She heard him come home, saw the light go on in his bedroom as he changed out of his dress uniform.

She saw, through the cottage's living-room window, that he also stopped to talk to Joe.

And then he headed out across the driveway.

She closed her eyes, picturing him using the kitchen door to get inside the big house, picturing him finding the note she'd left for him in her bedroom.

'Meet me in the tree house.'

She couldn't bear to be in the house alone. It seemed so empty and quiet without her father. Yet at the same time, she could feel Charles's presence. In the living room. In the kitchen. On the deck.

Particularly on the deck, where he'd sat day after day, just watching the ocean. Loving a woman who had preferred death to living without him.

The ladder creaked under Tom's weight. He knocked on the door before he came in, which was absurd, considering this was a tree house.

'How's Joe?' she asked, suddenly nervous about

everything she'd said to him yesterday, wishing he hadn't had to leave right away for those meetings in Washington, DC.

'He's feeling pretty lost,' Tom admitted. 'You don't spend nearly sixty years as someone's best friend and then not notice when he's gone.'

'Best friends for nearly sixty years.' Kelly shook her head. 'It seems as if it should be some kind of world record.'

'Yeah. He feels good about talking to that writer, though.'

'That's good.'

There was silence for a moment, and then he spoke again.

'You know, I got another thirty days of convalescent leave,' he told her. 'This time I'm really supposed to rest. Actually, I don't think I'll need a full thirty, because the dizziness isn't happening so often anymore.'

'You were dizzy yesterday,' she pointed out.

'Yeah, but it didn't leave me unable to function. I didn't black out. I'm taking that as a good sign. And now with this extra time . . . I'm going to be okay. I know it.'

'I'm glad.' She could feel him watching her in the darkness. 'I used to come out here to spy on you,' she told him. 'There's a clear shot from here into your bedroom window. I can't tell you how many times I've watched you walk around in your underwear. Or in less.'

'You're kidding.'

'Tonight your boxers are blue.'

Tom laughed. 'Holy God, you're a degenerate.'

Kelly nodded, pleased he should think so. 'That's right.' But then she sighed. 'Actually, I'm not. If I were a real degenerate, I'd go around looking into everyone's window. Frankly, the only window – and the only underwear – that interests me is yours.'

'Still, you get extra depravity credits for longevity.'

'Good,' she said. 'Yeah, I'll take 'em. At the very least, they'll help counteract my damned good-girl image.'

'Personally, I find it intensely fascinating – your combination of good and, well, evil, for lack of a better word.' His voice was like velvet in the darkness, surrounding her. He moved closer, and she could feel his body heat.

'Do you love me?' she asked, needing to know, and dammit, asking was the only way she'd ever truly find out. 'I mean, the real me? Not the me you want me to be, but the one who says bad words and likes having sex in closets?'

He laughed softly. 'How could I not?'

'I'm not trying to make a joke. I'm serious. Bad example.'

'*Good* example.' He kissed her, pulling her close. 'How are you with tree houses?'

'Tom—'

He kissed her throat, his hands already beneath her shirt. 'Because, you know, it's already been five minutes, and—'

'Oh, God, you're never going to let me live that down!'

'That's right,' he said. 'Until the end of time, I'm going to give you only five minutes of conversation, then I'm going to be all over you.'

Oh, God. 'It's going to be interesting when we meet in a restaurant.'

His laughter was soft and very dangerous. 'You bet.'

'Or on the beach . . .'

'Uh-huh.'

'Or an airport. I have a feeling we're both going to be seeing a lot of airports.'

He lifted his head. 'Unless you come to California with me.'

Kelly was silent. Was he asking her? . . .

He cleared his throat. 'I was thinking we could, you know, try to break Charles and Joe's record. Go for sixty-five years . . .'

Oh, God. 'You mean, as best friends?'

Tom nodded. 'I know the M-word makes you nervous, but yeah. I'm talking about the big, permanent friendship. A little different from what Joe and Charles had, though. See, I want to be the kind of best friends who make love every night, who share all their darkest secrets and favorite jokes, and maybe even someday make babies together. I know that kind of friendship requires hard work, but you know, I'm pretty good at hard work.'

Kelly laughed. 'My God, this is like getting propositioned by Mister Rogers. But then again, you always were a good neighbor. You're much more like Mister Rogers than, say . . . Satan. Wasn't that your nickname in town for a few years?'

'So ten thousand people were wrong about me. It happens.' He pulled her with him onto the blankets she'd spread on the plywood floor. 'Ten thousand people were wrong about you, too,' he said as he kissed her again. 'You're nowhere near as nice as they

498

all thought. Most of them have absolutely no clue that you can do that amazing thing with your mouth.' He smiled. 'But I do.'

Kelly smiled as she looked up at him.

Despite the shadows of the night, she knew he saw her clearly. And in the same way, she saw through all the labels and facades and the pretense to the real man that was Tom Paoletti.

'I love you,' he whispered. 'I know we can make this work. At the very least – as two very wise people told me – if it doesn't, we'll know it won't be from lack of trying. Marry me, Kel.'

'And become the wife of a Navy SEAL?'

'Yeah. Never a dull moment. Of course, I'll be the husband of a highly esteemed pediatrician. It's hard to say whose pager will go off more often.'

Kelly sighed as he kissed her. 'I'm afraid of marriage.'

'I'll protect you.'

'Do you promise?'

'I promise. I swear. I—'

'I want us to be the kind of people who are still crazy in love when we're seventy-five years old.'

He kissed her again. 'Definitely. Still doing it in the tree house at seventy-five. I promise.'

'I love you,' she told him. 'I have since I was fifteen. But I don't think I can marry you unless you agree to let Joe live with us. We can get a place with an attached apartment and—'

'You *are* as nice as everyone says.'

Kelly pushed him off her, wrestling him over and pinning him down onto his back. 'If you're not careful,' she warned, 'I'm going to have to prove you wrong by doing that thing, you know, with my mouth? . . .'

Tom just smiled.

Dark of Night

Suzanne Brockmann

In a dangerous world some people make
all the difference.
TROUBLESHOOTERS
Sexy. Exciting. Addictive . . . Lethal Suspense.

As members of one of the most elite corporate security companies in the world, the men and women of Troubleshooters Inc. face death on a daily basis, but even they are not immune to the loss of James Nash, one of their own. Blackmail, extortion, murder: the black-ops sector of Nash's previous employers. The Agency, will stop at nothing to silence their former operatives. But this time they've gone too far.

A team of Troubleshooters operatives, led by former Navy Seal Lawrence Decker and assisted by their friends in the FBI, band together to uncover the truth, and bring Nash's killers to justicce.

The stakes are raised even higher when Decker and Tracy Shapiro, Troubleshooter's Inc.'s receptionist, barely escape an attempt on their lives. It soon becomes clear that the hunters have become the hunted and the Troubleshooters are no longer just solving a crime – they're fighting for survival.

Praise for Suzanne Brockmann's novels:

'Sizzling with intrigue and sexual tension . . . with characters so vivid they leap off the page' Tess Gerritsen

'A taut, edgy thriller' Linda Howard

'Sexy, suspenseful and irresistible' *Booklist*

978 0 7553 5549 5

headline

Die For Me

Karen Rose

A SECRET CELLAR

A multimedia designer is hard at work. His latest computer game, *Inquisitor*, heralds a new era in state-of-the-art graphics. But there's only one way to ensure that the death scenes are realistic enough . . .

AN ISOLATED FIELD

Detective Ciccotelli's day begins with one grave, one body and no murder weapon. It ends with sixteen graves, but only nine bodies and the realisation that the killer will strike again . . .

A LIVING HELL

When it's discovered that the murder weapons are similar to those used in medieval torture, Ciccotelli knows that he's up against the most dangerous opponent of his career – let the games begin . . .

A killer obsessed with the past, victims tortured to death, and all in the name of a game – DIE FOR ME is Karen Rose's most chilling thriller to date.

Acclaim for Karen Rose:

'Karen Rose's COUNT TO TEN takes off like a house afire. There's action and chills galore in this non-stop thriller' Tess Gerritsen

'Rose delivers the kind of high-wire suspense that keeps you riveted to the edge of your seat' Lisa Gardner

978 0 7553 3706 4

headline

Now you can buy any of these other bestselling
Headline books from your bookshop
or *direct from the publisher*.

FREE P&P AND UK DELIVERY
(Overseas and Ireland £3.50 per book)

Dark of Night	Suzanne Brockmann	£6.99
Count to Ten	Karen Rose	£6.99
I'm Watching You	Karen Rose	£6.99
Die For Me	Karen Rose	£6.99
Nothing to Fear	Karen Rose	£6.99
Scream For Me	Karen Rose	£6.99
Kill For Me	Karen Rose	£6.99
Never Fear	Scott Frost	£6.99
Run The Risk	Scott Frost	£6.99
Point of No Return	Scott Frost	£6.99
Smoked	Patrick Quinlan	£6.99
The Takedown	Patrick Quinlan	£6.99
Stripped	Brian Freeman	£6.99
Stalked	Brian Freeman	£6.99

TO ORDER SIMPLY CALL THIS NUMBER

01235 400 414

or visit our website: www.headline.co.uk

Prices and availability subject to change without notice.